Also by Niccolò Tucci

Before My Time (1962)

Unfinished Funeral (1964)

IN ITALIAN

Il Segreto (Viareggio Prize, 1956)

Gli Atlantici (Bagutta Prize, 1968)

Confessioni Involontarie (1975)

THE SUN AND THE MOON

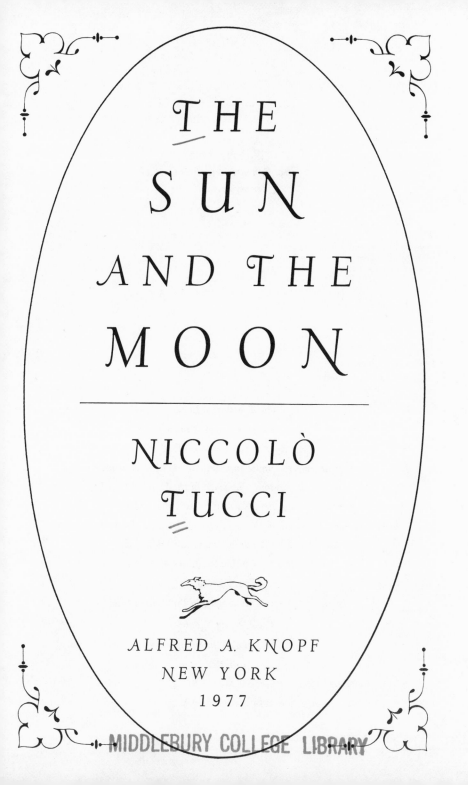

THE
SUN
AND THE
MOON

NICCOLÒ
TUCCI

ALFRED A. KNOPF
NEW YORK
1977

*With my thanks
to Carol Janeway and Bob Gottlieb,
my editors*

This is a Borzoi Book
Published by Alfred A. Knopf, Inc.
Copyright © 1977 by Niccolò Tucci
*All rights reserved under International and Pan-American
Copyright Conventions. Published in the United States by
Alfred A. Knopf, Inc., New York, and simultaneously in
Canada by Random House of Canada Limited, Toronto.
Distributed by Random House, Inc., New York.
Manufactured in the United States of America
First Edition
Library of Congress Cataloging in Publication Data*
Tucci, Niccolò [date]
The sun and the moon.
I. Title.
PZ4.T886Su [PS3570.U23] 813'.5'4 76-39918
ISBN 0-394-46640-3

For Lizzie,
and her basic ingredients,
Maria and Bob

THE SUN AND THE MOON

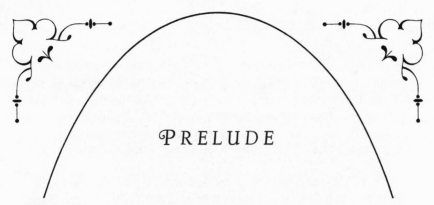

PRELUDE

T his is a fairy tale for children between the ages of six and
ninety-six, and adults between the ages of three and six. It is
the story of how the sun fell in love with the moon. Or was
it the moon with the sun? No one can tell, because this fairy tale
is different from all the others in that its characters never stay put
in their roles for more than a few days—hours at times, minutes,
seconds. They both claim to be the moon, but want to be worshipped as the sun, and if by any chance they begin to suspect that
they are not receiving the right tribute, or that the neighbors may
think so, they become very angry and say: "Do you think that my
light comes only from you? If I decided to shine elsewhere, where
would *you* be?" This is typical moon language, because the moon
does receive all its light from the sun and therefore lives in constant
fear, while the sun, the great source of all light, is by this very fact
both blind and generous, and this angers the moon all the more;
anybody can be a moon. But still the question arises: Who is the
sun or the moon *here*? Adults will never ask such questions, but
children will, and since they are in the majority, and many of them
too old ever to grow up, we might as well invent an answer for them.
Here it is: With every thought, word and action, everyone in the
whole world takes part in the old quarrel between reality and illusion, which divides all philosophers and unites all historians. The
philosopher will say: "I am the sun and everybody else is either a
moon (my pupil) or a speck of dust on my path towards earth."
And the historian will assign him a short period of history (or even
a long one: fashions change) in which to enjoy his claim to solar
clarity, thus humbly suggesting that, while thinkers are beautiful
comets, the real sun shines from History. As for the rest of mankind,
it may be so awed with Truth as to become its Prophets and Preach-

ers (woe to the thinker who has followers: they turn him into a criminal), or it may feel totally excluded from all access to the Truth in any form; still, in everyday life, even the most ignorant person will continue to believe that the only reality is his own ("clear as daylight," he will call it), while everybody else's reality is to be rejected as belonging to the lunar world of dreams or the real world of lunatics.

To us idle storytellers it seems that what escapes all these scholarly or unscholarly contenders for solar clarity is that dreams beget reality, while illusions are sterile. Thus, *in reality*, the only test of truth is fiction, which describes not only people's actions, but their dreams, their illusions, gossip about them and their gossip about others. If it makes sense in fiction, it's a *fact*, if it doesn't, it's . . . *fiction*. This is why we have decided to tell this story as if it were no fairy tale, but a fairy tale it is.

FIRST DAY

S he was called Mary, and he was called Leonardo. She was fifteen
and he was twenty-three, she was from snowy Russia and he
from sunny Italy; they met briefly in a museum in Naples on
February 3, 1893, saw each other again three times more, always
very briefly and in public, but did manage to tell each other: "You
are my sun and without you I am nothing."

Then cruel forces parted them, and they lived unhappily ever
after. Here their fairy tale ended, and reality began.

Now, in reality, you may live as if you were really alive while
really you are dead. This is one thing that you can't do in fairy tales,
so it is not true that in fairy tales anything is possible.

Unless you are a fairy tale character yourself, you don't open the
book of fairy tales, and that whole world is never born.

Which is where their ways parted. Leonardo closed not only
THAT imaginary book, but *all* his books, in order not to be disturbed by illusions, and began to live seriously in the world of
reality, as if he were alive. Mary instead kept THAT book open and
opened many new ones, and since the words of others were not
sufficient to keep her illusions alive, she chose books without any
words in them, white books with hundreds of neatly trimmed pages
all gilded along the edges, and very special spines and costly leather
bindings, and on each volume was printed in gold letters the title:
TREFEB. Which was her code word for February 3: the date when
she had met the sun. These books she filled with quotations from
famous poets, or even entire poems if they deserved to be lifted
from the printed page, redeemed from public print and received
into the private, loving, almost sacred home of personal calligraphy,
as was customary in those days among people of high culture. And
through every one of these poems or long tracts of prose, she felt in

daily contact with Leonardo: these were her letters to him even
though they were mostly in languages he did not speak—Russian,
German, French, English, even Norwegian. Every now and then,
she couldn't help inserting some prose of her own into those learned
books, and it was always in Italian, the language she was least familiar with, and then her love came pouring out, not too openly however, because the Evil Force that had torn her away from him
constantly supervised her cultural activities. One of her outbursts
read: *Love is blind, but only to such things as are foreign to it. This
blindness is, as Darwin would say, a form of amatory self-preservation. Because what love preserves with this blindness is a power of
eyesight so strong that it can penetrate all barriers of languages, and
even recognize a star invisible beyond three galaxies and seven milky
ways as the sun that governs* OUR *day.* WE DON'T LIVE ON THIS
PLANET. *This is what all poets and all people in love are saying with
every word, and to call them mad dreamers or deluded fools is like
denying the very existence of a universe of planets, suns and moons
beyond our own.*

   Such a beautiful way to stay faithful to a dream, and faithful
Mary stayed, at the expense of her reality (which caught up with
her as it does with everyone on earth, dreamer or not). She lived in
the constant illusion that she could manage reality as we manage
dreams: going back to them whenever we want, and for as long as
we want, without accounting to anyone for our daydreaming activities; whereas we cannot treat reality this way, because reality we
share with others and dreams only with ourselves. Thus for example
she believed that whatever she did was in defense of her "reality"
(alias "Leonardo"), and the actual consequences were none of her
concern, because this was her dream, indeed her constant nightmare, and hadn't Calderón de la Barca said that Life Is A Dream?
She was so pleased with Calderón for having written a whole poem
about this One and Only Truth, that she began to learn Spanish in
order to be in touch with him, too. But then this nightmare was not
always a nightmare; at times she even found it beautiful as a *real*
dream, and to this dream she came back again and again, AS IF IT
WERE HER PRIVATE REALITY. But hadn't Shakespeare also said "To
be, or not to be"? She wrote essay after essay in English on that

famous sentence, and became, in her own unscholarly way, quite a
Shakespearean scholar, as her secret books amply testified.

Now, in her private reality or public nightmare, there lived a
husband and a son: the husband she relegated to the realm of bad
dreams and the son to that of good dreams, thus uniting him with
Leonardo, whom she made his foster father on her dream planet.
And on *that* planet in bliss, or on *this* planet in horror, we shall
leave her for the moment, to see how Leonardo fared with *his*
dream and *his* reality.

"*Non c'è male,*" he would have answered, which means not too
badly, considering that this was not the ideal world, but not too
well, either, considering that there existed, somewhere, perhaps still
in Rome, an ideal girl called Mary. He relegated her to the same
world of dreams and prayers to which he had relegated her namesake, the Holy Virgin, seven years before meeting Mary, when he
had lost his faith and closed his books on theology, to open books
on archaeology and history, then closed these, six years before meeting Mary, to open books on medicine, then these, one year after
meeting Mary, to open the Big Book of Nature—human nature,
that is—as a physician for the poor, then opened the newspapers, to
see what the Camorra (continental Mafia) was doing to health on a
national basis, while he was trying to do the opposite on a personal
basis, then closed the newspapers, because they were too bookish,
too verbose, and ran for mayor of the town of Laterza (30,000
inhabitants, no water), but before running for mayor he ran for a
wife and chose the girl chosen for him by his great-uncle the Monsignor (hoping the Monsignor would forgive him for abandoning a
career in the priesthood), then started fighting him in politics.

The great issue at that time was the Apulian Aqueduct, on which
many politicians, both on the lowest local and the highest national
level, had grown rich by pocketing the millions earmarked for building it, minus the lesser bribes to lesser politicians for not building it.
The Monsignor believed that honesty means accepting the reality
of other people's dishonesty and staying as far away from them as
possible, while always holding oneself ready to convert them to
honesty and educate their children after the fruits of dishonesty
have been reaped and invested to a profit. "But you are living in the

moon," said Leonardo. "Honesty is not a private dream to be ashamed of: that's the definition of dishonesty. And it's the crooks who always try to seduce us after the fruits of honesty have brought us power."

"It's you who are living in the moon," said the Monsignor. "No honest man is elected to office."

But Leonardo was, and thus, sometime in March 1902, we find Don Leonardo Claudi (pronounced "cloudy"), doctor, surgeon and mayor of Laterza, on his way to Rome to address the Senate of the Kingdom and Tell All about the famous aqueduct. With him were two aldermen: Peppino and Liborio. Peppino was the cousin of Leonardo's wife Giovanna, and had been invited to join him so he wouldn't have to invite Giovanna. Peppino came in handy to persuade her that this was no pleasure trip: grave political reasons made it necessary for the three men to stay together every moment of their visit, and thus no one could accompany Giovanna to see the monuments and the elegant millinery shops of the capital. Liborio had been invited because he was a cousin of a person who had persuaded a most influential Senator to let Leonardo speak in the Senate. The Senator was a hard-core realist and an "honest" man like the Monsignor, and the man who had persuaded him to let Leonardo speak was a true representative of that ugly reality from which both the Senator and the Monsignor stayed aloof.

Sixteen hours in a tiny compartment of a third-class railway car were quite a test of Leonardo's faith in honesty, but he went on preparing his speech to Their Excellencies the Senators of the Kingdom, and paid no attention to the dirt and the noise and the coal dust, while Peppino and Liborio felt demeaned in their dignity as aldermen on their first trip to Rome by the closeness of illiterates whose feet had not been washed since the last time they had made wine in big crates, and who were not even going to the capital. At almost every station, with a quick gust of fresh air, fresh illiterates with fresh dirt under their boots and a slightly different accent assaulted the train, pushing their luggage and their baskets full of smelly cheeses and fragrant oranges into the compartment, while the outgoing illiterates were trying to get off with their dirty belongings, leaving their orange peels and cheese rinds behind. Poor Peppino and Liborio couldn't stand it any more, and to console themselves, they tried to imagine the great city—the Eternal Caput Mundi or World Capital—not in terms of monuments or churches, but of naked women on beds, presumably in whorehouses, but maybe even in private homes, you never can tell when you go to a metropolis; they're all corrupt.

They emerged from their train like three chimneysweeps in the cold morning air, and stood there motionless for a while, blocking travelers and baggage porters, and unable to make a decision, because only the leader could decide for the group. (He was not only the mayor, but also the man who was paying for the whole trip out of his own pocket.)

"Why don't we walk to our hotel?" asked Leonardo, and his assistants answered as one: "Because we don't know the way."

"We can always ask."

"Ask for trouble you mean, Don Leonardo. How can three Apulian Cafoni compete with Roman citizens?"

"Don't call us Cafoni. Or at least leave me out."

"Why you and not us? Do you mean to imply—"

"I mean nothing. I mean to get to my hotel as soon as possible and have a nap before I go to the Senate."

"Then let's take a cab."

"A cab? God knows where the hotel is, and Roman coachmen are famous for their dishonesty. I'm paying for this trip."

"All right, let's share the cost."

"Very good."

So finally they chose from among the many coachmen assembled in front of the station the one who looked most honest and trustworthy and whose carriage looked solid enough to get them where they were going without any major accidents such as collisions with electric tramways, notoriously the most dangerous vehicles on earth, owing to their speed and to the deadly electricity they are in contact with. Also to the fact that they cannot change course.

They spent almost the entire trip trying to establish amicable relations with the coachman so he wouldn't fleece them too badly; that is, Leonardo did this, while his assistants were staring at all the women they saw, and imagining them naked on beds.

The coachman had five children and an ailing mother at home, but he seemed aware that his children's future could not possibly depend on the riches these three Apulians had hidden away in their pockets or their miserable-looking suitcases, and he charged them what would have been a reasonable price in Naples—not in Laterza however, where for half that money they could have traveled all the way from the station to the town: three miles of uninterrupted climb on the most primitive of roads, all dust in summer and a sea of mud in winter.

The hotel looked filthy enough to seem reliable financially if not hygienically; Leonardo had brought his own pillowcases from home, to avoid contact with tubercular or syphilitic pillows. The three men washed six times in the icy cold water of the small available basin before the water ran clear again as they rinsed and the hotel owner protested. "If this goes on all the time," he said, "I'll have to hire a special water carrier for you, and it will cost you money."

"Be patient," said Leonardo. "We just arrived. All travelers are filthy with soot."

"Not if they travel first-class."

"But this is a third-class hotel."

"I beg your pardon, this is the hotel where Dante Alighieri stayed when he came from Florence."

"Dante Alighieri was used to hell, and besides, that was a long time ago, and if you call this a modern hotel . . ."

"We have electric lights, which cost a lot of money and are definitely modern. If you want a primitive hotel, I can tell you where you'll find one, but it will cost you just as much as here, because I'm too honest. If I were dishonest, like most people today, I would charge you ten times the price I'm charging, and you would have to pay it."

"All right, we're glad you're honest, and we promise that we'll need much less water tomorrow than we did today. I am here on a matter of water. Do you know that we, in Apulia, have no water? This is why I, as the mayor of Laterza, have come here to address the Senate about this scandalous situation: our Camorristi keep the population in abysmally unhygienic conditions, and steal the funds allotted for the aqueduct by the government. But no longer, just wait and see after I've spoken to the Senators. . . ."

"You wait and see: nothing will happen."

"You're a pessimist."

"And you are living in the moon."

After a few hours spent on his bed without being able to sleep, because he was too excited, Leonardo decided to reread his speech once more; in fact, he declaimed it, pacing the little room between the three beds, the washbasin, the chest of drawers, and the window.

"Your Excellencies, and distinguished ladies and gentlemen in the gallery! It is the first time in my life that I have the honor to address the National Laticlavium, and of course this is a great honor. . . ." He paused here and changed the last three words to "the source of deep emotion. . . . May I therefore be allowed to read my speech, instead of improvising. To begin:

"Whatever woes and hardships the proud Roman Legions spread over the entire globe in their epoch, they also brought two good things: Roman Law and Roman Aqueducts. I purposely omit the Roman Roads, because without water there is no civilization. The Barbaric Invasions destroyed all traces of Roman culture in Italy; all they left, as sad reminders of a great past, were these huge arches in red brick, surmounted not by an elevated stream of clean water, but by an absurd dirt road in the sky, with a strange vegetation of bushes and even trees, seeded up there by the winds, together with the handful of sand they needed in order to grow. Now they serve only to still the thirst for historical knowledge in the minds of German archaeologists, who, in good Germanic fashion, pursue only one subject at a time: 'How did the Ancients live? Where can we dig the barren clay to find their bones and the jewels with which they were buried?' Never, not even by mistake, do they ask themselves: 'How do the modern inhabitants of this beautiful country live, without water or food, and why are they so stupid, so suspicious of each other and so unsuspecting of any foreigner who tosses them a coin to be led to the site of the nearest Etruscan tomb?' If they ever asked themselves this, they could find the answer simply by studying the living with the same interest they apply to the bones of the Etruscans. And here, Illustrious Senators of the Kingdom, is what they would find: that the living are more fit to be buried than to be kept alive. Their eyes are the breeding ground for flies from the day they are born, so they catch trachoma long before they can catch a glimpse of the blue sky of Italy, so dear to foreign tourists, and therefore to the Swiss hotel owners who paste colored pictures of Sunny Italy with their Grand Hotel in the center on the suitcases and trunks of foreign visitors. Illustrious Senators, why don't you pass a law forcing the hotel owners to pay two thirds of that money to the victims of trachoma—not directly to them, or it would go into the pockets of dishonest fathers who gamble and drink in the local taverns—but indirectly, earmarked as follows: half to the local administration, to be spent only for medical care of the poor, and half to the Senate of the Kingdom, so that it may make genuine progress towards the building of the aqueduct, without which no care of the sick will ever be possible? But let me continue with my picture of what the learned German archaeologists would find if they studied the living and not the dead. Worse than trachoma, Illustrious Senators of the Kingdom, is the Catholic Church, that stinking carrion polluting the air of this Eternal City, *where Christ is being traded all day long.** It is in the interests of the Church to keep people suspicious of one another, so they will never air their views in public nor decide on public action as a spur to public education. Mazzini said: Now that we have made Italy, we must make the Italians. But what we are seeing in Italy is nothing but the repetition of ancient patterns based on ancient class differ- ences. Correct Terminology would ask that we re-examine the terms RICH and POOR, REFINED and RUDE, NOBLE and HUMBLE. And, once we have done that, we will discover that the rich in our country, and especially in the South, are poor, rude and humble, i.e., poor in judgment, rude in manners and humble only before the Camorra or the rich foreigners whose daughters they marry, if the foreigner is stupid enough to let them do so, while the poor are only poor in cash or political influence, but rich in judgment, rich in am- bitions for their children, whom they want to educate, . . . and again let's examine this TERM *educate*, which in this particular case means TO LEAD OUT OF—OUT OF THE MORAL SEWER OF OUR FEUDAL NOBILITY, SPANISH IN ORIGIN, CATHOLIC IN EDUCATION AND PREDA- TORY IN NATURE. The poor day-laborers in the fields sweat blood to send their children to school, and if these children don't end in the Holy Latrine of the Catholic Clergy that gives them the perfect

* He was quoting Dante, *Paradiso*, XVII, v. 51.

education for a future life of crime, they may and often do become real erudites (again, this TERM means REFINED, MADE GENTLER, CLEANSED OF THE DIRT FROM WHICH IT SPRANG), from which I conclude that our destitute are perfectly well endowed with what it takes to make real NOBLES, real GENIUSES; real ITALIANS in short.

"This being the situation in Apulia, and in the rest of the former Spanish Colony, wrongly called the Kingdom of the Two Sicilies, I most humbly submit that Apulia, like the rest of the Kingdom, needs a moral aqueduct first and foremost, the waters of which must come from ANYWHERE but Rome, where moral waters drain from the river Styx! The *clear, sweet and fresh waters* (Petrarch) we need are to be found in those high towers of Modern Science, which rise mostly in the North, especially, I am ashamed to say, in our former Roman Colonies Gallia, Anglia, Batavia, Lutetia, Aquitania, Germania, and Pannonia, from which the Barbaric Hordes came to destroy our beautiful country. Yes, gentlemen, and may I add that this has been made possible thanks to Italian Emigration to these lands. Let's encourage our scholars to stay home and take care of their parents, figuratively speaking, restoring Italy to what it once was.

"Coming down to practical measures, I propose that Italy be closed to foreign tourists until the Bordello is demolished and from her ashes the PROUD WOMAN OF PROVINCES WITH HER CROWN OF TOWERS arises again. A curse on archaeological finds and their finders, who expropriate the farms and houses of the poor without compensation, to favor a few dusty Etruscan Corpses for so-called Cultural Reasons! On the eve of the war that will liberate our enslaved brothers from the barbaric Teuton monarchy, our Reasons for everything we do must be purely Patriotic!!"

When Peppino and Liborio came back to take Leonardo out for lunch, they found him smiling and nodding to a huge audience of Senators and select Roman citizens, who were all over the room, from way under the beds to way up on the ceiling. In vain did the two aldermen try to bring him down to the solid reality of what *they* had seen: fantastic women everywhere, and all willing to be approached, some even winking at them, and restaurants where the most unbelievable delicacies were being served at reasonable prices, and the white Roman wines, half-sweet, half-dry.

"How can you talk to me about such things," he asked indignantly, "when I must keep my mind clear to meet the greatest challenge of my life? In less than two hours, the fate of our aqueduct—"

"We know, we'll come with you, but we must eat, you especially."

"You go and eat, I'll eat later, this evening. And I shall go to the Senate alone."

They seemed a bit disappointed at first, but since he was the mayor, and they were only his assistants, there was nothing they could do but obey him, and as they closed the door behind them, they heard him answer some inaudible question by some invisible Senator, obviously a Socialist: "The sun of the future? Science, Your Excellency, Science, Progress, without it your Sun of the Future is the same moon of the past that made the Pope write his idiotic encyclical RERUM NOVARUM, against all Things Modern. Both you and the Catholics are Ptolemaic lunatics. Our modern Galileos are Koch, Pasteur and other such foreigners. Why are they not Italians? Is our national genius dead? Not at all, but we need special telescopes to discover the firmament of the infinitesimally small, and these are called microscopes and are all made in Germany. We can't afford them in the provinces, and yet our poorest villages can afford to spend the equivalent of a hundred microscopes in one day, the day of the local Patron Saint, who consumes our entire budget in a single hour of firecrackers, Bengal fires and rockets. Give us the money for microscopes, give us hospitals and water and disinfectants, and we shall have no need of your bloody Marxist midwife of History. Revolution is not new, but Science is."

Peppino and Liborio stopped listening from behind the closed door and went in pursuit of their luscious gastronomic and sexual realities, certain that Leonardo would never wonder why the "Senate" was so small and had so few Senators in it.

And they were right. Leonardo went to the address given him by Liborio, met the appointed Senator who was waiting for him, addressed a large reading room filled with elderly gentlemen snoozing in their armchairs or hiding behind open newspapers, and shamed them, shook them from their slumber, whipped them into patriotic action for the poor province of Apulia, all with his beautiful speech.

Proud as a magpie for having really shaken up the minds of the
illustrious Senators and sown the seed that would grow into aqueducts and great political reforms, Leonardo regretted that he had
asked his two town councilors not to accompany him to the Senate.
He had felt this would be unfair to them: they were such good
people, but ignorant, and they had only just reformed under the
influence of his relentless teachings in the correct terminology that
makes for correct thinking. To make them sit as silent witnesses
while he delivered his speech on a truly adult level to people truly
capable of understanding truly intellectual arguments, would have
been a concession to his vanity, thinly masked as part of his effort at
reforming them. Now he regretted it, because the echo of his great
words (especially the quotes from *The Divine Comedy*) exalted
him on his lonely walk through the streets of the Eternal City. He
had never been to Rome, and he had allowed himself one extra day
in his schedule for sightseeing, knowing that he might never come
again. He had avoided Rome on his honeymoon, because in Rome
there lived, or HAD lived, the girl he had met in Naples on that
now distant morning of February 3, 1893, when he was still a student in medicine, and she a fifteen-year-old blond and pale apparition from the fabulous North. They had met the first time through
the glass cube of a museum showcase protecting a beautiful Greek
amphora, and the second time in the same museum; a third meeting in front of her hotel had been arranged at the end of the second
and had been violently interrupted by a uniformed hotel doorman,
who had shooed Leonardo away like a cat from a banquet table. He
didn't care to remember this unpleasant detail. But his decision to
eschew Mary was part of a much wider decision to rise from that
sewer of mankind that was Naples and any other city, town or
village of the defunct Kingdom of the Two Sicilies, and become a
Citizen of the World, which, in those proud years of scientific
progress, could only mean a Citizen of the Century of Exact Sciences, a Futurian, ready to descend upon Earth from the Heaven of
Scientific Truth like a new, but not lone, Messiah: ONE OF A HOST
OF MESSIAHS, the Better Humanity of the year 2000.

Consolation of Science, how much truer than *The Consolation of
Philosophy* that had helped Boethius overcome the despair of his
long years in prison! Leonardo did not regret his decision of Febru-

ary 1893, but of course he had to keep reminding himself of all the good reasons for such a decision and of the false reasons he had given the girl, even though these false decisions, because they were so closely connected with the true decision, were also, in correct terminology, true. It was true he couldn't afford to abandon his unmarried sisters, he being the head of the family, after the death of his parents, it was true he had a moral obligation not only to his defunct parents, but also to the kindly priests of the Jesuit college where he had so brilliantly completed his studies a few years earlier, it was true he could never marry a Russian Orthodox AND Protestant, but it was equally true that money cures everything, even the scandal of heresy, if a few thousand gold rubles are thrown into the mouths of the hungry. BUT WASN'T THIS LIKE ADMITTING THAT HE WAS LIKE ALL THOSE OTHER ITALIANS FROM DOWN THERE? So, if he wanted to rise from the sewers and become a real man, he must sacrifice everything and say nothing.

These were the thoughts that came to him as he walked aimlessly through the mysterious streets of that beautiful city in the yellow light of sunset. There is something in the yellow sunsets of Rome that makes for melancholia, almost for madness. A strange solitude spreads over the whole city; even now, towards the end of the century, at the end of all ancient solitudes, in this coma of noise and pollution, those who remember Rome as it was at the beginning of the century still recognize it for what it is. Even those who at this moment are inhaling the cancers that will kill them around the year 2000 feel that this golden sky is too sumptuous for their poor small hearts, and withdraw from it in sadness, like dirty plebeians or the famous filthy cats of the Forum, shooed away from the spectacle of Caesar's Triumph by his armed legions. Rome is a city of death and not of life. The Roman conquest of Greece could only bring death to that great civilization, and the Christian conquest of Rome could only bring death to Christianity, by turning it into another false religion of power, cruelty, ignorance and waste. Dante could never have been born in Rome, nor could Giotto, while Michelangelo died just in time to avoid the ultimate degeneracy, which was achieved by his pupils and is known as the baroque. Dante's violent hatred of the papacy should have earned his poem the honor of being Number One on the Index, IF THE CHURCH OF ROME BELIEVED

IN WHAT IT PREACHED. But then one should never forget that the best in Protestantism was Tuscan, and came long before Luther. Giano della Bella, Fausto Sozzini and Dante himself were the only true Protestants: Luther was a tactless German with a definite taste for the baroque in his sick scatological style. . . .

Such were the thoughts that accompanied Leonardo that evening in Rome. He felt nostalgic, not for his books or his home or his patients and disciples, least of all for his wife, although she was young and attractive, but for some violent and NEW sensation, such as only the few married women in his hometown who were willing to do so could give him. They were not young, alas, and certainly not new, but at least they were trustworthy, they betrayed their husbands only with their physician, and the illegality of it all, plus the ever-changing circumstances and risks, made up for the lack of novelty. In Rome there were endless streets filled with whore-houses, but he stayed away from them. "Moral reasons," he said to himself, and repeated to his sons many years later, "are, in correct modern terminology, reasons of hygiene, and these alone allow you to abide by the Christian dictate: 'Do not do unto others, . . .' namely, don't spread venereal disease, or in Dante's great words: 'One must only fear those things that may harm others. . . .'" As for the danger of having the same kind of morality applied to him by his wife, any man worthy of the name knows first and foremost what he marries, which accounts for the great proverb *"Moglie e buoi dei paesi tuoi"* (wife and oxen from your own country), and secondly it is not a matter of will power but worthiness. None of the husbands he had cuckolded wanted their wives to betray them, but if they were betrayed, what could their will power do about it? Women, he said to himself, *have* no will power, they are utterly instinctual, which is why they need our support and direction; by the same token, we need theirs, because their instinct tells them whether a man deserves the sacrifice of all their impulses, when they are free to act as they please, without fear of detection. That is the supreme test: a woman's decision *against her own freedom* AND *instincts,* in favor of a man who deserves supreme respect, no matter how boring, ugly, cruel or impotent he may be. And man HAS it in him to overcome all his worst defects (just think of Dante, the most impossible character who ever lived), and be worthy of that sacrifice, *even if he is inspired by another woman.* See Dante again: for him Beatrice had become Muse, Holy Virgin, Essence of Woman-hood AND Knowledge. And I am sure that Mrs. Dante Alighieri, the mother of his nine children, who goes unmentioned in *The Divine Comedy* or elsewhere in his verse, NEVER betrayed him, because she felt the marriage of his spirit with the spirit of Beatrice to be above human judgment. She stayed faithful to both, thus forming a new trinity with them. No other man could have given her that glory. She must have guarded his empty bed as it is guarded now, six hundred years later, by the superintendent of fine arts, as a national monument. . . .

These thoughts, too, were in his mind, on his mind, in the fore-front, in the back, at the edges of his mind, circling and whistling and tearing the motionless gold of the sky with sudden black shapes that were no sooner seen than gone, right before his eyes, gone again, then back in the very same place, but far, far away, much smaller now in a sky even more sinister and streaked with orange and deep purple.

They were like birds at sunset, and this heightened his solitude, because even the birds were happy and he was not. He passed tavern after tavern, all with their chairs and tables crowding the streets and squares like stage props before the play begins—and slowly now it was beginning: people were moving the chairs, sitting on them and inserting their legs under the tablecloth as they pulled the table towards the chair or made the chair perform a funny frog-dance under their buttocks to reach the table. Beautiful ladies and well-dressed gentlemen, sitting next to poor day-laborers and shep-herds in their dirty costumes, all indifferent to one another except for their partners in the orgy. Nowhere in the cafés or restaurants of his hometown or even of the great city of Naples had he seen such a mingling of classes and means: poverty and wealth seemed to pale into insignificance because all shared in the triumph of Caesar, of Bacchus, of Venus, of Mammon, the invisible gods speaking through the tinkling of glasses, the color of wine, the perfume of tomato sauce, fresh bread, frying eggplant and roasting lamb. If only he had his wife with him . . . HOW HE WOULD HATE HER was the silent ending of his thought, and it surprised him, be-cause this was the first time since his marriage five years before that he had dared think of her with hostility. And now a sudden realization of a deeper unhappiness came surging to the fore: he could have spoken for hours about her and against her, with the same eloquence he had used in the Senate, but this time to any of those audiences in any of the open-air theaters behind blossoming pink oleander trees in tubs. He knew that if she had been with him, she would have been his only audience; not a chance of saying anything new, clever, deep or even superficial: only the trite conversation of a provincial husband with a provincial wife, not talking for each other's benefit, but for a wider audience they must pretend to despise and to shun. This wider audience is well aware of the comedy and is bored, because it knows the script by heart. The audience of a provincial southern Italian restaurant or café is eternally the same: every member of it a policeman of *mores*, a controller of the fortunes and honor (manliness, in correct terminology) of their fellow human beings WHEN ACCOMPANIED BY THEIR WIVES, because, when the male is alone he must join the Supreme Court that sits permanently in judgment of the absent citizen. (A man seated with his wife is *absent*, even though loud and cordial greetings are exchanged between the couple and the Supreme Court, and precautions are taken by the Court to use the language of physiognomy or speak in whispers, so that the female creature be spared what she has no right to hear anyway.) This of course is well-known to the husband, because he was doing the selfsame thing a few minutes earlier, before he went home to pick up his wife because it was her day to be seen in public, and he will do it again, the moment he comes back after having taken the beast to the stable and made sure that the beast-keeper (or female relative) is now in charge. He rushes straight back to the Supreme Court and is greeted with joy; he may even sigh with relief, without betraying his inner opinion of his wife: does one have opinions about a bed, a nightshirt or a coat hanger? And he expects to receive compliments, either directly or in the form of greater respect, if his wife has been wearing the silk dress or the jewels that testify to his success. In correct terminology it is *he who wears the wife who wears the dress and/or jewelry*. As for the honor, it is shown in the expression of utter disgust *she* registers on her face, whenever she catches a glimpse of other males, plus the expression of ecstasy her face must register whenever she looks at her husband. This means "he is terrific in bed, and I can't control myself in public." Whereupon the Rule prescribes he should frown at her and whisper words of reprimand, or be seen to blush like a little child. If at that moment he catches a glimpse of his colleagues on the Bench, a slow, almost imperceptible bowing of the whole Supreme Juridical Body notifies him of the Court's congratulations. Respectful jokes will be made about this later, upon his return, and they must all be accompanied by much laughter and violent pats on the back. Someone may even say (in jest, of course): "If only you were dead, . . ." meaning one knows that only death could ever separate him from his beloved wife. Which is a great incentive for him to live a long and healthy (in correct terminology, sexually active) life. Leonardo had no children, and didn't want any, but he hated to think that the Supreme Court might be wondering: Is it *he* or *she* who can't? . . . And how often do they, anyway? Dangerous item of legal conversation this, between judges. The childless citizen lives under a heavy cloud of suspicion. Venus in heaven only knows: does he have a venereal past that makes him sterile or impotent? And is it IMPOTENTIA COEUNDI or IMPOTENTIA GENERANDI? Leonardo hated such thoughts, and yet they came to him, just like the whistling swallows of Rome, flying low above the tables of the open-air cafés and restaurants.

Now suddenly he became aware that the absence of his two councilors would make it impossible for him to dine, hungry as he was. With them, he could have commented on the beautiful women seated at other tables, and on the pompous asses with them, tried to catch a glimpse of their eyes and read the Truth in them: in the men fear of the "horns," upon seeing what dashing males were seated so close to their wives or mistresses (or sisters, or daughters; all potential horn-breeders); in the women fear and/or desire of decorating the male's head with horns. But how could Leonardo play such a game all alone? He could of course concentrate on religious thoughts about the Harmony of the Spheres in Pythagoras or on social thoughts of reform, or clinical thoughts about the right diagnosis for this or that patient. But not in Rome. In Laterza or Castellaneta or Montescaglioso or Acquaviva delle Fonti, he was known and respected. Here in Rome he was a nonentity. Not that

he cared, but it disturbed him to be mistaken for just another
scrivener or accountant or merchant, like the ones he saw seated at
other tables, all illiterates, from the way they spoke, and all dressed
like him: all from the South, all distinguished by the fact that they
wore mourning, either because they had lost a relative in the course
of the last ten or fifteen years (the suits showed the length of their
suffering), or because they had never had the money to buy themselves two suits of clothes: one black for mourning, and one gray for
all occasions. Those who could afford a third white suit in summer
must be at least university professors or high government officials.
Or nobles who had married a rich wife, or terrorized their tailor into
fitting them for free. Leonardo felt the eyes of the women on him,
but especially the eyes of the men, who were judging him as a
nonentity. He even thought he had heard the words "Some puny
provincial pharmacist or notary public from Down There." Had his
two councilors been with him, he would have spoken knowingly
and loudly on matters of such beauty and depth as to charm any
woman and shame any man on whatever social level. But alone?
How could he hope to be known and respected, with no one to talk
to? Since he couldn't eat dinner, how was he going to spend the
evening? After winning such a great moral victory in the Senate,
shouldn't he celebrate in some way? Dante provided the right quote
for the occasion:

> *Come cadesti, o quando,*
> *Da tanta altezza in così basso loco?*

(How did you fall, or when, from such heights to such a low place?)
He tried to escape the restaurants, but there were too many. The
happy tinkling of glasses, dishes, forks and knives, the laughter, the
song, the rehearsed speeches made for an audience of ONE DIVINE
WOMAN tables away, reached him and made him feel like crying.

Like Dante, describing his moral degradation in the middle of the
journey of "our" life. Why *our* and not *my* life? he kept thinking.
But why even think of this, since I never became a Dante scholar?
He dismissed the old regret, and went on repeating under his
breath Dante's description of how he had met Virgil who had been

sent him by Beatrice, to show him the road to heaven. And, lo and
behold, miracle of miracles, he found himself in front of a theater
reading the title of a play in huge red letters:

R E S U R R E C T I O N

B Y

C O U N T   L E O   T O L S T O Y

Tolstoy . . . his favorite author (after Dante, of course). He had
read none of Tolstoy's books, had not the slightest intention of
reading any, first of all because novels (except for *I Promessi Sposi*
by Manzoni, or *The Golden Ass* by Apuleius,) were not for men (a
poor substitute for the whorehouse in the years of dwindling sexual
power), and, secondly, because he had learned from a relative who
taught foreign literature in a "modern" (in correct terminology,
INFERIOR) school, that this man Tolstoy, whose patronymic was
Tolstoyevsky, had written about the scandalous adventures of an
unfaithful wife and a stupid cavalry officer, then about the great
Napoleon (and Leonardo hated Napoleon), then about degenerate
people, epileptics, anarchists and the like, and in the end had set
himself up as a new Messiah, the better to spread his gospel of civil
disobedience and anarchy. And yet despite all this Tolstoy was his
favorite author, especially tonight, coming to his rescue in a way so
similar to that of Virgil rescuing Dante in the dark forest of midlife.

How providential and how modern, compared with Dante's rescue! For a very modest price (as a substitute for an abundant evening meal with plenty of good wine to make him forget about sex, it
was a mere nothing), he could kill time until midnight, being resurrected from the pitfall of gloomy or dishonest thoughts with the
help of his adored Tolstoy. How many precious images the divine
name evoked in him already!!! If I were a believer and this were a
beautiful cathedral with music and all that, I couldn't feel more
purified than I already do, and this is only the beginning, he
thought, as he sat down in a comfortable orchestra seat such as he
wished he had in his living room at home, which his stupid wife had
filled with the wedding present requested from all her combined
relatives: the ugliest and least comfortable living room furniture

ever seen. And how she insisted on using it, now that he had become mayor! No longer could he sit in the kitchen, sipping coffee
after dinner before going to bed: the living room it had to be,
AFTER the dining room for meals; a double torture twice a day
makes four sessions of hell (to her it was heaven). . . . But then,
why think of her? All wives are stupid, in fact, all women are,
EXCEPT FOR MY MOTHER AND MY SISTERS. With this classical Italian
conclusion, the few remaining clouds of discontent were gone, and
his thoughts were all of Tolstoy.

And of the girl who had first made him aware of Tolstoy: Mary,
heavenly apparition that had lasted but a day or two and even then
only for less than an hour each time. The first day they spoke at
that museum in Naples, her third sentence to him had been: "Have
you read *Anna Karenina?*"

"Who's that: a Russian writer?"

"No, the writer is Tolstoy, the same man who wrote *War and
Peace.* He also wrote *Anna Karenina.* Great writer . . ."

"I don't care. After reading that smile on your face, I don't need
any books ever again: I need you to guide me as the sun or the
moon guides the lost wanderer on the long road of life, until he
reaches its conclusion."

He had spoken these words without really meaning them, yet
with all the passion of belief (in correct terminology, RELIGION,
from the Latin RE-LIGERE, binding in book form the best of our
knowledge) hoping to God his words might come true in the
future. He had in fact thought of Dante and Beatrice, lost loves to
him already, because he was studying medicine, not *Lettere e Filo-
sofia.* Had he told her what he knew, it would have further dampened the effect of the divine apparition she most certainly was.
And since he also knew that she was not alone in the museum, and
that in a matter of seconds the idiot who was with her (a Neapolitan widower-idiot he knew only too well) would come to rescue her
from him, why not make the best of it and speak as if she really
were the One and Only in the whole Universe?

And what did he know, that had already dampened the effect of
that knowledge in which *faith* brings to *fact* the confirmation of its
factualness?

Two things:

I. A foreign girl who choses that type of Italian is no wife for any man worthy of the name.

II. A foreign girl who can betray the man she has already chosen with the first man who smiles at her in a museum is *definitely* not worthy of any man worthy of the name. And now he also knew that she read novels, and a girl who reads novels is capable of anything. God only knows what kind of parents she has, if they allow her to read novels and to marry that kind of an idiot!

So, in conclusion, he could only thank God that she would soon be gone from his sight forever, and also for the victory God had allowed him to win over the widower-idiot. Now that he had made him a cuckold, he didn't envy him any more. Let him go blindly to his fate, which was that of growing horns so huge *da non passare le porte* (as to be unable to get through doors).

These were the memories that came back to him as he watched the dazzling spectacle of a theater filled with elegant people. He decided to concentrate only on the boxes, because there the display of bejeweled ladies and dignitaries was at its highest; the whole audience in the orchestra was watching the rich people perform, and would watch them again after the intermission. Which intermission, Leonardo concluded, in correct terminology is the play. As he glanced at the various boxes, his eyes fell on a young lady whose décolletage he found most exciting. There was a grace of movement in those shoulders, in those long, white gloves encasing almost the whole arm, now abandoned on the red velvet of the balustrade. His eyes were glued to the movement of hands and shoulders in the box. The lights were now dimmed and finally extinguished, because the curtain was about to be raised and the play to begin. Slowly, unwillingly, with sighs, even murmurs of protest, the audience in the orchestra turned away from the play of wealth and manners in the boxes and faced the "false" play on stage, already prejudiced against it because here the pretense was poorly sustained by poor voices, false jewels, cheap tailoring and stilted manners. Leonardo had never been to a play before, except the Passion Plays in his hometown and in the Jesuit college later, and he thought he knew everything about the theater, namely that it was silly, because the great Greek tragedians were dead and could only be enjoyed with the help of footnotes, Shakespeare was all in that colonial language

the Romans had allowed to grow because Latin clarity is impossible
in the fog and the rain, and French theater was only for whores and
syphilitic aristocrats from the Twin Kingdom, who spent their last
coins in Paris each year on the latest creations in syphilis, then
boasted with their inferiors at the café back home that they knew
life!

Only in the opera did Leonardo like the pretense and the cheap
props, because music redeems everything. This Tolstoyevsky Tolstoy
was just as bad on stage as in his novels, and he was glad of this
sobering reminder, because he was already too upset by the resur-
gence of memories, staring at those naked shoulders and those glittering earrings under that double cloud of blond hair and black lace
on top of it, surmounted by a diadem of blond hairpins.

Resurrection indeed! he said to himself, sneering. She served her
purpose as my muse when I had to pass all those exams and stay
chaste, but now that I am a doctor and a mayor in charge of real
people and real issues, I don't need all that sentimental marsh-
mallow.

But the devil has ways with nonpoets that cannot be circum-
vented and, once the lid has been lifted on the sweet memories of
youth, there is no sealing it again on Pandora's box. The *nonpoet*
Leonardo groaned in his seat; he now wished his wife were with
him. How he would throw himself on her body in their hotel room
after the theater. . . . And how grateful she would be, and how
unsuspecting of the real cause of such effusions. Now he regretted
he hadn't sent her a postcard on arrival, saying: *Rome is beautiful,
wish you were here, passionate kisses.* He couldn't do it if it was
only *she* he had in mind; he had been back in Naples for five days
in the third year of his marriage, for purely professional reasons, and
had stuck to these same reasons for five days, thinking of her only
with terror; namely, with the normal reaction of all husbands after
the first years of infatuation. The last day, shortly before leaving
Naples, he had caught a glimpse of a young woman just his type
and this had finally evoked lascivious images of his wife. It would
have been impossible to follow the girl: first of all, it was late, he
was already seated in his third-class carriage, with his heavy suitcase
stored away on the rack, under other suitcases and baskets, and,
secondly, even if he had been able to jump down from the train at

the last minute, what was the point of such erratic behavior? He would have missed his train, spent money to get out of the station, more for another night at the hotel, still more to send a telegram saying: OWING TO UNEXPECTED DELAY NOT COMING TODAY LETTER FOLLOWS PASSIONATE KISSES LEONARDO, and all assuming the right outcome; namely, that the girl could be approached and conquered—and how was such a thing possible? She seemed to be alone, but there were two factors to consider: (I) she was probably waiting for her husband (fiancé, brother or father) on the express train that was about to arrive from Rome, or (II) her father, fiancé, brother or husband had just gone to the latrine or to buy a newspaper. A woman as strikingly pure in her beauty COULD NOT BE A WHORE (namely, a woman who goes to the station alone), and IF, BY SOME IMPOSSIBLE HYPOTHESIS, SHE WERE ALONE AND RESPECTABLE, would she give in to him so easily? Not for at least ten days of intense courtship. AND EVEN THEN, how could he be certain she was not a syphilitic whore? A woman who gives in as easily as all that can be nothing else, AND BESIDES he was a married man, AND BESIDES he had duties, important public duties to perform as a mayor, AND BESIDES he had his Aesculapian ministry awaiting him, and could he ruin his reputation, his family life, his public career, his profession and his conscience, AND HIS FINANCES, on such a doubtful hypothesis? Never. So he had stayed on the train, wishing, indeed praying to God she might soon be joined by the most forbidding father and/or etc. The train left, AND SHE SMILED AT HIM, no mistaking that for a smile *to herself*, SHE HAD GIVEN HIM THE SIGNAL, and for the whole trip, twelve hours on that hard seat, Leonardo had suffered all the pangs of hell, and even back home he had thought of her for days and nights on end, but to no constructive purpose in bed, because the nearness of his wife and her insistence had repelled him beyond belief, and she had even questioned his virility to make him function, with the result that he, at the late age of thirty, since arrangements could not be made so suddenly to alert one of his women patients and see her in a safe place, had been forced to masturbate in the latrine, his eyes closed, his mind fixed on that girl at the Naples station. Aaah, he concluded, moaning with shame at the memory of that ultimate fall, if only women were not so foolish as to fall for the first idiot the moment they are left unguarded, life would be so much easier. But then it isn't their fault. God knows what kind of a family she came from. With these modern trends towards freedom and sentimentality, CAUSED ESPECIALLY BY NOVELS, there is no limit to wickedness. . . .

And now, for the first time since his spectacular victory over his basest instincts in 1893, which had won him the *summa cum laude*, he allowed himself to re-examine Mary and dismiss her forever from his memory.

Yes, there was a resemblance between Mary and that girl at the station (although Mary, being Nordic and blond, was far more beautiful); the resemblance (and he had never thought of it) was between their characters. Let's see, let's study her, let's anatomize Beatrice, now that I am no longer the most erudite man of my time, nor a Dante scholar. Mary, too, was the first to smile through that glass case, perhaps more innocently than the other girl, but no less dangerously for me, and I was easily fooled by her story that the widower-idiot Gennariello Martirana didn't mean anything to her. If he didn't, why did she agree to go out ALONE with him? And to be seen by all his acquaintances ALONE WITH HIM IN A MUSEUM? I didn't ask her, and why? Because I was already infatuated to the point where she could have cuckolded me without my knowing the first thing about it. How lucky I was to be rid of her in such a short time. . . . And how clever, to use the excruciating pain of surgery performed on my own live flesh with my own hands, to strengthen my will and overcome so many obstacles to my doctor's degree. . . . But the pain. . . . I could not do it again now. Thirty-two is not twenty-three. . . . Blessed youth, rich in temptations, but also in strength . . . where art thou gone? . . . But let's not dwell on sad thoughts. The only thing I can do now is to clear my overloaded memories of the last remnants of youth, and say, ADDIO GIOVINEZZA. . . .

He had tears in his eyes, and the spectators next to him admired him for being so involved in the play. They were still craning their necks to catch some activity in the boxes, despite the lack of light, and Leonardo became angry. What right did they have to look in that direction? Could they have a rich past such as he was remembering? Did they know foreign girls as intimately as he had known Mary? No, they were young and obviously uncharming. Which

made him still angrier, so he stared at them furiously to remind
them that they were supposed to look *that* way, not *elsewhere*,
causing disturbance. It worked: the two young men seated on either
side complied, blushing and muttering insults under their breath.
But now he himself felt tempted to turn his head and look at the
box. "The Malignant One (namely, the devil) is forever ready to
lead us astray," he murmured to himself inaudibly, so as not to be
mistaken for a defrocked priest. But he could only look at the stage
if his thoughts were retelling the drama he had cherished, untold,
for nine years. Thus an old banner, kept folded in camphor for centuries, will turn to dust the moment it is unfurled again, even
though it has been given every protection against moths. The moths
of time are deadlier, they leave nothing intact.

Memento quia pulvis es, et in pulvere reverteris, he recited to
himself, folding his hands like a priest, and now his ancient drama
unfolded before his eyes, and he relived things he had entirely
forgotten in the space of a near decade: he had seen Mary *four*
times; the whole story had lasted *four* weeks, perhaps longer; it had
almost killed his future, by making him lose all interest in his
exams. Oh, how much braver he had been than he had thought he
was, and how much more foolhardy, challenging gods that do not
forgive. . . . Here are the four scenes he saw on stage:

Scene I. Sudden letdown in the tension of study, caused mainly
by the season. February 3, even in the North of Italy, is the turning
point. And in the Year of Our Lord 1893 winter was definitely over
on February 3. Had it been a cold day, winter would have lasted
another forty days, according to tradition. So Leonardo and the
other three honor students in their last year of medicine—Peppino
Luccibelli of Naples, Donato Civetta of Cerignola in Apulia, and
Giulio Calace of Bengazi in Libya—have decided to stroll lazily
along the Bay of Naples; that is, along Via Caracciolo, basking in
the sunshine and looking at women.

Scene II. Suddenly, from the entrance of the best hotel in the city,
the Hotel Vesuvio, they see a fantastically beautiful blond girl,
probably English or American, emerge in the company of none
other than the thirty-five-year-old Professor Gennariello Martirana,
an archaeologist who had always been provided with enough money
by his lawyer father to study what he wanted (archaeology was even

less lucrative in those days than psychiatry); he had only managed
to become a professor through Daddy's political influence: a junior
Camorrista, *figlio di papà,* or Daddy's boy (in correct terminology, a
rich idiot). He had then married a very rich girl, again only because
of Daddy's connections, and been fortunate enough to lose her after
only three years of the usual Neapolitan marriage: wife at home,
husband at the club or the café, when not at the casino (alias the
whorehouse). And of course he would only marry again if he found
a girl much richer than his first wife, owing to the proverb that says,
"He who loses his first wife and remarries is unworthy of his loss"—
meaning not indeed that he should mourn her, but that he doesn't
know how lucky he is. What could be better than childless widower-
hood with a good dowry still intact, because your defunct wife has
had no time to spend it all on house and children? (Or even on you
but definitely not for the "casino," making it harder for you to justify your secret expenses?) Obviously the blond beauty must be rich
enough to tempt Gennariello, who did have enough brains to
understand the proverb and a few other bits of Neapolitan wisdom
on the same near-animal level. The four medical students despised
him especially for that, as they despised all Italians with that mentality; but then they also despised the Socialists who were trying to
oppose people like that and whose only manifestation of freedom
consisted of setting fire to school benches, laboratory equipment
and official records, and shouting obscenities at their professors in
the name of Marx, Bakunin and Proudhon. The four students had
ideals, even though their fortunes differed. Civetta and Luccibelli
were very rich, Calace a little less so, but still quite well off, while
Leonardo was not only poor, but poor with a heavy atavistic obligation towards a nonexistent wealth: there had been a severe crisis in
1884; at that time Leonardo's father had lost all his money and
therefore his position as a *galantuomo* (or gentleman) with three
generations of wealth to set him in a higher class than the horse-
dealers, bull-tamers and administrators of other people's estates, and
the sailors and clerks for their fishing fleets. His seven daughters
would therefore be eligible only as the future wives of people beneath him, perhaps even (perish the thought) of illiterate day-
laborers, because he had no title. And his one and only son could
not afford to let this happen to his sisters while *he* completed his

studies in letters and philosophy (with a view to specializing in
ancient history and/or archaeology). He owed it to his ancestors to
put the family back on that high level from which they could despise the absentee landlords as they deserved to be despised, but
then he owed it to himself to do something for the poor, on whose
toil the absentee landlords whored and lived, so he gave up letters
and the study of the dead to take up medicine.

Now that Leonardo's parents had died he had become a new
Gulliver in Lilliput: tied to the ground by every hair on his body
(namely, his sisters and the infinite links between him and his
ancestors)—and the puny Lilliputians were all the people, rich and
poor, titled or untitled, learned or illiterate, who had no ideals.
Therefore his hatred of Gennariello was both personal and prin-
cipled.

Scene III. Gennariello and the blond beauty stroll along the Via
Caracciolo while the four medical students follow him from a distance, trying not to be seen by him, in order not to give him too
great a satisfaction, but trying at the same time to overhear their
conversation; they can only hear *him. She* is obviously in love with
the whole city of Naples, the blue sky, the blue sea, the gray-blue
shapes of islands and mountains in the distance, the white-gray
pinnacle of smoke peacefully rising from the crater of Vesuvius, and
Gennariello is trying to appear as if he alone were the cause of so
much love. The four students comment on the cheapness of this
trick and liken it to those of poor beggars, who hire starving and
crippled children by the day on a commission basis, and they conclude that Gennariello's trick is far more reprehensible, because he
should know better in that he belongs to a better class, whether he
deserves it or not; a classical education is a form of knighthood, that
is the whole point of humanism: knowledge is nobility, hence the
Latin proverb

> *Quo doctior*
> *eo nequior*

(the more one knows, the more evil one becomes).

The four friends always sounded like four ascetics discussing the
meanings and modes of their mystical experiences, even when the

occasion for their dialogue was as unascetic as the pursuit of a beautiful blonde for the purpose of cuckolding someone and then dropping the girl because she wasn't worthy of their further attention. In this case she was doubly unworthy, because she was going around with a man unchaperoned and because this man was Gennariello. Would any of them want to be known as his successor in love? They were appalled by the very thought. Yet they had to admit she did look so angelic as to deserve to partake of God without confession (in correct terminology, she was by nature incapable of evil, i.e., like the Holy Virgin). But then to trust appearances . . . The more angelic they look, the more sinful they are. . . .

To this they also agreed, although with a certain reluctance, because the girl did seem extremely innocent, so their ultimate defense against temptation was in that proverb: "Wife and oxen from your own country." And thus, without noticing where they were going, they found themselves in front of the National Museum and saw Gennariello and the girl go inside.

Scene IV. "Let's go back to work now," said Donato Civetta. "We've had enough of a break in our work. If we go in here we'll become interested in something that really is interesting, and it'll be the end of our day."

"What?" said Giulio Calace. "Do you want to give up right now, just when it's getting exciting? I want to shame Gennariello at his worst; namely, while he is producing the finest gems of his great knowledge for her. I have never heard him lecture, and I bet you anything that he knows less than we do, and *we* aren't professors of archaeology."

"Giulio is right," said Peppino Luccibelli, "and I think we can really give him the lesson he deserves, then take the girl out to a café, where everybody will see us, and then take her back to the hotel, and make an appointment with her for the first day after our exams—an hour after—less, ten minutes, the time it takes to run from the university to the Hotel Vesuvio."

"No," said Leonardo. "That won't do. I agree with Giulio, provided Donato comes, too, but I don't think we should take the girl to a café, even if she accepts our invitation, because that would put us in the same category as all the other Italians we so despise; in fact, you, Peppino, have revealed that you belong to it already, and I defy you ever to go near that girl or speak to her."

This unleashed all hell between Peppino and Leonardo, and it took Giulio and Donato's good offices to make peace again, and that only when Leonardo had everybody against him for a more serious reason than just the dubious honor of a girl whose stupidity was beyond doubt, because (as Leonardo had repeatedly agreed until then) she had agreed to go out with an old man of thirty-five, who was also quite obviously an idiot and a vulgarian. The "more serious reason" was a more serious reason indeed, more perhaps in Leonardo's own opinion than in the opinion of his three friends; namely, that he couldn't afford to waste one more minute of his time in thoughts that might lead him astray from his exams.

Peppino had taken offense at Leonardo's accusation and Leonardo had asked him to apologize for offending the girl's honor, and their voices had become quite shrill, their gestures quite threatening, their faces quite ferocious, when Donato came up with *his* more serious reason.

"Just a moment, gentlemen, just a moment, before we transcend to ways of fact" (*"trascendiamo a vie di fatto,"* a typical Italian expression to describe the passage from words to blows). ". . . I am the eldest here, it is my right to have the last word. And in my opinion we all owe ourselves an apology for allowing such trifles to mar our friendship and disturb our serenity of mind which should belong only to our work until we have passed our exams. We are all equally guilty and this is why we go off on a tangent and get unnecessarily excited over nonexistent issues. This said, I agree with Leonardo on one point only: it wouldn't be decorous for us, both as *men* and as *Italians*, to show disrespect for the girl by approaching her as a group. One of us should give Gennariello a lesson, and it is better if it is one who can also catch Gennariello's blunders in archaeology. Peppino is not interested in the subject; I am, but am afraid of spending the whole day in the museum and going back there tomorrow again, so the choice is between Giulio and Leonardo."

Giulio took one glance at Leonardo and said: "I can see that the girl means more to Leonardo than she does to me, so I gladly surrender in his favor."

And Leonardo blushed and said: "Oh, I really don't care about the girl as such, only about us as Italians, and our reputation with foreigners in general, no matter what their sex or age. . . . And of course I hate to see ANY rich woman taken in by that unworthy Camorrista."

Donato paused a moment to observe Leonardo more closely before he gave his consent, then said: "Tell me, on your word of honor, Leonardo, have you seen the girl before?"

"Never, I swear," said Leonardo, blushing even more.

"You don't have to be afraid of me. I'm not the Father Prefect at the Jesuit monastery where you grew up. I am a friend and a colleague, and a human being like you, with the same weaknesses and passions. Tell me if you have played a trick on us all by leading us to the Hotel Vesuvio this morning." A chorus of laughter from the other two greeted Donato's words, and Leonardo, out of his wits with anger, shouted, "You are an idiot, Donato! What reason could *I* have to do such a stupid thing?"

"I don't know . . . but I can think of one: to enlist our help in your fight against temptation, without telling us—"

"*Me?* Are you *crazy?* Why wouldn't I have *told* you the whole truth, if THIS were the truth? I'm not a Jesuit!!!!"

"That remains to be seen. You WERE one, and you rebelled against them, but psychology teaches—"

"Psychology teaches my ass!!!" yelled Leonardo in his face, then looked to the others for approval, while trying to appear defiant of them at the same time. He had betrayed himself and was ashamed of it. But little did they know how much he had already struggled in the last four days against that very temptation, and how many times in the course of an hour he had changed position, from one extreme to the other. It was either clear as sunshine that this was the woman of his life, and a life without her meant nothing, or that a man must live his life alone with his God or his ideal (same thing), and woman must be no more than one of the ribs outside his heart. This is what the Jesuits had taught him, and this was the knowledge he had found himself cursed with upon leaving their rule. They had broken his will before the age of seven, as was their method, but it had been broken at home before even the Jesuits had done so, by the sight of a violent alcoholic father whose every absurd command had been humbly heeded by a meek and self-sacrificing mother, always in full control of her reactions but also in full possession of her judgment, and the child had seen everything and had learned. He had remained with the dream of a mother like his, to whom to atone for his father's misdeeds by serving her as if she were a goddess. What the Jesuits had done was to make his confusion still greater, by strengthening the image of that mother with their own cult of the Mother of God, and Leonardo remembered their theatricals only too well: thundering sermons by the most eloquent of his teachers, accusing the students of masturbating (in Jesuit terminology, committing acts against Purity) and thus defiling the Mother of God. "Defilers and murderers of your own mother! Repent, ye worms in the service of Satan!!! Hear her cry for her lost sons. See her in tears!!!!" These sermons were always held at night, in almost complete darkness. At that precise moment the doors of the lecture hall would be opened, and a statue of the Virgin in tears carried in by chanting priests while more chanting clerics, the youngest, the purest sons of bitches and liars in Holy Confession, carried huge candles, like burning pricks sputtering sperm at the top. "Kneel!!! Kneel in front of Our Mother and implore her to forgive you!!!!" And the whole class would kneel, and moan and sob aloud, some of the students would faint, others have convulsions, it never failed, even though the trick was familiar to all of them from many such previous experiences. These were the emotional hangovers that made Leonardo unable to decide whether *any* woman should be shunned as a prostitute or worshipped as a mother. Which is why he had led his friends into a secret trap on February 3, 1893, without telling them that he had met the girl four days before at the museum: the clever little bitch had cheated her own mother to talk to him, beckoned by his first smile. . . . He had seen her again, minutes later, in an open horse carriage. He bought a rose from a florist in front of the museum, rushed to the carriage, gave the rose to the girl and fled before her mother could see him. Thus (he concluded now, March something 1902, at the theater in Rome), thus it CANNOT have been February 3, 1893, that I saw Mary with Gennariello, it MUST have been February 7, therefore

the SECOND time, and here I have forgotten such important details
in the most important episode of my life, and why?

CUI BONO?

Not for my own good, certainly, but for hers.

PARCE SEPULTO

(Ye shall forgive the buried.)

DE MORTUIS NIL NISI BONUM

(Ye shall speak nothing but good of the dead.) Two holy precepts
I did abide by, but the Lord only knows at what price. . . . And
now new scenes began to unfold before his eyes, scenes of horrible
temptations he had yielded to, because his three friends had let him
go into the museum, instead of rebuking him. They had egged him
on, in fact, and told him in so many words: WE TRUST YOUR JUDG-
MENT. YOU ALONE ARE THE ARBITER!

SUAE QUISQUE FORTUNAE FABER EST

(Everyone is the blacksmith of his own fortune.) Such a stupid
expression, this, only remembered because it is the classical example
of the first oddity one encounters in Latin syntax: the use of
quisque (everyone), which can never be put at the beginning of a
sentence. Thus, in any modern language this reads: *of his own
everyone fortune blacksmith is.*

And Donato, that fool, had washed his hands of the whole thing,
because he himself was tempted by the girl, and so *pretended* that
the ancient artifacts were what would constitute a danger to him, if
he entered the museum. . . . Thus he (and the others with him)
had simply delivered Leonardo *into* the hands of the devil, rather
than *from* them.

Leonardo was in tears over his most glorious resurrection from the pits of satanic temptation *nine long years previously.*

ADDIO GIOVINEZZA

he mumbled to himself once more, sobbing freely into his handkerchief, as the first (or second?) act ended, and the audience applauded.

The young vulgarians who had almost caused him to create a scandal before the first act were now so awed by the sight of his tears that they rose from their seats and actually helped him leave the row, then volunteered to help him get out of the theater and call a carriage. He thanked them with a brotherly smile and a kind word, grateful that someone in Rome should treat him with the respect due a *sacerdos asclepii* and a mayor who had addressed the Senate of the Kingdom that same day. He alone knew the real cause of his sobs: HUNGER. And as a reward for that long day of great trials and great solitude he allotted himself an extra sum to be spent now *in the best restaurant in Rome.* But the young vulgarians wouldn't leave him alone. Perhaps they thought he was one of their own class, who might enjoy their company for the rest of the evening . . . perhaps they had decided he was the typical provincial pharmacist or country doctor who could be cleaned out of his money on his first evening in Rome. This thought sobered him up at once. "Thank you," he said curtly, "I need no company." He wished to God he could introduce some tiny reference to his political connections in the Senate, something like "You don't know whom you're talking to," but recoiled in burning shame from the vulgar temptation, which, alas, is almost irresistible in that cesspool of filth, the so-called Eternal City. But nothing seemed to scare those vulgarians away. THEY WANTED HIS ATTENTION.

"What is it?" he shouted, shaking their filthy hands away from his shoulder and pretending to brush it clean, so as to convey the message to all around him, many of them obviously distinguished people, who were beginning to protest because he and HIS FRIENDS were blocking their way. But now not only the vulgarians, even the most distinguished gentlemen and ladies were talking to him: "Someone's calling you."

He looked up, and THERE WAS MARY, BECKONING TO HIM WITH
BOTH ARMS AND CALLING HIS NAME ALOUD!!!!

The reasons he waved back with such enthusiasm and shouted,
"Vengo, vengo" (I'm coming, I'm coming), were ALL VULGAR.
Hunger and solitude again were responsible for his giving in to such
a cheap temptation. And yet . . . and yet . . . As he ran up the
stairs to reach the box in which he could find Mary, guided by the
very vulgarians he had treated so badly (he would never have found
that box without their help), he was ACTUALLY apostrophizing
Virgil, _Purgatory_, Canto XXX, verses 46–48:

> Men che dramma
> Di sangue m' è rimaso che non tremi;
> Conosco i segni dell' antica fiamma

(less than a drop of blood is left me that doesn't tremble; I know
the signs of the ancient flame). He thanked his friends (honoring
them with that title) as he hurriedly shook hands with them before
ordering them to leave, so as not to have them around Mary now
that he had found her again (one never knows), and again was
briefly tempted to tell them about his address to the Senate of the
Kingdom that very afternoon, but forgot all this as soon as he
knocked on the door and heard a strong female voice say: "Come
in." What he said, what he did to survive the actual heart attack he
felt had been sent him by the fates to punish him for his trespasses
against the Law of Moral Geometry, he could never remember as
long as he lived. He thought of Dante again: the splendor of the
silks, furs and jewels bedecking the two ladies, the white lace at the
neck, and the white leather on the arms, and the white ostrich
feathers of their fans, could only be compared to the intricate
Chariot of the Church on which Beatrice appeared to Dante, after
Matelda had addressed a long speech to him. He remembered
Mary's mother talking to him much too long, so that Mary never
had a chance to speak to him at all. He recalled trying to impress
the two ladies with the story of his speech to the Senate, and never
even being able to broach the subject, and so uttering silly things
that were meant to convey his total independence, even indifference, to their splendor and poise (Mary's poise was nonexistent, but

he couldn't notice that, because he never dared once look in her direction), but what he actually said he could never remember. The next thing he could remember was Mary's mother asking him to go back to his seat in the orchestra, because the second (or third?) act was about to begin, and he was creating a commotion by talking too loud. "Good night, and see you tomorrow for tea. Via Gregoriana forty-two."

He found himself back in his seat, greeted like a great dignitary by the vulgarians he had so curtly dismissed in front of the box, and kept asking himself why he hadn't gone out to dinner as he still intended to do. Dinner? Dinner? Whose dinner? he was trying to remember, then again: forty-two . . . Via Gregoriana forty-two . . . tea. Why tea, for God's sake? Who needs such exotic medicine? Now he recalled saying as much to the old lady and hearing her laugh and offer him coffee instead, and himself refusing the coffee too with a stupid remark that had made her laugh again. All of this in Mary's presence—but where was she? Did she exist? Oh yes, she existed, she even had a child. Her mother had said so, in connection with tea or coffee, and who in God's name could want anything from anyone any more when Mary had a child? The horror of the news hit him only now, as the actors went on chatting stupidly on stage. Mary was a widow. . . . A *merry* widow, obviously, because she wasn't in mourning, and her mother was procuring for her. What sort of people are these? Foreigners of course are capable of anything, but how about me? Why should I obey their injunction and be sitting here again, when I am not interested in this goddamn play? Resurrection indeed, from the bottom of hell!!! *Giovanna, aiutami tu.* (To the rescue, Giovanna.) It was the first time he had invoked his wife's name since he had known her. And it seemed to work. He got up from his seat, slowly and defiantly put on his overcoat and hat in spite of loud protests from the spectators seated behind him, and was about to leave, when his glance fell on that box up there, and he caught Mary's eyes. She signaled to him: her first sign of life since he had answered her first signal from the orchestra, and he sat down again with his overcoat on, only taking off his hat and apologizing to everyone he had disturbed before.

No resurrection for him now, no hope of stilling the basest instincts in him with food . . . If only I didn't love her . . . he kept thinking again and again in between spells of sensuousness and the wildest visions of orgies he saw on stage in spite of what the actors were now doing and saying. The play itself now had a new name:

TOMORROW IN THE TEA HOUSE

OF

VIA GREGORIANA 42

Dante was lucky that Beatrice had died, so he could forgive her and forget that she had been another man's wife after he had first seen her, aged nine, walking along the Arno River in Florence, with her two female companions. I forgave you, Mary, for Gennariello, and even for myself, and don't you forget that you betrayed me with myself, you responded to the worst in myself, the dishonest, sensuous, Neapolitan self that smiled to you across that crystal cube encasing that Greek vase. . . . I forgave you and forgot, because I had to remember who I wanted to be, not who I was. I wanted to be a real man, meeting my obligations to my dead parents, my living sisters, my barely existing compatriots, doomed by the government Mafia to die of hard work, underpaid, undernourished, left without water for their fields, without medical care for their starving, tubercular children . . . I had neither time nor TALENT for your charms, and your luscious Russian novels. My exams and my conscience: those were the objects of my love, in correct terminology, STUDIUM, and how right the ancients were in calling love a study, for a study it is, and towards knowledge it tends: carnal or spiritual, knowledge it is and remains. . . .

He was preparing his speech to be delivered the next day to Mary and to her mother, in front of that cup of tea he would refuse to touch. How neatly it tied in with his speech to the Senate. . . . He only wished Donato, Giulio and Peppino would be there to hear him tomorrow, as he had wished they had been in the Senate today. Because he still begrudged them their neglect. They had refused to help him on February 7, 1893, and had tacitly conspired to sacrifice him, because they were afraid the blond beast might devour them instead.

Suddenly it dawned upon him that when the enemy is internal, the best proof of courage is flight, BECAUSE NO MATTER WHO WINS,

YOU ARE THE BATTLEFIELD! If the enemy is external, things change entirely and fighting strengthens you, BECAUSE IT CORRESPONDS TO PHYSICAL EXERCISE. Thus abstract philosophical debate develops your reasoning powers and your influence on others, be they your pupils or your public, or even your enemies. Because abstract means, in correct terminology, *tracted ab* or *taken out from* the body of your feelings. YOU ARE NO LONGER THE FIELD. Therefore:

VADE RETRO SATANA

(get thee behind me, Satan), and if Satan is in your every limb already,

PERINDE AC AEOLUS

(like the wind god), filling your every sail, use strategy and not force: borrow as little of the wind as you need to keep the ship from capsizing, and turn the wheel away from dangerous waters. Away, away, Leonardo, away from Evil Rome . . .

QUO VADIS, DOMINE?

"Where are you going, sir?"

These words, spoken harshly in the crude Roman dialect he hated so much made him aware that he had got up from his seat in a trance and left the theater, his head low, so as not to look at the Evil Gorgon, like Dante with his eyes closed twice, by his own and by Virgil's hands. . . . Safely outside, he had gone quite mad and hired a carriage to go back to his hotel, but, once seated in it, his bereaved soul had carried him away from cold pagan mythology, to seek solace in the Passion of Christ.

"What's the matter with you, sir? Drunk or asleep? This is no bed, this is a carriage."

"Oh, sorry." And he gave the name of his puny hotel, trusting that the cabbie would know where it was located. "*'cci tua*," answered the cabbie, which in correct terminology means, "*alli mortacci tua*," or "curse those filthy dead of yours," but Leonardo knew at once he must not take offense and beat the vulgarian to a pulp,

because this was the surest way to land in jail and stay there, Senate
or no Senate: a Roman cabbie is more sacred than an ancient
Roman Senator. The thing to do was to give him the correct address, but he couldn't remember the name of the street for a while;
finally he blurted out:

"VIA GREGORIANA FORTY-TWO"

"Whaaaat? You must be really drunk, that's a street for distinguished people, not for shitty provincials like you. No hotel by that
name in Via Gregoriana. . . ."

"Oh, I am sorry . . . you're right . . . but I can't remember the
name of the street . . . I can teach you how to get there. . . ."

"YOU, TEACH A ROMAN FROM ROME HOW TO GET AROUND IN
ROME?" And, chasing him out of his cab with more curses against
his dead ancestors, and personal wishes that Leonardo might be
murdered at once (in correct Roman terminology, "*Te possino
ammazzatte*" or "*Va a morì ammazzato . . .*"), the cabbie proceeded to offer his services to some of the elegant ladies and gentlemen who were coming out of the theater. Leonardo couldn't see
Mary in the crowd, so he walked to his hotel still sane of mind, and
more determined than ever to leave hell as soon as possible.

Back in his room, he began to pack his suitcase and "plaid," blushing belatedly at the thought that the vulgarians he had so favorably
impressed during the intermission might have seen him in front of
the theater being abused by a cabbie. Perhaps even the Senators
who had admired him in the afternoon had been there, perhaps the
very cause he had almost won in the afternoon had been now lost,
because of a stupid and now impure woman, a widow, or whatever
she was, who left her child at home to go to the theater with her
procuress mother. . . . Away, away . . .

"What are you doing, Leonardo?" asked two voices. His councilors had come into the room.

"I'm packing. We're leaving tomorrow by the first train."

"But why? Tomorrow night you are invited to—"

"I am invited nowhere and neither are you, my friends and aldermen. We are invited to resume our duties in the administration of
the town, that's where we are invited. We have a meeting of the

Board of Estimate the day after tomorrow, and we shall arrive just in time to get some rest before we begin our debate the next day. Don't forget, sixteen hours on the train are no joke; those third-class seats are murder on your back, and we still have a two-hour ride by coach after that, so the only train that fits our timetable is the five thirty-three a.m. It is now almost midnight, let's go to bed as quickly as we can, so we get at least a few hours of rest before we set off."

"Goombà Leonard'" (from the Latin *Cum-Pater*; that is, co-godfather; in correct terminology, male member of the same family of interests), "you are invited by the Senator who asked you to address the Senate today, he is offering us dinner in a tavern outside Rome, on the Via Appia, and our political opponents will also be there, so it is in our interest to accept the invitation, or the whole project you have so forcefully presented today will be fucked out of existence before any of the guests have time to put Parmesan cheese on their macaronis."

"The Senator, you said? And why didn't he tell me anything today?"

"Because he was so deeply shaken by your beautiful words that he didn't even think of it, and when he did, a few minutes afterwards, you were gone. He didn't know where to find you. We met him later at the house of a common goombà and he asked us, but all we could tell him was you had forbidden us to attend the meeting, because you probably felt we were incapable of appreciating your high culture, we don't know why, but the truth is—"

"The truth is I didn't want to bore you with my long speech, and that's all there is to it. And so I missed a unique chance to say a few other things to the Senator, things much more important than the ones I mentioned in my speech, and if our opponents are there tomorrow night, I won't be able to talk freely. Goddamn it . . . And after I spent a stupid evening all alone, and didn't even have dinner."

"Your fault, Goombà, and you missed going to bed with a perfect creature, breasts like this . . ."

"Yes, and getting gonorrhea or syphilis or both. Thank you very much, I think it is a disgrace you behave the way you do, both married men."

"Just a moment. We didn't go to a whorehouse. These were virgins."

"Whaaat? Where? I don't believe it."

"Virgins, we tell you, from the estate of the Senator's brother-in-law in Calabria: women from our part of the world, and he had one for you, too."

"Who did?"

"The Senator."

"But isn't he a married man?"

"Of course, but he's a man, not a degenerate. . . . And not a Jesuit priest like you. If you come with us tomorrow night, chances are you can still have her. No longer a virgin, but she only went to bed with the Senator's son who is eighteen and was a virgin himself until last night. . . . How about it?"

Leonardo had been just about to tie the leather straps around his "plaid" and he couldn't decide to change his mind so suddenly, just because a new temptation had been insinuated into his ear. He decided to leave anyway, but to give up his few hours of sleep in order to have dinner and discuss the whole matter with his two councilors.

They went out to a very good restaurant, the others paying for him; he refused at first, then accepted, and so he felt relieved of at least one cause for remorse—that of spending money on frivolities, and during dinner he made a full confession because after all they were "cousins," so it was also a good occasion to teach them a lesson. They had sinned and were ready to sin again, while he had sacrificed such an innocent pleasure as that of seeing Mary for tea the next day. But to his great surprise, they knew more about Mary than he himself knew, only it was all a lie, invented by his wife and circulated secretly in public *a cani e porci*; that is, to dogs and pigs. In correct terminology, just about everybody in town except him. It irritated him immensely and saddened him, too. He felt betrayed by his wife, whose stupidity he had never really seen in action before, avoiding it on purpose out of respect for her, and not allowing her to talk in his presence, for fear she might say something too stupid for endurance. The story she had invented was that Leonardo, when just about to get his medical degree, had become engaged to the daughter of the Czar of Russia and India, who was traveling across Europe with her mother by elephant, wore a huge diamond on her forehead inserted into her frontal bone, a diamond on either side of her nose, more diamonds on all her fingers and toes, also wore sandals and greeted her guests with a belly dance, showing the biggest diamond of all in her navel.

"Wait a moment, Goombà, wait a moment," shouted Leonardo in a rage, "this is nonsense."

"Come on, Goombà, everybody knows it, what's the point of denying a truth that's been public domain for almost ten years?"

"Public domain, my arse, this is calumny pure and simple."

"Calumny? This is what your wife says: are you going to accuse your wife of calumniating you? Watch your words, Goombà, you're supposed to defend her honor, not undermine it, and if you do, there are people right here who are ready to bring you back to your senses and remind you of your first sacred duty under the sacrament of matrimony."

"But Giovanna can't have told you any such fairy tale; she's too intelligent for such nonsense. I'll have Giovanna tell you and anyone who cares to hear that the girl never wore a diamond in her navel, never."

"Just a moment—"

"Just a moment yourself, let me finish my own story: never diamonds in her navel, nor in her nostrils and forehead—"

"So what? Are you making an issue about the number of diamonds she wore? Even if she only had ten instead of twenty—"

"But that's not the issue at all—the whole story is ridiculous."

"Watch your step, Goombà, you're siding with our enemies. Is this the kind of reward we deserve for helping you address the Senate?"

Leonardo lowered his voice and, fuming with anger, said: "To begin at the beginning: I was never engaged to the girl, I met her and spoke to her four times in all, always in the street. Secondly, she was not the daughter of the Czar of Russia and India, not only because she wasn't but because there is no Czar of Russia and India."

"Okay, hairsplitter, why didn't you stay a Jesuit instead of becoming a married man? You loved the girl, didn't you? And you gave up her diamonds and elephants for Giovanna, because Giovanna was more beautiful, more intelligent."

"I met Giovanna four years later at home, she had never even been to Naples before that."

"Wouldn't it be much more reasonable if you admitted to us that you were carried away by your ill temper tonight, obviously as a result of the lack of food and women, and you said things you didn't mean? We would forgive you, because we're human, too, and besides, you are our relative and our mayor and everything. But not you, oh no. That university graduate's pride of yours means you can never be taught a lesson by two ignoramuses like us, with no academic titles. What you are trying to sell us doesn't make sense, it's just as phony as the glass arses those Indian gypsies sell our peasants at the country fairs."

"Or as phony as the diamonds of the phony daughter of the phony Czar of Russia and India."

"So now you go and discredit yourself, by saying that the girl's diamonds were false."

"Not false, but invented by you, which is even worse."

"Is that so? Then explain to us how she managed to pay for such an expensive hotel and for traveling by private railroad car. We know all the details, too, don't forget: we know the whole truth."

"You do? Well, then you should know that she was the daughter of a rich Russian industrialist."

"Rich Russian industrialist? But do you really imagine that rich Russian industrialists can't buy all the diamonds and elephants they want? We don't know the price of elephants or diamonds, but we know the price of that kind of travel and hotel living: it's astronomic. Don't try to make out these rich industrialists are paupers like you or us. We have our honor and prefer that to their riches, but that's all we have, or we would pay for the aqueduct of Apulia out of our own pockets, wouldn't we?"

"You're always changing the subject."

"Show us that you aren't, by answering this last simple question, before you change the subject. Wouldn't we, in your opinion, pay for the aqueduct out of our own pockets, if we had Mary's money? Wouldn't you?"

Leonardo was so shocked at hearing that sacred name pro-

nounced by others (he had never even spoken it aloud to anyone
but Giovanna, and that just once, to explain why they were not
going to Rome for their honeymoon) that he blushed and felt ready
to cry. Patting him on the back to give him courage, the two councilors laughed, then kissed him on the mouth as only trusted relatives will, and said: "We knew your intellectual vanity was only a
veneer, and that it would soon melt in the presence of the truth.
Don't take it badly now, or we'll have to admit that your enemies
are right."

"My enemies? Who? How are they right? What are they saying
about me?"

"They say you are so stubborn that you always think you're the
sole repository of the truth, because you've learned a few facts written in books. Books are written for fools by fools, but people who
know life don't need books to get ahead of the others. Now we can
tell you that your vanity with numbers and dates and Dante Alighieri and philosophy and all that crap almost cost you your election, and it was saved by us, the two of us: WE told your
opponents that you didn't really believe in the things you go trumpeting about, scaring voters away—and they believed us, because we
gave them our word of honor and also because we are known as
people with practical minds, who know fire from smoke. Even the
Senator last night said you were too much of a scholar and you
sounded like a priest."

"He did? But he thanked me and said I had opened his eyes."

"These are the things you say in senates and in parliaments and
even in town halls, but not at home, later, or in restaurants, with
trusted friends."

"That's the worst news anyone could ever give me. So I bungled
the whole issue and nothing will come of the aqueduct."

"See how extreme you always are? You won a great battle, the
aqueduct, the hospitals, all the reforms you proposed have already
made you famous in Rome, and if anything comes of them, they
will make you even more famous."

"What do you mean IF ANYTHING COMES OF THEM? Then you
know that nothing will come—"

"Don Leonardo, you are incorrigible. These are the things one
says: IF means, as you always remind us, GOD KNOWS WHAT THE

FATES HAVE IN STORE FOR US. . . . Isn't that your standard phrase?
See what faithful followers and admirers you have? We even know
your words by heart. You should be grateful you have us to keep
you in harness. And a wife like Giovanna, who admires you and goes
around telling everybody what a great idealist you are. She hasn't
forgotten that you gave up the daughter of the Czar for her. What
other man would have done such a thing? And now you despise
her, probably because you've seen Mary again today. Better watch
out . . . you're a married man and a mayor, you can't afford to
behave like a lovestruck adolescent."

Leonardo blushed and blushed and blushed until his ears burned.
To justify himself he said in anger: "You don't have to remind me.
Why do you think I had decided to leave tomorrow morning?
Exactly because I am a married man and . . . well, I still love . . .
that . . . *widow.*"

"You don't have to tell us: we understood that when we saw you
blush because we mentioned her name. Do you think we don't have
eyes? Or we haven't been young ourselves? Do you think you are the
only one to find an ideal girl he couldn't marry? Life, dear Goombà,
is different from the ideal. . . . Now, let's celebrate and tomorrow
we'll go our ways while you go to see Mary."

"No, I won't."

"Why? If she's a widow, you go safe. No one to knife you, and
she can't lay claim to you, because you're married. Perfect formula,
made to order."

"Please don't talk that way about her. And you don't have to tell
me what is safe and what isn't."

"Well, then, come with us and see the sights in the afternoon,
and in the evening we'll have dinner with the Senator and afterwards the girls. Safer than this you couldn't get from the Lord God
in person. No danger of diseases, and no danger of involvement,
because they are lower-class. We are sure Giovanna would prefer
this to the other. But this is no reproach to you: we know you are a
man of very high principles and impeccable morality."

Leonardo felt so disgusted he could have vomited in their faces.
Words were powerless against such vulgarity. And what made it all
the more disgusting was the priestly tone in which these last words
were spoken. For all my hate of the Jesuits, he said to himself, they

have respect for knowledge, even heathen knowledge, while these people here are not even heathens: they are the scum of the earth, and they still speak of a class lower than theirs: where is that class? The day-laborers whose daughters become the concubines of rich Senators before being sold on the white-slave market?

He claimed he was too tired to talk, which justified his longing for solitude while he solved the moral riddle he was facing the next day. But once he found himself in bed, he fell into such a deep sleep that when he woke up the sun was high and his companions gone. They had left a note for him, urging him to join them for lunch in another famous restaurant as their guest again.

He didn't even consider it, tore the bit of paper into so many tiny shreds and threw them on the filthy floor of his filthy hotel room. He felt soiled by the entire experience of the previous night, but in contrast to the conversation with the councilors in the restaurant the image of Mary and her mother seemed as intimate and innocent as his childhood dreams of worlds unknown, which could only be guessed at through the ruins of Sybaris and Croton, or the poor illustrations in his books of history. He was determined now to go to Via Gregoriana 42 for tea, and hoped he could resist whatever temptations might beset him there, without having to fall into the pit of immorality with his companions and the Senator later. But he *did* plan to have dinner with them, in order to find out for himself what sort of a person the Senator was, and what sort of relationship the other two had with him. He couldn't believe they were his friends. As for the idea of the girls, he dismissed it *in principle,* preferring not to think of it because he knew how dangerous such thoughts can be when based on nothing but hearsay. And so, with these nonthoughts in the back of his mind, and clear thoughts of antiquity in the front of his mind, he courageously climbed into a cab and ordered the coachman in no uncertain terms to take him to the Vatican Museum.

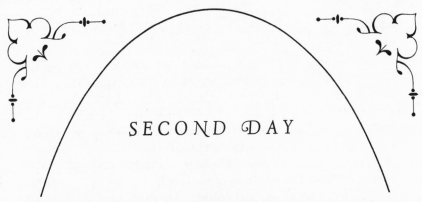

SECOND DAY

"First of all it is museumS, not museuM, which shows that you have never seen them before or you would remember, and, secondly, have you been to the Basilica of Saint Peter?" the coachman snapped back at him, to put him in his place.

Leonardo didn't answer, and the coachman drove him lazily through filthy narrow streets, until, all of a sudden, the cab emerged into a huge desert of glaring sunshine; it took Leonardo a few seconds before he could see that it was only a square, and he was faced with the most spectacular flight of columns he had ever seen, fiery fountains filling half the sky with white clouds of water, and the noblest of cupolas rearing up there on top of the world under the other blue cupola of the sky, to prove to Leonardo what the Florentines could still do, after giving Dante to the world.

When he consulted the big golden watch with the big golden chain he wore as a constant reminder of the time in his life (namely, the time allotted him after his father's time had been all spent), it was twenty minutes to four, and he was still in the Vatican Museums, no longer knowing whether he was walking through volumes in a library or rooms of art. His neck and his back hurt from the constant effort either of bending forwards to catch a glimpse of some microscopic object under glass, and *not* the reflection of the Cupola and the Vatican Gardens and the distant hills of Rome and the white laundry on roof terraces, and the white vapors on the white terraces of the blue sky, or bending backwards, to see some dark painting on the wall, and *not more reflections of more cupolas more hills more roofs more laundries more clouds on more windowpanes between more dark walls.* Statues and vases and jewelry and household utensils and *more* statues and *more* vases, jewels, household utensils from *more* serial numbers of B.C. and A.D.

civilizations were all trying to deliver some message to him and to the other tourists, mostly foreigners, who seemed resigned to die without mementos, serial numbers, glass cases or gilded frames, and no one seemed to know how to get forwards from Greek to Roman to Medieval to Renaissance to Baroque, without going back again. And now that golden watch reminded Leonardo of something else—God only knows how he was to reach the frightening Via Gregoriana from this labyrinth of centuries, this carnage of muscular mythologies on canvas and ceilings, this glitter of blinding views from open windows. He ran and ran as in a dream, away from everything, with a feeling of ignorance in his own past, as great and frightening as his ignorance of his own future from the next twenty minutes onwards.

Another cab was the answer. Thank God I don't have time to eat, he thought, and suddenly he realized that, no matter what happened in Via Gregoriana, he would have to eat afterwards, too, even if he didn't eat with the Senator, so somehow his hunger helped him dampen his emotions. It is true that it did so at the price of a terrible starvation headache which seemed to him a much better defense against Mary than all those long and impassioned speeches he could hardly remember.

But it was already 4:05 when he got to a cab in front of the museumS, and he humbly implored the driver for *advice*, in the same contrite tone he had always used in confession: "I am a poor provincial, lost in this big city: PLEASE help me, my situation is almost desperate: I am supposed to be in Via Gregoriana forty-two at four, it is five past four already, I'll pay you anything to get me there on time, I mean, with the least possible delay. Will you do me this great favor? I'd be so obliged to you."

"Leave it to me. Are you new in the service of these people?"

"Service? These are . . . friends, they expect me for TEA."

"Tea? English people?"

"Russians."

"Same thing. But in Rome time doesn't count, and if they haven't learned that yet, *you* teach them, *che cazzo*" (what the prick), "and if they don't want to learn, so much the worse for them: let them go back to their savage lands where people break their necks to be on time." He still hadn't let his horse know that it was time to wake up: the animal had fallen asleep in front of a blank wall, like a reader in the library, and Leonardo's impatience was making him perspire abundantly, with disastrous effects (he knew) for his white starched collar, now getting as stained as an old manuscript, and as wrinkled as an old man's neck. Also the cuffs were beginning to look like the map of a coastline, with inlets and brooks and estuaries of larger rivers flowing down from the dark caverns of his armpits, across the thorny meadows of his hairy arms. And his white waistcoat was beginning to sag under the weight of his gold chain and his grandfather's watch. He had already made the mistake yesterday in the Senate, and this morning in the Vatican MuseumS, of soiling his white waistcoat by fumbling nervously with the pink coral bullhorn there against the evil eye, or *malocchio*, and the long gold toothpick there against the *mal-alito*, or bad breath, both these amulets expensively encased in eighteen-carat gold and hanging on their chain. Both were unfailing signs of identification all *galantuomini* from the Twin Kingdom wore on their golden watch chains, without it ever dawning upon them that city people could tell their origins—almost their professions—by these trinkets, these trinkets which were helping him keep his inner eye on his forthcoming speech, while his outer eye read with mounting anxiety the mounting numbers on the electric meter (a great technological innovation) installed by the coachman on the side of his cab. He saw his money go down the drain of the *Gran Fogna della Cristianità* (great sewer of Christianity; namely, Rome), while his time went the way of all things and all men on the watch that had marked his own parents' last breath, while the powerless Son and Doctor was holding their pulse and waiting for their last word.

Il tempo seco porta
la fine di ogni desiderio

(time carries with it the end of all desires), and he didn't even remember whether it was in *The Divine Comedy* or in some anonymous piece of folk wisdom, but he did remember obsessively the one desire that Time, the Great Tyrant, makes bigger instead of smaller: the supreme desire he had been unable to satisfy in the Vatican, because obviously the sewers are devoid of latrines. "*Ovver-*

rosia le fogne son orfane di cesso" (the sewers are orphans of the toilet), he mumbled to himself, while the coachman was having the time of his life noticing his excruciating pain and taking him round and round Via Gregoriana.

In the end, even a Roman coachman is a Christian, which was the thought expressed by the beast from the height of his driving seat, as he finally entered the steep Via Gregoriana Leonardo had seen *three times* from the same end in his circular meanderings through hell.

It was exactly five o'clock. Leonardo's necktie and waistcoat were so wet from perspiration that his next supreme desire after the one already mentioned was to relieve his body of its clothing and throw himself on a bed and sleep. His headache had killed all hunger and thirst. There he stood now, in front of a somber Roman palace, in a street all made of palaces; the palace next door to his had a huge granite door in the shape of a dragon's mouth, and the horrible face of the dragon, eyes and all, protruded from the yellow façade, rendered more frightening by the sharp angles of afternoon sunshine cutting strange shapes on the plaster with the projection of roof edges and gutter pipes. A gaping dragon under a guillotine, that was what Leonardo saw of the palace next door, while the palace he was about to enter offered him solace in the form of a freezing cold draft, which at that moment, in his present condition, could have spelled pneumonia for him. The doctor in him remembered his own father's death by pneumonia, caught the same way. It is true that his father had also suffered from cirrhosis of the liver, but pneumonia is pneumonia all the same, and THIS MIGHT BE THE PUNISHMENT FOR HIS SECOND SIN OF THE DAY, THE FIRST ONE BEING HIS FAILURE TO TAKE THAT FIRST TRAIN.

He gladly paid the whole sum, postponing the financial regret to a later time, IF A LATER TIME WILL BE GRANTED ME IN WHICH TO WORRY ABOUT MONEY, he concluded, then looked desperately at the wall, as if to take aim before unbuttoning his fly, but the coachman warned him: "You're being watched; if you want to piss, I'll take you to a public urinal down there in the square for free," and Leonardo recognized to his horror the face of Mary's mother peering like a true Italian woman through the shutters of a window on the *piano nobile,* or noble floor (in correct terminology, the second floor, which is the first in correct Italian terminology).

"Thank you, my friend," he said to the coachman, "I accept your kind offer." And he climbed back in.

"It will be a pleasure," answered the coachman, turning his cab and whipping his horse so that it galloped away noisily on the gray cobblestones as it had never galloped in the entire course of their long, hellish journey from the Vatican.

In a triangular square only a hundred yards away Leonardo was able to relieve himself in the dark Temple of Vespasian he had beheld with such longing three times in the last half hour. After which, a completely new man, he walked slowly uphill to Via Gregoriana 42, feeling almost happy that his clothing was so messed up. Who cares? he thought. This is the way the fates have decided that this adventure should end, so let's thank them for displaying me the way I am: a provincial servant of the people with little time or taste for the romantic luxuries of the idle rich and their courtiers.

As he approached the palace, he saw the same figure at the same window, but no longer trying to spy behind closed shutters: now the shutters were wide open and the old lady in black was staring defiantly at some distant point above the roofs, her hands, in dark gloves, placed on the windowsill as if she were playing the piano and trying to decipher the score. The yellow light of sunset was reflected in her eyes perhaps more brilliantly than seemed normal from such a distance: could she be crying? The same noisy birds of last night were brushing the sky and diving down in long black ribbons from the red roof tiles and the yellow chimneys above them, to the gray cobblestones and the black human shadows treading them patiently uphill. Leonardo was glad he was one of those shadows, and that she wasn't looking, because her pale outlandish face with its slanted eyes was depriving him once more of all self-assurance. How strange that he should have forgotten in the space of a few hours how paralyzed he had been by that face and how unbelievable it now seemed to him that she be anything but a great lady with rather unconventional views about Italians.

They're all alike, poor foreign romantic fools, he concluded, and they'll never know what unromantic pigs we are, all of us, not just those who haven't gone to school.

Just as he was about to disappear into the archway of the palace, she noticed him and waved happily with both arms outstretched, as Mary had done the evening before, then disappeared and closed the window.

The tall, uniformed doorman with gold buttons down his long overcoat, and an admiral's cap, scanned Leonardo with contempt and asked him in his coarsest *romanesco* where the hell he thought he was going. "This is a private palace, what do *you* want?" "*Nothing* is what I want, and *I know* this is a private palace, you don't have to teach *me!*" Then he pronounced the old lady's name, tossing it as a password, and it worked—or almost. "Are you expected?" asked the doorman, staring at that golden chain with its trinkets, as if he were about to add: "A Burino* like you?"

But Leonardo promptly stopped him, snapping back: "*Ask her*, she's up there, at the window, waiting for me. EXPECTED is not the correct term: I am LATE."

"Then run along, don't waste your time with me! I don't want to be responsible."

Leonardo sneered at the man (he was beginning to learn the ways of the big city), and slowly entered the dark stairway, so typical of Rome, so contemptuous of the lowly, and yet so ungenerous even with itself: here was all this huge space, offering to the hurried foot of rich and poor alike only one third of the normal elevation *per step* any human stairway would offer, so that the waste of time and shoe sole would be greater, and for what logical purpose other than that of keeping social distance? Way up there in the dark archway, there was a lantern so huge it could have illuminated a basilica, yet within that intricate cage of iron and glass, there was one tiny electric bulb, so small it would hardly have lit a book in a library, a thread in a tailor shop, a nail under a shoe sole, a pot on a kitchen stove. So why all that pretense? Another clerical trick to keep you humble, he concluded. The Church is everywhere and of course these rich foreigners don't notice it. They may even find it charming. God knows what their houses are like, up in the Protestant North.

* Literally: dirty shepherd. Pejorative expression used to describe Southerners.

As he emerged from the stairway onto the *piano nobile*, a very noble butler all dressed in white like the Pope—white hair, white gloves, white breeches, white stockings, black shoes with golden buckles, then gold buttons all the way up to his neck—was holding the door open by a gold doorknob as big as a shield. Leonardo entered the hall and gave the butler his felt hat and his *chemiss'* (from the French *chemise:* a gray linen overcoat worn by all traveling Southerners to protect their black suits from the dust of railroad cars and the red of tomato sauce in taverns; typical of furniture movers in big cities). The butler showed him into a huge picture gallery with furniture and rugs and books lying open on tables under electric lamps, and needlework on other tables, and music sheets on a grand piano. The windows opened onto the same view he had seen from the Vatican; this time, however, the Cupola was smaller, owing to the great distance, and the Villa Medici was nowhere to be seen because it stood on this same side of the city as the Via Gregoriana. It all made sense, and he felt almost grateful to these foreigners for making Rome human again. There was one drawback: he didn't fit into all this; all this was a parenthesis, a visit to the museum of his own past . . . which happened to coincide with his country's. It's just as well, he concluded, that in a couple of hours at the latest I shall be dining with those two savages and the Senator, and who cares what happens afterwards! At least I'll have left *this* sacred vessel where she belongs: on an altar. Widow or no widow, she is a respectable lady to be worshipped from a distance, not to be loved, any more than I could love a Greek vase.

And at that moment, Mary came in, looking extremely pale, and so beautiful that he forgot everything, and as he stared at her, he heard himself make the most incredible blunder; he asked where her husband was. And so it was that Leonardo learned she was not a widow at all: the husband was away that day on a trip. His next blunder was to ask whether the butler would tell the husband that he, Leonardo, had been there that afternoon. Which made Mary indignant. HER MOTHER'S BUTLER? HOW WOULD HE DARE DO SUCH A THING? AND EVEN IF HE DID, WHAT OF IT?

Leonardo replied, logically enough, that he didn't think this was honest, and Mary asked him whether it had been honest of him to come to her box the evening before. His head was spinning, he was

deeply attracted by her, but the feeling he had so clearly registered
before that HE DID NOT BELONG HERE was even stronger than his
attraction. Now Mary was coming closer, stretching out her hands
to him, and he was recoiling from her, as if he knew this was
all a dream: he was still in the museum, and a statue was suddenly
moving about and speaking to him. The next thing he did to save
his composure was to ask her, stupidly, about another of the statues,
a white bust of a lady mounted on a black column; and he heard
Mary reply with a nervous laugh that this was her mother.

"But she's alive," he exclaimed, and this shocked Mary so greatly
that her whole face suddenly was flushed; she seemed bloated, ugly.
But she quickly regained her composure (and her beauty) and
made a joke of it, reminding him that he had seen her mother at
the theater the previous night. But her father was dead, and HIS
bust, the same size, mounted on the same type of column, stood
right there, separated from the bust of his living widow by a grand
piano. It all seemed unearthly. Leonardo now asked whether her
father was buried in Rome, and Mary said no, in Berlin, and
showed him the photograph of a huge, obviously very expensive
marble group with an angel hovering over something. Leonardo
made another stupid remark about the insanity of spending so
much money for tombstones and began to quote from Foscolo's
famous poem "The Sepulchers." This seemed to anger Mary, so he
asked her bluntly to tell him what on earth she expected him to say
to her . . . "you are happily married, best wishes etc.," . . . and
she simply replied, in the most natural voice, that she was NOT
happily married. But what sort of a woman was this? How could she
dare say such a thing to a stranger, in her husband's own house?

And so he learned that this was not her husband's house, that she
lived with her husband in Via Sistina, the street parallel to Via
Gregoriana, one of the very few streets of Rome Leonardo knew
well, thanks to the dishonest cabbie who had taken him through it
three times in the course of the last hour.

Mary seemed to come closer again, and again he recoiled and
defended himself by making some unpleasant remark, which was
meant to shock her and fortunately did. This, he felt with great
relief, was the right moment to go, and so out of politeness, he
asked her whether she wanted him to leave, and she said no, which

left him feeling immensely tired and anguished; even angry. But she didn't give him much time to feel anything. "Tell me about yourself instead," she asked bluntly. "Of course *you* are not married. *You* knew better."

Here, at long last, was his great chance to bring her back to her senses—and then run away.

"But I AM married," he began, collecting all his forces to make a long, sensible speech, because she seemed so disturbed, and then, without any change in his voice, he knelt in front of her and made his full confession: married, no children, no desire to have any with that fool, no meaning in that kind of life, he had been living in hell since February 1893; now, thank God, it had all ended: she was the Resurrection and the Light. And suddenly the light of that long day was gone. The stars were huge; an invisible hand reached from a great distance to knock softly and repeatedly against the two windows now closed. It was the Campanone of St. Peter's. When her hands lifted his pale face from her knees, he kissed them passionately, but as her face came down towards his for the first kiss, a tiny sound from the corridor made her stiffen, and she rose instantly, pushing him away, so that he found himself in danger of falling backwards—but her strong hands held him by both arms, as if she already knew exactly how to calculate all the risks of muscular imbalance caused by such an awkward situation, and then she smiled happily at him, WINKED AT HIM, as she called out, in perfectly controlled tones: "Bernhard?"

Bernhard was not the husband, as Leonardo had feared, only the butler, and they spoke quickly in German, while Leonardo walked towards the table with the open books on it and pretended to be absorbed in his reading. The electric lights that had seemed so wasteful in the yellow sunset light now came into their own on this table, on the table with the needlework, and on the piano. Bernhard lifted a huge silver tray from a low table that had been near Leonardo all this time; only then did he notice the huge teapot, the smaller silver containers and pink porcelain teacups that were being taken away, and he vaguely recalled that he had eaten nothing since the previous night. But he hardly cared. What was absorbing all his attention was the thought: This woman knows too much about the calisthenics of adultery not to have had a long training. . . . How

quickly she rose from her seat, how her voice hardened as she called
the butler, how she rescued me from falling after causing me to lose
my balance, and how she *winked* at me . . . MANY BAD SIGNS, NOT
JUST ONE . . . I don't like it. I am too infatuated with her; but
is *she* with me, or is this only my first taste of Woman's Dia-
bolical Arts? He sought to learn more about her from the book
on the table and the notebook in which she had been writing, but
he couldn't. Both were in Greek. Or perhaps Russian. He vaguely
remembered that the Russian alphabet was partly Greek, and so
all he learned was more about his present state of ignorance.

Dejected and irritated by the continuing conversation between
Mary and the butler, he walked to the window and stood there,
searching the darkened horizon for the last fragments of daylight
now nearly entombed under impending night. The Cupolone, true
to the cultural function of the Church of Rome, absorbed all the
daylight that had been and continued to linger. It was strikingly
beautiful, yet sad; it weighed more heavily on the heart than the
dark night itself. In Leonardo's heart, the extreme happiness that
had crowned his long day was now already in ruins, and he foresaw
a night without end for his soul. Months, *years* perhaps, of humiliating comparisons between the joys of love allotted him and those
obtained by unknown others before him. He wished he had never
allowed such great happiness to blind him, because now by comparison everything seemed black and he only wished he were still
able to desire the company of his old friends and share in their low
pleasures. All sensuousness was gone from him: his only wish was
for death—not his own, but the death of all the men who had
preceded him in Mary's love, unless she were suddenly to disappear
from the world—not by dying, but by miraculous assumption into
heaven. And again he envied Dante for losing Beatrice so cleanly
to his superior world of poetry. Which means that life is one thing
and the ideal another, he concluded.

Suddenly, from inside the huge porcelain trinket that soared
above the roofs of Rome toward the stars, another deep, raucous
sound rang out and struck Leonardo in the stomach. This was not
the voice of the Angelus, the last chime before total darkness, which
was so dear to Leonardo in his hometown: this was the voice of
Power. Two hands were softly placed on Leonardo's shoulders, and

a warm cheek was laid along his cheek. "Whatever you are thinking of," said Mary, "your thoughts are also mine and mine are yours. Nothing can ever separate us again. Isn't that true, my love?"

He nodded and placed his hands above hers by way of a reply, and it was immensely beautiful to be able to pretend that all this was so, but deep inside him the daemon of correct terminology was already replacing "separate us again" with "join us again."

"Soon we shall leave together. . . ."

"Mary, be realistic, *please*. I am here as the mayor of my home-town and must leave in a few hours, by the first morning train."

"All right, then we'll go south instead of north."

"That would be madness!"

"That's exactly what my mother would say."

"Does she know about us?"

"Not about *this*, yet . . ."

"And won't for a long time, I hope."

"Why? She's gone out for a short walk, but the moment she comes back we'll tell her together."

"The moment she comes back I will be gone, my love. And the sooner I leave, the sooner I'll come back, on some other . . . so-called mission. Not an honest one this time, alas! Gone are those days for me!!! But love is blind, and we had better close our eyes to everything else . . . until the fates . . ."

She was sobbing now, and he had to console her; thus their first kiss was filled with their first tears. He, too, was crying, but he soon stopped and urged her to follow his example. "If you want our love to last, let's start by protecting it from your mother. I'll find a solution, perhaps I could postpone my trip for twenty-four hours. . . . Let's talk about it. Let's be practical, for the love of God." And to humor her, he corrected himself cheerfully: "That is, for the God of Love . . ."

"What love?" she demanded, suddenly cold and forbidding. "What kind of love is yours?"

"Eternal love, my friend, the kind that kills . . . For almost ten years it has resisted all my efforts to kill it."

"And now we are together and nothing can separate us again."

"But you are wandering in the moon, my love. EVERYTHING AND EVERYBODY can and will separate us, if we are not very, very careful.

The Law, the laws, the customs, the husbands, the wives, and in the end our own consciences. There is no solution. . . ."

She laughed and cheerfully kissed him on the nose. "You are still so Italian, my darling. . . ."

"*Still?* As if twenty minutes with you could change me into a Russian!"

"I don't want to change you. I only want you to know that there *is* a solution!"

"Yes, there is, but it is not one to jump and laugh about. Aeschylus said, *pathein-mathein.* To live is to suffer. Carry the cross and try not to be crushed by it. . . . Don't cry, my love, your mother may be back any minute. . . . I'll write to you, and I'll give you an address where you can write to me."

"The solution is divorce!"

"DIVORCE? You *are* living in the moon."

"I am not living in the moon: I AM the moon, and you are the sun whose light I reflect."

She couldn't look at him now, but as an added precaution against the supreme impropriety of a direct glance, she closed her eyes and said: "The moon is blind. The sun is merely blinding. Blinding and ignorant. But the moon knows. Knows yet can't act. The moon is our conscience. It shines on silent battlefields, where heroes are the food of vultures and worms, but it also shines here, while Brunelleschi sleeps, and Michelangelo sleeps, but Goethe and Keats and a few others cannot. They stand at their windows and watch, and when the night is dark, they sit on their beds of torment and weep. Look, Leonardo, this is not a night for tears." He looked as he was bidden, and now the Cupola ruled like a second moon over the silent city.

"Let's open the window."

All the birds echoed inside the room as they swooped almost invisibly in front of the house, and down on the street each polished cobblestone reflected a flash of moonlight.

"Here she comes."

From the upper end of the Via Gregoriana, a closed carriage with two pale lanterns behind a dark horse was slowly coming. It stopped in front of the door, and Mary's mother was extracted from it with

much care by the uniformed coachman and the uniformed doorman. Leonardo was pleased, even though this meant yet another
confrontation and God knows how many more hours of fasting. But
it was the solution: speak openly to the mother, if possible not in
the daughter's presence. He trusted his sincerity and the violence
of his love to make her understand and perhaps even give her
consent to a long epistolary relationship between him and Mary,
which would make it a lot easier for both of them to endure the
sadness of their reciprocal duties towards their own unloved companions, in correct terminology, *con-juges*, or those harnessed like
oxen by the same *jugum*.

"I am sure you'll love my mother," she said. "You were frightened by her last night, but she loves you already, and you will see
what an extraordinary person she is. Do you want to wash your
hands before dinner?"

As if these words had been spoken through walls and down corridors to the butler, he suddenly appeared and, motioning to Leonardo, ordered him in a very Germanic Italian: "This way, please."

At long last Mary had come down to earth! Gastric and intestinal
cravings had been competing with love and with the moon for the
last hours, but what alarmed him now was that he couldn't tell the
butler what he wanted in front of Mary. But Mary, who had been
married to an Italian for eight years and knew that even in the
richest Roman palaces the toilet was miles away from the washstand, which could only be found in a bedroom, said to Leonardo:
"Don't worry. It's just a euphemism. You will find everything in the
same room."

Which reawakened in Leonardo all the daemons of jealousy. She
speaks too freely about these things, he said to himself, following
the butler down the corridor. As they reached the entrance hall,
the doorbell rang and Bernhard opened the door. Mary's mother
stormed in and seemed happy to discover that Leonardo was still
there.

"Oh, how lucky," she said, stretching out both hands towards
him. "Please stay for dinner, since our tea didn't scare you away
after all."

"Of course," said Leonardo, blushing and bowing awkwardly, as
he began to walk back towards the drawing room with her.

"This way," insisted the butler, touching his arm. Leonardo looked at him with indignation and, resigned to his sad fate, continued to follow the old lady.

"Just a moment, Mamachen," said Mary. "I had already taken the liberty of inviting the doctor, and he was just going to wash his hands when you came in."

"Oh, I see . . . I see. . . . Well, then," she motioned to him, "we'll be waiting for you in the dining room." And she walked alongside him towards the bathroom, without saying another word, as if he didn't exist. At the end of the long corridor their ways parted: the butler opened one glass door for his mistress, and another glass door for Leonardo, who thus found himself in a smaller museum, but no less of a museum than the rest of the house, and again he was the only thing out of place in it. First of all, there was no privacy: that glass door let all the outside noises come in, which meant that all the inside noises could be heard outside too. Secondly, the toilet was too close to the door, and, thirdly, it was part of a set of pink porcelain pieces all beautifully painted with pastoral scenes: toilet, washbasin, floor tiles, wall tiles all the way up to the ceiling, porcelain vases and jars on a porcelain mantelpiece, porcelain handles to the faucets. There was a comfortable fire with two comfortable armchairs in red leather at either side of it. There was even a small library with rows of gilded leather-bound books. Only the bathtub was all white, but it was huge, and had such huge gilded bronze faucets that they seemed far more fitting for the baptismal font of St. Peter's Basilica than for a private dwelling. Plus huge palm trees, as in the living room, and the same view over the same majestic Cupolone from another huge window with huge curtains and all the frills. Beautiful tiny rugs, beautiful gilded tables with baroque legs and pink marble tops (rows of perfume bottles and all the paraphernalia of a ladies' boudoir on one; all the paraphernalia of a gentleman's dressing room, razor and shaving brush included, on another). Add a bed to this place, and you could live in it like a king, thought Leonardo, as he waited for the crashing of the water to subside, but it seemed to go on forever, and he couldn't make up his mind to open the door, lest people discover that he had used the room for unmentionable purposes. He was rescued by the butler, who knocked gently and asked whether he needed towels.

And so it was, on Bernhard's suggestion, that he discovered a whole deposit of towels and bathrobes in a closet near the window.

He couldn't wait any longer for the damn waterfall to subside: they were all waiting for *him*, behind their chairs like statues, illuminated by the reflection of multifaceted crystals, bulky pieces of silver, huge white porcelain plates, each carrying a sharp white pyramid of shiny cloth of the same strange texture as the tablecloth, so shiny that it looked like a snowfield in sunlight, crisscrossed by large rivers and small streams. There was the old lady, there was Mary, there was a little graying, ugly woman and a very pale child with beautiful dark eyes, the picture of misery, obviously because he was suffocating with asthma, as Leonardo diagnosed at once. Behind them, a whole family of servants, three uniformed brigands in blue silk, white breeches and white gloves, ugly Roman faces, quite obviously the sons of brigands like the doorman downstairs and those coachmen everywhere, headed by that Teutonic imbecile in white. And these ones were calling him Burino with those ignorant but intelligent eyes of theirs.

In the distance, cheerful voices of women in the kitchen, and that damn waterfall in the toilet.

The old lady spoke a few words in German to the little gray woman, which the butler instantly took as being addressed to him, because he answered them with an instantaneous smile addressed first to her and then to Leonardo, and the little gray woman came forwards and shook hands with Leonardo, then made the child bow to him as if he were the Santissimo (Holy Sacrament), stiffen again to attention and stretch out his pale little hand, which Leonardo shook, blushing, because of his dirty and wrinkled cuff. Both the woman and the child had impeccable white cuffs of starched lace. The child was dressed in black velvet and had shoes like the servants (and the Pope).

Now the old lady was translating her message: "Leonardo," she said, in a voice charged with emotion which made her foreign accent much more noticeable all of a sudden, "allow me to call you by your first name, since we are related. This is Miss Luther, Mary's governess for twenty years, and now my grandson's governess, and that is my grandson Kostia. Let us pray."

They all folded hands (not the brigands) and mumbled a short prayer in German, then the huge chairs were pulled out from the table by the brigands and the butler, and everybody sat down and was pushed closer to the table until they were almost tucked in under the heavy tablecloth.

Now everybody grabbed a white pyramid and unfolded it, placing it on his knees. Leonardo laid his diagonally on his chest and tucked one corner into his collar, as he had always done. The brigands smiled and winked to one another, the butler stared wildly at the green fringe of the lamp above the center of the table (a huge silver monument filled with flowers); the two ladies suddenly appeared pensive, and the governess had an expression of disgust on her face. Only the child seemed happy. He was looking at Leonardo with loving eyes, and then, slowly, he picked up his napkin from his knees and tried to imitate him. But now the bony hand of his governess squeezed his wrist until he moaned and gave up, letting the corner of the napkin fall back onto his knees. She took the whole napkin away from him and gave it to one of the brigands, who had already slipped another open one onto the child's lap.

Discreet noises of spoons roving through yellow lakes of boiling hot soup, all crossing the saucer from chest to center table, except for Leonardo, whose spoon came in from the center towards his napkin, and again there were the same smiles, stares, sad glances into the void, the same contempt and admiration respectively from the two lesser creatures at the table, and Leonardo blushed up to his ears. In the distance, the same noises from kitchen and toilet.

"*Ma che cazzo je ha fatto a quer cacatore?*" (What the prick has he done to that shitter?) Leonardo heard one of the brigands mumble in very tight *romanesco* to his neighbor.

"*Ecchiedijello allui.*" (Ask him.)

Leonardo was trying to strike a balance between his appetite and the things that were conspiring to kill it. Never before had he tasted such good food and such fine wines, but never before, not even in his worst years in college, had he been scrutinized in every movement of his arms, hands, jaws, by so many different mentors and enemies, with the exception of the child who was the opposite of both: a pupil and a friend. As for Mary and her mother, they sat like goddesses beyond all reach of human eyes, on top of Mount Olympus, in the full glare and glory of their sunshine (obviously emanating from him), but who was he—what was he, rather? Certainly not the sun whose twin moons they were pretending to be: just a trapped animal in their heavenly nest. How could he argue himself free after she, the chief god(dess), Juno Jupiterized (there could be no Jupiter in a world of such women), had spoken as she had, breaking down all barriers by making him her son and the head of the family? And he was happy to be trapped, it was a dream of the most perfect beauty, but could it last? Didn't they know no divorce existed in this Eternal City and Papal See? And even if there had been a way: didn't they know what it would cost him? He could never let them pay for it and become worse than the widower Gennariello (another sudden enemy of his appetite, this name), nor could he . . .

"So you are here on an official mission, Leonardo. Tell us about it," said the old lady, from now on to be thought of as Sophie.

"Yes, I am," he said, realizing that she had given him back his weapons, and that they were still good. "I have come as the mayor of my hometown, with two of my assistants, to plead for the Apulian Aqueduct, a question of the greatest importance that the national government cannot keep postponing as it has for much too long, if the honor of Italy is to be saved. This is no longer a matter for the corrupt papal kingdom, despite all the illiterate and unprincipled dregs of that corpse which linger on. This city of parasites from all classes of society cannot go on sucking the lifeblood of the new, liberated, independent Kingdom of Italy. Not for this did so many of our best people die heroically, fighting the Austrian oppressor. *Italy is made*, said Mazzini, *now we must make the Italians*. . . . This was in essence the spirit of my address to the Senate of the Kingdom today. But I told them much more than these generalities. I had and have a very clear, detailed list of reforms, of which the Apulian Aqueduct is but one lesser detail, its vital importance to our exploited and impoverished populations notwithstanding. . . ."

He was now watching the brigands and their foreign leader whom they obviously despised as much as Leonardo did for his lack of intelligence, while a deep racial and cultural bond existed between him and the brigands, and he knew how to handle them for they were very little different from his two councilors and from many of his constituents: all born serfs, who needed to be shaken out of their moral slumber and shown the way to self-respect and freedom.

He was speaking for the two women who worshipped him, translating their strong feelings against Italy into an Italian language they could never have spoken, because they didn't know what made the Italians so contemptible and lovable at the same time; this was a guided tour through a museum of souls, a panorama of history, a labyrinth of ancient fears and crushed bones, and it showed on the faces of the brigands: they became honest, young again; gone were those wrinkles of suspicion and cunning that are mistaken for maturity by people of no hope and no faith. Dinner had come to a stop; no one wanted to be served and everyone wanted to serve: roles were reversed and there was a sense of deep moral communion Leonardo had never experienced before, nor perhaps had anyone else in that room. The cook and his two female assistants, the chambermaid and even that terrible doorman who happened to be in the kitchen, tiptoed towards the dining room to listen. And Leonardo noticed it and was proud.

"Yes," he said, "but now all these things have to be done, not just discussed. Anyone can make speeches, especially in this country, as Dante puts it so well:

> Che le città d'Italia tutte piene
> Son di tiranni, ed un Marcel diventa
> Ogni villan che parteggiando viene."

(That Italy's cities are filled with tyrants and anyone who takes up party politics becomes a great spiritual leader.) This was the limit he shouldn't have transgressed, but he did, and the enchantment was broken. He didn't notice it, but Mary did. "Tell us more," she said. "We all want to learn from you."

"Action, not words," he said, "and no one can teach action. All we can do when we act is to try and remember what we were teaching others with our words. Action may give you what you want, but it also makes you forget what you want, because so many desirable things you have never known before come to stop you on the road. This is what makes Rome so dangerous to any politician from the provinces. Those born here are corrupt anyway, so Rome is

to be avoided at all costs, not only by the believers who don't want
to lose their faith, but by the good citizens who don't want to sell
their souls to the devil."

"How well put," said Mary's mother.

"Words, again, Madame. But I hope I won't disappoint you, and
when I am not here, you'll hear from me very frequently, through
Mary. I shall write to her every day."

"What do you mean?"

"Exactly what I say: starting tomorrow, or rather the day after
tomorrow—" He stopped and made a gesture of disappointment:
"Oh my God, I have forgotten to send a cable to my office: we have
a plenary meeting of the town council and I won't be back for at
least another thirty-six hours. . . . Well, I'll send one tonight,
when I go back to my hotel. It will never get there in time. . . .
But, as I was saying, the first thing I'll do after the meeting is over
will be to write to Mary and to you and keep you informed, since
you have shown such interest . . ." He couldn't continue, because
the two ladies were not showing any interest whatever in what he
was saying. Mary was sobbing and leaving the table, and her mother
was pushing back her chair, prior to elevating the massive pyramid
of her presence and following her daughter. The governess and the
child also got up from their seats and left the room in a hurry, while
the brigands, turned brigands again, were beginning to clear the
table and Bernhard, whose stupid face had registered nothing, was
standing there like a statue.

"Leonardo!!!" called the old lady from the next room in a voice
that boded no good.

He obeyed, followed by the cold and inexpressive glance of the
brigands, and by their judgment too, he knew.

"Leo-naaardo????" the voice called again in a much higher and
angrier tone.

"Here I am," he mumbled, entering yet another museum, smaller
but no less lined with paintings from floor to ceiling, and crammed
with furniture. The moonlit Cupolone was still the centerpiece,
even though dimmed by the reflections of the various lamps on the
windowpanes. Mary was sobbing uncontrollably on a sofa and her
mother was pacing the room in front of her, like a sentinel in front
of a royal palace.

"What is this nonsense? What do you mean: writing letters to Mary?"

"I thought . . . I thought there was nothing wrong in it. We love each other."

"Thank you very much for informing me. I thought I knew, but I am beginning to entertain serious doubts as to the existence of this love."

"Why?"

"WHYYY?"

Mary answered her for him, with great violence: "He never loved me. He doesn't want to leave his wife."

"That's a lie, Mary. There is nothing I would want more, but I am a married man."

"And I am a married woman and we agreed we were going to get a divorce. . . ."

"But . . . *no such thing exists* in Italy."

"That's why Mamma has arranged for us to leave tomorrow night and go abroad."

"But . . . I have my duties, I am the mayor of a town of thirty thousand souls. . . ."

"YOU," shouted Sophie, "YOU, with no soul of your own?"

"You can't say that of me, Madame," he said, his voice beginning to tremble. "My soul has belonged to Mary since I first met her all those years ago. . . . And I swear I'll never look at another woman, ever, not even at my wife."

"Your *wife*? What is this: bigamy?"

"That's exactly what I was trying to say."

"Yes, and you seem to like it. No bigamy in my house, young man. This is your wife now."

"Ideally speaking, yes, Madame, but in terms of real life . . . The power of the Church . . ."

"Are you a Catholic?"

"God forbid, but—"

"Now I understand: the power of the Church is indeed supreme if it can stop a free spirit such as yours from asserting its fundamental rights."

"What fundamental rights?"

"The right to your own happiness."

"Oh . . . THAT . . . But . . . is there such a right? I only know
of a right to be true to oneself, and that, alas, involves a great
deal of unhappiness . . . of self-sacrifice. . . ."

"You Italians are so used to suppressing your best instincts that
you continue the work of debasement begun by the Church when
you were still children. You mistake humiliation for humility. How
can you be true to yourself? Where ARE you? If it's money that
deters you, we are rich, it means nothing to us."

"Thank you, but I am not the kind of Italian who debases himself for a place at the table of the rich."

"You are worse than those leeches, because they deserve to be
pitied. They are incapable of higher ideals, but you seem to me—
and certainly are—incapable of anything but the highest and most
noble ideals, and yet you intend to continue on a path of lies, puny
betrayals, not just of one, but of two women now, for a place in the
heart of a person who loves you more than anything else, a person
you too claim you love more than life itself. . . ."

"But I do," he moaned, getting down on his knees. "I love her
and I respect her."

"But then what is this? Is it love? Is it respect? Or is it one more
instance of that Italian dishonesty we know only too well, since we
find it right here in our midst, in the so-called man in our family,
the father of that unfortunate child there?"

Mary was so surprised that she stopped crying and sat there in
frightened admiration of her mother. Leonardo was not only surprised: this was the twelfth or seventeenth or thirtieth great surprise
of that day. He was admiring her too, quite without fear: his admiration ran deeper than his love for Mary, who was after all a
woman, therefore incapable of making sense, while this woman here
made sense, she said the things Leonardo had always wished someone would say to him, for despite all his moralizing (which had
gone deep enough to ruin his life), his constant self-reproach was
not unpleasurable. This woman here had the voice of a mother, the
authority of a priest, the strength of a man. Not the strength to kill
a bull with a bare fist, as Leonardo's father did in his youth, but the
strength to grab a dilemma by the horns and push it aside, so one
could pass without having to solve it.

"Mammà," said Leonardo in Italian, in southern Italian, with the

accent on the last vocal, and that did it for them both. He recognized his mother (a spiritual mother, because his real one had been
a squeezed lemon rind, a broken eggshell, a dirt-rag in his father's
hands), and she recognized a son she had never had, because her
own two sons were two beaten dogs, but dogs all the same, so they
had to be beaten again and again, lest they bite you. So to his call
for his dear mother, she answered with hers for her dear son; they
embraced, crying, and Mary joined them, feeling almost excluded,
exactly as she had in her early childhood when Father and Mother
reaffirmed every day their right to their own happiness against the
stern authority of that terrible grandfather, who had forced his only
daughter into a marriage of convenience from which she had fled
with a poor, upcoming, self-made man. This, just to explain that the
problem of divorce was nothing new to Mary's mother. New it was
and remained so for a long time to Leonardo that his new-found
mammà was herself a divorced woman, or he would never have
fallen into the trap (a phrase he never uttered aloud but tossed in
secret back and forth between his better and worse selves).

Up to that very moment, Mary didn't quite believe that her
mother would not suddenly withdraw her consent to her divorce
and marriage, but now that she saw Leonardo in the function of a
father, it all made sense to her: Mary's father had been dead for
years, her brothers had been regarded as dead, which was still deadlier for them, because every single time they were recalled from
death for a new test of their worthiness to live, they failed so badly
that their next death thrust them deeper down the rungs of hell
than any sinner in Dante's Inferno. Now, with the winds of suspicion subsiding, Mary suddenly basked in the warmth and felt it in
her whole body. And so did Leonardo.

"Children," said Sophie, "I know you are impatient to consum-
mate the triumph of your star-crossed love, and since I was the only
cause of your long odyssey, I hate to delay that consummation for
even one more minute, but let us not forget that we are still in
enemy territory, and the enemy is out there, looking in at every
window. If you become man and wife here, the servants will know,
and that other woman who claims that she, too, is a grandmother,
may take the child away from us and send us all to jail. So let us be
reasonable. Tomorrow night we're leaving for Switzerland, and that

will be your honeymoon, but now let's accompany the future husband to his hotel—I mean to our hotel."

To Leonardo it was cold again: two millimeters away from him
there was warm sunshine, but over him hung a huge, black cloud,
one of those that take so long to pass you never know where the
wind is blowing from, and in the meantime you know you may
catch pneumonia and die.

"Let's be even more reasonable," he said. "Let's wait a few weeks,
so I can go home and settle all my pending affairs and . . ."

Mary was in anguish again, waiting for her mother's reaction.

Her mother smiled and said: "Absolutely not. If we let you go
home (and I am surprised that you should still use that word), you
will never come back."

"I give you my word of honor. . . ."

"And I give you mine, if we must use these pompous Italian
expressions, that you must be protected against yourself. I saw you
run away from our front door this afternoon, and it was the only
time in my life I have prayed to your Catholic dolls in the heavens
to help me, and I must say they did. I couldn't believe my eyes
when I saw you come back, serene, proud, erect, a real man who
knows he is doing the right thing. For once. Not that I mistrust
you, Leonardo, but I know human nature. Try to tell me you didn't
run away from the door. . . ."

Leonardo stared straight ahead, blushing at the thought of what
he should have said to her, but also hesitant because he knew that
she was right. He had known all along that a strange force was
driving him to that house in spite of his fears, and, while relieving
himself in that square nearby, he had told himself aloud: "Well,
this may be my last chance to do the right thing. What do I have in
common with these people? Why am I going there?" And he had
gone. And it had been his last chance.

"I see you are an honest man, my son," she said now, interrupting
his inaudible answer. "You have nothing to say, and you are no
longer trying to treat me like a stupid Italian woman. I don't mean
they *are* all stupid, your women: they make themselves so, to cope
with your stupid philosophy of life. Stupidity is a career; you can
become a genius at it, if you work hard enough. All a matter of
perseverance. Mary, get dressed to go out." She waited for Mary to

leave the room, then continued: "I must tell you something. I am dying. Not visibly yet, but in my bones I feel the cold air of the tomb into which I am descending invisibly. Roentgen in reverse, my friend. You, as a physician, may answer my question: is it believable that X-rays have existed only since that German professor found them and used them to look at our skeletons while we are still alive and well? In my modest opinion, they have always existed and been available to any human being who applied himself to learning how close he was to his tomb. I have long periods in which I don't want to know, and I don't know. But I also have periods when the question presents itself to me with obsessive insistence, as all questions of knowledge present themselves to the minds of scientists. A year after I took Mary away from Naples because of you, and she married this terrible monster to spite me (on the advice of a woman I trusted, because she was the daughter of my closest friend and adviser), I asked myself that question, and the answer I received was: 'Within ten or fifteen years.' So I left Rome to go and die alone, in Germany. Then when I felt a new life warming the air from a distance, I came back. I knew Mary was pregnant, and although I was horrified at the thought of the Monster who had unleashed that cellular process, still, I felt, this is my life, my blood coming to life again, I must go back. And I came back, and I knew instantly that Mary's marriage was a mistake: it was killing her. And I also knew that it was all my fault, because you were still on her mind, but I said nothing. I soon realized that the Monster was unfaithful to her, and again I said nothing. But of course I applied my reverse Roentgen again, and I saw, from my skeleton, an outside world extending only until 1908. Beyond that date, an impenetrable wall: my tomb in the calendar. And I worried, oh, how I worried, scanning the horizon for a man, someone like you, who could bring Mary back to life. She herself never knew she was dying, because she didn't want to know, and also because she was living on me. We had always been very close, but this kind of closeness between mother and daughter is always fatal to the daughter, because her life extends beyond her mother's, even if the mother lives to be a hundred. For the daughter it means living in death. A living person cannot be sunshine for another living person. The sun is eternal, we are not. Mary, my moon, was going to be lifeless, dead, the moment

I died. So life has been hell for me these last eight years. And last
night, God bless Tolstoy, it was real resurrection for both of us.
When Mary dropped her opera glasses on the head of that vulgar
individual—"

"Mary? When?"

"Last night, before the play began, I thought you'd noticed it.
There was a great commotion in the theater, and some stupid person came up and started complaining that it would cost him a
thousand lire to be cured of the bump Mary had caused him on his
forehead with her opera glasses."

"Unbelievable! I trust you got rid of him."

"At once. I said we'd pay him his goddamn thousand lire."

"But you can't do that! Not even an appendectomy would cost
that much."

"Who cares? I had other worries on my mind, and it's worth any
sum to get rid of such leeches."

"Has he been paid yet?"

"I don't know. I gave him the name of my administrator."

"You must stop this at once. I'll see to it—"

"Look here, young man, it is my money and I am still alive. Will
you stop interrupting me? Or are you more interested in . . . Well,
I don't want to lose my temper."

Leonardo had lost all interest in anything else, and was also
extremely embarrassed, but she didn't notice and went on. "And
. . . so I knew something very exceptional must have caused Mary
to drop her glasses, so I focused mine in the same direction and
recognized you at once. Yet I had never seen you before. Isn't that
symptomatic of something?"

"Yes."

"I always knew there was *something*. You may call it God, Destiny or whatever, but there *is* something. So I knew this was a *sign*,
and felt better, because now I could die in peace."

"Yes."

"What do you mean: YES???"

"Oh, no, I mean no, you can't."

"I can't die in peace?"

"You can, but you must not die, that's what I meant."

"Thank you, my son. I knew you cared for me. And you do know,

I hope, that I care for you. So few people care for me, that when one does, and he is the right person, I am infinitely grateful to God, or to Something, and can even pray. As I did this afternoon, when I watched you run away from your true happiness. For eight long years of hell before this blessed resurrection, I used to say to Mary: 'Not a second divorce in the family. One is enough.' "

"Why, was Mary married before?"

"No. I was."

"You???"

"Here comes Mary. Let's go. Yes, I was, it's a long story, but we will have plenty of time for it during our honeymoon, I mean YOUR honeymoon."

"My honeymoon?" he gasped and mumbled under his breath: "And how long will it last, *my* honeymoon?" He looked at Mary, radiant and beautiful in her big hat with a gray feather circling it like a cloud and coming down on her left shoulder, and he knew: no aqueducts, no thirsty peasants, no governments; there were no mayors in the world, no duties, no suffering populations and no Mafias betraying them, no Senators, no wives, no sisters and nephews and no simple medicine: this woman, yes, and no pride for him either about accepting money: she needed him and she needed her pride in his love and if she ever weakened, he would kill her, kill her mother, kill the butler, the brigands, the maids and the cook and the coachman and the doorman and the horse and then himself.

"Let's go," he said, as the head of the family. "But you will not come with me. We will now take a short walk to that terrace up there I saw from the window, we will have a look at Rome in the full moon, then I will walk you back, and I will go alone in your coach to my hotel, where I will pack my suitcase and go to whatever hotel you have found for me, and tomorrow morning at eight, no, better make it seven, or perhaps six, the coachman will pick me up again and bring me here."

"Can we trust you to go to your hotel alone?"

"Of course you can."

"Won't you have second thoughts the way you did a few hours ago?"

"Madame," he said, "once a decision is made it is made. Mary is mine now, and I won't let go of her as long as I live."

"God, or SOMETHING be praised," said Sophie, crying with joy. "Now I know I can die in peace—but before dying I must un-invite all those bores who are coming to dinner tomorrow night. Twenty-six of them."

"No," he said. "Before doing that you must stop payment of those thousand lire to that bastard. A thousand nights at my hotel, that means."

"A thousand and one nights," said Mary, dancing like an actress on stage, her parasol open and her hair tumbling down from under her hat.

"Mary, Mary," shouted Leonardo angrily. "Mary, for God's sake, your dignity . . . And that parasol . . . be careful . . . it's dangerous."

Mary embraced him and Sophie laughed happily, saying: "Leonardo, we are alone. . . ."

"Yes, but that parasol . . . for God's sake, close it. . . . Close it at once."

"Why, darling? Why, my love?" And she resumed her mad dance.

"It is extremely dangerous, a parasol opened inside the house."

"Dangerous? Why?"

"It brings bad luck."

"Are you superstitious?"

"Of course not, but the danger exists all the same. . . . What do we know? . . ." And, seeing the two women wide-eyed with the kind of surprise that could explode into either anger or tears any moment, he said: "Something may happen."

"Now come on, Leonardo," said Sophie, "don't be Italian with us. Admit that you're superstitious, and try to break away from that nonsense in your past. The Monster is exactly like you in this, and you don't want to resemble him, do you? Mary was so happy a minute ago, and now she's on the brink of tears. Let's reason it out: WHAT can happen? NOTHING. So it is something atavistic and, as such, unworthy of a scientist."

"Perhaps," said Leonardo. "Perhaps it is something in me that doesn't like it. Call it atavistic, call it unworthy of a scientist, call it just SOMETHING, but it is something that can harm us, so we had better try not to behave as if we were the masters of our destiny."

Mary was smiling. She didn't seem at all on the brink of tears, but now her mother was. She threw herself on Leonardo with all the weight of her huge person, almost knocking him over. "You are so right," she sobbed, "so frighteningly right. . . ." When the crisis was over, she concluded: "We must always, always obey you, Leonardo."

A moment later at the front door, the butler handed Leonardo his felt hat and his *spolverina*, all neatly folded like a precious ceremonial garment, which made the *chemiss'* look even more like a dirty rag, and Bernhard even more like the Pope. What could he do? He was no longer the master of his destiny. He had to obey His Holiness. With that garment he had arrived there, and with that garment he left.

But even more significant was his behavior under the moon. For all the authority he had been given by Sophie, and intended to use, he couldn't obey his own body which had exhausted all possibilities of participation. Courtesy dictated that he let the two women under his orders "do the honors of the house." They "showed" him all the marvels of a Rome he couldn't see, because Rome was submerged in a cold sea of fog except for the Cupola of St. Peter's. What energy these Russian women have, he kept saying to himself as they prodded him for evidence that he had understood how incredibly unbelievable, how fantastically superhuman it all was.

"Yes, yes, yes, oh yes, oh no, I do, I do, it is *perfectly* perfect . . . *superlatively* superhuman . . . a fantastic dream. . . . Too bad we have to leave tomorrow night." How he regretted this!

"Then do we have to leave tomorrow night?" Sophie said. "The Monster isn't coming back until next week. Tomorrow night we could tour Rome, the next day the Via Appia, and we could also look at museums in the daytime. But then tomorrow night we couldn't *pretend* we had left, so why not have the dinner party as if nothing had changed? You will meet the most extraordinary collection of imbeciles and crooks and Cardinals and Senators and men of letters you ever saw. . . . And also some extremely nice people we shall be seeing again in Paris and later in Baden-Baden, and in Ouchy, and in Moscow. . . . Why not, Leonardo? Why not? Of course *you have the last word:* you are the head of the family and we must *always* obey you, but don't you think that *we* might also *suggest* something to you? In this one area: Rome and the sort of people who will be part of our milieu in the future? . . ."

Postponement was his only way out and he took it. "We'll talk about it tomorrow. I'm rather tired now."

"But then why go to your hotel? You may meet your two assistants, and God knows what they will do to you, if they find out! And, knowing you, with your sincerity, even if you don't talk, your happiness will show . . . or . . . isn't it strong enough? Love and a cough, says your Italian proverb, cannot be concealed."

"I have to see them."

"Why? Since you have severed all connections with that terrible past of yours? Look at us: we are leaving *everything,* abandoning the house . . ."

"Whaaaat?" He was waking up again. "Who . . . who will take care of it?"

"Bernhard. He may not be a genius, but he is the most trustworthy servant we ever had. And then the Avvocato Tegolani, our administrator . . ."

It turned out that even the brigands, even the doorman, even the coachman were the most trustworthy servants they had ever had, not to mention the cook, who had only been there three days. "Such a marvelous person, and so *lustig.*"

"What does that mean?"

"Amusing, witty."

"But . . ."

"In fact, we may ask him to join us on the train. We do need a good cook wherever we settle down."

"But . . ."

"But of course you are right, we can talk about it tomorrow. And, if we may suggest, just suggest, mind you . . ."

"No, I have to go. I must pay the bill. I'm still the mayor."

"Do you have the money?"

"Of course I do." It was the last time he could give such an answer, because it was the last of his money. The return ticket he

had, and who would use it now? I am kept away from my own
world . . . no, just KEPT, . . . a kept man! In vain did he try to
delude himself that this was not so. No, not a kept man. I am the
keeper of this treasure. . . . The better self of a self-employed
eunuch. . . .

"What are you thinking, my love?" asked Mary.

"Nothing!"

"You are tired, my love, I can see it in your eyes. DO go to bed.
And, if you MUST go to that hotel, have the coachman go in with
you, just in case you need protection."

"Leave it to me."

"Mary," said Sophie in a tone of command, "remember, we
must obey him *at all times!* Good night, Leonardo," she said, as
they reached the front door again. The coachman stood in front of
the closed carriage, ready to open it upon Leonardo's order. He and
the horse and a few happy strollers who were going to sleep in their
own beds tonight were witness to this parting scene. He couldn't
kiss Mary in front of them all. Inside the dark doorway, the doorman stood ready to notice whatever was about to take place, so
Leonardo had to use the full strength of his arm to keep Mary at a
distance as he said to Sophie, not quite daring to use the familiar
form yet:

"*L'affido a voi.*" (I am entrusting her to you.)

And, like a real sovereign male, he stood there until he saw that
they were far beyond reach of the doorman's impertinent eyes.

He paid the entire hotel bill plus one extra night for his assistants
and it proved more of an effort than he had imagined, but he felt
this was the only thing he could do to earn their future understanding and asked the hotel owner not to tell them until the next
morning. He also gave him a large tip, which proved even more
painful, because now he was almost in the same condition as a
criminal embarking for a penal colony with his personal belongings
in a filthy bag on his back. His suitcase was neither filthy nor small,
in fact it was quite large and in keeping with his mayoral dignity. He
even owned a "traveling plaid" tied with brand new leather straps; it
was his father-in-law's wedding present, which had looked quite
Scottish in Laterza, but he knew that it would look unutterably

Apulian in that carriage, where there was a real Scottish plaid and even a Scottish rug. As for the mayoral suitcase, it would look as puny, cheap and dirty as he himself did. Should I leave them behind? he asked himself, as if I had been run over by a streetcar? But this opened up the new problem of buying new clothes and new suitcases, just when he was giving up his salary, his mayoral dignity, his profession, his freedom, his bank account and his good name. The image of Sophie as the fatal streetcar crossed his mind in a flash, and he shuddered, thinking of his empty bed at home, his empty office with the surgical instruments waiting for him inside the sacred glass cabinet, while his derelict patients waited outside in the corridor, before learning from a tearful Giovanna that the doctor was no more. His thoughts wandered onwards through the streets of Laterza and visited his empty office in the town hall, then hurried back home again, unseen by all the malignant people who were commenting on Don Leonardo's betrayal of his duties, and he found himself alone with his horse, whose honest, affectionate eyes seemed to be asking: "Why have you forsaken me?" and then, after a long, painful silence, "Why have you forsaken that poor little boy dying in that hut on the road to Acquaviva delle Fonti?" Too late to think of these things. The "Streetcar" was waiting for him to carry him off to an enchanted country of limitless wealth, from which he might come back and help everybody in the village, even Giovanna. . . .

He forced himself to stop thinking and ran upstairs. One thing he hadn't taken into account at all (how easily one forgets) was the reassuring smell of poverty and dirt that hit him as he climbed the dark and filthy staircase to his room. Only a few hours earlier he had been kept awake by that selfsame smell because it was NOT reassuring, as compared with the clean, good, prosperous smell of his own bed and his own kitchen, which determined the smell of the whole house, according to the day of the week: Monday the smell of laundry soap in boiling water, but on any other day the warm smell of whatever the convent is passing, as the old saying goes, against a background of permanently cold smells, such as salted hams and *caciocavalli* (cheese on horseback; so named because the two roundish provolone cheeses are held by raffia strings so that they can be strung across the backs of donkeys or horses). There were also the

varied smells of burning thyme or laurel leaves, warm near the
hearth, cold in the smoke that floated up from the hundreds of
chimneys in the pyramid of streets below that formed all Apulian
towns—and all this blended with the smell of goat and donkey
manure from more streets both above him and below. Plus on
Sunday of course, incense and oil burning in front of holy images,
mixed with the smell of wine barrels, dirty socks and humid earth in
front of taverns and churches.

Here in Rome some of the smells were still agricultural—though
not in the sinister palace which was now his future home ("My
tomb?"). He entered his hotel bedroom, and now the smell of
peasant perspiration that had physically nauseated him the previous
night suddenly invited him to sleep. Impossible. The temptation
became so strong that he had to stand away from the bed and look
at it with his hands behind his back, like a mourner before a freshly
closed grave. If Mary and Sophie could only die now, he thought,
not out of hate, but out of genuine love, the only possible form of
love he could share with them. He didn't want the coachman to die.
He would go home after being kicked out by the doorman on
Leonardo's orders, but would never be able to make his report, because the two ladies had died. He almost prayed for such a miracle,
but knew that there are limits to God's generosity.

"Here he is . . ." sounded the cheerful voice of one of his companions. "Don Leonà, was it you came out of that elegant carriage half an hour ago? We were sitting at a tavern nearby and saw
it pass, then stop here and I am sure I saw you get out of it. We
argued about it for ten minutes, made a bet and here we are. Who
wins?"

"It wasn't me," said Leonardo gloomily.

"Oh . . ." The other assistant seemed so happy that Leonardo
almost blurted out the whole truth, but he was tired and too sad to
talk. He loved them both, they were part of his world.

"*Tè andata male?*" (It didn't go well?)

"No, no, TOO well," he replied with a sigh.

"Let's go to bed, you'll tell us all about it tomorrow."

He couldn't answer. He was trying to think. If he waited for
them to go to bed before taking his suitcase and plaid and collecting
his razor, he would fall asleep and not wake up until noon the next

day. If he just said he was going out for a stroll, he would lose the very things he had come to pick up: all his belongings for God knows how many years to come.

"It did NOT go well at all—tell us, we're your brothers. No shame in admitting defeat. We were stood up by the Senator, had no girls, just sat there and paid our own bill. So you see . . . *mal comune mezzo gaudio*" (shared misfortune is half a pleasure).

He didn't even hear them. What would happen to her if I never showed up again? he thought, knowing already he could never do such a thing, because he didn't want to. So he concluded that the only solution was even more impossible than the previous one. It WAS THAT HE HAD NEVER SEEN HER AGAIN AT ALL, NEVER GONE TO THAT DAMNED THEATER. Whatever happens is fatal, if not fated. Nothing ends well, ever. Aeschylus was right again. And Dante was wrong:

> *Nessun maggior dolore*
> *Che ricordarsi del tempo felice*
> *nella miseria, e ciò sa il tuo dottore*

(no greater pain than remembering happy times in poverty, and your doctor knows that). YOUR doctor knows the opposite. No greater unhappiness than remembering poverty in wealth. That's what YOUR doctor knows. . . . "By the way, Don Leonà, you should thank us."

"Yes? Why?"

"First thank us, then listen to us, but please don't get angry."

"What is it?"

"Promise?"

"Promise."

"Remember your cousin, Don Crocifisso Di Santo?"

"Yes, he lives in Bari."

"No, he lives here. But that's not the issue. Anyone can live. HOW you live, that's the thing. You should see how he lives. . . . Sybaris never saw such splendor. Two divorces he has been offered, not one, two."

Leonardo felt his blood rush to his ears, and was glad they couldn't see it in the dim light of the room. When he could manage to speak, he said: "How is that possible, if he hasn't even been married once?"

"Leonà, you're a real ignoramus, for all your celebrated knowledge! You don't have to be married to be offered a divorce. In fact, it's if you *are* married you can't receive such an offer, because in Italy there is no divorce. But if you are a bachelor, and a rich woman is ready to divorce her husband and marry you, what the hell would you call that, if not an *offer of divorce?*"

"But . . ."

"But nothing. You're still so provincial. You don't know life. Such things happen, but only to the daring, to the men of the world, like your cousin, not to the timid like you, who can only make fine speeches and find fault with the way others talk. You belong in a hermit's cave on top of a mountain, while Don Crocifì belongs in the great international world of power and money. We're telling you: Don Fifì received two offers of divorce, and turned them down, both of them. Just like that. Two of the richest women in Rome were ready to create international scandals FOR HIS SAKE, and he said to himself: wait a moment, cards on the table: what do I gain from this divorce? He tapped all the possible sources of information he could get, and decided that it was more convenient for him to refuse than to accept."

Leonardo was disgusted, but more so at himself than at these liars. He knew his cousin well enough to discard all these tales as pure fabrication, but how could he defend him now, when he himself was going to give them such terrible things to gossip about?

"Enough of this nonsense," he shouted. "What are you trying to teach me now?"

"That your cousin knows how to live and you don't."

"To hell with my cousin, I haven't seen him for ten years, I didn't even know he lived in Rome."

Peppino, who had not spoken, felt it was his turn to act as arbiter. "Don Leonà," he said, "be reasonable, please! And you, Liborio, don't talk that way to Don Leonardo. First of all he's married to my cousin. And here he is our mayor and you a member of the administration on an official mission. And since after all I am here too, with the same prerogatives as you, let me have the floor now. Agreed?"

"Agreed," said Liborio, and Leonardo felt his heart sinking, because Peppino was far worse than Liborio.

"The reason I said you must thank us, Don Leonardo, is that I— please note: not Liborio, but I—remembered to send a telegram to the mayor's secretary in Laterza and say that the meeting of the Board of Estimate was postponed until after our return, because you, the mayor, had extremely important revelations to make, which, because of their importance, could not be revealed in a telegram, which necessitated the furtherance of our presence in the capital until further notice."

"And who authorized you? . . ." stuttered Leonardo, blushing up to his ears and feeling great pity for this fool who didn't know how right he was and what troubles he himself was getting into.

"Who authorized *me*? I *knew* you hadn't sent a telegram until this morning, and I knew you wouldn't remember to send one today because of Mary, and when we saw your cousin sitting at a very elegant café in the company of a very rich lady, obviously a foreigner, we approached him. . . . Don't look so angry, Don Leonà, this was a foreign woman, they're not like our women, with them you can do anything, in fact, they expect it. It was she who said to him, Look, you have friends who are trying to catch your attention. And it was she who motioned to us to come and sit down, after he just waved at us and shouted, Hi, how do you do? So we sat down with them and told him all about you, he was surprised, didn't even know you were in politics, was very pleased to hear you were mayor, we told him about your triumph with the Senate yesterday, we told him everything—after all, he is your cousin and he wouldn't betray you—and besides, he never comes to Laterza, and doesn't know our family at all. So when she left, because she had to rush home to her husband—swear to God she did, she even said so, this is how immoral they are, these foreign women—so when she left, he told us all about her and about the other rich woman who had offered him a divorce, and he said that he was making more money than they could offer him, and he could get any woman he wanted. . . . By the way, do you know that he is the eye specialist for the Pope? And the King, too? He makes so much money that he could buy any Roman palace and become a nobleman, even a Senator: anything.

You should see the cigarettes he smokes . . . and the rings on his fingers . . . thick gold, with a coat of arms . . . Don Leonà, why are you so furious? Okay, don't tell us, we don't care, but let's get some sleep now, because tomorrow Don Fifì is going to take us on a tour of the Via Appia and of the Vatican Palace, he even has the right to take us through the museums, which are open only to the most privileged intimates of the Pope—did you know that?"

"You idiot," shouted Leonardo with a gust of contempt, "the Vatican Museums are open to cats and dogs for the price of a cup of coffee. I spent the whole day there."

"You did? So you didn't see Mary at all?"

"No."

"Aaaah, that's why you're in such a lousy mood. You're upset about not seeing Mary. . . . Well, don't blame us then, it was your own doing. If you prefer to spend your days in museums looking at pictures of naked women, rather than in real life, probably in bed with a naked woman you love, it's your fault."

"Will you shut up, you bastard? I'll break all your teeth and your nose too, if you say another word. And I demand an apology, right now."

The two men stood aghast, they had never seen him in such a fury. "Right this minute, or I'll move out of here to another hotel. And I mean it." He was about to pick up his two pieces of luggage, when there was a discreet knock on the door.

Leonardo paled, and the other two men felt greatly relieved by his embarrassment.

"See what you've done? You woke the neighbors with your shouting." Then, to the door, in a loud voice: "Okay, sorry, we'll be quiet from now on. Good night."

There was a silence, in which Leonardo, still frowning and avoiding their eyes, picked up his two pieces of luggage and made for the door.

"Don Leonà, what's the matter now?" said Peppino, trying to block his way. "Come on, cousin, we didn't mean to insult you. Come to bed now, don't be a silly fel—" Another, more determined knock interrupted him. Leonardo dropped his luggage and rushed to the door, but not quickly enough to prevent it from being shaken gently as if someone were trying to force it open. Liborio and Peppino promptly leaped in front of Leonardo, pushing him back, and shouted at the closed door: "Who is it? What do you want?"

Deep silence followed. Leonardo stood there, pale as death itself, as a timid voice from the outside called his name, preceded by the title of Excellency.

The two men were thunderstruck. They turned to Leonardo and at once understood that he must know something about it. And before anyone could speak another word, his name with that heavenly appellative was pronounced again. Leonardo moved to the door and shouted firmly: "You may go."

"But we have orders from Our Lady. . . ."

It sounded as if they were heavenly messengers sent by the Holy Virgin, no one else is called by that name in Italy, and Leonardo, who had recognized the voices of the two brigands in silk stockings and breeches, knew that there was no sending them away now. He shouted: "I'm coming. Go, please."

"Our Lady said we should help you with the luggage."

Defeated, Leonardo opened the door and tried not to look as the two heavenly messengers in white gloves rushed in, and, withering the two assistants with glances that boded no good, bowed before Leonardo and picked up his luggage without waiting for his orders.

But instead of leaving, as Leonardo had hoped they would (his last hope in the world), they stood there.

"Go, go," said Leonardo. "Wait for me in the carriage."

"Our Lady ordered us not to leave without you."

"And I order you to wait for me in the carriage."

They heeded his order for as long as it took them to go two slow steps out of the door, but their eyes remained fixed on the trio, to make sure Leonardo would follow them without any interference. But even they had underestimated the power of the splendor they presented—and represented—because Peppino and Liborio were beginning to follow along after them, while Leonardo stood stock-still and didn't seem likely to move at all. Obviously, with Burini one had to be more specific, and so they were; resorting to gestures and glances rather than words, they simply shooed the two un-wanted elements away, and moved back to stand by their designated but reluctant new master.

"Don Leonà," said Peppino, shaking him by the arm, "why are

you so gloomy? Don't tell me you're more of a priest than even we thought. This is the chance of your life. . . ." Then, to Liborio, on Leonardo's other side: "Right?"

"A thousand times right . . . Hey, Don Leonà, what's wrong with being so lucky? God knows what joys await you. Thank the Lord God on your knees for your luck. Are you afraid we'll talk to Giovanna? Never, but never, never, never, on our word of honor . . . You tell him too, Peppino."

"But he knows it," said Peppino, "he knows it . . . and if he doesn't, it's an insult to us, as men of honor. These are secrets for men, wives have nothing to do with them. Listen to me, Don Leonà, with a mistress like Mary you can do whatever you want. It's a blessing not only for you, but for your wife. You can stop nagging her because she spends too much, you can pay for all her dresses and hats, bring her jewels, buy her a villa. And you can help Laterza . . . build hospitals, aqueducts, a railroad station. And how about the church? That needs restoring. We bet you anything Don Ciccio Paolo your uncle will be the first to congratulate you if Mary helps him. My God, money is MANNA, and what the Church says about being faithful to wives has never had any real meaning except of course that we must do things intelligently, to avoid scandal. And as to that, trust us. . . ."

While this was going on upstairs, a crowd had assembled in front of the hotel and inside. The hotel owner in his filthy apron (he was also the owner and cook of the tavern next door), his wife and children, elderly people from the neighborhood, a couple of beggars, monks, priests, even a few German globetrotters in their leather pants and hairy legs, all were watching the fabulous horse carriage across the narrow street and whispering among themselves, as if to court the invisible owner of such wealth with their approval of the way he kept his horse ("very well-fed; well-groomed, too . . .") and his carriage ("beautiful varnish, perfect colors, look at those wheels"), but the coachman seated on his throne seemed to despise them all.

Finally, the two uniformed brigands came down, carrying Leonardo's miserable-looking suitcase and plaid. To the great surprise of the crowd, they didn't even go near the big carriage, but walked towards the ends of the street, where another carriage was waiting for them. They put the luggage into it and rushed back, exchanging whispers with the coachman, but refusing to talk to the plebeians who were besieging them with direct questions.

Now Leonardo appeared, flanked by his assistants who were actually holding him by the arms, not because he needed them to, but rather to impress the crowds with their own importance. Leonardo did look pale and distraught enough to justify the suspicion that he might be someone very sick, and he made a gesture of impatience when he heard this possibility aired. Instantly, his assistants chased away the crowd with harsh words that failed to obtain the desired results, because their directness, more even than their accent, marked them at once as outsiders to the fabulous world of the rich, whose servants were either very cordial or very dignified in their contempt for the lowly.

And these lowly being Roman, they were not going to accept such bad manners from a couple of Burini and said so. This threatened to disturb the dignity of the coachman and his assistants, who intervened, but not against their own countrymen, rather against the two foreigners from the Twin Kingdom who had no business to be in the capital anyway. "Who are you?" asked the coachman, probably interpreting their intervention as an impediment to Leonardo's freedom of action.

"They are my assistants," shouted Leonardo, with all the authority of which he felt capable. "And I am here on an official mission to the Senate of the Kingdom. Watch your words, please."

"I'm sorry," said the coachman, jumping down from his throne and taking off his top hat, as he bowed and opened the coach. "I thought you alone were expected. . . ."

This embarrassed Leonardo so much that he began to apologize. "Never mind explaining, please, my good man. You are doing your duty and we are doing ours. In life everybody does what he can to do what he must."

"Oh, there you are right, you are perfectly right," said the coachman, becoming very amicable all of a sudden.

"Bravo, bravo," shouted the hotel owner, giving the signal for general applause. "Well said . . ." And the crowd, which had

grown even thicker by now, moved massively around the coach,
making the horse begin to shift nervously, so it was now the two
brigands in breeches and white stockings who stepped in, pushing
away the mob and using very bad language as they did so.

"Just a moment," shouted Leonardo, "that's no way to deal with
people. Do you think you can act that way just because you are
dressed up like clowns?"

"Sir," they snapped right back at him. "We are acting on orders,
and Our Lady was very worried in case these two men tried to
prevent you from leaving. We are doing it to protect you."

"I'm sorry, I'm sorry," Leonardo kept repeating, to stop them.

But how could he leave now, without giving at least a hint of an
explanation to his friends? Had he been more of a city man he
might have used the freshly coined expression all the men of the
world were beginning to use in those days: "I'll telephone you." But
neither he nor they had ever even been near a telephone and,
besides, to admit he had such free access to one would only have
made him appear even more of a kept man than he was appearing
already. Unfortunately for him, Peppino now asked the coachman
directly: "Can you wait another minute, so we can put on some
decent clothes and come with him?"

The coachman blushed, which in turn made Leonardo blush because this meant the coachman knew too much, but Peppino took it
for granted that he could join Leonardo. "What are you waiting
for?" he said to Liborio. "Get dressed and we'll go too."

"No, no and no," shouted Leonardo angrily. "Are you insane?"

"But we'll only go as far as the door of Mary's palace at Via
Gregoriana forty-two . . . then come back." Leonardo had entirely
forgotten he had mentioned the address the previous night in a
moment of weakness, but to the coachman and to *his* assistants this
was evidence that all three Burini were dangerous people: one word
of complaint from them, and the Old Lady would dismiss them
from her service.

"We are going as far as Via Gregoriana, then you will drive us
back here," said Peppino to the coachman.

"Are you insane?" whispered Leonardo, withering Peppino with
his angriest glance and pinching him in the arm until he whim-

pered. It took a moment for this not-so-secret communication to
sink in, but when Peppino and Liborio realized that there was
nothing to be done about it, they tried at least to save face in front
of the crowd.

"As you say, Leonardo, as you say. We'll see you tomorrow with
your cousin the eye specialist to His Holiness and to His Majesty.
And bring Mary too, she will enjoy meeting your cousin. Remember
us to her. . . ."

He stopped, because Leonardo was about to explode, but made
his exit in great style, winking sordidly to Leonardo as he moved
away from him, then turning his back and disappearing into the
hotel. But Liborio was still there and he seemed to have a different
kind of face-saving exit in mind. Leonardo made angry glances at
him to go away; Liborio smiled stupidly, then whispered in his ear:
"Don't be angry, Leonardo. Peppino isn't a man of the world like
you or me. I understand the delicacy of your position."

"Thank you," said Leonardo, and embraced him affectionately.
Tears were rushing to his eyes and he was eager to get away before
anyone noticed.

"And by the way," said Liborio, who had been greatly pleased
with this show of affection. "One more thing."

Leonardo was already inside the carriage so it was easier for Liborio to speak without being overheard. "Does Mary have a sister?"

No answer came from the dark interior that smelled of wealth
untold. "Don Leonà, . . ." Liborio's voice began to sound like a
prayer in front of a holy image, "do me this one favor, Don Leonà,
don't abandon your friend and cousin. Even if there's no sister—a
cousin . . . or a friend . . . Rich people only know rich people
. . . so a friend will do. Please, please, Don Leonà, I shall be
grateful to you till I die . . . I'll pray for you day and night. And
you know I can be trusted . . . I'm not like Peppino. . . . Please,
Leonardo, please . . ."

Suddenly Leonardo moved, pushed Liborio so that he almost
landed on his back, leaped out of the carriage and ran into the
hotel, shouting to the coachman: "I'll be back, I've forgotten something."

A few seconds later he reappeared with his hat, and his dirty *spolverina* on his arm, jumped into the carriage, the coachman closed the door, mounted his throne and Cinderella's golden coach began to move away.

It took Leonardo a few seconds to recognize the palace. He had fallen asleep almost instantly after leaving the whole world behind. Then he recognized the door and the doorman and shouted: "But this isn't the hotel."

"No," said the coachman, "but I was ordered to take you back here."

"That's not true because I heard the orders when I left with you."

"Yes, but new ones came when Madame was so worried about you and sent the two footmen to find out where you were."

At this juncture the two footmen appeared and nodded in chorus to the coachman's last words; they had just been upstairs to report the safe delivery of their captive and now all four servants stood there surrounding their new master and giggling nervously because they were all men and all Italians and all from the same social level, financially speaking at least. Leonardo was eager to put them at their ease, but *he* wasn't at *his* ease with these ridiculous flunkies dressed up as clowns. He had always been at ease with his servants back home: they were his father's trusted farmhands, servants of course, but almost part of the family; in fact, the correct term for them was still the Latin *Famuli*, and the *Familia* could never have functioned without them. And besides, they had been under the command of men, these were commanded by women, which subverted everything. This was the myth of Cinderella (a stupid, Nordic myth)—but Cinderella turned upside down, backside up, mirrored in a matriarchal society. The prince was a woman and Cinderella a poor orphan boy living in the political kitchen of Laterza, where his stepmother/great-uncle the Archpriest had tried to prevent him from going to Rome (*he* favored the Mafiosi who were opposed to the aqueduct). . . . And instead of being taken back to that kitchen in the golden coach with the glass slipper, he was being taken *away* from it with his battered suitcase, plaid, felt hat and *spolverina*, the symbols of his poverty.

"Let's go," he ordered suddenly in his manliest voice, and sank back into his portable museum of rare fabrics, silver trinkets and perfumes: a mere object among objects. Oh, for a *man*, to reassure him that *he* was still a man . . . There *was* the coachman up there, but all he could see was that bulging behind in those precious white trousers: he, too, was dressed up as a clown, and maybe laughing to himself at Leonardo . . . an unbearable thought. But then he was overtaken by a more worthy perception: If I want to be treated as a man, I must treat other men as men, and not as slaves. He tapped repeatedly on the glass partition that separated him from that white backside, and the coachman stopped his horses, opened the window and asked him, not at all deferentially: "What do you want?"

"Ride with you up there."

"Up here?? But this is for the footman."

"Lucky footman, but since he isn't there, may I ride with you?"

"If you want to see the view, I can take you through the Borghese Gardens. . . ."

"I want to talk to you."

There was a moment of hesitation, then: "But it just isn't done. . . ."

"Why?"

"People might think I'm giving a ride to a friend instead of doing my duty."

"I *am* a friend, and your so-called duty is to take me to my hotel."

"What will Our Lady say?"

"Leave it to me." And without waiting for further comments, he stepped out of his china cabinet, put on his *spolverina* and climbed up there, happy as a boy. This was in fact a dream version of his first ride on the village stagecoach, at the age of eight, and with the timid smile of those faraway days, he asked: "May I drive the horses?"

"Nossir. What if something happens? It's my responsibility."

"But I know how to drive. I'm a country doctor, except that my battered old Sunday trap is nothing like this. I usually ride my own horse, . . . nothing like these beautiful animals."

Not a word from the coachman. After a few seconds he stopped his horses and said: "This is the famous Pincio. If you care to see Rome in moonlight, there it is."

"No no, thank you, I want to talk to you, and first of all to apologize for insulting you in a moment of impatience."

"You had every right to."

"No no, I had no right at all, and I intended to apologize, but then, you see, those two friends of mine—they're not really friends, they work for me, and I paid for their trip—are totally uneducated people . . . I mean, education doesn't have to mean a doctor's degree, it means first of all being considerate towards others and restraining one's impulses. As the Delphic Oracle so wisely says . . ."

He was interrupted by the appearance of a very tall and very distinguished gentleman accompanied by a lady no less tall and no less distinguished, who made it a point to smile at the coachman, and the coachman became all smiles too, and took off his hat to them. But they were already gone.

"Who's that?" asked Leonardo, a bit jealous, because he now realized that the coachman had never greeted *him* so humbly.

"His Excellency, the Prince of Teano, Fondi and Bassiano, Duke of Sermoneta, the Honorable Onorato Caetani, former mayor of Rome."

This was all chanted like responses in catechism class.

"I am a mayor, too," said Leonardo resentfully.

"Oh? Of what city?"

"Laterza in the province of Brindisi. I'm in Rome to plead for an aqueduct. I addressed the Senate yesterday, and . . ."

He was interrupted again, this time by the sudden appearance of the very Senator who had invited him to speak, and who now winked at the coachman, without giving him the time to reply, because he was running after an elegant lady.

"That is the Senator who invited me to talk yesterday."

"Yes?"

"Yes. And you may wonder why I . . . I . . ."

"I never wonder about anything. I'm a Roman."

"But you *should,* because you must have noticed that Miss Mary and I . . ."

"It's getting windy, don't you want to ride inside?"

"No no, not at all. You see . . . without being indiscreet, and I do trust that you will keep this a secret, Miss Mary and I met at the

theater yesterday evening after nine long years of separation. We
were almost engaged to be married nine years ago, and then . . .
well, I said no, because of the obvious difference in wealth. I'm an
honorable man, I'm not one of those . . . you know . . . Anyhow,
this meeting was a miracle, and so now we're going to get married
after all."

The coachman stared at him with big eyes for a second, then
whipped the horses, shouting warnings to the crowds to make room
for his carriage.

"I know this may seem strange to you"—Leonardo was now
shouting too—"because it entails a divorce, or rather two. But we're
both unhappily married, and divorces are less scandalous than the
adultery these corrupt Romans practice without a second thought."

"EEEEEH-YUP . . ." shouted the coachman to the horses, making them gallop dangerously down a steep road.

"But I intend to continue in my profession, and I know I can
repay my future mother-in-law for the huge expenses all this entails."

They were now in a large square, and the coachman said: "That's
your hotel. The Hotel de Russie."

It was *such* a splendid hotel, with so many private carriages in
front of it—even two automobiles—and many, oh, so many elegant
people, that Leonardo felt it all as a reproach, thinking of the
battered suitcase that would soon emerge from what was now almost *his* coach. "I am a simple man like you," he said. "This is not
going to corrupt me. In fact, I can even be useful to my mother-in-
law, by helping her save money on all these useless trinkets, like
private carriages and uniformed servants."

Silence from the coachman.

More uniformed servants, dressed up like soldiers, stormed the
coach and practically dragged him out of his hiding place, exposing
him and all his symbols of poverty to public ridicule. At the glass
door of the hotel, a group of dwarfs in red uniforms and white
gloves took charge of the prisoner and ordered him to stand in front
of a civilian judge in morning coat, who asked his name, nodded
and rang a bell, which was answered by a very elegant jailer with a
huge key in his hand, who in turn ordered him in a polite but
authoritarian whisper: "Follow me." Leonardo tried to pick up his

luggage, but the jailer hissed, "No!" and signaled to a man in a green apron to help the gentleman. Gentleman . . . what gentleman? thought Leonardo. Am I a gentleman?

He passed several palm trees and reached a staircase so large that for a moment he thought he was in the Senate again, except that this was more elegant: a light-brownish rug with two wide red stripes on the sides, overlaid with a lighter white rug that seemed like a bedsheet, covered every step and was anchored by a thick golden bar at the base of each riser. As he gradually put more and more distance between himself and the inquisitive eyes of his judges, he felt more confident, and could begin to think about the one thing that had seemed so infinitely distant for such an infinite number of hours: the chance to undress and lie down. And right beyond this thought, he saw and felt an infinity of riches all his own: Mary's love and the promise of a new life, Mary's mother as a new and intelligent mother for him too. But this whole world was sinking in a haze under the moon of his shadowy memory, and it could well wait for the new day. To bed, to bed . . . He unbuttoned his boots and threw them away into the huge room that had been opened for him, then collapsed on the bed without even dismissing the servant or taking off his jacket.

THIRD DAY

When he woke up he knew it was late; he had known it for some time in his sleep, and Giovanna had told him to get up, but he had turned his back to her because he was too tired and just couldn't leave his bed. He knew he couldn't justify the long delay and his failure to notify the city council that he was not coming back in time for the meeting, he knew it all, but still he could not get up. And he had fallen from dream to dream, always believing that he *had* got up and gone to the meeting, but the first time the meeting had been held in Mary's library, and she was always hiding behind curtains and pianos and statues of her parents. It had been a relief to be shaken out of it by Giovanna, and to get up at long last. But the next dream had always been as bad as the preceding ones, and always ended in the illusion that this time he really had got up and gone about his business, but if it wasn't the city council it was his waiting room filled with dirty patients, some with bandaged arms or legs or swollen faces because of a sore tooth that had to be pulled, others with children whose eyes were bandaged because they had trachoma, and there were also pregnant women who had come in for a checkup and still, every single time, the scene had been Mary's dining room, or that fantastic bathroom, but much wider than anything he had ever seen in his life, in fact, it had always been the square in front of St. Peter's, and there had always been two toilets with two water jets as high as the two fountains in front of St. Peter's, and the moon, and the sun and the doorman and the coachman and the theater and the restaurant, and both hotels—all so vivid and yet so confused that he had woken up exhausted, only to fall back into the same kind of confusion, to feel even more anguished and tired. At long last he woke up in his dormitory at the Jesuit college of Matera, because the alarm clock

had been ringing and ringing so loudly that he couldn't ignore it
and he jumped out of bed to stop it once and for all. But there was
no such object in the whole room, and yet the alarm went on ringing and ringing, and then finally he really did wake up and he recognized the origin of that terrible sound: a black telephone of the
strangest make ever seen, not nailed onto a wall, but placed like a
huge stethoscope on his night table. He grabbed the two big receivers and out of habit put one to his ear and the other on his chest.
When he realized what he was doing, he began to laugh convul-
sively, with high soprano shrieks whenever he had to gasp for
breath, followed by more gusts of choking laughter, and so he paid
little attention to the voice rattling inside the stethoscope, imagining
that it was Mary, and feeling confident that his laughter would suffice for the moment to reassure her he was well and happy. Which
in fact he was, to his surprise, for the first time in his whole life. So,
without even saying so much as "I'm coming downstairs," he put
the receivers back on the hooks. Before running out of the room to
find the toilet, he first tried to find his boots, and it alarmed him
that he couldn't remember where he had thrown them. He did recall it had been somewhere in the distance, but he searched in vain
behind thick and thin curtains at either side of the two windows,
behind armchairs and dressers; the damn boots seemed to have
walked out by themselves. In despair he opened the door and was
resigned to walking to the toilet in his stockinged feet (doubly disturbing, first of all because such a thing isn't done, and secondly,
because he had holes in his socks). He began to call loudly: "Where
are my boots? Hey, someone, anyone, waiter, where are my boots?"
A chambermaid appeared at the end of the corridor and said: "I'll
call your steward," then was gone. By that time he had seen his
boots in front of another door and grabbed them, but was in too
much of a hurry to put them on, and besides there was no chair on
which to sit for such an operation and he didn't have the appropriate
instruments, so he proceeded to open one door after another, but
not one of them opened on a toilet. He was in such pain he didn't
even notice the commotion he was causing and the number of
people who were protesting. Finally a tall foreigner, speaking a
language he had never heard, grabbed the boots from him, calling
him all sorts of names in his strange tongue. He fought for his boots

shouting: "Thief!!! What are you doing?" and when the concierge
arrived with a number of stewards and chambermaids, they were
at great pains to separate the two fighters and explain to Leonardo
that his boots were right at the entrance of his own room. This
calmed him down, but only for a second: he was still trying to find
the toilet, and still angry that someone had dared take his boots
away from his room while he was asleep.

"What kind of a hotel is this," he shouted, "where they take your
boots and leave them at your door?"

"But sir, this is the rule—"

"To hell with rules, where is the toilet?"

"In your *suite*, sir."

"In my *what*???"

"Here, sir."

And he was shown the door leading from his bedroom to his
bathroom.

He was so happy to find himself where he wanted to be that he
slammed the door in the face of the steward and gave way to his
happiness. After which, he began to observe his private bathroom,
the bathtub, the faucets, and then began, like a child, timidly to
experiment. Suddenly, above his head, he heard a terrifying explosion, and saw a whole surface of blue flames rise from a screen
under a huge copper boiler, and dance merrily, while a thick vapor
emerged from one of the two open faucets and from the bathtub
into which the water was falling. What reassured him (but not
quite) was that all this fire looked like the gas flames he had used in
the chemical laboratory at the University of Naples while a student—but why this waste to heat the water for a bath? He had
never taken a bath, although he had used sitting baths, but then
only on such solemn occasions as justified the waste of water, burning wood, and endless ado: women going to the fountain for water,
warming it, pouring it into the sitting bath in the opposite corner of
the kitchen, and then washing and scrubbing the bather with a long
brush. Babies of course require these services at least once a week,
but as one grows older one does not expect to be treated like a baby
by a doting mother. Only a married man has the right to exact these
services from his wife, unless she feels too citylike to perform them,
and Giovanna had made it quite clear on the day of their wedding

that she would never give him a bath. "I'm descended from Saint Thomas Aquinas on my mother's side and have five monsignors in my father's family, all five active and quite likely to become bishops, perhaps even Cardinals before long. I am not going to give you a bath."

"And I don't wash in holy water," he had snapped back, thus making it clear that he was, at heart, anticlerical. He swam in summertime, when cold water is a pleasure, but how about this now? Why not try it?

He studied the situation, saw that there was a rubber cork at the end of a chain in the tub and that it fitted the waste hole; he mixed hot and cold water until it seemed perfect, and then he flung his clothes into the bedroom and jumped into the first "tub" of his life. Sitting there, he was transported once again, but this was more of an enchanted coach than Cinderella's horse-drawn carriage. Oh, the joys of ablution, "the correct term for which," he said aloud to himself, "is absolution, and, in fact, *Ego te Absolvo* means: I wash thee from the filth of sin. . . . Baptism by immersion is the truest form of redemption Christ wanted for his followers . . . hence: an AQUEDUCT for my people, made impure by filth and disease for lack of water." This thought somewhat clouded his joy, but, as he was a realist, he told himself that there was no going back now. He must pass through the whole process of redemption from subservience to a world of hypocrisy and cunning he had always detested, so that he could return to Rome in triumph, married to the woman he loved, surrounded by his own children, and established (why not?) like his cousin Crocifisso, as a leading physician, with enough power, coming to him from his wife's money, to influence the government without having to associate with shady figures from the Camorra, in order to obtain that damn aqueduct and lots of other things for the underprivileged. And again he departed towards the enchanted shores of fantasy in his white porcelain carriage . . . "the correct term for which is *ship*, because I *navigate* . . . but no, this is not navigation, this is contentment, the correct term for which is *containment*, because this is a *container* and I am traveling *in the space it contains* . . . a *humid* space, in fact, solid matter, not solid enough to be impenetrable, but solid enough to move as part of my body, in fact, if I move slowly enough to imitate a body as large and heavy as this whole body of water, I can impart the impulse of my own muscles to this body, and make it move with me."

He tried, and it worked. Moving his arms and legs under water without making a ripple, he slowly imparted their movement to the water, and soon enough the water was going right overboard and falling onto the marble floor with the same noise as the waves on a very quiet day on the white rocks of Capo Miseno or Santa Maria di Leuca, back home . . . all mixed with the suds of a soap so divinely scented as to remind him of the wild lilies growing on the beaches of Apulia. These waves breaking on the rocks became so true that tears came to his eyes while he was watching them and basking in the warmth he could receive from the faucet by a mere twist of his fingers. More and more waves splashed out of the tub, more and more warm water came in from the source. Oh, the joys of Sybaritic wealth! Now he knew what had stopped him from studying archaeology: the lack of documents. Death is no document for the study of life. Obviously, the real sites to excavate are the great modern cities, which are still above ground and still functioning. You are learning more about Pompeii from this one bathtub than from all the fragments of bathtubs you have dusted and classified and put under glass. Accept, Leonardo, accept your new condition as a challenge. Pretend you are plunging into this blessed water of wealth for the sheer pleasure of gratuitous daily ablutions, and learn how to move these waves until you can displace as much weight as your whole body, and— Splash! He watched the waves fall on the marble floor and spread until only a thin sheen of humidity remained, because the bathroom was so large that it would have taken a whole tubful to wet it all. Some of the water reached the bedroom from under the closed door, but Leonardo didn't worry: he knew that brick floors absorb water so quickly that before you can sweep the wet dust with a broom, the whole surface is almost dry. "Eureka!" he shouted suddenly, laughing again as he had laughed when he mistook the telephone for a stethoscope. "Eureka!!!" He had discovered Archimedes: the MAN behind the discovery: "What guided Archimedes to discover his law? The comfort of a hot bath, such as they had in all our ancient cities before the great Mediterranean cultures disintegrated, and the Nordic barbarians brought us the poverty and filth that are still with us, after all these many centuries of superstition, degradation and foreign rule. Hygiene is essential if modern man is to advance towards worthier goals. It all depends on *who* is sitting in the bathtub, and why he wants to displace his weight in water. Specific weight? No, specific *purpose*: that is the correct term. So: Eureka! and Eureka! again, I am the Man behind the Law!"

After his bath, time for the finishing touches. He emerged a new man: clean-shaven to the very edges of his superb goatee, his mustache soft and curled, as if to guide the admirer's glance towards his fiery eyes, so full of purpose and . . . why not?—genius.

". . . for what is genius but perseverance and focused effort?" He donned the white bathrobe lying ready, tied its white belt around his waist, and what he saw in the tall, *masculine* mirror (not Giovanna's tall mirror, half hidden by her stupid veils and cheap cosmetic bottles and hairpins and picture postcards of the places they had visited during their honeymoon) was a real Roman Senator, marching forwards with dignity towards his reflection, then away from it. . . . But at this point another startling discovery presented itself to him: The tall mirror came in three sections, two of which could be moved like windowpanes. This was a triptych, and it showed Leonardo as he had never seen himself—from the sides, even from the back, and he liked himself even more. Which led to a third discovery: *This* is what was at the root of my unhappiness yesterday: cheap suit, crumpled collar and cuffs, and above all, the smell of stale sweat all over me after two days of frenzied activity: pleading with bureaucrats, running up and down the stairs of huge public buildings, that long talk at the Senate, the evening at the theater, then the restaurant, and the next morning in those museums, and then the anguish of the ride. . . . How could I offer myself to the woman I love as something even vaguely worthy of her presence? Oh, why don't I have enough money to go out and buy myself a shirt and a necktie as splendid as the ones Mary's servants wear?

Suddenly he perceived the horror of the next few days, which were supposed to be the happiest in his life: would she GIVE him the money to buy himself what he needed, to regain his lost face with her servants? And if so, even if they didn't guess, wouldn't he lose face with *himself* forever? Oh, if only this second Archimedes could tell himself he had made a real, scientific discovery in his bathtub, one applicable to all mankind, not just to his particular person, wouldn't he feel release from this anguish? . . . But let's be realistic: let's go back to the wardrobe I have and see if the shirt I wore on the journey is still in better condition than the one I had on yesterday. And how about my socks? There is another pair of dirty socks in that suitcase, not clean (hardly, after sixteen hours on that train), but at least they have no holes. . . .

He opened the door to his bedroom and was blinded by sunshine from two large windows he hadn't observed before, because the room had been dark and he had had to turn on the light, and the corridor, too, had been lit by electricity. This was no longer the view over the Cupolone: this was an entirely new Rome he had never seen before: a steep cliff, like those back home, but so full of vegetation that no countryside he knew bore any relation to it; oak trees growing almost horizontally out of the cliff, stretching out their green arms towards his room. And hidden birds singing and flying from branch to branch. And swallows circling the deep blue sky above the trees . . . children shrieking in the distance, playing in open spaces he could not see . . . a beaded haze of water from fountain jets above the cliff, like so many heads of nymphs, shaking their vaporous locks in the wind. . . . Closer to him, deep inside the dry body of the cliff, a huge fountain mask: an ugly old god. Father Jupiter pouring his discreet thread of water into a huge marble ear lying in front of him: the ear of Mother Earth. . . . Leonardo was beginning to fall in love with Rome, and the thought that he might have to leave Italy tonight struck him suddenly as grave news. But perhaps those old foxes in the Vatican . . . their casuistry was such that they could grant him a divorce under the guise of Special Dispensation.

Suddenly, from deep inside the natural theater beyond its curtains of branches and nymph heads and voices and sounds, the deep, sinister voice of the Cupolone echoed so frightfully that even Mother Earth and Father Jupiter seemed to be silenced by it. "DONG . . . DONG . . . DONG . . ." Leonardo counted twelve, and he couldn't believe his own ears. But a hundred other chattier church bells from all over Rome came crowding into the cavern in search of echoes of their own, all chiming midday, though in less dictatorial terms, all responding to orders from the Vatican. Other signs that it was noon came from a source Leonardo had missed until now: the cadence of brick-dropping from the pushcarts of masons in some nearby construction site, and the cadence of songs, interrupted by giggles, curses and the breaking of bricks under a hammer. All this came to a stop and Leonardo knew: These are the lazy Romans stopping whatever work they are doing at twelve noon sharp, to eat their bread and anchovies or cheese and drink their wine in the sunshine, then go to sleep stretched out precariously on top of thin walls, covering their faces with their hats. If there is one law the Italians trust, it is the law of gravity when they're taking their midday nap. With what deep faith in its authority they give their bodies to the surface supporting them in sleep. . . . And again he noticed that he was procrastinating. Ah, I know why. . . . To reach that world out there, which is now my world, I must dress up like a slave, the lowliest of them all; namely, a slave of his ideals, who refuses to be a Mafioso or Camorrista, and is too educated to don the honest uniform of a coachman or a cook, the two categories of servant I would choose for myself, if I were not an educated person, with a responsibility towards my parents, who sacrificed their last savings to give me an education. . . . Be a realist, Leonardo, this is your temporary role in the fairy tale; CIN-DERELLO IS YOUR NAME!

Only now did he realize that his gold watch was on the dresser between him and the window. He couldn't recall putting it there or taking it off his white waistcoat, and he had slept with it in his pocket on purpose: too lazy to leave the room and wash his hands (he had seen no trace of a washbasin), he had known that one more handling of the buttons of that waistcoat would have made it totally unpresentable for the next day, and his other waistcoat, the one he had worn on the train, was so dirty it had had to be wrapped in an old newspaper, lest it contaminate the "other" shirt with the greasy soot of sixteen hours' uninterrupted travel.

"Strange," he said aloud, "I didn't put it here, but perhaps I was too tired to remember what I was doing, or I wouldn't have slept so long. Let's see, where did I put my only presentable waistcoat. . . ."

But he couldn't find it.

"Let's see . . . I undressed HERE and put my waistcoat HERE . . . and my shirt HERE . . . and my socks HERE . . ." No traces of anything anywhere. Now frantic, he went to his suitcase where his "other" suit was packed, and the suitcase was EMPTY.

"Madre di Dio . . . Madonna del Carmine . . . " (his two most solemn swear words).

Suddenly, there was a knock on the door and a servant in a green waistcoat appeared with a rag in his hand.

"Where is everything? Who stole my shirt, my suit, my socks? Who dared to open my suitcase?"

"Not I, Your Highness, . . . I have come to—"

"Highness, my ass, you imbecile, don't you dare use those servile words with me."

"How shall I address you, . . . Highness?"

"Call me Mister Mayor. I am the mayor of the city of Laterza in the province of Brindisi."

The servant, who had already revealed his Tuscan origins, now revealed his knowledge of Leonardo's birthplace by laughing in his face, as he said: *"Bella harriera!"** (What a brilliant career!)

Leonardo hesitated for a moment before reacting. Used as he was to giving everybody a chance to air his opinion, he couldn't quite imagine such cold irony, which, more even than the accent and the Etruscan C, is the true essence of Tuscan speech. No Roman would have made such a comment: he would simply have asked: *"E a me che me ne fotte der sindaco de Laterza?"* (And what fucking use is the mayor of Laterza to me?) And no one in the Kingdom of the Two Sicilies would have been so mild. He would have come forward with his own social weapons, always preceded by the sinister warning: "You don't know who you're talking to," and *then* have mentioned or, in correct terminology, *brandished* the names of his powerful relatives or masters. Thus a lowly servant like this one, who was obviously good for nothing except to wash floors or repair leaking toilets, would have insisted he was an intimate of His Excellency, Highness or Majesty whose personal toilets or floors had been

---

* The Tuscans still pronounce C as H, as did the ancient Etruscans—a whim satirized by Horace.

his own family's privileged area of work for three generations.* Not a Tuscan, however: whether plumber or Pope, a Tuscan stood forever on his linguistic privilege, which he had inherited from the greatest user of the satirical whip, Dante Alighieri. Leonardo understood this, so he gave himself time to interpret this appraisal of his career (which he *did* consider brilliant, since he had become mayor without using any of the local Camorristi to win the election, and despite the opposition of the entire local clergy). And while Leonardo did his thinking, the servant most disrespectfully brushed him aside, to go and mop up the water off the floor all along the edges of the thick carpet and even underneath with a filthy rag, wringing it again and again into his equally filthy pail. Suddenly it dawned upon Leonardo that *"Bella harriera" must* have been meant as an insult, and he cast his first fulminating glance of moral and sociopolitical indignation deep into the mirror, where, in some forlorn corner of that large room, he saw the backside of his enemy, and the green strings of the apron tied around his waist. At the same time he couldn't help noticing the reflection of the handsome Roman Senator in charge of National Science and Future Redemption of the Italian Character, so he let the Senator have more of a voice in the matter than the humble mayor of Laterza would ever have dared claim for himself, and thus, for the first time in his life, he used the word "serf" in an utterly disparaging tone, shouting: *"Servo ignorante ed arrogante, t'insegnerò io a mancar di rispetto ai tuoi superiori."* (Ignorant and arrogant serf, I'll teach you to talk disrespectfully to your superiors.)

"A me tu, sindaho de' mie' hoglioni, nun insegni un bel cazzo" (you don't teach me a beautiful prick, you mayor of my balls), and Leonardo, despite his unspeakable anger over the familiar *tu* and the great anguish caused him by the notion that he would lose face forever if he actually grappled with such a low creature, couldn't fail to notice yet again that in certain cases the Etruscan C becomes a

---

* This explains why since the days of the Teutons and Goths the Twin Kingdom alone had kept such underbrush of the heraldic flora as: *Count of the South Gate of the City*, or *Marquess of the Third Door of the Second Floor of the Royal Palace* (in correct terminology, *Guard at the South Gate* and *Valet in Front of That Third Door*).

very hard H, and wondered what the phonetic rule was for such a
sudden change. The low creature in the meantime had resumed his
verbal attack by saying that he, on the other hand, could teach the
mayor of his balls to take a bath without flooding two rooms: his
own and the room below, where a distinguished lady had been
awakened by rain falling on her bed.

"It's obvious that you've never had a bath before," he concluded,
still mopping and giggling disrespectfully.

Could Leonardo take advantage of his strategic superiority and
kick the bastard in the ass, as he felt inclined to do? Never! So he
tried to elevate the tone of the quarrel, by restoring the serf to a
social dignity he had denied him in a moment of anger, and began
by apologizing: "I am sorry I called you a serf—I apologize—but
you forced me to do so. Yes, of course, you could teach me to take a
bath, and I am sorry I caused such inconvenience to people downstairs. Yes, it is my first tub bath, but does that put me on a lower
social rung, or justify your passing from a servile attitude unworthy
of your dignity to an even unworthier impertinence towards another
human being like yourself?"

"*Essere umano homemme? Tu, un Burino hafone, sporco me-
ridionale figlio di troia?*" (Human being like myself? You, a rude
Burino, filthy southern son of a bitch?)

This was too much, and Leonardo decided that a kick in the ass
was the only possible answer for the moment, pending the several
social sanctions to be taken by the man's employers but he found
himself confronted with a madman threatening him with a shower
of filthy water from his pail, and how could he ever have answered
that, without bloodshed?

During the brief moment of hesitation a maid and two other
servants entered the room behind Leonardo's back, which he noticed only when he saw his enemy put down the pail and laugh
disrespectfully in his face, as he explained the situation to the newcomers.

"Look at him . . . just look at him, the bloodthirsty Burino.
Next he'll take out his stiletto and plunge it into my heart. . . . Do
you know what he did? He accused me of stealing his shirt and his
other filthy rags."

"Shame on you," said the maid, using the respectful *Lei* and speaking almost with affection: "I'm not pleased with you, young man, not pleased at all. Don't you know that in *any* hotel, anywhere *in the world*, the staff polishes your boots and washes your laundry and brushes and presses your suits? We're no thieves, we're all honest people who work hard for our bread and have our human dignity, just like yourself."

"And I apologize to you too, but you should have heard him insulting me, after demeaning himself by calling me Your Highness!!"

"He was doing his duty! He didn't know you were here. This room was occupied until last night at nine by a foreign royal highness who did very strange things, and looked very much like you, but he was nice and you are not."

"Not nice . . . nossir . . . not nice . . . nossir," she kept repeating, as she put Leonardo's newly pressed suit on the back of a chair, and his ironed and neatly folded shirts, waistcoat and socks on the dresser. "Here, they're still wet, wait at least an hour before you put them on. I did the best I could, trying to wash them and dry them and iron them too . . . and mend your socks. Not nice, sir, not nice . . ."

The men were all silent, but snickering disrespectfully at Leonardo, while he stood there, no longer a proud Roman Senator, as the mirror informed him instantly, but a very embarrassed little boy, whose naked feet were exposed for everyone to see and which they seemed to disapprove of as much as his manners. How would he ever explain to Mary's mother—now—that he was worthy of her daughter and of the huge sums of money she must spend in order to obtain a Burino like him for a new son-in-law?

"Here, I'm finished," said the serf he had so unjustly provoked, and Leonardo heard him wring his dirty rag into the pail once more, but didn't dare turn and face him. And yet he knew the only decent thing he could do would be to stretch out his hand and say: "I'm sorry, let's be friends." The maid probably expected just that, thought Leonardo, wondering what made her smile at him after having so justly accused him of the worst crime he had ever committed against his own dignity.

He felt he did not deserve such easy forgiveness. The warm sunshine reflecting in his face from the glass top of the dresser was almost lulling him to sleep. His eyes were closing, an unexpected snoring sound came from his nostrils, bringing a sneer to the faces staring at him from invisible points in the deep shadow. . . . Suddenly a door opened behind him (since yesterday afternoon there were more and more doors in his life) and shrieks of delight from everyone in the room isolated him even more cruelly from the joy of that beautiful spring day. He didn't turn around; but the loud and authoritative voice of Sophie paralyzed and moved him at the same time, as if his whole body were rotating on an invisible pivot, after being turned to stone.

"I'm so happy to see you have made friends with my dear, *dear* friends, Leonardo . . . I knew you would. . . ." And without paying any further attention to him, she embraced the maid, kissing her on both cheeks, then shook hands with the men, and especially with the serf, who apologized, because his hands were wet.

"Oh, come on, Dante," she chided him in her strong Russian accent, "if you have shaken hands with my friend Leonardo, you can't give yourself such airs with me, you *bizarre Florentine spirit.*"

Leonardo was thunderstruck by these three words from the Eighth Canto of the *Inferno.* Could this Dante be a Dante scholar? But Sophie didn't give him time to go on wondering. Unfortunately, she reverted to French, this being her usual signal for the servants to leave, and Leonardo, who thought he knew French because he had read many medical texts in French, found himself at a loss, but tried to make up for his ignorance by feigning great attention and seriousness, as she said: "When I settled in Rome, after my husband's death, this was my bedroom. The next room, where we are going to have breakfast, is still ours: we keep that and the rooms facing the square for occasional guests when the house is too full. This room I had to give up, because it is famous the world over, and people who have been in Rome even once, have either lived in this hotel or been told about this fabulous view. I came here yesterday afternoon, when you were having tea with Mary, and asked for it, knowing you would like it. They said it was occupied but I see now they were able to make the Shah of Persia leave. . . ." She began to giggle, then continued: "I'll tell you later what a swine he is. . . ." The servants, who all understood French, began to laugh nervously, but when they saw Leonardo's stern face, they thought he was still angry at them and not merely that he was ignorant of the language, and so they stayed on, making Sophie quite edgy. Two facts made their situation particularly alarming: that their beloved mistress had addressed him in the most familiar terms, and that she had come down from her palace to have breakfast with him so late in her day, which always began punctually at six. Finally, noticing something strange in the atmosphere, Sophie became really upset and said: "I'm terribly sorry, I hope you all understand, but I must discuss some very serious business with my friend here, who is the mayor of . . ." She looked at Leonardo for help, but that was the one word he could not bring himself to pronounce again, and his embarrassment alarmed her even more. "Help me, Leonardo. What is the name of your hometown?" There was a rapid, frightened glance between Leonardo and Dante, then Dante took the initiative and said, bowing deeply in Leonardo's direction,

"I believe . . . if I am not mistaken, that this gentleman mentioned the town of Laterza in the province of Brindisi."

"Yes, yes," said Leonardo, blushing with relief. "He's right. Laterza in the province of Brindisi. It should be in the province of Taranto, in Latin Tarentum . . . but it is not."

"And neither is he the mayor of Laterza any longer," said Sophie, obviously delighted. "As you have become such good friends, I might as well tell you that he and my daughter Mary are going to get divorces from their respective illegitimate wife and husband, and they will soon be married."

As in a comedy of errors, when the final *colpo di scena* shifts the embarrassment from the one victim of everybody's contempt to his oppressors, now appalled by the memory of what they have just said, so now these people lost all their spontaneity and looked as unhappy as Leonardo had until then.

Sophie understood nothing about Italy or the Italians, because her atoms were combined according to a different chemistry, but she had a keen sense of the dramatic, and she noticed at once that she was on stage, and that the audience wanted to be anywhere but in that theater. They were all equally terrorized by her presence. What could it be she had done to them, or *would* do, *once the terrible truth became known?* Asking them was no solution and she knew it: she had employed Italian servants much too long not to

know what they feared most—the testing of their beliefs, the asser-
tion of their rights. As long as they could wail behind closed doors
that their beliefs had been betrayed and their rights denied them,
they could be summoned from inside those doors to humiliate
themselves even further and then be kicked out again to cry in the
cold, but let no honest master dare help them to help themselves
rise in the world on his advice; they would instantly leave him and
find a more discreet master, one who didn't eavesdrop. And her
Protestant, Victorian conclusion was always the same: *These charming Italians don't want to rise in the world. They invest in our pity,
to conserve and develop their own capital of filth and laziness.*

"What is it?" she asked, distressed and pale, but no one answered. Left to her own deductions, which could only be based on
personal experience, she realized that the one element she could not
rely on was Leonardo, because she knew him least; in fact, she didn't
know him at all and had trusted him blindly. This famous Leonardo, this mythical person whom Mary had seen three or four
times perhaps, but briefly, nine years before, and only in the street
or in museums, *who was he? On what knowledge of him and of his
past* had *she* given him *her* daughter, *her* grandson and *her* personal
fortune? Instantly she too fell prey to inner upheavals that could
neither be expressed in action nor in words, and thus the comedy of
errors turned to a high tragedy that now reached into real life.

"What is it?" she asked again, in a tone of command her former
servants had never heard addressed to them, only to Mary or to
Mary's governess in moments of crisis and/or high drama, from
which they had dutifully fled, out of discretion, to take shelter in
the kitchen, where the woes of the rich are forever reviewed as
comedies or completed as tragedies, by the addition of the Chorus.

"What is it?" she asked again, in a shrill voice that made shivers
run down five identical Italian spinal cords. But now she could
perceive a difference between the eyes of her servants and those of
the Mythical Character, and knew at once: he must have told them
things they couldn't help listening to, because they were doing their
duty, but he must have been boasting, as most Italians do, probably
without mentioning names, and her arrival had suddenly revealed to
these kindly, honest, simple souls just *who* was the victim of this
Burino's filthy schemes, and of course they didn't dare speak, be-

cause they had added their own comments to his boastful vulgarities, so they were guilty too and frightened of his retaliation, but
they had an excuse and he had none, so it was for him to speak.

"Mister Mayor," she said, in the iciest tone she could summon,
"would you deliver yourself of one of your great speeches to this
auto-physio-psycho-logical Senate I have the honor to represent?
What vulgarities have you been telling these good, kind, honest
people? What indiscretion have you committed, Mister Individual?
Can you to tell me?"

Leonardo, whose greatest unhappiness at this point concerned
first his naked feet and legs, then his loss of face in front of his
enemies, and only in the ultimate instance his loss of Mary (happiness is forever an illusion), looked at her reproachfully and muttered: "You don't say, 'Can you *to* tell me,' you say, 'Can you *tell*
me.'"

"All right, I am a foreigner and I make my mistakes, but you
understood me well enough to be able to answer, before giving me
an Italian lesson, Mister Individual!"

Meanwhile, Leonardo was thinking: Cinderello's carriage broke
down on the cobblestones of reality and he found himself confronted with an insane foreign female. In correct terms, she suffers
from a progressive disintegration of the thinking processes, as indicated by her incoherent speech. Let's hope Liborio and Peppino
have enough money left for me. Perhaps Crocifisso will help me. At
least I got my laundry done for free and my pants pressed. I must
manage to put some of that perfumed soap into my suitcase. Will
they let me?

"All right. You won't answer, but you, my friends, will. Did he
say he wanted to take advantage of this crazy Russian woman, but
was going back to his wife?"

At that moment the door opened again, and the director of the
hotel stormed in, bowing to Sophie and saying: "We will have this
man arrested, Madame."

Sophie looked at him and shouted: "Have you been listening
behind closed doors?"

"I?? Never, Madame, I swear . . ."

"Get out of here, you came in without knocking."

The director looked even more distraught than Sophie, and Leonardo couldn't help smiling, but the servants were now completely at a loss. They didn't dare stay and they didn't dare leave. "You. Come with me," said the director. They all started leaving.

"No such thing," said Sophie, in French now.

"But, Madame . . . they are working for me."

"Here they are working for me and you get out at once. Understand?"

He did and closed the door behind him.

Now Leonardo felt like a Roman Senator again, in charge of public sanity. "You," he said to the maid, then, pointing to the others, "and you, and you, and you. Please answer the question Madame asked you. And you, Madame, calm down, please. Nothing is ever gained by losing your temper."

"Madame," said Dante, with his hand on his chest: "it was all my fault."

"Yes," said the maid, "and he can tell you that this gentleman never said anything about you or Miss Mary."

"Not a word," said Dante. "The soul of discretion. What happened was . . ."

But Sophie didn't let him go on. She embraced first Leonardo and then the maid, crying and giggling with joy, and this brought tears into the maid's eyes, and now Leonardo was crying too, and kissing the maid on both cheeks and receiving kisses and blessings from her and handshakes from the others, even embracing Dante, as in a great family reunion.

"Let's have breakfast," said Sophie, "I'm ravenously hungry."

"I . . . would like to get dressed," said Leonardo, who had regained his timidity with his happiness. Only in despair did he know how to behave, and even found pleasure in displaying that *savoir-faire* typical of the medical profession in poor countries, where there is nothing to be done, short of curing the social ills of centuries.

"You want to get dressed? Of course you want to get dressed, my poor friend, how inconsiderate of me to have entered your room while you were in your bathrobe. But don't get dressed yet. Here, come into the dining room and let me show you something."

Leonardo didn't dare protest, and followed her obediently like a little boy. The dining room, which was next to his bedroom, had a large table set for three, and the rest of the tablecloth was occupied by large and small packages tied with red ribbons. On each package were tiny envelopes, all addressed to him in beautiful calligraphy and with such endearing appellatives as *To the Sun, from the Moon*, or *To my love, from his wife*.

He was both moved and embarrassed to be reading such messages in Sophie's presence.

"Well?" she said, showing fresh traces of anguish. "Why don't you ask where Mary is?"

"Oh yes, where is she?"

"At home, crying."

"Crying? Why?"

"Because she thought she had lost you."

"Lost me? How? When?"

"When she called you this morning to tell you that you would find a new shirt, collar, waistcoat and a new pair of socks in this room, you laughed at her, then hung up."

"Ohhh, THAT . . . But let me explain. . . ."

"I know and I told her: he's laughing because he's happy, and because he is shy, and because he is amused at the idea that you can buy shirts and collars without having the right measurements, let alone neckties, which no man ever accepts from his wife."

"Not at all, I didn't understand a word of what she was saying, I laughed because—"

"I know, and I told her: he probably hasn't understood you and—"

"No, no, I didn't even listen, I laughed because—"

"Eat first and tell me later."

"No, I'll get dressed and rush . . . home, to console her. I cannot bear the thought of her crying."

"All right, take these packages to your room and get dressed, but I have to eat, because I'm ravenously hungry, and we'll be having lunch in a few minutes."

"I'll eat when Mary comes."

"No, we are going to eat lunch at home with Mary."

"But isn't this lunch?"

"No, this is what we call *small lunch*."

"A whole roast beef? Potatoes? And fish? . . . My God, this is a banquet!"

But Sophie wasn't listening to him. She was devouring fish and salami and lobster and heaven knows what. Leonardo had never seen such a rage for eating, and his clinical eye noticed at once that there was something childish, and at the same time almost senile, in this passionate way of attacking masses of food. He had seen it in psychiatric wards and read it in diagnoses of a form of despair in those whose stomachs had never been filled—but here? What could it mean? And for the first time he realized that, whatever it might mean in a medical textbook where the patient is classified like a fossil in a museum, it acquired a new medical significance if regarded as medicine to cure the doctor of his pride. He must learn to pity the rich just as much as he pitied the poor.

He was devoted to this woman now, even more so than the evening before: her absurd outburst of jealousy and suspicion made her at long last understandable beyond all her clear reasonings that were so unfeminine in nature, yet not even masculine: merely professorial. Now he knew that she cared for her daughter; she was therefore cleared of all lingering suspicion that she might be a *cocotte d'alto bordo,* as the Neapolitans call those women who trade in rich men and train their daughters in the ways of the profession after they have secured them the shield of a respectable marriage. He could afford to call her Mamma without offending the sacred memory of his real mother, but, this done, he could *not* afford to let her have her way. He was the master of the house now, he didn't want any of her money, and whatever she was to pay for his divorce would be repaid by him tenfold, from his own earnings—but she could not expose her own intimate fears and his dignity to public censure and ridicule, as she had done that very morning in that very room. Oh no. And neither could he let his future wife dress him up like her new doll, just because she had the money to do so.

"Sophie," he said, calmly but authoritatively, "stop eating for a moment and listen to me."

Sophie seemed struck by lightning upon hearing herself addressed in this way and yet pleased, because she smiled and stopped eating at once.

"What is it, Leonardo?"

"First of all, calm yourself. Don't eat so fast; the only train you'll miss by eating slowly is the Orient Express to the next world."

"How right you are. . . . You're a great man, you're like Gladstone. He always told me the same thing. Do you know that he used
to chew every mouthful eighty times before gulping it down?"

"And who is Gladstone?"

"I can't believe you don't know. . . . But that is unimportant."

"Quite right. Especially to you, who haven't learned the one
lesson he had to teach. What I wanted to say is, first of all, *eat
slowly,* then: *don't eat so much,* if you are to eat lunch afterwards,
and, thirdly, I am *not* going to wear a new shirt or new socks, when
my own things are clean and must be dry by now."

"But Mary will be very disappointed. She came here at nine this
morning, waited for you to wake up, then went out, bought shirts in
every size for you to choose from, came back and waited again, and
then had to go because Kostia and I were waiting for her in the
park, and I persuaded her to come home and call you from there."

"All right, one more reason to go home at once, but let me get
dressed first. I'll see you in a minute."

Back in his room, he found the maid busy airing his sheets and
beating the mattress on the windowsill.

"I'm late, Mister Mayor," she said, in a familiar tone that made
the appellative sound particularly sweet, the way it did from his true
followers back home, "but I took the liberty of mending your socks
and fastening those buttons on your trousers and here," she said,
showing him his waistcoat, "here it was coming apart at the seams. I
repaired it just in time."

"Oh, thank you, dear friend, you shouldn't have wasted your
precious time on me," he said, taking her hand and pressing it
against his heart.

"It wasn't wasted," she said, "you are a good man and I know
that you are a friend of the poor."

"Oh, come . . ."

"Yes, Mister Mayor, you are their protector."

"First of all, don't call me Mister Mayor. And then, how can I be
their protector, if I am practically one of them. Self-preservation
would be more accurate: everyone does what he can in our great
human family. You beat the dust out of my mattress, I beat the
microbes out of your blood, you keep my rags together on my body,

so it won't be naked, I keep the body on your soul, so *it* won't be
naked."

"Oh, but your knowledge is far greater than mine. . . . You save
my life."

"And what life would this be, if I lived in filth and lost my pants
and my waistcoat? My knowledge would be useless without yours,
and yours without mine. Only God has true knowledge, said Socrates."

"He must have been a saint. If we had more Socrateses in the
government, the Pope would still be king, instead of being a prisoner, deprived of his last penny. How can he help the poor, if he
can't even feed himself? You and I know who's responsible—those
heathen liberals. . . . Here, see? Your *spolverina* was coming apart
at the seams as well and had two buttons missing. I found two the
same color and sewed them on."

"Oh, thank you, you shouldn't have done all that. . . . I really
don't know how to thank you."

"You don't have to. Give a few microbes to those anticlericals,
and I'll kiss the ground on which you tread," she said. Then, as he
picked up his belongings and headed towards the bathroom: "No,
no, Mister Mayor, don't go in there. My son is washing the bathtub
and mopping up the floor. You can get dressed here, while I shake
these blankets out of the window. I won't look."

"But if he comes out?"

"My son? Oh no, not as long as he hears you talking in here. He
said so himself when he heard you coming in. He said: 'Mother, I'll
lock myself in the bathroom, don't let him come in, I don't want to
see him.' Not that he dislikes you, Mister Mayor, on the contrary,
he sees you as the teacher his father never was, and he's ashamed of
his ignorance. It's a good sign, Mister Mayor, God has finally answered my prayers. I'll have to tell Father Mansueto of the Capuchins about this as soon as I get out of here . . . he's my confessor,
and he's been praying for my son, and also, let me tell you confiden-
tially, for the conversion of Mary's mother, who's a saint without
even being a Catholic at all. And let me tell you about my husband,
while I'm at it . . . poor man, the Lord called him to His bosom to
give him his last chance to enter Purgatory before it passed him by,

and that's where he is right now. He was the devil incarnate. He
drank, he gambled, he squandered all the money I was sending him
to keep our son in school, so the boy never finished his education,
and I, who thought he was getting his degree and coming up in the
world . . . I wanted him to become a good priest, we have such
need of them, now that the Heathen have occupied Rome and
usurped the Holy Throne of Christianity. . . . So I wanted him to
become a real priest, but he wanted to study medicine, and nothing
came of it, because he never got his degree to enter the university.
He still could, but now he doesn't want to. I even sacrificed my
fondest dream of offering a real priest to our Church, I said never
mind, go ahead, study medicine if you prefer, but go back to school.
My brother, who is a saint, but has a family of his own to feed, said
he would gladly pay for his years in medical school, but he said no
and no and no. He prefers to work as the humblest of servants in
this hotel, where, if he only wanted, he could work in the office and
become the director, especially with your mother-in-law (and may
the Pope bless that union very, very soon, after he has given you
and Miss Mary the annulment you deserve); with her help, as I was
saying, he could soon rise to the top in this hotel, but he says no,
he'll mop the floors and wash the toilets, and that's what he prefers
to do. He's very proud."

"Let me get dressed," said Leonardo, "and I promise I'll look into
this matter and talk to your son, and also to my future mother-in-
law."

"Will you? Will you really? Do you mean it, or are you just trying
to get rid of me?"

"*Quanto è vero Iddio*" (as true as God is true), "I mean it. But
I'm also in a hurry, because Mary is at home crying, she believes I
don't want her any more, and I'm anxious to go and console her."

"You're a saint, you are. . . . Let me kiss you and bless you, my
dear, and I'll rush to church to pray for you both."

Before leaving she stopped in front of the dresser, where Leonardo's wallet, housekeys, keys to his office in Laterza, and a few
coins were piled up in a corner. Leonardo understood only too
clearly and said, much against his better judgment: "Take those
coins, please, and forgive me if I can't give you more. I have to cash
a check in the bank, there is nothing in my wallet."

She left in a hurry, mixing thanks to him with prayers to the Lord, as if to give him proof that she really did mean to pray and was in fact as urgently in need of the relief as he was to use the bathroom.

"Dante, get out of there, I need the bathroom," he said, shaking the door handle, and when Dante came out, apologizing like a beaten dog, he smiled and said: "All right, all right, no need to apologize, I'll see you soon, I want to have a long talk with you."

This was not only a way of apologizing for not having any money to give him, but also his most serious intention. He had understood Dante's situation and had every reason to become personally involved; indeed, Dante's problem was now second only to Mary's and Sophie's, because Leonardo had a sister, whose personal lot had been very much the same as this poor maid's, and if his sister had never been a hotel maid and her sons had never been hypocrites like Dante, Leonardo himself had been a hypocrite with his mother, for very much the same reasons as he detected here: she was terribly religious, a born martyr in need of constant martyrizers around her, and she had aggravated her husband's disposition to drink by her iron resignation to what he, in turn, came to accept as his own destiny: to be the God-appointed villain in his wife's Passion Play. She was the Female Christ on the Cross, as was now her daughter, whose very name seemed to have been predestined for such a part in her own Passion Play: Addolorata (the Bereaved One).

Addolorata had married her great love and both families hoped it would be the most perfect of marriages, but lo and behold, he turned away from her and became a public scandal by drinking, gambling—even philandering, but that only when she refused herself to him in disgust because of his drunkenness, and reproached him for spending all her dowry and leaving her penniless, burdened with three children (fortunately males, because a girl born of such a father would never have found a husband in all of Apulia). He had then gone off to live in Naples, taking two of the boys with him, and in Naples he had gambled and liquidated whatever money she could send him for educating the two boys (and it had been Leonardo's hard-earned money), until he died of cirrhosis of the liver and delirium tremens. Only then did Leonardo discover that the two boys had never gone to school, because there was no money either for tuition or books, but they had studied all the same, alone, borrowing the books from other boys in the class that should have been their own. And who had given them the moral strength to do such a thing? Uncle Leonardo, by sacrificing Mary (he had told them the story to give them moral strength), and their dear mother, by her exemplary devotion to her husband. She had never complained to anyone, always defended her husband's reputation in the family by pretending to believe all his lies, and the two sons in Naples had done the same with her, pretending that their father's lies were the truth. Back in Laterza with the two boys after the funeral, Leonardo had continued the sacrifice by paying the huge debts his brother-in-law had left in Naples, and by sending the two boys to the same school where he had once been so thoroughly trained in the classics. This was all past history, but of a very recent past. No resemblance between his nephews and that vulgar Florentine servant Dante, of course, but what shining example had *he* received from his mother's only brother? None at all: one more reason for Leonardo to save this lost sheep if he could, in expiation of his present sin towards the two nephews who were now studying at the University of Naples, and paying for their own tuition. They would certainly be shocked by the news that Uncle Leonardo had betrayed their mother (more than Giovanna, his own wife) because Addolorata, old and sick now, and with her third son still in public school, had no one to help her but her saintly brother Leonardo.

"Ready, let's go," said Leonardo, all dressed up, combed and dignified, with his *spolverina* on his arm and his hat in his hand, as he burst into the dining room.

But Sophie paid no attention to him. She was so engrossed in her conversation with the director of the hotel that she had not even touched the large triangle of chocolate cake on her plate, and was poking tiny holes in it with a thin, two-pronged fork, to mark the highlights of her orders. Their recipient, indeed, seemed to receive them and memorize them in the body of the same cake, nodding and promising obedience every time a new double hole was poked into the chocolate.

"Yes, Madame, yes, Madame . . . Right . . ."

"But is it definitely right?"

"Yes, Madame, it is."

"Clear?"

"Yes, Madame, perfectly clear."

"Repeat with me . . ."

"It isn't necessary, Madame, I remember every word you said, and I can swear on my honor—"

"None of that Italian swearing on your honor. I know what it's worth. Just repeat after me. Let's begin with this"—she pointed towards the first two holes on the upper left corner of the triangle, as if it were an agenda—"what did I say here?"

"You said we should ask your lawyer to be present as the estimate of repairs was made by our architect."

"Perfect. Now this: what did I say here?"

". . . er . . . er . . ."

"See? You've forgotten already."

"Oh no, Madame, I haven't. You said—"

"So much for your solemn oath: I said"—and the two tiny holes were carefully enlarged to make them clearer—"I said . . . NO, . . ." and she waited like a teacher for the pupil's reaction. "Cavaliere Pellacchia, you disappoint me again: I said NO FIRING OF THE MAID, OF DANTE OR OF THE TWO OTHER MEN."

"Oh yes, yes, of course, but that was out of the question."

"It was not, because you seemed quite determined to make them responsible for the whole scandal in front of your superiors."

"That was under the stress of emotion, Madame. . . . We had just lost our best client, Madame."

"You haven't lost anything, since I am your best client, and I said I would pay for that apartment until someone else rents it for the same length of time. And that brings us to this point here: what did I say here?"

"You said . . . you said . . . er . . . er . . ."

"Cavaliere Pellacchia, you should be fired on the spot. I said and repeat that under no circumstances should I be charged with the bills of other people. Understand? My lawyer tells me that he has uncovered certain strange repetitions of charges for rooms I am supposed to have occupied when I wasn't even in Rome, but in Baden-Baden. None of that nonsense again, understand?"

"Yes, Madame."

"Say you have understood."

"I have, Madame."
"All right, you may go."

After bowing very deeply to Leonardo, the man disappeared.
"Sit down, my son, won't you have a slice of this excellent cake?"
"A cake, at this hour, before lunch?"
"What's wrong with that? It's even better than after lunch."
"No, no, absolutely not. You eat it, I'll see you at home. . . ."
"You're not leaving me alone!"
"But Mary is crying. . . ."
"Mary stopped crying hours ago, when I sent her a messenger saying everything was the way I thought it would be—that is, perfect—and that she could either join us here, or wait for us there. She answered by the same messenger that she preferred to wait there, because the animal was sighted in the streets this morning."
"What animal?"
"Her illegitimate husband. I am sorry to have called him an animal, I owe an apology to the whole animal kingdom, bacteria included, I meant the Monster."
Leonardo had slumped into a chair and seemed to have become insensate, a sitting corpse. This finally WAS the end. . . .
"Leonardo, did you hear me?"
"Can't you see I did? How could I not?"
"Why so pale, all of a sudden?"
He gave no sign of life.
"Come on, Leonardo, don't be silly now. You won't even know him if you see him."
"If what?"
"If you see him—unless you've seen pictures of him elsewhere; there are none to be found in my house."
"But . . . HE? . . ."
"He what?"
"He . . . is here."
"Here? Are you crazy? He wouldn't dare."
"In Rome . . ."
"Rome is a large city, you know."
"His wife . . ."
"Please, no inaccuracies—YOUR wife . . ."

"MY wife? My wife is . . . in Laterza."

"Not again!!! Leonardo, are you or are you not ready to take up your new responsibilities in the eyes of the world?"

"What world? What responsibilities?"

"There is only one world, as far as I remember. Or do you know of other worlds? Up in the sky, of course . . ."

"Sophie . . . this world . . . has laws. . . ."

"The laws of science, you mean? Well, those work for you, they commanded your biochemistry to recognize your true and only wife, and Mary to recognize her true and only husband. They are part of the laws of Creation, God, if you prefer, and I hope you won't tell me the fairy tale that He, or It, the Great Something, resides in the Vatican."

"Will he be home?"

"God? I hope so. We couldn't live without Him. Or It."

"I mean her husband."

"You."

"No . . . HE."

"The illegitimate husband, you mean? Of course not. He knows he's not welcome there, any more than Mary would be welcome in the hangouts where his many mistresses live. No problem, my son, none at all. You wouldn't meet him even if you wanted to. He must have been called back by one of his mistresses who found out he was away in the company of a new one, but their squabbles and priorities don't interest us. Come, sit here and have some cake."

"No, thank you."

"Then let me finish mine, or I won't have any appetite for lunch." And she began to consume the cake on which she had marked her orders, sipping tea between mouthfuls. To him, watching her, it was as if she were devouring his will power, his logic, his entire world. But she seemed unaware of anything but the cake. He hated her now, he could see himself having to wait there for another two hours, unless he was blunt with her.

"You eat alone, I can't wait for you. I'm going home, I want to see Mary. Do you understand or don't you?" She cringed like a child afraid of a beating, the fork fell from her hand, she hurriedly wiped her mouth, threw the napkin on the table and pushed herself back until she could rise from the chair, which fell over against a china cabinet, breaking the glass. "Oh," said Leonardo, "I'm so sorry."

"No no, it's nothing. Let's go."

The first blow to Leonardo's self-assurance was given him by the entire hotel staff, from the uniformed directors and subdirectors to the last porter busy taking out luggage and then waiting for a tip before the clients entered the stagecoach bound for the station. They all bowed deeply to Sophie, the despicable bastards, but they straightened their backs again instantly to have a good look at him, and it was he who lowered his head and quickened his step, hoping at least to reach the door before the comments started.

But alas, awaiting him right outside the glass door was a second blow far worse than the first one, even though it came from nature: unpredictable March with an icy wind that lashed only him, leaving all the others untouched. Instantaneously it was doing damage to his body, and in the immediate future, as he knew, it would be doing the same to his social position. But alas, he had left his precious *spolverina* in his room (his first clever diplomatic calculation: It's almost spring, we're going to ride in that stuffy china cabinet: why expose my reputation to the eyes of those idiots who have never even seen a *spolverina?*). But neither had they ever seen such a fine gentleman come shivering out of such a fine hotel and continue to stand there shivering with no more protection than a ridiculous felt hat instead of rushing back inside at once to reappear almost immediately in a thick shield of armor against the sneak attacks of the retreating army of winter. All the coachmen and even their attendants, who stood by the horses to whisper soothing words, while the coachman stood by the open china cabinet and helped the precious china figurines climb into it—*all* of them wore long coats that reached almost to the ground, and shorter coats on top, to cover their shoulders, and thick white woolen gloves, and shiny top hats that made them look like great gentlemen so that only their physical position, their slow, deferential movements, and their solemn faces distinguished them as *undistinguished*.

"*Che ventaccio . . . che tempo da pazzi avete a Roma*" (what ugly wind, what crazy weather you have in Rome), he said to the coachman of some other rich lady, while Sophie's coachman was

being summoned in loud tones by the master of departures (also a
uniformed servant in white gloves, blue and white breeches, high
boots, blue overcoat with gold buttons and a top hat with a black
shaving brush on one side).

No one answered him, and even Sophie seemed indifferent to
him now. Finally, when her coach arrived, she seemed to rouse
herself from a daydream and said: "Sorry, I wasn't paying attention
to what you were saying. For some stupid reason I was afraid the
coach would never arrive, but here it is, thank God, so I can talk
again. What were you saying?"

"Nothing," he answered rather stiffly now, because her coachman
was standing in front of her and holding the door open, while one
of her brigands was holding the reins of the horse from up there on
his high seat, but neither of them was taking off his top hat to greet
her, and Leonardo was absolutely sure they were doing this to spite
him publicly, and if this involved insulting her too, they probably
felt they could get away with it because she was always so absent-
minded. Both men had their huge shields of wool-armor against the
wind, and an air of defiance he didn't at all like. He tried in vain to
seem superior and smile gently to remind the coachman that they
had met the previous night: the serf raised his eyebrows impertinently as if to remind *him* of the rules. "Rules, my arse," muttered
Leonardo, making sure the man wouldn't overhear him. Then, in
complete silence, he concluded his thought: I may not yet have any
right to consider myself a member of this family, but I am still a
public official, *and* a physician in *my* own right. He climbed into the
coach behind Sophie with as much dignity as the icy winds allowed
him, and sat down next to her, as she gestured to the coachman not
to close the door yet.

"Not the short way," she ordered, "take the long way, out of the
city gate, then down the river port of Ripetta, then . . ."

"But Mary is waiting for us . . ." said Leonardo, to no avail.

". . . then back by Palazzo Borghese, Quattro Fontane, Via
Condotti and stop for a moment on the foot of the Scalinata, so we
can have a look at it."

"Very good, Madame." The coachman slammed the door as
gently as he could, and only after doing this did he bow a symbolic
gesture of salute that embraced both passengers.

Leonardo was pleased that at least one humiliation had been spared him, but he was hurt by Sophie's open disregard of his wishes in front of someone else. Obviously, that must be the rule with top hats, he thought to himself as the coach began to move, but I'll be damned if I study these codes, when I intend to have no servants, ever, besides a cook if Mary doesn't want to learn. Let's hope she'll be better than Giovanna.

"I wanted to show you some of the beauties of this part of Rome," said Sophie, "before we leave for good, and also I wanted to talk to you about certain things, without having Mary interrupt us all the time. She has no practical knowledge worth speaking of, knows nothing about life, and is not very prudent. She will blurt out whatever comes into her head on the spur of the moment, and in Rome you just can't do that. You must be on your guard with Italians, except of course with people like you, but how many are there, in this whole country? Your own brothers, of course, and your father, that I will grant you. . . ."

"I have no brothers, and my father is dead."

"Oh, what a tragedy. My heartfelt condolences."

"He died ten years ago."

"Oh. And you have no brothers? Mary told me you had seven brothers."

"Seven sisters."

"The same thing. They can be trusted, but they're the only ones perhaps in the entire country who can."

"May I say something before we reach home, since we are on the subject of prudence, and Mary is not part of our conversation?"

"Of course, my son, you are the head of the family now."

"Well, first of all . . . or perhaps last . . . no, perhaps first . . . yes, we'd better make it first . . . because . . . frankly speaking, even though—"

"Look at the river, please, look! And now look at the ancient wall from the outside! See the goats and cows up there? And the wonderful shepherds with their traditional footwear, the same the ancient Romans and Etruscans used to use? Aren't they fascinating? And look at their hats, those conical hats, like brigands—and perhaps they *are* brigands, like most Italians . . . I've always tried to learn the secret of their psychology, but haven't found a single

Italian who could be open with me about this. You of course are
the one, because you don't tell lies . . . so rare, in Catholic countries, but especially here. . . . And now look at the barges loaded
with goats, and flowers, and fruit and vegetables . . . Shall we stop
to listen to the cries of the fruit vendors? No? All right, let's not
. . . But look now: see those beggars in front of the church rushing to buy something from that fruit vendor? Just a moment . . ."
She lifted her umbrella, inserted it into a narrow opening of the
window separating them from the coachman, and aimed right at the
poor man's bulging white trousers with three brisk prods. He
stopped the horse without even bothering to turn around. "Three
times to stop him, once to get him going again," she said, as if she
were teaching Leonardo how you train a horse. "And look at that:
they've bought themselves flowers, not vegetables. Isn't that peculiar? No fruit, either. And yet they beg for *bread* all day long! That's
the Romans for you."

"Also the Neapolitans."

"How true! Also the Neapolitans . . ."

"And the Swiss, the Germans . . ."

"No no, please, there are no beggars in Switzerland, and hardly
any in Germany."

"But if there were, they would ask for bread, not fruit or vegetables. Bread is a symbol, it is valid all year long, while fruit and
vegetables vary according to season, and, besides, bread sits on your
stomach and stills your hunger, while fruit goes down too quickly
and helps the digestion: that makes you hungrier, it may even give
you diarrhea, and vegetables have to be cooked: those people don't
live here, they work here."

"ᴡᴏʀᴋ? Do you call begging work?"

"What else? They even pray for you."

"Begging, again. On the assumption that you are superstitious."

"As if you Protestants weren't superstitious. You want to impress
God by working, on the assumption that He does. Since when has
God worked?"

"Don't be childish, Leonardo, do you believe in a personal God?"

"No, but—"

"Then I am right. Nature, or that Mysterious Something we
know exists, works all the time in mysterious ways that challenge

our minds to discover It, or at least imitate It, as long as we fail to discover how It works."

"What's so mysterious about the way merchants and industrialists work?"

"Leonardo, you're right. I'd never thought of that. Let me write it down." She took out a booklet from her purse and began to scribble into it with a tiny pencil, while Leonardo started to feel sick with impatience.

"There it is: nothing mysterious about their way of working. But do you include scientists in that category of simpletons?"

"Of course not, but—"

"Then I am right again. By the way—"

"Just a moment. Can we go now?"

"Yes." She punctured the white backside, and, as the horse began to trot again, Leonardo said: "Speaking of prudence . . ."

"Oh yes, speaking of prudence: we're definitely not leaving tonight."

"We aren't? Why?"

"It wouldn't be prudent. If I called off all my dinner guests at the last moment in order to catch the Paris Express with my grandchild and another guest, the papers would print it at once. All my movements· are in the papers. . . . I know this makes you unhappy. Mary is unhappy too, but one cannot be too prudent in these things. After all, we are doing something that, in the eyes of these idiots here, is against the law, and the police can stop us even in Turin, at the border, and put us all in jail. This is why I haven't spoken about Mary's happiness to anyone, and I beg you to be just as prudent as I am, *even hypocritical!* Tell Mary we *must* be, as long as we are here. She refuses to follow my example."

"Your example? But you revealed everything to the maid and her son and those other two men. That's very dangerous."

"Nonsense. Those are friends. They're not going to be shocked, whatever we do."

"But they are."

"How do you know? It's the first time you've seen them. . . ."

"I speak their language, they consider me one of their own, they're Catholics."

"Who isn't in Italy? Even you are! And yet . . ."

"The maid believes Mary is going to get an annulment from the Pope."

"She knows perfectly well it isn't true, but she must invent some explanation for what I do. That's the Catholics for you."

"I'm sorry, Sophie, but you don't know the first thing about these people."

"I don't? But they've been in my service for twelve years, off and on. And they have relatives in hotels in Naples, Sorrento, Taormina, Cairo, Pegli, Venice, Nice, Lausanne, Baden-Baden—wherever I keep an apartment. It's in their interest to explain my conduct to themselves, and as long as I don't do anything against morality—"

"But to them whatever the Church says *is* morality. And then the laws—"

"Come on, you and your laws . . . Oh! Look at that peasant boy with his branch of a peach tree in blossom. Isn't he the quintessence of this heavenly country, where beauty is everything?"

"That's not a peach tree, that's an almond tree, and he's probably taking it to the nearest church as an offering to some local Madonna. And that includes offerings of gossip to his father confessor, who wants to make the same offerings to his superiors."

"Do you mean to insinuate that my maid is disloyal to me? There, my friend, I draw the line. She is as loyal to me as to her local Madonna, I tell you. And the same holds true for her son and her brothers-in-law, those two men you saw. I know my servants, and I defend them."

"And I know my relatives and I defend *them*."

Sophie's eyes went wide; she gasped and stuttered: "I'm so sorry. Are you . . . related to them? Not that there's anything wrong with it, on the contrary, I am proud of—"

"Absolutely not!" shouted Leonardo, who already hated himself for speaking that way, but couldn't control himself. "They are illiterates, and in my family we are all university graduates. But we're part of the same cultural tradition. And I know that these people's first loyalty is to the Church. In fact, speaking of flowers, the sacrifice of their loyalty to an employer, in order to report in confession whatever they hear from him or about him, is a duty, especially if it implies the risk of losing their job. In correct religious terminology, this duty is called a Little Flower. This means that at this very moment Father Mansueto of the Capuchins is being informed by your maid of our plans for divorce. He's her confessor, and he's praying for your conversion, so she told me."

"Nonsense. She thinks it's an annulment, you said so yourself a minute ago, and anyway Father Mansueto's an idiot, a kitchen priest, a Scagnozzo,* as they call them here. So he'll believe it too."

"One more reason for him to rush to his superiors and tell them he knows someone important enough to get one of those unheard-of concessions from the Pope—an annulment. It may be the best thing that ever happened to him: he may become important by spying on the true motives for seeking an annulment, and one thing leads to another. . . . And don't forget that you used the word DIVORCE with your maid; even if she doesn't know what it means, Father Mansueto will."

"I wouldn't worry. My maid knows better than to blabber about me to a priest. In fact, I meant to tell you that. . . . Oh, look at the laundry hanging over that dark street: it makes it as bright as a stage . . . these people's instinct for the theatrical—just look at it! Wait, this deserves a halt."

And she poked violently at the coachman's behind, then shouted: "Back up a few steps, we want to look at that street. Open the door."

Leonardo was so horrified he couldn't even utter a word. He had recognized his own hotel right there before him: in fact, even the women sitting in front of their houses seemed familiar to him.

"I prefer not to get out," he said.

"Why?"

"It's so late, and I'm so anxious to see Mary again. Please understand."

The coachman was already at the door, opening it, offering his left arm to Sophie.

"Never mind," said Leonardo to him. "We're leaving."

The order was obeyed, slowly, after a brief arching of the eye-

---

* Scagnozzo is the lowest type of priest, usually a serf in the kitchen of Roman princes. Hence a term of insult applicable to the entire Catholic hierarchy.

brows, as the coachman realized that Sophie was not going to insist.
When the coach was beginning to leave, she said, with deep resentment: "As you wish. I was only trying to call your attention to
something deeply significant and beautiful, but you Italians always
think you know your country so well that no foreigner can teach
you what is really valuable about you as a culture. Not your goddamn museums or excavations, not the dead, but the living, especially the illiterates. I'm sorry—but even your university graduates
are a bad imitation of the Germans. What interests me in Italy are
the simple people who hang their bedsheets and all their intimate
linens across the street, like banners, like garlands for the procession
of a patron saint of painted wood and plaster. I wish I could venture into these filthy little hotels and see what savages stay there
overnight. . . . But my coachman, who is a goddamn snob, never
allows me to do it. He says the people who sleep in these places are
all unspeakable. Perhaps he's right, but still . . ."

"Unspeakable? *He* is unspeakable, if you want my opinion. To
tell the truth—"

"He's a good man and does his job perfectly well. The horses love
him and trust him, and even if he cannot always be trusted by us,
we employ him for the horses, not for his conversation."

"You're wrong there. I had a very good conversation with him
last night."

"Him? You do surprise me. I wonder what . . . Oh, here we are.
Let's buy those roses there, before that stupid lady in black gets
them all. I know who she is, and . . ." She poked the coachman
again, and ordered Leonardo: "Open that door, quickly!!! and buy
them all, no matter what the price. I'll wait inside, I don't want the
old fool to see me."

Leonardo paled and pretended he couldn't open the door. What
else could he do, except admit to her that he didn't have a cent in
his pocket?

"Let me open it!" she shouted, but the coachman was already at
the door, and this time she accepted his help, brushing Leonardo
aside, but she wasn't quick enough in reaching the florist, who had
abandoned his displays at the bottom of a huge white staircase, to
rush to the old lady in black with all the roses he was trying to sell
and offer them to her. The lady, who was surrounded by two coach-

men and two servants in uniform, as against Sophie's one of each, had already indicated what flowers she intended to buy, and Leonardo was delighted to see his problem vanish so quickly, but Sophie was not. She stood there, angry in defeat, but seemed resigned to getting back into her coach and leaving when the "old fool" turned towards her and said in a very studied voice: "Beautiful day, isn't it?" Leonardo recognized her at once as a person he had seen in Naples, but wasn't quite sure whether she was the mother of his friend Peppino Luccibelli or the wife of the Magnificent Rector of the University of Naples, Professor Luigi Miraglia, in which last case he could not really speak to her, because he had only seen her from a distance. In the meantime he observed Sophie and was amazed to discover that *she*, of all people, was fidgeting and embarrassed, and when he realized that she had given up all hope of buying the flowers, he ran after the lady, calling: "Your Excellency!"

At once two solemn-looking gentlemen who resembled him so much they might have been his brothers grabbed him by the collar and took manacles out of their pockets, shouting, "You're under arrest!" *in his own hometown accent of Laterza.*

"What do you mean?" he shouted back. "How dare you put your hands on a town mayor and free professionist?" (*Libero professionista* is any man who, having become a full citizen by virtue of his classical studies and consequent *laurea*, exercises freely the profession of which he is a "Doctor.")

But a Black Maria had already appeared from nowhere, and a plainclothesman and six Carabinieri in high uniform were moving swiftly to close the circle around Leonardo, whose necktie and collar had now been torn askew.

"I am the mayor of Laterza, a city of thirty thousand inhabitants," he shouted in a voice that could be heard way up on top of the steps of the Trinity of the Mounts.* All the windows filled with people fighting to get a front row view of the scene. Sophie, pale as death, was being prevented from falling by the coachman and his assistant, and the plainclothesman seemed hardly less disturbed than she was, because his hands were trembling, and he had inter-

---

* The steps of the Trinità dei Monti, incorrectly called the Spanish Steps in all American books.

rupted the manacling of Leonardo, but his assistants could not let go of him, because he seemed in a fighting mood, as he went on shouting his attributes, even going into such details as his having addressed the Senate of the Kingdom only two days ago. Seeing that nothing helped, he finally yelled: "I am the first cousin of the personal eye doctor of the Pope and the King!"

This did it. Not only was he at once released by the plainclothesmen, and begged in the most operatic vibrato to accept the apologies of the Questore, but the coach of the lady who had started the whole trouble suddenly stopped and she herself emerged from it again, accompanied by two very tall and distinguished-looking gentlemen, whom Leonardo had noticed before; this pair came towards him and confabulated with his captor then hurried over to Sophie and asked her something, bowing deeply to her. After which, Leonardo, having been released and led back towards Sophie again, saw Her Excellency Miraglia come towards Sophie and heard her ask: "How are you?"

Sophie regained her composure at once and (unbelievable sight!) curtsied to Her Excellency, blushing as she mumbled that she was very well indeed, thank you. Whereupon one of the gentlemen came forwards with the bunch of roses Sophie had so coveted before, and offered it to her.

This was the moment for Leonardo to speak, and he did. "Your Excellency," he said, to the lady in black, without noticing that he was creating a commotion again, "I recognize you. You are the wife of the Magnificent Rector who gave me my Laureation as Physician and Surgeon, in the name of His Late and Much Lamented Majesty King Humbert."

The lady stared at him with horror, then quickly addressed herself to Sophie in a language he didn't understand. Sophie answered in the same tongue, blushing abundantly and curtsying again. In vain did Leonardo try to repeat his remark; Her Excellency was gone, whisked away by the two tall gentlemen, and the whole attendant group was running towards the other carriage, with the police behind them, while Sophie stood there somewhat aghast, again fidgeting with her gloves. Only the coachman seemed to smile.

"What is it?" Leonardo asked. "Why all this mystery?"

Sophie gave a little chuckle, which she tried to repress, but it grew wider on her face and wilder, until she turned her back to Leonardo and climbed into her coach, laughing out loud. Now the coachman was laughing too, *quite disrespectfully.*

Leonardo was about to put the man into his place, when his captor came running to him, put a card into his hand and ran away again, shouting: "See you again, Mister Mayor, that's my address, don't ever hesitate to come and see me. We shall have a good visit to our fatherland!" (The correct term is *rimpatriata,* and it means a friendly chat about things of local interest.)

He looked at the card before he climbed back into the coach, and immediately recognized the name of a man whose youngest brothers had been in elementary school with him: neighbors, almost relatives, in fact, although at a certain remove, because they were of an inferior class (no one in the family was a university graduate). But what was printed in block letters above the name at once promoted its bearer to the honor of a full relative (again a great exaggeration in the opposite direction):

S. E. IL QUESTORE DI ROMA

(His Excellency, the Chief of Police of Rome). And in pencil, above the address: *Dear Mr. Mayor, I hope you remember me. Please come and see me. I saw your cousin yesterday, and shall be seeing him again soon to tell him about our meeting. Yours devotedly . . .*

"I knew he must be from Laterza," said Leonardo to Sophie as he sat down beside her. "But who the devil is she, if she isn't Her Excellency Miraglia?"

Sophie burst into laughter again. When at last she calmed down sufficiently she said, still choking: "The Queen Mother of Italy."

"The . . . what?"

"Yes . . ."

Leonardo was so pale with emotion he could hardly hold the card in his hand. "Of course, of course," he mumbled, in a trance. "Of course I've seen her before—*on postage stamps!*" These words brought Sophie's hysteria to such a pitch that the coachman stopped the horse and rushed to the window to see if she was sick, in time to overhear her—"Then you've even licked her back to put her on envelopes!" *and his stupid answer:* "I never do such a thing! It's unhygienic!"

In the gloomy few minutes that followed, caught between the laughter of the rich and that of their servants, Leonardo realized sadly that he had been wrong. There were no stamps carrying the image of the Queen, only of her husband the sovereign. But he had seen her sweet face and concentrated on it with more anguish and for many more hours than even on the dear face of his mother. In a religious college the crucifix stands in front of the pupils above the two ruling sovereigns, and between looking up words in the fat dictionary and deciding in what tense and context to use them, a quick glance at the crucifix is in order, provided there is neither amusement nor resignation in that glance, because amusement may mean dirty jokes and resignation sleep. Like all schoolchildren of his time, Leonardo had never been interested in the crucifix. But the two ruling sovereigns did live in Italy, and vague news of them did pierce the thick walls of monastic life every now and then. To see her suddenly in the flesh made her come true so vividly he could no longer recognize his own knowledge as being based on nothing more than paper currency.

These were the thoughts that occupied his mind for the rest of the ride between Piazza di Spagna and Via Gregoriana, while Sophie tried to pull herself together and stop laughing, without success, and it angered him that he couldn't explain these interesting facts to her. He punished her, as they got off the coach, by not making the slightest attempt to help her with the flowers, but she not only failed to understand this, she understood the opposite and tried to prevent him from doing what he was so obviously and defiantly not doing in the first place. "Don't touch them, please," she ordered, becoming serious all of a sudden. "I want to carry them myself." Thus he followed her humbly all through the long, dark entrance hall, feeling himself pursued by the glances of the doorman and his wife, whose curiosity, he knew, would soon find a great outlet in the same laughter he had received all the way up from Piazza di Spagna, and the scent of those roses in that cold air, in that dark place, mixed with his own mood of humiliation in a world so foreign to his own, brought back the feeling of loss he had experienced at his mother's funeral. Except that then there had been reason to cry, especially in public, for every show of weakness in front of death is also implicitly a show of strength: back in those sad but glorious days there had been no doubt of his strength in any human (that is, Laertian*) mind, for everyone in the whole world, namely in Laterza, had known what a model son and brother he was.

"Smile, my son, smile, don't return to your bride with that funereal face! I never saw my husband gloomy, or suspicious, or jealous, and you seem sick with these three maledictions that affect everyone in this uncivilized country except for the very poor. Chin up and smile before I ring the doorbell or I won't give you these roses to offer Mary. The reason I didn't want you to carry them up here was that you looked like a mourner at a funeral, and I'm superstitious about these things: we Russians have our superstitions too, and they are better than yours, so smile now, I order you!"

They had reached the front door and it was so dark that Sophie had to take out her *lorgnon* and examine Leonardo's face like an object in a shop. He smiled, and she hardly had time to put the flowers in his arms before the door was flung open, and an obedient Bernhard stood there, offering his new master his own perfect smile.

He's obviously heard every word, thought Leonardo, as he tried to avoid glaring at the man because Mary was standing there holding her son by the hand, but that evil German governess was not far behind, and eyes and ears could be felt behind curtains and statues and closed doors.

"We're late," shouted Sophie, embracing and kissing her daughter, "because we had some difficulty in securing these flowers Leonardo wanted to buy for you, darling, but he was a real hero: do you know what he did?"

"No," said Mary, advancing dangerously towards Leonardo with a passion that flickered through the air like sheet lightning.

"I did nothing," said Leonardo, turning sad again, with a voice that trembled with emotion. "It wasn't my fault."

---

* Laterza having been founded by Laertes, Ulysses's father, the citizens still proudly call themselves Laertini (Laertians).

"Fault, he calls it!" shouted Sophie, exploding again into those shrieks of laughter that had so amused two of her servants earlier and were amusing the rest of them now, for they all suddenly appeared from behind everything.

"He gave the old fool her first lesson in humility! He called her . . . hihihihi . . . hihihi . . . I can't even tell you what he . . . hihi hiiii . . . I can't, I'm going to choke. Hihihihiiiiiii . . . hihi . . . And you know what she did? She . . . hiiihi—hihi . . . She . . . hihi . . . hiiiii . . . she asked me in German if . . . if my guest, that is, Leonardo, liked Italy and if he could speak Italian. . . . Hihihihi . . . And I . . . hihihi . . . I re . . . hihi . . . I replied . . . he is . . . hihihi . . . he is doing his best . . . Your Majesty. . . . Hihi . . . hihihi . . . But the whole story is so funny, you'll . . . hihihi . . . you'll die . . . hihihi . . . when you . . . hihihi . . . hear it. . . ."

Mary wasn't listening at all: she was staring at Leonardo and he was staring back, and now they seemed so removed from everything that even Sophie noticed it. It not only calmed her down, but instantly made her gloomy and dangerous again.

"Has Kostia eaten his lunch?" she asked, including everyone in her question. No one dared take it as addressed to him or her, including Mary, who was looking to the others for help, as they were looking to her.

"I asked a question, but never mind, I SEE the answer in this child's face." She paused to glower at everyone, then continued in German: "And you, Fräulein Luther, don't you try to hide behind Mary and make eyes, pretending that _she_ is to blame, for she is not and you know it. What a mistake I made, to think I could take you into my confidence! All right, don't stand there like damn fools, all of you. Bring the food for the child to the dining room at once, I'll feed him myself. Our lunch can wait."

The Italian servants had understood enough to take shelter for their own good. Fräulein Luther at once took Kostia to the dining room while Bernhard rushed to the kitchen to give his orders and execute hers. Mary alone seemed at a loss, but not so Leonardo. He was delighted, only unable to understand what was happening. After a few vain requests for an answer to his eloquent Neapolitan gesture for "What's the matter?" he frowned terribly and asked: "What's the trouble now? Will anyone inform me?"

"Nothing," said Sophie in a very loud voice, so as to be overheard by her Italian subjects too. "That's exactly what always happens, the moment I take time off to look after my own business in this house. Kostia has been kept starving for hours. And yet my orders were quite specific: he was to have his lunch the moment I began to be late, which I so rarely am. You can't expect a child to suffer because we grownups have our problems, our worries, our good or bad reasons for neglecting our own nourishment. A child, as everybody knows and a doctor knows better than the rest of us, must be fed at regular hours, or he will get asthma, not to say rickets or worse. Don't you agree? But I don't want you to waste your precious time with these trifles, when there are so many people here to whom they shouldn't be trifles. If I am incapable of making my own servants work for me . . ." The rest of the sentence was in a language he couldn't understand, so she promptly embellished it in Italian: "as Shakespeare so wisely says about the state of Denmark!"

Leonardo was only too happy to find himself in authority again, and he instantly smiled and said soothingly: "Calm down, Sophie, please calm down! Everything will be all right. *Late is late* and cannot be made *early* by shouting, no matter what your Danish doctor says—I imagine he must be a pediatrician: everybody is a specialist these days—we don't need *him* to understand what you have put so clearly in plain Italian."

It was her turn now to frown terribly and blush, as if she were about to explode. "My fault! All *my* fault! I haven't been clear at all! What I meant was that *you*, of all people, shouldn't waste *your* time with *my* problems, when you and Mary have such important things to discuss. Go now, go to the drawing room or to the library and discuss quietly what we were discussing before! I shall sacrifice *my* lunch, as usual, to feed that poor, neglected child!"

"No! no! please!" said Mary in a state of extreme agitation, "I'll do it . . . it's my fault . . . I'm so sorry."

Sophie stopped her with a cold glance. "If *you* were to blame, I would have *told* you so! I *never* speak obliquely, you know *me*!!! Don't stand there like a goose. Go, *I order you*, go and discuss *our common problem* with Leonardo."

"But why should you starve because of my stupidity?"

"Mary," said Leonardo, placing his hand on her arm and smiling with the greatest detachment. "Mary, please stop it. Your mother is not starving, she can very well feed that child without the *slightest* sacrifice to herself. *On the contrary*, it combines a positive pleasure, i.e., feeding that poor little darling, with a much needed *hygienic* measure, i.e., eating a little less herself. That is *one* of the things we must discuss in private, the three of us. . . ."

Sophie stood aghast. She didn't know whether to betray her resentment or conceal it, and Mary felt obliged to come to her rescue. "Mamachen," she said, flinging herself into her arms, "please don't be angry with him. He didn't mean it unkindly."

"I know, I know," said Sophie, wiping her tears, but beginning to sob, so that Mary began to sob too. "I . . . know . . ." (sniff, handkerchief, smile amid the tears and sniff again) . . . "He is *so* good!!! He didn't mean it unkindly."

Leonardo was amused. "Unkindly? What a silly word to use!!! It's *your mother* who is unkind when she overeats! Even your Danish pediatrician would agree with me, if we asked him, I'm sure. Come, Mary, let's talk about *our* business." He took her by the hand and dragged her towards the drawing room.

"No," said Mary, timidly, ". . . the library."

"Oh no," he said, "not in the library."

"But . . ." and she didn't dare continue, because her mother's eyes were on her.

"But nothing," said Leonardo, becoming impatient. "What's wrong with the drawing room?"

"And what's wrong with the library?"

"I don't like it." Then, seeing that Sophie was still standing there: "Sophie, please tell me: is there any objection to our talking in the drawing room?"

"None at all. And I think Mary should obey her husband."

"Good. Thank you, Sophie. Did you hear that, Mary? Come."

After the first few moments of bliss came the struggle for more, and finally he lost patience.

"But why not? Aren't you in your own house, under your mother's eyes?"

"Yes, and she's watching us."

He was so frozen with terror that he didn't even dare look in the direction of her hand, so that she had to be more specific.

"Not literally, but look—" And she pointed towards the marble bust.

"Oh, you goose! Really!"

And he rose from the sofa, going towards the mirror to see if he still looked presentable. "Let's eat."

"Eat? How can you think of eating?"

"All right, let's not." And he stepped closer to the mirror, adjusting his necktie and assessing the damage done by the police to his collar.

"I . . . thought you wanted to talk."

"On an empty stomach?"

"*Gospody!*" she shrieked, covering her ears with both hands and looking terrorized.

"What is it?"

"You talk like the Monster!"

"Mary, don't be a child."

She shrieked again. "These are his words too! Stop, please stop! It was all a mistake . . . I knew it. . . . Oh, how can I go on living?"

And she burst into tears.

It took him a long time to make her stop, and even longer to make her lift her eyes from the contemplation of her fingernails, but he was cheered by the discovery that her famous independence of mind was all pure nonsense.

"Look, my love," he said, "I am quite willing to talk, but not before I have a list of all the words that have not been used by the Monster, so I can avoid them. Fair enough? Or are these also among the censored words?"

"You're being cheerful," she said reproachfully.

" 'Cheerful' is not the correct term. 'Happy' is the word."

"Happy to see me in tears?"

"Happy to see that you have stopped."

"But especially happy to discover that my famous independence of mind is pure pretense."

"Nonsense!"

"Nonsense if you prefer. But this being so, I lose by comparison with your illegitimate wife, and your great infatuation is over."

"How can you say such stupid things?"

"My God!!! Not again!!!"

Now he really felt cornered. After a pause she began again.

"You have nothing to say, not one good argument to prove me wrong. And I can see other symptoms. . . ."

"Of what?"

"Of . . ." She began to sob again, then muttered: "You're not even wearing my shirts and my neckties."

"Darling, how can I know which one fitted?"

"There were shirts in all sizes, two of each, and neckties don't have to fit. Obviously, I didn't choose right. You despise me even as a purchaser of neckties."

He was rescued by Sophie's voice, calling loudly from the corridor: "Mary! Leonardo! Lunch is ready!"

But he had grown wise enough not to show his relief, and stayed seated, refusing to take her hand and follow her.

"Darling, aren't you hungry?"

"No."

"But Mamachen is hungry, we can't keep her waiting."

He jumped to his feet, hoping that this was the right gesture, and followed her without a word.

There was no one in the corridor, no one in the library, no one in the dining room. Mary seemed so distraught that Leonardo asked her if anything was wrong.

"I hope not," she said, clasping her hands and looking tragic.

"Then let's sit down and eat."

"Before she comes?"

"I hope she won't eat when she does come, so we might as well begin."

"Why do you hope she won't eat? Do you think you can love me, if you hate my mother?"

"I love her almost as much as I love you, darling, but if you had seen her at the hotel, eating (no, sorry, the correct term is *gorging*) caviar, lobster, roast beef, potato cake, chocolate cake and bread, you would say that only her worst enemy could want to see her do it again *now*."

At this moment Bernhard entered the dining room and said: "Madame wants you to eat, Miss Mary. She is writing a note to Mr. Schultz and the messenger is waiting for it. She will eat later. With your permission, Miss Mary." And he was gone.

"What did he say, that German marionette dressed up like a general?"

"He said she's writing a note to an old friend who has just arrived in Rome. You'll meet him. A most wonderful person. Let's sit down and eat. She says we must."

"All right, let's eat," he said, and kissed her passionately, then quickly withdrew from her and they sat facing each other across the table, next to Sophie's monumental empty chair, but they seemed unable to do anything but stare at each other in ecstasy. Every few seconds Mary had to close her eyes and gasp, and Leonardo used these moments to open his eyes even more widely and study his surroundings, partly with suspicion, but mostly with awe. The whole dining room seemed more splendid now than it had seemed in artificial light the evening before, and he knew why: the silent opulence of objects now stood out frankly for what it was, and whether he liked this or not, felt guilty or not, these were his private reactions to it all, while on the previous night the emanations had not even come close to him, they had been absorbed by all those men standing between the furniture and the table. What the hell were they? Part of the furniture or native inhabitants of that opulent room? Today on the other hand, he could let his worst instincts run loose, and the pleasure he experienced had almost something sexual about it, which he didn't recognize for what it was: the same primordial greed that makes thieves of us all in childhood. He channeled it towards nobler regions of the conscience as men channel their desire for a woman into the dream of making her the mother of their children. And Mary being the woman of his dreams, he felt he loved her more spiritually for seeing her surrounded by her material possessions.

Everything in that room was part of her body, and the thought that anyone might covet it, awoke in him all the devils of jealousy. Oh, why hadn't he accepted her love nine years ago, and kept her from falling into the hands of the lowest and most useless of men in the whole modern world? A *painter*; a man permitted *by law* to undress women and look at them (and certainly also touch them), for no scientific purpose at all; that is, not for *their* good but for *his* own pleasure. What kind of a husband and father could that make?

"Mary," he asked, choking with emotion, "Mary, why did you fall so low?"

"I?"

"Who else exists in the whole world for me?"

"But when? How?"

"You married a *painter*! Did he ever paint you in the nude?"

"Are you insane? He never even saw me in the nude."

"But he possessed you."

"I was his wife. . . ."

"Oh, that word!! How can I go on living?"

"My poor darling . . . But you were married, too."

"Not to a prostitute."

"Oh, . . . which means you respected her. You still do!!!"

"But *you* . . . were *faithful* to him."

"I should *say* so."

"And you are still *proud* of that faith you kept for eight terrible years."

"Oh yes, they were terrible. . . ."

"For me, not for you."

"How can you say so? What do you know of my sufferings? You had forgotten me completely."

"How can you say so? Were you inside my heart?"

"Were you inside mine? You, too, were faithful to your wife."

"Never!"

"Oh . . . that's the kind of man you are, a pleasure-seeker . . . another *Italian*."

"I did it out of despair . . . I never loved her. I *married* her out of despair."

"What despair?"

"How can you ask such a question? The despair of ever falling in love again."

"But you were unfaithful to her, after swearing to God you would be faithful."

"I *was* faithful to her."

"What do you mean? You just said you never were."

"I was, I was. To the person I had married without love, to that fiction of love that is called kindness. I was always very kind to her."

"So was I to my husband. I never loved him, not for one day."

"So you *did* betray him. Confess it!!!" He gasped, looked threatening, rose from his seat and pointed a terrible finger at her. "Confess!!! Be as sincere as I am!"

"I have nothing to confess. I was never faithful to *him*, but . . ."

"Oh, so you weren't? Oh my God . . . Oh my God . . ."

". . . but to the promise I had made before the altar."

"What altar? You have no altar. You have no God. . . . Don't be a hypocrite. You Protestants worship only money and power . . . nothing else."

"I became a Catholic."

"You did? Thank God!!! I hope you still are. . . ."

"How can you say that? You, who pretend to hate the Church?"

"I hate the Church, but I don't hate Christian Morality, especially in matters of human behavior."

"Morality *is* about behavior, not about the Ontological Argument, Parthenogenesis, or Transubstantiation."

"Who taught you theology?"

"My mother. Certainly not that *fottuto cazzaccio*" (fucked foul prick) "who converted me to the True Faith."

"Mary!!!! Mary!!!!" he cried, wringing his hands. "Mary . . . such language. Did your mother teach you that, too?"

"She never uses such words, but everybody else does in Rome, especially good Catholics, when they're speaking about the Pope."

"Who, your husband?"

"The Monster you mean? Yes, he did."

"And so you speak like him. You, who accuse me of speaking like him when I say the most innocent things."

"Innocent things? Your speaking against ME??? Thank you! And now tell me, please, how do *you* reconcile your respect for Christian Morality with your fucking around???"

"Mary, that language . . . I forbid you ever to use it again."

"We are *alone*, we are *adults*, and we have both been married for years."

"Yes, but *that language* . . ."

"And *that behavior* . . . I only give it a name, you do it."

"I *did*, out of despair. A man must live."

"And a woman must not?"

"A woman isn't exposed to life the way a man is. A woman lives at home, she is exposed in a different way, to purer pleasures, purer eyes: those of her children. She is exposed to worship, like the Mother of God in the temple . . . she *is* in fact the temple; *more*, the Fatherland, and this *is* the correct term: land of the Father, that no outsider must invade. Imagine a man walking the streets claiming worship from the crowds."

"Not worship, but love. Why can't a man lead an exemplary life, like a woman?"

"That's what priests are for. But can every man in the world live like a priest?"

"Outside the house, yes: *his* temple is the world."

"But this is a Protestant concept: the priesthood of every believer. If we all lived that way, the population of the world would disappear."

"Are you so concerned about that? How many illegitimate children do you have? Confess!!!" She was becoming hysterical.

"Calm down! None, Mary. None."

"You only fucked around out of despair."

"Mary, that word . . ."

"All right: you cried on other women's shoulders out of despair. And then fucked them out of duty, to help them play the Madonna in front of their husbands and children. Is that better?"

"The cynicism . . ."

"Whose?"

"I had no home. . . . I went home to a wife I detested."

"That's why you were so anxious to go back to her last night, because it was your duty before the law to detest her and cry hot tears and hot semen all over town."

"Mary . . . my ears . . ."

"Don't put your hands over your ears. That's what women do. Be exposed to unpleasantness as you are to pleasure. What guarantee do I have that you won't do it again out of despair, three months after our marriage?"

He folded his hands and said, with his eyes to the ceiling: "I swear to God . . ."

"Yes, just like you did in church."

"I am not a Catholic."

"But you want *me* to be one! Why?"

"I didn't know you until this very moment, Mary. . . . You are *so* intelligent!!! You know *so* much!!! *Our* women are *stupid,* and the Church provides them with the knowledge they need to circulate amongst the traffic of ideas without being run over by the false arguments of those who are after their vessel, their honor. Once the vessel is broken (in correct terms, the honor is lost), a woman is finished."

"Yes, and a man is begun, initiated, *confirmed. His* honor consists in dishonoring as many women as he can, and still being preferred by his wife, because he is such a real man. The 'correct term' in Roman is PRICK! If you men knew how little we care for your manliness, you might begin to care more for your honor up here, inside your head, not down there inside your fly. Tell me: isn't 'prickhead' the correct Roman term for imbecile?"

"Oh yes, not just in Rome, in all Italy."

"Then why should your honor be rooted in your prick?"

Leonardo didn't answer, not only because he didn't know what to say, but because he was ashamed for her in front of the chairs, the china cabinets, the paintings on the wall, the lamps, the objects on the table. And yet a feeling of pride such as he had never known before insinuated itself into his chest, making him breathe more deeply. That such a woman should love him was indeed a true honor, even though she had no sense of propriety. What other woman in the world would be concerned with correct terminology in argument? And more even than this, she had said that women didn't *care* for masculinity in sex! Of course she was wrong, but this meant she wasn't sensuous, thank God! A real, honorable woman at long last . . . He could even imagine her saying all this to the creature she had married. Oh, bliss! To be finally free of those tormenting images of her in bed with him!

"Why don't you answer me, Leonardo?"

"Because you are right and I repent having spoken as I did."

"And I absolve you, but you must mend your ways once and for all. A man's honor consists in never telling a lie, and he doesn't have to take oaths in front of a painted wooden doll to be believed, or say: 'I swear to God.' Or, even worse, 'God is my witness.' That's pure blasphemy. As if God, or the Something we call Justice or Harmony of the Universe, were not there all the time. Understand?"

"Yes."

"God is within you, says Tolstoy, and my mother, in her infinite wisdom, adds: therefore whatever you do has a sacred character, and you are a priest. And now let me make my confession to you. God sent me the Monster as a punishment for lying to my mother about you all those years ago. I lied three times: the three times I saw you. First I said that the rose you gave me in her presence had been given me by a woman who put her arm into our carriage while she wasn't looking. The second time I lied was when you walked past the hotel and I came out without a hat on, telling her I wanted a breath of fresh air. The third time was when you came to Sorrento. And God returned my false witness, first by sending me a horrible suitor, an old man, the husband of a friend of ours, who tried to seduce me."

"His name, his name at once, and his address . . ." shouted Leonardo at the height of indignation.

"Why?" asked Mary, who was obviously pleased by his reaction.

"Because I'm going to kill him."

"No need, my love, he never touched me."

"But he tried to . . . His name, I order you . . ."

"Carlo Tempi . . ."

"Carlo Tempi? All right. If I ever see him, he'll have to apologize to you on his knees for what he tried to do, and if he should refuse, he'll have to die. On with your confession. Who came next?"

"A young painter who volunteered to accompany me on a tour of the Via Appia with that old lecher. And the third punishment was that God made me bring the young man into this house in spite of my mother's precise orders, and when she asked me what kind of a butcher I had invited for tea, God made me say in a fit of blind anger: 'Not a butcher, but the man I am going to marry.' From then on God heaped his wrath on me: He made the wife of the old lecher tell me I had done the right thing and should marry the 'butcher.' "

"She did? The bitch. Was she trying to recapture her husband's love?"

"She knew nothing about his low habits."

"And you didn't tell her?"

"Tell her? Are you insane?"

"I am not, but God certainly was, if he didn't force you to shout it from rooftops. Go on with your story. What else did God make you do?"

"He made me convert to Catholicism, which is like those places in Dante's Inferno where the sinners curse God, their parents, the human race, the time, the place, the occasion for their insemination and their birth. Remember?"

Leonardo sank to his knees. "Mary, you even know *The Divine Comedy* by heart. . . . How did you manage it?"

"I memorized the little I know."

"That's easy for a man, not for a woman. And, on top of it all, to be able to comment on it intelligently. You're a genius. You're better than the Holy Virgin."

Mary was in tears. "Come," she said, "don't kneel in front of me. Kiss me."

"May I?"

The honor was too great. He almost fainted, but as soon as he began to recover himself, he pulled away from her in fresh horror and asked, threateningly:

"Do you ever see these Tempi people?"

"Occasionally."

"And your mother accepts this situation?"

"But there is no situation. There never was one."

"You are married, and it's obviously his fault."

"Nonsense, Leonardo. It was my fault alone. Everyone acted blindly on God's preordained plan, so leave them alone."

"But my honor demands of me . . ."

"Your honor demands only one thing of you: that you never tell me a lie."

"I swear. God be . . . Sorry, I . . ."

"Say 'I promise.' That will be more than sufficient."

"I promise, I most solemnly promise . . ."

"No. You just promise. Leave the solemnity to the Catholic Church."

"I . . . yes, but . . . this is a solemn moment."

As if evoked by his words, Sophie appeared at the door with all the Queen mother's flowers in a large crystal vase, which she set down in front of her, on her empty plate, without looking at either Leonardo or Mary, who were now quickly composing themselves in a more suitably social manner.

"What a heavenly smell," she said, hiding her face in the flowers and inhaling avidly. "It has almost made me forget that I haven't had lunch. But we must not become too ascetic, children. Aren't you hungry? Come, Mary, help me make room on the table for these. They make me think of (sniff) Capri, (sniff) Sorrento, (sniff) Amalfi, but perhaps even more of (sniff and resniff) Egypt and Greece."

"Oh yes," said Mary, "Egypt and Greece especially." And she closed her eyes the better to evoke these beautiful places, as she, too, began to sniff. Leonardo did nothing and said nothing, but the flowers had said and done more for him than any human could: they had restored his lost self-confidence. The reason for this change, both sudden and extreme, was that the cold winds of March had killed their scent in the street, while the heated apartment had reawakened it at once. Up to the very moment Sophie had come in, Leonardo had been oppressed by unfamiliar smells of furniture polish, French perfumes, tea, confectioners' sugar, marmalades, liqueurs, lobster, roast beef, spicy sauces, hot buttercakes, cold leather-bound volumes and moist ancient books, a crazy combination of things beyond his reach and taste, in which only the furniture polish, the books and their bindings bore some resemblance to places he had seen in his youth. But now suddenly this invasion of flowers made him feel the nearness of his whole family, his patients, his constituents. He could finally begin to perceive the intense experiences of the last two days as his own, unbelievable though they still seemed. Leonardo closed his eyes and put his face into the bunch of flowers and began to breathe with such force and to exhale

such heavy sighs that the two women withdrew, at first in fear and
then in awe, as they watched him, until his sighs turned to deep
sobs and he murmured: "Mammà . . . Mammà . . ."

And thus he told them amid tears that in Apulia spring exploded,
saturating the air with the perfume of flowers. Only in kitchens,
near the fire, was this heady scent watered down by the smell of
simple foods, such as bread in the oven and tomato sauce in the
frying pan, which were the real perfumes for women who wanted to
impress their men. No need of fine French perfumes for them any
more than of flowers in vases for their living rooms: *the kitchen* was
their living room and temple. There the Vestals officiated and the
men came to worship: outside, the gods were different. Cruel Mars
and shameless Venus roamed the streets. Only in temples could
men find shelter from this struggle for salvation. Venus and Mars
existed in homes, too, since they were gods and had free access
everywhere, but ever since Christ had arisen, Mars was tempered by
charity at home and Venus by motherly love. And what was more
charitable and less crassly egotistical than the care of a woman for
the child that was not yet implanted in her virginal body, from
being stirred and awakened to life by the wrong sperm and the
wrong catalyst or male organ in the female vessel? These were the
correct terms and only a priest of the medical science had the right
to use them in polite society. And therefore Mary was wrong when
she reproached him for living *in the world*, where she had never
lived, thank God, because that was no place for honest women.

Sophie and Mary were deeply impressed with his countenance
and the dignified tone of his voice, and they apologized for even
daring to think of him as anything less than the most truthful of
humans under the sun. They didn't know that they were not the
only women present in that room at that moment. His mother and
his sisters were present round that fireplace, and they too were
proud of him, so he went on, for *them:* "Of course, as an honorable
man, I must make full confession of my sins and I shall frankly
admit that I have lied to you, Sophie, less than an hour ago, but
only by omission, not by commission, when I failed to tell you why
I was in such a hurry and didn't want to look at that street with the
laundry hanging up there and the small hotel for *unspeakable*

people right in front of us: *I* am unspeakable, and that was *my* hotel until yesterday!"

The effect of these words was such that Leonardo mentally allowed his two nephews and even some of the neighbors to come into the kitchen and join his mother and his young sisters in their mute admiration of the scene, to see with their own eyes that Uncle Leonardo was not to be classified as a kept man, even though he was about to marry a millionairess. Before Sophie and Mary found courage enough to speak, Giovanna's spirit had arrived too. And Giovanna of course was far more interested in the expensive clothes and the beautiful jewels of the two women than in the blatant fact of adultery to be followed by divorce. He braced himself for a new master blow in the International Tournament between the Burini and everybody else in the whole world of kings, queens and bankers, but he hadn't counted on the resilience of his competitor, who began her counterattack with the following words:

"And I, as an honorable, Protestant woman must also make a full confession of my sins and admit frankly to you that I lied when I defended my coachman whom you had branded as unspeakable. I should have told you humbly that you were perfectly right: he *is* unspeakable, he is not even a human being, he is an INDIVIDUAL!"

"What do you mean by INDIVIDUAL, Sophie? We are all individuals."

"Oh no, I know my Italian colloquialisms by now. When you say of someone, *that individual*, it is as much of an insult as it is for us in Russia to brand anyone as *Celoviek*. I called you that myself at the Hotel de Russie, remember?" Leonardo remembered and blushed, because he didn't want his spirit audience to be party to *that* scene, so he interrupted Sophie with a quick move.

"I had noticed already that you had a tendency to go from one extreme to the other in your dealings with people beneath your social and financial level, Sophie. All the rich foreigners who come to Italy commit the same mistake: they are either too friendly or too insulting; they have no sense of measure and no notion of the confusion they create in the minds of the poor."

"Look, my young friend," said Sophie. "I have dismissed the servants so we can eat alone and talk about the things I wanted to discuss with you last night when I sent word for you to come upstairs before going to your hotel and you refused. We were both disappointed. You see, Leonardo, what we wanted to tell you was that *all* our servants, here and at the hotel, could overhear our conversations and we would still be safe, *except* for the coachman, that is. He is the only one who could and would harm us: he is the real spirit of Judas incarnate, he belongs to that evil race of self-appointed spies for governments we all know so well in Russia. Here they spy for the Vatican, of course. I hope you didn't tell him about Mary's divorce."

"I???" said Leonardo, blushing.

"I'm sorry," said Sophie. "I shouldn't have asked you. I knew you could be trusted. Aaaah," she sighed, and added a few words in Russian, making the sign of the cross (the wrong sign, of course: from right to left), "thank God we have found ONE Italian who can be trusted!! I realized it yesterday, when I saw you come back after your momentary flight. I knew what that meant, for a person like you: once you have crossed the Rubicon, there is no going back: you can be trusted to stay faithful to your decision for the rest of your life. You are not like the Monster. . . ." She took his hand with both of hers, as if to join them in prayer, then said: "Mary, let's give thanks to the Lord, or to the Something, because our woes are over. We have found peace: you to live, I to die. And you, Leonardo, open this bottle of Champagne!" Leonardo obliged, staring intensely at the fireplace to make sure the kitchen of Laterza had not assembled there again, and when he kissed Mary and Sophie three times, in Russian fashion, before toasting to the success of their endeavor, he felt like Judas.

From that moment on he stopped fighting for his own independence of mind with these two strange creatures from a different planet and their servants in this one, to concentrate solely on the task of fighting for his own sanity. The thought that he and he alone, for no logical reason, had shattered his own dream of happiness and caused these two wonderful creatures the greatest harm in the world was too much for him to bear. He was alone in a world he detested, after learning to love it in the short space of two days and one night . . . or was it one day and one night? Yes, one afternoon and one morning, with one happy night in between. All of it gone, because of that mania he had to be on human terms with all other humans at all times. Lazily, listlessly, without the slightest interest, he let his mind wander all the way back in history to the sinking of Atlantis, to the earthquake on Crete which had sent King Minos underground to become the gatekeeper of hell, and while letting his mind wander thus aimlessly from one impotent thought to another, he watched the two women eat and drink until they could hardly breathe, and began wondering whether it wouldn't be a blessing for them to die of apoplexy now, rather than in a filthy Roman jail next morning, or perhaps even this afternoon before their infernal tea.

They noticed his silence only after they had eaten up the last crumb of chocolate cake on the dish (he had helped them stack the other dishes and hated them for considering this an adventure: changing dishes without the help of three uniformed servants in white gloves! "How independent we are!"). He was thinking of the final act of his personal tragedy: suicide, of course, what else? Could he ever go back to Laterza after the scandal in the papers? That unspeakable coachman would of course make a star witness. But perhaps the coachman wouldn't talk, perhaps he hadn't believed him, *perhaps they were exaggerating* . . .

"I have it," he exclaimed cheerfully. Then: "Is there any cake left?"

"We'll ring for more," said Sophie, "can you tell us your EUREKA?"

"I must see my cousin, who is the personal oculist of the Pope and the King, as you heard me say this morning on the square."

"No, I didn't."

"Didn't you? I shouted it, that's what made the police treat me with greater respect; in fact, it may even have been the reason Her Majesty came back and gave you those flowers, now that I think of it. Well, it so happens that my first cousin Crocifisso is the personal oculist of the Pope and the King. I want to see him before this evening."

"Why don't you ask him to dinner? Is he a good man?"

"A most excellent man."

"But how interesting! We can talk about the eye. What a great mystery of nature it is. . . . Vision . . . how fascinating. Oh, Leonardo, Mary, my beloved children, isn't it wonderful that the three of us can finally do something useful for mankind? I have been hesitating for months between care of the insane and that of all those derelicts who contract trachoma because they haven't learned the ABC of hygiene. Now, if this cousin of yours is a good eye doctor, he can't go on curing the Pope and the King and their servants at their damned courts forever: they are all blind by choice anyway, and if they get trachoma for a change, it would serve them right. But the poor, and especially their children, just imagine *how many* we could rescue and train and then launch into the modern war against ignorance and superstition. . . . But now go, and please be back in time for dinner at eight. And by the way, now that we know you haven't spoken with that awful individual, this is what we can do: tonight late we all move to the Russie, and during the night, Mary can join you and no one will be able to say a thing. Here I wouldn't trust myself to do such a thing. The spy lives here, it's better to be prudent. But if I move to the hotel, because I want the furniture changed in my room here, who can find anything strange in that?"

"Thank you, Mamachen," said Mary, pale with emotion, but Leonardo, who had turned just as pale, said somberly: "No. I don't think it would be prudent."

"But I told you, my servants can be trusted: he is the only exception."

"All the same," said Leonardo, "I think we would be safer if we waited until we are out of the country."

"*Your* decision, and I must respect it. And so must you, Mary: this is between the two of you from now on. I must go now and write a few thoughts in my journals, then do some reading. This has been a most fruitful day, for which I thank the Something, or let's be frank and say the Lord, but I haven't done any of my homework yet. I have given nothing: I have only received, and received, and received again. . . . From you, my dear son." And she kissed him on the forehead, then on both cheeks, then kissed Mary the same way and quickly was gone because she had tears in her eyes.

Mary looked at Leonardo very sternly, then, staring at the floor with an expression of fixed distress, she murmured something he couldn't hear.

"What was that, my love?"

"am I your love?"

"Oh, is that what you were asking me? What an absurd question."

Mary shuddered and closed her eyes, then asked, slowly, almost in a whisper: "Then I can tell my mother that we accept her . . . offer?"

"Listen, my love, do you know that the maid at the hotel, your mother's own trusted maid, promised me to go and pray for the success of our divorce? She was going to talk to Father Mansueto about it."

"Whaaat?"

"Yes, she calls it an annulment. . . . Now, Father Mansueto may or may not be a trustworthy priest, but, as I told your mother, if he believes such a story, he will be eager to let his superiors know that he is intimate with people rich enough to buy themselves an annulment. And since an annulment is so rare an event that the whole body of Cardinals, the whole city of Rome would know about it, it is easy enough for his superiors to find out that this story was either a lie, or someone's mistake. And then? And then come the police to take us all to jail, and your husband gets a separation from you, and deprives you of your child. Would you want to take such a risk? Not with *my* help! You do it alone. . . ."

"*Gospody Pamilyui* . . ."

Leonardo wasn't moved by his usual curiosity to learn what those words meant. She seemed terrorized at the peril implied in her mother's daring plan, and that sufficed; he felt that her inquisitive stare had been deflected from him for the moment, and he was eager to leave before it was turned again on his filthy soul.

"I must go, Mary, I'm anxious to find my cousin before he leaves the hospital."

"What hospital does he work in?"

". . . er . . . hm . . . I . . . I know how to get there, but I forget the name."

"Be quick, take a cab."

She didn't say "Take our carriage," nor did she ask him if he had any money for cabs. That's the way the rich are. They always think that other people are as rich as they are . . . except when they suddenly remember that they are richer than everybody else. And woe to him who, being less rich than they are, thinks of himself as their equal because he has been given a tiny glass of sugary liqueur and a dry biscuit on a small plate with an embroidered napkin on it. Soon will come an embarrassing question such as: "When were you last in Paris?" or "Did your horses race at San Siro this year?" To which the answers are: "Never" (in more correct terminology, "Never been out of Italy"), and "I never owned a horse that wasn't heavy enough to pull a cartload of rocks up a steep mountain." He knew these things from his rare associations with those rich cousins of whom Crocifisso was the eldest: some were married to titled nobodies, others to untitled somebodies with money, but all claimed descendance from St. Thomas Aquinas, just like Giovanna.

He was already halfway down the dark staircase, hat in hand, when Mary's voice called: "How can you know how to get to a hospital whose name you don't know, when you have never been to Rome before?"

"What a question," he answered. "Instinct, medical instinct."

"You can't tell *that* to a Roman cabbie, my love. He'll curse all your dead ancestors. Why don't you give it up and stay with me? There are so many things we must discuss."

"We'll have the rest of our lives."

"So you don't want to talk to me! Are you afraid?"

"No, of course not."

"I like that OF COURSE. . . ."

"Mary, please, . . . someone may overhear us."

"Come back upstairs, I don't talk on staircases, it's not my habit."

"But . . ."

"You still haven't answered my question about how you will find him."

"I'll just go to one hospital. . . ."

"Yes, but how do you find that?"

"I'll ask."

"Very well. Good luck. But take a cab, don't walk."

He would walk, of course. What else was there for him to do? Walk, in search of a solution. But already on the first turn of the huge, vaulted staircase away from Mary's reach, he found the same unfriendly winter wind that had made him so miserable in front of the hotel earlier; what a change in his future, between then and now . . . Then, he was waiting for Cinderello's golden carriage and going towards his love, his new and comfortable kingdom, plus lunch and a fireplace he longed for at this moment more than he longed for Mary. And now? Now only towards the tomb of his short-lived illusions. He didn't love her the less for her unbearable questioning, indeed he loved her more, because that, again, even more than her belief in the basic frigidity of women, was a guarantee of her innocence, but he loved her as a Princess of the Moon, not of this world. "A man whose every word is true: *Hai detto 'na parola,*"* he said aloud, speaking to Emperor Augustus (or was it Trajan? Or Caesar? He couldn't make out the features of the dusty marble statue that emerged from a niche at the end of the landing). A blast of air, and a lot of cold, bitter dust met him halfway towards the second landing. He was freezing, and again his thoughts flew to Laterza, where his only winter coat lay, deeply buried in mothballs, and the thought that he would soon be able to reach it, while having no need for it, was like another lesson from On High. I trespass, he wrote in his mind; here I am the head of an immensely rich household, and have not a penny in my pocket. Here, everybody is tough and inhuman, and these two women discover a deep kinship with me, because we in the South are softhearted and human—and I turn out to be their worst enemy, because I behaved as I would at home. Here, it is still winter, but I am dressed as if I were back home. Oh, why didn't I make a full confession half an hour ago, and walk straight to the hotel, pick up my luggage and walk to the station and go home, where I wouldn't have to explain anything to Giovanna, because she always sees me gloomy and aloof, the moment I'm back with her? Once I'm gone, the coachman's denunciation will fall into the void: with the end of my trespass ends also all evidence of these women's wrongdoing. It was all an illusion. Cinderello is back in his kitchen, and the princess in her castle in the moon. So, why don't I go to the hotel, write a one-sentence letter: I LIED TO YOU, BUT I WILL LOVE YOU FOREVER AS I HAVE IN THE PAST, then pick up my suitcase and plaid and go home? Why?

---

* Neapolitan for "You said a mouthful."

His question was now addressed to another ancient Roman, whom he recognized as Cato the Censor because there was a dusty window next to that particular niche; it also showed palm trees and laurel bushes, tormented by the wind, and a beautiful garden, and a sky torn into shreds of white and gray, against a background of blue. "Cato Uticensio," he said, with sobs in his throat, "you, who committed suicide rather than submit to political servitude under Caesar, and were forgiven by Dante, who had Christ come down to Limbo and take you up to Purgatory, you, the most righteous of politicians in Rome, you understand my plight, I know you advise me to go home."

But Cato didn't answer him, and he walked past the dusty statue, farther down towards the entrance hall and the street, knowing that he would never be so courageous as he had been nine years before. "What am I going back to? Peppino and Liborio know, and they will laugh at me every time they see me looking gloomy, and they will tell on me at the café, and everybody in town will know, except for the usual stupid wives, who have no right to know anything. So Mary's name will be dragged in the mud too, and that, again, will have been my doing. But how will I ever forget these two days in the moon?"

He was now speaking to an urn, a poor Renaissance copy of some ancient Grecian urn, in a niche at the end of the staircase. He had noticed it before, on his way up with Sophie and the Queen's flowers; ah, the sting of his last humiliation: another lesson from On High, that, too. . . .

He passed the doorman, trying to look dignified, but the doorman WAS dignified in his huge winter coat, and the doorman said cheerfully: "Winter's back, eh? You better wear your winter coat, if you don't want to catch pneumonia. Rome isn't like the South."

"I know, I know," he said, pretending to laugh as he put on his poor hat, "but I'm not afraid of this weather. . . ."

Another lie. Nothing but lies to mark the road of the trespasser. At least, back home, he could afford to be truthful in public, as befits a man: lies are for women only. And these two women here . . . or rather, THOSE TWO WOMEN UP THERE, think they can set the rules by which a man should be truthful at all times. . . . How can you be truthful most of the time, if you can't tell lies some of the time?

He was now walking past the façade of the palace, and decided to head uphill, towards Trinità dei Monti, because that way he would soon reach a corner and turn either right or left and be out of sight of those windows up there.

Sophie's words came back to him: Once you have crossed the Rubicon, there is no going back. You can be trusted to stay faithful to your decision for the remainder of your life. . . .

He laughed bitterly, remembering what Rubicon he had crossed down there, in that public urinal on Largo Crispi. . . .

He had now reached the staircase of Trinità dei Monti, and began to descend, stopping at every step and looking back. The palaces of Via Gregoriana gradually came into view above him, taller and more forbidding at every step, as he himself was carried downwards and ever closer to his natural equals . . . after the Fall: the beggars who were huddling in their rags against the wind. A bony hand stuck itself out of one of the many holes in those rags: "Penny for the blind man . . ." Leonardo stared at the white steps in front of him, to hide his shame. How could he say: "I don't have a penny in my pocket"? Another lesson from On High.

"Sir . . . sir . . . look at my hungry child . . . he's sick . . . he's dying with fever. . . . Won't you help?" Leonardo looked, because the voice reminded him of his mother, and the child in her arms had the typical eyes and short breath he would have seen in Laterza today at this very hour. . . . He remembered the name of the sick child back there, and wondered how it was, and worried. Of course Peppino and Liborio had notified the mayor's office that the mayor was detained in Rome by urgent business, but who would notify that poor woman? And who would trust the substitute physician to go to her hut today? She was not a paying patient, and Leonardo knew the contempt in which these derelicts were held by his ambitious younger colleague. And I allowed myself to be shielded by that telegram . . . Urgent business . . . unforeseen circumstances . . . What if that child dies today? He felt a new impulse to return to Laterza immediately, without even going to the hotel, in order not to miss the next train (Why not lose my luggage, since I know that the child may lose his life?), but he knew very well that it was an impulse he would never heed. In the meantime the sick child here was whimpering, and the mother sobbing aloud: "Help me, good sir. I'm all alone in Rome, abandoned by my husband."

He paled. Her accent was unmistakably Apulian. He stared at the child, and she misunderstood his stare as being directed at her bosom, which was still partly uncovered after nursing.

"What are you staring at?" she asked. "Aren't you ashamed of yourself?"

"I am a physician," he said, apologetically. "Perhaps I can help you." And he touched the child's forehead, but she misunderstood this gesture too, and pushed his hand away.

"You? A physician? You're a pig, that's what you are. And an *Apulian* pig on top of it all! I know your kind! Physician, my ass! . . . If I need a physician, I know where to find one. Give me the money and I'll go to the hospital right now."

"You won't need money, if I take you to the hospital. All you will have to do is tell me where the hospital is, I'll walk with you, and recommend you to the best doctors."

"You will, will you? I want your money, I don't want you."

"I have no money, that's my trouble. Look." And he took out his wallet, to show her its contents, then pulled out the lining of his pockets, to show her they contained not a cent, then showed her his stethoscope, and said: "This proves I am a physician . . . but, owing to unfortunate circumstances, I find myself penniless today. I have a cousin at the hospital, who can help both you and me. Come along."

"Oh no. I know your story. You're a married man from down there, this is your first trip to the big city, you went for the whores, and they robbed you. Perhaps they didn't even let you fuck them, which is why you're trying to get me, because I'm obviously a fallen woman. Give me your gold watch and chain, and I'll let you come with me, but I need money more than you do. Your cousin can help *you*, he wouldn't help *me*."

"My cousin will help us both, but I swear to you I haven't been robbed."

"Oh yeah? Poor little boy, wasn't robbed by a whore, eh? What was she? The Holy Virgin? Is that why you haven't gone to the police? Nossir, you haven't gone to the police because you are afraid of the scandal back home, poor Burino. Your wife will beat you up, the town paper will make fun of you. They're all alike. And the whores here know it: safe game. These people can't go to the police. Southern Honor forbids it. Go fuck your mother next time, it's safer."

He turned from her and ran, a gust of wind blew off his hat, he chased it and was almost run over by a cab at the foot of the steps, while the hat fell into the fountain. A little beggar boy jumped in after it and came back with the hat in one hand and the other hand open under Leonardo's nose for money. This time Leonardo had no reason to apologize. He grabbed the hat from the boy and said, "Sorry, little boy. Next time. I have no money on me."

"No money? You were gypped by that whore up there? *A-cazzac-cio . . . A-burino . . . Abbuciardo . . .*" (you prick, you Burino, you liar). With every new profanity, the feeble voice of the beggar child gathered momentum, attracting a wide audience: servant girls and elderly people at the windows, people of all ages from the streets across the square, except for those in the company of ladies, who rushed away to avoid hearing what they couldn't help hearing anyway. Leonardo decided it would be better to pretend that the words weren't being addressed to him than to quarrel with a child. He tried to be a tourist and looked at the blue Roman sky with great intensity, thinking: Where can I go? What can I do? His most urgent desire at that moment was for a cup of real Italian coffee, and a warm place and a MAN, an ITALIAN MAN, to talk to, one who didn't believe that other human beings are perfect. A liar! An honest-to-God liar! he prayed. A few drops began to descend, causing umbrellas to be opened by well-dressed men over the hats of well-dressed women, while the beggars welcomed the chance to look even more pitiful than in the sunshine.

Then, a miracle. "Sir, may I be bold enough to talk to you for a moment?" said a timid Apulian voice, which came from a gray-haired little man dressed in mourning like Leonardo, with the same white vest and watch chain, even the same amulets dangling from it, although everything about him, even his stature, even his gold chain, even his amulets, were of a slightly inferior quality.

Leonardo felt so happy to see his prayer answered that he laughed aloud, saying: "Small world, indeed! . . . Two poor Burini lost in the woods of the big metropolis!"

"Not me!" snapped the small man. "Not Luigi Schillasi. I'm a proud Roman citizen with thirty-one years in His Majesty's service, added to fifteen years in the service of His Holiness the most regretted Sovereign Pontiff Pius the Ninth. . . ." Then, seeing he had scared Leonardo, he added, with a condescending smile: "Sicilian-born, of course, as the name tells, but raised in Apulia; to be more precise, in Acquaviva delle Fonti."

"Acquaviva delle Fonti," muttered Leonardo, paling as if he had met his Maker on Judgment Day, "my wife's hometown . . ."

"I'm sure I know her: what was her maiden name?"

And humbly, against his will, the doomed sinner confessed: "D'Aquino."

"A descendant of Saint Thomas, no doubt."

This resurrected and disgusted the sinner all in one. He could almost hear Giovanna's hated voice answering proudly: "Of course I am, I even look like the Great Family Saint."

"Dogs and pigs are called D'Aquino in Apulia . . . a name even more common than Claudi!" he shouted, to silence both the internal and the external goad at once.

"Still, a most illustrious name, my dear sir. Not everybody is called D'Aquino."

"Thank God for that!" And with these words, Leonardo was gone in the rain. "Sir! . . ." shouted the proud Roman citizen, "Your Excellency . . . Your Highness."

"No such demeaning appellatives for me," shouted Leonardo, stopping to deliver his lecture: "Call me Doctor, if you have to call me anything, but what the hell for, anyway?"

"Only for the honor of being near you in your distress. . . ."

"What distress?"

"Weren't you looking for the police?"

"Me, for the police? Nonsense!!!"

"But weren't you just robbed by that prostitute up there?"

"Robbed? Not at all, thank you very much, goodbye."

"But, Doctor, please, let me talk to you anyway. Don't reject a compatriot in distress. . . . For I, too, am in distress, despite my

many years of honorable service to the cause of our National Resurrection, Culture, Morality and all the noble, positive values I have
always protected and defended singlehandedly, with such dedication, abnegation and pride. . . . You were lucky . . . you had
money to get yourself an academic title, and I had none . . . perhaps the mindlessness of youth was also to be blamed for my bad
luck: I should have recognized my rare cultural talents much earlier
in life. . . . Too late, too late to think of it now, in my fifties . . ."

"It's never too late," said Leonardo, feeling it was certainly too
late for him to be wasting any more of his time with this knave.

"It is, it is. You're lucky, you have a title, and I am nothing.
. . ." The knave obviously knew he had made a dent in Leonardo's heart, and went on, looking pitiable: "The trouble with me
is, I'm too generous and too honest. I never cheated, never tried to
use my high personal connections to get what others, less worthy
than I am, have got for themselves . . . I even stooped so low as to
accept the most menial employment in museums—about which I
knew more than all the museum directors and experts put together.
Italy is a cruel stepmother to her best sons, dear Doctor. The place I
occupied in the Vatican Museums for fifteen years was called the
Chair of Ancient Greek Sculpture, and the chair I later occupied in
the National Museum is still called the Chair of Renaissance Painting—but not by Italians, nossir, only by foreigners who appreciate
my culture and call me the Professor."

"Too bad. Well, good luck to you and perhaps we'll meet again
sometime."

"No, no, don't go, don't leave me alone with my bleeding heart
in my hand. Allow me to offer you a cup of coffee."

"Thank you, I can't. It would be for me to offer you coffee . . .
but, owing to unforeseen circumstances . . ."

"Never mind . . . in Rome you are my guest, if I may be so bold
as to think of you in such terms. You are a doctor, and God knows
what other important things that I don't even know about . . .
and I am nothing. It follows . . ."

"No, nothing follows, because the premises are wrong," said Leonardo, who was already following Schillasi across the square,
through a dense crowd of umbrellas, finery, top hats, horses and
carriages. Why am I doing this? he asked himself. Do I need coffee

that badly? Or do I need further proof that I'm still a better man
than this fool? He couldn't answer these questions, yet he knew he
was wasting his time and perhaps making an even greater mistake
than he had made the previous night with the coachman; he soon
realized how right he was, when he heard the knave calling from the
sidewalk: "This way, Your Highness."

Suddenly he found himself alone: traffic had stopped around
him, people were looking at him in awe. "Schillasi," he shouted,
"what nonsense is this? I'm no Highness. . . ." But Schillasi was
still calling: "Here, Your Highness . . ."

"Nonsense," he shouted back; then, addressing his admirers:
"This man's a liar, I'm a nobody, I am a country doctor. . . ." And
yet he went on following Schillasi instead of turning his back on
him and fleeing. In his confusion, he bumped into a paunchy little
man in Homburg hat and white gloves, who lifted his cane to hit
him, but here was Schillasi again, rescuing him in the nick of time
with magic words that turned the threat to a gentle smile: "To the
Supreme Poet of all times, Gabriele D'Annunzio, greetings and
salutations!" and the Poet smiled gently and was gone. But Schillasi
was *not* gone, and Leonardo shouted at him: "You Are A Liar! . . ."

"He calls me a liar," said Schillasi, addressing the crowd: ". . .
but earlier today he was seen here on this very spot in the same
carriage as Her Majesty the Queen Mother, and she even gave him
flowers as he left. . . ."

Leonardo tried to escape into a side street, but this time he found
himself surrounded by a group of young men who began to chant:
"This way, Your Highness," then, as he turned the other way: "No,
not that way, Your Highness . . . this way. The Professor is awaiting you in the Caffè Greco around the corner."

Thus Leonardo found himself in the café before he even knew
how he had got there. All the customers seated around their marble
tables had turned their chairs in the direction of Schillasi, who was
already settled in a corner on a red velvet couch. Mirrors and gas
lamps illuminated the scene. A tiny cup of black coffee was steaming
in front of him and the solemn-looking waiter who had brought it
was still standing there, listening to *his* version of the *incident* with
the mysterious friend of Her Majesty the Queen Mother.

"All our nobles look like provincials lost in the great city," Schillasi was explaining to the waiter, for want of a better audience, "and so do our best minds in every field: we all look a bit like most provincials, and in a way we are, but we are lost in modern *times*, not in modern *cities*. No wonder we feel lost. . . . But we still stick together, we *recognize* one another even hundreds of miles away from home. This great gentleman, who is also a great scholar, and of course a great friend of Her Majesty the Queen Mother, *recognized me* in a vast crowd, and in a moment of distress, when he needed to confide in someone from his own background . . ."

At that moment he saw Leonardo and froze into appalled silence. Leonardo pretended to have heard nothing, sat down in front of him, planted both elbows on the cold marble surface, cupped his hands around his mouth and whispered: "Imbecile."

"Me, imbecile? *You* are the imbecile, allowing that whore to rob you of your last cent, and then complaining to her, instead of calling the police."

"I *told* you, I wasn't robbed at all, and in any case that's all beside the point. You, on the other hand, are robbing me of my dignity by calling me Your Highness, and spreading it far and wide that I was in the Queen Mother's carriage: all lies."

"You're calling me a liar, are you?"

"If you tell lies, that's the correct term to describe you."

Schillasi had tears in his eyes; Leonardo had spoken loudly enough to attract everybody's attention.

"No one, ever, in forty long years of honest work, has called me a liar."

"I only just did, so what are you complaining about?"

Leonardo had not meant to be funny, but the audience applauded. He felt sorry for Schillasi, whose quivering cheeks were lined with tears, which wetted his gray mustache and beard before dripping into his cup, causing their equivalent weight in coffee to splash onto the saucer and the table.

"You break my heart," said Leonardo, stretching out both arms and caressing Schillasi's face. "Stop it or you'll make me cry too."

"You've ruined my life!" Schillasi sobbed.

"Goombà, you ruined your life yourself when you didn't take your degree in letters and philosophy all those years ago. Too late to think of it now . . ."

Schillasi cast a side-glance at the audience and, seeing that it was still very much present, he said: "But you're a liar too."

"I? And what lies have I told you?"

"I heard you say to Her Majesty that her husband had usurped your throne. So you must be the King of Naples."

The audience was delighted again, but at this point a very aged man, who looked like God the Father in an El Greco painting, rose from his table shouting: "This is a slur on both monarchies: that of the Piedmontese usurper and the legitimate one, my ancestors' . . . I demand a public apology, since I cannot challenge you to a duel; for you, Professor, are not a gentleman." Then, to Leonardo: "Are you a nobleman?"

"I don't know. If a nobleman is one who slashes human flesh, then I am not one because I sew it up, I mend broken limbs, I am a physician. Yet mine is the noblest of professions, and so it would seem to me that the correct termin—"

"We are not interested," said the Royal Pretender. "Tell us, rather: Were you really in Her Majesty's carriage?"

"No, I was in the carriage of a friend of Her Majesty's."

"And who is that?"

"A distinguished Russian lady . . ."

"Who? Name and predicates of nobility."

"I can only tell you that she lives in Via Gregoriana number forty-two, and that she honors me with her confidence and friendship. Any further details would be highly indiscreet because this lady and I—"

"We are not interested," shouted a red-haired man who was seated not far from Leonardo with a beautiful woman and several of the noisy young men who had caught Leonardo in the side street and pushed him into the café. Then, turning to the El Greco: "Cecè, don't waste your time with those Apulian Cafoni." And the Descendant of the Caesars, whose real name obviously was Caesar, seemed instantly reassured against all further loss of regal dignity by that demeaning diminutive. Not so the two recipients of the insult, who were blushing at each other and not daring to look anywhere else but into each other's eyes, lest they see things that would make them blush even more.

"See what you've done to our good name in the nation's capital?"

mumbled Schillasi after a while, and Leonardo felt impelled to shout at the red-haired man: "Who the hell are you anyway? And how dare you?" But these words were supported by so little breath that Schillasi himself found it difficult to hear them in the general din.

"I should really go and beat him up, that's the only argument you can use with such a CAFONE," commented Leonardo, putting a great deal of emphasis on the last word, as if to make it clear that it was *his* insult, not his rejection of someone else's.

"Don't make more trouble than you have already," said Schillasi, looking at him with contempt, and then with infinite sadness at the red-haired man, because *he* was now telling a joke, and even the waiters were allowed to take part in the general laughter: not so Schillasi.

"I'm sorry," muttered Leonardo. "I may not know the ways of the great world, but I do know that a man of your culture can find no solace in the friendship of such vulgar and immoral men. History repeats itself, even on a very small scale: we scholars are the descendants of the poor Christians in the Colosseum, and these are the descendants of the mobs at the courts of Caligula or Nero."

But Schillasi was no longer listening, nor in need of consolation. A tiny, bald man with a goatee had just appeared at the entrance of the café and was undecided whether to come in or not. It seemed to Leonardo that his reason for coming in was the group around the red-haired man, and Schillasi his reason for running out again. Suddenly he was spotted by the red-haired man's mistress; "Pirandello, come and join us," she called, and everybody else got up to reshuffle the chairs and include one more table in the group.

"No, no," shouted Pirandello, trying to avoid Schillasi who was just as obviously trying to be noticed by him.

"Yes, yes, come in," they shouted back, and Pirandello made it quite clear with his gestures that he was afraid of passing Schillasi's table.

"Goombà," whispered Leonardo, "don't make a fool of yourself."

But Schillasi was determined to get his revenge; he rushed over to Pirandello and seized him by the arm, saying: "Pirandello, you can't disappoint your friends, and you don't have to be afraid of me. I only want you to shake hands with a gentleman who is most eager to meet you. He is a great scholar and a personal friend of Her Majesty the Queen Mother."

"But I really can't," pleaded Pirandello, trying to disentangle himself without being too impolite.

"One handshake and a word, and you will make him happy. He is a great admirer of your work. . . ."

"Delighted to meet you," said Pirandello, shoving his hand into Leonardo's face, as Leonardo was rising from his seat with the words: "It's not true."

"It is," insisted Schillasi. "He came to Rome expressly to see you."

"Good luck to you and I hope you have a nice time in Rome," said Pirandello, withdrawing the hand Leonardo had not found time to shake, because his own hands were still up in the air, sketching the meaning of his remark, and before Schillasi could explain things any further the Great Man was gone.

"Now you've done it again. Are you pleased?" asked Schillasi, with tears in his voice.

"It's you who've done it again. Why did you have to say I was a great admirer of his? I'm not. I read one story of his once while sitting on the toilet, hated it, and used it for what it was worth. So I would *never* come to Rome expressly to meet him. . . . What is all that nonsense?"

"All right, all right, don't try to attract attention just because I made a mistake. I did it to please you, I thought you'd like to meet a celebrity. But you could have been a bit more understanding. Writers are vain, they have to be flattered all the time, and now you and your stupid sincerity have made me lose another friend."

"A friend, you call that a friend? He seemed desperate to avoid you."

"What do you know about my friendship with him? What do you know about *anything*?" He was now really close to breaking down; Leonardo had scored a success among his enemies, while he, once more, was free game for the onlookers, even for the waiters. But Leonardo realized it too, because this was the fate of all village idiots in all the cafés of Italy, and he felt he must defend him. The first measure was to get rid of the waiter. "Two coffees," he ordered, feeling he was pronouncing his own death sentence, then in a louder voice: "And two small cognacs, please."

Schillasi's face brightened; he promptly called the waiter back, shouting: "Make it two large cognacs, the best you have."

"No, no," shouted Leonardo, "only one cognac. I've changed my mind."

"You are my guest, Goombà." Then, to the waiter. "Two large cognacs, and a tray of pastry."

This dispelled the curiosity of the crowd, and Schillasi resumed his patronizing tone: "Sorry I was a little harsh, but this is Rome, this isn't home, where everybody knows you and you can even afford to dress up like a nobody. Here, unless you exhibit your title and dress up according to your rank, you *are* a nobody, and the Romans are cruel, as you've now learned both at your expense and my own. I understand your reluctance to exhibit yourself, because I'm exactly like you: I *never* exhibit my knowledge, *never* talk about my wife, who was born a baroness, but I've paid very dearly for my natural restraint. Ah, well . . . Life isn't easy for an honest man without a title—of nobility or studies—any title at all." Here he sighed and then resumed his lecture: "I *saw* you talking to Her Majesty and I *saw* her embarrassment. And only a couple of hours later I *saw* you being robbed by that whore, and I *knew* why you didn't go back to your mistress and ask for more money: it is embarrassing, it would be the same for *me*, if I had to ask *my wife!* We are both noble creatures, you and I. Now let me explain about Pirandello. I don't admire him any more than you do, but our detractors admire him, I mean these foreigners who come to Italy because our ruins are so pretty in the moonlight, and our beggars so picturesque. To them we are still a nation of beggars, thieves and prostitutes, who pose in the nude for so-called painters and sculptors. And Pirandello encourages these delusions. Apulia has no aqueduct, our sons must emigrate to America, where they lose their identity as descendants of the Roman legions that conquered and civilized the whole world, we *still* have no colonies; now Rome is our national capital again, thank God, but we *still* don't control our natural frontiers: our brothers in Trento and Trieste are *still* being hanged, if they dare affirm their desire to be reunited with us—and what does this internationally renowned writer do? All he can find to write about is degenerates, ineffectual dreamers, deluded fools, paraplegics, gigolos, unwed mothers, cuckolded husbands, ITALIAN

cuckolded husbands, I want you to know: *all* of his ugly characters are Italian—not *one* of them is a foreigner. Is this a writer
from the same noble country that has given us Dante, Julius Caesar,
Mazzini, Garibaldi, Galileo, the whole Renaissance, everything that
makes up modern Progress and Civilization? Why doesn't he write
a patriotic novel? No, he claims that is beneath his dignity. Then
why not a novel about an ineffectual dreamer and deluded fool like
myself, a man of immense culture, of high moral and patriotic
principles, married to a noblewoman from an illustrious family of
patriots? A man never accorded recognition by his fellow countrymen, because he had no doctor's degree, while all the greatest foreign scholars still come to him for advice and venerate him as their
master? Now with one foot in his grave, this man still pursues his
old dream and preaches the Gospel of the Sacred Goddess Rome,
which says: The New Italy needs a New Italian, a man worthy of
his Imperial Past, of his Great Christian Tradition, modernized by
scientific progress, to re-establish Italy's primacy over the whole
civilized world."

Here Schillasi stopped to ask: "Do you see what I mean?" Leonardo saw what he meant. "Then spare yourself the effort of informing me that Pirandello is not my friend. Of course he tries to
avoid me, because I am the Voice of his Patriotic Conscience. And
of course now he has the perfect excuse for not heeding that voice,
because you insulted him."

"I'm sorry," said Leonardo, made humbler by the arrival of
coffee, cognac and pastry.

"Tell *him*, not *me*," said Schillasi, lifting his glass to toast his
friend. "Write him a nice little note, saying you were a bit confused, or angry with me for other reasons—anything—but *do* confirm that you admire his work and want to see him again, and invite
him to your mistress's palace for dinner."

"I can't do that."

"Why? Because you'd have to invite me, too? Not true. I'm self-
effacing by nature, one more sacrifice for the good of the Fatherland
won't hurt me much."

"No, no, if I could invite him, I would insist on having you too,
but . . . I can't. I'm leaving tomorrow anyway. I only came here to

address the Senate on the question of the Apulian Aqueduct, and
my task is done." He sank back into a deep, mournful silence.

"Well?" asked Schillasi, drawing patience from his cognac. But
Leonardo was also drawing patience from his, and was in no hurry
to talk. He had a great deal of thinking to do: how to explain his
departure to Mary. A letter, yes, a long, eloquent letter, which
Sophie would appreciate before Mary could, and Sophie would see
to it that Mary didn't do anything foolish this time. . . . Even that
husband of hers would unknowingly come to Leonardo's assistance:
Mary would not want to risk a second bad mistake, and so, after a
few months of despair, she would be resigned to the fact that this is
not the moon—and, besides, there was every reason to be "pessimis-
tic" about the aqueduct. One official trip to Rome would not suffice:
in less than a month Leonardo would manage to come back
. . . and in the meantime so many things could happen. . . .
Perhaps Sophie could be persuaded to seek an annulment from the
Pope. A woman who knew the Queen Mother so well could easily
arrange to meet the Pope and, faced with so large a fortune, the
Pope would know what to do to avoid the scandal of divorce.

"I know you're not leaving tomorrow," said Schillasi.

"But I am, I swear I am."

"That's a lie. You're only saying so because you're ashamed that
your mistress is old enough to be your mother. But that's idiotic:
these things happen. . . ."

"What do you mean? Not to me!!! I am *not a kept man*!!! It's the
daughter, not the mother, who—"

"Come on, Goombà, restrain yourself: the daughter has a husband, he comes here every day."

"Oh my God: is he here now?"

"Not any more, but all his friends are."

Leonardo paled, cringed, grabbed Schillasi's hands across the
table and asked, in a whisper: "Do you think they heard me?"

"Of course they have. You were shouting."

"Oh my God . . . But you don't think they may have interpreted what I said about the Russian lady the way you did?"

"They most certainly have, if *I* have."

"What shall I do? I can't pass for a kept man."

"Come on, Goombà, where are you living: in the moon? If you aren't being kept by the mother, you're being kept by the daughter, unless you're much richer than they are, and that's impossible. But, as I said, this is perfectly normal."

"For corrupt people like you, yes, not for people like me, I want you to know!"

This last outburst was accompanied by the sudden arrival of a gentleman in the Renaissance uniform of the Sovereign Military Order of Malta, whom the waiters greeted as Your Highness, and many customers as Coco. Leonardo closed his eyes and said very humbly, "I must ask you a question, and I expect you to answer me with the utmost sincerity, regardless of the pain it may inflict on me. Can you swear you will tell me the truth?"

"On my honor."

And Leonardo, in a whisper: "What is the reputation of the two ladies in Rome?"

"What two ladies?"

"The one you mistakenly believe to be my . . . you know what, and her daughter?"

"Absolutely above censure."

"How can you be so sure?"

"Goombà, be logical: would Her Majesty the Queen Mother deign to talk to a lady whose reputation is not absolutely immaculate? Let alone offer flowers to her reputed gigolo?"

And now that Leonardo had been reassured as to Mary's morality, now he must reassure the whole café as to his own and hers again, because he alone had stained it. But unfortunately the whole café could not have cared less: His Highness Coco and the El Greco Royal Pretender had joined forces at a nearby table, and the crowd at the red-haired man's table was now focusing its attention on a very elegant woman who had entered the café quite alone and seemed undecided among several tables from which to command attention. Leonardo knew these tactics from his early café days in Naples: the tactics defined the type. This was obviously a very high-class prostitute who didn't have to court the men; she had come to shatter the reassurance of the women, and when she made for the table next to the red-haired man's, Leonardo and the whole café knew that this was a personal challenge to him, more than to his mistress. All the occupants at the other tables felt exempt (the women with relief, the men with envy), and became active spectators at a tournament between the red-haired man and his friends. He had three challenges to meet: he must keep holding the fort in conversation, keep his mistress from making a scene and win over the challenger.

"No," he began, apparently addressing no one but his mistress but talking very loudly with all the mimicry and pathos of an opera singer: "No and no and no! Love is not a human passion: *my* feeling or *your* feeling, *my* devotion or *yours*: love is outside us: a supernatural force that makes fun of us, torments us, surprises us, tears us away from wife and mistress, parents and children, just like the infernal hurricane Dante speaks of . . ."

"Right," shouted Leonardo, with a sudden gust of affection for his worst enemy of a minute ago, but his approval was drowned by the operatic contralto (the tenor's mistress): "Don't you shout NO at me! I wasn't even talking, let alone talking any such nonsense!" This angry retort brought laughter from the audience and the tenor felt he had lost face. "Darling," he said now, trying to soothe the contralto: "My *no* was rhetorical, I was talking to *myself*, not you, reproaching *myself* for being tossed about in the infernal hurricane that never rests . . ." A quick, fiery glance in the direction of the new woman delivered the message: "You are my hurricane."

She acknowledged it with a languid smile, and said, in a thick French accent: "How delightful . . . How true!" Then, " 'Le coeur a des raisons que la raison ne connaît pas,' as our poet . . . er . . . de Musset says."

The red-haired man was so excited by his triumph, he could hardly restrain himself: "De Musset is my favorite poet: may we invite you to join us?" "If Madame doesn't mind . . ." she said, coming over to their table, without even waiting for Madame's invitation. And Madame, the poor, fiery contralto of a minute ago, was so shocked by this utter disregard for her feelings that she simply withdrew, like a whipped servant, whose only revenge consists in belatedly muttering all the proud retorts she failed to think of at the right moment. There she sat, entertaining the audience with cheap stunts the winning rival could neither hear nor see; the other men at her table could, however, and they made it a point to displace their chairs and form a new circle around her. Leonardo was transfixed by the scene, because he had suddenly discovered that, in a certain vulgar way, the woman looked like Mary. How dare a whore do such a thing to him? His Highness Coco and the Royal Pretender were now transfixed too, because, in her anger, she had crossed her legs and lifted her skirts.

"What lack of respect for this place, where my own mother used to feel it was safe to drink coffee until eighteen seventy!!!" said His Highness in a shaky voice, without taking his eyes away from the dark tangle of white lace and black silk.

"Say what you will," said the Pretender, "but if my Lusignano Dynasty had been offered the Kingdom of Italy, I know they would have left Rome to the Pope. We learned our lesson with Justinian and Theodora, we would never repeat the error of moral permissiveness now. In my opinion—and after all I am the Roman Emperor—in this age of free love, free heathen science and free primary education, only the Pope can police our capital." And he angrily pushed his unlit cigar off the edge of the table, then went down on his knees to grope for it blindly, his eyes still fixed on the scandalous view.

Three waiters threw themselves on their knees in the same blind search, foiling Coco's generous effort to do the same (his red cape, his *fraise* and his sword had slowed him down). "And they want to conquer Libya," he snapped as he gave up.

"There I disagree with you," said the Pretender, back on his seat, rolling his cigar with trembling fingers. "I need Libya, too." Then, lowering his head towards the table, because the whore had lifted her skirt even higher: "Let's consider these veins in the marble as a map of our coasts and those of Africa. This is north" (he was using the cigar as a pencil, pushing it towards the Unspeakable), "namely, Sicily and Italy. And this here" (he was withdrawing, lowering his head under the table again) "is Africa. As the Teuton hordes are attracted by the South, so are the Moors by the North. We are their historical compass. So, unless we descend on them in self-defense, the traditional enemy of Christianity will aim at Christian Europe, as he did when your ancestor Godefroy de Bouillon stopped him at Roncesvalles."

The descendant of the Liberator of Jerusalem made a heroic

effort to look away from the Unspeakable; he had noticed that people were laughing. "But we are not militarily equipped to take Libya," he concluded, with a sigh of supreme resignation.

"We are not *morally* equipped," shouted Schillasi, who was instantly admitted as a peer at the strategic conference.

"Right!" said Coco. "A dynasty that usurps the Throne of Christ is not morally equipped to defend Christ!"

"That's not what I meant," said Schillasi, who had kept his eyes off the Unspeakable but very much on the sordid onlookers: "I meant to say that the Dynasty now happily reigning by the Grace of God and the Will of the Nation is more than equipped to defend Christ from Moslems, Socialists and Protestant proponents of Divorce, but not from the Italians themselves, who crawl on all fours to satisfy their sinful curiosity."

If Judgment Day had come, the catastrophe could not have been more complete: no one spoke, no one looked, everyone seemed to have been caught in prayer, except for the whore who blushed and pulled down her skirt as if she hadn't known what she was doing all along, and the Pretender, who rose like a ghost from a tomb, shouting: "Are you trying to insinuate . . ." But Coco stopped him, also shouting: "Don't, Your Highness, don't, he means the proponents of divorce, not you."

"Of course," said Schillasi, trembling in every limb, "the proponents of divorce . . . YOU!!!" he shouted at Leonardo, "who haven't answered my question yet: Are you in favor of divorce?"

"No," whispered Leonardo, blushing.

"And how about your Russian friends? They must be in favor of divorce, if they're Orthodox."

"How do you know?"

"Oh, they are, are they?" And he looked at his audience triumphantly but the audience was lost again: only the whore, like a new Magdalen, seemed ready to repent and follow the Master, and for her alone did the Master now speak, in exemplary terms, to his only pupil:

"A few minutes ago you called me immoral for suggesting that you had a rich mistress. Now it turns out that she believes in divorce. Would you marry a divorced woman?"

Leonardo didn't know what to say. In the space of a few minutes he had first accused this man openly, then admired him secretly for not looking at the whore, then worshipped him secretly for coming out openly against the lowest of all creatures on earth, the so-called Highnesses, then decided to be even more of a hero than Schillasi and defend the poor whore, who, in her distress, had been totally unaware of what she was doing, and here, all of a sudden, the great hero Schillasi turned out to be the lowest of the low. What could one do with such a man? Beat him up? He, a thirty-two-year-old, athletic healer, beat up a frail old man? No: the only thing to do was to talk openly and honestly, regardless of the consequences, then leave, write that letter and leave again, this time for good . . . until the slowness of Roman bureaucracy asked for another official visit from the good mayor of the waterless town in the Deep South.

"Before accepting your challenge," he began in a very soft voice, "I shall accept your advice of a few minutes ago and a few hours ago: DON'T SHOUT. And now: the truth. First of all, Mary is not my mistress. She was my first and only love, and if I didn't marry her nine years ago, it was only because I didn't want to become a kept man, and so I married my Cause, which consisted in being of service to mankind as a doctor. Mary was the second love I gave up, to be absolutely truthful: I had first been engaged to the study of archaeology, history, letters and philosophy: the same engagement you broke when you married your baroness, or perhaps earlier, I don't know and don't care to know."

"You mean to—"

"Don't interrupt me." Leonardo's voice was already rising. "I mean to tell you that Mary may even talk about divorce without losing one inch of her purity, dignity and saintliness. . . ."

The whore blushed and rose from her chair, advancing towards Leonardo and staring at him, while pretending she was looking somewhere else. Leonardo stared back, their eyes met, and he knew he was in love.

"No woman here, no woman anywhere on earth can replace Mary in my heart, because no woman can come even vaguely close to that model of perfection, intelligence and nobility called Mary." The whore was very close now: she had found another whore to talk to, and was using this excuse to brush Leonardo's hair with the back of her crinoline. He stared into his empty cup, scraped the sugary blob

with his spoon as if to find her there, and called softly: "Mary . . ."
Then, to Schillasi: "Nobody has the right to judge Mary, because
nobody knows what she is like . . ." (he certainly didn't: the more
he searched that blob, the more he saw of the prostitute whose
vulgar chatter was now filling his ears) ". . . I would have to be a
poet like Dante to recite her virtues and her beauty. . . ." And
again he plunged his gaze into the cup, to exorcize the evil force
that stood between his words and his feelings. But again, all he
could see was the face of that whore. "I'm no Dante, as I was
saying, but I *can* and *must* sing the praises of MY Mary: she is *not*
like these women who betray their lover at the first sign of infidelity,
to court a perfect stranger, without even knowing whether his heart
belongs to someone else. MINE DOES, and MY MARY, who married
a Roman painter out of despair, was never unfaithful to him,
even though he was never faithful to her. Why? you may ask.
I'll tell you why: because she was faithful *to me* all these years, yes,
to me, and yet she didn't even know if I was still alive. So, if she
talks about divorce—" An acute pain in his left arm interrupted his
speech and made him cry out. He turned around, and saw Mary's
stern face and fiery eyes, the TRUE Mary's. But no. Thank God it
was still only the whore, but by God, she did look like Mary now,
and what broke the spell was her coarse voice, as she hissed into his
ear: "Shut up, you fool! Mary doesn't want you spilling all her
secrets!"

"Mary, you said? Do you know her?"

"No, but, as a woman, I *know* she is *exactly* like me. Don't make
such big eyes. . . . I may be a whore and she may be an angel, but
when it comes to defending our secrets, a whore is a much better
friend to an honest woman than her fearless champion and wor-
shipper." Then, to Schillasi, in a tone of contempt: "I didn't know
YOU were such a fool, Professor. Get out of here, quick, both of
you!" And before they could say anything, she was out of the café,
arm in arm with the other whore, both of them giggling and chattering and provoking the men with their usual tricks.

The waiter, who had heard everything, stood next to the table
with his portable blackboard and chalk. Leonardo followed with
terror the long line of items consumed, their exorbitant prices, even

their sum total, which he had quickly calculated in his mind while the slow knave was still painfully getting there, finger on nose. But Schillasi gave no sign of having noticed all this. He was still reeling under the blow of the ultimate insult, and Leonardo was just asking himself: Who will pay? when the waiter asked *him:* "Who will pay?"

"Oh," said Schillasi, suddenly noticing the waiters and the rest of the audience: he pulled out his wallet, let a few large banknotes fall on the table, picked up one and threw it at the waiter, then began to walk out, slowly putting the other banknotes back into his wallet, so everyone could see them.

"Sir? . . . Professor?" shouted the waiter, "it's too much."

"Keep the rest as a tip."

"Are you crazy?" asked Leonardo.

"You're perfectly right, Goombà, but that's the way I am: NOT JUST TOO HONEST BUT TOO GENEROUS. . . . We're all punished for our virtues: you for yours, I for mine."

And with these noble words, he showed his guest the way out of the premises.

"You first . . ." said Leonardo.

"No, you first . . ."

"I insist . . ."

"All right, age before learning. May I walk you to Via Gregoriana?"

"I'm not going there, I'm going to my hotel."

"Which is? . . ."

"The Hotel de Russie."

"The Hotel de Russie? Why didn't you say so before?"

"Why should I?"

"It would have made everything much easier." Then, in a tone of veneration: "You know . . . I have NEVER met anyone who stayed at the Russie."

"Neither have I," said Leonardo, heavyheartedly, under his breath.

They left the Caffè Greco, Leonardo walking in front and determined to lose Schillasi, who was panting behind and calling out in despair: "Please slow down, please stop for a moment, please wait for me . . ." But his words were broken by asthma, by the noise of horse carriages and the din of a thousand church bells calling the faithful and the faithless to prayer: women with their daughters who didn't dare disobey them, and all the young men who felt so much more attracted by the show of obedience and restraint in a woman than by the reality of all the flesh offered them so freely in the cafés and on the sidewalks. And yet some of these men who were running to church were no doubt married, and the church-going girls were far from elegant or beautiful or bright, and the whole venture would consist in a long, boring wait on the steps of the church, to exchange a few glances—often no glances at all, just a few words of wishful thinking between the men, as the girls paraded in front of them without lifting their eyes from the ground. When he was certain he had lost Schillasi, Leonardo stopped briefly in front of a group of churches and almost joined the young men, but what drove him away was the voice of his persecutor surging again in the distance.

This city was so utterly different from Naples (the only other city he knew). The elegance of the carriages filled with beautiful ladies and gentlemen, the general atmosphere of joy and peace on every face glimpsed in the flash of a streetlight, the glow from a shopwindow, the last pale reflections of the most golden of sunsets he had ever seen: a sunset that had definitively ended the most golden of dreams he had ever had—these were the elements he needed to write his letter and then go to bed, rather than back to Mary.

Now the sky was all dark, and the air cold again, and full of scented smoke from a thousand kitchen chimneys and a thousand restaurants. Oh, how he wished he could stay and see Rome with Mary, and then travel with her to distant countries and return again, a happy husband and father—because he did feel an attachment for Sophie he had never experienced in his life: as for an intelligent mother, a mother who loved science and archaeology and the classics *like a man*, and had more courage than any man he had known in his life (or perhaps only more money?, in which case money was a real blessing); namely, the courage of her own disbelief in the Catholic Church. . . . He hesitated at a crossing. Did we come this way or that way with the carriage? He knew he was taking the long way back to his hotel (he couldn't take the short way because Schillasi might be preceding him), but now his famous sense of direction was beginning to betray him. He asked a passerby, who was too poor to know the Hotel de Russie. He asked another, and the answer was discouraging: "The Hotel de Russie, you said? But the Hotel de Russie is way back there, in the opposite direction. If you don't want to lose your way you have to go back to Trinità dei Monti and then, once you're in the Piazza di Spagna, you turn left. . . ."

"And if I go this way?"

"This way you get to the Tiber."

"And *that* way?"

"Worse still: you get to Saint Peter's."

"Well, can I walk back to the Hotel de Russie *without* going this way?"

"Absolutely not. You'll never find your way in the Old City."

"Thank you."

The stranger was gone, and he looked at his watch. God, it was late . . . surely Schillasi must have gone home by now. . . . He decided to go back to Trinità dei Monti and he began to run, but the next thing he knew, he found himself in front of his old hotel. The owner recognized him at once. "Have my friends left?" he asked.

"No, they're leaving tomorrow morning. They've gone out to dinner."

"Where?"

"I don't know."

He remained silent for a while, trying to think. Besides, how could he go back to them for advice? What did they know about sacrifice? Absolutely nothing. Whom to ask, then?

"How long will it take me to walk back to Trinità dei Monti from here?"

"Walk? Are you crazy? At least an hour, if you go up that way, then turn left—"

"No, *that* way."

"Nossir. Do you think you know Rome better than I do? If so, go ahead, but that way you get to Saint Peter's."

"I thought it was *that* way you went to Saint Peter's."

"No."

"Thank you."

And he turned the corner, to be out of sight, then stopped, feeling like a lost child. Destiny had decided for him: the best thing to do was to go back to HIS room and disappear without a word. Then, "*Quo vadis, domine?*" shouted a well-known voice from way above his head. He cringed, he could hardly believe this was real, but yes, there at a window in the filthy old building was Schillasi's face. "Don Leonardo," he giggled, "you told me a bunch of lies. I heard you talking to the owner of YOUR hotel just round the corner. . . ."

"I haven't told you a single lie, not one. . . . Please come down and listen to me."

Schillasi obeyed.

"How can you call me a liar? Didn't you hear me asking the way back to Trinità dei Monti?"

"No, I didn't. I was in the toilet, which overlooks the other side, when I heard you asking about your friends, so I rushed back to the kitchen to tell my wife you were here, and I was coming down the stairs when I saw you from the window on the landing and called you."

"Well, then let's go back to my hotel *here* and the owner will tell you the truth, but let's run, because—"

"We don't have to run. Let's take a cab, I'll pay for it."

"But you can't . . . you already paid for three coffees and the cognac."

"I can and I will. Just let me tell my wife. Annunziataaaaa," he called, and a raucous voice answered in a grunt that never seemed to end; it was joined by the sound of feet stumping on stairs, until the most horrible, bearded, cross-eyed, gray-haired and parchment-skinned face appeared at the window.

"That's him," shouted Schillasi in a triumphant voice that made Leonardo quail. Already the hotel owner and all the women who had witnessed the first scene less than twenty-four hours before were staring at Leonardo and listening. Once more Leonardo found himself being exhibited like a rare animal: "He knows the Queen Mother and he's the lover of one of the richest women in town: a Russian lady who lives in Via Gregoriana."

"That's not true," said Leonardo, furious again, this time without the slightest respect for his unwanted audience. But it was true enough for some of these people, who were now telling each other how they had seen him the evening before, what a fantastic carriage he had appeared in, and how HIS servants were dressed.

"To hell with you," shouted Leonardo to Schillasi. "You're a dirty liar and I won't have anything to do with you."

And he fled again, choosing the first street that was empty. "Where do you think you're going?" shouted Schillasi. Leonardo stopped instantly, in despair, then muttered, "You could at least show me the way."

"I will, I will," answered Schillasi with a sneer. "You've already shown me just what a provincial you are."

"Provincial or no provincial, I completed my degree and you never completed yours." The blow was so hard that Schillasi blushed and hung his head.

"Here comes a cab," he said in a funereal voice. He opened the door, said something to the coachman, climbed in after Leonardo, sat down, then slammed the door noisily and sank into a gloomy silence, while Leonardo divided his attention between the lively streets he was seeing for the first time, and the listless creature slumped next to him in the seat.

They had penetrated into the thick of the Corso, just at the hour of the daily parade of carriages and pedestrians which transformed the whole street into a social gathering: carriage after carriage after carriage, filled with ladies who all looked like Mary and Sophie, and with gentlemen who all looked like the men at the Caffè Greco, plus more of the same ladies and gentlemen on the sidewalks. He was tempted to keep looking at them, and then tempted to hide as deep as possible inside his carriage, but the cheerful voices and brilliant figures outside kept driving him back to the show like a child to the window when the procession of a patron saint is passing. The carriage was moving too fast, and in a few more seconds this final parade of Cinderello's fairy tale would come to an end; the carriage was moving too slow, and anybody could look inside and see him seated next to Schillasi, two sorry clowns who were already the talk of Rome.

They finally arrived at a square so huge and splendid that Leonardo's worries and fears were dwarfed by it for a brief second, long

enough to make him feel that to live in a city as gigantic as Rome
might in itself perhaps set everything right in his life, Mary or no
Mary. At the end of the square there was a monument of marble,
still unfinished, which glittered in the full moon as if it were composed of the selfsame material. How was it possible that he had not
seen this marvel of all marvels on his way to the hotel the previous
night or that same morning?

"What's that?" he asked, and Schillasi proudly answered: "It's
the monument to King Victor Emmanuel the Second, the Father
of the Fatherland."

"Of course," said Leonardo, "I've seen pictures of it in magazines, now I recognize it, but how come I haven't seen it before?"

"Because you are a provincial Burino, in spite of all your academic titles: you come to Rome and deliver a speech to the Senate,
taking the Fatherland to task for not giving your province an aqueduct. This *is* the Fatherland, my friend, and in a modern world, the
World of Nations and of Progress, these are the Public Works we
must ask for from the Senate or the Chamber of Deputies, because,
in the Concert of Nations Italy alone must be the conductor. The
aqueduct can wait, my friend, and the Senators you addressed
yesterday should have brought you here and shown you this, by way
of a reply to your puny requests for puny people in the backwoods
of Apulia. You know what lies behind that? The Colosseum. Have
you seen the Colosseum?"

"No, I haven't, but . . . if I'm not mistaken . . ."

"Coachman," shouted Schillasi, "on to the Colosseum."

"Just a moment," said Leonardo, then to the coachman: "Where
are we going?"

"To the Colosseum," answered the coachman condescendingly.

"Weren't you given orders to go to the Hotel de Russie?"

"Of course, on our way back."

"On our way BACK?"

"These were the orders."

"Not mine."

"Who's paying for this?"

"I will . . . tomorrow."

"So tomorrow I'll take orders from you. If the person paying me
now orders me to go to the Colosseum, I go to the Colosseum

unless given counterorders by him, because he promised to pay
double fare. Clear?"

"Absolutely clear and logical, my friend," said Schillasi to the
coachman, with a glance of contempt at Leonardo, who seemed
more confused than angry. He was in fact debating with himself
whether to include this visit to the Colosseum in his memories of
Rome. Wasn't he going to come back? Yes, but when? And how
would he pay his debts tomorrow, if in a few hours he was to leave
Rome like an empty-handed thief? A childish curiosity pushed him
towards new sights and new experiences, but with it came the realization of what he had lost. But was it really lost? Couldn't he wait
another day before the storm broke? And, come to that, WHAT
storm? The fears that had tortured him since he had left Mary
seemed so exaggerated now, even his sacred professional duties
seemed puny, in the face of this greatness and the patriotic duties it
demanded. He pulled out his watch and looked at it for a long time,
as if he were reading a page.

"Well?" asked the coachman; Leonardo concentrated on his
watch even more. "Listen to me, sir. If you're in a hurry, so am I,
and the longer you wait, the more you'll have to pay tomorrow,
because by now we would almost be at the Colosseum."

"No," said Leonardo. "I have no time for sightseeing. I'm leaving
first thing tomorrow morning and I still have a lot to do."

"All right, let's hope we make it. The traffic is so thick by now it
will take us at least half an hour. In five minutes we can reach the
Colosseum, and by the time we're back here, the traffic will have
eased on this end of the Corso, so it will come to the same, and
you'll have had more for your money. It's very rare to see the
Colosseum in full moonlight, even for those of us who live in
Rome."

"No—please let's get going."

"As you say. It's your money, not mine."

They turned their backs on the beautiful monument, and Leonardo wished he could give it a last loving glance, but he didn't
dare. Schillasi's eyes were fixed on him from the depths of his
corner, and he owed himself a certain consistency of style, before he

justified his conduct to this pathetic creature who had spent so much money on him and was willing to spend more. Yet the poison of Rome was slowly taking hold of him; the scent of humid earth and fresh flowers, the elegance, the ease, the apparent happiness of the rich in their carriages and the poor watching them from sidewalks and windows, the strange reflection of the moon on that man-made (or rather government-made) mountain of marble, the very effrontery of building such a thing which had certainly cost hundreds, if not thousands of aqueducts to the southern taxpayer, made him feel powerless to oppose it, and eager to be part of it, even as a passive onlooker. He felt the way he had always felt in a church since he had lost his faith—on vacation from prayers and penances, therefore hopelessly exposed to the spiritual comforts it offered (more so than back in the days when he had sought that comfort without finding it).

"Goombà, I don't want you to feel that I'm insensitive to your kind efforts. . . ."

"Forget it. You're in a hurry and that's that."

"Oh, but I'm not in a hurry any more; or rather, I'm in a hurry to ask your advice."

"My advice? The advice of a nonentity who hasn't even completed his studies?"

"Don't say such things."

"I'm merely repeating."

"I know, I know, and I apologize."

"No need to apologize, you were right, and I—"

"Not at all, I was wrong and I *must* apologize, but please try to understand, and help me. Do you *really* think I should leave tomorrow morning before dawn, like a thief, without seeing Mary again?"

"You're a man of high principles, and you know what you want."

"Of course, and that *is* what I want; I can't stand the thought of being a kept man. I'd forgotten to tell you that I'm not paying for my room at the Hotel de Russie. . . ."

"I know."

"How do you know?"

"My wife saw you from the toilet last night while I was asleep, and I left the house this morning before she woke up, so when I

came back she said: 'I bet you that's the man who was kidnapped in
a beautiful carriage last night.' And she was right. You heard me tell
her so."

"Yes, so you can see why I am in a hurry to leave: my situation is
untenable."

"Right."

"Ah, it is, is it?"

"If you say so. You're a man of high principles."

"Yes, but doesn't it seem . . . considering the fact that Mary is
an exceptional person, and so is her mother . . . doesn't it seem
rather . . . well . . . *cruel* to you?"

"Decisions based on principle are always cruel. There are no two
ways of being just. Think of God: He's always cruel, but He knows
what He's doing. . . . Kindness is a form of compromise—it's typical of those who don't know what they want."

"How true. And how profoundly philosophical. I didn't know
you were so intuitive."

"I do what I can. I told you I'm not just a museum guide. But
you are so much more knowledgeable than I, because you always
know what you want."

"Well, that's where you're mistaken. I did the right thing nine
years ago, and the result is I married a woman I didn't like, and
Mary married a man she didn't like, either. Yet, to repair this
mistake which came from doing the right thing, I'm now supposed
to break the law, create a scandal, betray my mission, become a kept
man, help her betray her husband and take his child away from
him. . . . Is this *right*, I ask?"

"No, it isn't."

"Well, you see? Then I should leave her, without seeing her
again, because . . . you don't fight temptation, you flee it."

"Right."

There was a deep silence. Leonardo was on the brink of tears, but
Schillasi seemed utterly indifferent. Leonardo became angry.
"Which means, in other words, that I should pack my belongings
right now, and go to yet another hotel—not the one I came from,
because they would look for me there. But I don't know any hotels
in Rome."

"I can help you find one."

"But I have no money."

"It goes without saying that you would be my guest."

"Your guest again . . . is that right?"

"When principle is involved, my last penny goes to defend it. That's the kind of person I am."

"I can't tell you how grateful I am, but now consider the element of time. Had I been back at my hotel two hours ago, I could have written a letter to Mary, explaining the reasons for my decision, but now . . ."

"You have the whole night to write it from another hotel."

"Yes, but . . . they have twenty-six people for dinner, and it's late already, and imagine the havoc if I suddenly disappear without a word of explanation. Can I afford to be so cruel to these two women, when I'm their only hope on earth?"

"Twenty-six people for dinner? And think how important they probably are. . . ."

"I don't care about them, I care about myself. What should I do? What would *you* do in my place?"

"I wouldn't care about myself. That's egotistical. What good are you, with your high principles intact, but with no influence and no money? Just think of the good you can do with that wealth and those connections. An occasion like this . . . my God . . . you heard me attack the two ladies as Protestants . . . but that was when I still didn't really know them. Now that I know them so intimately . . ."

"Since when?"

"Since you described them to me in such moving terms. How could anyone fail to understand that these are exceptional women? In their case, even divorce, even abduction of minors, *anything* is justified before the throne of God."

They had reached the hotel and Schillasi was already exhibiting a large banknote, before giving it to the coachman. Leonardo cringed with shame in front of the uniformed servants.

"You're in the same moral position as the father-in-law of your friend the Queen Mother," Schillasi went on, tipping the coachman so generously that the poor man almost went down on his knees to thank him. "King Victor Emmanuel the Second, the Honest King,* did not hesitate to wage war on the Vicar of Christ and usurp His throne with the troops of the atheist Garibaldi: he was doing it for reasons of higher morality, alias patriotism. So you see, you're in good company."

Leonardo cringed even more, not just with shame, but with hatred and contempt, and yet he, too, was tempted to go down on his knees in an outburst of gratitude. His will had been so broken by the Jesuits that he could never do anything he wanted (in this case go back to Mary), unless ordered to do so by someone he despised and feared. Now he finally understood why he had married Giovanna: because moral cripples such as himself often mistake the things they do under orders for those they would do of their own accord. Oh, how happy he was, and how anxious to tell Mary why he had lived so immorally until now; because, again, a man whose will has been broken must consider every personal impulse to be bad on principle (an act of singularity, in Jesuitical terms), there-fore something to be cultivated in secret, and, conversely, anything truly immoral becomes a true manifestation of his secret freedom.

Away, Leonardo, away from this terrible country!!! Rebirth, Resurrection, Tolstoy's Resurrection!!! Oh, how anxious he was to *obey* his worthier masters!!!

"My dear Schillasi, thank you for everything. It was so good to be able to discuss all these matters with a man like you, but now I must go and change for dinner."

"Can't I come upstairs with you?"

"No, but I'll repay my debts before I leave."

"Just for one minute???"

"No," answered Leonardo firmly. He had a strange foreboding that, if he allowed this little snake to come into his room, it would turn into a viper and bite him to death.

But Schillasi, too, seemed possessed by a strange foreboding that if he didn't follow Leonardo into the hotel, he would lose him forever.

"Please, Goombà, remember, you owe your whole future to me.

---

* *Il Re Galantuomo* in Italian, i.e., the gallant king, which has nothing to do with the concept of chivalry, only with a bourgeois concept of reliability.

You had already given up Mary when I forced you to accept her as a
gift from heaven. . . . Let me see your room."
"I know, Goombà, but not tonight. Come tomorrow morning,
early . . ."
"Tomorrow I won't have time for you. I don't see why you—"
"Professor!!! Professor!!!!" shouted a foreign-sounding voice from
a carriage next to the one they had just left, and Schillasi jumped up
with joy, shouting: "Mister Azzeltini!!! My friend!!!" Then, dragging Leonardo by the arm: "Come and meet the famous American
sculptor Azzeltini, he's one of my greatest admirers."
"I can't," protested Leonardo feebly, "let me go, I'm late. . . ."
But the famous American sculptor jumped out of his carriage and
came over to shake hands, followed by three beautiful young
women who were obviously foreign, spoke no Italian and looked
somewhat like Mary, every one. Leonardo was dazzled, and
strangely excited when he heard Azzeltini say: "These American
beauties saw you at the Caffè Greco with the Professor and have
fallen in love with you, all three. Come with us, we're going to have
a glass of wine at my place."
"Thank you, but I have a dinner party and I'm late already," said
Leonardo blushing. Azzeltini translated his refusal, bringing a
chorus of lamentations from the three beauties, while Schillasi
fumed with impatience, because no one was listening to him.
"Azzeltini, tell my friend the mayor-doctor who I am." Then, to
Leonardo: "Azzeltini is the one who says I know more about Greek
sculpture than any university professor." Finally Leonardo took pity
on him and said to the sculptor: "Our friend here knows a great
deal, it seems," and Schillasi began to recite dates and names as if
he were a schoolboy in front of his examiners. Azzeltini laughed.
"Great man, our Professor. He deserved a chair at the university,
not in a museum." "Too late," said Schillasi. "Do you want to hear
me tell you about the Renaissance?" "I must go," said Leonardo,
waving goodbye and shouting to Azzeltini: "Tell him it's never too
late to go back to school." And with these words he fled back to his
happiness, but the moment he saw the carriages reflected in the
crystal door of his hotel, the image of Mary's coachman rose forbid-
dingly before his eyes and he suddenly remembered why he had let
Schillasi talk to him in the first place. He turned back in time to see

Schillasi climbing into Azzeltini's carriage. "Schillasi! . . ." He shouted, "Schillasi! Stop! . . . Stop! . . ." But Schillasi couldn't hear him, and the carriage was rolling away amid so many others in the flicker of gaslights under the first evening stars.

How he avoided being run over by a streetcar, then another, then a horse carriage, he couldn't tell. He was no longer running after Schillasi, he was running away from his bad luck, from the ruins of a dream that had lasted long enough to shatter all reality forever; he wasn't even calling any more, just panting and sobbing aloud in despair, until he knew there was no point in trying, and walked slowly back to the square with the big obelisk in the middle, knowing that at the other end of that dark mass of indifferent humanity, indifferent horses and indifferent gaslights, he would find the Hotel de Russie and probably be arrested, or insulted by Mary for what he had done to her dream. But what else could he do?

He didn't even look at the door as he entered the hotel, his eyes glued to the red rug he now knew so well. He began his last pilgrimage on that symbol of an ascent that was no longer his, when he heard the voice of the hotel manager: "Doctor Claudi, someone is looking for you."

This is it, he thought, and closed his eyes, standing there motionless on the staircase to receive whatever blow Moral Geometry had decided was due him.

"Goombà, what happened?" asked Schillasi, and Leonardo burst into tears, sobbing: "I'm ruined. It's all over. . . ."

"Why?"

"I told Mary's coachman about the divorce last night. I didn't know he was a spy or that he'd have us arrested at the station tomorrow, or whenever, perhaps even tonight."

"Nonsense, these things don't happen."

"How do you know?"

"Because I know. And I repeat: it's nonsense. Things don't happen that way in Rome."

"Why don't they?"

"Because they don't. This isn't home, where the betrayed husband kills everybody involved and then himself. Here he just waits for the police to arrest them, then he negotiates. He names the price for his consent, and he only resorts to public scandal if his wife refuses to pay. Now if the wife is foreign and rich, things don't even go as far as involving the police, because the police are always around anyway to give protection and be paid for it."

"The police, you said?" he asked, smiling with sudden joy. "But I know the chief of police here, and he said I could always go to him if I needed help."

"Never mind. Don't go to him. Never go to the big boss in this city for small things. It's an insult to his dignity, and he would have to go to his underlings anyway. *I* know the underlings, I know them all, I have a son in the police in Sardinia, so if this coachman is a traitor or a spy (and I don't believe he is), he, too, will have to go to the police. And the police will comply with his request—with a little delay: to be precise, the time it takes for you to leave the country in peace. Enough of that. Let's see what you have in all those boxes on the table."

An hour later they emerged from the Hotel de Russie like father and son. They even looked alike, although they hadn't previously, deepening the sense of *trompe l'oeil*—same shirt, same cravat, with breast pocket handkerchief to match, same yellow gloves, which in .those days constituted a status symbol comparable only to the car in our times (people spent less on status symbols: the whole economy was sounder, and yellow gloves were very expensive), same white waistcoat (on which glittered the first, barely perceptible dissimilarity between them: Leonardo's old chain was elaborate, Schillasi's gilded one puny), and of course the same proud smile on their faces. And yet, if the eye had not been cheated by these and other easy terms of comparison, it might have noticed dissimilarities that spoke for past and future trouble between these two men so different in outlook and temperament. And they might walk arm in arm, they might look ferociously defiant of any Roman who passed them, but it was Schillasi who was dragging Leonardo unwillingly towards his happiness, and not for the reasons already given: there were new reasons, graver reasons, that made Leonardo realize he had been right to suspect Schillasi's motives for coming upstairs.

Why had he shared Mary's beautiful presents?

Because Schillasi had asked for them; calling him a miser when Leonardo had said: "These are Mary's gifts."

"And Mary is my gift to you. Or have you forgotten?"

And Leonardo had had no answer, so between two shirts of the same make, one in plain cotton and one in the finest silk, he hadn't dared take the silk one for himself, and Schillasi had instantly reminded him of the fact that he was older, had been generous, had no hope of getting another such shirt in the short years that remained to him, while for Leonardo it would be the first of an endless series. "You'll come to my funeral in a new shirt like this, so why not honor me now instead of regretting it then?"

Thus even the socks had been divided between lion and lamb, and at a certain point Schillasi had said: "Your gold chain would look far better on my silk waistcoat than on your cotton one. If you weren't such a damn hypocrite, you'd give it to me. Of course, the watch belonged to your father."

"So did the chain."

"One chain is just like another, it's the gold that counts, and you're going to marry the richest girl in Rome. Will you give it to me?"

"No, I can't."

"Miser! Hypocrite! But never mind, we can't change human nature."

"But . . ."

When it came to the cufflinks, of which Mary had bought three different sets, two of them went to Schillasi and one to Leonardo.

A deep feeling of sacrilege and the fear of being found out fell like a shadow on his love. At the last moment before leaving the room where these ignoble transactions had taken place, Leonardo said: "Oh my God, I mustn't forget to take my *spolverina* with me." And he took it.

"Oh no," said Schillasi, "now that you are a rich man, you can't walk through the streets of Rome and appear at your wife's palace wearing that symbol of provincialism."

"I certainly can and will. This is no symbol, this is—"

"It is a symbol—and the worst, in our case."

"Nonsense!"

"You leave that thing here or leave *me* here."

"But the dust . . ."

"There is no dust in Rome, not between here and Via Gregoriana."

"But it's cold, I was freezing all day."

"That won't protect you against the cold. Sophie will buy you an overcoat, especially as you're going north from here in a day or so."

Sadly, Leonardo laid his *spolverina* down over a chair. Then his eyes brightened. "At least there's my hat."

"All right. Make yourself ridiculous. Warm your brains and lose your dignity—I don't care."

. . . So here they were walking arm in arm, with almost the same smile above the same shirts and almost the same white waistcoats.

They did not meet the beggar woman with her child on the steps.

At the door of the palace they embraced and kissed on the mouth, like brothers, blocking the way to the elegant guests who were arriving in their horse-drawn carriages.

"Goodbye . . . Good luck . . ." shouted Schillasi several times, trying to attract the attention of as many people as possible.

"Thank you for everything," Leonardo shouted back. "I owe everything to you."

"Then follow my advice, and if you're tempted to repeat your mistake, think of me."

"Thank you, thank you, thank you . . ."

Leonardo ran inside while Schillasi walked off, hesitatingly, stopping at every step to look back at the doorway, smiling and shaking his head as if to say: This is the way they all are, young people: happiness makes them ungrateful. . . . But no one was there to appreciate his feelings or to realize that he was connected with anyone living in the palace, so, with a last glance at the windows, he gave up his private comedy and merged into the shadows of the night.

Alas, he wasn't aware that someone had been observing him with the greatest attention, registering his every exchange with Leonardo from behind the closed shutters of a window above the large *portone*, the same window, incidentally, from which she had studied Leonardo's first hesitation twenty-nine hours and seventeen minutes earlier: Sophie withdrew from the window, sat down at her desk and marked the time in her journal, just to give herself something to do while she waited in an agony of impatience for the doorbell to ring in the distance. When it finally did, she drew a deep breath and hid her large face in her hands. She had been worrying herself sick from the moment she had last seen Leonardo in the dining room, exactly four hours earlier, but that was a figure she did not mark down.

As these concluding notes of Sophie's long anguish were being written, Mary was still unaware of Leonardo's nearness, not because her impatience was any less than her mother's; on the contrary, it was so much greater that she could not afford to look out of the window without besieging the whole street right and left. Each person appearing at either end of it, be it man, woman or child, instantly looked like Leonardo, but still quite vaguely so, because of the great distance; then more and more clearly, until, halfway between the end of the street and the house, the delusion created by anguish could not be kept up, and Mary could not repress a wild impulse to punish the trespasser for daring to look like the person she was waiting for.

Sophie considered herself solely responsible for letting Leonardo escape again, but this was her own private affair with the Punishing Powers That Be, and the sight of Mary's suffering seemed almost an intrusion on her own guilt, a reproach she couldn't accept from her daughter without feeling her own wild impulse to assault her. She knew of course that this was all absurd, as Mary knew that her urge to assault the passersby was absurd. Leonardo's new flight had not been mentioned by either of them, but it had begun to dawn upon them as a vague possibility after he had been gone a whole hour, and increased until it had become such a reality that they didn't dare look into each other's eyes for fear they might see what was evident anyway in the wringing of their hands, the marking of the pages of books or of the tea tablecloth with their sharp fingernails, and the frequent, sudden lifting of their faces towards the clock in the dining room, which they would look at unbelievingly for a few minutes, only to move away suddenly and stop in front of the Sèvres clock on the mantelpiece in the library, or the small watches on their night tables. What can he have to discuss with that cousin of his, to keep him away from his love? This consideration, plus the fact that she had asked him specifically to take a carriage, and also to invite the cousin to dinner . . . How long does it take an impetuous Italian to tell his cousin that his long-lost love of almost a decade has reappeared on his horizon and is now waiting for them both? He must have told him all this, but only as a preface to other things that had destroyed in a matter of minutes a dream of nine years, such as, "She doesn't believe me, she accuses me of lying to her mother." Leonardo must have been hurt by that sentence as he said it; it had marked him, it had in fact confirmed his own doubts, and he was now willing to have them strengthened, in order not to fall for a love that was frowned upon by the Law and the Gospels. Add to this Leonardo's sense of duty towards his patients and his city and his goddamn aqueduct, and what do you have? Leonardo goes to the station and asks his cousin to do the explaining. . . . He may even be writing her a letter that the cousin will deliver by hand tomorrow morning. Yes, he is writing it. He has tears in his eyes, exactly as he had nine years ago, but he keeps writing, because he wants to be a strong man. . . . And why should Mary wait for him tonight? Why not go to the station and ask which platform for the next train to Laterza, and wait for him there? And then, if he comes, will she go with him to Laterza? He would never let her, but the train wouldn't leave either, because, like Anna Karenina, Mary knows exactly what to do. . . .

Now Mary is waiting, no longer for him, but for her mother, who should but doesn't go to the drawing room where the first guests are waiting for them both. Dinner is waiting, the servants are waiting, even Kostia, in his playroom, is waiting for his grandmother's kiss before going to bed. Even the Italian guests, who can never be on time, are beginning to arrive and they, too, are surprised that the two ladies of the house should be so late.

Such was the state of the house when Leonardo, later than anyone else, came to the enchanted palace like Prince Charming in the fairy tale, and broke the spell by kissing Sleeping Beauty. Only in this fairy tale, Sleeping Beauty was very much awake, sleepwalking along the dark corridor between her mother's bedroom door and the door to the drawing room, from which so many cheerful voices

could be heard, and she hated them so, she could have gone into
that room brandishing a sword to punish them all for having looked
like Leonardo at either end of the Via Gregoriana as they walked
towards the house in the light of the full moon.

"*Amore!*" gasped Mary, emerging from the dark; pushing away
Bernhard, who had just opened the door, she grabbed Leonardo and
dragged him into a corner to kiss him passionately, without noticing
that they were visible to everyone through the drawing room door
her mother had left open. Bernhard discreetly hurried into the
drawing room to fetch a tray and closed the door behind him.

"Oh, my love, how happy I am you didn't write me that letter. . . ."

"What letter, my love?"

"The letter telling me you had decided to go back to your duties
and not to marry me."

"Who told you?"

"I was right then. . . . Did your cousin advise you to leave me?"

"No."

"He didn't? But you wanted to leave me. Confess it. . . . No
matter, you're back now and you'll never leave me again."

"No, I won't."

"If you ever tried, the train wouldn't leave without cutting me in
half first."

"Oh no. I would kill myself too, on your grave."

"This way, please," whispered Bernhard, pushing Leonardo
gently towards the dining room door and opening it for him. Mary
was grateful, she hadn't realized that all the new guests were standing near the entrance watching them with amusement, instead of
walking towards the drawing room door, which another uniformed
servant had opened for them, allowing still more people to take part
in this intimate scene. "Oh, look at you, how beautiful you are,"
said Mary, closing the dining room door behind her and watching
Leonardo in the glitter of many electric lights reflected in many
mirrors along the walls. "You did open my presents, darling, and
they fit . . . but why didn't you choose the silk waistcoat instead of
this one? You didn't know, my darling, of course you couldn't,
you're a serious person, a scientist, and these are stupid notions for

stupid, empty-headed, society people like the ones out there . . ."
and she pointed towards the other door, behind which one could
hear voices. "Never mind, darling, no one will notice the difference,
but tomorrow night you will wear the silk one. And the silk shirt,
too. Oh, you did choose the cheapest of my cufflinks . . . I must
apologize for buying them, but I was sure you would want something very inexpensive. You are right, your strong, honest hands are
the jewels that decorate the cuffs. But tomorrow you'll wear one of
the two other pairs. You'll do it for me, won't you? Promise you
will, my love? They are family jewels!"

"We'll see . . . we'll see."

"Let's parade in front of this mirror."

They walked towards it, arm in arm, putting their heads together,
then kissing and trying to catch a side-glimpse of the kiss in the
mirror; they failed to notice that the other door was now open and
Sophie was triumphantly preceding her guests into the dining room.

What embarrassed Leonardo was not the scandalous situation
itself, but the ease with which it was buried at once in the general
chatter and then even more deeply in the comedy of formal intro-
ductions. Mary introduced him to people who were obviously her
intimates as if he had just walked into the room: no difference in
her attitude. Could this mean that such occurrences were normal in
her life? That they were so in the lives of the others he could see,
and he felt deeply offended by their forgiveness. They seemed to
say: "You, too, have fallen under her fascination." And that "you,
too" hurt and kept ringing in his ears as he sat down before a
beautiful decorated menu bearing his name in Gothic characters.
Mary's name was on neither of the menus next to him; he was
stunned. While he was actually sinking into his seat, head low, eyes
gloomily scouting the horizon of chairs—some still empty, some
already concealed by elaborate coiffures and bright, naked shoulders
and a wealth of pearls, earrings and bracelets, fluffy silks and thin
laces—Mary's sweet voice reached him from amid all the glitter and
the noise: "Your health, my friend." Then, in whispers loud
enough to be overheard by everyone: "The seating arrangement was
not my choice."

He searched the table and recognized Mary's arm and part of her
face between two silver vases, but the rest of it was hidden in the

thick of the flowers above, and the glimpse of her one eye was not sufficient to dispel his deep resentment against everybody, Mary included, for the noisy comedy they seemed to be playing against him. Were *these* the people who had delayed Mary's decision to leave this kind of life for his sake? She didn't seem at all out of place here, whereas he was. In fact, this seemed to be the kind of dinner party where you would meet people from the famous Passeggiata at the Corso. And then indeed he recognized some of them among the male faces above the same white silk waistcoat he had given Schillasi.

"Someone is trying to attract your attention, and you're not even looking at her."

These words were spoken so kindly, and in such an angelic voice, that he felt instantly consoled, even before he saw the face of the lady who had spoken them, and when he did, it was the first aristocratic face in his life for which this adjective was not an insult. All those he had seen before, even in Crocifisso's family, were the faces of degenerates, with effeminate voices if they were men, and ultrafeminine voices if they were women, and he had always regarded them as illustrations of the moral dictate that says: "Do not covet riches or power, nor wish them on your own children." But this woman was a woman, and yet she looked like one of those ancient goddesses he wished could be found in reality, but exist only in marble or granite. Whether Greek or Egyptian or even Roman, they are idealized, therefore purely hypothetical statements of feminine nobility. In actual life (and Leonardo had a theory about this) they are all *Greek Beauties*, namely, *prostitutes* and *carriers of syphilis*, for the logical reason that men are evil, women weak, and *no such beauty can ever escape notice*. Thus, by virtue of the same logic that guided all of his actions, he formulated the hypothesis which instantly became a conclusion: God knows how rich this woman's family must be, to protect her against the onslaught of men.

Such lofty thoughts took rather more time than the mere registration of her beauty and nobility, and this made her uncomfortable. She blushed, blinked, shook her head disapprovingly, then, seeing that these warnings didn't seem to break the spell, she said, in a voice clear enough to be overheard across the table: "Not here—you should be looking across the table." And her hand pointed to where Mary was blushing and frowning, very close to tears.

"Oh," said Leonardo, as he detached his stare from her face and attached it to her hand, which was so beautiful that he took a little more time to admire it, before he decided to obey its gesture. Only then did he realize that Mary had leaned to one side of the flower vase the better to see him, and that she didn't like what she had seen.

"You have nothing to fear," he said to her, looking into her eyes with passion, and tilting his entire head towards the left to indicate: *I don't like this woman at all.*

Mary's two male neighbors burst into loud laughter, while she answered Leonardo's gesture with an equally eloquent message that read: *You fool, we'll talk about that later.* After which she turned to her neighbor on the left, and gave him all the loving attention and smiles and the whispers Leonardo no longer deserved.

This was too much. "Mary!!!" he cried, causing the whole conversation to stop and bringing even the waiters to a standstill with their trays dangerously slanted towards the shoulders of the guests. Mary shrugged her shoulders nervously and stared into her glass without daring to move. Everyone, suddenly, seemed to have something interesting to say, and a chorus of loud voices drowned the incident; isolating Leonardo so completely that he began to look for friendly faces around him and found none.

He tried to arouse Mary's attention again, and was about to stretch his arm across the table to do so, since all his mime and loud coughing had gone unnoticed, when a soft, manly voice on his right whispered into his ear: "If you want to alienate the lady's love forever, you're going about it the right way." He turned around and what did he see? No, he couldn't have, this must be something else, and yet . . . certain signs are unmistakable. The priest's collar, the frock, the thick gold chain with the cross on the chest . . . probably a Protestant high prelate, probably a Russian Orthodox . . . archimandrite . . .

"May I introduce myself?" said the man smiling gently: "Bistolphe, Cardinal d'Escarande-Lalande."

Leonardo's first Cardinal. Instinctively, he bowed his head in search of the pastoral ring to kiss, and it was graciously extended to him above the tablecloth. While he kissed it, he thought: This is the end, and Mary was right to react as she did, but she was wrong before, when she kissed me within sight of all these people; she should have warned me. There was still the problem of justifying himself in front of the Living God who had caught him in mortal sin, and he didn't dare lift his lips from the ring; in fact, he held the hand for fear that it would slap him on both cheeks, once it was free again.

"Enough, enough, my son," said the Cardinal, "we're not in church here. My warning was offered to a man of the world on worldly matters by a complete outsider, both by choice and chronology. You are still very young and inexperienced, as anyone can see, and I repeat to you, that is no way to conquer the ladies, or to keep them, once they are yours."

Leonardo was humbly waiting for more, but so confused by this sarcastic method of priestly censure as to be unable to lift his eyes above the golden cross on the Cardinal's chest. He saw it shining triumphantly as it would on Judgment Day against the dark background of Eternal Night, now and again beclouded by the passage of huge clouds of guilt over the sun. This effect was produced by the Cardinal's own hand, as it beclouded the glitter of the candles every time he lifted his spoon to put it into his mouth, and then lowered it again to scoop up more soup from the bowl in front of him. He seemed to have forgotten Leonardo and his sins with a calculated cruelty that not even the worst censor in Leonardo's days of novitiate had ever been able to master for more than a few seconds. Perhaps, he thought, this is the Gallican Church's way of talking to sinners, which would make sense, because all Frenchmen are such devoted gourmets.

"Here," said the Cardinal, putting down his empty spoon for the last time, so the waiter could take the bowl away from him and replace it with a new dish for the second course.

"Aaah, what a perfect *bouillon.* In no other Roman household does one eat so well as here. Not even at the French embassy. Aaaah, a real delight." And he let Christ on the Cross tremble with hunger and thirst and cast fearful reflections of His Divine Glory into the faces of all those sinners at the table, then shrouded Him again, this time with a white cloud of linen, as he wiped his mouth with the large napkin that was spread on his knees.

But when he realized that Leonardo's bowl was being removed untouched (which of course required slower movements on the waiter's part in order not to spill it), he asked: "Whaaat? Don't tell me you don't like it, or I'll have to conclude that your lack of style with the ladies is a symptom of an inferior taste for all the good things this vale of tears has to offer to us sinners. It is an axiom that men who don't like good cooking don't like beautiful women either. They are content with the lowest in flesh, like wild beasts in the forest. I see that you seem somewhat disturbed. Have I offended you with my remarks about the lady of your heart? If so, I apologize most humbly and beg you to take it as a piece of good strategic advice, coming from an old hand in the ways of the world, for that is the spirit in which it was meant, I can assure you."

"Advice?" asked Leonardo almost in whispers, as if he were kneeling in the confessional and talking through the tiny holes that so conveniently shield the face of Censoring Divinity from the face of Censorable Humanity and the other way about.

"Yes, advice. I see that your eyes are fixed on your wedding ring, as if to expose your sinful soul to me without constraint, and this touches my old priestly heart very deeply. An unusual occurrence in this kind of a gathering, my young friend. Remember the Fifth Canto, where it describes the behavior of the newly dead in front of King Minos, whom Dante has made a high functionary, indeed THE highest, in the new theological bureaucracy? Quite a promotion, that, for a demoted heathen half-god. But what is your sin, may I ask? Marriage? Early marriage, probably. But marriage is always early, even when it comes late, for it is a decision made in the worst moral condition for the preservation of your faith. If woman is a vessel of Evil—and she is, just as men are—then all marriages except perhaps one in a million are made with strong mental reservations, or otherwise so vitiated before they are decided upon that they should be considered void by the Church as a matter of course, and our care should be in deciding which marriages can pass the test and be seen by us priests as fulfilling the conditions needed to make them into real celebrations of a Sacrament, not in trapping souls and virtually condemning them to regard marriage as a fatal mistake. In this, you see, our Greek and Russian Orthodox brothers are right and we are wrong. They have divorce and we don't. As a result, they lose fewer believers than we do. All those Italian Popes are the curse of Christianity. This secondhand, provincial country with no history to speak of since the end of the Middle Ages keeps the Church on the level of the most ignorant and rapacious village priest, just at a time when the Church needs new forces, modern attitudes, to keep abreast of the progress of science and the final disintegration of Luther's delusion into a religion of things and of crude violence. If a great ecumenical gathering was needed, and it certainly was, the first item on its agenda should have been our attitude towards Marx and Communism. The Church should have taken the wind out of that Jewish economist's voice, and what did the Church do? It debated the stupidest, the most artificial of theological questions ever raised: that of Infallibility, and to do so they pushed the most provincial epileptic in all Italy onto the Throne of Saint Peter's. He didn't even want to be a priest, he wanted to become a Noble Guard, the puny Count Mastai-Ferretti, and he was rejected because of his seizures. Can you imagine the Gestatory Chair being thrown off balance by one of the four bearers any time he had a fit? Well, a family doctor with the magnificent name of Concionofrio Concioni persuaded him to opt for the priesthood, promising him the papacy—and he was right: a rare occurrence for a doctor, wouldn't you say? But the first major pronouncement from His Asinine Holiness was a well-staged (well-staged by the Jesuits, that is) *motu proprio* of the Immaculate Conception. If ever there was a stupid dogma, that is it: Saint Anne experienced no sexual gratification when she became pregnant with Mary. And how about her own mother? And who cares, anyway? The Lord God certainly didn't, for His aim was to have His Son born a man; namely, of weak and sinful flesh. Had He intended it otherwise, He could have bypassed human frailty altogether and made His Son appear on earth as full-grown God on the same noble level as the heathen Olympians, or the same coarse level as the vengeful Hebrew Jehovah—but that was precisely the purpose of the New Tidings: to lift the disinherited of the earth to the level of those who thought they would inherit it, a kind of French Revolution *avant-la-lettre.* No Bonapartes in heaven to set the clock back again and create a new bourgeois feudalism, that Marx must try to undo with his new, atheistic religion . . . But no matter, you are an intelligent man and you understand me very well. The world is on the brink of ruin: European Civilization is about to be wiped out by either of the two threatening monsters: a return of Jehovah with Protestant industrial support from Germany and Russia (and mark my words, Russia is far more advanced industrially than England, and to give you an example of the alliance between Germany and Russia just take a look at our hostess: a Protestant-Russian steamroller with German-Jewish advisers. Look at the gentleman presiding over this side of the table, his name is Schultz, a German who pretends to be English and does private dirty work for Russian grand dukes, such as adopting their illegitimate daughters by French prostitutes whom he has proudly married, and I know what I'm saying, for the French prostitute he married is, alas, the black sheep of one of the best families of France (namely, my own), so, as I was saying, on the one side we have these modern Tamerlanes and Ostrogoths descending upon Catholic Christianity, and on the other Doctor Marx with his Golden Calf for popular consumption. The new spirit of the times is, alas, a spirit of dissolution, in the etymological sense of the word: the very granite of the temple dissolves, the pillars melt away, the ancient ties of the family are loosened, authority no longer binds servant to master, wife to husband. To the Protestant mind this appears to be progress: divorce as an expression of social responsibility, the so-called Duty To My Own Happiness, Egotism as a virtue. . . . What could be worse? Any French parish priest, elected Pope, would have done better."

Leonardo was so fired with enthusiasm that he tried to grab the Cardinal's hand to kiss his ring again and tell him how happy he was to have met an intelligent priest at long last but the hand of His Eminence was now busy making circles in the air to convey his encyclical thinking to an elderly gentleman beyond his right-hand neighbor, a very imposing lady who seemed eager to prove that these were all her own arguments, and therefore right. Leonardo had never thought it possible that a woman dare have opinions of her own in a discussion between men, but it was absolutely incredible to see a woman *stealing* the opinions of two learned men (one a high prelate, the other, so it seemed, a famous professor), from their very mouths, without being told to be quiet. Did this lady have a husband? And was he present? And if so, why weren't the others laughing at him for his subservience? In Leonardo's world, a woman who behaved that way could only be a prostitute of the most aggressive type, someone like Semiramis or Messalina, unless she be a very old woman, far beyond the temptations of sin. His eyes were fixed on the talkative lady. And the better to study her case and imagine himself in the role of her husband, he stared at her from behind the Cardinal's back, then leaned forwards when the Cardinal sat back to stare at her from the front. He became so intensely absorbed in his study that he didn't even notice Mary, who was equally focused on him, and who also didn't like what she was seeing.

How can I ever trust a man like this? Mary was thinking. First he falls for the lady on his left, then for the lady on his right, the first two ladies he has met in my house, or, to be more precise, in *his* life, after meeting me in a public place nine years ago. And how dare he say to me: You have nothing to fear? My husband said the same thing to me the first and last time I cared; namely, in those five or six days before we got married. I'd completely forgotten, but now that I remember, I'll never forget it again, because this time I love the creature, and how I wish I didn't. . . . He knows it, too, but I'll make him suffer just as much as he's making me suffer, IF I STILL CAN. To be, or not to be capable of making a man suffer. This is indeed the question. What other proof of love can there be for a woman in this terrible country? She turned to one of her two neighbors and said: "Do you have paper and pen in your pocket?"

"Of course I do," said the young man on her left, who was a society columnist with vague ambitions of becoming a real independent writer. Leonardo saw Mary take the young man's fountain pen and notebook and write furiously in it, the young man looking over her shoulder on the obvious pretext of reading what she was writing, while in reality trying to look as deep as he could into her décolletage.

"Who is that man?" Leonardo demanded, pulling the Cardinal by the sleeve without any respect for the red silk peeping discreetly

from under the black silk, a few inches from the ring he had just
kissed with such devotion.

The Cardinal was so appalled by this lack of civility that he stared
at his sleeve as if it were a human being who had begged his
protection against some mad beast, then he stared at Leonardo with
feigned surprise but also with real anger, then again at his sleeve,
and polished it lightly with his other hand. Only then did he consider Leonardo's request and answered it in a tone Leonardo knew
only too well not to be instantly terrorized by it, because it was the
tone of his ecclesiastical superior in college: "And who are *you?* I
should answer, if I were not aware that your judgment is blinded by
jealousy. One does not pull on a Cardinal's sleeve, young man, even
a three-year-old child knows that, but you are a mature man who
must have spent years at a good clerical college, and I assume that
you are now what all Italians of your type are, if they don't become
priests: an active anticlerical. But no matter, young man. I shall
answer your question, because I like your innocence, and I realize
your plight. You are a three-year-old beggar for the favors of a young
goddess—you Italians have this ridiculous image of yourselves as
charming creatures who combine Christian morality with pagan
common sense, and then you cry like babies all over the map of the
world, because other nations don't take you seriously, but the fact is
that you are no serious nation, you are a bunch of provincial bad
boys, whose only interest is in your mirror, not even in your love
affairs. Leave those to the French, who alone know how to deal
with women because they know how to deal with everything else in
this vale of tears. You ask me who that man is next to the woman
you love. Once you've learned his name, what are you going to do to
him? You should do to her what HE is doing to her because YOU
didn't: charm her with your politeness; don't cut it off like a supply
of bricks and cement once the building is finished. A love affair is
not a *thing*, my friend, no human relationships can be treated like
things: they are creatures, they need food and drink and a great deal
of care, especially while they are being born. Plus many new kinds
of care as they grow up. The pagans knew this very well, the Christian heathens don't. It's still the same old misunderstanding. Misunderstandings are always intentional: you don't understand

manners, because you don't want to understand yourself. *Know Thyself*, said the Delphic Oracle, and then *Nothing in Excess*, not even the kind of soul-searching that will destroy the Protestants in the end. Leave that to your confessor, my dear friend, he alone knows where you should stop, because he learned it all straight from the Pythian priestess after God was reborn in a different province of history. Does that answer your question?"

Leonardo said yes, because he didn't dare say no as he should have. In fact, the Cardinal had not only failed to answer his one question but pushed him back, as only a good confessor could, beyond a whole barrage of questions the sinner thought he had answered already. And as no one was talking to him now, he had only himself to converse with; no light table talk to help the appetite and distract the attention from the intricate movements of the hands between serving plate, plate, mouth, plate, mouth, napkin, glass, mouth, napkin, side plate, mouth, plate again, all with instant transitions from fork to spoon to knife, always making the right choice from the battery of surgical instruments lined up alongside the plate, and using each in the right way, then replacing it in the right way on the dish and not on the napkin, so that you almost have to steal your meat from under the knife that has cut it, to say nothing of the salad on the side plates, which must be shoved into the mouth without letting it fall onto the dish or the tablecloth again—and, as if this weren't difficult enough, there is the problem of avoiding the nose and the chin and the sides of the mouth with that damn oily lettuce leaf, and then disentangling it from the prongs of the fork without having to pursue it so far that the prongs hit your throat. It is an actual duel that you fight with your fork, and all for what? The duel is renewed with each mouthful, with each sip of water or wine—for the glass, too, must not be lifted too quickly lest half the liquid go down your neck. And what of the constant interruptions from your neighbors or from across the table? The conversation is a whole orgy of duels, you are being challenged unceasingly and the ladies take part too, so it really is a free-for-all. No refuge in authority: the mayor cannot silence his constituents, nor the physician his patients, not even the Infallible Pope his own clerical servants; this is Rome, this isn't home, Leonardo kept repeating to himself, while the most delicious foods were being put

right under his nose, and he kept hoping that the waiter at least
would answer his hesitant "no" with a cordial rebuttal, such as,
"Come on, don't think twice: eat up, it'll make you feel better." He
went so far as to ask the waiter: "Do you think I should accept your
kind offer? Well, since you keep coming back with more and better
dishes, let's reconsider. . . ." But he had hardly spoken the first
three words before the waiter withdrew the long platter from under
him, and he found himself speaking the rest of the sentence to his
neighbor on the left, but she dismissed the verbal disturbance with
a stern glance as if to ask: "How dare this stranger talk to me?"

"Help is coming to you from Jupiter in person, the Great God of
Thunder," said the Cardinal, suddenly pulling him by the sleeve.
The finger with the pastoral ring pointed in the direction of Sophie,
way at the other end of the table. Sophie was smiling joyfully as she
lifted her glass, urging Leonardo to do the same. Leonardo did so,
and drank a sip of the good wine on an almost empty stomach,
without smiling, still following Mary's every move with wide open
eyes.

"But at least be kind to Jupiter," whispered the Cardinal, and
Leonardo lifted the glass again and smiled at Sophie, who was obviously talking about him to a German professor; the German professor obeyed her orders and lifted his glass to Leonardo. So
Leonardo produced another smile and drank another sip, taking his
eyes away from Mary long enough to acknowledge yet another
friendly glance and smile and lifted glass from the powerful lady,
the one who owned all the learned opinions of the two illustrious
guests.

"You see—it works," said the Cardinal now, pointing towards
Mary, and indeed Mary was now actually smiling and lifting her
glass and looking at him with real passion again. Then the beautiful
young man did the same, and the lady on Leonardo's left joined in
with her glass, and pretty soon everybody was toasting Leonardo,
who was forced to swallow more and more sips, which so enhanced
his dormant appetite that for a moment he felt like calling the
waiter and asking for the meat he had so stupidly missed. Unfortunately for him, the Cardinal felt like talking again.

"Why don't you ask me now who the German professor is?"

"Yes, who is he?"

"Theodor Mommsen. Does that name ring a bell?"

"A bell, you say? Bells and firecrackers and salvos, plus a few gunshots from snipers," answered Leonardo joyfully, while Mary winked at him in between nods of acknowledgment to her talkative neighbor, and this heightened Leonardo's appetite to such a point, that when the waiter pushed a huge ice cream under his nose, he said: "Oh no. I want some of that roast with potatoes." The waiter stared at him with fiery eyes and whispered in purest Apulian: "Are you insane? We're serving this now, and if you don't like it it's just too bad."

With these words he withdrew the plate. Leonardo's craving for meat was instantly replaced by a much greater craving for ice cream.

"Have this," said the Cardinal, taking his empty plate away from him and replacing it with his own.

"Oh no, I can't accept," said Leonardo, blushing but smiling with affection.

"Don't be a fool, take it. Too bad I took so little, but I only wanted a taste of it, and I shouldn't have given in to the temptation. I've eaten too much anyway. But you haven't eaten anything at all, you're like a schoolboy in love, and what have you gained by your silly games? Nothing. Worse than nothing, you've lost your independence which is so essential in love affairs if you are to find out what you want from your own feelings, not only what the lady of your heart wants from you, and so now you have a reputation to defend, instead of having a new province of life to discover. Have you ever read Stendhal?"

"Who?"

"Never mind, I should have known: Italians don't read anything but Dante, and then only in school. They treat their love affairs as a religion, and their religion as a love affair; in fact, they refuse to discuss it by saying: *I have my own private religion and I respect other people's private religion.* Which is all wrong, because religion, my friend, is *the* public activity by definition, more so than politics. While love is *nothing* if it isn't private. You Italians make love in public, so to speak. Your love affairs are the talk of the town, and that's why you have to be jealous: your reputation is what counts, not your feelings towards a woman and hers towards you. Those are all pure pretense, or pure ritual, which is the same thing. Well, I see we're in for a real toast this time."

There was indeed some commotion at table, disrupting the waiters who had to whisk away their trays of pastries in order not to find themselves squeezed between arms and silks and huge backsides, even chairs being pushed back to make room for the speechmakers and their eloquence.

"That idiot German would of course do the wrong thing," said the Cardinal, urging Leonardo to lift his glass. "Do as the others do, especially as you are not in Rome; here, you are in Russia, in Germany, even in France, I must say, to give the cook his due. But no Frenchman would toast with red wine after ice cream! Couldn't the fool wait for the Champagne to be served?"

The fool in question was a very rosy-faced and very blond and very young German of very huge proportions—Mary's right-hand neighbor, whom Leonardo hadn't tried to inspect until now because he hadn't seen Mary turn her face in his direction, and anyway he had been hidden by the flowers. His manners, gestures and language were highly militaristic and at the same time innocent, as if he were trying out different styles for his voice and his muscles.

"And to think," said the Cardinal, "that he's half French and a relative of mine. His mother is the daughter of my namesake and distant cousin Bistolphe, whose second wife is Roman. I celebrated the wedding in 1881. It was quite an occasion, because the bride's father, Prince Scarandogi, perhaps the most ignorant of all Roman princes (and that's saying a great deal), always pretended that he was the only true d'Escarande, and so did my cousin, and so did my own father, the head of the d'Escarande-Lalande branch, and so did this boy's father, the head of the German branch, called Sandroxyll zu Greifenegg und Brucholtz und Jeglar. They were all eager to prove their point and all even more eager to refurbish their finances. And Scarandogi was the only one who had any money, a great deal of it, too. And a daughter to give away, but then he was also a noted homosexual; it's said that his lover was also the girl's father: a stable boy who had been at the sexual services of Scarandogi's mother, before serving his wife, so chances are that . . . Oh, Mommsen is answering, let's hear what he has to say."

Mommsen was indeed answering, and his short speech made
everybody roar with laughter. The Cardinal remained serious, then
translated in whispers: "He said it was the first time in many years
that he felt no sadness upon hearing his great friend (namely, the
boy's grandfather) mentioned, because he knew that the old man
would prefer to be dead than hear himself praised in such terms. A
bit cruel on his part, but then Germans will be Germans, whether
we're speaking of the greatest scholar or some poor adolescent ignoramus. But here comes a second helping of ice cream and cake for
you, don't miss it this time."

But Leonardo missed it again, because now the young German
was proposing a toast in Italian to Mary as the most beautiful
woman present, and this caused a certain consternation on the part
of Sophie, so Mommsen himself lifted his glass and said: "I drink
not only to her beauty but to her literary talent." Which made
things easier, so immediately someone else, an elderly gentleman,
proposed a toast to Mary AND her fellow writer on the pages of a
literary sheet called Il Fanfulla della Domenica.

Mary and the young man on her left toasted each other and then
together thanked the public, all with Sophie's obvious sanction.

And the beautiful lady on Leonardo's left, who seemed more
enthusiastic than anyone else at the table, asked him in her angelic
voice: "Why don't you drink? Are you jealous?"

"No."

"Then drink with us."

"No."

"How rude you are," she said, turning her back on him in a way
that attracted everybody's attention. Mary frowned at Leonardo in
reproach, and then, with a loving smile, asked: "What is it?"

He frowned back, staring at her so terribly that she lowered her
eyes and caught her breath.

"And I propose a toast to Medical Science," cried the Cardinal,
lifting his glass and pinching Leonardo's arm hard. From the way
Mary toasted the Cardinal and smiled and winked in gratitude,
Leonardo understood that she still cared more for him than for her
fellow writer, and this relieved his pain, but he still intended to get
a clear answer from her to the question, Why haven't you told me

about this man and the newspaper in which you and he are united
as only husband and wife can be?

Dinner was over. "Look at her, look," whispered the Cardinal
again, as he remained seated. "If you had ever been to Russia this
would remind you of a snowstorm rising above the horizon of the
holy city of Kazan. Look at the shadow she casts over the tablecloth,
the silver, the porcelain, the glasses. It's all calculated for effect, or
she wouldn't have those strong lights behind her on the wall. I must
say our female Jupiter could teach Madame Sarah a lesson in stage
settings and stage presence. But let's get up. We can't be too impolite to the rest of the company. I just wanted to anger her a little,
and I am satisfied that I have."

And the white table did look like a mountain plateau with so
many black shadows crowding in on it from all sides, then moving
slowly away, as if pushed by high winds, to reveal long cliffs all
around between the displaced chairs and the invisible legs of the
table, way, way down in the dark.

Leonardo couldn't wait another minute. He tore away from the
Cardinal, who had been leaning on his arm to raise himself more
easily, and it was Bernhard who rescued the poor arthritic old
gentleman just as he was about to collapse onto the table. Some of
the guests noticed but couldn't run to his aid, because a jittery
Leonardo was directly in their way.

"Young man, young man, young *barbarian!*" called the Cardinal
now, putting both hands on Leonardo's shoulders to liberate his
rescuer. "This is not the rape of the Sabines! I told you, when in
Rome, don't do as the Romans do. . . . Come, just stand here by
me, don't go on making more of a fool of yourself than you have
already." Leonardo blushed and glowered at the waiters and at
Bernhard, all of whom were smiling. The Cardinal conducted his
social rescue by saying to everyone: "What is this? Get on with your
duties, all of you," and to Bernhard, quite condescendingly: "Thank
you, my good man, you may go now. Your assistants need your help
more than I do."

When they were gone, he pulled one of the chairs to him, and
with its high back lodged under his armpit like a crutch, he let go of
Leonardo and stared at him in anger. "Now, now, now . . . forgive

me for my tactlessness in front of the servants, but you deserved
it. . . . And you were lucky I didn't fall and break my hip. Or
don't you know how brittle one is at my age? As a physician you
should, and let me warn you: if I *had* broken my hip, you would
have been a social cripple for the rest of your life. It's true that
these Russians are impervious to public opinion and, as Protestants,
they might even have found it amusing that their best friend should
cause their best enemy to break his hip in their house, but then I
don't know. . . . On the one hand, they are utterly barbaric, and
on the other, very civilized, while you are neither: the typical Italian. How low this country has descended . . . And to think that
you once gave us so much. All of Europe has benefitted from you.
But then it's true that the elderly fall into childhood before dying.
. . . How long will it take you to die, that is the question in my
mind. The French are still suffering from growing pains . . . and
so are the English, not to speak of the Germans—but you? Is this
noisy New Italy the final stage of your arthritis? And if so, how long
will it last? The trouble between Mother Italy and us, her growing
children, is that some of us, individually, represent the submissive
child, and others the lively rebel who is just beginning to discover
those great ancestors our mother has forgotten for centuries. But
you still live in the ancestral house and we don't. Who will inherit
it? It's not the house that counts, for it's unlivable by now, it's the
garden, the fields and the forests beyond . . . all these forests of
the spirit, that we would keep intact and you are destroying to make
room for this new generation of barbarians who invade it from
within . . . rats from the sewers . . . What do they call them
here? Burini . . ."

"What do you mean?" shouted Leonardo so that even the servants in the corridor and the guests in the next room could hear
him.

"Calm down, young man, and don't behave like one of them."
The Cardinal was speaking in whispers, and smiling, and holding
him by the arm, so what everybody who rushed back into the room
saw was two intimate friends exchanging a most secret joke. "I
mean exactly what I say and let me finish my sentence. Look at
these Roman princes destroying their own villas to build in the
center of this ugly, vulgar, pretentious, provincial little town. Lucky

that the Villa Medici is in French hands, or they would have raped that part of their history too. Lucky the Vatican Gardens are in the Pope's hands, and this is the one instance in which I can only praise the Pope's backwardness. Have you seen the monument they're putting up to Victor Emmanuel the Second? I'll take you there and you will see two things: on the one hand, the rising marble symbol of what the Italians call *Risorgimento*, because they can't use the true word *Resurrezione*—words are dangerous, you know?, they are ALL THERE IS TO THE WORLD, my friend, because the Word gave life to the flesh, not the other way about—and on the other hand, you will see the very core of the ancient city of Rome demolished, and its ancient inhabitants dispersed, exiled from their own homes. This is not the first time such a thing has—"

Mary's entrance was so sudden, and her anguish so visible, that the Cardinal couldn't even pronounce the word "happened." Mary was trying very hard to master her feelings in front of the Cardinal, and he was incensed to see her on the brink of tears. He took her by the arm and said: "Don't mind me, I'm leaving. Young people should be left alone . . ." then, turning to Leonardo, "when they deserve it. You are a real barbarian, you don't deserve the attentions of this charming young lady."

Far from being embarrassed by these words, Leonardo was himself incensed by the sight of the Cardinal's arm around Mary's shoulder, and the Cardinal, who was aware of this, removed his arm and walked away as briskly as his arthritis permitted, saying "*Quel barbare!!!*" and other words in a very loud voice, until he disappeared into the next room to join the guests.

"Well, we're rid of him," said Leonardo with a savage smile. "If I ever catch that lurid heathen putting his arm around your shoulder again, that will be the end of his immoral life. He believes in free love, he criticizes the Pope, the sacraments, the liberals, there isn't one thing in the world that's safe from his poisonous attacks." Mary grew pale and tears began to form in her eyes. "Do you object to my attacking your admirer?"

"He is not my admirer and you ought to be ashamed of yourself for suspecting me."

"Then why are you crying?"

"Because that's what the Monster says about him."

"Well, for once the Monster is right. And now answer my question: WHO ARE THOSE TWO MEN?"

Mary's face lit up suddenly as she answered with a smile: "Two complete nonentities."

"Then why do you accept their impudent courtship?"

"I never did."

"You did a few minutes ago right in front of me; you even encouraged them."

"I did not."

"You did too, and you even flirted with them."

"I? I never spoke a single word to the German."

"But you allowed him to toast you and you smiled with real love as you drank to his health. . . ."

"I—"

"Let me finish. And you flirted with the other one too, you whispered to him, it was a real scandal."

"Nonsense, I did it all to anger you, because you were flirting with those two ladies."

"I was not."

"Oh yes you were. And besides . . ." She stared at him with angry eyes, and before he knew it her lips were on his for a long, passionate kiss that the noise of a door, the buzz of voices from the next room and a cough advised Leonardo to interrupt, because she hadn't heard a thing.

"Mary," he asked in a whisper, without daring to look at the door, but pretending to be laughing: "Can you swear on your child's head that you never kissed anyone like this before?"

"I swear it on my child's head and on my father's grave. I never did, not even my husband, nor ever will."

"That's better," he said, pretending to be laughing at some joke of hers, so as not to be caught in an embarrassing situation, which was the only tribute to the rules of the game he felt society had the right to exact of him. Mary on the other hand felt so embarrassed that she said: "Darling, now that everything is clear between us, let's do something for the others. They deserve it."

"Yes, my love, let's. What is it, and who are these others who need our help?"

"Let's go in there and behave in a civilized manner. You pretend to court the two ladies I accused you of courting, but do it well, please, and use all your charm. It won't be easy for me, I assure you, but you must. WE must. And I'll use all my energies to seem pleased, even amused."

"By what?"

"By the sight of your seeming infidelity. Promise?"

And with a quick, perfunctory kiss on the tip of his nose, and a wink of the eye, she turned her back to him and hurried towards the next room, from which more and more faces were beginning to appear and disappear in quick succession, accompanied by discreet giggles.

"Say you!!!" shouted Leonardo, grabbing her by the arm and almost making her stumble. "What is this immorality?"

"Immorality?" she shouted back in her best soprano.

"Yes, immorality is the word."

"Darling," she whispered quickly, taking advantage of the fact that the guests were beginning to retreat into the next room, "of course I won't do the same. I swear it on my father's grave and my child's head, too. Or don't you believe me? If you don't, I'll open that window and jump."

"You silly goose," he said, managing another social smile. "Of course I believe you, but you don't seem to know that women don't have to court men; it's men who court women."

"You're right," she said, pretending to be very amused, and then: "I swear I shan't allow any man to court me tonight."

"Only tonight?"

"Ever. Until I die in your arms."

"Let's not presume to know who will die first, but if it's you, I won't survive more than the time it takes to thrust a knife into my heart."

"Wonderful," she said, "so now we don't have anything to fear from anybody, except my mother, if she's noticed that people are talking about us. Let's go back in there, please."

"You go first."

She did, and he went the other way, into a dark corridor, to be alone with his happiness. But happiness means health and life, and he hadn't had enough to eat, so his steps led him straight to the kitchen, with its enticing smells that were beckoning him on.

As he approached the kitchen, he heard cheerful voices that seemed more human to him than those of all the refined people he had eaten (or rather, NOT eaten) dinner with, the Cardinal included, and this encouraged him to open the door like a neighbor dropping in for a chat.

"May I?" he asked, without waiting for an answer and extending his hand for the handshake that follows the normal, "But of course you may, come in, dear cousin." (In Laterza, as everywhere in his world, everybody was a cousin or a cousin of cousins.)

He was so happy to be among cousins again, that he didn't notice the consternation of his "neighbors," none of whom would even look at him after the first frightening glimpse. They were all looking to the family elders for guidance in this terrible emergency, while the family heads, namely the cook in his tall cap and Bernhard in his beautiful uniform, were looking to their inferiors. A most unusual state of affairs, but then in all emergencies the first thing one forgets is social standing, to rediscover human solidarity in face of the enemy. The confusion was so great that while some of the servants could afford to look to Bernhard and the cook for guidance, because they were close by, all the others could only duck or pretend to be so busy as not to have noticed anything at all. Serving plates were broken, a great deal of silver was noisily dropped on the marble table by the lesser servants busy drying it, hot water was inadvertently poured out of the kitchen sink onto the feet of the two women who were busy washing pots and frying pans. Things never happen in silence.

And now Leonardo suddenly realized the truth: the coachman had been entertaining his friends with the story of the rescue of his new master from Peppino and Liborio. He stood for a brief moment in the doorway, then, broadening his smile and his whole attitude of studied naturalness: "How are you, my dear friend?" he said to the coachman, pretending not to notice the giggles that had followed the breaking of dishes and the crash of solid silver on the table and the floor.

Of course the coachman was broken, his moment of glory forgotten, but the poor devil couldn't muster the courage to climb back into life by grace of a brotherly handshake. Leonardo knew this *non sum dignus* attitude from his recent experience with the Cardinal, so he withdrew his hand to scratch his nose, then took out his breast pocket handkerchief to wipe his brow and his neck; in so doing dropped his stethoscope and bent down to pick it up and see if it was broken. This was the magic wand everyone recognized and obeyed, and he knew it without even having to look beyond the tool of his trade, but still he insisted on wiping it and feeling it before putting it back behind that kerchief, and only then did he speak again:

"Thank God it isn't broken. What would I do without this little instrument? Six years of medical school and nine of daily practice would leave me worse off than . . ." (he quickly discarded naming any of the trades represented in the audience) ". . . than . . . than a BEGGAR, that's it, my friend, a beggar, that's the only valid description of my worth without this instrument and all the others that cannot be carried in this pocket of mine, such as my microscope, and my whole arsenal of weapons, not to mention the hospital pots and pans, and china and silver we civilized cannibals need to spice and burn and slice our fellow human beings on kitchen tables like this one." Then, to the coachman again: "You haven't told me how you are, so let me do it. You're not too well, which is because you feel only *too* well with all this superb food and wine in front of you. Who wouldn't? But we should always remember the uninvited guest who waits behind the kitchen door: the heart attack. You should eat less and move about more. Learn from your horses and let your inner coachman whip you into running: it will do you a lot of good, just as it does them good not to be locked up in the stable for months at a time. You may learn from him, too," he said now, pointing to the cook. "He can flatter all of us into eating more than we need, for he is such an artist that we all wish we had stomachs as big as this room, to be able to gobble up all the good food he prepares. But he doesn't fall for his own flattery. Look at him, how lean he is: I can see that he eats very little. Perhaps the idea of eating what he makes is unthinkable to him, as it would be for a painter to eat his own canvases." Then, to the cook: "Tell me, my friend, what are your eating habits?"

"Oh, I have no eating habits," said the cook. "I eat very little."

"I can see that, but very little of WHAT?"

"Oh, nothing in particular. Bread and cheese, or bread dipped into one of the sauces I'm making at the time. But I assure you, sir, that it isn't because my cooking tastes like canvases: ask Miss Mary's husband, ask any of the great painters who are invited here, they all love my cooking, even if you don't."

"I know, I know," said Leonardo, "and I love your cooking too . . . but . . ."

"You didn't even taste it, you hardly swallowed a spoonful of my soup."

"But it wasn't my fault, I was talking. . . ."

"So was the Cardinal, but he ate plenty and he loved it. He always comes in here to shake hands with me after meals."

"And I would have done the same, if I'd been given a chance to eat your sauce. I asked for it, it was flatly denied me. . . ."

The din of silver and china being dried and thrown on the table and the whole orchestra of pots and pans under running water was making this conversation rather difficult, but the cook didn't seem too interested in Leonardo's replies. It was the coachman who called the lesser servants to order: "Hey, you, will you stop that racket? We're talking here." Then, to Leonardo: "Are you serious about my heart? Because I—"

"And besides," said the cook, after a moment of silent meditation, the content of which was flashed to Leonardo in angry frowns and much rotating of eyeballs—but again the din prevented Leonardo from capturing the rest of the sentence.

"Say, you, are you deaf?" shouted the coachman, and the din came to another brief halt, during which he said to Leonardo: "I'd like to ask you a few questions, but these turds here have no respect for anyone. Let's go into the next room where you can listen to my heart, if you want. I'm sort of worried about my heart."

"With the greatest of pleasure," answered Leonardo, and then, to the cook: "With your permission . . ."

"You don't have to ask my permission. The coachman is as much at home here as I am. You may go. . . ."

"No," said Leonardo with as much authority as he could muster, "I meant to ask your permission to dip a slice of bread into the sauce I couldn't touch, because that young man there refused my request . . ." And he pointed to the young waiter, who blushed up to his ears.

"Go ahead," said the cook, "but the sauce is cold by now, and you won't understand a damn thing about it anyway. That kind of dish must be tasted with *that* kind of red wine, but perhaps you don't know anything about French wines, so . . . Well, if you want to try it, you're welcome to it." And he turned his back on Leonardo to give orders to one of the servants, but this obviously had nothing to do with Leonardo's request, as became embarrassingly obvious after a few seconds. At this point the coachman shouted his own orders to the whole assembly of serfs, and in a tone of voice that hurt Leonardo more than it did them: "Say, you, get going and obey this gentleman, and make it quick, too."

"Not for me," said Leonardo, smiling broadly and making a generous gesture towards the crowd. "I'm sorry I interrupted everybody's work; please forgive me." Then, to the coachman: "Let's go."

The next room was the servants' wardrobe; an elderly woman was starching and ironing a whole pile of servants' collars and shirts and waistcoats on a large table covered with a white cloth that had turned brown in the center, even black in spots burned out by the hot irons, which stood on another kitchen stove of lesser proportions.

"Clear out of here, the doctor's going to examine my heart," said the coachman in the usual rude Roman way, and the little woman ducked and said humbly: "Let me just finish this and put away the iron."

"No," shouted the coachman.

"Yes," said Leonardo, "she can even stay here while I examine you." Then, to her: "I'm sorry I'm interrupting your work. My name is . . ." But he stopped, because he realized that by being too polite he was going to lose face. He coughed, spat into his handkerchief, cleared his throat, and, pretending he didn't notice that the little woman was leaving her ironing undone in obedience to the coachman's signals, he took out his stethoscope and waited for the coachman to strip to the waist and sit down on the table. And as he auscultated his first patient in Rome, he was also auscultating his own heartbeat and his own breath, bursting with happiness.

"You have no reason to worry, my good man," he said. "Which is to say: you have a very good reason to worry, and that reason is yourself. Mend your ways, my good man, honor God in the things he has given you; namely, in your health. Court your own favors and not other people's. In correct terminology, this means: don't fill your mind with hate and contempt, because they alter the blood so that it corrodes the walls of the heart; but it can also corrode the walls of the stomach and give you an ulcer. And in the scar of an ulcer, cancer is frequently born. Remember the maxim: *Servire Dominum in Laetitia.* The masters of this world are not gods, but that is for you to decide. If you prefer to consider them gods, then serve them happily, don't judge them, as your horses don't judge you, and you'll have no reason to worry. Second recommendation: wear wider collars, don't strangle yourself in order to look more distinguished. Third recommendation: when you have to spend hours waiting in front of houses or theaters, don't go to the next tavern and drink, but either sleep inside the coach, or walk around it. Or, if that is too boring . . ." He was going to say: "Read a good book," but then, looking at that face again, he decided that the only thing he could honestly tell him would be: "Die and be reborn a better person, because for you there is no hope, and neither is there for the people who came in contact with you." This of course he couldn't say, but he hadn't counted on the rage to live he had aroused in his patient.

"Well, if that is too boring? . . ."

"Oh yes, of course . . . If that is too boring . . . let's see . . . er . . . read a good book."

"You're joking. You live in the moon. I'm not a person like you: I'm a shit, I'm no good to anyone. Have you ever waited for hours in front of places where other people live and enjoy themselves while you just wait and wait and have nothing to do? Why am I even asking? The right question to ask is: *Have you ever been me?* You haven't, so shut up, because if you were me, you would drown yourself in wine or in water: no third solution."

Leonardo had started to nod and nod and nod, like a doctor, except that the doctor usually hears his patient's nonsense before auscultating him, not afterwards.

"I must go now," he said.

"Just a moment," said the coachman, getting dressed again. "I hear the voice of the French Cardinal out there in the kitchen.

Don't trust him. First of all, he's a Frenchman, and, secondly, he's bitter because he has been a Papabile* for years, but nothing came of it and nothing will, thank God for that at least."

"May I come in?" asked the old woman, timidly opening the door.

"No," shouted the coachman, and the woman disappeared before Leonardo could say yes.

"She will, she will," said the coachman, noticing Leonardo's intention. "Let me just give you a piece of friendly advice, because you and I are like brothers: TWO ROUGH DIAMONDS, and I tell you, this is Rome, this isn't your hometown in the provinces. You've got to be careful in Rome. Don't trust ANYBODY, especially the people who say they're your friends. They're the worst. Tougher than diamonds, but NO DIAMONDS they. Impure of heart, that's what they are. You may think I'm a fool, because you are a doctor and I had no schooling whatever, but the Apostles were no doctors either. Christ was a doctor, and from him all doctorship descends. And I can tell you—"

"May I come in now?"

"Yes, you may," said Leonardo, nodding to the coachman and smiling as if to mean: *I agree, and thank you for the advice.*

The coachman was hurt, but he had to pretend he hadn't been slighted, in order not to lose face in front of the old woman, so he shouted at her: "The doctor has no time for you, he must go back to the drawing room."

"But I, too, have something wrong with my heart. It won't take long, Doctor, I swear. . . ."

"Yeah, you swear. Don't you know one shouldn't swear? Especially when you're trying to cheat people." Then, to Leonardo: "Don't let her get started with the story of her woes, or she'll never finish."

"You liar," she shouted, "ask my doctor, he'll tell you there's plenty wrong with me."

---

* A Papabile is a Cardinal likely to be elected Pope. The saying has it that no Papabile has ever actually succeeded, yet the Romans continue to select their Papabili and shower them with favors so as to be favored in turn if one of their candidates ever ascends the Throne of St. Peter's.

"Then go to your doctor, don't pester my friend here."

"But my doctor doesn't understand a damn thing. He's a doctor for the poor, he's poor himself, he's unable to make good, and he's deaf, he puts his ear on my back and doesn't hear a thing, but there's so much wrong with my insides that even I can hear the noise. You, Doctor, you have good hearing and a modern machine, please use it on me for a second, and you'll hear noises you've never heard before. . . ."

"Tomorrow," said Leonardo, "I promise I will see you tomorrow and give you plenty of time to tell me your whole story, but now I must go."

"Then don't go through the kitchen," the woman said, "there are five servants who want you to hear their noises with your machine. And they're all young and healthy."

"I'll see everybody tomorrow, you can tell them that from me."

He had hardly spoken these words before he heard them being repeated by the coachman in the kitchen: *"I'll see everybody tomorrow, you can tell them that from me."* Then the coachman explained: "Words of the doctor to me, and you can trust him: a great diagnostician!"

Leonardo had some difficulty explaining to the old woman that he preferred to go back through the kitchen rather than to follow her down a dark corridor, but the coachman came back to rescue him.

"You go that way," he said to the old woman, and as soon as she was gone, he took Leonardo by the arm and whispered into his ear: "Don't trust her. She is a hypochondriac, as you may have realized already. I know some medicine too, and I can tell you she's not only a faker, she's a thief—a real thief too, for your information. . . . Tell the ladies. I can't, they wouldn't believe me."

At this point Leonardo would indeed have preferred to follow the old woman through the dark corridor, but he knew he could not allow this low creature to turn into a second Schillasi. And he was angry, because his first motives for passing through the kitchen had been so good, so brotherly, that he had been willing to face even the Cardinal again with the same Christian love he felt towards the whole world, and now . . . He entered the kitchen and everyone except the cook and the Cardinal was ready to strip to the waist and

tell him all their secret pains, but not of course in public: "In
there," they said, beginning to push him back towards the ironing
room while fighting among themselves. This was so different from
what he had expected that he meekly accepted the coachman's help.
What further dismantled his plans for an exemplary show of Christian love in action was the presence of the two men talking French
and looking at him with such contempt. And they were not without
an audience, either. Bernhard was nearby, and although he didn't
talk or show anything on his mummified face, he obviously understood what they were saying, and was probably enjoying it too, in
his Germanic way. Around them gathered the crust of the servants;
namely, those dressed up for the show and ready to appear on stage
at any moment and speak their brief but impertinent lines, without
which the play could not continue. Whereas around the proverbial
good doctor were gathered only the lowly, those whose very existence in the pyramid of Service is usually unknown to the masters.

But there were also two leaders in the two groups, and these were
the Apulian waiter who had so rudely reprimanded Leonardo and
been so rudely attacked by him, and the coachman. The Apulian
waiter was obviously scared of the cook and would never have tried
to usurp his authority, while the coachman was doing exactly that,
and, far from being scared by Leonardo, he was in fact protecting
him, so that everyone could see how scared and submissive the little
doctor was.

What tipped the scales in his favor was a tactical mistake by the
cook, who thought he could humiliate both his enemies at once, and
amuse his noble guest at the same time. "Say," he shouted to the
coachman, "stop playing Napoleon: the doctor doesn't need your
protection. And you, there," he shouted to the Apulian waiter, "get
busy and give the doctor some of the meat you refused to serve him
at dinner."

Everyone looked at Leonardo aghast, and that gave him the courage of a lion. "Thank you most kindly," he said to the cook in a
voice trembling more with fear than with rage, "but I don't need
anyone's protection in this house. If I want to taste your cooking, I
can give you my orders tomorrow. And I don't want this boy to do
any extra work now. With your permission."

His only act of cowardice was to retreat through the wardrobe, in order not to face the Cardinal, who had already retreated through the main door. "Show me the way back to the living room," he said to the little old woman, but the coachman was quicker than he, and said: "Just follow me." Thus, in the end, Leonardo obeyed his self-styled protector, and even had to thank him, in order to put an end to the long list of people he shouldn't trust in the household. Well, anyway, he said to himself, as he reached the main corridor again, I must not forget that I'm happy.

But he was hungry, oh, how hungry he was, and how the scent of that meat haunted him in the empty dining room. Hungry and sleepy, and shivering, and with a headache. He looked at his watch: almost midnight. In the whole civilized world (that is, in Apulia) sleep, silence and darkness were the rule at this hour. He didn't miss his lawful wife, of course, but he missed having the chance to turn his back on her. Suddenly, the door opened, but it was not the door to the drawing room, and a procession of uniformed servants marched past him, carrying trays with cakes and ices and refreshments over their heads. He couldn't let them know that he was not at home in the Throne Hall, whence orders for all that godsend had come, and so he followed them to play his role in the comedy, but he soon realized that no one, not even Mary, had eyes for him. She was behaving well, thank God for that: she was surrounded only by women—that is, she was one of the ladies who surrounded Sophie and the professor, together with a few of the elderly gentlemen, while all the "dangerous" young men and some of the sillier ladies chatted in smaller groups everywhere else in the room. The Cardinal was presiding over one of these groups, and a lot of new faces were present. But no one paid any attention to him; not even the people he had met before dinner seemed to remember him. There were a few unoccupied chairs along the walls and he sat down wearily on one of these, but couldn't accept the servants' offers, as they lowered their trays in front of him. It would have been a repetition of the offer he had so bravely turned down in the kitchen: how could he let them go back and report that he was eating all alone in a corner? Yet his hunger was so great that he pretended he had heard and was enjoying one of the jokes that was making some of the younger people laugh, and this gave him a chance to accept one servant's offer, but he was careful to insist that he give him only a tiny bit of cake and the tiniest portion of ice cream, "so as not to offend the cook," he said, with an understanding wink and a smile that won him some attention from a human being at least. But when he joined the laughing group, he realized that they were speaking French, so he went back to his chair along the wall and ate his meager serving of ice cream and cake, smiling sadly to himself, to save appearances in front of the same servants. But once the servants were gone, he sat there in gloom, staring straight ahead and thinking of his bed in Laterza.

Suddenly an old gentleman detached himself from the group and sat down next to him, as if he, too, were tired of the whole thing. Leonardo noticed him from the corner of one eye, but didn't turn in his direction because he was so tired that he didn't even care to find out about the young man next to Mary at dinner; yet he knew this might be his best source of information, because this was the gentleman who had proposed the toast to them as fellow writers. I am happy and Mary loves me, he kept saying to himself to stay awake. And this is our last evening in Rome. But won't it always be this way, even in Switzerland? Don't these two women know everybody everywhere, have houses everywhere, family everywhere, don't they speak every language under the sun?

Yet the mere fact that he had seen the whole world of the servants, on which this world rested for the very privilege of ignoring it, made it seem incredible that Sophie should even think of leaving it forever, without worrying about its future or the future of her money, because in her absence these people could only live as the masters of the house, which was dishonest. And, if they were honest, then they should stop eating and drinking the moment they stopped working, because Sophie couldn't feed an army of parasites, simply because they had done some minor tasks for her while she was living on Italian soil.

"You must think that these people are very stupid," said the old gentleman, suddenly turning to him.

"Who? Our hostess?"

"Lord no! Thank God for her . . . she's one of the most intelligent, illuminated persons in this city. . . . How could you say such a thing? How could you even think it?"

"I wasn't thinking it. Why, does it show?"

The old gentleman blushed, as did Leonardo. They stayed still for a second, looking at each other and then away, until the old gentleman said: "I thought you meant these young people making silly jokes about the Cardinal. I thought their utter stupidity had driven you away in despair. It has me, after a few attempts to establish some kind of contact with them."

"Oh. No, I left because I don't understand French very well."

"I see, I see . . . Well, you haven't missed anything. But you must think very highly of the Cardinal. I saw you engrossed in conversation with him during dinner. Don't you think he's an extraordinary person?"

"Oh yes, he is."

"May I introduce myself: my name is Lumbroso."

"The criminologist?"

"Good Lord, no, most definitely not. We have nothing in common. I am a student of ancient history, and of course a most devoted pupil of Mommsen's, who honors me with his friendship. I am Giacomo Lumbroso; the criminologist is Cesare Lombroso." A long pause, then the gentleman continued: "Do you know what the Cardinal said to me one day when I asked him, point-blank, whether he was trying to convert me to the Catholic faith?"

"Why, are you a Protestant?"

"A Jew."

"A . . . WHAT?"

"A Jew." And the gentleman blushed again, while Leonardo stared at him in horror. He had never met a Jew before, and the thought that these people, who had not yet accepted Christianity and who were still waiting for the true Messiah to come, should have anything good to say about a Cardinal appalled him.

The gentleman giggled to overcome his embarrassment, and went on as if nothing had interrupted his story: "He said: 'I wouldn't dream of it. It's for you to convert me to the true faith. Then alone will I know that you have discovered it, because all converts lose their sense of proportion, as is only right. They are reborn, like children, whose first conscious activity consists in teaching their parents that the world exists.' So I answered him: 'My dear friend, you Christians are the children, it is we who dare not remind you that the little you know comes from us.' "

But Leonardo was no longer listening. He had seen one of his two rivals, the Italian one, leave the group of the Cardinal's critics and make straight for Mary; Mary seemed to welcome his interruption, while her mother seemed to resent it, so here was a new and extremely disturbing element of fact: Mary pleased by something that displeased her mother.

"Do you know that man?" he asked, without even bothering to notice whether Professor Lumbroso was looking in the right direction.

"Of course I do," answered the professor, greatly surprised by Leonardo's tone.

"What is he to the daughter of our hostess?"

"A very precious friend; in the years when her mother had broken off all relations with her, he represented her only spiritual support in Rome. He always had a special affection for her."

"And she for him, I suppose."

"And she for him, of course. People accuse him of being a social butterfly, but that isn't true. He has what very few men in his social class have today; namely, a way of putting people at their ease and slowly lifting them to his own level of intellectual and moral distinction. It is a modern version of the Socratic discourse—what the French call the art of conversation—and very few Italians have it, unfortunately for our country."

"But he does . . ."

"Oh, definitely. As I was telling him the other day, if I were young, I would allow myself to be tempted into writing a book called *Grandeur et décadence de la politesse dans le monde*. And he reminded me of something I had read in Voltaire years ago, but completely forgotten; namely, Voltaire's definition of politesse: *La politesse est une force de la Nature*. How true that is, and how I wish all those who are fascinated by the so-called natural sciences today read more of Voltaire than of Darwin. They would stop trying to discover the ape in themselves, and justifying it in the mob, and they would rediscover the moral science, which is the science of politeness and conversation, or, as the Cardinal so aptly put it the other day, politeness IN conversation. He said, 'If we replaced the word "freedom" with the word "politeness," we would have Politeness of the Press, Politeness of Thought, Politeness of Worship, and the Socialists, the Anarchists and all those other hooligans would be deprived of their best weapon.' "

"I am not interested in what the Cardinal said; what I want to know is, if he's such an exceptional man and loves Mary so much, why didn't he marry her?"

"He? Who?"

"The social butterfly . . ."

"What social butterfly?"

"Oh my God, the man accused of being a social butterfly, who is instead the greatest man of culture and politeness et cetera you have ever met in your life et cetera . . ."

"You mean the Cardinal?"

"Dammit, no! I mean *that man there, see?* I pointed him out to you when I asked my first question ten minutes ago, and you obviously didn't even look!"

The old gentleman's surprise was such that he sat there staring at the floor and shaking his head, then stopping and then frowning and making faces as if to say, "I don't believe it," and then shaking his head again to express this silent disbelief. Leonardo was now physically torn between the violent, visceral curiosity of the jealous lover, and the vague, social curiosity of the educated person who wonders whether perhaps he has hurt someone's feelings without meaning to. But he could satisfy neither, he was trapped like an animal. This silly little Jew who was so impressed with that old lecher of a Cardinal barely deserved the most perfunctory attention, *if and when* the situation was normal. But the situation here was far from normal, for the rules of mutual respect were not the rules of men, they were the rules of animals: women are animals, and Protestants are women of some sort, or merchants, which is saying the same thing. And if Jews are not merchants, what else are they? Mary was not responsible if she accepted the courtship of these same men she had promised not to court (again, how can a woman promise anything? Hadn't she recognized the absurdity of her own promise?) but her man was responsible for creating around her that aura of unapproachability he himself, as a man worthy of the name, would never have respected, unless it were present in force. And how could it be present, if no one here knew the real facts? To all intents and purposes, Mary was free game: she had no master to respect and obey—worse, she and her mother lived by Protestant, Nordic, matriarchal standards in the most corrupt capital of a whole universe of men.

Laterza may be a province and Rome a metropolis, but politeness without honor means nothing, so I'd rather be provincial than a cuckold.

With this clear conclusion in mind, Leonardo left the little Jew to his thoughts and made straight for Mary, pushing several people aside, to ask her, in a tone that boded no good: "Are you going to introduce me to your friend?" She shook and paled, as if she were about to faint, then with immense self-discipline, she smiled and made her introduction: "Count Jahn-Rusconi, Doctor Claudi."

The young count shook the hand that was thrust like a knife at his stomach, because he could do nothing else to stop it, and said, with visible effort, in a slow, deep whisper: "You could be a little kinder."

"I am being kind, I am being very kind in fact," answered Leonardo withdrawing his hand and wiping it with disgust on his trousers.

At this point the Cardinal grabbed him by the arm and said very loudly: "How about a little music, Mary? Our friend Doctor Claudi probably doesn't know that you are an accomplished musician, especially as a singer. What will you play for us tonight?"

"Oh no," said Mary, "I would never dare play in public."

"Why not?" "Yes, why not?" "Please, do," "Yes, do," came the echo of cheerful voices, one of which even asked Leonardo: "Why don't you insist? She won't do it for us, but she will for you."

And again many voices joined in, so that Leonardo found himself suddenly at the center of the friendliest attention, in which, however, he detected more than a shade of fear. But, to his great surprise, he couldn't utter a word. His heartbeat was too violent to permit an untrembling voice to emerge, so he smiled stupidly, trying to hide his hands, because hands betray even more emotion than the voice.

"Can anyone here play the violin?" asked the Cardinal, but no one answered. "There is a violin here," he went on, "a Stradivarius, and I'm sure that the lady of the house would not object to having it used."

"Of course not," called Sophie, interrupting her *tête-à-tête* with Mommsen. "Klagonov promised to turn up later with a friend, he plays the violin very well; in fact, he often plays here with Mary: they adore each other, they make a perfect team."

This blow was too much for Leonardo. He just stood there, smiling. In the general animation Mary had managed to walk past him and whisper into his ear: "I love you as the moon loves the sun: you are the source of my light," and Sophie's first words had caught him in that kind of stupor caused by an excess of happiness, but when her whole sentence slowly began to take shape through the thick rosy fog that had hidden the world from his mind he was so quickly precipitated into hell again that he left his smile behind, as you leave your eyes open when you die. And sure enough, the bell rang in the hall, and, before Bernhard could open the door, deep Russian voices were heard through the thick walls, out on the landing, awakening a corresponding chorus of Russian voices inside the crowded living room, thus establishing a clear-cut division between cultures. The Italians were all very loud in the range of tenor and baritone, and their women all very faint soprano; the Germans all extremely soft-spoken, the English all very noisy, but in their typical English way—making English noises, something between speech and song, aimed at destroying both, so that neither emotions nor thoughts could disturb the physiological privacy of the true English Subject. In contrast to all these, the Russians were so outspoken: they outsang and outfelt to such an extent that everyone withdrew towards the walls to make room for these extraordinary actors. A natural stage thus came into being. To his surprise, even Leonardo withdrew to the wall in awe, becoming more aware of the show than of his own emotions. But not for long.

There was a stormy general embrace between the Russians running out of the drawing room and those running in from the outside. Suddenly, a huge, apelike man with slanted eyes and a red nose threw himself bodily on the crowd, pushing everyone aside to lunge at Leonardo and grab him by the necktie, shouting in Russianized Italian. "Thief! what doing here are you?" Leonardo, who had instantly recognized the Russian whose boots he had taken by mistake that morning, fought back until the giant had to let go of the necktie, and at that point Bernhard and several other servants who had come in from the kitchen were able to pull the two combatants apart, until the other Russians took care of their man, while Mary dragged hers into the dining room to protect him and to talk to him in private. But she didn't have much time because, after only a few bars of an all-Russian chorus in the anteroom, the Russian giant rushed into the dining room and threw himself on Leonardo, this time to kiss him on the mouth and hug him, shouting: *"Fratellissimo carissimo fedelissimo amicissimo,"* and other such Italian *issimis* against which there was no defense. They walked back into the drawing room arm in arm, and Leonardo realized how popular Klagonov was, even among the non-Russians whose general rush to greet him eliminated the difference between audience and stage. But Klagonov, who had been told in the greatest secrecy what only the other Russians in the room knew, felt he must help his new friend in distress; at the same time he knew he must keep the secret he had sworn on his honor not to reveal.

"Meet my great, old friend, scientist-surgeon, diagnostician, discoverer and scholar, archaeologist et cetera . . ." at which point he kept having to ask Leonardo for his name, which he seemed unable to remember. Leonardo felt like a clown, being reintroduced to all the guests he had met before dinner and spoken to during dinner, but it surprised him and comforted him to see how smoothly the convention of *politesse* functioned in real society. Here was the key to all the contradictions that had baffled him and angered him during the last two days! And what made his surprise even more pleasant, if possible, was that Klagonov had brought with him the only person he had truly liked in Rome so far: Azzeltini, who turned out to be called Hazeltine.

Everybody in the house, including the servants out in the kitchen, was now taken into Leonardo's great secret, without revealing it, of course, because Klagonov was discreet, as he himself explained in his *basso profondo* with sudden darts into the highest falsetto when he laughed: "Lieff Franziscovich" (his version of Leonardo, a name he couldn't possibly remember) "here in the Rome city for secret reason scientific discovery with his colleague-discoverer scientist Sophie Julievna is, and for certain-uncertain time period no one must about this know because scientists have secrets and you no scientist, you just poor idiot like me, but he old friend of mine and way, way back Darwin's monkey days, isn't that true, my friend Lieff Franziscovich? And now he also friend of yours, please." Then, introducing Hazeltine to Leonardo: "This man sculptor-horseman crazy American Hazeltine by name. . . ."

"But we know each other very well," said Hazeltine, patting Leonardo on the back.

"What? You-you very well know? Where and when have you-you met?"

"First I saw him at the Caffè Greco, where he was fascinating all the women and making all the men jealous, then I saw him again this evening, this time fascinating three American beauties who . . ."

"What's that about the Caffè Greco?" asked Mary from the opposite corner of the room, where she had been summoned by her mother with a severe glance of those frightening eyes, to be told in Russian whispers that she must not always stay where Leonardo was.

Klagonov shouted something in Russian, then explained to Hazeltine: "You fool, don't you know Caffè Greco Mary's husband hangout is?"

"What's wrong with that?"

"And Mary love this man?"

"So do all the ladies, it seems."

"But this love secret is and tragedy may come."

"You Russians are such babies, with your love of conspiracy and tragedy. Thank God everything in Rome is done in the open, and for fun."

Klagonov was so angry, he couldn't talk Italian any more. Leonardo understood that Klagonov wanted to run away from all those people, probably to tell him some big secret, but only because the strong hand of his friend was squeezing his arm and dragging him into the dining room where more Russian noises were delivered loudly into his ear, as if they were whispers, and it wasn't until after the opening theme of the symphony that he was able to interrupt him with his timid: "I don't understand Russian."

"Eeech, vot horror, poor *carissimo fratellissimo*, I sorriest for you feel, Russian is onliest language where you can expand thought and feeling freely like running horseback-on for hundreds of miles in big infinitatious endlessness of countryside and forests, because Russian without effort spoken is: musicality of language helps to becoming you its speaker, and you help language to its becoming your ownerly personal language. Italian is language for *walls with ears*, and *people without walls and without infinity*, because they in village square and in Caffè Grecos and cathedrals all their time spend."

"You are right."

"Don't contradict me by you saying I right am, and then running away into different argument of conversational subject. Let me finish: I saying was a question: WHAT DO THESE THEYS DO IN THEIR CATHEDRAL-CAFÉ-SQUARE-CITY-VILLAGE-STREETS? I ask and I answer that they make fun of poor devils like Professor Schillasi, who not a professor is, because no school sat in for years he, but knows more than all professors. . . ." Leonardo was about to agree with him, but was warned by a threatening finger in the air; after a long pause, Klagonov said. "He."

"He . . . what?"

"He more than all professors, although not in schools for years has sittened himself, knows."

"I see."

"You don't see: you hear, but I see, because seen for many years I have this good man who in museums recognized pig from gentleman, art-lover from fuck-lover, if such medical language using with permission yours I may. Many young Romans take honest foreign girls to museums under pretentiousness of art history interest showing examples of sculpture and painting, and then them statues without figleaf show and explain forbidden and indecent thought of prick growing bigger and bigger and bigger, and giving woman body all greatness of immensity of mysterious joy that excite honest girls and to try this new experience with young man decide, and then to Via Appia go, under same pretentiousness of other ancient archaeological art learning about, and then, in high grass, first with one kiss, then with two, then with Italian comedy that big prick hurts, and their responsibility it is, because they kissing of themselves permission given have, they young man to touch underwear permission

give, and then I cannot even tell you what happens, but you probably have intuited enoughly to no further explanation need."

Leonardo had intuited more than enoughly for his own peace of
mind, and asked: "Do you know a Marchese Carlo Tempi?"

"Which one? Old one or young one he?"

"Whaat?" he asked, feeling the dagger in his heart. "Is there also
a young Carlo Tempi?"

"Is old man's grandson he."

"Grandson, you said? The only grandson?"

"No, two: Carlo and Alberto they."

"And the father is dead, of course."

"Oh no, very much alive he."

"Very much alive, you said? And what does he do: go to
museums?"

"Never he! Goes to be astronomer he. Tries to discover new stars
he. Great collection telescopes he."

"And shows them to innocent foreign girls?"

"No he! No swine like himselve's ownish father he. So goodish
man he, that only original telescopes of Galileo and Kepler and
Koppernigh uses he because Pope, imbecile he, pronounced infallible enciclica against modern machines he, and so Marchese astronomer Benedetto Karlovich of name he, him Pope asked of permission to use old machines he."

"I am not interested. And the grandchildren know Mary?"

"Yes, great friends of Angelo and Mary they."

"Who is Angelo?"

"Mary's husband he."

"Don't call him her husband!"

"Ex-husband, I am sorry, did I bleedily dagger your heart?"

"Never mind. Tell me, does he go to museums?"

"Must! Painter he."

"I know, I know . . . goddamn all the painters on earth. And he
met Mary in a museum, of course. I know that, too."

"And *you* met Mary in museum she!"

"Oh, you know that, too? Who told you?"

"She."

"In a museum?"

Klagonov unhooked his arm from Leonardo's, crossed both hands on his heart and said, looking at his *fratellissimo* with deeply honest eyes: "I am sorrow . . . yes!"

"Oh. So ʏᴏᴜ also met Mary in a museum."

"No, I met her when child she and child me."

"But you took her to a museum."

Klagonov gulped, detached his hands from his heart to plant them there again in a new demonstration of his truthfulness and said: "Ask Professor Schillasi. Tell you he I never stopped in front indecent statues or paintings. Never. Other things in museums they: Madonnas, Jesuses on Cross, landscapes they."

"I know museums, and now I know you too, and I trust you. We are brothers. So tell me, Angelo took Mary to Via Appia?"

"No, no. Didn't have to he. Took him to Sophie Julievna she, and said she to she—"

"I know the story. But how about Carlo and Alberto? . . ."

"No . . . ridiculous to imaginate it you! Alberto cows, pigs, wheat, vineyards, soil agroculture uniquely interested of he, and Carlo only arms of coats he."

"Women's coats?"

"No, sorry. I mean coats of arms. Nobility, because Tempi family not Tempi family anciently descended from is. Real Tempi family turned off, I mean extinguished, much o'clock ago, 1776 of year, and old Carlo Tempi, who nobody was, but ambitioned himself for to be known and somebody, bought of extinguished Tempi family omonimous castle he, and thusly—"

"Damn *him*! So Carlo is not interested in women, either."

"Oh yes. Very much he of, and, to tell truth, tried marriage with Mary he."

"He ᴅɪᴅ???????" Leonardo staggered and fell backwards, but Klagonov rescued him in midair, saying: "*Ask of to,* I meant, you never finish me sentence let. Asked Sophie Julievna he."

"Oh, he did. Thank God. And she said no."

"No, no, said, *ask my daughter she,* she."

"The fool!!! But then Mary said no."

"Mary laughed she. Oh, how laughed she!" And they both laughed aloud, but Leonardo suddenly turned gloomy again and muttered: "But she didn't mention this Carlo Tempi at all. . . ."

"Probably not given enoughly o'clock you she."

"That's right . . . but still . . . And tell me about Count Jahn-Rusconi. Does he go to museums?"

"Art historian he, henceforth obliged."

"Who is an art historian?" asked the Cardinal from across the dining room, "and what obliges him to do what?"

The two of them were speechless, and the Cardinal went on. "I am asking you, Doctor Claudi. You have no right to keep our friend here from playing the violin. We are all waiting for him, our hostess has dispatched me to rescue him from your claws. Let him go, and you stay here with me."

As soon as Klagonov had closed the drawing room door behind him, the Cardinal said: "Now, now, now! You really have obtained the impossible." And he stared at Leonardo with a devilish smile that reminded him of his worst Jesuit censors. "The *impossible*. She asked me, her archenemy, who converted her daughter to Catholicism, to rescue you from that fool. But after this, what follows can only be what may seem impossible to you, my young Burino; namely, that our Protestant hostess will kick you out of her house to save her Catholic daughter's marriage. You smile like a fool, you don't seem to realize the gravity of your behavior tonight—you and that Russian prince, who comes here whining like a dog that's been kicked out of the house, since Mary's sister did just that to him."

"Mary's sister? Does Mary have a sister?"

"*Does* she have a sister, he asks!!! Hahaha . . . what a joke!!!! *Does* she have a sister!!! She has *three*, my young friend, and the eldest has been put away in an insane asylum in Berlin, because she dared to divorce her Mamma-appointed husband and wanted to run off with an obscure penniless pianist, an Italian probably. . . . The second sister seems to be a perfect goose, who obeys Mamma and is now engaged to marry some solid Protestant industrialist or banker, I don't know which, but she comes after our darling Mary, who married a Roman painter to spite Mamma, who had prevented her from marrying a rich Neapolitan widower, then comes darling Ludmilla, the pet of all these Roman good-for-nothings who frequent the Caffè Greco and Aragno . . . Ludmilla the amazon, Ludmilla the mistress of that other silly fool you were talking to, that American sculptor who owes his fame to the fact that he goes up the steps of Palazzo Altieri on horseback. . . ." Leonardo heard all this and a lot more about the stupid Hazeltine, the stupid Romans, the stupid Protestant Jupitress, and the not-too-stupid, but totally confused little doctor from down there—namely, himself—who might still not lose Mary's affection and her mother's approval, if . . . and if . . . and if . . .

And Leonardo accepted all these ifs like a good little pupil really intending to learn from his great teacher, indeed worshipping him as he had never worshipped any of his teachers before. But what the teacher didn't know was that the fairy tale in which Leonardo was living had been suddenly transformed. Simply by mentioning the wealthy Neapolitan widower, the Cardinal had turned Cinderello into a toad. No time to cry now about spilled milk that had never been his, but how it hurt to realize that she had loved not him, but that bereaved clown of a Gennariello, a totally forgotten figure in his life. Of course, Leonardo had won Mary's heart on that famous February 3, 1893, in the museum of Naples, but this also meant that she had lied to him today and yesterday, several times. Would I have given up everything as I did had I known it two days ago? he asked himself, while still trying not to lose any of the Cardinal's advice. Too late to think of it now, he acknowledged with horror. I am trapped for the rest of my life, and would still be, even if I were to learn the worst about her. All I can do now is become so famous as a scientist and so attractive as a man that none of these people here, nor anyone anywhere in the future, may mean anything to her, *ever*! I know I'm a poor Burino from down there, a donkey lost amid sounds, as the Cardinal would say, but I must prevail. Let's listen and learn.

". . . So now you understand what kind of hornet's nest you've fallen into," said the Cardinal, squeezing Leonardo's arm, and Leonardo smiled tragically. "You don't have to look so despairing, young man. This is life, and learning how to live in the best circumstances—namely, when you are well and happy—is the completion of your medical science, which concentrates only on how not to die. *How to live:* that is the question Shakespeare understood and you don't. But let's join the musicians. I suppose you're going back to your hometown tomorrow, but the next time you come to Rome, see me before you see anyone else. Promise?"

"Promise," said Leonardo, trying to look a little less sad than before, and so they entered the drawing room just as Mary and Klagonov were beginning to play a new piece.

Leonardo didn't like difficult music, chamber music, music for piano and violin; he only liked the pianola, or the piano as accompaniment to Neapolitan songs. He loved the village band, especially when it played Italian operas, but then of course he loved Italian opera—and church music, and the tarantella, which he danced very well. Here he instantly recognized difficult music, but more instantly even than that, he recognized Mary in love, and, again, not with him, this time with Klagonov, and he had to restrain his first impulse which was to go and smash *his own* Stradivarius (wasn't he still the master of the house? What bitter irony . . .) over the traitor's head, and then throw the traitor himself out of the window, because that is the least one can do with a man who has made you *cornuto*.* After which, bang the piano shut and send Mary straight to her room, shouting: "Enough of this nonsense! Get out of here, you stupid girl. . . . I'll teach you to play music . . ." (or some even stronger phrase to that effect), but this whole second part of his revenge he kept vague, because it was to come after the first part had left everyone aghast, and *really* so, not just pretending, as they did now, to prove how deeply they were affected by the music. He knew these were all dreams, because the reality was, as expected, God's punishment for all his sins. Oh, how he hated everything, beginning with himself . . . and ending with Mary!

He tried to look away from the piano, and it was even worse. The whole room seemed to have been transformed into the Caffè Greco, or the street in front of it. He recognized D'Annunzio, who seemed to recognize him for a moment and turn his face away in disgust. But the others . . . oh, the others were all talking about him, and, in a way, this did him good. At least they weren't listening to the musical conspiracy between those two, who kept exchanging amorous glances and smiles, as if no one could see them. Every time Mary and Klagonov exchanged a glance to agree on the moment of her entry into the act, after his *solo* flight into the highest regions of musical rapture, Leonardo tried to warn her with a dirty look that this was becoming a scandal. But he was too far away from them, so

---

* Cuckold.

he decided to stop all this nonsense, cost him what it may, and was walking angrily and noisily towards the piano when the Cardinal noticed and forced him back to his place along the wall, pulling him by his coattail like a naughty child, while the scandal went on, Mary nodding more and more tenderly to Klagonov and he almost falling over her as he tormented his instrument to make it whine more amorously to the soft heartbeat of the piano. His eyes were full of tears, and his sighs were obscene.

"What a whore," whispered the Cardinal into Leonardo's ear.

"Who?" snapped Leonardo, making everyone turn in his direction, except for the musicians, of course.

"Beethoven," answered the Cardinal, and Leonardo, in extreme anguish, cried: "I don't understand French."

"You should say German. French he was not, but a great genius anyway, even when he became a whore. Just listen to this . . ." And he looked at him with all the mimicry of a woman at the height of passion. Leonardo's eyes turned right and left to avoid him, but everybody else seemed to be having an orgasm too: elderly ladies staring at the leg of a chair, or at the highest point on the ceiling, elderly gentlemen staring at the hat of some lady in front of them, young men and women closing their eyes and slowly rocking like ships in a storm. Only the two conspirators were still counting and looking at each other with the utmost attention, to lead the whole audience deeper and deeper into the pits of sin. Then that devil of a Cardinal whispered into his ear again: "No wonder Tolstoy saw this as the symbol of woman's perdition!"

Thank God it stopped then, and everybody was applauding. Not I, he thought, as he made for the dining room door again.

"Where are you going?" asked the Cardinal.

"To piss. May I?"

"Of course, of course. But come back, and be nice to the Baron."

"What baron?"

"Baron Lumbroso, who was very hurt by your bad behavior. And also—"

"I will, I will."

"Let me finish: the cook is also hurt. You praised his metabolism. Stop in the kitchen on your way back and praise his cooking."

"I will."

"All right, go now."

Leonardo was in a great hurry, but not for physical reasons. He had noticed that Mary was looking for him in the crowd, and he wanted to be seen to ignore her. Yet, as he left, he felt so sorry for her being slighted by him that he was ready to burst into tears. He was sobbing so loudly as he entered the dark bathroom without turning on the light that he heard his own sobs echoing from the walls, and this sobered him at once. Him, not the echo, which acquired a terrifying physical form and embraced him and kissed him on the mouth, wetting him with a whole gust of hot tears. Klagonov.

"*Fratellissimo carissimo,* you alone understand me could, if knew truth of my sorrow."

"I do. Ludmilla."

"*Gospody Pamilyui . . .* don't that name speak!!! You make me cry."

"Well, you're crying already, so what?"

"Oh, cruel those who happy are they! Mary crying was because happy of you, I because unhappy of that *innamable* creature."

Leonardo felt better. He turned on the light and forced Klagonov to wash his face under the faucet, then sent him back to the drawing room, but decided to let Mary suffer a little more, while he went to the kitchen to praise not only the cook's food but everything about him. Aaaah, how good it felt to be untoaded again.

"Sir!" he said, as he saw a white form standing in front of the kitchen range.

"God, you frightened me, sir. . . ." It was a girl's voice.

God, he felt like answering her, you do anything but frighten me. . . . She was so beautiful, so bursting with sensuousness, so young, and so little covered by a very short nightgown, that his whole body went up in flames, inside, outside, from head to foot to fingertips, rotating like a great wheel of fire.

"You are the doctor who's going to see us all tomorrow," she said, and he gulped without answering because his voice had abandoned him.

"I have a pain here in my chest. Do you want to see me now?"

He gulped and gulped, and managed to ask: "Here?" with his eyes on the door.

"In there, where you saw the coachman," she said, "it won't take
long."

"But . . ."

"No one's coming. I can assure you."

He followed her, staggering, and she had hardly closed the door
behind them before he fell into her arms, panting and biting and
sucking all over that hot cushion of flesh. When they reached the
summit, which was soon, and every social shell was broken, she
called him by his first name, and he let her do so without asking for
hers, because in that ignorance was the last rampart of his rank.
Suddenly a faint noise from the kitchen made them instantly withdraw into their social separation.

"What shall I do?" he asked. "Shut up," she ordered, "and don't
move until I call you."

By the time he heard her whisper his name from outside the
door, he didn't dare answer, because he had reached another summit, one more familiar to him than the summit of sexual desire; it
had been his one constant experience since the earliest days of his
childhood and all through college: the summit of total humiliation.
"This *little* child, this *big* child, this *little* boy, this *big* boy, this
adolescent, must be locked up in the dark closet and stay there until
his teachers are satisfied that he has seen the light." And his teachers were all priests, as friendly to him as the Cardinal tonight: they
had all been attracted by something sacerdotal in him, and hoped to
shape him into a fighting priest, perhaps a Pope, who knows? "Are
you there, Leonardo?" she whispered again. "Yes," he answered.
But when she appeared, he turned his eyes away from her and
apologized in shame. "Oh, . . . sorry!" Because what she had
found to cover up her nudity was far more obscene to him than even
her wild sexual prurience: she was wearing a chambermaid's uniform
—long black dress, white apron, hair up, and the white crown of
slavery on top of her head. These two white items in starched linen
were the only things that distinguished her from his mother or his
aunts, while her attitude was so typically theirs that it made him
even humbler. Now this obedient maid assumed the same air of
submissiveness to a distant authority. His personal feelings were not
supposed to exist. But they did, the moment he was freed from
humiliation and fear. He touched her breasts, but she withdrew,

quickly, saying: "The bathroom is out there, to the left. I must prepare the drink for the little boy."

Leonardo obeyed again, feeling more guilty for having touched a servant's uniform than for having possessed the whole servant, in defiance of Mary's rights. Who is the liar here? he thought, remembering his angry tears of a few minutes earlier in the selfsame bathroom. And yet, as he hurriedly rid himself of all traces of sin, his conscience seemed to be washed clean of all ugly feelings of jealousy. He was impatient now to go back to the drawing room, in order not to make his absence seem too long, but, just as he was crossing the corridor, he saw the maid opening a door in the distance, and he heard her say: "Here, here comes the medicine, now I know my little darling will stop feeling sick."

Instantly he felt hurt and conscience-stricken. The mention of sickness touched him, but that maternal tone was an insult to Mary, and this of course he couldn't tolerate, so he decided to follow the maid, and if Mary discovered him there, what better place for him to be, so late at night?

He barely had time to enter the bedroom before the German governess, in a long white nightgown and with curlers all over her balding head, pushed him out, cackling protests in a broken Italian he could hardly understand. The maid laughed, and he heard the little boy laugh too, but couldn't see him behind the maid's back. "Shut up and go to bed," he said to Fräulein Luther, pointing the way to her corner. "I am a doctor, d'you think I never see people in their nightgowns?"

After which he said to the maid: "Cover him up, I'm going to open the window. This room stinks of German perspiration."

But Fräulein Luther jumped out of her bed again to shoo him away from the window, shouting: "Malaria, malaria . . . night air brings malaria."

"Come on, what nonsense is that? *This* is malaria, not what's outside." And he walked towards the window, which was hidden by two sets of heavy brocade curtains. The maid rushed to his help and found the wires to pull them apart, then he opened the window and the shutters, letting not only a gust of clean air come in, but also the full moon in all its glory. A silence followed. Out there, in the center of that huge still-life, was a round, white shape surmounted by a tall white crown and a glittering ball: the Cupola of St. Peter's. On either side of the moon, which seemed to have devoured all the stars in the sky, two invisible dogs were measuring the night, barking to one another their position in the ocean of eternity, like ships at sea. Leonardo had frequently seen these ships along the Ionian coast, blinking at one another in the dark, and had imagined the fabulous ruins of ancient Greece beyond the roundness of the watery world. Between the Cupola and the windowsill: the subdued shapes of slanting roofs, broken lines further broken into so many tiny round waves; the curved tiles of the ancient city and the occasional squares of painters' attics, all mirroring the moon. The street below: a dark river of silence. Suddenly the silence was broken by the voice of the Pope; namely, the clock of St. Peter's, striking ONE. And all other church bells in Rome seemed to acknowledge that infallible papal dictate. "My God, how late," he said aloud. He hadn't been up that late since the night before his wedding, five long years earlier. Heavy with thoughts of guilt, he turned his back on the moon and what he saw frightened him more than if he had seen the devil in person, ready to grab him by the throat and take him straight to hell: the little boy had also been attracted by the moon and there he stood, transfixed by what he saw, his face serious, almost angry, as the faces of children often are when they dread adult interference with their adoration of the miraculous, and this face, mad with murderous jealousy, was one Leonardo knew very well. Now the truth was out: the red-haired man at the café had been the father of this boy! Instantly, Leonardo replayed the whole late afternoon scene, to retrace the words he had spoken and try to discover how much he had revealed of Mary's secret to her husband. "Everything, everything," he concluded aloud. "It's a matter of hours, and then the fairy tale is over. Finished forever!"

The little boy looked at him and smiled. Now he looked like his mother.

"What fairy tale?" he asked, in her voice, and with a heavy Russian accent.

"What fairy tale? Oh, . . . any fairy tale."

"I want to hear it."

But the maid interfered. "You'll catch cold, go back to bed."

"No."

"Yes!"

"She's right," said Leonardo, "go back to bed now."

"But I want to see the moon."

Before Leonardo could answer, Fräulein Luther shouted from her bed: "Malaria! Asthma!" as if ordering the maid to fetch them.

"No malaria and no asthma," said Leonardo. "I am the doctor here."

The little boy laughed, and asked: "Will you tell me the fairy tale?"

"I'll sit with you and talk to you, but you must get into bed, because it's getting cold."

An icy wind was blowing in now, lifting the curtains like huge ghosts in the moonlight. Leonardo shut the window, without shutting the curtains, and the little boy called from his bed: "I'm in bed now. Come and tell me the fairy tale."

And just as Leonardo was sitting down and taking the little boy's hand into his own, the door was flung open and Mary stormed in, shouting: "*Gospody!!! OODJASS!!!* Is my darling little bird very ill?"

"Not at all," said Leonardo, and the maid confirmed it: "He had a seizure but then the doctor came in, and now he's fine again."

"*Garnicht!*" shouted Fräulein Luther, adding her usual order for Malaria and Asthma in staccato German.

But Mary wasn't listening. She stood in awe before that vision of family happiness, like a child in front of a Christmas tree, shaking her head in wondrous disbelief, and when she had been sufficiently awed, she walked slowly to the bed and knelt down in front of it, to kiss first Kostia's hand and then Leonardo's.

"Bless my two darlings," she said. "And the moon too, our dear, full moon. . . . Let's go and thank the moon," she said, getting up and dragging Leonardo to the window, to ask him in whispers: "What is it? Tell me the truth, no matter how frightful."

"Nothing. Your child is perfectly well."

"But you? What happened to you?"

"Nothing."

"I know you even in the dark. I can feel disaster. Or is it the child?"

"Neither the child nor disaster. I couldn't be happier."

"On your honor?"

"On my honor. I'm radiant with happiness." Then he added: ". . . if you are."

"Tell me frankly, what is it? The Cardinal said you had gone to make peace with the cook, so I ran to the kitchen and looked for you even in the wardrobe, but found no one there, so I came here. Did you have a fight with the cook? Or was it the coachman? It must have been the coachman. Tell me the truth."

"Oh no. The coachman and I are on the best of terms. Like brothers."

"You spoke to him?"

"I gave him medical advice, and all the servants asked to be examined by me tomorrow. The cook was angry, it seems, because I praised his metabolism instead of his cooking. That's all." Leonardo tried to sound casual and to hide his face from the moon, because the thought of what might have happened if Mary had looked for him in the wardrobe only a few minutes earlier gave him that delayed shock of terror that makes mountain climbers faint when they have reached the other side of the precipice.

"Mamma," wailed the little boy. "I want to hear the fairy tale."

"Quiet, we're talking about important things." Then, to Leonardo, in whispers: "I worry about this familiarity with the servants."

"Why?" said Leonardo, trying to sound even more casual.

"They're ALL Italians, except for Bernhard and the cook."

"So am I," said he, now very cheerfully and loud enough to be overheard by the maid.

"*Gospody!!!*" Mary replied, in a shriek of horror, then, in whispers again: "Promise me on your mother's grave that you will never, never say that again."

"Why?"

"Because that's what the Monster says."

"I swear," said Leonardo, feeling suddenly relieved of all his previous terrors.

"That's better," she said. "Because you are not Italian, thank God."

"No? What am I?"

"You're . . . a saint."

"Mamma . . . the fairy tale. It'll be too late."

"It will not."

"The doctor said so."

"He just assured me it will never, never end. Isn't that true . . .
Doctor?"

"It is, but it's also very late, and now let's go to bed. You, little
boy, what's your name?"

"Kostia."

"Kostia? But that's a woman's name."

The little boy was indignant: "No, it isn't. My Grossmamachen
wouldn't have given me a woman's name."

"I apologize, I know nothing of Russian names. But the correct
term for that other word is grandmother."

"Oh no. Grandmother is somebody else, isn't it true, Mamachen?"

"It is, it is, but your . . . your new—" Leonardo stopped her by
pinching her arm. "Ouch . . ." she said and Kostia stared at her in
the dark, trying to understand what had happened.

"Lie down and sleep now," said Mary, kneeling next to him and
kissing his hand again.

The little boy obeyed, but the moment he heard Leonardo say to
his mother, "I'm going to leave now too, I'll see you all tomorrow,"
he began to breathe with difficulty, and Mary rushed to his bedside
again. "*Gospody*, another attack!!!"

Leonardo rushed back too, and put his hand on Kostia's forehead.
Instantly, the attack disappeared.

"Asthma, Malaria," mumbled Fräulein Luther from her dark
corner.

"Quiet," said Leonardo, and Kostia laughed. "And you, Kostia,
you are a man, with a real man's name, you obey your doctor now
and go to sleep, or I won't be back here when you wake up, but if
you obey me and sleep quietly, I will also go to sleep, and the
moment you wake up, I'll be here."

"And you'll tell me the fairy tale?"

"I will."

"Promise?"

"Promise."

Mary and Leonardo waited silently in the dark for a few minutes before daring to leave, and the boy seemed to be breathing normally, but then Fräulein Luther, who had slipped out of bed without being seen, pulled the curtains shut and Kostia instantly began to wheeze again and muttered something in German, to which Fräulein Luther answered in the same language.

"What are they saying?" asked Leonardo.

"He wants to see the moon and she says he mustn't, because the full moon is dangerous. It makes for sleepwalking."

"I'm glad to see that ignorance and superstition are not Italian prerogatives. Northern barbarians have them too. Tell her to shut up and go to bed." Then, before Mary could translate, he snapped at the governess: "Let him have his moon if he wants to, and don't fill him with your silly nonsense."

After a few more minutes of silent watching, he and Mary left and quietly closed the door behind them.

"Do you think I could leave without saying goodbye?" he asked, as they reached the entrance hall.

"Absolutely not. Mamachen is quite angry at you for the way you behaved, both at dinner and afterwards."

"But it's one in the morning."

"So what? You have no duties in Rome. Your duty is to pretend that you're just another guest, so that no one will suspect anything."

"After what they've already seen and heard?"

"Why must you be so cynical? Or don't you care if someone goes and reports to my husband that I have a lover?"

"You never used that word *husband* before, and we are not lovers yet, so why are *you* turning cynical?"

"Darling, let's not have a fight. Lover is the first word these awful Romans will use when they see a married woman showing a preference for one of her guests. This will be especially noticed in my case, because I never, never showed any preference for anyone, all these years."

"Except for Gennariello."

"And who is Gennariello?"

Leonardo hesitated for a moment. An inner voice was warning him that he might be making the mistake of his life, but moral considerations prevailed: either her flesh was as weak as his, and he must forgive his own trespasses to stand by her, a weaker vessel of sin, or it was not, in which case she needed a still stronger guardian of her virtue than he did of his.

Mary was standing in front of the door, terror-stricken by the prospect of his leaving in defiance of superior orders.

"Who is Gennariello?" she asked, more timidly.

"Who is Gennariello? I notice that your voice is wavering, though you insist on pretending you don't know. Well, let's pretend I haven't noticed. Gennariello was your bereaved suitor when I met you in that museum."

"Was *that* his first name? My God, you're right, it was! Thank you for reminding me! I've been wracking my brains *for years* to remember it, and *all* I could think of was his *last* name!"

He didn't like her flippancy, nor her wracking her brains for years, all those years she had made him believe belonged to him.

"So I was right: you did prefer Gennariello."

"Darling, how can you be so illogical?"

"You don't wrack your brains in pursuit of a fact you don't prefer over others that are stored in your memory."

Mary kept looking at him, and then closing her eyes and turning her head away from him, and now he knew why: his logic was the same as her husband's, for whom he was beginning to develop a sense of kinship and also a strange gratitude—obviously he was not a man to let his wife AND his mother-in-law get away with their ideas of women's independence, and he regarded her present confusion as evidence of her good faith. Obviously he, Leonardo, had scored two victories: one over Gennariello in 1893, and another one now, over her husband and whatever was left of her confused images of the past, and in due course, who knows?, he might even make her accept the fact that he was a real Italian man. For the moment he accepted her plan to have him stay on and act like just another guest, absurd though this plan was, and what made him even more lenient was the sight of the Cardinal's robe moving slowly towards them from the end of the long corridor. "Enough now, love, the past is the past and the future is what counts. Don't turn around, and behave normally, because the Cardinal is coming to find us."

She smiled and whispered: "Do you still love me?"

He smiled back.

"Would you still love me if what you said were true?"

"Of course. Alas, nothing on earth would make me love you less."

"Me too, but I assure you that it *isn't* true. I never, never could stand that idiot of . . ."

She didn't dare pronounce the name, so Leonardo generously helped her: "Of a Gennariello, I know, and I also know that you were unaware of any deep desire to find it out. Women usually don't know what's happening to them until after it has happened. My advice is: consider yourself lucky it hasn't, as I do. Let's think only of the future, and build our own nest, away from all that moral filth, and . . ."

"Well, well, well, that's where they would be, two little pigeons, cooing together in the dark, to escape from their bad consciences. . . . Children, children . . . *children*, that's what we all are, until we reach old age . . . so, don't strain your father's willingness to understand and forgive."

Mary blushed and lowered her head like a guilty child, and this pleased Leonardo so much, that he decided to show her how much authority he had gained in those few hours. "Come, Mary," he said, "His Eminence is our friend."

She looked at him incredulously, still trying to avoid the Cardinal's eye, and the Cardinal said: "Friend, yes, of course, I am everybody's friend, as long as they behave . . . so, don't mistake my goodness for laxity! Mary knows where to stop, but you don't even know where to begin. . . . All right, follow me now, and you, young man, be nice to the Baron, will you?"

As soon as the Cardinal had walked a few steps ahead of them, Mary asked in whispers: "What is he up to with the Baron? Do you know?"

"Why? Don't you like the Cardinal?"

"I don't know. Mamachen hates him, because he's the quintessence of all that's wrong with the Catholic Church, and he hates her, because she's Protestant, but recently he has been so nice to us that we have both had a chance to admire him for his culture and his philosophical *finesse*. The Monster hates him, and he hates the Monster, which is also a good recommendation."

They couldn't continue, because they were now inside the drawing room, secure in their happiness, and therefore more than eager to be hypocritical with everyone, without the least sense of guilt. This is what happiness does to lovers, besides making them sincere and kind: it is their indifference that makes all the difference.

Leonardo knew this too, and he felt kindly towards the Cardinal, especially because of Mary's doubts about him. As master of this palace again, he felt he must impress everybody with his goodness, especially the Cardinal, and, through him, the Pope. If only I were my cousin Crocifisso, he thought, I would open the Pope's eyes to the beauty of Progress, and of all the New Things he seems to fear so much, because that is, as the Cardinal says, the culmination of all medicine: *mens sana in corpore sano*, and to stay healthy, the body must live in a healthy world, a world of universal politeness and love. But where love isn't possible, because circumstances forbid it, reciprocal gratitude must take its place. And he hoped the little servant girl felt grateful to him for the joy he had given her, as he was grateful to her for the sense of well-being she had given him. How good it felt, to be rid of that sting of repressed desire. By taking that burden from him, she had allowed him to exercise that honest and courageous *pursuit of the facts*, which had made Mary see the light. Oh, what an endless future of happiness he saw in front of himself and Mary!!!! Always be truthful, always push your logic to its ultimate consequences, and others cannot fail to see the Truth, he dictated to himself as his rule of moral guidance.

"Darling," said Mary, whom he hadn't seen rushing towards him through the room, "Mamachen says you must join her circle the moment Mommsen is through with his discussion on the political situation in Germany. But remember: tomorrow you must wear either of the other two sets of cufflinks, because she has noticed that you chose the new ones, and she would be so happy if she saw our new man, our true man in the family, wearing the cufflinks of the last true men in our family: her father and mine. Promise? And, in case I forgot, you should also wear that other white vest: this one is cheap, and it shows. I must go."

And she disappeared to tell her mother that she had delivered her message.

My God, how complicated life is in society, he thought, imagining the scene he would have with Schillasi the next morning. I can

only get these things back and keep his good will if I make him a
positive offer, something he will value more than moonstones and
gold. . . .

With these generous thoughts, he hurried towards the Cardinal,
who was hunting from group to group for listeners and feeling
slightly unwanted, for the moment he approached, the conversation
froze to a standstill and the group began to dissolve.

"Your Eminence . . ."

"Oh, it's you again. What is it now? Have you spoken to Baron
Lumbroso?"

"I will, in a minute, but I have a great favor to ask."

"What is it? Tell me quickly, I have no time to waste."

"Oh, . . . then I won't."

"No, tell me, but be brief."

"It's about that professor of art history. He's a great unrecog-
nized scholar who's the victim of his own lack of self-confidence. If
your good offices could procure him an honorary Ph.D. by the
Vatican—"

"Is he a serious scholar?"

"Very serious, but, as I was saying—"

"Go and tell the Baron about him. He's a professor of ancient
history and a pupil of Mommsen, and looking for just that type of
person. It will make a perfect excuse for you to approach him again.
Go now, and don't forget to tell him that the idea comes from
me."

Leonardo went straight to the Baron, who was engrossed in conversation with a very tall, solemn-looking gentleman and an equally tall
and solemn-looking lady who were obviously brother and sister. The
Baron being very short, his two listeners seemed to be atoning for
their excessive height by bending towards him—over him almost—
like trees in the wind. The old gentleman's foliage was his white
beard, and his sister's, the long green feathers coiling around her hat
and sweeping down almost onto her left shoulder.

"Mister Baron," said Leonardo, "I understand from the Cardinal's hints that I wasn't very polite to you, and I have come to do
my little duty; so, letting bygones be bygones, I hear that you need a
scholar. I have just the man for you. . . ." He couldn't go on. The
trees had stopped moving, and the little Baron seemed transfixed by

real terror, as if he had heard not a human voice, but the roar of a lion coming to devour him. *Heard,* but not *seen*: he wasn't looking, and neither were the two trees but their paralysis seemed to spring from a different cause; they were immensely amused. After a short silence, in which Leonardo participated as a curious spectator, the Baron said to the big trees: "I deeply apologize for this untimely interruption."

"Oh, not at all, not at all," said the two trees, trembling up there in a flurry of hilarity, "do go on, it's most interesting."

The Baron was about to resume his interesting tale, but Leonardo interrupted him again and said: "They're right, it's not for you to apologize, I can do it myself, I'm not a child."

This time the Baron did look at Leonardo, pleadingly, like an early Christian trying to melt the lion's heart, having lost all faith in the hearts of his compatriots who have paid their tickets for the circus and don't want to miss the show. But Leonardo interpreted this look as encouragement, and said to the big trees: "I'm sorry I interrupted the Baron, but he can go on now, I know he must have an interesting story to tell."

The trees began to be shaken by different winds: the white-beard-tree by anger, and the hat-feather-tree by joy, while the poor little Baron seemed to have been transformed into a frightened dwarf, caught in a fairy tale bigger and less friendly than his own.

Again, Leonardo read the change in the winds as favorable to his ship, and said: "I know: I've made another blunder and I must correct it at once: I failed to introduce myself. Leonardo Claudi from Laterza. And you?"

The white beard shook so violently that his roots began to creak—indeed, the old gentleman began to walk away in anger—but his sister stopped him and said to Leonardo: "I am Ersilia Lovatelli, and I know your whole family."

"You do? That's good news . . . tell me all about them."

"Aren't you the Marquess of Navarrete?"

"God forbid, no. Do I sound like a pipsqueak? These degenerate aristocrats with their Spanish roots, bloated with Spanish pride and stupidity, they all have voices like pipsqueaks. How could you mistake me for one of them?"

Now the trees stood firm, and the little dwarf almost sank into a rabbit hole. Luckily for them all, the Cardinal came sailing from the other end of the room, heralded by his sonorous voice pouring jets of warm honey over the entire scene: "Look who's here: Prince Caetani, the Duke of Sermoneta, and dear Donna Ersilia Lovatelli. . . . What a surprise to see you. You must have come to fetch Mommsen. If I'm not mistaken, he's staying with you this time."

"Yes, he is," said the Duke, still shaken by anger and red to the ears, but standing bravely in the storm like the proudest of oaks. Lightning was visible through his thick white eyebrows and Donna Ersilia's green feathers.

"And of course you have found the right company here: our dear Baron is, as you certainly know, Italy's greatest epigraphist, and Mommsen's closest associate."

"We know, we know," said the Duke and his sister at the same time, which gave the Baron the strength he needed to resume his own tale, in spite of the hurricane.

"We were speaking about laziness, and I was saying to the Duke that it is so much a part of human nature we may say it is present in the entire universe. It only gives way to feverish activity in those rare human beings who have a precise goal in their life—a positive stimulus, if I may borrow the term from modern psychology."

"You may," said Leonardo. The Cardinal stopped him with a cold glance.

"Mommsen *is* one of those rare human beings, however. I have been trying for years to find out if and when Mommsen had been in Florence between 1865 and 1870. A few days ago I happened to be in Florence myself . . ."

"Lucky dog," said Leonardo, "I've never been there yet."

". . . MYSELF, and went to see if the famous Laurenziana Library had any records of his passage. They didn't . . ."

"Too bad," said Leonardo, under his breath this time. Lightning flashed upon him from all sides.

". . . they didn't, because no record of people studying there or of the subject of their research exists previous to the year 1870. But the librarian regaled me with an interesting episode. It seems that a few months ago, Mommsen arrived in Florence on a Saturday night, and asked permission to spend a couple of hours in the library on Sunday. The librarian took upon himself the responsibility of keeping the library open, in defiance of all the rules for public buildings, and the next day Mommsen arrived at eight in the morning, sat down with the precious manuscript he had chosen to consult, and got up at five in the afternoon; nine hours without any interruption whatever. Extraordinary what one may do, when moved by a deep interest."

"That's me, when I was young."

"That's all of us, when we were young," said the Baron with resentment, "but Mommsen is eighty-five."

The two trees nodded seriously, the Cardinal bowed deeply and left, and the Baron went on, looking after him:

"There is the only liberally minded priest I have ever met, and he has read everything."

"Granted, but then he destroys everything with his mania for the paradox."

"There I beg to disagree," said Leonardo. "He is the only priest I ever met who is openly in favor of divorce."

"Impossible!" said the Duke and the Baron together.

"What do you mean?" asked Leonardo, getting angry. "Why the devil should I invent such a thing? He told me that, in so many words, during dinner."

"Another one of his stunts to impress the simpleminded," said Donna Ersilia, with an air of timidity that charmed Leonardo, even as he replied, "We might say the same thing about his antiliberal stunts." The feather-tree shook as in an earthquake, and so did the poor little dwarf, but the Duke just looked on, smiling benevolently, as he commented: "Yes, yes, indeed we might. This is a very valid hypothesis."

"But I am certain he wasn't performing stunts, in either case," said Leonardo, "because that would make him the simpleminded one. An intelligent man wants to impress intelligent people, not fools. And whether you or I are fools is not the subject of our present discussion. We were discussing the Cardinal, not one another."

There were no trees and no dwarf any more; they had metamorphosed into a stunned audience which attracted all the other small groups in the room. People flocked around the performer and asked

for more, without bothering to go through the formalities of personal introduction. But since the Cardinal was among the first to
arrive, the original audience re-botanized itself at once, and now
even the little dwarf began to act like a tree and asked Leonardo in
a very artificial voice, "Weren't you telling me about a scholar you
wanted to introduce to me? I'm so sorry I interrupted you."

"The scholar," said Leonardo very slowly and nervously, "showed
great promise in many fields: in history of art, archaeology, ancient
history, et cetera, but he had to devote his time to the servile and
humiliating work of guiding rich foreigners through the museums of
Rome, because he was too poor to complete his academic training.
A very sad life, when you think that this man knows *everything*, he
is a walking encyclopedia, and is very highly thought of by all the
greatest foreign scholars, but he's quite unknown here, because Italy
is always a cruel stepmother to her best sons. I wish someone would
get him a degree, or some sort of recognition for his services to
Italian culture before he dies. He is an old man. . . ."

"Oh, what a heartbreaking story," said Donna Ersilia. "What can
we do for him?"

"I have the answer," said the Baron triumphantly, "I can send
him to my co-father-in-law Marco Besso; he's about to build the
biggest and most splendid private library in Rome, and the services
of an art historian will certainly be needed; if he's more of an
archaeologist than an art historian, his services will be needed too."

"How wonderful, and how kind of you; such an ideal solution,"
said Donna Ersilia.

Most of the newcomers, except for the Cardinal, were now moving away murmuring all sorts of scurrilous things about the poor
Burino and her, calling her an old goose, and even worse. It was so
embarrassing that the Duke simply walked off and the Baron felt he
had to catch Leonardo's attention, to avoid some major explosion.
The first warning signs were already visible in Leonardo's flushed
face.

"How do you like Rome?" the Baron asked.

"As a city I like it," said Leonardo, "but let me tell you quite
frankly, the population is hostile."

Both the Baron and Donna Ersilia couldn't help laughing at this,
which gained them the approval of their detractors in other groups,

while poor Leonardo felt all the hostility concentrated on him, and he looked really helpless now.

"Why don't you come to my house tomorrow night for dinner with your scholar friend?" asked Donna Ersilia.

"I can't," said Leonardo, "and I can't tell you why, because that would be indiscreet toward third persons."

"Oh," she said, "but your protégé will come, I hope."

"I imagine he will, if he has nothing better to do."

"Send him to me first," said the Baron, handing him his calling card. "Any time between eight and twelve in the morning, not one minute later."

His face was flushed with anger, and Donna Ersilia, seeing this, smiled kindly to Leonardo and said: "Now let's join Mommsen, we had promised to come and get him before it was too late for a walk to the Pincio in the full moon. He loves this part of town: who wouldn't? Of course the Roman population is hostile, but in a way you must understand: it is the kind of hostility that replaces real war. Rome has conquered so much and lost so much and kept so much of what she lost, in the sense of historical experience, that the Romans still behave as if they owned the world, and this prevents them from wanting wars with anyone, ever. That was the first infallible mistake of the first infallible Pope: to believe that the Romans would fight the excommunicated King of Italy just because the Pope had called them Defenders of the Faith. But here is Mommsen. Let's hear what he has to say."

Mommsen was at the center of a lively discussion with a group of young men, all newcomers to the party.

"That's a delusion," Mommsen was saying. "There are no traces of prehistory in this country. On the other hand, there is plenty to be learned about the beginnings of Europe from the prehistory of the Scandinavian countries."

"That's a lie," Leonardo interrupted, staring at Mommsen, who smiled gently and said: "Don't get excited, young man. I know you don't like such a statement, and I myself doubted it before I completed my volume on the southern Italian dialects. But I don't see why you should object to it. After all, you Apulians are closer to Greece than to Rome, in character, in philosophical tradition and in language. You always hated Rome, the predatory instincts of the

Romans, and their pernicious rhetoric, which found its highest expression in that notorious windbag, Cicero."

"When Cicero was windbagging in Rome, you Teutons were grassing in the forests of Germany," said Leonardo.

"Correct, but that doesn't prevent us from realizing today that Cicero was a windbag, so perhaps we were lucky to be grassing instead of being corrupted by his ideas.

"You're right," said Leonardo, in an outburst of joy. "I confess I've never read a word of Cicero—except in school, when I was learning Latin, but that was at the age of sixteen. And I want you to know that I have always detested Rome and loved Greece. And I gave up the study of archaeology and ancient history in order to study the living in everyday history, and I have become the mayor of my hometown. . . ."

The Duke of Sermoneta touched Mommsen on the shoulder and dragged him away from Leonardo for a whispered consultation. When Mommsen came back, Leonardo noticed something in his expression he didn't like, and asked bluntly: "Has that man been saying things against me?"

"No," said Mommsen, blushing.

"Are you sure? I think he has, because now his sister is angry with me."

"Is she? Why?"

"Because she's stupid. Just a moment ago I began to explain to her why I had abandoned archaeology, but she didn't even let me finish my first sentence and ran away."

"Never mind her. Why don't you tell me about your political fights? You are the mayor of your hometown, I hear."

"Who told you?"

"Never mind. Tell me about yourself and your work. You must be a friend of Salvemini."

"Salvemini? That pig?"

"Why is he a pig? He's a man like you: an Apulian who fights for his own people, and has great courage."

"Courage? He's a Socialist."

"What's wrong with that?"

"Socialists are pigs. All leftists are pigs."

"Oh . . ."

"I mean: present company excluded."

"I'm not a Socialist, but I *am* the founder of the leftist progressive party in Prussia that opposed Bismarck, and in Italy I respect the Socialists as being the only honest and constructive party you have."

Leonardo felt utterly destroyed. In the distance he noticed Sophie and Mary looking somewhat disturbed after a brief word with Donna Ersilia. Mommsen noticed too. Taking Leonardo by the arm, and pretending to be engrossed in a highly intellectual discussion with him, he swept past all the people who were now uniting against this provincial doctor. "Let me put it this way," he began. "Now that religion and philosophy are dead, and the liberal arts, which are the true exercises in freedom, are dying too, technique emerges as the substitute for culture. Take archaeology, for example. In Goethe's day it was still sheer destruction of whatever had been preserved intact underground for dozens of centuries. Not now: the modern archaeologist knows that love is more deadly than death to whatever still lives of ancient cultures, so he proceeds with the most delicate techniques and greater precautions than even a surgeon would use: he first identifies a possible site, then excavates as slowly as he can. One might say he erodes, or reverses, the process of nature that works in man and soil at the same time: in man, by burying the visions and techniques that had kept him at peace with his equals for centuries, and in the soil, by letting dust and rain and organic substances take back—"

"The correct term, Professor Mommsen, is, if we may use a neologism, to *in*-ducate what man had taken out, or *e*-ducated. . . ."

"Perfect, perfect!" said Mommsen, laughing and squeezing his arm: "Inducate is the word: make mud forget it was once clay, and pottery, painted amphoras, and do the same to iron and bronze and marble and gold. I like your image! But this is all off the real subject. What I meant to say was that you are clearly a gifted archaeologist by instinct."

"Thank you." And Leonardo blushed and bowed.

"And also a good historian . . ."

"Thank you."

"And a good man . . ."

"You are too kind!"

Leonardo was radiant: his enemies had heard! But as soon as Mommsen had propelled Leonardo beyond the crowd his tone changed: "But, in your way, you are more suicidal than all the archaeologists you so hate."

"I????"

"You. After identifying what is wrong with this modern nation, you extract it from under its layers of national hypocrisy and pride with such haste that instead of arousing curiosity and enlisting all the help you need, you use your pickaxe to destroy everything your vision had intuited underground."

"Er . . . umm." Leonardo gulped and coughed and pretended renewed attention.

"You have insulted *everybody.* Donna Ersilia, the only truly serious woman scholar in Italy and a member of the Accademia dei Lincei, her brother, Prince Caetani of Sermoneta, a great liberal thinker who, as mayor of Rome, did more for his city than any political figure has ever done or any great idealist has ever dreamed of doing, . . . then you have insulted Baron Lumbroso, the Cardinal, and even me. Now I am ordering you to apologize to every single one of these people except for me."

"But . . ."

Mommsen had shut his mind to any further contact with him, as Leonardo well recognized, for he had seen it happen day in, day out with his best teachers at the medical school of Naples: the world-famous teacher of clinical medicine, Cardarelli, the world-famous teacher of psychiatry, Leonardo Bianchi, and Rummo and Rubino —all people from whom he had learned things that had made him a good doctor and a good man. Not one of them could bear to hear or speak one more word after they had delivered themselves of a lecture, for each lecture was a piece of live inspiration, and not mere repetition of what they knew they knew.

Suddenly he felt Mommsen's hand on his head, and heard him say: "Forgive me for what I said, but now pull yourself together and don't act like a fool." Leonardo kissed the hand and placed it against his heart. "All right, all right, now behave like a man. Go and wash your face before you show yourself again out there, and be a good boy."

"Thank you, Professor. Must I apologize to those two?"

"Lord, no . . . not now . . . A little sense of occasion, by God . . ."

And he pushed Leonardo quite gently out of the room by the door opposite the one they had come in, making sure first that no one was there outside it. "Thank God, this is a corridor," he said. "Do you know your way around here?"

"Yes," said Leonardo, and then he hurried towards the bathroom. When he emerged from it, he felt refreshed and restored, but when he appeared in the crowded drawing room again, he was hit by such a violent headache that he couldn't help putting his hand over his eyes.

The first person to approach him was someone who hadn't been there for dinner and hadn't come with the after-dinner guests, Leonardo was sure, because such a disgusting face could not have escaped his attention. So he must be part of the household, and the mere thought of this unlikely possibility made him rise to the defense of Mary and Sophie. The first words he heard from him, indeed the man's very voice and servile expression, confirmed him in his suspicion that this must be the Roman equivalent of a Mafioso. Leonardo knew what to do: instead of eliminating him with a stiletto, eliminate him with your contempt, look through him as if he were thin air, and he will know just how far he can go with you, because all criminals need a margin of respectability. Leonardo had proven to his constituents that an official who doesn't want to be corrupted can stay clean and even get publicity without doing anything but treat the Mafiosi with open contempt. They will flee from him the way a dishonest servant flees from a master who has caught him stealing.

"May I introduce myself," said the man, pushing a flabby and perspiring hand into Leonardo's, "my name is Pio Tegolani, nobleman by birth, lawyer by profession, and administrator of estates by necessity. I am Mrs. von Randen's lawyer and man-of-all-trades, so . . ." and he lowered his voice to a whisper, but in the typical way of a Mafioso; namely, pretending to be so breathless with laughter because of the joke he had just told that he had no voice left. ". . . you can talk freely to me, because I know everything. I am in charge of organizing your flight with the two ladies tomorrow,

and since that implies two crimes under the Italian penal code—to
wit: desertion of the marital roof and abduction of a minor—you
can easily understand what prudence this requires. No fear: I am
the ideal person for the job. The only field where I cannot be
trusted is when I try to protect my own interests, because my one
defect is that I'm too honest." (Typical Mafia talk, this, too.)

Leonardo looked at him with disgust, long enough for the bastard
to get the message, and the bastard did, and turned the tables on
him. "Well," he said, suddenly earnest again and holding out his
hand, "congratulations. You put the sonofabitch German professor
in his place, and the sonofabitch Roman prince and his bitch sister
in theirs. As for the little Jew, he's such a rabbit, he never dares
peep out of his hole, and that's how it ought to be. I heard you, and
a lot of other people did too, and I can tell you, you scored a big
success, so, once more, congratulations, also in the name of the
fatherland. After all, you and I are Italians, and we can talk without
hair on our tongue. I can tell you, I was about to become honorary
professor of history (Roman history, to be more precise) when my
father lost his entire fortune and I had to go into litigation to help
him, the poor man. I couldn't do much to save him, because we
were two of a feather: too honest to get ahead in a world of exploiters and bootlickers of the foreign exploiters, but I did manage
to save something, and then I went on working, so now I'm an old
man, and still I'm working. I understand you are not rich yourself,
but with me you can talk openly, as if I were your brother . . . a
much older brother, alas, almost an uncle, but an uncle who feels
like a father. You come here from the backward provinces, and in
one evening you put them all in their place. And you chose the right
persons, you picked them out as a good prosecution lawyer would
pick out the criminal in a huge crowd. I really wonder why Mrs. von
Randen, who is no fool, keeps inviting them. I'll tell you why: she's
like me: too good, too unsuspecting. We're like brother and sister, I
always tell her, and she laughs. Wonderful person, and she must
also have been a beautiful lady in her youth, not now, of course, but
who is, in old age?"

Leonardo realized that no one in the room knew this knave except
for Mary and Sophie, who nodded embarrassedly when they saw
him, but it was clear that they hadn't expected him and that he

knew he hadn't been invited, for he blushed, bowed several times, winked and said, exhibiting Leonardo to them as if they had never seen him: "See what I found? A brother under the skin. We think the same way, feel the same way, only he's more courageous than I am, because he's young and we are old, isn't that true, Donna Sophia?" Then, to Leonardo: "Mrs. von Randen is younger than you are, because she has the blood of civilized barbarians in her veins . . . that's what the Slavs are, my dear friend, so she will always stay young and react with the typical generosity of her eternal eighteen years, but we Romans are born old, every one of us is two thousand years old on his first birthday. With your permission, ladies, I'll release your friend in just one moment, and I'll see you" (another wink) "tomorrow late in the day, so I'll say goodbye for now."

And with another deep bow he withdrew from their crowd, which was composed mostly of Russians, and went on whispering into Leonardo's ear: "And let me warn you against that traitor to his class, Prince Caetani and Duke of Sermoneta, a man whose father betrayed his own sovereign, the Pope, to organize a plebiscite here, in papal territory, in favor of the usurper King Victor Emmanuel the Second, and went to Florence, then capital of Italy, to invite the King to liberate Rome from the pontiff. LIBERATE, do you understand what that means? As if the Vicar of Christ could be regarded as a tyrant. That is atheistic Communism, if you ask me. And he opposed papal Infallibility: the usual thing a liberal would do. . . . Now of course we have a united nation, respected the world over, and I, as a good citizen, obey my King and would never side with the enemies of law and order. Never. How I wish these degenerate Roman princes reasoned as I do, instead of opening their palaces to German detractors of our history, and even to divorced women . . . which is really going a bit too far."

"But . . . Mrs. von Randen is a divorced woman. . . ."

"WHAAAAT? Not she, oh no, not she . . . Mary is going to get a divorce to marry you, and to help you get one, because that's the only way we can arrange the problem, and, although we don't like it, we're realists . . . but Mrs. von Randen is not a divorced woman. Where ever did you pick up that slander against your future mother-in-law?"

"She told me so herself."

"She . . . she, WHAT?"

"She told me so herself."

"Where? When?"

"Right here, last night."

The lawyer now looked on the point of pronouncing instant ex-communication. Then something suddenly changed behind that pontifical forehead, and the next face Leonardo saw was that of the same slimy Mafioso he had been hating for the last quarter of an hour.

"You are lucky," said the Mafioso with his Mafious grin, "that you said this to me and not to a total stranger, because in Rome you cannot keep a secret for a minute—the Romans are terrible gossips—which explains why I seemed upset just now: it was fear, fear for your safety in carrying out our little project, fear for Mary, fear for Donna Sophia as well. . . . And don't you volunteer any further indiscretions about her personal life when you talk to me: I refuse to hear them. Because I don't HAVE TO KNOW ANY MORE. I know enough: she is a saint, and some day, with God's help, she will be a Catholic saint, but even if she doesn't make it before dying, I know she will go straight to heaven." (No Mafious wink here, only closed eyelids and a bent head for a moment of deep silence, hands folded on his cravat.)

It was the ideal moment to flee from the fool without seeming impolite, and Leonardo took it, retreating backwards as one does in church when the service is too long or the sermon too boring. But a man who is *too honest* is also too sensitive to dishonesty in others not to feel it even with his eyes closed, which Tegolani instantly did. Changing his tone, he grabbed Leonardo by the sleeve and pulled him back to him: "Well?" he asked, clearly enough to be heard by the others. "Is this the way they teach respect for old age and experience in those provinces of yours down there?"

And it worked, because Leonardo was instantly apologetic: "I . . . I thought you'd finished . . . I assure you . . ."

"You do, do you? And you thought I'd finished. I hadn't, but the best way to find out is always to ask." And when he was sure that his authority was not going to be challenged again, he said: "Just one more piece of advice, and I swear it won't take long: beware of the Cardinal, and don't listen to Mary or to her mother when they praise him. It's a new fashion in them, because the old fox knows how to flatter people, but he's a most dangerous influence . . . yes, a most dangerous influence, proof of it being that he ruined his chances for the papacy all by himself. The man was exceptionally brilliant a few years back, so brilliant in fact, he had risen to the top of the list of Papabili. Then, one day, suddenly, he tumbled down to less than nothing and turned against everybody. . . . That was just at the time when Mary was studying to become a painter."

"Mary? When was that? And who was her teacher?"

"My brother."

"Your brother? And did he make her paint nudes?"

"Oh no, he's a priest!"

"Another Cardinal?"

"Never!!! God forbid!!! My brother the Monsignor is like me: too honest to wave a little finger to obtain for himself the slightest portion of what he so richly deserves: a red hat. But God forbid that he would ever be regarded as just another Cardinal like the one here: cynical, crawling like a worm in front of anyone who could be useful, and of course profoundly immoral."

"But didn't the Cardinal convert Mary to Catholicism?"

"He? God forgive you for saying such a thing, no! My brother did. The Cardinal just talked, that's all he can do. Now that he's lost every chance to become Pope, he talks his head off to break the Tripartite Alliance, in the hope that he'll be made Archbishop of Paris, so that if the French win the next war he may name himself the next Antipope and start the whole thing of Avignon all over again. The poor fool doesn't know that history never repeats itself the way we want it to: only the way God wills it, and God's will is of course unpredictable. . . . But here he comes, *lupus in fabula* . . . *water in your mouth!!!!*" And with a deep bow to the Cardinal and another deep bow in the direction of Sophie, who was aiming her *lorgnon* at him from afar, the lawyer Tegolani bowed out of the room.

The evening was finished and the guests were beginning to leave which meant that the servants were beginning to arrive from all ends of dark corridors, carrying fur coats and overcoats and cylinder hats and gloves and walking canes and even, for the pessimists, an occasional umbrella. In the crowded anteroom the rightful owners of all these things were trying to recognize them amid the others, and accepting a servant's assistance in this formal restitution of personal property as they glanced at themselves in the mirror to make sure that everything was there and hadn't been damaged during these long hours of separation. The servants in the meantime waited like criminals in court for the final dismissal of each case and the dropping of all possible charges against them, before they rushed to the next courtroom to be heard by the next judge, and it was only after the end of each case that the judge turned human again and paid the witness, more or less generously, according to his judgment of the pleasure it had given him to do justice.

Leonardo stood there, transfixed, and not entirely without envy, seeing all the beautiful black overcoats lined with soft fur which showed only around the collar, the same kind of overcoat he had seen on his new friend the coachman yesterday and today while he had nothing to shield himself against the bitter Nordic climate of Rome. And what would the climate be like farther north, in Switzerland, in France, in Germany, his new homes for God knows how long, as of tomorrow night? Blasts of cold wind were coming into the house every time Bernhard held the door open for a new group of guests to leave, and what made Leonardo even more envious was the sight of the gold coins, some of them large gold coins, Bernhard was collecting from the departing throng. At a few steps from the butler, his own underlings who brought in the coats were paid in tiny silver coins, and with contempt, while he was being paid in gold, and smiles—why should there be such class divisions even amongst these nonpeople?—and the guests accepted his comments on the weather and his orders to pull their furs up to their ears.

Every now and then Mary and Sophie made an appearance in the entrance hall, to accompany some foreign friend with whom they still had so much to discuss that it interfered even with Bernhard's little comments, which were also uttered in various languages. But as they didn't include Leonardo in their group, no one thanked him or even spoke to him before speaking to Bernhard. Of course this is all part of our plan, he kept telling himself to comfort his hurt pride, but it didn't help much because he was the only one who knew that—and how can you believe anything in total isolation, especially when it bears no resemblance to your former experience?

What made it even more confusing was the sudden metamorphosis of all the guests into shopwindow dummies or drawings for fashion magazines, faces hardly showing behind heavy veils or in the narrow space between a thick fur collar and the rim of a shiny top hat so tall that, if it were a totem pole, there would be room for five more faces on top. And whenever a thin overcoat without fur or sartorial distinction suddenly appeared on the body of a person with whom they had been most cordial all evening, all the thick fur coats would consort in one corner. When D'Annunzio appeared, he was first offered a very shabby brownish raincoat with dirty black gloves and a dirty gray beret (the only one so far) that didn't match, and his anger was such that he threw the raincoat on the floor with a glance of cold hate for the knave who had dared help him into it while he wasn't looking.

"This isn't mine!" he cried, recoiling from the gloves and the beret as if they had been snakes.

"Whose are they then?" asked the servant, and D'Annunzio, who had identified his walking cane in the meantime, brandished it in the air and said: "How do I know?" Then, noticing Leonardo's smile, he pointed his cane almost into his face and said, *"That* person's, perhaps," loudly, to invite the audience to laugh. But no one did.

"Are they yours?" asked the servant, coming humbly towards Leonardo, and Leonardo said quietly: "No, I'm sorry, I wish they were." In the meantime another overcoat, not as shabby or as inadequate, but still not opulent enough to claim equal rights with the ones already mounted on their knights and waiting in a secluded corner for the signal to retreat, was offered D'Annunzio, and rejected again with contempt.

"Mine?" he said, "this dirty thing?" and the servant who had brought it, this time a woman, ran away with it without daring to seek out its rightful owner, and two other women arrived; namely, (oh, horror!) Leonardo's "adventure" and the old woman he had seen in the wardrobe. They were carrying an overcoat which seemed more opulent than all those lined up near the door, but much too

big for the small poet, and with it came a Homburg hat, which of
course was completely out of place with the overcoat. It was clear
that they must have discussed it before bringing it along, but there
existed reasons to believe the coat and hat did actually belong to the
same person. Bernhard, who had meanwhile disappeared, thus de-
laying everybody (because a real gentleman cannot just open the
house door by himself, like a butler, and leave like a thief; that is,
without tipping the butler), reappeared walking alongside the two
women, to handle the whole matter personally with the guest (it
would have seemed highly inappropriate for the guest to discuss
such things with one of the lowest servants). When the trio presented themselves to the poet, he made it an occasion for an im-
promptu theatrical, saying to his assembled friends, "Anus et Puella
. . . the two pillars of the Ewig-Weibliche, the feminine power
that was, and the feminine power that is, these two custodians of
our male frailty and force come to bring me my shield against the
bitter winds that have stripped the night-virgin Hecate of her
pudibund veils. . . . How appropriate for a poet."

He took out a small black notebook and a gold fountain pen to
catch more such poetic pearls for future reference before they were
lost to posterity. Some of the guests complimented him, but Leonardo noticed at once that this base flattery did not seem to please
the great man, which was confusing. But next second the riddle
was solved by D'Annunzio himself. He couldn't have been more
explicit if he had betrayed himself in so many words. The whole
message was contained in one extremely rapid side-glance at the
wider audience out there, beyond the chorus of his cronies—the
audience of fur-lined coats and top hats and the extravagant feather
hats married to the fur coats and hats. It was *their* applause he
sought, and he hated his cronies for standing between them and his
Act of Nativity ("I am the Angel Gabriel and the Holy Virgin in
one, for I give birth to the Word," one of the cronies had quoted
him as saying on another such occasion), especially as these cronies
were wearing cheap ready-made overcoats and held soft, greasy felt
hats in their hands. And what made things worse was that Bernhard
was trying to make things easier for him by taking the overcoat out
of the two women's hands and holding it up himself. The poet
grabbed the coat away from him and returned it to the hands of the

two women, who were instructed to hold it, while he turned his back on them and, after acknowledging with a slight bow his cronies' applause and the awed silence coming from out there (especially from those who didn't understand Italian anyway), he offered one arm to the old woman, saying: "To thee, O dream-image of my mother's loving care for a hundred and a thousand and a hundred thousand anguished minutes in one night, the Angel Gabriel offers this arm in flight from the heavenly shores of inno-cent childhood." Then, again acknowledging a second gust of ap-plause and awed silence, he put the other arm into the sleeve held by the young girl, saying: "And to thee, O dream-image of future womanhood and potential motherhood, the fallen Angel Gabriel offers this arm and leads you by a hundred and a thousand and a hundred thousand burning promises across the River Acheron, to-wards the painful shores of sinful adulthood."

After which, acknowledging a third and last gust of loud praise and awed silence, he took advantage of his triumph not to tip either the two women or the butler, as many in the awed audience pointed out the moment they recovered themselves.

What destroyed the poet's triumph in a single second was that the dirty raincoat and beret were claimed by Prince Caetani, and the other battered overcoat by Mommsen.

And now prince after prince, duke after duke, diplomat after diplomat, poet with cronies after cronies without poet having gone, and, the most frightening of them all, the Holy Pontiff and Field-Marshal Bernhard having gone too, Leonardo felt this was truly his home and not just a public theater even worse than the one where his fairy tale had begun two nights previously (ONLY two nights? WAS that possible?? YES, only two nights), and he wished some-one—but not the coachman—some magician would transport him to his hotel and straight to his bed without passing the desk and all those other comedy characters, because he was falling to pieces, and his headache was getting much, much worse.

He also wished someone would close the front door Bernhard had left open, but he soon realized that it was being kept open for him by the one person in that whole fairy tale world who represented truth to him: the little chambermaid. He didn't dare look at her, because they were alone now and she might have called him by his first name. I must go home. HOME? Home. What am I waiting for? he thought. And like an echo in a dream: Yes, what am I waiting for? Then, the same inner voice came again, from a still greater distance: I'm waiting for that silly girl to leave. How can I tip her if I have no money? And how could I if I had all the money in the world, and all the diamonds, rubies, emeralds et cetera, what's the name of all those things more precious than gold? Moon-stones, yes, moonstones. How could I tip her if I had pocketfuls of moonstones? I couldn't. I don't want to hurt her, and I don't want to thank her, and I don't want to see her, and . . . oh yes, I want to say goodbye to Mary, but what is it that frightens me about saying goodbye to Mary? Oh yes, I know: her mother, and what's her name again?

What *was* her name again? He sat down on a high-backed chair and instantly began to snore; the cold gusts of wind coming up from the staircase brought distant noises of laughter, even more distant noises of water, and from the drawing room distant tinkling of glasses and dishes which made him feel that the party was still going on, but no, these were noises he knew, these were the noises of waiters clearing a Neapolitan restaurant late at night, while the students still lingered on, discussing their future and pounding on the dirty tablecloth and drawing diagrams of their future with toothpicks, now that all the forks and knives had been taken away. But no cashier, no angry wife of the restaurant owner, no stray waiter was shouting: "Get going, the lot of you. . . . This is clos-ing time. . . ." What were they all waiting for? They were waiting for him to go to bed in his own home, but up there in the drawing room Mary and Sophie were discussing with Giovanna where she would sleep tonight, now that she was no longer Leonardo's wife before the law. WHAT LAW? The law of the JUNGLOFF, that's what Russia does to names, it makes them all end in OFF, and once they have ended in OFF, try to rescue them again and make them end in A and O and INI and UCCI and ACCI. . . . Mommsen knows them all, he's written it down for eternity in that fat book DIE UN-TERITALISCHEN DIALEKTE. But you can't use that sentence to greet people and to take part in conversation, and I must go to bed. UN-TERITALISCHEN DIALEKTE . . . (shake hands and smile)

(gobble gobble from Mommsen)

"*Ja, ja,* UNTERITALISCHEN DIALEKTE" (Leonardo's answer)

(And here comes Sophie with rolling eyes of fire, shouting UNTERITALISCHKOFF DIALEKTOFF: otherwise known as "YOU MUST HURRY UP AND COME WITH US. THE CARDINAL IS WAITING.")

"But I'm going *underitalici dialetti* to bed."

"Oh no. You're come-off with us Cardinalofski Klagonoff Tolstoy-off Resurrectionoff Fullmoonoff.

Leonardo yawned and Mary pinched his arm hard, saying: "Mamachen is ready, she has just gone back to the drawing room with the Cardinal. Let's go. Where's your overcoat?"

"OH . . ." He yawned again and rubbed his eyes, and now the door was closed, thank God, and the maid was right there in front of him, with Mary, saying: "My sister's still trying to find it."

Only at this point did Leonardo realize that the little girl at the door had not been the little girl in his arms, all naked and dripping with juices and devouring his kisses, oh no, God forbid, this was an ugly, gray-haired, cross-eyed, bearded, fat woman, the image of that little girl in another ten years or perhaps less. She was wearing the same black uniform with the white apron and the white crown; that was why he had mistaken the rest of her for HIS woman.

"What does your overcoat look like?" asked Mary.

"Like nothing, because I never had one."

"Oh yes you did. You had a beautiful gray summer coat in silk, I remember quite clearly."

"You're living in the moon, my love, if you remember it as beautiful and silken. It's the ugliest, cheapest *spolverina* ever seen, we call them *chemiss'*, the correct term for it being nightshirt in French, and I left it at the hotel, because this wasn't the occasion to come here with that thing on. Your butler, who looked disgusted when he handed it to me yesterday, would have kicked me out of the house tonight, with all those distinguished fur coats coming in on princes and dukes."

Mary and the maid laughed, and Leonardo yawned again and said: "I must go to bed now, I have a terrible headache and I'm falling asleep, as you can see."

"But you can't go to bed, darling, you just promised Mamachen you would join us at the French ambassador's party."

"What? Another party? I never promised any such thing, I never even heard about it."

"But my soul," she said, happy to be able to use that expression in the presence of the maid, "you heard Mamachen call Giovanna and ask her where she had put your overcoat, and you shouted at her: 'In the bedroom, where else?' Isn't that true, Giovanna?" And the bearded Giovanna was happy to prove her total devotion to the new master of the house by being slightly disrespectful: "Of course it's true, but he wasn't listening. Men are always that way." At that moment Bernhard appeared again, followed by the two women and holding a huge fur-lined overcoat on his arm, which he presented to Leonardo. "No and no and no!" he cried, "this isn't mine!" and he tried not to look at *his* little girl. But *she* took it from Bernhard's hands and just put it on Leonardo, then came around him and buttoned it under his chin, saying: "Stay put for a moment, Doctor, we just want to see how much the sleeves and bottom must be shortened."

It was an absolutely gigantic fur coat, and Mary allowed everyone to smile by roaring with laughter herself, then saying with obvious pride: "My darling love looks so funny in my brother's fur coat, doesn't he?" No one dared answer, they just smiled a little more openly while the little girl, putting a few pins into her mouth, and taking them out one by one, proceeded to fold up the sleeves around Leonardo's wrists, and then left the rest of the job to her mother, who quickly sewed in the actual hems after removing each pin and putting it in *her* mouth, while her daughter, kneeling at Leonardo's feet, pulled up the bottom of the coat and prepared that part of the job for her mother. "Looks perfect on him, doesn't it?" she asked, placing herself next to Mary, who immediately hugged her and kissed her on both cheeks, saying: "My little dove, I'm so grateful to you for having thought of this. . . . You're like a sister to me."

After the older woman was through with her work, she too was kissed on both cheeks and called a dear, dear friend.

Leonardo felt completely excluded from their world and, to give himself a certain countenance, said, "I didn't know you had a brother."

"He didn't know I had a brother, my poor darling," answered

Mary, speaking to her servants again, before answering him. "I have two, one worse than the other." Then, addressing the servants again: "Tell him it's true."

Bernhard of course was also excluded from answering, but the older woman said: "There are no bad people in this family, and we are all bad people now and then. I say it's like those who say the world is bad and those others who say the world is good. The world is never bad, it's the worldlers* who are bad. Isn't that right, Doctor? Of course, you must excuse my ignorance."

"You are perfectly right," said Leonardo, "and you couldn't have put it better. What's your name?"

"My name is Michelangela, because I was born in the household of Prince Michelangelo Caetani, and my three daughters are Giovanna, the older one there at the door; Adriana, this one here, who is Miss Mary's chambermaid; and Cefala, who doesn't work here. And we love everybody, because we are not in this world to judge others, only to live with others. If you are interested in learning what other people are made of, turn your back on them and look into yourself, don't put yourself in their clothes. When they come knocking on your door and strip naked in front of you to ask for understanding, it's other things they want you to understand, believe me, it's other things, especially with women. So don't you go getting into other people's clothes. Clothes don't live, but they talk."

"Just like you, Mamma," said Adriana, and everybody laughed.

"Who's talking now? You are, so be silent and let me finish. Clothes talk, but only on the surface, and only to fools. . . ." Here she suddenly realized she had made a mistake and was stitching it into permanence: the pins had fallen out and the hem was no longer horizontal, but rapidly descending towards the floor. "*Te possiono* . . ." She quickly corrected herself: "A curse on the four ancestors of electricity! I can't see a damn thing, sewing here in the dark. . . . Bring me a candle, Adriana. Electricity is the stuff lightning is made of!" Adriana lit a candle and knelt on the floor to help her mother, who wasn't pleased. "Just leave that candle there and go make coffee for the doctor, but make it black, and bring a

* In Roman dialect, *li mondaroli.*

headache powder. He's not used to staying up so late, doctors don't stay up late unless their patients can't sleep. People who stay up late, unless they have to . . . here," she concluded in a minor key, lifting the hem of the coat as if she were about to kiss it, but only bit off the thread. "Here, now you look as if this had been tailor-made for you . . . and will its rightful owner shit when he sees it!!!" These last words had been spoken in such thick *romanesco* they were lost on Leonardo, but not on Mary, nor, as he suddenly realized, on Sophie and the Cardinal, both standing behind him in their huge overcoats, and both immensely amused.

"See you in front of the Villa Medici or inside," said Sophie, "so don't gulp your coffee. We're going." And they left.

"That's good," said Michelangela, "now I'll have time to press the alterations."

"Oh, come on, Mamma," said Adriana, "can't you leave people alone when they want to be left alone for a moment?"

"Yes," said Giovanna, "Adriana is right. Let's go to bed."

"Oh . . . oh . . . I hadn't realized," said Michelangela, taking back from Leonardo's hand the cup he had emptied in the meantime. "But you haven't taken your headache powder."

"He needs no headache powder now," said Adriana, and she ran out like an actress who has overstayed her scene, humming snatches of a cheerful tune to herself, as the other two women followed in silence.

Now it was a pleasure to inhale the cold air of the night, and to slam a door behind you as if you were in your own house, and to kiss your bride in the dark with no fear of intruders. All due to a warm overcoat. A new day was beginning. Two o'clock, said some lesser church nearby. Mary was shivering, so they didn't linger too long on the landing and soon reached the huge front door, where the wind seemed to be at its angriest, driving icily through all the fissures, even through the keyhole. "In your interest and in your mother's interest, speaking as a family doctor," said Leonardo, "I forbid you to go outside in this tempest. Let's go back upstairs and wait for her there."

"Oh no," Mary said. "We've said we would go, and—"

"We didn't—*she* did, and—"

"It's the same, and—"

"Oh no, it isn't, and—"

Mary opened the heavy front door herself, and there outside stood the moon. In the distance, the violent waterfalls were now no more than a single thread of liquid that spun itself slowly from the marble fountain mask to the basin beneath. The wind had become a mere shadow of itself on the pavement, expanding suddenly from a flight of whirling ghosts into static rectangular shapes, to contract just as suddenly again into shapes even crazier than the first ones: Leonardo and Mary looked up and saw a line of bedsheets hanging out to dry over a terrace roof, flashing when they caught the moon, and dark when they shrank from it. There was even a sideshow of trees, knotty with buds, but too thin to cast their dancing shadows down on the cobblestones far below.

"Wasn't I right?" said Mary. "I learned it from my father. He always used to say that people who live in palaces have more room for their fears than for their pleasures. God punishes those who are afraid of leaving their safe little corner to meet the great challenges of nature raging wildly out there in search of a master. Isn't that a beautiful thought?"

"Y . . . es," said Leonardo.

"What do you mean *y . . . es?* If I hadn't taken the initiative, we would still be standing in there, shivering and frightened."

"No: we would be back upstairs, unshivering and unfrightened. There are OTHER challenges, too. Nature is with us all the time."

"Yes, my love, I know. But if it had been up to you, you would have gone back to your safe corner in Laterza this morning, and we wouldn't be leaving tonight for a new life all our own."

"Sssshhhh. The echo is very strong here."

DONG . . . DONG . . . DONG . . . echoed the voice of St. Peter's.

"Goddamn it," Leonardo said, "three o'clock." DONG . . . ". . . four?" DONG . . . DONG . . . DONG . . . DONG . . . ". . . it couldn't be eight." . . . DONG . . . ". . . or nine?"

"No, it's the death-knell. Perhaps the Pope has died. Who cares?"

"Oh."

They both listened as the bell merged into the voice of the wind, at moments very distant, at moments very close—and, indeed, no one seemed to care. The street had become an extension of the drawing room: small groups were still standing together as they had stood upstairs, only now they seemed denser with overcoats and taller with top hats, or poorer with raincoats and felt hats, but they were still discussing the same subjects that had brought them together.

Leonardo and Mary began to walk slowly on the whirling shadows, listening to the bronze voice of the wind. As they reached the top of Via Gregoriana, where the twin belfries of Santa Trinità dei Monti become visible, the distant hills and all the lower city with St. Peter's spread out before them, and the wind resumed its own voice and its bad manners, blowing dust into eyes and slapping top hats away from gentlemen's heads. It couldn't do this to the ladies, because their faces were protected by fish nets and their hats tied like sailboats to the moorings below, but the sails fluttered and the ropes creaked, feathers reached under the rim to wound the eyes, and lace collars came up from under fur coats to lash them from below. Leonardo pulled his felt hat over his eyes and ears, and burrowed down into his fur coat like a rabbit into the ground. He looked something like a bandit trying to hide from the police.

"Don't do that," said Mary, "you frighten me."

"Never mind, this way I can keep my hat on without using my hands. I have no gloves."

"But you were wearing yellow gloves when you came in."

"Yes, but they're either upstairs somewhere, or someone has stolen them."

"Poor darling, I'll buy you some tomorrow."

"This *is* tomorrow, and you won't buy *anything!*"

He had seen a few beggars bundled up in the dark corners of the Scalinata and was wondering whether the Apulian woman with her child was among them. Oh, how he wished she could overhear him and appreciate his moral solidarity with her, since for the moment he couldn't offer her anything else. . . .

Ahead of them Sophie and the Cardinal had also stopped to gaze at Piazza di Spagna and the whole majestic spectacle of the city. Two fountains could be heard in the wind: one down in the piazza and the other hidden by trees in front of the Villa Medici, on their right. "I don't want to see her and hear her nonsense," said the Cardinal, "let's wait until she's gone."

"Do you know what they're talking about?" whispered Mary.

"No."

"The great scandal of the season: the Saxony divorce."

"What kind of a divorce is that? The one we're going to get?"

"Darling, Saxony is a kingdom in Germany, and the Saxony divorce is the divorce of the Queen of Saxony from the King. She's going to marry an Italian songwriter, Enrico Toselli, and the scandal consists of the fact that he's a musician. If he were a diplomat, or a plain stupid landowner with a great title, it wouldn't *be* such a scandal. The King will do anything to prevent her from obtaining her freedom, but she has a good lawyer in Geneva: the same lawyer we're going to have. Mamachen has already sent him a retaining fee to handle both our cases. Don't look now, but she's right behind us."

"Is she?" asked Leonardo, turning around at once. "She looks radiant. One can see she's happy."

These loud words put everyone to flight: the Cardinal seized Sophie by the arm and walked away; the two gentlemen who were with the Queen did the same and walked away with her. Mary alone stood where she was, cringing and leaning over the parapet to look at the beggars crouched in corners down the steps, but now suddenly the Queen disentangled herself from her protectors and came straight towards Leonardo, her hand outstretched. "I am so glad you think so," she said.

Leonardo shook her hand without taking off his hat. "One doesn't have to be a genius to understand it. Mary and I are also getting a divorce, and we share the same lawyer, it seems."

"You do? Why, I have never heard anything so amusing," said the Queen.

"Amusing is not the correct term, Madame Queen, but we're going ahead with it anyway, because we love each other more than I can say."

"Then why get a divorce?"

"Because we need it. In fact, we're getting two."

"TWO?" cried the Queen, laughing hysterically.

"Exactly. What's so funny about that? We're both married, so we need two divorces. You see?"

"Oh . . . oh . . . I'm sorry. . . . Of course you do. Good
luck, and thank you for the compliment."

The next moment, the Queen was gone, and in her place there
was only the moon on a white square with an obelisk in the middle
surmounted by a flower and a cross, and a star in the sky. All around
the obelisk, the same small groups as before began to gather, standing in their own shadows because the moon was so high.

"Darling," said Mary, "why don't you look at me?"

"I must apologize to the Queen. I was a fool; I didn't even take
off my hat. I never, never did such a thing in my life, but . . ."

"Don't give it a thought."

"Do you think I made a fool of myself? But she started it all."

"You never make a fool of yourself, because you're honest, and
that's what I love in you. All these Italians are . . ."

She was interrupted by Sophie, who had emerged from the dark
of the trees in front of the Villa Medici. "I love you, Leonardo,"
Sophie said, stifling her laughter. "You did the right thing. You are
the only person I know who treats royalty the way they should be
treated. Louise of Saxony is a fool, and so is the Queen Mother you
met this morning."

"THIS MORNING?" asked Leonardo. "YESTERDAY MORNING, you
mean."

"As you wish. But now listen, children. I have persuaded the
Cardinal to let us go. He was eager to show you the beauty of this
villa, Leonardo, and he was right, but I see that you're tired, and we
have a million things to do before we leave for Switzerland tomorrow; that is, . . . tonight. Too bad you won't see the Villa Medici.
The Cardinal lives in a small apartment on the . . ." She was
suddenly attracted by a lady who was walking all alone, followed by
another lady. An almost total silence from the small groups, and
their spontaneous withdrawal, as if to assure her the greatest privacy, betrayed her as a great public figure. "See that sad-looking
woman in black?" whispered Sophie. "She looks exactly like the one
member of royalty I have always respected and loved: the Empress
of Austria, always traveling alone, under an assumed name, always
hopelessly miserable. Just like me. She didn't lose the most wonderful husband on earth, as I did, but perhaps her plight was worse.

The Emperor is such a damn wooden fool I cringe at the very thought of spending twenty minutes alone with him. And that poor woman married him! She found him a mistress, before taking to her travels, but she never looked for the ideal man: there is no such thing when you sit on the pinnacle of power. Your equals are the birds that fly around pinnacles, but not even they can nest there! What a terrible life . . . Of course, these poor people almost always end up associating with the worst vulgarians on earth, musicians, actors, painters . . ."

"Do you know her well?" asked Leonardo.

"She was murdered by an anarchist four years ago, in Geneva. Do you remember her, Mary?"

"Yes, very well," said Mary. "She stayed at our hotel in Ouchy."

"Of course you knew her," said Leonardo.

"No, we didn't," said Sophie.

"What a pity!"

"Why?"

"I don't know."

"Well, try to explain why you think it such a pity. Are these people any better than the rest of mankind?"

He was glad he didn't have to answer, because he had discovered in himself a very undemocratic, unmodern, unscientific trait and hated himself for it, since he couldn't hate her. What saved him from answering was the sight of the Cardinal running after the lady who resembled the dead Empress. Everybody witnessed his embarrassment; it was a rare view, and one that all the members of the various groups enjoyed and exploited at once with loud comments and giggles, thereby embarrassing the poor Cardinal even more. The ghost Empress just looked at him in amazement, nodded silently in reply to his attempt at claiming acquaintance, and fixed her head again in an upright posture, as if to affirm her right to regal aloofness, then, as soon as she had rid herself of the disturber, she was back in her loneliness, stooping, as if in search of some lost object in the dust.

The Cardinal stared into the distance, smiled and resumed his own dignified pace, but the self-satisfied nature of his smile was lost on the crowd, because his face was totally blackened by the shadow of his large hat.

"She certainly taught him a lesson," said Sophie, with obvious satisfaction. "But who is that woman? It can't be the Empress of Austria."

"No," said Mary, "definitely not."

"Nor a Bonaparte."

"Absolutely not."

"Then who? Help me, Mary. That face intrigues me."

"Bragancia?"

"Mary, how can you say such a thing? You know the whole clan, not one of them looks that distinguished."

"One of ours?"

"We would have heard about it from our chatterbox of an ambassador." Mary volunteered a few more names, but Sophie rejected them all, saying: "Nonsense. That is a Royal Highness, most likely a ruling sovereign. But which one?" And Leonardo couldn't help thinking: If these people are no better than the rest of mankind, why is she so curious about them?

"Oh, what a fool I am," said Sophie. "Of course we know her— that's the widow of the Cardinal's cousin, you know, the one who died in Paris three months ago."

"That's it, Mamachen, she's Giovanna Scarandogi, that prostitute who—"

"Exactly—who was the mistress of her own grandson."

"whaat?" shouted Leonardo, but Sophie just laughed and said: "No reason to be shocked; she's only thirty-seven, her husband was ninety-six when he died, and the grandson, whom you met tonight—he was the one sitting on Mary's right—was in danger of becoming the lover of his uncle Alain, who's this woman's son, and three years his junior. So the whole thing was a blessing for the boy. . . . It was his grandfather who thought of it all."

Leonardo was wide-eyed with horror, and wanted to say something, but their conversation was interrupted by the sudden appearance of the Cardinal a few steps away. He was looking at the majestic view of Rome, and seemed lost in meditation. It was clear that they couldn't move in the direction of Via Gregoriana without passing behind him on purpose, and Mary was dispatched by her mother to thank him again for his kind invitation and repeat the excuse that their guest was very tired. "Ah," said the Cardinal, answering Leonardo instead of Mary, "that means bad news for you, young man. You expected to go abroad tonight for the first time in your life, and you won't go. Higher authorities have decided against it."

Leonardo saw the two women's fear and felt afraid himself. "I swear I didn't tell him a thing," he said in response to their unspoken question.

"What's the mystery now?" asked the Cardinal; then, seeing he had been indiscreet, he said: "None of my business, of course. What I meant was I had invited you to cross into France" (and he pointed to the Villa Medici) "but Madame here said no, you were very tired."

"I'm not tired at all," said Leonardo, "and I would like to see the villa where Galileo was held prisoner by the Inquisition."

"A prisoner? A most honored guest of the Florentine ambassador, you mean. Galileo was a prisoner of his habit of talking, like all Italians. Copernicus, who truly displaced the center of the universe and rocked the throne of man, dedicated his astronomic fantasies to the Pope and *no one*, except for Luther, Melanchthon and Calvin, called him heretic. The Jesuits had been teaching the Copernican system in Japan long before Galileo came here and created a scandal among the lesser clergy by telling his mathematical fairy tales. As the Florentine ambassador wrote to his Grand Duke: *Mister Galileo should know that this is no place to talk about the moon.* And don't forget that if Galileo's trial was a formality and his punishment nil because he died in his beautiful villa surrounded by his daughters, it was all due to the great liberality of the Medicis to whom he had made the present of a few stars while the Grand Duke reciprocated by rescuing him from the stake. We in France have inherited some of the Medici tradition. Don't forget, we had two Medici queens. But I always talk too much."

"He certainly *does!*" shouted a youngish male voice nearby. "The only reason Galileo wasn't roasted was because the Pope was afraid of war with Florence! So much for the French liar!"

"And priest," shouted another voice, and the first voice echoed: "And priest!" with a loud catcall.

"Let's go, quickly," said Sophie, grabbing Mary by the arm and walking in the direction of the villa. The Cardinal hurried after

them and Leonardo walked behind, but more slowly, because he
didn't want to seem afraid. He turned his face towards the dark
mass of cheap overcoats and cheap felt hats from which the noise
had come, and was smiling broadly in full moonlight when he heard
the first voice ask, very politely: "Are you going to cross into
France? Long live Italy! Down with all foreigners!" This was too
much, so he ran and caught up with Mary in front of the fountain.

"We have higher ideals than anyone here," Mary whispered into
his ear, close enough to breathe into it and almost touch his cheek
with her lips. "We're *modern*! We believe in Science, and the true
freedom of Progress! And we can help ALL mankind, even these
idiots here!!!"

"It's exactly what I feel, now," he said, kissing his words into her
ear and sniffing the scent of her hair like a dog. But a few angry
words in Russian from Sophie separated ear and lips so suddenly
that it was obvious to all the onlookers (or so it seemed to Leonardo) that he had been put in his place. An imperious glance from
Sophie seemed to be saying, "The whole thing is off!!" and to the
others, through him, that he was a Cafone of the worst type. The
Cardinal, who had seen everything, anchored his eyes and his
thoughts onto the shores of Eternity, namely, the Cupola of St.
Peter's, exactly as he had done earlier after the slight from the
mysterious non-Empress of Austria.

Suddenly, the same DONG . . . DONG, the same chime of the
dead surged from inside the Cupolone towards the sky, and everybody's gossip went to church, so to speak, hypocritically asking, "Is
the Pope dead?" No one seemed to know the answer or to care,
except for the Cardinal. For him it might be the death-knell of his
whole career, or perhaps its coronation in glory, one couldn't tell,
but the word *Conclave* whispered behind him by the various groups
fixed him as the center of attention.

"Hey, you, Mister Red-Hat!" called the same youthful voice that
had taken him to task on Galileo, "you better go to bed, because
maybe in a few hours you'll be locked into the classroom and won't
be allowed to leave until the winner of the finals is declared!"

A chorus of giggles, some less discreet than others, but none
inaudible, greeted the speaker. "That's the Italian INDIVIDUAL
again," said Sophie in French, "shame on him! They're such indi-

viduals, these Italians. . . ." Leonardo couldn't understand her, but
he did understand that the young man was now proceeding to give
her a lesson in logic, responding in perfect French.

The Cardinal rose to the occasion once more and courageously
translated, for Leonardo's sake: "This young man who speaks
French so well, says—rightly, I think—that the word INDIVIDUAL
is not an insult, especially when it comes from a Protestant, because all Protestants are individualists. They believe in personal
initiative and not in God's Grace. To quote him verbatim, he
said that our kind hostess believes in certain select individuals, such
as bankers and industrialists, and not in others, such as poets and
prophets of the New Religion of Speed. And he claims to be *the*
one and only such prophet blessing the sacred soil of Italy at this
moment. Which of course—"

"Just a moment, Your Eminence," said the young man coming
forward and taking off his hat. "May I first of all apologize to this
kind lady for not taking off my hat earlier, but my Italian pride had
been so wounded by her that I forgot my manners. And now that I
have discharged my social duties, may I take you to task again. . . ."

"Young man," said the Cardinal, "this is no language to use with
a prince of the Church, and, besides, you have not introduced
yourself."

"My name is Marinetti."

"No one invited you, so, please, spare us further noises, onomastic
or otherwise." Then, turning to Sophie and offering her his arm:
"Madame?"

Sophie took his arm rather unwillingly, and ordered Mary to
follow them to the villa, but with a cheerful smile, which wasn't
altogether for family consumption. Mary and Leonardo stayed
where they were, both fascinated by the young man, but for different reasons: Mary, because she was always fascinated by the frankness of "genius," and Leonardo, because the young man was the
mirror-image of his ideal self, without all the elements that had
made of him what he now was: an unrepentant rebel against the
Church, who had not strayed much farther than his first step outside the gates of the theological seminary and was far more paralyzed by his freedom than he had been by his shackles. In contrast,
this man Marinetti, so much younger than himself and with so

many other obvious moral impediments (namely, his elegant clothes and hat, and his knowledge of French), had gone so far beyond all possible horizons of the impossible that the word *prophet* he had used to describe himself seemed to Leonardo much too modest.

Marinetti's next words did seem to encourage the hypothesis of superhuman infallibility. "I agree with you one hundred per cent," he said, and Leonardo, while baffled, since he hadn't actually uttered a word, felt like kneeling in front of this genius and asking for his blessing. "Yes, I most emphatically, revolutionarily, futuristically, electrically, speedily, superspeedily, fulminologically agree with you."

Mary folded her hands as if in prayer, and tears came into her eyes. She, too, felt like kneeling in front of this Messenger and asking him to celebrate their marriage right then and there.

"BUT," Marinetti went on, "your genius, so like mine in essence, origin, propulsiveness, violence and explosiveness, is corrupted at the core by passivism, dustiness, deathiness, stayputtiness, antielectrical countergenius, such as one always finds in those who have not deloused, disinfected, desickened, deputrified, devaticanized themselves."

"How do you know so much about me?" asked Leonardo, head low, hands clasped and very contrite.

"I heard you earlier this evening, when you were putting that Germanic bookworm in his place. You did it splendidly. You also put that green-feathered traitress to our national heritage in her place, along with that Jesuitical red-hatted snake, that Bore Constrictor, who—"

"I must interrupt you," said Mary, putting her begloved white hands into Marinetti's begloved yellow hands, in a gesture that made Leonardo leap like a tiger ready to pull down the God from His Heavens, but he did nothing of the sort because Mary understood and looked at him with infinite tenderness before resuming her interrupted interruption: "Yes. I must interrupt you to apologize in my mother's name for not telling the Cardinal that you were our guest. She has so many worries these days that she must have failed to recognize you, and so did I. Please forgive us both but, let me explain—"

"Nothing to explain, nothing to apologize for, my charming Nordic beauty. I never was your guest."

"But then . . . how could you . . . you MUST have been there, to . . ."

Leonardo was speechless. Had Marinetti answered: "I can see through walls," he would have said: "Of course, forgive her for not knowing." But Marinetti answered: "Genius can always find its way into the house of beauty."

Mary gasped and frowned for a fraction of a second, then blushed with pleasure while Leonardo closed his eyes, then reopened them to take leave of the moon, which was no longer his.

"Your mother is calling you," said Marinetti, as Sophie appeared at the entrance of the villa, but hesitated to come out; it looked as if the Cardinal were holding her back.

"Oh yes," said Mary, "let's all go, and I'll tell the Cardinal that you are now MY guest, OUR guest."

"No thank you," said Marinetti. "The Cardinal has no power to stop me, if I want to go, because I am ALWAYS invited by the French Academy, while he is invited only every now and then. Don't forget that the so-called French Academy is the Villa Medici: OUR Villa Medici, not THEIRS, as he was implying a few minutes ago. If the Medicis gave the French two queens, it is we, all Italy, that gave them two teachers in good manners and good taste. I prefer to stay here."

Now Leonardo put his ungloved hands on Marinetti's arm in a hypocritical gesture. "I'm so sorry you're not coming with us. How can I get hold of you? I still want to hear what's wrong with me."

"I can tell you right now, that's why I don't want to go in there."

"But I can't stay with you, I MUST go."

"Why?"

"Because . . . because I am inv— I mean, because I MUST."

"No, you MUST not. You WANT to go, and that's a different matter. In that case we'll say goodbye here, and Merry Christmas."*

"But . . . don't take offense."

"I'm not taking offense, but you should, because I have insulted

---

* Euphemism for "Go to hell."

you, and if you choose not to ask for an explanation, so much the worse for you. None of my business."

"Mary," said Leonardo, "will you please insist that he come with us?"

"We both want you to come with us," said Mary.

"Well then, I'll have to say no to both of you."

"Why?" asked Leonardo pleadingly, seeing that Mary was getting upset.

"Because there are matters that men should discuss only among themselves." He bowed away, saying: "I'm sorry."

"YOU stay," said Mary to Leonardo, "I must go!" Then, offering both hands to Marinetti for a cordial goodbye: "I do hope we'll meet again, if not here in Rome, elsewhere. And very, very soon." She ran off, but before reaching her mother, she turned back and called: "Don't keep him too long."

Marinetti bowed deeply to her from a distance and shouted: "Your wish will be honored."

"What a fantastic woman!" said Leonardo, as if to celebrate his return among men of his own type, namely students and great idolizers of womanhood, but in reality to hear himself flattered in the same words that would, inevitably, praise her to high heaven, this being the tradition.

"That's what's wrong with you," said Marinetti, squeezing his arm. "You are a slave of women. And you bask in their praise. All wrong. You should *despise* them! Be *yourself*, be *alone*, be *free*, be *violent*, love something worthier of your manliness, love war, as I do. WAR IS THE ONLY HYGIENE OF THE WORLD: MILITARISM, PA-TRIOTISM, THE DESTRUCTIVE GESTURE OF THE LIBERTARIAN, THE BEAUTIFUL IDEAS FOR WHICH ONE IS READY TO DIE!!! I despise women! Women and culture and museums and libraries: same trash!"

There was a long silence, during which Leonardo took refuge in the moon, knowing that Mary was looking at it too and thinking of him. He wanted to tell her what a low creature this was, and especially to warn Sophie, who had been so impressed by him because he spoke French.

"You are looking at the moon, you rotten old romantic. The moon should be destroyed, defiled, beshitted, torn away from the sky of Italy, and replaced with a motor, a locomotive, something

that burns the coals of hell to produce speed, force, power, the
FUTURE!" And he shouted: "FEW . . . FEW . . . FEW, FEW, FEW
. . . TURE!!!" like a child imitating a choo-choo train.

Leonardo abandoned the moon to look at this silly child who had
been his god only a few minutes earlier.

But instantly the child became mentor again. "You look like a
Jesuit and, by God, I know them. That stupid Cardinal didn't give
you a straight translation of my speech in French: he was afraid of
hurting the ladies, but he hurt them much more with his attack on
Protestant individualism. I was very specific in defining my message
to mankind: the Future, invented by me, and a future for men only.
Yes, that's what I said, and the old lady liked it. So did the young
one. Women always look for their master. But they represent the
past. They cherish it, they hold it for nine months in their belly,
how can they escape their fate? We sow the seed and leave, we have
better things to do, we must beget the world that will make heroes
of our sons."

There was a long silence, then Marinetti laughed. "He didn't
know I had gone to a Jesuit school, but he felt it, without my telling
him. Do you know that I was kicked out of their school in Egypt,
because I brought Zola's novels into the classroom? And did you
notice how their attitude changed, the moment they heard me
speak French so perfectly? I'm a well-known poet, and an Italian
poet, too. But these foreigners . . . Our past is sacred to them, but
they despise our present so much that the moment they hear us
speak our own language, they brand us as ITALIANS!!!!! And what's
wrong with being an Italian, may I ask? I tell you what's wrong:
they know—they *feel*, these exploiters—that one Italian is worth
one thousand foreigners. We have genius, and that's all you
need in the world. They know it, because in fact they buy it, they
purchase our poor emigrants like slaves in the marketplace, and
their countries grow rich and powerful with the genius of our
workers."

"Perfectly true," said Leonardo, happy to be able to agree on one
thing at least.

"What a horrible house they have . . . all that trash . . . those
terrible old paintings and statues, that mass of silver . . . gold . . .
museum pieces, what a horrible house."

"Not horrible, but a bit too opulent, when you think of the poverty of our people."

"Admit you were impressed with all that trash."

"Me? Not at all."

"Come on, don't tell me you're used to that kind of opulence where you live."

"Of course not, but . . ."

"Be honest: I saw you gaping every time you looked into those china cabinets." Leonardo was about to say something, but said nothing. "You were like a good Italian schoolboy, raised in the worship of the past, to please our foreign masters." Again Leonardo hesitated, and Marinetti tore at his fur collar, ripping it inside, but Marinetti didn't seem to care, in fact, he laughed and went on: "Admit you worshipped that silly Cardinal and that pompous German pedant like gods. . . ."

"N—no," said Leonardo. And it wasn't unwillingness to lie that made him hesitate, it was the very poverty of the Italian language which places everything absurd or fabulous in Egypt. He knew no answer but *"Macchè dei d'Egitto,"* or *"Macchè tesori d'Egitto."* But this man *came* from Egypt, he was the *first* Egyptian in Leonardo's experience, and that, at the unending end of an endless day in which he had met his first Jew and his first Baron, all in one, his first D'Annunzio, his first Pirandello, his first descendant of the Emperors of Byzantium, his first Cardinal, his first and second Queen, and almost his first Empress, besides countless Counts, Princes and Dukes . . . all of them firsts—and of these fabulous characters, the only one who had awakened any feelings of worship in him was this vulgar individual here. Yes, now he knew: what tied him to Marinetti like a pupil to his master was a certain resemblance between this conversation and those of 1893 with Peppino Luccibelli, Giulio Calace and Donato Civetta, who had persuaded him (without ever saying so) to leave Mary the first time. None of those three had been as rich as this young man obviously was, but their passionate concern for sincerity and honesty and for the good name of Italy was exactly the same.

"I see my words have troubled you: good sign," said Marinetti, leaning over the balustrade and looking at St. Peter's, whence the chime of the dead was now coming much more feebly, because the wind had changed. "They tend to regenerate people who seemed completely lost to the Cause of the Future. Think what a torrent of my eloquence will be needed to devaticanize Italy. That thing there is the biggest and oldest piece of excrement blocking our national intestines." He then turned to the Scalinata, where two men with large felt hats and the typical black bowtie of the Socialists were gesticulating and talking about the revolt of the masses, the Socialist experience, as the only thing that could unify Italy, etc.

"Just look at them. See what the fat one is doing?"

"What's he doing? I can't see."

"He's leaning over that sleeping beggar and putting banknotes into his pocket, so the poor wretch will believe that God or the Holy Virgin has come down from heaven to single him out and reward him with money. And when you think that these two are Members of Parliament, you wonder whether this country can ever be saved. In Parliament the Socialists rave against the government as reactionary, and in their papers they incite the people to revolution and mass murder and the desecration of churches et cetera, then they come here and work for the Vatican. And that's the second piece of shit that will have to come out, after the first one's gone, or perhaps simultaneously. I hate the Socialists."

"So do I," said Leonardo with passion. "Now I *know* we're brothers! . . . But for the moment, goodbye. I'm going."

"You are not."

"Mary's waiting for me."

"Oh, is that her name? Well, she is NOT waiting for you. NO ONE is waiting for you, that is a concept of the rotten past, which must be eliminated from our thinking habits, if we are to become citizens of the Future. Only the Future is waiting for you, and since *I am the Future*, you'll stay here and answer my questions. What is Mary, your mistress?"

"No, my future wife."

"But you're married."

"Yes, and so is she, but we're getting a divorce, two, as a matter of—"

"Oooh, aaaah, ooooooh, I see . . . you believe in marriage. Marriage must be abolished. Love is free, quick and contemptible. The only love both permitted and permanent is love of our own heroic destiny, therefore of Speed, Motorization, War, metallization of the human body and the human environment for the complete mastery of Nature. The earth will finally give all it can. Clasped in the vast electrical hand of man, it will express all the juices of its wealth, like the beautiful orange that has been promised our thirst for so long."

Leonardo was so angry, he couldn't help answering: "Perfect analogy: no longer a tree to be cultivated, but a fruit to be squeezed. Thus the earth will be deprived of everything it needs for the renewal of its forces."

"Petty-bourgeois thinking: the little provincial landowner worrying over the renewal of nature's capital in the soil—rural capitalism at its worst. The future belongs to industry, the tree of future life is the smokestack, and the forbidden apple a bomb in our hands, which the enemy will get in his teeth. That'll teach him to steal apples from this Garden of Eden, our Divine Fatherland!!! But we—unlike Adam and Eve—we, the true children of the gods of Science plus Industry, will eat our own apples and acquire more and more knowledge towards the complete mastery of Nature. Carnal life, in the futurism my genius is beginning to shape, will be strictly limited to the function of conserving the race, which will be all to the good for the growing stature of man. We, the men of the future race . . ." Leonardo wasn't even listening carefully enough to catch the logical sequence, if any. "You don't agree, you man of little faith?"

"I really must . . ."

"We've heard that tune before, and we're not interested. You're supposed to answer my question: do you agree or don't you? You're speaking to a new Italian, a Futurist: total sincerity, and no Jesuitical ᴅɪsᴛɪɴɢᴜᴏ. Those who are not with us are against us. If you don't agree, beat me up."

"I don't agree that the ᴅɪsᴛɪɴɢᴜᴏ is entirely Jesuitical. It is Aristotelian, and, even more distinctly, Socratic. And besides, I don't agree that arguments can be settled by blows."

"But if you are confronted with a man who answers your Jesuitical jelly with blows, what are you going to do then?"

"I can't betray my argument in order to defend it. It's lost on you, but neither you nor I will last forever. The future belongs to no one, but the illusion of our future belongs to our children, and the illusion of our fathers' future belongs to us. I'd like to hear *your* father on the subject of your being kicked out of school."

"All right, you asked for it, you'll get it." And he slapped Leonardo in the face, but all he got was Leonardo's hat, because Leonardo had ducked and was now crouching on the ground. Marinetti lifted his leg to kick him in the face, but two strong hands grabbed him from behind, and Leonardo saw himself rescued at the last moment from what might have been a fatal blow by the one person in Rome to whom he hated to owe anything at all: Tegolani, the lawyer.

Thank God . . . now they'll both get the beating they deserve, thought Leonardo, getting up and dusting his overcoat with his hand. But to his infinite surprise, Marinetti seemed instantly tamed, even pleased to see the lawyer, and they walked off together like the most intimate of friends. The only remnant of Marinetti's fury showed itself in his feet, treading Leonardo's hat while he and Tegolani talked, until the poor object lost all trace of identity.

Leonardo gave it up for dead and walked quickly in the direction of the villa. There in the entrance hall, so much like the hall in Sophie's palace, only even bigger, he found Mary and Sophie in a state of extreme agitation, being reassured and almost physically sustained by the Cardinal.

Mary and Sophie both threw themselves on Leonardo to protect him from whatever danger he had already incurred; when they saw him hatless, covered in dirt and obviously upset, they lost all self-control, kissing him, hugging him, babbling Russian to each another and to him, but obviously even more to God, as their skyward glances and dramatic gestures clearly showed.

"What happened to you? Where's your friend?" they finally managed to ask.

"My friend?" he said. "He's not my friend, he's the worst Italian I've ever met. I'm not for burning books, destroying museums, dishonoring women and beating up anybody who doesn't agree with me. He tried to slap me in the face, and when I ducked, he tried to kick me in the teeth with his boots, and he only didn't succeed because someone came along and stopped him."

"Poor Leonardo," said Mary, very unconvincingly. She DID NOT say poor love, because her mother had given her a hard look and hissed something in Russian he did not like one bit, although he didn't understand it.

"Leonardo," said Sophie coldly, "the *someone* who rescued you is our lawyer Tegolani, who happened to be passing by while we were trying to decide whether or not to come and separate the two of you ourselves. You did see him and recognize him, and I think that, since you couldn't thank him then, you might at least now acknowledge his part in your rescue. Thank God you're not hurt, but since you are well enough to complain, you are also well enough to make light of the whole matter. And what makes it still worse is your branding your opponent as ITALIAN, as if you were not one yourself. There are no Italians or French or Germans, there are *people*, and now let me apologize to you for saying these things, but I believe in total sincerity, as you know."

"Let me apologize for him, Mamachen. It's my fault if he used the word Italian that way: I had used it with him earlier this evening, and he answered my stupid argument with the same words used by you. Please don't reproach him if he made a mistake. Poor darling, he's so upset, and he's very, very tired. Don't forget that he's usually getting up to begin his daily work at this hour, and we kept him in that whirlwind of silly people for hours and hours. . . ."

Sophie was instantly transformed. "Come here, my son, and give me a kiss. . . ."

Then, to Leonardo: "The coachman is waiting for you right there in the dark, you see our coach? But please" (and she lowered her voice to a whisper) "PLEASE don't talk to him about anything, least of all about you and Mary, or he may understand and go and tell everybody in Rome. Don't forget, he's an Italian. . . ."

"But . . . don't you think he's heard plenty already, in the last five minutes?"

"He never listens, he's so stupid. And besides, he's certainly sound asleep inside the coach. I don't mind, because I never ask my servants to stay awake when they don't have to, but be careful on your way to the hotel. He may feel like asking questions. You're in Rome here, don't make the mistake of believing you're in Berlin or Saint Petersburg, where you can talk as you please and no one is

going to report you to the Vatican. Good night, my son. And don't
have any scruples about waking him up. Just shake him: it's all
sheer pretense with him: the usual Italian comedy."

All this was said in the presence of the doorman, who bowed
deeply in front of Leonardo before shutting the big *portone*. Leonardo crossed the street, and from the dark the coachman's voice
asked: "Hotel de Russie?"

"No, thank you. I'm going to walk. You go to bed. I'm sorry you
had to wait so long."

"At your service, sir," said the coachman, in a tone that hurt
Leonardo very deeply, because it was so different from the tone of
brotherly friendship he had used earlier in the kitchen.

Who the hell cares, Leonardo thought, walking away. That's the
way they are, these Italians.

It wasn't so much the chirping of the sparrows over the roofs or
the calls of "Milkman!" followed by the yawning voices of doormen
and the cheerful tinkling of tin pails that marked a new day for
Leonardo, but simply the fact of being away from all that fairy tale
world he didn't understand. Even his love for Mary became greater
the moment she was gone, because she had returned to her accustomed place on his mental horizon, in her accustomed shape and
dress of nine years earlier. So this is the woman who is that woman,
he concluded with a feeling of infinite triumph. Then he corrected
himself: Or, to be more precise, THAT is the woman who is THIS
woman, and Giovanna has nothing to do with either of them. A
deep intake of fresh morning air, with all the healthy scents of
winter, water, dust and stars, plus of course goats and cold metal
and cooling perspiration, boots, socks and stale breath. If he had
closed his eyes, he would have been able to put his hand on the
dirty piece of string that kept the straw door closed on the one-room
stone hut where the sick little boy lived in Laterza, and he would
have gone straight to his bed to see how he had fared in the doctor's
absence. But this was Rome . . . Remember, you're in Rome, not
in Berlin or Saint Petersburg. . . . —and not in Laterza either, so
he kept his eyes open to fight off the seductiveness of the familiar
noises and smells that used to stay put while he rode by on his
horse; here, it was he who stayed put, while they rode by and tried

to call him back to his duty. Another cloud of sheep and goats was
tiptoe-dancing onto the monumental stage from way under the trees
of the Villa Borghese. Other troupes, preceded and followed by
their shepherds, were coming back from Via Gregoriana and Via
Sistina, where they had stopped in front of every house to fill the
housewives' jars and pots, right from the taps in their bellies. They
all crowded together at the top of the steps, where Leonardo was
now standing, and soon began to dance lightly down, by one, by
two, by three, as Dante says, and where the one goes, the others
go . . . timid and quiet, and they don't know why. . . .

"Hey, you, milkman," shouted an Apulian voice from under the
heap of torn blankets in a corner, "here, fill this." And an arm was
raised from the heap, holding a tin cup for the shepherd to fill. The
shepherd did so, with the help of the goat closest to him. "Thanks,"
said the woman, "wait till he's finished it, I want some too."

Both the shepherd and the goat were way down at the end of the
steps by now, but since more shepherds and more goats were coming after them the woman didn't even bother to look or to repeat
her question: her cup was filled again, and she went back to sleep,
while two male voices grumbled at her under the blankets for taking
too much room.

Leonardo stopped, undecided whether to speak to the woman or
not, but his experience of the previous afternoon and his opulent
overcoat made him prudent. He also wondered whether he should
announce to the woman that the two men sleeping at her feet had
Socialist money in their pockets, but again he didn't dare.

A strong scent of fresh bread came up from under the trees on
either side of the steps to meet another strong scent of coffee from
farther along the road, probably from the Caffè Greco. Scents of
burning oregano, thyme and pine needles came down from the
roofs and chimneys of Via Gregoriana, and there was even a faint
scent of incense from the church of Santa Trinità, which was just
opening its doors for first Mass, while the Infallible voice of the
Pope spoke again from St. Peter's and struck five against the moon.
"Go to bed," it said.

As he entered the hotel, he saw Klagonov. He was in the deserted
dining room downstairs, crawling towards the corridor on the thick

carpet, moaning: "Metallization!!!" Someone began helping him to his feet, when from the garden terrace several young men came in and joined forces in lifting the tall, heavy Russian. "Metallization," he kept moaning. Another voice shouted. "And Champagne!" and someone brought him a bottle, which Klagonov grabbed with both hands the way a child grabs a cup of milk and started sucking at it, but it was empty, which sobered him instantly. In a thunderous voice he demanded a new one. The waiter came; at this point Klagonov caught a glimpse of Leonardo. "*Fratellissimo carissimo,*" he shouted, falling all over him and kissing him on the mouth. "Flesh weak is, but metal strong. Flesh cry after Ludmilla, but Marinetti says woman contemptinudinous she, woman belongs past, war and metallization to future belong they, war only hygiene of world he, and . . ."

Leonardo tried in vain to disentangle himself from the huge mass of revolting flesh, but Klagonov was too strong and kept saying: "Not to abandonate me you please is, drink to repentance of Russian nobility for sins against working class."

At that moment Marinetti arrived from the garden, accompanied by more young men who were obviously sober because they were drunk on his eloquence; he grabbed Klagonov from behind and pushed him towards an armchair shouting: "Shame on you, disgracing yourself like that in public!"

"Come on," called Klagonov's friends, "stop talking and drink with us."

"No, thank you," Marinetti said drily, in a way that impressed Leonardo deeply. More voices and glasses were lifted and offered him; as he turned them down in anger, Leonardo became their next target.

"Don't bother *me,*" he said, hearing his own timid voice echoed by Marinetti's strong one, except for the word *me* instead of *him*— and his heart melted, only to freeze again before he could stretch out his hand in gratitude, as he caught Marinetti's next words: "I caught you, you slimy Jesuit: you're out betraying your future wife."

"Never! I would never do such a thing!" His own stentorian voice was back once more.

"Oh, come on, what's wrong with that? I bet you a thousand lire right now that you're about to do it, un—"

"And I accept your bet."

"Just a moment. Let me finish: unless you've already done it earlier and you're tired."

"You disgust me with your cynicism! Certain values are sacred. . . ."

"Yeah, in the name of the Father, the Son—"

He was not allowed to continue. "Please, PLEASE, no blasphemy," shouted the quintessential, clerical voice from the back. It was the lawyer Tegolani, who had been sitting in the night clerk's office and was now making his surprise entry into the play. There was a long silence. Leonardo took advantage of it to say, "Good night," and leave.

"Don't tell me you *live* here," exclaimed Marinetti, and everybody laughed.

"I do," Leonardo called back, feeling this was a great mistake.

"You do? Then don't try to tell me a woman isn't paying!"

And again everybody laughed, while Leonardo disappeared into the darkness of the staircase.

FOURTH DAY

He locked himself in, undressed in a hurry and threw himself on his bed, but Marinetti had got there first, and was laughing at him in hieroglyphics under the Egyptian moon. He ran away in his nightshirt and took refuge in a pyramid, but Marinetti ran around it, and encircled the pyramid with four cardinal points marked by four hats in the sand. He lifted the lid of a tomb and there was the Cardinal with two black hats on his breasts and one on his pubis, and it was Adriana. "You can't make love to me," she said, "because Marinetti is outside and this is the Pyramid of Jupitress Sophie."

"I *can* make love to you," he said, "because your name isn't Giovanna, so everything's all right."

And he made love to her, and she was Mary, but she was also Adriana, Giovanna, *and* the prostitute with the sick child, *and* the mistress of the red-haired man, *and* Adriana again, but the moment he finished making love to her, she turned into Kostia, and the real Adriana was running out of the room, while Mary was standing in front of the window and talking to the moon. He woke up, loving Adriana as he had never loved any other woman, but he was glad that he had Mary as a pure angel to give him refuge against jealousy, because he still couldn't help despising Adriana for seducing him. She was obviously a whore and would do it again with other men, and how could he let such a creature become the mother of his children? A man's first duty to his children is to give them a respectable mother: the rest doesn't count, or, rather, it counts only as part of his duty to protect her against her own nature. Essentially there was nothing wrong in Adriana's impulse, but her parents were wrong in not guarding her properly, or in not finding her a husband at the age of fifteen, even earlier if possible, given the undeniable fact of early womanhood in people who live so close to the earth.

A man who tries to behave like an angel, because he loves an angel, is not worthy of becoming her guardian: the guardian angel of an angel can only be the devil, or, in correct terminology, that mixture of devil and man who knows all about the mixture of angel and woman he has for a companion. But Leonardo was happy with his dream, and remembered the observation of his psychiatry teacher Leonardo Bianchi: "In dreams the experience of the day is sifted and purified like the particles of gold from sand, and the strange links between things we would never put together in our logical mind are revealed as the quintessence of logic. We may not live according to our dreams, because we are not alone on earth, but we may never live in a civilized world and tell right from wrong if we do not dream our lives as well. The dream tells us where to go and what to look for, and reality tells us when and how and if at all."

Now he saw why Sophie was the pyramid; she had given him everything, but without understanding anything about the nature of her gifts. Nor should she ever be told. You don't speak to the walls of a house and thank them for what they contain. Elderly people become empty but, for that very reason, capacious, and the space their dry organs no longer occupy must be used by the young for what it is worth: sheer protection from the onslaughts of nature, human and otherwise. Thus the Cardinal, too, had given him much: Adriana was his present. And the last image in his dream had given him something worth getting up for: the exercise of his profession on that asthmatic little boy.

Happy with this truly scientific absolution for all his sins, he turned on the light, rang the bell and got up to open curtains, window and shutters. And the happiest day of his life, his wedding day, greeted him with the most brilliant sunshine. It flashed at him from windowpanes, glass table tops, his gold watch on the dresser, the mirrors, even the shiny wooden floor. He looked at his watch: it was 7:12—shamefully late for him, even on special holidays, but this reminded him again that he was now on holiday, and a permanent one at that, unless he could find himself a new function in a society larger than that of Mary's family or her servants. And only now did he finally realize that he had slept no more than an hour and a half,

if that, considering the time it had taken him to come back to the
hotel from the top of the steps where he had heard the Infallible
Voice striking five, and the few minutes of his encounter with
Marinetti and the other fools. He was about to hurry into his
clothes and out of the hotel, when an unfamiliar object stopped his
whole course of thinking and deflected it into more modern, not to
say futurist channels: the telephone. Why not use it, since it was
there and it had been used by his new wife to awaken him the
previous day? Wouldn't she be pleasantly surprised by his call? And
by the knowledge that he was up already and rushing out to do his
duty? Sophie would be pleased too.

He grabbed the two receivers, put them to his ears, and called:
"Can you hear me?" No one seemed to have heard him, so he
shouted even louder. This went on for a few minutes, until someone knocked on the door. He put down the receivers to open the
door, and there stood the night concierge, surrounded by several
angry ladies and gentlemen, whose stature, checked tweeds and
strange voices made them recognizable as English even to Leonardo,
who asked: "What is it?"

"Why are you shouting so much, sir? Everybody can hear you,
and this is no hour . . ."

"I was trying to telephone."

"I know, sir, I was *at* the telephone."

"Then why didn't you answer?"

"Because I thought it must be a faulty contact or something, so I
unhooked the receiver to avoid a short circuit, but then I heard you
shouting from upstairs, and I came up to ask you not to disturb the
other guests. But I arrived too late." And the concierge proceeded
to apologize to the others, who thanked him and withdrew to their
bedrooms, saying God knows what in English against Leonardo.

"It's all your fault," said Leonardo, "if you had answered the
phone I wouldn't have had to shout."

"But, sir, you don't seem to realize that this is no hour to use the
telephone."

"You're wrong, because yesterday at this very hour someone telephoned *me*."

"Maybe, sir, but you probably received it from abroad."

"I don't know anyone abroad, I received it from the household of Mrs. von Randen."

"Oh . . . but that's a different thing. She calls Moscow and London and Berlin all the time; there are special operators who are trained to stay awake for such calls. But the local operators are asleep at this hour, and no one uses the phone in Rome before ten or eleven in the morning."

"And how did you know I wasn't going to call Moscow or Berlin?"

"Because people who do don't shout that way."

"All right, I'm sorry, but now you go downstairs and call Mrs. von Randen for me."

"I can't, sir, she went to bed so late, she must be asleep."

"How do you know she went to bed late?"

"Because her maids and her cook were here a few minutes ago, to pick up one of our maids and go to church with her, and I heard them talking about it."

"And this is Rome, you said? This is a village, if you ask me. Was it Dante's mother who went with them?"

"Yessir, it was."

"Is Dante here?"

"He's busy washing the staircase."

"Send him to me, please."

"At your orders, sir."

When Dante arrived, Leonardo was almost ready to go out. In his hurry to rush to the bedside of a patient, he had not even thought of shaving, which was as it should be. "What a joy to see you, my dear friend," Leonardo said. And, indeed, it felt like being back home, after such a long time and so many great events that had filled every minute since yesterday.

"I want you to do me a favor, while I rush over to Miss Mary's to see her child, who's sick."

"Sick? Her child? Little Kostia, you mean? I heard he's perfectly well."

"When did you hear that?"

"Minutes ago, from Adriana and her mother. They went to Mass

with my mother and said he had been so well taken care of by you
last night that he was asleep, and they were sure he would sleep late,
the way he loves to."

"Oh. Then probably I shouldn't go right now."

"No, you shouldn't."

"If only that damned fool of a night watchman had let me telephone."

"He was right not to let you. That would have been a great
mistake. Mrs. von Randen hates being telephoned, she always
thinks it's a call from her sons in Moscow or her brother in Paris,
and she hates to hear from them. And then, at this hour, in fine
people's houses, the servants are either at the market, or in church,
and there's only the foreign personnel to answer the phone. Mr.
Bernhard can't speak Italian over the phone. Why don't you wait
until ten?"

"Me? I'm a farmer, a shepherd, a man of the earth, my dear
friend. At this hour I have usually finished my morning calls to the
neighboring villages, and my horse is already worn out."

"Well, here in Rome at this hour even the goatherds take a nap.
They've finished their tour of the city and milked their goats dry,
you can see them asleep under their blankets in the Villa Borghese,
even from here. And you can hear their goats grassing in the
meadows near Villa Medici. Why don't you have breakfast? Or take
a bath?"

"That's an idea. I could even shave. Wonderful. Bring me a cup
of black coffee and leave it here on the table, I like to drink it cold,
and I never eat breakfast, but I want you to do me a great favor, if
you have a little time."

"I will, after I finish washing the floors in here."

"Why should you wash the floors in here? You washed them
yesterday, and today I won't let the bathtub overflow, I promise. So,
if you have nothing else to do, you are free now."

"Yes, thank you, I am."

"Do you know that small hotel in Via dei Sediari?"

"Yes."

"Don't go there, but go to the house behind it, beyond the big
double urinal, you know the one I mean?"

"Yes, I know the urinal."

"Well, the house that has windows right on top of it . . . go upstairs or call from the street for Professor Schillasi and tell him to come here at once, dressed as he was last night, and to wait for me here, if I'm not back. Tell him it's very, very important. Here, I'll write down the name."

"I know the name."

"You do?"

"Yes, I know the man, too. He was a museum guard, or a doorman or something; he's now retired."

"He is NOT a museum guard or a doorman! He is a man of great learning who abandoned his books early in life and sank into the gutter, but I can help him get back where he belongs, among respectable people."

Dante at once became very respectful, and very, very sad.

"At your orders," he said, bowing out.

For a moment Leonardo felt like running after him and apologizing, but then he said, aloud, "Absolutely not. Why should I? Learning is, after all, the only true aristocracy, and it is open to all, so if he feels hurt, that's his fault, and it may even do him some good!"

With this thought in mind, he undressed quickly, donned his robe, paraded in front of the mirror, and then quietly walked into the bathroom, where he ran himself a bath with all the expert knowledge he had acquired the previous day, feeling very proud because, after all, it was only the second such experience in his life. The sun was shining on the water and through the clouds of vapor, the rounded edges of the bathtub were as white as the marble of ancient Greek ruins after the rain; the window was open, the trees visible directly and indirectly in triplicate in windowpanes and mirrors; birds and goats and human voices in the distance completed the illusion of being back in the South on top of that hill where the last columns of Sybaris were still defying time, but what made it all so strange was the hot water, which allowed for daydreaming and even for the sweet afternoon nap of a hot summer day. What's so bad about wealth, he asked himself, when it's associated with true artistic appreciation and knowledge? I'm a Sybarite, and it feels better than being a Spartan all the time. The Spartans after all were only good for fighting, for destroying life and property and shunning the liberal arts, which alone led us to the discovery of science.

It all depends on what you use your wealth for: if you use it to let yourself sink into a sea of sensuousness and other physical pleasures, you are of course a degenerate Sybarite and your softness is disgusting, but if you use it only to steel yourself against all the comforts that allow the inquiring mind to play with new ideas, then you are a degenerate Spartan, and your softness is just as disgusting, if not more so, because it doesn't show, clad as it is in muscular fitness and unquestioning discipline. Archimedes's EUREKA came to him in hot water: his discovery of a good use for his apparent laziness was one of the most important laws of physics. This being so, it's no shame for me to marry a rich woman, if she can help me help mankind, and luckily she can. What better luck could I ever have wished for myself? It follows that I must not even think of Adriana any more. Dreams are dreams and reality is reality. And the reality here is that what happened last night was not my fault and it did me *and Mary* a lot of good. But if it happened again, I would be worse than all the Marinettis of this world. So I must not even think of it again, and besides, even if, *in the craziest hypothesis*, Mary *didn't exist*, and Adriana *were* pure, and I were *not* yet married, *still* Giovanna would be a better wife for me. She comes from a good family, she went to school, is of course a complete goose, but at least can pretend respect for knowledge, while Adriana is much too earthy to do any such thing, and also too intelligent. Besides, I never loved Giovanna at all, so she could never be an impediment to my work for the people (nor to my scientific research, if I were rich enough to pursue it), while Adriana would absorb all my thoughts and my energies; I would have to be constantly on guard, lest she cuckold me, but I would also be constantly ashamed of her manners and her origins, so, consequently . . .

A faint knock on the bedroom door made him aware of a detail he had forgotten. Dante was a lazy good-for-nothing and if it had taken him this long to bring him coffee, while he had nothing else to do, it might take him until noontime to find Schillasi, and that wouldn't do for many reasons: the cufflinks, and, more important even than those, Schillasi's future and his appointment with Baron Lumbroso that morning. "Come in," he shouted angrily, "and wait for me." He was determined to ask the hotel administrator in person for a carriage and a servant to accompany Dante on his errand, for by now he had learned that money was not to be mentioned at all, since Sophie paid for everything, and always paid too much.

He half dried himself and put on his robe to give Dante his orders, but when he opened the bathroom door what appeared in front of him was not Dante, oh no, it was Fate, Bad News, in the worst sense of the word: a young princess, almost a child, barely fifteen, probably Russian, or English, or German, certainly not Italian, and so beautiful that for a moment he was not even aware of his naked feet, his hairy legs and his wet body dripping water on those feet and on the carpet like urine. But the child-princess was embarrassed and trying to look away from it all. "I'm sorry," he said, "I'll be back in a minute. Do you understand Italian?"

"Yes," she said, in the roughest Roman voice, "I'm Cefala, Adriana's sister, and Adriana sent me here because she couldn't come herself: she has to iron all Miss Mary's blouses and help her get dressed, and my mother couldn't come either, because she has to do the same for the Signora. So they sent me, and Adriana said, 'Make sure you tell him such a thing has never happened before in my life, and I'll be damned if I know why it happened,' and she hopes you'll forgive her. Mamma is angry and says it was all Adriana's fault, but I don't believe it."

She was still looking away from him, now revealing her truly noble profile.

"I . . . I don't understand what this is all about, but there's no reason for Adriana to apologize. Please tell her so, and . . . I'm sorry I came out of the bathroom this way, I thought it was Dante. . . ."

His eyes fell on the cup of coffee Dante had left on the dresser, and this was the match that sets the haystack aflame: he knew Dante wouldn't come back, so he was all alone—safely alone—with this angel.

"I'll tell Adriana and I know she'll be pleased. Are you sure you're not angry because of what happened last night?"

"WHAT happened last night?"

"People laughing at you and hissing as you came upstairs, because you were dragging your overcoat in the dust?"

"Oh . . . was I???"

"Yes, and when my mother heard it this morning from Dante's

mother, she said it wasn't her fault, she had rushed her tacking because it was late and you were going out for a short walk. I see you're angry, and I'm sorry it all happened. But I can repair it now, if you want."

"Yes," he said, totally resigned to the loss of his soul. "I'll put it on and you can work on it. . . ." His voice was trembling, and she must have noticed it, because she blushed and said, still not looking at him: "Get dressed. I don't like to work on you this way."

"Oh . . . I'm very sorry . . . I . . . I'll be back in a moment." And he locked himself into the bathroom, but she knocked on the door and said, in an angelic voice now: "Here are your shoes and socks and clothes."

He opened the door wide, but she stayed on the threshold and handed him his various things as if he were a child. Another new and most humiliating experience, which he tried to use instantly, in a renewed fight against Satan.

Forgive me, Lord God, if I have appeared to deny Thy existence, but I was only trying to translate into modern scientific terms the eternal truths that are Thine, as they have always been and always will be. Amen. And help me overcome this new temptation, as you helped me in 1893, and, by God, that was a mistake. If I had married my true love then, I would never have felt tempted to betray her, please believe me. Strengthen in this girl the detestation of sin—since I can't detest it, in my base nature—and make her as reluctant as I am willing. Amen.

He was trying to shave while repeating this prayer and other ones besides, but his hand was shaking so that he cut his face in several places, and left parts of his cheek totally untouched. Which, for a man with a thick beard, is terrible. But all his thoughts behind these words were a current carrying him away from the shores of salvation. The current was *in* him: in vain did he try to button his pants and shirt collar and tie his cravat, and then his high boots . . . he had to stop several times and try to calm himself and imagine what would happen if the girl told all. She was clearly not like her sister, and she might go straight to Sophie to denounce Leonardo's unspeakable dishonesty. And then? What then? Yes, but what *now*? That was the question. When he finally emerged from the bathroom, his face all lined with red scars and his neck almost bursting

in its starched collar, Cefala looked at him calmly and came towards
him, holding his overcoat like a shield in front of her body. And
what else could he do in front of that shield but turn his back to it
and stretch out his two arms behind him to have himself all
wrapped up in fur and thick wool, two more long steps away from
the nakedness that his whole body craved?

"Let's do the whole thing again," said Cefala, lifting the hem of
the overcoat and tearing at it with big scissors, to undo all the
stitches her mother had sewn into it.

Now, with the coat returned to its normal size, he looked like a
Spanish Dominican monk in one of those primitive pictures of the
various Grand Inquisitors that had hung in the sacristy of the
church of Matera. The same black beard and upturned mustache,
the same accusing eyes, the same long tunic taking up so much
space on the floor for so small a man, whose head seemed even
smaller, perched as it was on the top of such a pyramid of black.

He looked at himself in the mirror, and saw her blond hair shining transparently in the sun against the blue sky and the green of
the oaks on the cliffs of the Pincio. She did look like Mary, he
realized now. Or was it only the blond hair? Perhaps only the hair—
yes, certainly the hair—Mary's face was much sweeter, less yellow,
less Mongol-like. Thank God: one element against this girl, thought
Leonardo, and he tried to concentrate on the blond hair, Mary's
most miraculous trait (Mary had so much of it that her large tor-
toise-shell pins could hardly keep it all together, while this young
girl had very little, and it was all held up above her neck by one
dirty celluloid comb. But what a neck . . .).

Now her preliminary work was over, and she put some pins into
her mouth, just as her sister had done a few hours earlier. Thank
God she looked ugly right now. But now she was kneeling in front
of him, and again he saw only her hair and her hands, and the
hands were also like Mary's, but much more like Sophie's, thinner,
but better than Sophie's, younger, much younger, of course,
younger than Mary's hands . . . years younger.

"How old are you?" he asked, in the same cold tone he used in
his consulting room, the tone used in hospital wards by all doctors
with illiterate patients.

"Fifteen next week."

"You're too young," he said, as if she had offered him her body.

"Too young for what?"

"For being exposed to the perils of the world."

She shrugged her shoulders impatiently, and didn't even lift her face, which made him wonder whether she could be blushing down there or just playing coy and waiting to see how far he would go.

"Or don't you think so?"

She was biting off the thread, and couldn't answer. When she had finally rescued the needle from the thick cloth, she looked at it, then lifted it again to her mouth for a much closer contact with her lips and bit it several times, with passion, it seemed to him, and he decided this was a clear signal.

"Do you or DON'T you think so?" he asked, with irony in his voice.

Now she was sucking at a new piece of thread, to stiffen it so it would enter the eye of the needle, and her lips made kissing noises that excited him unbearably.

"Did you hear my question, or . . . didn't you?"

"Of course I did: what was it you were saying?"

"I asked you: do you think you are too young, or don't you?"

"I don't know," she chanted, like a child bored by a parent's insistence.

"That's very bad, if you don't know. Some ill-intentioned man might think you're old enough for any kind of . . . thing, and when you discover you are too young, it's usually too late."

"These buttons are loose. Let me secure them." And she proceeded to unbutton the coat, which also seemed indicative of her clear intentions, because she was kneeling in front of him, and the back of her left hand inside the coat was only a few inches away from the part of a man that doesn't think. He pushed his body forward, to make her feel the truth, and she quickly withdrew both hands, looking at him with innocent eyes.

"It'll be easier for you if you take off the coat. You can sit down and rest, and I'll be finished in a minute."

"No, no, I'm sorry if I disturbed you, I'm in no need of rest, I just . . . I thought you were finished, that's all."

She resumed her work without acknowledging the apology, which meant she knew it was due her, and he thanked God for this

providential reminder, trying to comfort himself with nobler
thoughts. This is my wedding day. What I renounce this morning
will be given me tonight lawfully and for life. This despicable impulse, had it been allowed to succeed, would have ruined tonight's
joys with remorse, and God knows what consequences it might have
had for this innocent creature . . . or for me, if she turned out not
to have been so innocent after all. Syphilis can be a curse for generations, long after it is gone from the blood; if I rely on the moral
character of this weak creature, more than on my own, I may be
safe from syphilis and conceive healthy children, but God may give
me nothing but daughters, all as beautiful as this one, but all as
rotten as their father, and at the age of fifteen or even earlier, they
may dishonor themselves and their parents, just to teach me a
lesson.

"Your mother told me you don't work in the household. Where
do you work?"

"Here and in other hotels."

"Why doesn't your sister Giovanna do that?"

"Because my mother wants her to stay home."

"And Adriana?"

"Same reason."

"But wouldn't it be wiser if they went out to work in hotels and
you stayed with your mother?"

"Lift your chin, I must fix this button here. I don't want to sew
your beard into the cloth."

"Wouldn't it be wiser for them to go out into the world and for
you to stay home?" In his peculiar posture it seemed as if he were
addressing God.

There was a silence, then she whispered: "Perhaps."

"What does your mother say?"

"She doesn't want me to stay home."

"Why?"

"Because I like to sing."

"And what's wrong with singing? You have a beautiful voice."

"You haven't heard it. When I talk I have an ugly voice, but
when I sing, they can hear me down in Piazza di Spagna from the
kitchen of Via Gregoriana."

"Has Miss Mary heard you sing?"

"Oh yes, and she sent me to her singing teacher, but he said I must study music and learn how to read, and it takes years, and I want to sing now, in the taverns, during Carnival, or in the streets on Saint Peter and Paul's night, when the Cupolone is all lit with oil lamps and there are men with mandolins and they sing too. And then I like to dance on tables like the Spanish women with the black veils, and the singing teacher says that's no singing, that's . . . something else."

"Something else, what?"

"Just something else. I don't like to use the word he used."

"Did he use it in Miss Mary's presence?"

"Are you stupid? Of course not, but in my mother's presence he did. And my sisters were there too, and they said he was right and I should stop singing or leave home."

"And you left home?"

"What else could I do?"

"Where do you live?"

"Here with Dante's mother."

"I'm glad. She's a good woman."

"Yes."

"Do you like her?"

"Yes."

"Does she let you go out and sing and dance?"

"No."

"But you go anyway. You don't have to be afraid of me, I know human weakness and I won't talk."

"This button is fixed now. Let me sew the fur inside, it's been ripped. Just lift your arm, like this, yes, and don't move."

"You won't tell me?"

"No."

"Why, don't you trust me?"

"Oh yes, I trust you, I was answering your question. I don't go out and sing. Only with her, on Saint Peter and Paul's, and on Carnival."

"I am glad to hear that. You're a very good girl. May God bless you and give you all the happiness you deserve in life."

She kissed his hand, and his body was on fire.

"Don't," he said, "and promise me that you will never kiss the hand of a man."

"Not even a priest's?"

"His ring, if he's a bishop or a Cardinal, and you can't help it, but even there, be careful. They're all swine."

"That's what my father used to say," she laughed, looking at him with eyes that made his blood rush again.

"Why 'used to say'? Is he . . ."

"He's dead."

"Poor child," he said, patting her head with his hand, and it trembled so that his wedding ring became tangled in her hair. She helped him disentangle it. In doing so she lifted both arms, and a warm scent of perspiration rose to his nostrils. He felt her warm wrists against his, and closed his eyes, the better to concentrate on his decision: should I or shouldn't I?

"You should get married soon," he said.

"I'm going to," she replied with a smile that lifted him from the brink of the precipice of hell right up to heaven.

"Good!" he said. "I'm glad to hear it. Is your fiancé . . . jealous?"

"Oh yes, very."

"Good. Very good. You need it."

"That's what he says, but I don't pay much attention to all that."

"You should. Why? . . . Do you . . . give him reason to be jealous?"

"Not that I know of."

"The question is," and his heartbeat was pulling him down again through the hole in the clouds he had just reached, "HOW MUCH do you know?"

"All a woman needs to know." And she put her face close to his neck to bite off the thread.

"Tell me," he said, laying his hand on her cheek, "who taught you: your mother?"

She laughed. "You sound like a priest."

"No," he said, very hurt, "not like a priest, like a man, very much like a man, my dear child. . . ." And he couldn't go on, while she waited in a rather warm silence for whatever might come next, word or deed—or so he guessed and he knew she wouldn't help him.

"And a man who could like you much too much for his own good or yours," he added, in a trembling voice.

She was still silent, motionless, and blushing up to her ears. A girl blushing and looking so seriously at him, this was an experience he had almost forgotten. Mary of course had blushed in 1893 and then again now, but Mary was almost an old woman compared to this child. He was staring at her full lips, her neck, saw it pulsating with passion, lifted his eyes to meet hers, and they frightened him. There was something solemn, sacerdotal about this moment, and it hurt not to break through it and touch her mouth, only a few inches away. He was now breathing in her face and she in his.

"Is Dante's mother likely to come here?"

"No. She's at your house."

No further comment, no warning frown, no indication that she might reproach him or discourage him. Father in heaven, he thought, why have you abandoned me? This is my wedding day, lead me not into temptation, but deliver me from evil. Amen.

Finally she sighed and said: "You're a professor of medicine."

"Not a professor, only a humble doctor."

"But you know all the medicine that exists."

"There isn't much medicine, and there isn't much sickness, either. There are doctors and there are sick people, and the sick people must help the doctor just as much as the doctor must help them. We are all poor ignoramuses groping in the dark for a way out of this vale of tears without too much dishonor."

"You talk in a way that I like. I like likable people. You could also be a priest, and I don't mean that as an insult: a GOOD priest."

"A physician is a priest. In olden days, when medicine had not advanced at all, a priest was a physician."

"I would like to be a physician."

"Why?"

"To help mankind."

"Who taught you this phrase?"

"You hear it in church all the time, but how are you to help mankind? With prayers? With the coins that go into the Pope's pocket? Science—that's how you help mankind."

"You're a good soul. But you talk like a Protestant."

"That's what my confessor says."

"And what do you answer?"

"That he's a fool."

"You do?"

"Under my breath, and then I recite one more Hail Mary and one more Paternoster, to make penance. But he's still a fool, because he thinks he knows everything and he doesn't know nothing. The stupidest man in the world."

"Who is your father confessor?"

"You don't know him. His name is Monsignor Tegolani."

"The brother of the lawyer?"

"That's right."

"I think the lawyer is a fool."

She laughed, and her laughter was beautiful, raucous, sensuous, it did more harm in one second than all the silent allurements had done before. The old wanton spirit of evil was up again. The distance between their faces had not changed at all, which was of course painful, but it was also a good sign. Was this the moment to abolish it instantly, and kiss her while she laughed? It might pass for a momentary madness, to be apologized for if needed, without any loss of face. But he let the occasion slip by, feeling real pain in the parts that don't think, but still thinking, and that kept his arms and his neck muscles completely still.

"Isn't he a fool?" he asked, with a big friendly wink of the eye, but he knew this was a mistake. It confirmed a social distance that seemed to give her a new poise she had lacked until then. Her next words were purely conversational, and they hurt him very much, even though their content was not indicative of anything.

"I can't say."

"Why? We're all alone here."

This was meant to reopen the chapter that had been interrupted, but it did so only for him. She had stopped blushing, and moved imperceptibly backwards, reverting to social form, sighing with relief as she said: "Because he's the devil incarnate. He has the Signora wrapped around his little finger like this, and if he speaks one word against any of us, at home or even here, we're out. And once you are out with the Signora, there's no way back. Or even with

Miss Mary. Out is out, and the Lord have mercy on you. Do you know what they call you?"

"No."

"*Furbo.*"* She sighed again and stretched as if awakening from sleep, and he knew what this meant: it was the end of temptation for her. The blood no longer engorged the walls of the vagina, or the tips of the nipples, ready to receive him; it circulated freely, and fed ideas of purity into that most Protestant little head that believed itself so Catholic. Now she even yawned, as she said: "They're right. All Italians are *furbi.* That's what makes them so stupid. My two sisters are stupid, and my mother, poor fool, is also stupid, but that's what the Cavaliere likes. I'm differently stupid than they are, and that's what he's afraid of."

"Do you know the whole family?" (Why had he asked this question if it made the gesture of putting his arms around her shoulders NOT EVEN VAGUELY POSSIBLE?)

"Yes, I do."

"Miss Ludmilla too?"

"Yes, of course. She's like me: stupid. But I'm not completely out and she is."

"How? Why?"

"I can't tell."

"Why, don't you trust me?"

"Yes, but you're stupid like me, forgive me for saying so. . . ."

"Oh, you're right, you are perfectly right. . . ." And his arm slowly circled her back and came to rest on her shoulders, but she lifted it without even turning around, just as she would remove a dead object that had fallen on her from the ceiling.

"This is your last day in Rome," she said, "you must not do these things."

"You're right, but . . . if it were not the last day, it would be all right?"

"But you want to play *furbo* while you're not. Be stupid as you are, and you'll go to heaven. Miss Mary is also stupid, and I like her. Don't do these things to her."

"I'm sorry, you *are* right." Now it was for him to yawn and

---

* Clever, sly.

stretch his arm, as he said: "So the Signora alone is stupid in the other way . . . or isn't she?"

"No no, she's stupid our way too, and so is Miss Mary, but . . . they are stupid-English, not stupid-Italian."

"English? They're not English."

"We say English to mean people who travel and have houses everywhere and go to museums, but some English are German, and others are Russian, some are even French, and then there are the English who are American. The world is full of English people, and Italy is full of Italians. Too many of them for the loaves and the fishes on the table. Do you know what my father used to say?"

"No, what did he say?"

"He said: Christ spoke the word and was able to feed seven thousand loaves and seven thousand fishes to seven people. *That's* the miracle!!"

"How perfect! How wonderful!" shouted Leonardo. "And they were *all* Vicars of Christ at his table!!! Oh, Cefala"—and his arms reached out to her in a symbolic embrace that didn't dare come true—"your father was a genius!"

"No, not a genius, just stupid."

"One . . . two . . . three . . ." counted Leonardo, as the voice of the clockwork Pope vibrated in his empty stomach, "don't tell me it's ten!" By the time he found his watch, the Pope had told him so, and all the lesser churches were beginning.

"Well, it's too late now, even if we wanted to. Better this way." These words, spoken in *romanesco*, cut deep into his heart, and he cried out almost in a sob, his arms outstretched again: "Cefala . . . MY Cefala, my guardian angel. You saved my life, but God is cruel, to send me a messenger like you and then take her back."

"*Ce metto'a firma . . .*"* she said, and after a long sigh: "You should be a public scribe, you say things so well."

Almost at the same instant there was a knock on the door. The hotel manager was standing outside, very discreet but very curious, asking, "Is the seamstress Cefala here, by any chance? She's needed in the wardrobe."

Leonardo was pleased he had been caught with his coat on, and

---

* "I'm ready to affix my signature to this . . ."

Cefala busy brushing his hat and trying to give it some sort of a shape again after being trampled upon by Marinetti.

"That will do," he said to her, "I told you not to waste any more time on that hat, I'll have to buy another one today anyway." And he went out in style—not his own, of course, but the arrogant style of the rich, whose politeness is more offensive than a direct insult. But he was all torn to pieces inside, longing to turn and look once more at that beautiful face, and make the angel feel how much he cared. He followed the manager slowly downstairs, hoping she would catch up with him, but he didn't realize that servants use the service stairs, and when he reached the porter's desk, he heard the manager say to a bell-boy. "Tell Mr. Marinetti that his shirts will be ironed and starched within the next hour. The seamstress will bring them to him, and we have his tickets: one private compartment with sitting room on the Paris Express."

Again, summoning up all the most arrogant hypocrisy which was to be his only defense from now on and for the rest of his life, he asked the porter: "Is he leaving today? What time?"

"The Paris Express leaves at one twenty, sir. Do you want to speak to Mr. Marinetti?"

"Let's see," he said, consulting his watch, "no, I'm afraid I can't. But . . . I'll try to be back in an hour and . . . well, just let him know I have something urgent to discuss with him before he leaves. That's all. Oh yes, and say hello to him for me."

And out he went, under the heaviest overcoat that ever was.

The first weight he cast off his heart was that of Cefala's infidelity. He's not her type at all . . . I am, unfortunately for her, my poor little angel . . . and unfortunately for me too, and for Mary . . .

Careful now! The day was bright and very cold and very, very beautiful: the perfect day for some great celebration of happiness, such as the crowning episode of a romantic dream that had lasted nine years.

Marinetti is a swine. . . . God knows what slimy methods he will use to take advantage of her weakness. . . . He may promise her a career as a singer and dancer in Paris. Let's hope her religious convictions will be strong enough to see her through this terrible encounter. She loves me, anyway . . . and that's bad for both of us. . . . And for Mary! Enough of these fantasies now!

He tried to think of Mary, but he could only think of her *as living in Laterza;* that is, in the image he had nurtured in his heart for nine years. Here he saw her in the shadow of that huge mother of hers, those huge curtains, marble busts, china cabinets, bookshelves and books, rooms, corridors, kitchenware and silver, those weird, unpredictable opinions that changed every five minutes, or, rather, changed places, now coming from her mother, now from her. . . . Cefala on the other hand was so simple, so clear-thinking, so modest . . .

Marinetti is a swine, but if he knows that I'll be back in an hour, he probably imagines he has made a new acolyte of me, and his vanity is such . . . besides, she loves me, that's clear . . . Too young for me, of course, and then: how would I face the world, going back home penniless, dishonored and with a living scandal on my arm? But where else could I go? If Crocifisso were available right now to give me advice . . . But what about Mary?

And again he felt he could never betray his dream. It had become his true religion, his refuge against all things vulgar and stupid, the dishonesty of Italy, the monotony of life in Laterza, the lack of high ideals in the minds of his colleagues . . . And the true person Mary had not betrayed the true dream Mary; in fact, she was a thousand times better, and so was Sophie, with her love of mankind, her enthusiasm for Progress. . . .

Marinetti is a swine and a fool, but he's right about certain things. . . . But he won't fool Cefala, of course, because she loves *me.* . . .

Now he knew what was weighing most heavily on his heart: his failure to kiss her at least once. A chaste kiss, and she wanted it so . . . That last sentence of hers . . . What deep regret, what sadness in those words. Why didn't I do it? Only *one* kiss . . . her *one* night of happiness . . . Isn't it odd? She and those sisters and that mother . . . This is the true Cinderella. . . . How close I was to kissing her. Why didn't I do it? ᴏɢɴɪ ʟᴀsᴄɪᴀᴛᴀ è ᴘᴇʀsᴀ* . . .

---

* Italian proverb: every woman you don't pursue immediately is lost.

That of course is a very vulgar saying, but there's some truth in it. That one kiss would have sealed our experience. Now it's gaping open, bleeding like a wound. . . .

He had reached Piazza di Spagna and found solace in the sunshine. Up there directly in the sun was the same group of beggars, still under the same blankets, which were certainly warm by now. "Don Leonardo!!! Don Leonardo!!!"

No, it wasn't Schillasi, this was a Roman voice, and he soon knew which one.

"Wasn't it lucky that I was in time last night and again this morning to rescue you from Marinetti? But I want you to know that he's a good man. His father is the richest lawyer in Cairo."

"Oh, is that what makes him a good man?"

"Of course not, but . . ."

"But what?"

"You know . . ."

"No, I *don't* know. I only know that I don't think the way you do."

"But you and I think the same way . . . we're both superidealists, and fools—of course, God's fools, too honest, too pure. But the OTHERS reason that way—"

"Who are the others?"

"Oh, you know . . ."

"Yes, this time I do know: YOU. And I know a few more who are the likes of you too, and I don't care for any of them."

"Young man, you are insulting me. And I have saved your life—twice. I am your friend."

"I'm not insulting you, you are insulting me by teaching me lessons in morality that a child wouldn't accept. You never saved my life: I'll have you know that I've been in a fistfight before, and I can hold my own, even if I lose a hat and a few teeth."

"My God . . . you remind me of myself a few years back. . . . Youth, the great, generous idealism of youth . . . Wasn't my whole life ruined by it? But I would still behave as foolishly, if I were given a second chance. Because that's the way I am . . . *we* are, I should say. I'm older than you, and I do have greater experience—that, I hope, you'll concede."

Leonardo didn't know what to say, he was so eager to be rid of the worm.

"I see you're silent. This much I can be grateful for. Because I like you very, very much. Just as you are, difficult to handle, insulting, disrespectful . . . I only mentioned Marinetti's father because he's a wonderful person, and so is the mother, and the son is devoted to them. In this he's like me. I worship just one person in the world: my mother, God keep her in good health for another hundred years, she's ninety already. . . ." He wiped a tear with his sleeve. "The day she goes . . . I'm finished. . . ." He was now in floods. "Remember her in your prayers, will you? God listens to the pure of heart like you. . . . One cannot help liking you . . . I only mentioned money, because we all need it in life. You are about to become a rich man, but God knows what life has in store for us. . . . Great fortunes tumble like castles of cards. And a friend like Marinetti, in Paris, where your future mother-in-law has only enemies, may some day come in handy. . . . Goodbye, I must make arrangements for your trip. By the way, it seems you won't be leaving tonight."

"No? But why?"

"I don't know. I just obey instructions. It's not for me to ask questions. But you'll find out in a few minutes anyway."

And with these words he was gone.

"Why so late?" asked Mary.

"Why are we not leaving tonight?" he replied.

"Who told you? You don't seem at all displeased."

"I beg your pardon, I am very displeased, why do you assume things that aren't true?"

"If they weren't, you wouldn't seem so absent, so cold with me, so . . . I don't know, I only know that something has changed in you. And why don't you answer my questions?"

"That bastard Tegolani told me."

"Tegolani, a bastard? Since when? How can you judge a person who has saved your life twice? You, who haven't even spoken to him once?"

"I have spoken to him twice, and that was more than enough to form the most negative judgment possible. He's an extremely dangerous person."

"You seem to hate everything we like. And you still haven't answered my first question."

"What first question?"

"Have you forgotten it, or are you playing games?"

"I've forgotten it."

"Oh, so you have! My questions don't seem to interest you any more. I would much prefer to hear you say you were trying to cheat me, but obviously I'm not even worth that effort. Just forgotten. Finished! Is that because you found someone else? Did the little seamstress work in your room? You liked her, of course. Isn't she charming?"

"Mary, you should be doubly ashamed of yourself: first, for your insane jealousy—I never looked at a woman in nine years—and, second, for doubting my taste. That's no woman, that little scrawny monster. How she can charm anyone is a mystery you'll have to explain to me."

"You, on the contrary, have several mysteries to explain to me. First mystery: you never looked at a woman in nine years, yet in those nine years you had many, plus a wife. Did you always keep your eyes closed? Second mystery: how can you speak of taste if you never looked at a woman? That's like saying, I never drank a drop of alcohol, but let no one dare question my taste in wines!"

Leonardo paused to smile. It was only now that he remembered he hadn't kissed her at all, even though she had met him on the stairs outside the front door, on the darkest landing, where they had kissed that same morning.

"You're so aggressive, my love, you frighten me. Here I was, totally destroyed by the bad news of this delay, and you don't even kiss me. Why? And why this barrage of inquisitorial questions? Of course I'm upset, and I humbly apologize, but, having done so, I refuse to speak one single word unless I receive the first kiss of our wedding day."

She fell into his arms and cried. "I was so worried. I was sure you'd been taken in by that horrible monster of a Cefala, that little whore who throws herself at any man's throat the moment she sees

him. You don't know her, my love, but I do. I was so angry at
Adriana for asking her to go up to your room. Adriana trusts her,
thinks her sister couldn't be any worse than she is, and she always
accuses herself of being flirtatious, but she really is an angel. And
truthful like no other Italian woman, in all my experience. Do you
know that the Monster tried to seduce her? In my mother's own
house!!! But she spat in his face and came to me, crying. She's my
only *true* sister. If we ever have a daughter, I pray God she'll be a
second Adriana. Not a second Cefala, God forbid! The very thought
makes me shudder. That scrawny, pretentious little upstart, who
thinks she's got all the answers . . ."

"And didn't I call her *scrawny*? One glance was enough. Of
course I keep my eyes open. But there's a great difference between
seeing and looking."

Another kiss sealed this answer, and Mary laughed at her own
stupidity.

"Of course, my darling, I owe you an apology for thinking so little
of your judgment. That is the *correct term*, as you always say. Judgment, not taste. And you *do* have judgment, you sized her up at
once. Did she work in your room?"

"Of course not."

"But didn't she have to measure the length of the coat on you?"

"Of course she did, but that takes less than a minute."

"More than five, certainly."

"Right, but I'm repeating what I said to her. I was impatient to
see her go."

"And did she go?"

"I made her. I said: Come back when it's ready. She understood."

"You know how to treat women of that type. She's a dangerous
whore."

"Darling, I think you exaggerate. And you give her too much
importance. Here we have been discussing her for the last five minutes, instead of our own plans. Why is it we're not leaving tonight?
I hate to spend another minute in Rome."

"Mr. Schultz insists that we make a full inventory of everything
in this house before we leave. That's the bankers' mentality, you
know? Petty, obsessed with security, afraid of being cheated, and

unable to see beyond their noses. Poor darling, I'm being unjust to
him, because he's so devoted to us, but he can't help it, he's a self-
made man, after all, . . . and a Jew."

"So was your father."

"Not a Jew, please! Only a self-made man, but then Pappa was an
exception. He could *only* see beyond the petty details, in grand
lines, with a true Russian sense of greatness . . . that's why he died
almost in penury."

"He did? And how about all this?"

"Oh, this is nothing. We're poor."

"Who is rich then?"

"Everybody else."

"Who? Cefala's mother? Dante and his mother? The goatherds
who bring live milk from door to door at five in the morning and
then give milk for free to the beggars on the steps of Trinità dei
Monti? Your servants are rich compared to the goatherds, and they
are rich compared to the beggars, but the beggars are poor. I too am
poor, but let any of my patients in Laterza hear me, and they'd be
just as shocked as I am when I hear you say that *you* are poor."

He didn't give a damn about any of these things, which is why he
was speaking so joyfully: he was happy at the thought that they
would not be leaving Rome for another few days. Not that he had
changed his mind about Mary or his future, or especially about
Cefala: on the contrary, he wanted everything to be made more
acceptable by one chaste goodbye kiss. And he believed this to be
possible.

"Darling, you and I are so much alike that I can't get angry at
you, even when you insult our best friend Tegolani. But you and I
are like my father and mother: too honest, too generous, not to be
exploited by others, and we're very lucky to have friends like Tegolani and Schultz who are both idealistic and practical. They form a
shield between us and the world. What irritates both Mamachen
and me is that these two wonderful people should be constantly at
loggerheads with each other."

"I'm on Schultz's side. Tegolani is a shit. Sorry, but there's no
better word for him, and shit at least has a function in life, while he
has none."

They had reached the library, when they heard sounds of a violent fight being carried on between Sophie and Mr. Schultz in Russian. The voices were so angry that Leonardo paled with fear. He wouldn't have thought it possible that a woman and a man could fight so violently without coming to blows. Mary on the other hand seemed very amused.

"What's all this?" he asked. "Why don't you call your servants to rescue your poor mother from that wild beast?"

"Rescue?" she asked. "Wild beast? What do you mean? Can't you hear they're having a chat?"

"I don't understand Russian, as you know, but even so, it's the tone that makes the music."

"But the tone couldn't be more cordial, my love. They're discussing pacifism. Mamachen says that his point of view will lead him to lose his temper, and he says that her point of view—"

"Whaat? He hasn't lost it yet? We must stop him at once, before he does, or he'll kill her."

"Schultz? The meekest man on earth? That's not the sound of a man losing his temper. He's so phlegmatic, he's the joke of Russia. He tries to out-English the English at being softspoken. But it's a pity you can't follow the argument, because Mamachen speaks with great passion about nonviolence, and I wish you could hear the beautiful things she's saying in defense of Tolstoy, who is her god and also mine. Shall we ask them to continue in Italian?"

"Not now, I must see Kostia. I promised him last night I would see him this morning, and then I must rush back to the hotel to meet my cousin, who's probably there right now waiting for me."

"We can send the coachman to pick him up, and he will have lunch with us."

"No no, I must see him there, I have things to discuss with him. . . ."

"We can leave you alone in the library with him, no one will disturb you until it's time for lunch." And without waiting for his answer she rang the bell, and Bernhard arrived.

"No," said Leonardo in anguish, "please don't. I said I must see him at the hotel and not here. I know my cousin. He's extremely timid, and he wouldn't . . . er . . . he . . ."

His sudden embarrassment was covered by Mary's distressed face. "Why do you have to shout?" she asked. "Can't you talk quietly?"

"Me? Shouting?"

"You."

"But, darling . . ."

"You must have some mysterious reason for not letting us meet your cousin. What is it?"

"Me? Mysterious reason? *What* mysterious reason?"

"That's what I want to know."

"But there are no mysterious reasons!"

"Then he'll come. Very simple." And she gave orders in German to Bernhard.

"No," shouted Leonardo this time, running after Bernhard and catching him in the corridor. "No, Bernhard, NO."

And he came back to the library, to find Mary panting and pale, her eyes staring into space.

"What is it, my love?"

"I am not your love. I had asked you as a great, special favor not to use the words the Monster uses, and you seem to do it on purpose. I can't even know where you picked them up."

"What did I say now?"

She grimaced. "What . . . did . . . I . . . say . . . now . . . ANOTHER ONE OF HIS PHRASES . . ."

"I'm sorry. I shan't do it again. But what did I say before that that was typical of him? Please tell me so I can avoid it in the future."

"You said NO. He always says NO. Every second word is NO. And I, who deluded myself that we were like one soul in two bodies . . ." She broke out into sobs, and he paced the room, fumbling with his stethoscope. After a few seconds she wiped her tears and tried to smile. "Come give me a kiss and be good. Don't pout, for heaven's sake, he does that too. Obviously there's something in the Italian language that makes all Italians talk alike. At least you don't talk with a Roman accent, and you don't have red hair. Thank God for that. Come, let's make peace. . . . What is it you're playing with?"

"This? My stethoscope."

"Black and gold? I've never seen such a strange stethoscope. The ones our doctors use are all black."

"This was . . . made to order."

"Oh. It's a present, then."

"Well, in a way . . ."

"A wedding present."

"In a way . . ."

"May I see it?" She took it into her hand, kissed him again passionately and then said: "Shall we start a new chapter in our life?"

"But this is a . . ." He was quick at correcting himself: "Yes, of course."

"Then this wedding present, which obviously comes from *her,* must go." And she broke it, gashing her hands. *"Gospody!!!! blood!!!* The evil witch!! Even from a distance she casts her evil spell on you."

And while he rang the bell (the first time he had touched the levers of command in his new house), she rushed to the window, opened it and threw the broken pieces into the street.

"Darling," he shouted, "don't move, you're spilling blood everywhere."

"*She's* doing it!" answered Mary in a rage, and while Bernhard was throwing up his arms and running out to call for help, Leonardo cast a last glance at his beloved stethoscope and saw that it had fallen on the head of a small man dressed in black: Schillasi, who looked up and called: "Leonardo, I'm coming upstairs."

Leonardo didn't answer, and didn't even close the window. He rushed out of the room, almost stumbling over Adriana who was running in with bandages and disinfectants. He opened the front door and ran down the stairs.

"Imbecile," he shouted, as he met Schillasi on the landing, "who ever authorized you to come here? I said to wait for me at the hotel."

"If that's the way you greet your benefactor, go to hell and stay there!" Schillasi shouted back, loud enough to be overheard by everybody in the house, since Leonardo had left the door open.

"Please, please, Luigi, my brother, my friend, please listen to me, it's for your own good."

These words, too, were overheard, while Leonardo ran after Schillasi—the exact reverse of what had happened through the streets of Rome less than twenty-four hours earlier.

"To hell with you, to hell!!! My own good, he says . . ." Now Schillasi was haranguing the street, which included the doorman and the coachman and a few other persons of low origin and still lower understanding, plus, alas, the highest and the best, because Leonardo had left the window open and now Mary and Adriana were watching the scene from one window, and Sophie with Schultz from the other, using opera glasses to get a closer view of the actors.

"Yes, Goombà, your own good, I beseech you, listen to me, the reason I sent for you is I have found the solution to all your problems!!!! If you listen to me, the doors of heaven will be flung open to you, but you must act at once, or else. . . ."

"Hear ye, hear ye, ladies and gentlemen, the gigolo of a rich foreign woman, who has left his own lawful spouse for her! . . . And he owes his great fortune to me . . . for it was I who forced him to come back here, he was going straight to the pigsty he calls home, down in the back of beyond. . . . And now he denies his benefactor, because he's ashamed of me, I'm not a laureate and he is. . . . But I'd much rather be myself, illiterate and poor as I am, than a doctor like him, a sponger, a gigolo, and a traitor to his friends. . . . And to his wife . . . And to his duty . . . He comes here fr—"

The rest of this short word was smothered in a death rattle; Leonardo had grabbed him by the throat and was threatening to kill him.

"Shut up and listen if you don't want to die, you sonofabitch turd shit . . ."

And the final revelation was lost to the audience, because Leonardo was dragging his victim down the steps of Trinità dei Monti, talking to him in a monotone born of desperation.

"I have worked for you, faceless turd and shit that you are, and you are invited to dine this very night at Donna Ersilia Lovatelli's, an extremely—"

"Whaaat? Are you telling the truth?"

"The truth, so help me God Almighty and the Holy Madonna of

Pompeii, the saints Crisostomo and Giovanni Colasanzio, the truth, I swear on my own mother's tomb. . . . *Invited*, as a professor, and a French Cardinal will have you given the title of Professor by the French government in person, I mean the President of the Republic of France, but first you have to go and see Baron Giacomo Lumbroso, here is his address, go at once, before the clock strikes noon, he will explain your new functions as the librarian of Signor Marco Besso. . . ."

"Marco Besso, you said? The king of insurance? The one who's building that huge palace on Largo Argentina?"

"I know nothing about him, I only know this is the man you're going to work for. Quick now, go, but before you do, you must give me back those cufflinks and that white vest, instantly, because—"

"Are you insane? Or has the greed of the mighty corrupted you already to the point of no return? Look at your fur coat! Isn't that enough? These are presents, ʏᴏᴜʀ presents. And besides, how can I present myself to a baron, and then go to dine with a countess-princess-duchess without cufflinks and without a vest?"

"You'll be wearing mine. It's just an exchange . . . I'm going to give you these I'm wearing in the place of those you are wearing."

"But *mine* are better! If I am to meet all these important people, I must wear my best things!"

"Look, I was able to arrange all this godsend for you wearing these cufflinks and this waistcoat here, so you can wear them too." And he started to undress right there, in the cold wind. "Quick, give me yours and take this, I'm freezing. And be quick, it's getting late. All right, now the cufflinks."

"Not the cufflinks, leave me them at least. I'm used to them. I can't get used to the others."

"What do you mean ᴜsᴇᴅ? You've had them for less than one day!"

"You don't know me, I'm a man of habits. And at my age—"

"Nonsense. But let's waste no more time. You may keep them for today, but tomorrow morning, no later than seven, I want you to come to my hotel with these cufflinks *and* the others. Understand?"

"The others too? But they're no longer in my possession."

"What do you mean, they're no longer in your possession? Have you sold them?"

"Not quite."

"What do you mean NOT QUITE?"

"They're at the *monte di pietà*. . . . Don't look at me that way! You rich people don't realize that a poor man like myself needs money. What's wrong with that? Why do you keep making big eyes, as if you had never heard of poverty? I'll have you know another thing you rich people never realize: You cost *us* money. . . . You, Leonardo, cost ME a lot of money yesterday. Yes, you did! That was my monthly retirement pension I was spending, and I spent more than half of it, yes, and I couldn't tell my wife I had spent so much money in one afternoon—she would have given me a beating, you don't know her. So I had to pawn those cufflinks first thing in the morning, and I would have pawned these too in another few days. I know why you want them back: because they're more valuable than yours. Typical of the rich. I'm not surprised. Nothing can surprise me, at my age."

"Go, go now, don't waste any more time. I can't give you any money for a cab, because I don't have any, as you know. Spend the money you got from the *monte di pietà* and take a cab right now, I'm sure the Baron will give you an advance payment on your salary if you tell him you're poor, and, besides, I swear to God I'll have money tomorrow morning, and I'll give you more than you spent on me yesterday. I'm no sponger."

Leonardo was surprised to see Schillasi move away so meekly. He had been resigned to another outburst and was already steeling himself against the temptation to waste further good words in defense of a lost cause. He didn't know that Mr. Schultz had been passing behind him. Schillasi had seen him, and, as this extremely well-dressed foreigner seemed to be watching him with such admiration, Schillasi walked off, to savor the feeling of those rich, foreign eyes on his person, and especially on his cufflinks.

"By God, I was right," he said aloud, "these cufflinks are worth more than the others; in a pig's eye I'll give them back."

Mr. Schultz had good reason to be so fascinated by these cufflinks; he had seen them every day when he was a delivery boy in the bank of Sophie's father, a man of very Spartan habits whose one concession to luxury was these jewels, given him by his wife, who

had died at the tender age of twenty-four, after giving birth to those
terrible children: Jules, now settled in Paris and protecting failed
artists, and Sophie, traveling incessantly and protecting all sorts of
shady characters from Tegolani to Leonardo, her latest whim. . . .

Leonardo meantime was walking slowly home. He had reached
the steps and was about to climb them when the same beggar
woman who had caused all his troubles in the first place suddenly
threw her blankets aside, causing her elderly bedfellows to curse in
protest, and ran after him, grabbing him by the arm: "Hey, you,"
she shouted, "if you can be so generous with that bastard, why don't
you help me? I need money, he doesn't; he's married to a rich
woman, they own the whole palace where they live, you haven't
seen the palace where they live . . . two stories high, and a beautiful blacksmith shop too. They don't need your money, but I do, for
my sick child. Why won't you help me?"
Leonardo had hardly recovered from his shock, when the other
beggars began to whine and beg from their filthy beds or piles of
rags on the cold steps: "Good sir, make charity to us, poor old men
full of woes. . . ."
"Later, later," he shouted, "I haven't got a cent in my pockets
right now." And again he exhibited his empty pockets and his
empty wallet.
"The cufflinks, the watch, the chain, the empty wallet, anything
. . . we can sell them."
"No, I can't, but I swear to you on the Holy Virgin . . . just let
me go home and get some money for you, and I'll bring you plenty,
I promise. . . . And medicines for your sick child."
"Bless your heart, you're a good man," she said, kissing his hand
just as Cefala had kissed it, which made him think of her again in a
way that sent waves of joy and pain down his spine, and before he
could withdraw his hand, she was shouting: "And don't help that
sonofabitch Luigi Schillasi, he's an evil man, I know him, he's my
uncle, he's been trying to get me arrested and sent back home by
the police, because I had an illegitimate child."
"Really? And you don't want to go back because of the dishonor. . . ."

"Fuck the dishonor. Everybody in Acquaviva delle Fonti knows that I'm a whore, I couldn't care less. My mother's a whore too, and everybody knows and she doesn't care."

"Then why don't you go back to her? Or is she too poor?"

"She would be glad to have me back, she has a tavern and a few goats, and a small piece of land."

"Then *why don't you go back?*"

"Because this is where all the money is. This is the Great Capital of the World, the Pope is here, all the big people are here; you're stupid, my uncle is right, you don't know how much money there is here."

"And you do, I suppose."

"Of course I do. What would I be doing here otherwise?"

"What ARE you doing here is the question you should ask."

"Oh no, dear sir, the question is: what would I do back home? Even if I reformed, even if I got married, what would I do on holidays? Watch the people go by? They're all poor, they're afraid of us, they run like cats the moment they see one of us, yet we would never beg from them because we know them. Believe me, dear sir, once you're used to the life of the big city, you can't live in the backwoods again, no, never. . . . Here it's always Sunday, Easter, Carnival, Procession of the Holy Ghost. Here we only see the rich. Ask my friends over there, they'll tell you. On Carnival we have a lot of fun, and on Saint Peter and Paul's night, when all the oil lamps are lit and you can see the shape of the Cupolone from miles away, who would want to be starving in the provinces? You should see the traffic on these steps then. Once I even saw the Pope, and he gave me a gold coin."

"How much?"

"Five lire. I still have it, I kiss it every time I begin my day, it brings me good luck, it comes from the Pope."

"Why don't you spend it, and pay for a doctor? Or for medicines and food? Five lire can keep you alive for a month."

"God will take care of everything, don't worry."

"God yes and the Pope no?"

"But the Pope isn't God—he has so many expenses. Running the Vatican is no joke. Just a moment, don't go away, I'll be back in a minute, I've got work to do!"

And she ran to her child, who seemed completely comfortable, playing with the older beggars; she grabbed him violently, pinching him repeatedly until he started whimpering again as he had for Leonardo the previous day, then ruffled her own hair, and, with the child in her arms and an expression of infinite pain in her eyes, she came up the stairs again towards Leonardo, who was thinking: Doesn't she realize I've seen everything? This time I'll just tell her I agree with her uncle, but she didn't give him time, because, just as she passed, she winked and, before he knew it, here she was approaching THEM with the same gestures and look of pain in the eyes, reciting the same litany of the sick child that had proven so successful with him.

Very few people resisted, but not one of them had a kind word for her. Those who refused either treated her as nonexistent or dismissed her with insults, but those who gave generously were even more generous with their self-reproach.

"I always do it," said one kind lady, closing her purse and putting her begloved hand back into her mink muff.

And the husband: "When will you learn?"

Another one: "And to think I promised God in my prayers this morning to put an end to that child's woes and take him away from his mother, no matter what she said to me—but how can you do such a thing without causing a scandal? You never know if you can trust the police in this city. If they don't remove these beggars from the steps, they must have a reason. Perhaps they get a percentage."

Leonardo was so appalled by it all that he stayed where he was, not caring if he was late; home spelled the problems of explaining his behavior towards his "cousin" and in words unsoiled by the Monster, so he took his time, but in the process the sleep he hadn't had the previous night began to assert itself. He stared at the endless procession of elegant people passing between him and the old beggars, and stared and stared, but he stared as one stares at receding reality while being carried away into the land of dreams. Leonardo didn't want to fall asleep becuse this was a new day, and Mary was awaiting him with love, and everything in his future was promises, but the one promise that had always been faithfully kept at the end of each day had not been kept last night: the promise of as many hours rest as had been filled with work. So he stared and

stared, telling himself: "Just another few hours of this comedy—"
He had forgotten Cefala, Adriana, even Schillasi, in fact he had no
idea where he was: he knew there was sunshine, and that is all one
needs to know about the world before leaving it for a short nap.

It all became a beautiful dream. There suddenly was Mary coming down the steps in the company of a man who was her husband.
Dreams being what they are, it didn't seem at all absurd that she
should be with the Monster: wasn't he still her legitimate husband?
There they were, walking together, she looked at Leonardo with
love and he was talking to him, and, what is more surprising, cheerfully, jokingly, and everybody was laughing, even Mary. Oh, wasn't
this the ideal dream? To be at peace with both of them, therefore
with the law as well, and to know that Mary loved him and was
indifferent to her husband, just as Leonardo loved her and was
indifferent to his wife. . . .

He woke suddenly and was restored to unpleasant reality by the
sight of his hat hoisted on top of a stick and rotating like a weather-
vane, to everyone's amusement and his greatest dismay. There stood
the Monster, waving the stick in question and calling him a gigolo
of rich elderly ladies, and all around him were the people he had
seen at the dinner table the previous night: Count Jahn-Rusconi
with his sister and an older lady who was obviously their mother,
Countess Ersilia Lovatelli and her ducal and princely brother, and
maybe there were others too, but Leonardo didn't care to recognize
them. He had seen more than enough for his own peace of mind,
but what struck him most cruelly was the laugh of the Monster's
companion: she *did* look like Mary in some mysterious way that he
alone could see; in fact, she looked far more like Mary than the
vulgar mistress the Monster had exhibited the previous day at the
café. This was the *other* woman, the one whose attention the Monster had been seeking while his mistress was seeking Leonardo's
attention. How strange, he thought, or rather didn't: he couldn't
think much, but he knew that, in a more peaceful future, if such a
thing could still exist for him, he would think it rather strange that
he knew nothing of this man, yet he had a great deal in common
with him, because the same type of woman attracted them both. He
stood aghast looking at all these people, these citizens at the zoo,

looking back at him in his cage. But the good star of social hypocrisy, unknown in the low provinces, still ruled supreme in Rome:
the first to feel moved by it was Prince Caetani, who acknowledged
Leonardo's stare by taking off his hat and moving on, as if nothing
had happened. Second was Count Jahn-Rusconi, who had seemed
amused earlier and now was merely polite and bored. And of course
all the women followed the men without greeting Leonardo, because that had been done by their men, or was it that myopia also
belonged to the code of good manners? They all had a lorgnette
hanging over their mufflers, and didn't seem interested enough to
aim it at him. But the Monster's new mistress was more than just
interested: she was angry at herself for having laughed, and she
lifted her arm above her lover's shoulder, pulled down the stick and
grabbed the hat in time to save it from a gust of wind, then gave it
to Leonardo, and it was he who didn't dare acknowledge her politeness by taking it, so the wind got it after all, and it rolled down the
steps, just as it had yesterday, but this time Leonardo didn't run
after it. He was glad they were all gone, and would rather have lost
his hat forever than be seen by them again in some new clownish
act. And then his attention was caught by the Monster, who was
now having a loud scene with his mistress.

"What's wrong with my smiling at him?" she was shouting.
"He's nice, I like him. But I don't like you. One more stupid jealous
scene and I'll leave you."

"Jealous scene? Me! . . ." And the rest was lost in the distance.

But from the same point in the distance the hat now came back,
carried by the same type of young hoodlum who had rescued it
yesterday and given him such trouble. This time, however, Leonardo had better defenders. "Hold the child for me, will you?" said
the whore, and ran down the steps to meet the hoodlum halfway
and beat him over the head until he relinquished his prize. Then
she came back slowly, rubbing it with her sleeve, which was much
filthier than the dust it had lain in; when she reached Leonardo she
was completely out of breath.

"Here . . ." she sighed, puffing. "Thank you for . . . aaahhh
. . . looking after my child."

"Thank you, rather," answered Leonardo, who was somewhat

embarrassed at being seen in such friendly conversation with a beggar. "Goodbye, and thank you again. I'll . . . bring you something
from the house in a few minutes."

"I'll walk with you," she said. "What house is it?"

"Number forty-two, Via Gregoriana."

"The Russian ladies with the nice little boy, you mean? But
they're the most Christian people I've seen in my whole life. They
always pay in gold. Don't ask them for more money: they give
enough. And the boy is so nice: they always put the coins into his
hand and he gives them to me. A real angel. And he always asks
after my poor child. That's a good Christian, if you ask me. I
wonder whether the father is dead."

"No, he's not. You just saw him playing with my hat on his
walking cane."

"Oh . . . is THAT the father? See how people degenerate . . .
And they say: Like father, like son. Not true at all. I know that
man, he passes this way at least twice a day, usually with another
woman. This one is new: she wasn't with him yesterday morning.
But he's a beast, a monster. Just to give you an idea: he sees this
poor child, half naked, sick, almost dying, and do you think he ever
gives me one penny, even one kind word—me, the bereaved
mother? No, sir. Never. Cold as winter . . . Well, I see people
coming out of that house and I'd better get back to my work, or I'll
lose a great deal of money, so I'll say goodbye here and God bless
you. But you can do me a great favor: when you see my uncle, tell
him I don't want any of his money, even if he goes around with
barons and gets money from them, I don't want it, I won't touch it.
I only want one thing: to be left alone. I never bother him. You
saw: you passed right by me and I heard everything you said to him,
but I kept out of sight till he was gone. Why doesn't he do the
same with me? Why should he have all of Rome to himself, while I
have none? Tell him that, make him see that, and you'll do me the
greatest favor in the world. There's room for everybody in Rome,
that's what he still hasn't learned, he still thinks this is Acquaviva
delle Fonti. . . . Goodbye now." And caressing her child: "Say bye-
bye to the gentleman, my love . . . bye-bye . . . with your hand,
like this . . . bye-bye. . . . And now to work!" She pinched the
child's backside and arms, squeezed his wrists until he began to

whimper again and then made her great entry on that great stage. Her act was so good that Leonardo couldn't help swallowing a tear, especially when the deep voice of the Pope roared noontime through his twelve bronze throats, and the same song was intoned by all the lesser churches, and all the while the poor beggar woman with the sick child reminded the rich that their children were healthy and well fed, while hers was sick and starving.

Leonardo moved away from the scene because the stage was sun-lit from the first step in front of the church to the last one down in the piazza, while the two converging streets that ended in front of the Hotel Hassler were both in the dark, and the cold air whirled in them: even he felt it, in spite of his warm overcoat. But his heart felt much colder than his body. Mary had a husband and Mary had a child, and Mary had a palace and all the money in the world, Mary lived in the moon and knew so little about her beloved sunny Italy that she had lost a husband to those women, both looking like her, which was a sign that her husband loved her and no one else on earth. Just like Leonardo. Who else would recognize in that pair a likeness to Mary? Only one who knew the secret of her beauty. And who else would betray her, but one who knew the secrets of her arrogant character, which sprang perhaps from her wealth, or her foreignness, no one could tell? Leonardo had seen only three days of that wealth, with the result that he was penniless, had left an excellent position in politics and an excellent practice in medicine and an excellent house and landed property. The hard truth was that in three days of work, or even with three days of his salary, or three days of the interest on the small capital he owned, he could have given generously to the beggar and her colleagues, instead of himself being a kept man . . . kept on nothing at all. Angelo (he now called the Monster by his first name) was quite right: Leonardo *had* stared at his woman, today and yesterday. . . . I wonder whether he knows Cefala. He must . . . perhaps he loves her too. I only hope she was as adamant with him as she was with me. . . . But was she? These thoughts brought him to the door of the palace, and here reality hit him as it had hit Schillasi with the broken parts of Leonardo's stethoscope. . . . How much can she have heard? Schillasi was shouting, and I left both the window and the front door open. . . . How could I have been so careless? Luckily both the door and the window were closed on Sophie and Mr. Schultz. And their voices were too loud to let them hear a thing other than their own Russian nonsense. . . . I can still handle Mary. Adriana won't talk. But how about those cufflinks? And this vest? Oh my God, how could I have been such a fool? She'll see. . . . Can I say I ran back to my hotel to change and didn't find the cufflinks because I was in such a hurry to come back? Perfect idea . . . Leonardo, you're no fool.

With these thoughts he reached the front door and, in a state of extreme agitation, rang the bell.

Wealth hit him on the nose, with all the most alluring culinary scents and creature comforts, all of them so pleasant as to have become indispensable after only three days. The scents of freshly ironed table linen, freshly polished furniture, silver (how could one ever have imagined that silver has its own smell? Emperor Vespasian was wrong . . .), cigar boxes, flowers, but not the same flowers as come with a cold whiff of winter wind from inimical gardens beyond inimical walls or inimical iron gates guarded by inimical dogs: these flowers were tamed, they had learned to be soft-scented, socially discreet, living in the same room with the denatured essences of foreign flowers, treated with oils and alcohol and sold for exorbitant prices as ladies' perfumes. Even Bernhard seemed to smell good; his white uniform, his white gloves, the braids around his cuffs and on his collar, and more of the same around each button on his chest, were all part and parcel of Mary's personality: Mary, the center of wealth, but not, alas, its most attentive distributor. Only with titles was she lavish: "You are the master of the house, you are the sun in my sky, . . ." etc. As he relinquished his overcoat and hat to Bernhard's careful hands, he looked at himself in the mirror and tried to button up his jacket in order to conceal his waistcoat. Alas, the jacket was not so well cut as to hide it completely.

Bernhard opened the door to the music room, and more scents from rich women's evening dresses hit him in the face: the spirits of last night's party. By contrast with that vivid presence, the room seemed strangely silent, and the Cupolone framed in the window

more silent still. He wondered why he hadn't been shown into the
library, or into the dining room, and timidly he opened both doors,
only to *see* the same silence and almost the same spirits. Books and
table linen, even food asserted their pride of place. But why wasn't
anyone coming to greet him? Could they all be out? That idiot of a
butler, if Mary ever insists on bringing him along, I'll refuse. He
rang the bell, and the idiot appeared.

"Are the ladies out?"

"Nossir."

"In?"

"Yessir."

"Have you announced me?"

"Nossir."

"Why not?"

"Orders are to let you wait in here."

"But am I not late?"

"Nossir."

"Oh, so I'm not?"

"Yessir."

"Can you please be more precise: am I or am I not late?"

The idiot looked at him, frowning like a dog trying to interpret
his master's will, then said: "Nossir."

"Nossir you can't tell me, or nossir I'm not late?"

"Must ask ladies."

And he opened the dining room door again, went through that
room, opened another door to the right, which Leonardo had never
noticed before, crossed one more room Leonardo had never seen,
opened yet another door, and only then did Leonardo hear a torrent
of Russian voices. Probably another peaceful discussion on pacifism,
"Let's hope to God," he said, touching wood, and almost at that
very second the voices stopped altogether, as if everyone had died.
One could hear distant cries in the street, wheels on cobblestones,
the huge English clock in the dining room, but nothing else, not
even Bernhard's steps. He had probably turned into a pillar of salt.
Then the door was softly closed on that same silence, and Bernhard's passage was marked by a sudden flash of white light on the
glass that covered some photographs hanging on a wall out there.

Another door discreetly opening and closing was the only noise that
intervened before another very long silence, after which the door
opened again, and again the angry voices could be heard, then the
door was suddenly closed once more and once more there was total
quiet.

Well, at least they do have solid doors, Leonardo concluded,
thinking of Schillasi's voice on the landing and his own screams at
him to stop.

A long rattle, as of a sick man preparing to spit, then a deep
indoor church bell striking just once.

Twelve thirty, he thought, and looked at his watch. No: one
o'clock. From the Pope, nothing. Was he too part of the conspiracy of silence? Not the lesser churches, however; they were ringing—and ringing angrily, pettily, unpleasantly, making Leonardo
quite nervous, but no one else seemed moved to action by them.
Probably in the kitchen things were becoming impatient to be
served, because they were sending out warm reminders of their
incredible goodness, reminders that he himself had eaten almost
nothing in the last twenty-four hours.

When Mary finally came out, he wasn't even listening, or feeling
hungry, or worried about his problems any more. He heard the door
being opened and closed, but no sound of voices, and he picked up
the book he was looking at, to take it with him and place it on a
different table, so that he could continue examining it, after assur-
ing himself that nothing new had happened. He had just made a
major discovery, one that held the clue to many mysteries which
had been baffling him for the last three days, and this discovery was
the more important because it might help him avoid fatal mistakes
in his future life with Mary. The book was a family picture album,
one of those monumental albums only the rich can afford: huge and
bulky leather binding, pages as thick as wooden boards and gilded at
the edges, and the photographs inserted into the body of the page
so that they looked like paintings in frames within frames within
frames.

"I've made a great discovery," he shouted at her across the two
rooms. But she seemed very upset, and it took her the whole length
of those two rooms to collect herself under a mask of social hypocrisy that upset him instantly.

"You have?" she asked, offering him her two hands at the end of two stiff arms, which meant she didn't want to embrace him or be embraced by him. "I'm dying to hear. What is it about?"

"You."

"Oh," she said haltingly. "You too? This seems to be the day for great discoveries in this family. And where, pray, have you made your great discovery?"

"In this album here," he said, almost in a whisper.

"Poor darling," she said now, kissing him lightly on his forehead, "you can't have made just one, but many great horrid discoveries in that family zoo. We're all in it, bold as brass and twice as unrepentant. Mamachen calls that thing *The Criminal's Dossier*. Put it down on this table here and show me what *you* think is a great discovery."

"Darling, what is it? What's happened?"

"Nothing," she said, with a false smile, staring wildly at his waistcoat. (Damn fool, he thought, why did I unbutton my jacket again?)

There was a brief silence, which didn't seem to surprise her, and it freed him of all embarrassment, leaving only the anguished need to formulate his next words: "See? I haven't forgotten. That is, I must confess I had, but when I was almost here, I remembered I must not appear with the other waistcoat, so I ran back to my hotel and changed."

"You did? But you were already here with the other waistcoat, and you ran away again to catch your cousin downstairs. Or wasn't it your cousin? Mamachen swears it was: she saw him this morning and she had seen him last night, when you arrived so late for dinner and said you had been delayed by your cousin."

"Yes, it was . . . but let me explain what happened."

"Don't."

"Why? Don't you want to know why I'm not wearing the other cufflinks?"

"No, I don't want to know."

"But I want to tell you. It's amusing."

"And I don't want to hear it."

"Why, don't you want to be amused?"

"You are right, I don't want to be amused."

"Are you . . . angry with me?"

"No, darling, I am not. I could never be angry with you, because I love you. You could be anything and do anything, I would still love you. You could even be a . . . a Socialist. But at this moment I don't want to hear amusing stories, not even from you."

"What happened?"

"Nothing. Let's look at this album."

"Here or sitting down there?"

"Sitting down there."

They sat down there, and it was the same place where they had first kissed, so he tried to kiss her again, and she pushed him gently but firmly away. "Let's look at the album, please. Mamachen may come in at any moment."

"The time you wasted saying that could have been used for better purposes. Come on . . ."

"Please, I said. One isn't always ready for these things."

"You must have decided to hate me."

"How silly, I might just as well have decided to love you."

"Why? Did you have to decide that, all of a sudden? Did I do something wrong?"

"No, you just made a silly remark, but that is no reason not to love you. I hope you'll make many, many more in our life together. Isn't that what marriage is all about?"

"I don't understand you."

"Another silly remark. I could say the same thing. Understanding takes time. And the will to keep trying. But love comes first and dies last. So understanding isn't really necessary, though of course it's preferable to have a few of those thin intellectual bridges to throw across the sudden crevasses in the glacier of love."

"Glacier? Isn't love fire?"

"That's sensuousness, false love, because it kills itself. True love is timeless, like the purest ice that feeds eternal rivers down in the valley. You know who wrote that?"

"No."

"My mother."

"Beautiful."

"Oh. Is that all you have to say?"

Leonardo felt like sinking to his knees and saying: *Domine, non sum dignus.* And he knew that by not saying it, his silence would express it anyway and she would notice it. He was lucky: the distant door was opened again, and Sophie's solo voice filled the whole house. It was soft and persuasive, yet very violent, like that of a teacher who prefers words to physical punishment, because he knows that souls suffer more than bodies when they are the souls of intelligent pupils, and thus his voice cannot go unheeded: it carries praise on the edge of the knife, and goes on cutting with savage joy. Unfortunately for Leonardo, the words were Russian. But fortunately, they did seem to revive Mary. She listened, her face changed, her eyes lit up, and, like a dog obeying a distant whistle, she stalked, then jumped on Leonardo and kissed him with such passion that when Sophie and Schultz entered the room, they found Mary irreproachably seated at a distance from Leonardo leafing through the album, and Leonardo crouching, blushing and trembling, like the classic cat that has eaten the canary.

And of course when he saw these two people who had agreed to call a truce—a brief one, apparently, as the tension in their faces and gestures clearly showed—he felt even more fearful of the beating he knew he had earned and had avoided so many times since the beginning of his nightmarish fairy tale.

"How do you do, my friend," said Sophie, using the formal *Lei* for the first time since their first meeting, probably in total innocence, because when Mary flashed her a look she blushed in embarrassment and said: "Sorry, I meant THOU, not YOU, since we're so closely related now. I never used THOU with the Monster, as our friend Mr. Schultz here is about to remark, and he is right. By the way, have you two met?"

"Yes, of course, we met at dinner last night," said Mr. Schultz with Jesuitical mellowness in his voice, but with a truly Protestant shudder as he stretched out his hand to shake Leonardo's timid one, and it was at that moment that Leonardo felt this was truly the ending of the fairy tale and not a happy ending, alas. Just one glance at his cufflinks from those slanted green eyes had sufficed to deliver that message.

Bernhard suddenly appeared at the door without uttering a word, and Sophie said something in German that made him disappear at once. Did this mean lunch would never come? Leonardo felt faint, and he couldn't remember why they were all so tense. Hunger erased all guilt from his mind. Had they questioned him now, no threat of torture would have made him confess, because he could no longer tell the difference between any evil action committed by him and their unforgivable crime. One doesn't keep a human being from eating, after tempting him with such heavenly scents.

"Shall we look at these pictures of the old days?" asked Schultz hypocritically, trying to keep Leonardo from even coming within his field of vision.

"I think we should eat," said Sophie. "I have just ordered lunch to be served instantly. I'm very, very hungry."

"I'm not," said Mr. Schultz.

"Too bad," she answered, moving out of the room, and only now did it become obvious how much they all agreed with her.

Leonardo was so happy that he pushed Mary aside to enter the dining room together with Sophie, and before she even had time to sit down herself, he sat down on her right, Bernhard pushing the big armchair with obvious expert knowledge of how these things are done. Sophie settled herself down and smiled at Leonardo, saying: "I see you're hungry too. But today you must sit on my left. This chair is for the guest of honor—or, as the English say: age before beauty."

"Not the English, the Americans," said Mr. Schultz angrily, bumping into Leonardo behind Sophie's chair.

"Not the Americans, the English," said Sophie, even more angrily.

"I wager you it's the Americans. You've never been to America, I have just come back from there."

"If you say so. How is New York?"

"Splendid as usual." He flung these words at Leonardo, while staring at his hands. Leonardo had quickly changed places, grabbed the bread on the little plate next to him and eaten it all. Never had he tasted such good bread, and yet it was the common Roman bread, only sliced very thin. Now he looked for more and found it on another small plate, grabbed that and ate it all.

"That is Sophie's bread," said Mr. Schultz, slowly and somberly, still staring at Leonardo's hands (or was it his cufflinks?). Leonardo apologized.

"No need to apologize," said Sophie. "I always do the same thing."

"Here's more bread for you," said Mary, pushing her little plate across the table towards Leonardo, while Bernhard looked on very worriedly, shaking his head in disapproval.

"And here is still more," said Mary, laughing happily, and upsetting the arrangement of the remaining places at table.

Bernhard was now serving Mr. Schultz, but he couldn't help whispering something in German, which Mary instantly translated in an irritated voice, to make the serf aware that German was not the official language of the occasion. "Bernhard says he is here for this purpose, but since I see that he is busy, I have taken the liberty of doing some heavy work for once."

"Thank you," said Leonardo with a smile.

"How can anyone find New York beautiful with all those strange buildings?" asked Sophie.

"They're not all strange. And Fifth Avenue is the most beautiful street in the world, if you ask me."

"I didn't ask you, but I do answer that I think all this is insane."

"Also Moscow is a new city, if that is what you mean."

"I never said Moscow was beautiful, but I would say Saint Petersburg is."

"Right, right, perfectly right, Sophia Vladimirovna."

"And what makes Saint Petersburg so beautiful," she said, looking at Leonardo, "is that it was all built by Italian architects."

"Right, right," said Mr. Schultz, blushing. "Hard workers, those Italians, *when* they work."

"Why, are the Germans or the Americans hard workers even when they *don't* work?"

"I never said that. I said that the Italians—"

"Just a moment. Let me talk to my future son-in-law for one second." Then, to Leonardo: "Your plate is empty. Why? Haven't you been served?"

"I'm glad you noticed," said Mary, looking worried, and then to Leonardo: "Darling, what is it? Weren't you very hungry?"

Upon hearing the word *darling*, Mr. Schultz almost choked and started coughing violently into his napkin, but only Bernhard seemed concerned. Mary and Sophie were still trying to get a clear

answer from Leonardo, who had already said twice in whispers:
"Thank you, I'm not hungry."

The truth was he had not only forgotten his guilt, but his table
manners too, and to have that distinguished old gentleman stare at
his hands (cufflinks?) made him feel like a child being examined on
his second day in nursery school.

"Bernhard," ordered Sophie, looking very impatiently at Mr.
Schultz, who hadn't yet decided whether to choke to death or recover, "pass the serving plate here again, please." Then, to Leonardo: "You must eat. The cook told me you didn't eat anything
last night, because that fool of a Cardinal kept pestering you with
his verbal aerobatics."

"The Cccc . . . (cough, cough) . . . the CCCC . . . CARD . . .
(cough, cough) . . . ardinal is no fool . . . (cough, cough) . . .
he is the most br . . . (cough, cough, cough)."

Sophie sent out a huge arm and lowered it onto Mr. Schultz's
back, hitting him repeatedly and saying: "Look at the little bird
. . . Look at the little bird up there. . . ."

Mr. Schultz refused to look at the little bird and all the while
Leonardo was refusing to take food from the platter and Mary was
pleading with him in the tenderest tones: "Darling, you must eat.
The cook will be very offended if you don't. . . ." She raised her
voice now, because Russian thunders had begun to roar again on the
other side of the table: "He was so touched that you went into the
kitchen after dinner to have a bit of that excellent roast beef."

"He told you that?" asked Leonardo, quickly shoveling meat and
potatoes from the serving platter onto his plate, and then devouring
everything in a mad frenzy, because Mr. Schultz was now trying to
incinerate Sophie with his eyes, while *basso profondo* notes were
vibrating through all the silver dishes on the buffet and on the
contrebuffet—even through the windowpanes. "No," Mary had to
shout, "he didn't tell me that: Adriana told me. She told me everything in the greatest detail. I laughed so much. She's a real actress,
that girl, I adore her. Don't apologize, no, no, go on eating . . .
darling, I am so happy to see you eat. . . . They'll all be delighted
in the kitchen." Then, in a lowered tone: "And I am so ashamed of
myself for breaking that silly instrument. I'll buy another one today.
. . . Am I forgiven?"

"Ghm Ghm-hm-hn . . ." said Leonardo, speaking to the food in his mouth and not to Mary, but she understood this to mean, "Yes, my love, you are," so she went on: "And you must also forgive me for receiving you so badly this morning. I'd hoped you would be here to hear the story of last night as told by all the servants. Mamachen and I laughed so much. . . . But I have another horrible crime to confess: I was jealous of poor darling Adriana. She said she loves you, but I know now how she means these things. She's all impulse, but she's also the one person in the world who is incapable of cheating. I must apologize to her too, and I know she will forgive me. She is such a—"

"Mary!" shouted Sophie, very angrily this time: "Why weren't you listening to our discussion, instead of pestering him with your silly chatter and preventing him from enjoying his food? Now I'll have to retranslate it all for Leonardo's benefit, and that is something you could have done, if only you had been listening to us." She shook her head several times, then continued: "Always, always thinking only of herself . . ." Then, to Leonardo: "You're not going to have an easy time, taming a child of Nature like Mary. Other people just don't exist for her, which is bad enough when the others are strangers, but when they are your own mother, then I am at a loss for adjectives to describe such an attitude. Un-be-lievable. Innnnnnnncredible." She sighed, while Mr. Schultz and Leonardo seemed so profoundly united by the same unspoken opinion that, without even looking at each other, they were doing exactly the same things, in exactly the same order of succession, and the same rhythm too: first, staring at the tablecloth, then feeling the tips of a fork with the tips of their fingers, then blowing a crumb off their plates, then sighing, then looking at the ceiling, out of the window, at the door, from which Bernhard had just entered with the next course—and he, too, seemed to be having an opinion, if such a thing can be said of a servant: he clearly felt it better not to move one inch farther into the room or back out of the room until the storm had passed. And it passed soon enough, but it left a great sadness in its wake: "It's sad, it's sad, it's very sad," whispered Sophie now, staring at the tablecloth before she moved on to the next gesture, feeling the tips of a fork with her fingertips; but here she changed tactics: she didn't blow a crumb off her plate: she pressed it with her finger until it stuck, and then ate it, then frowned at her butler, setting him instantly into motion again. "Do you want to know what is really the saddest of all?" she asked Leonardo; and he said timidly: "No."

"Saddest of all is that a man like Mr. Schultz here, the dearest friend and adviser I have" (Mr. Schultz bowed his head without smiling), "a man whose sense of justice is so great that statesmen in all countries seek his advice on matters of the highest policy, and I mean matters of life and death, war and peace and the like, this man should fail to understand the beauty of nonviolence, as expressed in the writings of Tolstoy. This was what we were talking about in Russian, and now I will have to repeat it, because I want to hear what you think of this, Leonardo."

Here she stopped to serve herself abundantly, then asked Mr. Schultz:

"Didn't you say Tolstoy believes all humans are angels?"

"That's what I said and now repeat."

"But if this were true, then the whole argument of nonviolence would be void."

"And so it is."

"But Tolstoy's not so innocent."

"There you are right: he's a criminal, he's trying to subvert the Imperial Monarchy and its ancient religion, which, I admit, is just a heap of superstitious nonsense, but that's exactly what the Russian people need if they're to stay quiet and let the Czar govern them in their own best interest. Now here comes this criminal Tolstoy, and wants to give them ideas, and what ideas? Let the enemy come and enslave you, and the Will of God will be done. The best you can say in defense of Tolstoy is the opposite of what you said; namely, that he IS innocent, he DOES believe this is a world of fairy tales and not of crude realities, in which violence alone can help you stay honest, because everybody is a devil deep down and so the best of us crave a strong hand to restrain us from doing bad things."

"I see that you have never read Tolstoy. He *does* say that men are all devils deep down and barely human only for reasons of social hypocrisy or economic convenience, but at the same time most certainly tempted by the devil lurking behind all such reasons. That is why Tolstoy cautions *both* governments *and* individuals against the use of violence *at all times* and under *any* name. And may I add, as my own contribution to this argument, that angels are not the symbol of meekness, but of violence unrestrained and unforgiving, because they alone can use it for the good."

"Tolstoy can't have said that: he's not a Catholic."

"Neither am I, but I'm saying this to correct your use of the term, as our friend Leonardo here would put it. Angels come with a fiery sword, which represents the sharpness of ideas. The first and only refusal to use violence takes place long before you and your policemen appear on the scene. It is *my* refusal to do violence to *my own* way of thinking, and to replace it with *your* way of thinking. That you may kill me for refusing your ideas on patriotism, manliness, courage, et cetera, is secondary, a traffic accident that may be avoided, or perhaps only delayed, if I'm lucky, but what do I care?"

"Sophie, you should be a Catholic; you might even become a great saint if you can gulp down all that nonsense, because you are a fanatic, you love to suffer, to be martyred in public, and medical science has recently discovered that all those ancient saints were the victims of nervous aberrations."

"Me, believe in suffering? I'm so much a believer in health and peace and the good things of life that I believe I can convert even you! And when I see that I cannot succeed in making a civilized person of you, I know this is because you have done violence to your own way of thinking, which has to be the same as mine or anybody's who isn't terrorized by violence. And by violence I don't mean only military conscription, but also the silent threats of those who refuse you a good job unless you agree to steal and kill as they do, telling yourself that, since everybody does it, this is obviously *realism*, as you prefer to call it. Of course, if people are left to themselves they will do horrible things, but being herded into an army by licensed criminals doesn't redeem the horror, it only shows the criminality of your so-called realism. Idealism is what you need. Tolstoy has it, you don't."

"Your words are very, very violent."

"The violence of my words is not my own: it is the violence of Christ who came bearing not peace, but a sword: *the* sword: the sword of thought, brandished by the Good Angels who trumpet the Word of God throughout the Universe. . . . But what is it, Leonardo? Aren't you eating the second roast? This is the same dish we had last night, only much better, the cook tells me, because he has prepared it only for us. He will be very disappointed if you don't eat it."

"I'm not hungry, thank you."

"But you must be starving."

"No. I gorged myself already, as you probably saw."

"I didn't see you touch a thing."

"I did," said Mr. Schultz. "Leave him alone. He's probably used to more modest meals."

Leonardo registered the blow and answered with a smile: "I wasn't, at home, but I learned to be frugal from my daily contacts with the poor. We can learn so much from them."

"How true," said Sophie, her mouth full and her fork already loaded.

"We can learn nothing from the poor but suicide," declared Mr. Schultz rather impatiently.

"Suicide?" asked Sophie. "What a strange notion."

"Not strange at all if you consider that our whole life—mine, my government's, my Emperor's, our Emperor's, your family enterprises, therefore, even the life of your sons—is dedicated to rescuing the poor, day after day."

Sophie laughed out loud and so did Leonardo and Mary. She let them laugh freely for a few moments and then said: "I can hardly picture my sons rescuing the poor from starvation. If ever there were two dirty egotists on earth, they're the ones."

"Would you say the same thing about your late husband? Or your late father?"

"Never, but wouldn't you say there's a difference between them and those unruly idiots?"

"You don't have to be an angel to work for the good of mankind. Modern society is based on the premise that everybody must get richer, or at least less destitute in the future, if the world is to have a future at all. The very existence of money was something Tolstoy could afford to despise, because he was never without it, but since he hadn't earned it, this made him feel guilty."

"Please, we do not talk about money in this house."

"*He* was talking about money."

"I?" asked Leonardo.

"You. When you talk about the poor and what they have to teach, you talk about money."

"Oh no. I talk about frugality, which is a virtue, while money is a thing, or a convention about the value attributed to a thing."

"Frugality is no substitute for money."

"Nor money for frugality. Give people money, and they will gorge themselves to death or find other means of committing suicide."

"True, but you can't cook frugality in a frying pan or knead it into bread."

"No, but the frugal will survive and till the soil, and work, and even find rich people to help them. . . ."

"Another Tolstoy . . . The poor are angelic, the rich are too, everybody cries in mutual adoration, and they all live happily ever after." Here Schultz became purple with rage: "On what? I'll tell you on what: on the work of brutal realists like myself, like your father, Sophie, and your husband—two rare exceptions, individually speaking—but in the iron rules they constructed, everyone was forced to do good if only because they found it convenient. But let the rich learn from the poor, and they'll soon be joining them on the steps of Trinità dei Monti, begging for sick children who are neither sick nor their own. The poor are evil, and if you, Doctor, haven't learned this in your experiences with the poor, then you are another one of those saints who should be kept away from the world, because they can only bring poverty and havoc, encouraging idleness and branding honest work as theft, just as the Socialists do when they say, *ownership is theft*. You answer me now."

"Just a moment," said Sophie. "Before you answer, I want you to know that Mr. Schultz, who seems so eager to prove he is a devil, is in reality an angel such as has rarely been seen on earth. I have seen him being cheated out of huge amounts of capital by crooks, and he knew they were crooks, but he wanted to give them a chance to reform. And after he discovered they were crooks, he not only re- fused to take them to court, but went on helping them. Now, if this isn't angelic, what is it?"

"Practical, Sophie, coldly and cynically realistic, that's what it is. You're speaking about your own son, aren't you? Well, let me tell you: since his father and his grandfather were both dead, and you had no use for him, I could have taken him to court and ruined him, but this would have ruined the bank, and with it many thousands of poor people who had put all their savings into it. Credit is like a house of cards: you can only destroy it after you have photographed it, so you can circulate the evidence of a reality that is no more, and thus it will be reborn of that same evidence. Pierre was a crook and perhaps will always be one, but as far as the bank and cotton mills and other family enterprises are concerned, he is also a genius and can help many more people than Tolstoy or your friend here, the idealistic doctor—and this is no reflection on their honesty, only on their sense of reality. If I had sent your son to jail, he might have read books and become a perfect Tolstoian, but the thousands of poor workers or small investors would have benefitted little, while now they profit a very great deal—and concretely—from his financial genius, which I, or, rather, not I—the system—keeps in chains."

Leonardo was very grateful for this return to reality—not the reality of finance, Pierre or the afterlife of credit, but the reality of two large pears he had put on his plate and was extremely impatient to eat: a meager meal after being tantalized by the procession of fantastic roast, an *Intermezzo* soup, marked as such on the parchment menu in front of him, a fish, another dish of meat, and a salad with soft cheeses, the eating of which was probably the most dangerous feat of all table acrobatics, judging by the way the other three handled the lettuce leaves and cheese by means of special little forks he would never have dared touch. Pears in March were a contradiction in terms, he had never seen any, although he knew winter pears existed up North, but they had never reached Apulia. Now, pears are eaten whole, skin and all, after spitting on them and drying them on the seat of your pants to wipe off the dirt. He was never going to do that, because he was now a man of the world, but he was going to wash them in the nice little crystal bowl Bernhard had put on his plate, and he was going to dry them on his own napkin. All of which things he could never have done if Mr. Schultz had continued to stare at his hands (cufflinks?), but from the moment he had begun to speak to Sophie about her criminal son, his piercing eyes had been fixed on her face, and hers had been wandering all over the ceiling, as if she were hoping to see it cave in and kill her adviser.

"As I told you, I was in New York recently," Mr. Schultz began again and his eyes, too, left the earth of crude facts, to wander all across the ceiling. "Oh, what a city!!! Saint Petersburg is nothing, even Rome is nothing in comparison . . . Fifth Avenue! Palace after palace after palace, all the styles of the world, an open-air museum of architecture, and they don't clash, on the contrary, they blend. . . . My friend Andrew Carnegie, a man who really rose from nothing, built himself a modest but solid townhouse way out of the city on Fifth Avenue and he invited me to stay there for a few days, after I had spent a week at a perfect little French château belonging to a Mr. Frick, another remarkable person. You met him, he was here with me for dinner two years ago."

"Yes," said Sophie, "but what does New York, what does Mr. Frick, what does Mr. Carnegie have to do with the subject of non-violence? Be realistic, not lyrical: leave that nonsense to idealists like Leonardo or myself."

While waiting for his answer, she paralyzed Leonardo just as he was plunging the first pear into the crystal bowl and turning it, so that the water began to splash all over the tablecloth. He looked at her plate, and saw that the bowl had been removed from the center of it and was now standing on the side, for God knows what purpose. But what alarmed him even more was that she too had taken a pear and was peeling it with a small knife he had already used for the fish, but she was also using a fork of the same make and size to keep the pear in a standing position, and the whole operation reminded him of his first lesson in surgery, as delivered by a famous professor of the University of Naples. She wasn't even looking, but her knife cut through the white substance with not a second's hesitation. Leonardo had reached the same complete self-control on the bodies of his patients, but the mere thought of peeling a pear in front of this great teacher was too much for him. Could he remove the pear from the bowl and the bowl from the plate, and replace the pear on the plate? Only if Sophie were to look elsewhere again for a moment. As for Mary, he didn't even dare look in her direction, counting on her love to make her blind to his failings. But unfortunately not only did Sophie continue to look: Mr. Schultz also began to take an active interest in his plight, and he was speaking about his rich friends in their rich New York palaces, as if they were all in that bowl, swimming around that pear, or perhaps inside it. Or were they all hanging at the end of his cuffs? A most unpleasant feeling, anyway.

"Why don't you eat them with your hands?" asked Sophie, and Mr. Schultz, who thought she had spoken to him, asked: "Why don't I what?"

Mary burst into uncontrollable laughter, and Sophie tried hard not to do the same as she answered: "I was speaking to Leonardo, not to you."

But Leonardo didn't laugh. He blushed up to his ears, and pretended great surprise as he hid his hands in his napkin, not so much to wipe them as to conceal their tremor.

"What am I doing? I never meant to eat fruit anyway."

"Why, darling?" asked Mary, hoping to make Mr. Schultz cough again, but he did not. "Pears are good for you: you haven't eaten anything at all, my love."

"Don't interrupt Mr. Schultz, Mary, I find his story fascinating." Then, to Mr. Schultz: "So Mr. Frick, you were saying?"

Mr. Schultz showed a brief glimpse of gratitude in his eyes, then, seeing both Mary and Sophie (and especially the butler) embarrassed by something, he said to all of them, very slowly:

"Now, for example, you, who despise Americans because they put their feet on the table and their hands under the table, let me tell you that once you get used to these systems, you find they have their virtues. Putting your feet on the table (a thing I have never seen them do during meals, only at the office, and then when their inferiors are not present) is very restful for the feet—as the doctor here can tell you. And putting your hands under the table allows you to scratch your knees, which I also find very restful, probably for the same reasons: it favors circulation. At my age these things are important. Don't forget, I'm eighty-two."

Which made Mary and Sophie blush and sink their heads in shame, while the butler was trying to catch up with the last sentence.

"Now let me tell you what happened to me at Mr. Carnegie's—

not this time, years ago—but your argument about the poor reminded me of it. We were having lunch there: the Carnegies, a
Reverend Strong with his wife, who is the daughter of Mr. Rocke-
feller, and another couple who arrived rather late and excused
themselves by saying they had been delayed by a long conversation
with a beggar to whom they had given twenty-five cents. Mr. Carnegie lost his temper and said: 'Shame on you! By giving that
money to a beggar you have done a great disservice to me, to yourself, to our children, to America. You have encouraged vice and
corruption, alcoholism, and God knows what other unmentionable
things.' He went on like this for a while, until the Reverend Strong
said: 'Mr. Carnegie, Our Lord and Savior says we can only learn
from the poor.' To which Mr. Carnegie replied: 'I wasn't there to
hear His exact words and I know nothing about the economic struc-
ture of that ancient society, but let me tell you that in my experience, and in the experience of all those who have made this country
what it is, we have nothing to learn from the needy. From their
needs, yes, to satisfy them in a better life than the one in which
they are starving, surrounded by plenty. It is they, rather, who can
learn from us. Take the example of the drowning. They cry out for
help and we, who can swim, generously jump into the water to
rescue them. We are their only friend, the sea their only enemy. Yet
the first thing they do is try to drag us down with them, so the first
rule for us is to subdue them. Why? Because, unless you consider
life as a struggle and Nature as the God-appointed enemy to prove
your worthiness, you have already chosen death instead of life. So
have these beggars, so has Tolstoy, so have all those false Christians
who misread the message of the Gospels.'

"This said, let me add something else he always says: The Italians, he says, are our best laborers: never drunk on Monday mornings, always willing to work, always ahead of the foreman in devising
new ways to do more in less time and to improve the quality of the
product, while the Irish are always drunk until Tuesday and always
in debt. But don't forget that deep down in every Italian there is
also the *furbo*, one of those untranslatable Italian expressions, a
whole world in a single word."

"I must say you are right," said Leonardo, quietly but almost
aggressively.

"Well, well," said Mr. Schultz, getting up from his seat, "then we agree on everything, it seems. Excuse me for rising before you, Sophia Vladimirovna, but my legs do need stretching and moving a bit."

They moved to the library and Mary disappeared, to return almost instantly with the album in her hands. "Show me the great discovery you made in this album, darling."

"Leave him to me for just another second," said Mr. Schultz, then, offering a huge cigar to Leonardo: "Don't smoke it now, our hostess hates tobacco."

"No no," said Sophie cheerfully, "I love the smell of good Havana cigars, please go ahead."

"Then we will," said Mr. Schultz, grabbing the cigar back from Leonardo's hand, "and let me show you how these are trimmed before you smoke them."

He trimmed it with his golden cigar-cutter, then trimmed one for himself and said: "I have good news for you, young man. There is hope for the Italians, even in Italy: in Milan."

"My God," said Sophie, "I hate their accent."

"And I hate the Roman one," said Mr. Schultz, laughing. "But do you realize that when I was already an adult, I saw the Milanese still living like pigs, sitting in the sunshine or in their taverns, never doing a stitch of work, drowsy, dirty, reduced to begging and vice? My friend Princess Belgioioso wrote a whole book in their defense, a moving plea to the Austrian government, which had forbidden the founding of any industries in the whole northern region of Italy; she said: 'Give these people a chance to work, and they will stun the world with their activity.' Well, they have. Your son recently arranged for a large loan to one of the youngest cotton industries in Milan. Last year he was responsible for financing a small optical industry, now on its way towards becoming the largest in Europe. He is now financing the Italian automotive industry, while your former suitor Robert Boesch, Mary, has moved to Turin, where he makes carburetors, and he has already trebled his fortune, which was large to begin with, even by Russian standards."

There was a long, unpleasant silence, then Mr. Schultz turned to Leonardo again and said condescendingly: "See? Little Italy, the land of macaroni and barefoot mandolin players, is quickly joining the March of the Times. Aren't you pleased?"

"It is you who should be pleased, sir, you and Mary's dishonest brother and that former suitor of hers, for being allowed to march towards the shining goals of Progress way behind Little Italy. The transportation of electrical energy was made possible by an Italian: Galileo Ferraris, discoverer of the rotating magnetic field. Another Galileo, the only one whose name may have reached you so far away in Russia, was of course the inventor of the telescope, not to mention Leonardo da Vinci, who was well on his way towards discovering the ways by which men would be able to fly instead of using trains. The telephone was invented by an Italian named—"

"Nossir, not by an Italian, by a Scottish-American named Alexander Graham Bell. Mr. Carnegie took me to see the place where the great invention was made."

"Tell your friend Mr. Carnegie that the inventor of the telephone was called Antonio Meucci, a Florentine, and your Bell, or whatever his name is, stole the invention from him."

"That's not true."

"I'm not going to argue with you, if you are so uninformed. Go and find out the facts and then come back to me and we'll discuss them."

"Sir, I'll wager you—"

"I don't believe in gambling. I leave that to Mary's dishonest brother."

"But who told you these fairy tales?"

"History, sir, the same history you have no time to read, as I can see."

Mary walked away to conceal her sense of triumph, Sophie began to leaf through the pages of the album, making an effort not to laugh, and Mr. Schultz was nervously twisting his mustache and weighing his next move. Leonardo alone seemed relaxed, yet still not happy. The name of that rich former suitor of Mary's was clouding his skies.

Finally Mr. Schultz came towards him with outstretched hand: "Young man, I like your attitude. You stand up for your countrymen, and that is fine, even if I believe your facts to be wrong. May I

ask you where you picked up all that knowledge about things un-
connected with medicine?"

"In school, sir, in high school, to be exact. Don't forget that the
humanist tradition (another thing invented here) makes it manda-
tory for the student to learn physics, chemistry, mathematics, and of
course history, before he can enter university. And I have a cousin
who is an electrical engineer and knows these things."

"Oh, I see. You have a great many cousins, it seems."

"Sixty-five, sir. We all have large families in my part of the
country."

"I know. One of the causes of starvation. Have you read
Malthus?"

"No. Who's he?"

"He WAS a man who studied facts you ought to know and study,
down in your part of the country. But no matter. I still admire your
firmness. I want to have another talk with you tomorrow. Now I
must go. Sophie, may I ask to be driven to the Russian embassy by
your coachman?"

"Yes, of course," she said, and rang for the butler.

"You know what takes me there," he said.

"No, I don't."

"You mean you haven't heard! Our Minister of the Interior has
been murdered!"

"What? Not Katinka's husband."

"Precisely, Katinka's husband—and she's here in Rome with her
daughter, staying at the embassy. I must go and pay my respects to
her. And I think you should go too. With Mary, of course. Why
don't you come with me?"

"Not now, in a half hour. Poor Katinka, first she had to endure
congratulations for being married to that imbecile, and now she
must endure condolences for being rid of him."

"My dear child, you are not charitable. Poor man, he may not
have been the ideal husband for a woman of Katinka's intelligence,
but she was married to him, and the daughter sealed their pact, and,
besides, he was one of the pillars of the monarchy."

"Poor monarchy, if all the other pillars are *shliapas** like him."

---

* Russian for "flat hat," i.e., a man without character.

"*Shliapa* he was not. He was a believer in force and applied it."

"Force is a form of weakness. Read Tolstoy."

Mr. Schultz's shoulders rose and fell. "Have you read Tolstoy?" he asked Leonardo.

"No."

"Don't!"

"He doesn't have to," said Sophie, laughing. "He was born in *War and Peace*. His name is Platon Karatayev."

"Never mind her," said Mr. Schultz. "Read Andrew Carnegie, I'll send you that book."

"But I don't know any English."

"Learn it, then. It's the language of the future. Do you know why I admire America so much? Because it is the one country based entirely on truth. Does the name of Washington mean anything to you?"

"Washington, you mean the capital of Australia?"

"Australia???"

"Sorry, I mean Canada."

"Canada??? The United States, my friend."

"But . . . isn't New York the capital of the United States?"

"No, it is not, but never mind, I have no time now. This will be our theme for tomorrow: George Washington, the man who couldn't tell a lie. Nine thirty sharp, that's when the lesson begins. Here in this room." With these words he was gone, and Sophie sighed with relief before opening her arms to let Leonardo come back to her like a long-lost son.

Leonardo and Mary both ran towards that blessing, and during those heavenly moments there was peace. But the moment they all parted, one of them felt himself left out in the cold again.

Schultz and I are the same liars, Leonardo felt, we only differ in details, and now that I am no longer the weaker of the two men here, these two women will know me for what I am. As Sophie said, without knowing what she was saying: the voice of God rings out in silence. Silence is upon us, and I am guilty.

But the two women didn't seem to feel it yet. They were so proud of him, and said so. "You were splendid. He didn't give you an easy time, but your grilling was short. I had two hours of it, so perhaps I, too, deserve some credit, although my arguments in your defense were never as brilliant as yours."

DEFENSE. That was the word that broke the spell. Suddenly, the three of them were embracing again.

"Before we leave," said Sophie, trying to stay cheerful, "let's look at that album and see what discoveries you have made about us. I hope they are good ones, but I hope even more that the next ones won't frighten you away from us."

"Yes," said Mary, "let's, but not here. In the other room we can all sit together on the sofa."

They opened the door, and there it stood—the *corpus delicti*, a bottle of iodine Adriana had forgotten to remove from the scene. "Iodine?" asked Sophie with apprehension. "Who was hurt?"

Now Mary couldn't help showing the tape across her palm.

"It was nothing," she said, "just a small cut."

"Is she speaking the truth?" Sophie asked. "Tell me everything, don't spare me anything."

"There's nothing to tell, Mamachen," said Mary, blushing with pride, because here she was, defending Leonardo. But she looked at him desperately for support, and her mother noticed it.

"Children, you're concealing something from me: what is it?"

"Oh, it was nothing," said Leonardo. "She was playing with something and broke it."

"Something? Nothing? What are all these vague words? I want to know the truth, and the truth cannot be something that is nothing and yet causes bloodshed. Why don't you answer me, the two of you? Why this conspiracy against me? And just when we were all so united against our enemy?"

"I was playing with my stethoscope, and she wanted to play with it too, and she . . . broke it."

"A stethoscope? What is a stethoscope?"

Leonardo was shocked. How could this woman, who prided herself on writing articles on clinical medicine and taking the great clinics of the world to task, not even recognize the commonest tool of the medical trade?

"A stethoscope is that black instrument you apply to the body of a patient to auscultate his lungs or his heartbeat."

"Hm-hn," she mumbled, blushing up to her ears. "I understand. And I apologize for asking such an intrusive question, but you forced me to, and I mean both of you. You are husband and wife, and it is easy to say: 'Please, these are intimate matters.' I would never have dared insist. It is highly embarrassing for me to have to defend myself as if I had committed some indiscretion. Why didn't you tell me? *Gospody Pamilyui, isbavyi nass ot lukavavo . . .*" And after asking the Merciful Lord to deliver her from Evil, in the last words of the Lord's Prayer, she went to her desk, picked up a handful of pencils and broke them angrily, throwing the broken pieces at her own marble bust, as if to punish it in the presence of her husband's: he, who had already reached perfection for all eternity, must see how she punished her image, for daring to stand there, next to him, as if she deserved such an honor. And of course this brought about the catharsis of tears that had been slowly building in her heart during the struggle in defense of her future son-in-law. Here indeed was something that spoke to Leonardo's heart in his own moral language, despite all differences in geography and wealth. He read this act of atonement exactly as it was intended, so when Sophie ran out of the room sobbing aloud, and Mary rose from her seat to run after her, he stopped her: "Don't," he said. "She must be left alone."

"Why do you want to be so cruel to her, after she has done so much for you? What is this?"

"It's respect, not cruelty. You ought to understand. She worships her husband, she wants to be ready to die on his level of perfection, and she feels she has demeaned herself by her usual wild temper."

"Wild temper? How can you—"

"Let me talk. You know she has a wild temper, and you know she knows it and disapproves. On this particular occasion, I alone am responsible for the whole thing."

"Well, if you are, then why don't you explain a few things that she and I and Mr. Schultz have been wondering about all morning? First of all, for me: why did you run away from me when I was bleeding and in need of disinfecting and bandaging? And for us all: why wouldn't you let your cousin come here? Are you ashamed of him? I'm going to be asked again in a few minutes, and if I say I know nothing about it, she won't believe me, and rightly so. We are about to be married, and you are shielding from me so many things that I feel utterly left out, repudiated, on the eve of what should be eternal union. . . ."

"I am concealing nothing from you," he said, quietly, staring at her with fear, and hoping she would read it as strength, sincerity, even moral indignation. His familiarity with the soul-searching techniques of the Jesuits applied to both themselves and to others, and his profound belief in Divine Justice (which his loss of faith had not destroyed) had shown him certain things Mary could never have guessed. All these Protestants were stupid: they were upset by superficial lies and discrepancies, but had no flair for major trespasses, and were quickly reassured by the most blatant lies. Of course he hated to be found out about the cufflinks, the scene at the Caffè Greco and all that, but even if he were, he felt so fortunate to have concealed his major sin with Adriana, and his sin of intention with Cefala, that he couldn't take these other things too seriously. But now his conscience was showing him what happens to the liar who gets away with his lie: he can't get away from it, he wishes he were able to believe those he loves, as they believe him, but they are fortunate, because they are innocent, and he is unfortunate, because he has lost his innocence. Everyone is left with what he has: the truthful with their truth, the liar with his lies, and that is why the liar needs total honesty in others—if even they are as weak and confused as he is, who else in the world can he trust? Thus Leonardo, with the deepest sincerity and anguish, asked: "Tell me, my love, why should you and your mother care so much about my cousin? What is he to you? You say I'm shielding you from so many things, that you feel utterly left out and repudiated on the eve of what should be our eternal union. But these are *my own words*, that I never dare speak, because you always take offense, saying I talk like your husband, or, if you don't do that, you say I'm silly. But do you realize what I have given up for you? I have betrayed my duties, left my entire world, to follow you. And of course I always believe you, because the very tone of your voice spells purity, the sight of your face stills all doubt in my heart, but then I keep hearing more new names of men who have loved you or were after you, and again I have no right to ask any questions. Do you think this is fair? Can't you see how I suffer?"

"Oh, my poor love, you are right, and I'm a terrible egotist to treat you so badly. Ask me anything you want, I will answer you. And tonight, since we'll have to go out soon, we'll continue our general confession—*mine*, I should say, because you have nothing to hide. You're not like the Monster, who's a real Jesuit at heart."

". . . All right then, let's begin with Gennariello."

"Gennariello? Are you joking? That mad old idiot?"

"Well, this time you seem to remember his name quite clearly while last night . . ."

Mary blushed scarlet: "I remember it because you mentioned it last night."

"Then why are you blushing?"

"Because I'm ashamed of what I did last night."

"What?"

"I came after you in the kitchen and in the wardrobe."

"And what did you find?"

"Nothing, of course."

Leonardo sighed and felt better, but then, suddenly, he thought: And isn't that what I would have said in her place? How prompt she is, how sure . . . she sounds just like me. Then, aloud, with a sigh: "Did Gennariello ever kiss you?"

"He tried, but I said no."

"Oh, he did, the swine. . . . And he stopped because you said no?"

"Yes."

"Are you sure? I see you're trembling."

"Because I'm afraid you will leave me, if . . ."

"IF . . . ?"

"My love, I hate to see you suffer so. Can't we leave these archaeological items where they belong: buried in the mud?"

"Why MUD? Was there anything . . . deserving that strong an adjective?"

"Darling, mud is no adjective."

"Don't you try to sound like me, this is serious. What else was there that might cause me to leave you, IF I knew about it?"

"Nothing. Absolutely nothing."

"Don't tremble if your conscience is clear. I'm no ogre . . . I'm your only friend and guardian, since your husband—"

"Oh, don't speak about him, *please*. No obscenity in this room."
And her eyes wandered briefly towards the two marble busts, only
to withdraw instantly in shame. But that very word *obscenity* set his
whole mind afire with lewd images. He was so excited and, at the
same time, so crushed that he felt he was going to have a heart
attack.

"I'm sorry," he said, in a trembling voice, "but I must continue
with Gennariello. Did you ever kiss him?"

"Once, on the forehead, because he was so miserable."

Leonardo hid his face in his hands and moaned like a dying
man.

"Darling, see how wrong this all is? I was a silly little girl of
fifteen, not even fifteen . . . it was one week before my birthday. . . ."

He cringed and buried his head deeper in his forearms, while she
timidly caressed the backs of his hands.

"Don't touch me!" he shouted, and she began to cry. He instantly
melted and tried to kiss her, but she pushed him away, murmuring
amid her sobs: "I'm not worthy."

This put the Grand Inquisitor instantly back in his seat, and he
asked, very calmly: "Why do you say such a stupid thing . . . unless . . . there are REASONS?"

"There are no reasons, except for those you feel, and whatever
you feel is more important to me than my own life."

At this point, someone knocked timidly on the door.

"Who is it?" asked Mary, while the Grand Inquisitor sobered at
once and pretended he was just an early twentieth-century layman,
playing with a silver ashtray.

"It's me," came Kostia's voice timidly against the keyhole, as if he
had been peeping, but of course he had not, as Mary explained to
Leonardo in a whisper: "He loves to use the keyhole as his telephone. Shall I ask him to go away?"

"Come in, Kostia," shouted Leonardo cheerfully, and the Revised
Standard Version of the Red Man's face stood timidly in front of
Leonardo, under a Russian crown of colored feathers, and over a
beautiful medieval costume, with belt and sword and golden em-
broideries. Without even looking at his mother, he said, in German: "How do you like my costume? I have two thousand horses

out there and two thousand Cossacks tied under the horses' bellies with knives in their teeth."

"Your new daddy doesn't understand German yet, my boy, please speak Italian," she said, and he slowly translated, with many errors that made Mary smile. Then he knelt in front of his mother and took out a letter from his velvet jacket to give to her. She read it, laughed, and said to Kostia: "Tell your grandmother that I shall do as she says, and now say goodbye to your new daddy and be gone."

He shouted something happily in Russian, and ran away, while Mary was beginning to translate: "He wanted to thank me in the name of Stenka Razin, who asked Kostia to come with his two thousand Cossacks and help him fight off Genghis Khan, who is now at the doors of Moscow."

"Oh."

"And let me assure you I never had an affair with either of these two gentlemen."

Leonardo laughed, but warned her: "Don't use that expression: *having an affair*. It's not fitting for a young lady."

"This is Rome, my love, this isn't Laterza, and I have been married for eight years."

"All the same, Mary."

She sobered at the mention of her name in the place of *love* or *darling*, while he was trying very hard not to think about her kissing Gennariello.

"Don't you want to hear what my mother has written?"

"Yes, of course."

"She's such a darling. She says we can continue to talk here for another hour, then I should go to the Russian embassy. She's leaving now, because she is still so upset by what she did to us—and she hopes you'll forgive her—that her face looks just perfect for condolences. Let me translate the last sentences: 'It will help Katinka to see me cry: she will cry in my arms for the benefit of the Russian correspondents, and they will write a moving article about her and her daughter. Perhaps the Empress will read it too and order her husband to read it. And of course Pierre will get another decoration for helping his mother shed tears, and Mr. Schultz will make a million rubles on it, selling shares in the Demidoff mines to Carnegie. You never know.' Isn't that typical of Mother's wit?"

"Yes," he said, brooding. "Just one thing, my love, I hope you don't mind. Or do you?"

"No," she said, growing apprehensive again.

He noticed this bad symptom and asked, slowly, without looking at her: "Why does the Cardinal believe that Gennariello is here to settle down in Rome as your lover?"

"The Cardinal?"

"The Cardinal."

"Oh . . ." And she became pensive, then suddenly there was a flash of joy in her eyes and she said: "Of course he would. My so-called mother-in-law, who's always snooping and listening behind doors, must have heard me year after year mentioning this rich Neapolitan widower, and the fact that he was coming to Rome because of me. But there isn't a word of truth in it."

"Why did you say it then?"

"Because I was trying to make the Monster jealous."

"Which means that you loved him!"

"He was my husband, damn him, and the father of my child!!!!"

"Do you have to curse like a Roman servant?"

"Yes, I do; I so hate all that period in my life, that even to think of it makes me vomit."

"I'm sorry. Stop."

"Oh no. You asked for it, you'll have to hear it all. I was trying to save my marriage. . . . After making such a fuss to marry him that I estranged my mother and almost killed her with grief, what was I to do, all alone in this unfriendly city, in that unfriendly house, surrounded by priests and kept like a prisoner, and not one intelligent book to read? Do you know or don't you, that I could not even read Renan, because he was on the Index?"

"Who's Renan?"

"The author of *Life of Jesus*, a most beautiful book. You should read it."

"I'm sorry, darling. Please don't cry. I'll ask no more questions. Only one posthumous remark: see the damage you have done to yourself by telling lies to your husband? No wonder he betrayed you."

"He didn't give a damn about me anyway, and never believed one word about the rich Neapolitan widower. His mother did, of course, and was terribly shocked. But she was never shocked by the fact that her darling son had mistresses all over Rome. She had been trained that way by her husband, another saintly man who divided his days between the church and the brothel. He died last year, thank God. It was a great relief for her, too. Now she can worship him and cry on his tomb, instead of crying all alone at home while he was out laughing with his whores. And do you know what his name was? Teofilo: friend of God! Can you beat that?"

"Do you mind one more question?"

Again he noticed the same bad sign he had noticed earlier—an undue apprehension in her eyes—and again he lowered his, pretending he had noticed nothing. "So you never saw Gennariello again?"

"Never."

"And never thought of him with affection or regret?"

"No, because I had you in my mind all the time."

"Oh. BECAUSE . . . And IF you hadn't had me?"

"Then my aunt would be a chariot."

"What's that?"

"An old Russian proverb: *if my aunt had wheels, she would be a chariot.* Just to illustrate . . ."

"Very amusing," he said sternly. "And how about that Robert Busch?"

"Boesch."

"All right, Bish, Bash, how about HIM?"

"Oh, him? I was supposed to marry him."

"You were? When?"

"Since I was eight, or even earlier."

"Until?"

"Until I met you."

"Me, or Gennariello?"

"What's the difference?"

"Oh . . . OH . . . no difference? Same person? Remember: you met him first. Was it he who put an end to your engagement?"

"I wasn't engaged, it was a childhood fantasy created by our parents; they were related, you know."

"Did he ever kiss you?"

"Yes."

"On the cheek or on the mouth?"

"We always kiss on the mouth, even when we kiss our parents."

"You kissed Gennariello on the forehead, or so you say."

"Yes, I did, because he was like a poor child."

"Except he was twenty years older than you."

"But still a child."

"Anatomically speaking? How would you know?"

"Mentally, which is what counts. He didn't impress me as a man; I found my act extremely innocent."

"Innocence begets children, we say. Our proverb."

"I know, but still, I wasn't interested."

"Interested enough to break your engagement."

"No, my love, no. To feel I couldn't be a mother to a widower, which was his excuse for wanting to kiss me. I felt I wanted to be a woman in the arms of a man, and when I met you the next day, I knew this was it."

"So much *it* that you became a woman in the arms of someone else."

"You'd left me, what could I do?"

He cringed and hid his head in his hands, moaning so loudly that she had to stop him. "Darling, I know, I'm a fallen woman, but haven't we discussed this before? Didn't fate bring us together in that theater where the resurrection was being played out? Don't you see in all this the hand of God, acting through Tolstoy the redeemer of our corrupt times?"

"That's blasphemy. . . . Christ was not a novelist. Can you see Christ writing about a fallen woman? And getting royalties?"

"He could have used them, God knows. . . . And I wish we knew more about Mary Magdalen. But are we here to discuss the origins of the Russian novel, or our future?"

"How cynical you sound." And he looked at her sternly again, bringing back the same disturbing symptom of a troubled conscience. "What are you concealing from me now?"

"I'm concealing nothing from you," she said, looking at him exactly as he had looked at her while pronouncing the same words.

He felt trapped in the circle of his own secrets, yet he knew he must try to believe her, because she was obviously trying to be honest. But she was also quite obviously still burdened by something. "I prefer you frightened than defiant," he said, "because a sense of having done wrong is the first step to salvation, but why should you be frightened of me? How can I guard you in the future, if I am not allowed to enter the citadel of your conscience? Look straight into my eyes and recognize me as your defender, not your enemy. Now remember that the woman I love must be as pure as the Mother of God, and as truthful. Do you know that when I was told my mother had given birth to a girl and not to a boy, I ran to the kitchen and came back to her room with a carving knife in my hand, crying with rage?"

"*Gospody pamilyui!!!!* Were you trying to kill her?"

"No, to defend my sister against anyone who might come and attack her. That was the kind of brother I was!! . . . Say something, why are you so pensive? You look horrified . . . SPEAK! I ORDER YOU!"

"I'm afraid . . ."

"Of what?"

"That you might think me stupid."

"That's out of the question. And preferable in any case to an overintelligent woman."

"Ah. Then I'm not afraid, because my question is stupid: is southern Italy like Rome before the rape of the Sabines?"

"What do you mean?"

"I mean are there so few women that girls are raped at birth?"

There was a long, long silence, then Leonardo shook his head and asked: "Is this the question of a civilized woman? Do you think we're barbarians? Wild beasts?"

"No, no, of course not."

"Let me ask you, rather: where are all your Russian brothers, when you Russian girls reach the age of fourteen?"

"Where should they be? Around the house."

"Yes, but not in the room where their sisters are being kissed. Or did you kiss in public?"

"Of course not."

"*Of course not!!* The very premise of sin: a girl decides what she does with her body when the first devils of temptation call. Next question, quickly now: who else was there all these eight years of married life? Count Jahn-Rusconi, of course. Confess. You even wrote for the same paper."

"Ridiculous."

"Why ridiculous? I look ridiculous compared to him: he's Adonis personified. I wish I looked like that: blond, pale, blue-eyed . . . a fellow writer . . . a nobleman . . . Why didn't you ever think of him while you were writing?"

"Do you want to see what I wrote all these years?"

"Of course I do."

She moved towards a closed bookcase, opened it, and there on one shelf stood a line of volumes, some white, some green, some yellow.

"The white ones are my works," she said.

He picked up one; it was rather thin and luckily in Italian. The title was: *Last Message and Other Sketches*.

"Where's the name of the author?"

"Here."

"But here it says TREFEB. Is that one of your Russian names?"

"No, it was my name, between *February third*, eighteen ninety-three, and now. Now my name is Mrs. Leonardo Claudi."

He tried to kiss her, solemnly, as a king kisses a knighted hero after the accolade, but she pushed him away. "This is the first time I have spoken the oath that makes me worthy of this: 'The name of Monsieur et Madame Claudi will be next in the annals of that truly modern union of free thought in the service of a freer mankind, after the names of Monsieur et Madame Curie.' "

"And who are they?"

"Don't you know? The discoverers of the new element: radium."

"Oh yes, of course, but are you sure they didn't steal the discovery from an Italian?"

"Darling, how can you be so suspicious of all foreigners?"

"We've been cheated too often—ever since the fall of the Roman Empire, earlier even."

"Well, you're an Italian, the future belongs to you, so let's take it. But to do so we must both overcome our insane jealousy. It's a foul thing, a kind of *furberia*. And I confess that I'm very much like you in this, too. In fact, the reason I never could love the Monster was that he never showed any jealousy. I could have done what I pleased: he trusted me; that is, he didn't care. You care, but you care too much, you frighten me. Shall we declare this a sacred pact: never to be suspicious of one another again?"

"Yes."

"And I shall never ask you another indiscreet question. I BELIEVE YOU."

For the first time in his life (in his new life, that is), he was happy to be rid of Mary. There were many reasons. He was infinitely tired, his eyelids had been constantly shutting during the last part of their conversation, and he had been *furbo* enough to pretend a much deeper concentration than necessary, so that he could close his eyes and put his hand over them. Another reason was that he believed her completely, so why should she go on talking so much? But the gravest of all reasons (which might seem to contradict the one just now mentioned) was that *she* believed *him*. That destroyed everything, made all the long speeches unnecessary; in fact, it even slightly eroded the dream of all dreams, because who could want to be married to an idiot? Up to that moment he had never even vaguely dared think of her as an idiot—yes, here and there, now and then, a commiserating little smile never visible on his face, upon seeing how innocent she was—but never a real idiot. While now, this was the only way he could enjoy his peace and go to bed, as he so desperately wanted to. "SHE BELIEVES ME," he commented aloud, as soon as the front door was closed and he was safely down one flight of stairs.

How can she, unless she's a real idiot? She's honest, of course, that I can see. But if she isn't an idiot, then God doesn't exist! Of course God doesn't exist, what I mean is Moral Geometry, and if that didn't exist, then we'd be all dead.

Satisfied with his own intelligence, that allowed him, even in his present state of fatigue, to have such fine perceptions, he took in the cold afternoon air, which was wintry again, and started walking in the direction of the Scalinata. But he was in for great surprises at every moment, or so it seemed: he wasn't at all sleepy, on the contrary, he was wide awake, and wild with hunger again. And still not a penny in his pocket. Could he go down the Scalinata now and face the beggars, when he had promised them money? Of course not, so the longer way must be his: all through the Villa Borghese and down the Pincio hill by a long, winding road. I'll eat at the hotel, he thought, and that helped. But right next to the fountain he had seen and admired in moonlight that same morning at 3 a.m., there was a steep little road going down, he assumed, to Piazza di Spagna, and down he went. And the first thing he saw was a vendor of *porchetta* and fried potatoes, which smelled so good he ordered one at once, but before he could touch it, the vendor asked for money, and so he was forced to say he had left it at home.

"Where do you live?"

"Via Gregoriana forty-two."

"It's very near, go home and get it."

"No, it's too cold, and I'm tired."

"And you think you can get away with this? You tried to cheat me, sonofabitch. All alike, these rich people, that's their sport: try to cheat a poor man out of some fried potatoes and a piece of meat. This is the third time it's happened in four days. And I fall for it, because I can't spend my life being suspicious. One needs friends, one needs trust, that's the basis of all honest trade, but rich people like you don't understand, probably because you came by your money dishonestly. Sonofabitch bastard . . ." And he went on cursing every one of Leonardo's dead ancestors and looking up and down the street for someone deserving of the good fried potatoes and the meat. The fried potatoes especially hurt him—you have to eat them at once, they're no good cold, or fried over again—so he kept shouting, while Leonardo, transfixed by hunger and fatigue, couldn't move another step, and let the torrent of insults pour over him without budging.

"Can't you leave, sonofabitch bastard? Do you think I enjoy insulting people? At least the others leave at once and curse back. I don't like that either, but it's a game like all the other rich people play: cruel and stupid. But you? Move on, idiot, don't stand there like a beggar, what's the matter with you: are you really so hungry?* Come on, talk: did you have a fight with your wife and she kicked you out of the house? Does she beat you all the time? Tell all, it's

---

* *Affamato* (starved) is a terrible insult in the Roman dialect, surpassed only by *morto di fame.*

my turn to have some fun. If you open your heart to me, I'll give you these damn fried potatoes for free. But not the *porchetta*, that doesn't spoil."

Leonardo was thinking: What a barbaric country, where dying of hunger is an insult to your dignity, almost worse than being cuckolded. And how right this man was: he himself had seen enough of the rich in one evening to believe this was the kind of sport they would find amusing, especially people like D'Annunzio and Marinetti, but for very different reasons: D'Annunzio because he was truly a *morto di fame*, no matter how high his claims on luxury—a young man who lived on rich women, or tried to, using up part of his booty to cultivate higher tastes in everything, so that the next rich woman could believe him to be a decayed aristocrat and not the son of dirt-poor parents from the backwoods of Italy. He was sure that D'Annunzio belonged to that category, and now that he had the time to think of everything at leisure, Schillasi too must belong to that category, and perhaps all his knowledge was also some sort of make-believe. A third person he added without any further thought was Tegolani. Marinetti on the other hand belonged in the category of Klagonov, Schultz, Mary's brothers perhaps (he had seen their pictures in the album—but that was not THE discovery; he preferred not to think of that now), even the young Count Adonis Jahn-Rusconi, all so protected from any contact with reality by their mothers (who else would ruin a child to that extent?), and therefore capable of the most unbelievable cruelty without the slightest hesitation and remorse, and yet at the same time so extremely delicate and thoughtful when dealing with people of their own class that an outside observer was bound to be fascinated by the contrast. As for the insults this man was heaping on him, he no longer cared. And let the wind come down icily from the top of that wall, and let even the cold water of the fountain shower occasional drops onto his face. All deserved, all richly deserved.

Finally, when he felt he had suffered enough, he regained his composure and asked his chastiser: "Sorry, but why in God's name do you keep your stand here and not in a more open street? Or in the piazza right around the corner?"

"You're asking me?"

"Of course, who else could answer?"

"The police commissioner who ordered me to move from the foot of the Scalinata, where I was born, where my father and my grandfather had their business and where we made very good money. Ask *him* . . . Just a moment, let me throw away these fried potatoes, I'll be back in a second to tell you what the police commissioner would answer."

And he disappeared into a makeshift hut covered with straw that was so caked with dust it looked like a real roof. Leonardo was in real pain: his head hurt, his stomach hurt, and he reproached himself for not asking the man to give him the fried potatoes instead of throwing them away, probably into a toilet hidden inside that dirty tent.

"So here I am back to tell you what the police commissioner would answer: he would answer you, 'My dear sir, this is the nation's capital, the Eternal City, we can't have an open cooking place and a *porchetta* stand where all the most important people of Italy and all the English of every country pass every day.' Yessir, that's what he would answer you, and do you want to know what I would answer to that? I would answer, 'Dear sir, yourself, if this is the Eternal City under the national government, it was even more eternal under His Holiness the Pope, who represents Eternal God on Earth. Eternity is not modernity, and we, who have fried and sold *porchetta* for most of the Popes in history, and even for the French when they were English with Napoleon who was the father of the King of Rome—we have an eternal right to be here, for the English of every country in the world, and even for the national government and the Burini of Piedmont who are our kings. And one more thing, dear sir,' I would say, 'if I can't earn my honest bread by selling *porchetta* at the foot of the steps, why do you let all those beggars sleep there and earn their money dishonestly?' That's what I would answer him, but go talk to the police commissioner, if you're a poor devil like I am."

"I know the head of the Roman police very well," said Leonardo. "I met him yesterday, he comes from my own hometown in Apulia, we became friends and he said whenever I wanted a favor I should go straight to him. Do you want me to talk to him about you? I'll be glad to, because I know you're absolutely right. If the beggars can sleep there, you can work in the square down below."

At that moment a fat woman emerged from the hut with the plate of potatoes in one hand, a fresh potato in the other and her mouth full.

"You're a saint," she said, spitting out a few potato parts to make room for her few words, which came out garbled anyway, "and we should kneel in front of you and kiss your feet, instead of treating you like shit. Forgive my husband, he's a no-good sonofabitch with the brains of a mosquito." Then, to her husband: "Why did you have to call him names, when you could see that he looked like a saint? I can see the halo around his hat, so why couldn't you? Apologize to him at once and give him a plate of *porchetta* and fried potatoes, quick. . . ."

The husband obeyed instantly, cursing her dead ancestors under his breath, while the wife, wiping her mouth with her skirt after swallowing the last fried potato and stretching out her greasy hand, said: "Before we talk business, let's make peace and be friends. If you can get us back to our old place at the foot of the steps, we'll serve you *porchetta* for the rest of your life, every day you pass by. Fair enough?"

"Fair enough," said Leonardo, taking the plate from the man's hands and devouring all that was on it without even using the fork he was being offered, because it looked too dirty.

"He looks as if he hadn't eaten for ten days," said the wife, very suspiciously. "How can he know the head of the police if he's so hungry?" Then, to Leonardo, while her husband was muttering away: "Wasn't I right to put him in his place? . . . Don't ever listen to him, but now, since we're friends, just tell me: where the hell did you get that fine sable coat, if you have no money?"

"From a . . . future relative, who lives at Via Gregoriana forty-two."

"Future relative? You mean the fat lady who lives in that palace?"

"Yes."

"We know her. But we don't like her. The little boy always wants to eat the *porchetta*, and she tells him God knows what in some ugly foreign language, but it's clear she's against us. So, she's your future relative and gives you this kind of a present? She must love you."

"Yes, but don't ask me any more questions, because I don't want to be indiscreet. She's a good woman, that's all I can say. And I give you my word that tomorrow I'll go to the police headquarters and try to win your case for you."

"God bless you," she said. Then, to her husband: "Give him another portion, quick."

"No," he replied angrily. "Let him earn the one he's eaten already, before we risk more. What guarantee has he given you?"

"My word," said Leonardo, proudly, and then left, because he didn't like the stare of a woman standing at a window right across from the *porchetta* stand.

He hadn't moved two steps, when Avvocato Tegolani popped up from nowhere and stood there in front of him with his usual slimy smile. "What a coincidence . . . I was just thinking of you. Are you on your way to the hotel?"

"Yes," said Leonardo, without smiling back or even answering his greeting.

"Wonderful. I'll see you later, we can have coffee or tea together." And, without waiting for his nonreply, he was gone.

Could he be in the service of Moral Geometry? thought Leonardo with a sudden feeling of doom, which rekindled the headache and the ache in his stomach which had just been extinguished by the wonderful *porchetta*. He dragged himself to the hotel, and right outside he saw Klagonov, who was about to board a cab: "*Fratellissimo carissimo*," he shouted, "in hurry extremely greatest now, but later you in hotel see, wait for me, talk lengthily I want."

He didn't answer, just waved back and nodded, but the moment he entered the hotel, he went straight to the desk and said: "I'm not well, and am going to bed. Please don't allow anyone to disturb me, and I mean *anyone*, for *any* reason. Thank you."

"Sir . . ." shouted the porter, as he was already climbing the stairs, "your key . . ."

The thought of walking back down discouraged him, so he stood there, leaning on the banister, his eyes closed and his mouth open. "Let me help you upstairs," said the porter, holding him by the arm. "Do you want a physician?"

"I *am* one, thank you. I need sleep, that's all. And please, let no one come upstairs and disturb me. You may go."

Satisfied with this show of authority, he reached his room, leaving the key in the lock because he wasn't used to living in hotels, undressed, and, without even putting on his nightshirt, he climbed into the soft bed, and was already snoring as he slowly pulled the blankets over his head.

After hours of total unconsciousness, he stretched his legs, yawned, and opened his eyes into a dream, which was the same one he had taken leave of that morning, only in this dream Adriana, dressed like a lady, with a pretty little hat and a purse hanging on her arm, was picking up his clothes from the floor and putting them neatly on a chair next to his bed.

"Adriana, my love," he mumbled, and thus realized that he was wide awake, and naked, and instinctively he covered himself up, asking: "What are you doing here?"

"Miss Mary told me to bring you this letter and this package," she said, turning her back on him after giving him both, so he could sit up and read without being embarrassed.

"What time is it?" he asked, opening the letter in great confusion.

"Nine fifteen," she said.

"Nine in the morning?"

"No, at night."

"Oh." And he began to read: *My love, I tried to call and was told you didn't want to be disturbed for any reason. You are right and I apologize, not only for myself and Mamachen, but also for Mr. Schultz. He was beastly to you, and you were splendid, but don't be angry now, please understand him, I'll explain when I see you again, if you still want to see me, but if this is to be the end, let me know immediately, so I can kill myself while you are still* . . . He didn't want to read any further, because he instantly felt tired again, but he skimmed the rest of the long letter to know if she was about to visit him, and was greatly relieved when he read: . . . *dinner with Katinka and her daughter tonight, please understand, it is one of those things that* . . .

A quick glance at Adriana, who was still standing there, motionless, her back turned to him, then a last glance at the letter: . . . *Just ask Adriana if you need any medicines, or even a doctor. Our*

family doctor . . . The rest was embarrassing, so he put down the
letter and opened the package, to find a standard stethoscope, just
like the one he had used before his marriage. Another long glance at
Adriana, but an angry one this time, because he couldn't guess
whether she had been chosen by Moral Geometry specially to tempt
him, and thus the memory of last night was again rendered ugly by
fear. But at the same time he feared losing her again, so he thought
he could master both temptation and prudence, the two eternal
enemies of luck, and said: "Is this all you have brought me tonight?"

"Yes." Her voice was distant and harsh.

"I also meant to thank you for what you gave me last night."

"My pleasure."

"Mine, too. And . . . you did me a great deal of good."

"My duty."

"But . . . may I ask you a question?"

"Questions yes, favors no."

"I said *question*, not *favor*."

"At your orders."

"How . . . are you?"

"Perfectly well, thank you."

"I don't mean that, I mean: what you gave me last night . . ."

"Can't be given tonight."

"I never asked you that. I meant to say: what you gave me last
night, for which I have been . . . I mean WILL be eternally grateful . . . er . . . how sure are you that . . . er . . . that you
haven't given me anything I shouldn't give . . . to others?"

"You mean six hundred and six?"*

"Where did you learn that expression?"

"My husband is an orderly at the Policlinic Hospital."

"Oh, you have a husband."

"And you have a wife. So what?"

"But . . . since you don't seem to . . . care much for him, how
can you be . . . sure?"

"Because I never gave my cunt to anyone but you, since I last
gave it to him the night before our wedding."

* I.e., syphilis: 606 was the name of the cure in those days.

"Ah."

"May I go now?"

"Just a moment. May I ask just one more question?"

"Miss Mary said: *give him anything he asks.* I don't know why she said that, but she did."

"Just give me an answer, then you may go. My question is: why . . . did you give it to me, if you knew . . . that I was . . . I mean, if you had never seen me before?"

"Because when I see food on the kitchen table that isn't meant for us, and that has come to the kitchen by mistake, I eat it."

There was a long, long silence, then she turned slowly towards him while he wasn't looking, and, seeing his terrified eyes, his flushed face, and his gaping mouth, she asked, with real concern: "What's the matter? Aren't you feeling well?"

"I'm feeling well enough to make you feel well too, that's what's the matter."

"And I'll let you," she said in the most natural voice, then grabbed her hat with both hands and threw it into the distance, ripped off every bit of clothing in a rage, and came, all naked and sweating, towards the bed, where he made room for her, threw away the pillows to make space for her head, and then widened her legs, and he actually saw steam rising from that dark forest in flames. They reached many summits, flying upwards together and then falling together very softly into the deepest valleys of sleep, still always together and more strongly together with every part of their bodies down to the very bones. And then they loosened their embrace and became like two strangers who meet by chance on the street. "Why did I do this?" she asked, covering her face with both hands.

"That's for me to ask," he said, hoping she would remember that it had not been his fault, but hers both times.

"Don't be a hampotrick," she said, using the typical Roman distortion of the word that always amused him but not this time. Had Mary used such a word correctly, of course, he would have been very resentful, but with this young girl he couldn't be. She had detected his game, told him so, and the whole thing was forgotten.

"Easy for you," she said. "You love Mary" (he resented the use of that name without the servile appellative *Miss,* which is as far as a servant may go to prove she has known her mistress for years), "you're leaving with her tonight or tomorrow night or whenever, but I stay here, and I love you: that's the insanity of it all." (How well she talked: clear, simple and to the point.)

There was a silence, then she said: "Of course you can't say you love me, and I can't say I love Mary, but I know you love me, really very much—let's not be hampotrick—and you know I love Mary very much, but justice says we can't say what we feel, so that's the hampcracy of justice, not ours."

"Right," he said. "It will be very difficult for us to pretend, and yet we must, because she needs us, *as we are:* you as a friend and me as a husband."

"Well said, that's how a public scribe would put it."

"Don't you know how to write?"

"Of course I do, but with the wonderful scribes we have here in Rome, who wants to write his own letters? You can try for a thousand years and still not find the right words, but if you go to him, he listens to your woes and without even stopping to think, out he comes with the perfect phrases. That's one of the reasons I can never leave Rome: where else in the whole world would you find such great scribes? My mother had a scribe who was better than her confessor; in fact, she always confessed all her troubles to him. With confessors you can never be too frank: they will use it against you for years afterwards and even when they don't, they jerk off while you talk, which is why they insist on getting all the details of your sins, and you feel you've been a whore for free, plus the duty of so many prayers and penances, to add insult to injury. If you have a good scribe, and he feels yours is not the right letter to send, he will refuse to write it, won't charge you, and will spend an hour with you telling you where you've gone wrong, then he'll write a proof letter, and if you don't like it, he won't charge either. Honest people, and real friends. It's a mission, if you ask me. There are bad scribes too, but they don't stay in business for long."

"What happens to the bad scribes?"

"They become lawyers."

"Lawyers? Doesn't that take years of training and cost money?"

"That's for lawyers with a laureation; *doctors* we call them in Rome. Not doctors like you—doctors in tricks, who use go-betweens, procurers, thieves, spies, everything bad, everything dangerous for the poor. The rich don't know that kind of lawyer. Take the Signora, for example. Does she know all the sonsofbitches who go round and do dirty work for her lawyer? No."

"What do you think of Tegolani?"

"Think? You don't have to think to vomit. You just vomit, that's all."

"Have you ever told Mary or her mother about him?"

"I'm no fool. You can't do that, if you want to survive in her service. Tegolani is a saint."

"Why?

"Because he's a real sonofabitch, like most saints have been, since . . . I don't know, let's say since the sack of Rome, or the death of Jesus, anyway, the Church has gone astray for a very long time."

"You still haven't told me why Tegolani is a saint."

"Oh . . . because he loves his mother. He knows that with two . . . English persons like our two ladies, to love your mother is the thing that will send you straight to heaven. The Avvocato knows how to exploit that English way of thinking. They swear by him. Every time he mentions her name, he cries. And she isn't even dead yet. What will he do when she dies? Steal openly from the two ladies, because that, he'll tell them, is the only way he can forget his mother. And they'll let him do it. If we stole openly, God, what a scandal that would be!"

"But . . . do you believe in stealing . . . secretly?"

"I don't, and in a household like that you couldn't steal if you wanted to: you're too busy emptying the wastepaper baskets into your pocket: they throw away everything after using it no more than once or twice: brand new overcoats, furs, shoes, hats . . . the hat I'm wearing tonight was thrown out by Mary yesterday: she wore it just twice. And it was made for her in Paris by the best milliner: she wouldn't go to one in Rome. As for what goes into the ashcan in the kitchen, I tell you—the best restaurant in Rome could serve people like them on what they've thrown away the previous day."

"Does the cook steal?"

"Of course he does: he charges twice for the same food, by pretending he's gone to market again. But you can't touch him, because he's English too, and the English are all honest by decree of the Fathereternal."

"But isn't he French?"

"That's another way of being English."

"But Bernhard is German."

"As if the Germans weren't English. What d'you think they are: French?"

"And . . . how about Dante and his mother?"

"What about them?"

"Tell me about them."

"Hampotrick, you want to know about Cefala. Why didn't you fuck her?"

"How do you know I didn't?"

"She told me."

"Why, do you think she would?"

"Of course she would."

"Then she's no virgin."

"Of course she is. But someone must inaugurate the bridge, and you always choose someone important to cut the ribbon: the mayor or a Cardinal, or the King, if you're lucky. She chose you."

"Without seeing me?"

"I told her about you, and she asked me if she could have you, and I said go ahead and enjoy him."

He hated himself now, and hated Adriana too. She noticed it. "Why have you taken your hand away from my breast? You love Cefala."

"And you hate her."

"Nobody hates her, and she knows it, but that's the story she likes to tell when she's playing Cinderella."

"So she's a hypocrite."

"She's no hampotrick. Why do you have to insult her? Your fault, if you didn't take her. But she preferred it that way, I know that too."

"Did she tell you?"

"I haven't seen her since, but she will. I know my sister, after all: she likes to play the old game."

"What game?"

"*Show-it-to-him-but-don't-give-it*. She hopes to marry the Prince in the Fairy Tale."

"But she's engaged."

"So what? A prince needs no divorce: he takes her away and they live happily ever after. You're a prince, you should know."

"But I'm getting a divorce."

"Because you're not marrying a princess: you're marrying a Protestant bankress and industrialistess, and even if she has princes in the family, it's because they needed money and married it, that's the way princes work. With prick and cunt, the way we do with shovel and pickaxe, or kitchen knife and serving spoon. Why do you think poor Mr. Schultz had to marry that bitch of the duchess and pretend he was the father of the girl he actually wanted to marry? Because the real father of the girl, who is a Russian grand duke, and her mother, who is a whore and was his children's French governess, didn't want the girl to be married to a Jew, so the mother sacrificed herself and married Schultz so *he* couldn't marry the girl, who ended up in the hands of a false nobleman, worse than *generetto:** *marchigiano,* you understand? You know the proverb: better a death in the family than a *marchigiano* at the front door."†

"You mean the old Marchese Carlo Tempi?"

"Who else?"

"Didn't he court Mary at one time?"

"Mary and everybody else—me too, but I kicked him in the face and he had to stop."

"But Mary married the Monster to flee from him."

"To flee from dear old Mamma, if you want to know the truth. Only swear you'll never tell her, because she doesn't know it, and she would never forgive you for telling her. *The real deaf are those who don't want to hear,* says the dictate. Put that hand back on my breast, it's my first and last night of happiness, I too am Cinderella, but I won't ever find a prince, because I wouldn't want him. I'm happy as I am."

"Tell me about Cefala," he said, fondling the breast without the slightest pleasure.

"The tongue licks where the tooth hurts, eh? Another dictate . . . Well, have you noticed something peculiar about her?"

---

* *Generetto* is the petty bourgeois with social ambitions; *generone* is the bourgeois who has arrived.

† Marche is the most backward of all the Papal States.

"I know."

"Oh, did Mary tell you?"

"No, I discovered it in a family album: she's the daughter of one of the two brothers."

"Yes, the one on the left, sitting down with a sword in his hand: that's Pierre."

"Have you seen the album?"

"Seen it? What do you think we do during the nine or ten months on our own in that big house? We live in it. We know every family album, every family secret, every family heirloom, every family handwriting and almost every family language they speak. I know every letter in the Russian alphabet, I just don't know what they stand for, but I could recognize them in a newspaper if I saw one. I also know the sounds, even if I don't know the letters they stand for, but what I really know and we all know in the kitchen is the people in those albums and those paintings; we know them the way they really are, from one end of the day to the other, from snout to rump and backwards, from breakfast cup to night pot; for us they have no secrets, and not because we snoop, but because for them we have no eyes and no ears and no judgment. And I don't mean that our ladies are worse than other rich people, they're all alike—once they begin to be served, they consider the servant an object. Some love their objects, and our ladies do more than others, but objects we remain, and when you're with objects, you feel you're alone, and you hide nothing, and that's when we learn everything, even if we don't want to."

"So that's why Mary hates Cefala."

"No, Mary doesn't know anything about it, and if you told her, she would never believe you."

"But you thought she'd told me."

"With Russians everything is possible: one moment they understand everything and the next moment nothing. And Mary is more devilish even than her mother that way: she'll pick up signals from the air, but if she doesn't want to know, she won't, and no signal can help."

"Then why does Mary hate Cefala?"

"Because she looks exactly like her sister Ludmilla."

"And like Mary as a child."

"You're crazy in the head if you say that. No resemblance at all."

"Did you see that picture of Mary as a child in the album? The big one, taking up a whole page?"

"That's Ludmilla, not Mary."

"Impossible."

"Look, Leonardo, I know the family and you don't. Stop talking like an imbecile. You wanted that picture to be Mary's picture, because you love Cefala, and since she didn't give it to you, it still itches down there, but stop thinking with your prick and try to think with your head. Ludmilla and Cefala are no women for you: they would walk right over you to reach some higher goal, I know them both and love them, too, so you can't say it's a slander. I even envy them, and so does Mary, because we two are alike: faithful to one man and goodnight, musicians. You're lucky you got Mary, and the proof that you got her is that you got me too. We always liked the same men, it's almost a joke how much alike we are."

"What do you mean, you liked the same men? Tell me at once— and no nonsense. I have a right to know; she's going to be my wife and the mother of my children! And don't try to fool me: I went to school with the Jesuits!"

Adriana reared up like a snake ready to strike. She looked comical in that imperious position, all naked, her breasts shaking as if frightened of their mistress's voice and meekly agreeing to obey her, but the moment she put both hands on her hips, she was no longer a snake, but the classical washerwoman venting her full repertoire of vulgarity, as she started giving this upstart loudmouth what he deserved.

"*I* . . . what do *I* mean? I mean, *You*, what do *you* mean, and I know exactly what I mean, come on, Mister Bigprick, if you want to talk big, go jerk it off in the face of the Reverend Father General, I'm no little angel going to confession for the first time in her life, I'm a married woman who got rid of her husband right in church, on her wedding day, if you know what *that* means, and the priest never knew it, and nobody else knew it, and they all thought the laugh was on me, because they were all looking at my arse, and my bridegroom pinching it, and me trying to make him stop; even the priest heard me and was trying not to laugh, but I knew he'd heard, and I said to myself: I'm not going to give him the satisfaction of kicking me out of the church of my own Lord and Blessed Father-eternal, no, indeed, I'll go through the whole service of my arse and keep quiet, but just wait until we're alone, my little husband and me. . . . And now Adriana will tell you what happened to a certain sonofabitch I loved so much until he pinched my arse in church."

She was now so magnificent that Leonardo had only one desire: to make love to her again. But to do that, he had first to be forgiven, so he said, very humbly and sincerely: "I'm sorry, you're a thousand times right and I am rottenly wrong, forget my question and forgive me if you can, but now tell me what happened to you and your husband, how did you get rid of him if you said yes to the priest? Matrimony is a sacrament, and it binds you for life."

"You're teaching me? I'm teaching you that you can't say no to a priest. Excommunication is for the rest of your life; I don't mean that he can pronounce it, because God stands higher than he does and can see over his shoulder, but I mean all your relatives and friends who can laugh for the rest of their lives when they see you going to church on Sundays, and *that* excommunicates you from wanting to go on Sundays or even on the day of your own funeral, because you'll make sure that you die out of town. I loved my bridegroom, oh, he was so beautiful, you should have seen him, he looked a little like you, I told you Mary and I have the same taste in men, and of course I hadn't given it to him because I thought, let's let God bless the union, or God knows what will happen while the soup is being cooked for the next nine months, God may not exist at all, but we'd better not try to find out. That's what I told my bridegroom, and of course I always helped him with my hand when he was stiff, the way any self-respecting girl would before she gets married, and of course that morning he was so stiff he couldn't even walk and you could see the head of his prick pressing inside his new pants, and I hoped nothing would happen before he took them off, because cleaning those spots from black cloth is nearly impossible. But the idiot was trying to get himself even more worked up by whispering to me how he was going to tear off my drawers and . . . you know . . . Well, to make a long story short, he pinched my arse just as we were about to say yes to the priest. So I said, 'No,' under my breath to him, meaning don't touch me there, everybody can see, and he just went on doing it again and again, and we could hear the people laughing, as I told you. So I decided to do nothing, because I really felt like crying, and at the very moment I said yes to the priest, I said to myself, Up your arse, Mister Priest, if you think God hasn't seen you laughing, and in fact God immediately cut the wires connecting my body to my husband's. I just felt nothing: love was gone, and when love's gone, what can you do? Nothing. We went home and he did what he'd wanted to do for so long, and of course he didn't notice anything, because men are all prick and no brains, but I felt nothing, and the next morning I told him the whole truth and said, 'You find yourself another hole for a prick-hole, I'm shutting up shop and declaring a holiday. Goodbye.' "

"And did you ever see him again?"

"Oh yes, we're good friends, but if he were eighty years old, I couldn't care less."

"And if I made you pregnant, what then?"

"You'll never find out, because I don't want my child to become a great doctor after his father, only someone whose own son may want to take after *him*. If you were still a poor doctor, then yes, because your mother must be a woman like myself, with all due respect to her memory. But today you're a rich man, and you can't go back, because you've crossed the Rubbacon, now you're living in the moon, I've seen you looking lost like a babe in the woods, you didn't even know how to use a knife and fork, and I don't mean to say you weren't taught at home, but these are no knives and forks, they're the prongs of hell, and they have silver hairpins to cut fruit and dentist's pincers to eat snails, and they do it all so fast that a poor peasant like you doesn't know what to do. Don't you think we all know in the kitchen why you can't eat a thing in that house? Have you eaten today? I bet you anything you went out and ate *porchetta* like the real peasant you are. Am I right?"

"Almost, because I had no money, so I got into a fight with the *porchetta* man and he gave me some only after I promised I'd help him get his stand back in the piazza."

"And how can you do that?"

"Because I know the head of the Roman police."

"You do? How come?"

"He's from my hometown."

"Oh, I should have known: they're all from down there. But, first of all, you'll never succeed because he will say no, and, secondly, don't you get mixed up with those fucking sonsofbitches, you can only get yourself in trouble, listen to Mamma, she knows best. You and the chief of police . . ." She burst into shrieks of laughter. "I can just see you with him: what a pair . . . the wolf and the lamb. You know who's safe with the police? People like Tegolani: dog don't eat dog, but you? . . . Hahaha . . . hahahaha . . . Come on, let's make love again, it'll be the last time."

This was the moment he had hoped for so desperately, and he could hardly give her time to fall back into position and open her plump thighs, but before he could throw himself on her, she had closed her legs again and coiled up into a mass of quivering flesh—quivering not with passion, but with sobs. Their bodies collided, because he hadn't foreseen the sudden change, and she pushed him back so violently that he rolled over and fell off the bed in a fantastic somersault she didn't even notice: her fists were in her eyes, then in her teeth, then opening and closing on her hair, which she was pulling, trying to tear it out of her scalp, and all with such a crescendo of shrieks that he had to struggle in order to gag her with the bedsheet.

"Stop, stop it, for God's sake, what are you doing? Do you want the night manager to come up here?"

The shrieking stopped, but her sobbing became all the more violent, and now she was pushing the bedsheet into her mouth and biting furiously on it. She even looked like Mary in her tantrums: who was the teacher, who the pupil, and who cared anyway? After fear had killed all sensuousness, an immense pity killed the fear in his heart, and he himself began to cry—silently, because he didn't want to encourage her—but suddenly even pity was killed by acute pain, as she began to slap him across the face with such violence that he feared for his teeth and his eardrums.

"Swine . . . Pig . . . Shitheap, why did you let me do it to myself? You imbecile, heart of stone, monster . . . MAN . . . Aaaah . . ." and the shrieks began again. He hit her back just as violently. "Stop that, stop, this is madness . . ."

She stopped and looked at him with quiet curiosity, then smiled and finally laughed, sobbed for a moment again, then laughed again, then there was silence: a grave, funereal silence, while she looked at his body as if he were dead. Tears rolled down her cheeks in such streams that her whole face appeared lost beyond a closed window in a rainstorm.

Finally she covered her eyes and wiped them with both hands, saying, amid her last shudders: "That's life, Adriana . . ." And then, to his great surprise, a phrase in some kind of broken French he had never heard before: *"Bandie' de la Fransse, donnenn'u della pazianze. . . ."**

And with this the crisis was ended. Now she knelt there motionless and exhausted and she looked so pure and beautiful that Leonardo couldn't remember any greater intimacy with her than this sight of her tired nakedness. On her breasts he could see the marks of his fingernails, on her pubis the glitter of the glue, and it was with veneration now that he whispered: "Shall we?"

"No," she said quietly. "That was the end and that must be the end. No fear: your child will not be born; *this* child here is dead." And she pointed to her chest, like a Madonna in a painting: with the whole hand. She got off the bed, and turned her back to him to look at herself in the mirror, carefully examining first one side of her face and then the other; he could see that new sobs were beginning to shake her shoulders and arms, but they were discreet sobs, and when she turned to him again she was smiling. "Funny, how stupid we can be in life. . . . Cover up, you'll catch cold. And try to sleep now. What time do you have to get up?"

"Very early, five at the latest. What time is it now?"

"Two fifteen. But you mustn't get up before seven."

"Oh no. I have to go and find the person to whom I stupidly gave those cufflinks."

"I know: your cousin; and you'd better get them back quickly, because they're sacred objects."

He said nothing, and she went on talking as she opened a large suitcase she had obviously brought with her and removed her chambermaid's uniform and a black shawl. "You needn't go before seven. Do you know how to get there?"

"Not exactly, but I'll ask Dante to go with me."

---

* "God of France, give us patience."

"Take a carriage, here's some money."

"No, please, I can't allow you . . ."

"Stop talking like an imbecile. If I can't even do this for you, what am I good for?" Her words ended in more sobs. She blew her nose as peasants do, spitting out of each nostril while holding the other closed with a finger, then began to dress, put hat and gloves and purse into the suitcase and closed it, saying: "This is your suitcase, but until I have a chance to hide my things I'll leave them here. It won't be for long. I guess in two more days you'll be able to leave, and I wish it were . . . it we—" (a rebel sob, soon repressed) "right now." Now that she was all dressed up as a maid, she began to act like one: "Get up and let me change the sheets."

"No . . ."

"Don't be a child. I, too, would prefer never to have to wash again, but I'll have to, the moment I get to my room."

"Take a bath here."

"Oh no. That's for the masters: cold water and a small basin for us, and laundry soap. If I go in there, everybody will smell the perfumed soap on me tomorrow."

He got up, put on his robe, and when she came back from the bathroom with clean sheets on her arm, he tried to help her, but she pushed him away without saying a word and quickly changed his bed, then hid the dirty linen in the suitcase, saying: "These will be thrown away. I can't wash them in the servants' quarters, Dante's mother would notice, and I can't leave them here in the hamper. Now go to bed, my love, and sleep well. Cefala will knock on your door at seven, and please don't let her in, remember?"

"Yes."

"Promise?"

"Promise."

"Because she's dangerous. She wouldn't be loyal to you nor to Mary: only to her crazy dreams . . . or is it her crazy blood? Who cares? . . . I at least am loyal to Mary. It doesn't look that way right now, does it? But you know what? I say that loyalty begins when it's all shot to hell and you have to put it together again out of the wreckage. That's where loyalty begins. Before that it's all words."

She bent over him and caressed his face at length without kissing it, and he was grateful: their lips were tired, swollen and dry, and they had lost their function: they could no longer initiate a night of love, and, as for ending it, silence alone could do that, however unsuccessfully. Her last words were: "If you are ever disloyal to Mary, I'll come all the way to Paris or wherever you are, and I'll kill you." And without waiting for him to answer, she was gone.

When Cefala knocked he was in his bathtub, exactly like the first time, only it was much, much earlier: in fact, not quite five yet and pitch dark. He hadn't been able to sleep, or, rather, he had slept without knowing it, because instead of dreaming, his mind had never left the room and the sight and the smells and the physical sensations of her flesh around his. The temptation to answer "Come in" was very strong, and he decided to let destiny decide, by pretending he had heard nothing and turning on the water so as to justify his deafness. And after less than the time it had taken him to turn on the water, the bathroom door was flung open, and there stood Adriana.

"It isn't that I don't trust you or Cefala," she said, in a very tired voice, "but I had to see you again. Mary will have you for the rest of her life, and may God grant you happiness and a very long life together and many, many healthy children, all loving and well-meaning as I am to both of you. Amen." She was standing there like a servant, an old servant, who knows she can take her liberties, but will not trespass.

"We have time," he said, emerging from the tub and coming towards her, armed with the visible argument of his own passion.

"Go back into your element," she said, stretching out her arm like God chasing Adam and Eve from the garden. "And don't you think I didn't mean what I said at two fifteen this morning. I did, I do and I will forever, remember. But I couldn't sleep, I couldn't, Saintly Mother of God, I kept seeing those white shoulders of yours above me in my sleep all the time, all the time, so I said curse the . . . whatever it is to be cursed, and here I am. But now I must go back, or I won't be able to pretend I went to first Mass. Goodbye."

And she was gone again.

FIFTH DAY

A wet, wintry morning was beginning to form around the gaslights in front of the hotel, but only one element as yet was
actually present: the rain. All the rest was still night, even up
in the sky, where small samples of gray cloud-flannel were being
shown and then withdrawn again, to make room for a different
cloth, now fluffier, now more compact. It only looked like daylight
because it was ugly, but in fact it was obviously moonlight, shining
brightly above the sea of clouds. It reminded Leonardo of that hill
town where he had spent the best years of his life, getting up at
five and marching through the rainy courtyard to Mass in soldierly
formation with the rest of the college, under the supervision of the
Father Prefect. And why that image, when it hadn't come to him
for years? Because any other image of mornings like this was of his
ever-present reality: crossing the square of Laterza in the wet, either
on foot or on horseback, to see how his patients were doing after
another night of pain. The gaslights of Laterza were not as citylike
as those of Rome: they hung on the end of a short iron bar sticking
out of the corner of some church or municipal building, and there
were precisely three in all, while here alone there were at least
twenty, and they stood all around the huge square, with its huge
obelisk in the middle, the huge palaces across from the hotel, and not
one but three huge churches. And of course in Laterza there were no
horse carriages standing in line, waiting for rich customers: here
there were at least six. But the one image that was present in the
minds of both the doctor-mayor of Laterza and the kept man, kept
by two women and unfaithful to three, was the image of the comfortable bed they had both left, to go out so early into the rain. Except that in Laterza, if the doctor had been able to shirk his duty
and go back to bed, he would have been able to enjoy his warm

corner even though it was not much of a bed, and a detested wife could kick him any time and pull all the blankets off him as she turned in her sleep, while here in Rome, in the richest of hotels, in the largest, most comfortable and most private of beds, Leonardo could not even enjoy the sleep he so needed, because his conscience attacked him even harder than Adriana had. Thus he preferred to face the rain and do his duty. But what duty was that? Recapturing precious personal belongings to which he had no right anyway, from a person as bad as himself. No, he concluded, the only advantage is that here I have a warm overcoat, while in Laterza I have none, but my conscience is bad, no matter where I stand, sit or lie down, even this repentance is unhealthy; a useless escape from one sin into another, with no honesty ahead: I'm just committing incest with myself.

He told the night porter to call him a cab, and tipped him very generously, thinking that this was the one honest thing he could do: give back to the humble the money that belonged to the humble.

"Thank you very much," shouted the night porter, so that all the coachmen could hear him, and they all started towards the hotel, before he could so much as shout: "Cab!"

"Where are you going?" they asked Leonardo in chorus, and he, recognizing an old Neapolitan trick that is only used on foreigners, harangued them all in his best Neapolitan, with gestures. "I don't need six cabs, I need one!"

"You should have told us that," answered one of them for the rest, who laughed while Leonardo tried to shout through all the noise: "I didn't even call you, *he* did," he cried pointing to the night porter who was no longer there. "Porter!" he shouted now, making gestures in the direction of the hotel, but nothing moved from the dark regions, and all he saw were the skeletonlike horses being stripped of their rain blankets, while their owners pretended to fight among themselves for the privilege of serving what some called "His Excellency," others "Er Milordo" and still others "Er Zignor Principe."

Confronted with the choice between another humiliation in front of the same servants (HIS servants, alas), who had seen him ridiculed every single time he had entered the hotel, and this private humiliation at the hands of perfect strangers in the dark of the

night, he chose the latter; after all, he couldn't go anywhere without
their help.

"Whoever of you feels like getting a good tip is welcome to serve
me, but if you would rather spend your time in your own vulgar
games, you are perfectly welcome to do so, and I'll order my own
personal horses to be harnessed." This went so much against the
grain that his voice quivered as he spoke, and his words were not
immediately understood; also the hotel door was being opened
again, and some very expensive pieces of luggage piled up under the
awning and guarded by several porters, before the next rich customer or customers made their appearance on the square. This
attracted the attention of the six coachmen, who left their horses
and ran to the new source of income ripening out there in the dim
light beyond the rain curtain. And it rapidly became obvious to
Leonardo that he must act to protect the ill-gotten gains of his
many treasons and desertions; namely, the precious overcoat, which
was beginning to grow ever heavier with rain.

In the meantime he spied on the scene, feeling protected by the
darkness, out of reach of the next pool of gaslight. And he saw
Marinetti come out of the hotel, tipping everybody and being
thanked with bows, not with false words that were the signals to the
thieves in the night that the hunt had begun. . . .

He couldn't go back now, so he walked farther out into the rain,
to make sure he wouldn't be seen. But perhaps it wasn't Marinetti:
this man looked bigger, in fact he looked like Klagonov. . . . Well,
perhaps he could, indeed *should*, go back now: Klagonov was the
type to take him wherever he was going *and* pay for the fare, besides
making him known to those bastards as his *fratellissimo carissimo*.

He walked slowly out of the shadow, but no . . . oh no, this was
indeed Marinetti, and he was lecturing the thieves. . . . Back into
the rainy night, Leonardo, and now wonder why Marinetti didn't
leave yesterday. Could he have . . . HAD Cefala? A rush of such
violent sensuousness invaded him again that he began to moan
aloud in pain. He had been made *cornuto*, there could be no doubt.
O Cefala, O my real love . . . why should this happen to *us?* You
can't love him, you love me . . . O Cefala, my Cefala, you, the true
love of my life . . . And that liar, your sister, that whore, who stole

me from you . . . everybody is cheating me, this is Rome, this isn't home, they're right, all those people who keep warning me. . . .

But as quickly as this torment had come, it departed again to make room for a less painful picture: Adriana is no liar, she can't have staged the whole thing, her words were true, for if they weren't then Mary, too, is a liar, because they're such friends.

But then, what am I doing here, using the money I was paid by a whore for my services, to recapture those cufflinks in order to cheat Mary all over again?

And then it hit him like lightning: Mary didn't exist any more— Mary, HIS Mary, the Holy Image in the sky above the rain at five in the morning in Laterza, for so many years, at all hours, in all seasons and weathers . . . Mary, by definition Holy and Virgin, had fallen the first moment he heard from her that she was married and a mother. . . . So this was Moral Geometry.

But why wasn't Marinetti leaving, so he could go back and find shelter against this icy rain? Marinetti was waiting for someone, and here they came—SHE came . . . Cefala, of course, same size, same way of walking. . . . But no, this woman had a hat and an elegant overcoat . . . but hadn't Adriana worn a hat, that she hid in his suitcase? Probably Cefala, too, had received (RECEIVED? And why shouldn't Adriana be a thief too? She was a whore and a liar and a traitor to her closest friend . . . why not a thief?) . . . But no, it wasn't Cefala. . . . But who could be sure? . . . Now they were leaving in one of the coaches, they were coming his way. . . . Now the night, too, was going, it was gone and Leonardo walked away, quickly, turning his back to the coach and feigning interest in the sky: up there the deal had been closed between the purchaser of daily weather conditions and the Great Shaper of the Human Condition in general. He, or she (who but a woman could choose colors and curtains and wallpaper?)—SHE had ordered a very pale gray, and it was interesting to see how such a dead color could win over the warm and lively yellow of the gaslights. . . . All around the square the bright yellows paled and shrank to the size of dots in the rain.

Now the traitors were gone, he turned around and saw that the carriages were gone too. . . . Oh no, thank God, two were still

close by and moving slowly in his direction; he heard the coachmen
shout at each other, but couldn't understand what they were saying,
because the rain had turned to hail and it was dancing noisily over
the cupola and on the rim of his poor, battered hat. So he moved
towards them and now he could hear that they were discussing him,
weighing the pros and cons of serving him: "If he does, it means he
can afford to let the rain ruin his overcoat."

"Let's ask him."

"All right, but I have first crack."

"Go ahead, ask him."

"Sir," said the holder of the option: "The hotel porter says, if you
want to have the ladies' coachman alerted, he can send for him, but
I think it may be more convenient if you take me, instead of having
to tip him and wait a half hour."

"All right," said Leonardo, very pleasantly surprised to hear that
his shameful boast had been a statement of fact, one of the less
unpleasant facts of his present condition; remembering that he had
money now (this second new fact he had momentarily forgotten)
also struck him as not at all unpleasant, and he dispatched thoughts
of repentance and gratitude to both Mary and Adriana, in fact, to
all three women around his heart. "You are perfectly right, my
friend, let's go." And, climbing into the cab, he gave the name of
his erstwhile hotel, whereupon the other coachman, who had been
eager to find out where he was going, burst into laughter and said:
"Didn't I tell you he's a gigolo? How can you expect him to give
you a big tip?"

And his coachman, just as loudly, but very, very angrily: "The
porter says you can trust him." Then, turning to Leonardo from the
height of his authority: "Isn't he right? Aren't you the friend of the
fat old lady?"

"I am her son-in-law!" shouted Leonardo, "and stop asking indiscreet questions."

"Oh, I'm sorry, sir, I didn't know." Then, to the other: "He's her
son-in-law and stop asking indiscreet questions."

But the other coachman was seized again by uncontrollable
laughter: "The son-in-law? Then he doesn't pass the doors."

At the moment these words didn't bother Leonardo too much:

he had heard so many Roman idioms in the last four days that he had no interest in learning more about their despicable language, and besides, even if he had been insulted in his own dialect, he would have paid no attention to it. On the other hand, the question he should have been asking himself was: Why are we moving away from the center of the city and not towards the very center where I know my old hotel is. But the question actually on his mind was: Could any of these women coming out of church here be Cefala? An impossible question to answer, because there were three churches and so many women you couldn't count them all, and it was raining, so there were shiny black umbrellas hiding two, three, even four apiece, and there were nuns and monks and elderly cripples and goatherds with their tall hats that hid more of the scene, and that was changing so rapidly that one moment the entrance to the church was all blocked by a great dark mass, and the next moment it was empty and you could see all through the central aisle up to the altar, where the sacristan was extinguishing the candles with his big stick with the little iron hat on top of it. (Brief, very brief flash of memory: how many times he had done that in the mornings, back home and in college . . .) Too late, Leonardo, too late, and yet, what a chance you missed: because, if Cefala was up at that hour (another proof that Adriana had lied, because if Cefala *was* up at that hour, she would have gone to Mass right after waking him, so where was the time to go to bed with him?) . . . dammit, why didn't I think of that before taking this cab? Obviously they must go to the church right in front of the hotel. . . . But that church and the twin church next to it, and the three streets fanning out from them, were now empty, while the one next to the city gate was obviously of no interest, and yet it was so full that the coachman had to stop for a while and let the outgoing faithful leave. How Leonardo hated them all for their unchristian attitude towards a poor, suffering soul like himself. What would it cost them to let one of their black shadows be Cefala? O God, why are you so stingy with me? Or is it you, Moral Geometry, that keeps punishing me with my own temptations?

The coachman whipped his horse and the coach had started moving, when two women crossed its path and were almost run over:

one was Cefala and the other Adriana, they clung to one another in their thin shawls under their wet umbrella, and both looked very sad, but Adriana even sadder than Cefala.

They trotted and trotted and trotted out into the open country-side, and the mud was so thick that it shot chunks of clay right into the cab and onto Leonardo's overcoat.

"Where are you going?" he asked, in a sudden fit of anger.

"I don't know, you tell me where that hotel is, and how far from the city."

"Far from the city? It's in the very center of the city, you bastard, as you know perfectly well."

"I only know what I'm told, don't ask me for directions: you're the master here, you pay. I drive the horse, that's all. My duties don't extend beyond the fact of conveyance by animal traction."

"Goddamn you and everybody else in this den of thieves. Go right back and take the road to the right of the church."

"What church? There are two."

"The one to the right."

"The one to the right to the street to the right . . . what are you talking about? Can't you give me the name of the street?"

"I don't know it."

"Then learn it: it's called Via di Ripetta, and it is NOT the street that leads to your hotel, unless you want to make a long detour that would cost you more money. If you want to save both time and money, let me take you the way I know, and you'll be satisfied."

"Th . . . the . . . nerve, the . . . unheard-of . . . Well, enough said. Get going."

"That's what I think too. Say nothing, and as for advising me to get going, I've been doing nothing else for the last half hour, so what kind of advice is that?" And he went on cursing Leonardo's dead ancestors in his usual Roman fashion. It was only then that the expression "He doesn't pass the doors" came back to Leonardo's mind, and he began to wonder and wonder, and found the key to it soon enough in the image of a man with horns so high that he couldn't get through a doorway. This filled him with anguish again, but since he could do nothing now, he promised himself to question Mary at length as soon as he saw her, and no tricks this time. He hadn't finished formulating this plan when the carriage stopped in front of his hotel.

"Turn around and go into that narrow street behind us."

The coachman did so, and stopped right in front of the urinal, got out and relieved himself, while Leonardo turned into the next street and climbed the stairs to Schillasi's apartment. The shame, the degradation of these filthy stairways with their rich monuments framed at each landing, in the filthiest windowpanes . . . Was this the center of the world? Not even the most destitute lived that way in Laterza. And the stench of rats and cats and ammonia from the urinal . . . But Schillasi didn't live here. The name above the greasy cord to a bell, carved out in shiny brass on a black background, was CAVALIERE CORSELLI, and there was even a crown on top of it. And yet he knew this was the floor. Upstairs there was nothing: a door off its hinges, shaking sadly in the wind, but even there, beyond that pathetic sight, the gold cross and two arms in wrought iron atop a splendid baroque cupola. . . . After a brief hesitation, Leonardo took a clean handkerchief out of his pocket to pull the greasy cord without catching God knows what diseases, syphilis included, and all the churches of Rome, including St. Peter's in the background, began to ring angrily in the rain, calling the faithful to the second Mass of the day. Closer by, a chorus of cats began to meow from inside the filthy door, but no one opened it. He waited and waited, while the cats went on meowing and scratching the door, then rang a second time, and finally decided to call: *"Ehi, di casa!!!"** But the inhabitants didn't answer, so he opened the same window on the landing through which he had seen his persecutor two days previously, and called: "Schillasi!!!"

Instantly three dirty windows on three dirty floors of the house across the alley were opened, and three horribly decayed old women appeared to ask him what he wanted at that strange hour.

"I want Schillasi."

"Are you delivering a telegram or are you a creditor?"

"A friend," he said, but they couldn't hear him, because suddenly they were surrounded by cats answering Schillasi's cats. Finally one of them replied: "He doesn't live there."

---

* "Hey! Whoever lives here!!!"

"What do you mean he doesn't live here? I've seen him here."

"Seeing is one thing, living is another."

But now other neighbors, even some down in the street, began to offer their opinions: "He lives there," said one, "but the house belongs to the widow of Cavaliere Corselli, and no unpaid promissory notes can be protested here, because he owns nothing."

"And besides," said a third woman, "he's away on a trip."

"Yes, on a trip," said the first woman.

"On a trip? Where's he gone and for how long?"

The answers varied between three days and three weeks, some even spoke of months. Finally another crippled old woman appeared from the next street and they all said: "She can tell you, she's the maid."

"I'm the maid," said she, making her proud entry on stage. "He's gone to his hometown to introduce his wife to the family. He made money yesterday, sold some gold things to a rich jeweler, so the wife said now you've made money at long last we can take a vacation and you can introduce me to your folks."

"The swine!" shouted Leonardo, and they all disagreed, more or less violently, but all on the same assumption that a man who has spent all of his wife's money for years drinking coffee with friends and never taking her along must offer her a trip before she dies, especially if he's become rich all of a sudden.

"But that money is mine, those were my wife's family jewels," shouted Leonardo. "I'll have him arrested, wherever he is!"

This news left everyone speechless.

"Where is he?"

"In a place no one has ever heard of, somewhere called Laterza," answered the maid. "You can't catch him there, he's a prominent citizen, he's related to the mayor."

"The mayor? I am the mayor of Laterza, and he is no relation of mine. He stole from me, that's what he did, and by God I'll have him jailed this very day!"

This speech was delivered with the Ciceronian wrath of a pronouncement from the high judicial bench rather than from the dirtiest landing of a house in the slums.

After a moment of general awe, the Roman populace reacted as it always had in history: "Where's Laterza, and who the hell are you?"

Let the Romans hear a strange name long enough to place it in their language and it will become pure sound, "Laterza?" (the tone here was timidly inquisitive), "Laterza?" (here it was timidly ironical), "Laterza??" (here it began to fall apart into its phonetic components, and was no longer addressed to Leonardo, but to anyone down in the mob who was willing to play ball with it). Light gusts of laughter shook the atmosphere, and the sun, shining warmly through the clouds, helped everyone's spirits so the laughter began to grow louder and stronger, until finally a voice came out with the first joke: "*Laterza elementare . . .*" followed at once by "*Laterza classe . . .*"* and at this point the maid came in courageously, like the bullfighter after the picadores have blooded the poor animal and driven him insane with confusion:

"Mister third-grade mayor of my balls," she began, hands on her hips, belly protruding defiantly, "how dare you say such things about my mistress?"

"I never accused her, I accused *him,* he's always squandering her money and you know it. . . ."

"If she chose him, he's all right. She was married to a baron before, and she chose this one because he was called Professor. He has no degree, but his knowledge is immense. . . ."

"Don't I know that?" asked Leonardo, beating the windowsill to call the mob to order. "I was the first to help him, I put him in contact with a Cardinal, a baron and a countess, who is the sister of a prince and duke, I did all this for him, two nights ago, and he was supposed to become the librarian of a millionaire all because I recommended him. And now he abandons his good fortune, betrays my good faith, appropriates my wife's family heirlooms—which come from Russia, I want you to know: Russian gold, Russian emeralds—and runs away. . . . Is that an honest man?"

These words froze the crowd into attention. Leonardo now pointed to the maid, and went on: "I admire and respect this good woman for defending her mistress and I myself would do the same, AM, in fact, doing the same, because I caught a glimpse of her from this very window two days ago, and found her deserving of all

---

* Puns, based on the fact that *la terza* means the third one, i.e., third grade, third-class.

human respect: gracious, even beautiful, despite the cruel on-slaughts of age and disease, and therefore I . . ."

Alas, Moral Geometry made good use of the brief pause, by inspiring the kitchenmaid to repeat his last words and turn the whole thing into a rowdy insurrection: "And therefore I," she con-tinued, "appeal to you, Friends, Romans, Countrymen, and urge you to learn from our great third-class mayor . . ."

"Third-grade mayor," shouted a voice from the crowd, and that did it. "Voice of the people," she answered, "voice of God . . . we all must learn from our great third-grade teacher. . . . And I mean you too, pissers! Stop shaking your heads in disbelief, I mean your prickheads. . . ."

At this point Leonardo shut the window and was gone, but the coachman, who had taken no part in the scene because he didn't want to lose his client, saw that he would anyway if he didn't act at once, so he began to harangue the crowd in his stentorian, Roman voice; "Fools," he shouted, "you don't know who that is! He lives at the Hotel de Russie, and has his own carriage and coachman. His wife is a princess or something, and you are nothing—less than prickheads, the lot of you! Let me pass!!!"

Like the Red Sea for Moses the crowd withdrew in front of him, and when Leonardo emerged from the door he was received by his own coachman and greeted with the awe he deserved. Alas, he turned the tide against himself at once by refusing all honors with a smile: "Don't believe him," he said, "I'm nobody, a poor country doctor from that town of Laterza none of you has ever heard of."

Thus his departure, which was about to begin like the passage of Caesar Triumphant on his way home from the conquest of All Gaul, became a Roman Carnival, with jeers, obscenities and cat-calls. Leonardo directed the coachman to drive him to Via Gregori-ana and the trip back was filled with socio-philosophical considera-tions, which the privacy of a carriage and the comfort of a warm blanket over the knees easily evoke in the mind of the right-eous. . . .

When they arrived, Leonardo asked, "What do I owe you?"

"More than you have in your pocket."

"What do you mean: if I had a thousand lire in my pocket, would I owe you that?"

"More, as I said."

"Why?"

"Because I saved you from a murderous mob, at the risk of my own life. I have five children, yet I didn't think of them, only of your personal safety. What would have happened to you if I hadn't been there?"

"Nothing, I would have run away and no one would have seen me."

"And how about me? I would have lost the fruits of my hard work, I, a poor man with five children, a wife and a mother to feed."

"Of course, I would have looked for you. I don't know my way about in Rome."

"Priestly tricks and priestly language to match—listen to that" (he was now addressing the doorman and other servants on their way back from market). "Looking for me meant looking for trouble, I was in the thick of the crowd . . . sonofab—"

"That's enough, here's all I possess in the world."

And he reached in his pocket for all the money Adriana had given him. The coachman took it quite eagerly, but only to exhibit it to his audience: "Look at this: he left the Hotel de Russie with hardly more than the fare for the ride to his friend's rathole and back, so he knows his way about. . . . Keep it, I don't accept charity, I'm no beggar, I'm a worker and a Socialist—*and you are a gigolo.*" And with this he threw the money in Leonardo's face. This was too much. Like a lion, Leonardo was at his throat, strangling him with his left hand, while he boxed his ears with his right, shouting: "I'll teach you to live, you and all the other proud Romans of my arse . . . city of thieves, city of whores and procurers, all of you . . . from your shithead of a Pope to the last of your citizens. . . ."

They had to pull him off his victim by force. He was grateful to the servants who did this, because his victory was now complete: the poor coachman was bleeding from the nose, and the servants had picked the money up from the street and were giving it back to him. What spoiled Leonardo's revenge was the sudden arrival from the usual nowhere of the usual Avvocato Tegolani, who ran after the coachman, tipped him lavishly (as anyone could have guessed from the loud thanks he received), and then ran after Leonardo, who was running away from him into the palace and up the stairs. "Dear friend, I'm so sorry you had this inconvenience, I see he scratched your face quite badly, the beast."

"He did not. He didn't lay his hands on my face."

"Who scratched you then?"

"Nobody."

"How typical of you, and of me, needless to say, typical of us both, I so understand you. . . . Ah, my young friend . . . if only . . ."

"If only you stopped recognizing yourself in me, you might recognize yourself in that bastard I beat up."

No sooner had he spoken these words than he regretted them, because the worm didn't even pick up the challenge as Leonardo had so intensely hoped he would; instead, he defeated Leonardo at his own game.

"Of course you can do whatever you please, you're the master in this house and I have nothing to say, in spite of my old age which, I mistakenly believed, might grant me protection from such base attacks. I have nothing, absolutely nothing to say. I am in Rome as you are: a man of higher . . . aspirations, let's say, because the word *quality* is not the correct term for people who strive to be honest and humble, though they may never succeed; not everyone is endowed with such vigorous muscles as you have. I for one never was, not even in my youth, let alone now. May I suggest, without risking strangulation and a few broken teeth, that your generous impulses, though obviously prompted by an excess of enthusiasm for all things good and noble, are among the things you should fear most, because they do have the power to harm others; indeed, they have done so in this case: that poor man, whom I have known for years, is the soul of humility and kindness. He will pass through earthly life without leaving a trace worthy of mention in the schoolbooks—neither will I, for that matter, very few do. You of course will, and may the Lord assist you, but, speaking of the man you have so badly harmed, he will have to spend God knows how much money for doctors and medicines, and be away from his work for God knows how many days, and, even if he may have deserved such a punishment for being disrespectful to you, his children, his wife and" (out came the usual handkerchief with tears to match) "especially his mother, an ailing, saintly old lady, none of them deserve it. Forgive me for being so verbose, you've had a strenuous time, I see, you don't need any old chatterbox like me. Try to rest, and I wish you a good day."

These last words had been spoken as the Avvocato was turning the key in the lock, and Leonardo found himself pushed—gently, but pushed nonetheless—into the entrance hall, while the kindly old soul, bowing and smiling, sneaked into the house after him and made quickly for the kitchen.

Mary was already up and waiting for him, full of concern and somewhat fearful (he was beginning to know her), and he soon found out why: there stood Sophie, very obviously displeased, although she was hiding it quite well, according to the standards of this weird world of mysteries and silences. "Good morning," she said, "make yourself at home, you look wet and tired." And she was gone to Kostia's room (he was beginning to recognize the particular noise of every door, too).

"Darling," said Mary, caressing his face with trembling hands, "look what he did to you, that . . . monster! Come here, lie down, I'll go and ask Adriana, she'll know what your face needs, she's such a good nurse. . . . But you're all wet, Mamachen is right, come, let me help you take off your coat. . . . Why isn't Bernhard here?"

Before she could ring the bell, Bernhard materialized as if he had been hiding in the wall. He helped Leonardo out of his overcoat, removed the soaking hat with a flicker of distaste, then Mary noticed that his shoes were soaked with rain.

"Come, let's find a place where you can take off your shoes and put on some slippers. There are only women's slippers in this house, but Adriana will know what to do."

"Don't call her, please. I'm all right, I don't need anything. A cup of coffee perhaps."

"Of course, my love, but first your shoes. Come into the library and take them off in front of the fire. I'll go and see if Adriana has a good idea."

"No. Don't," he said, sitting down in front of the fireplace and warming his wet feet close to the flames.

"Why?"

"She must be tired too. She hasn't slept a wink."

There was a long, long silence, marked slowly and discreetly by the ticking of the big clock, while their eyes met in reciprocal anguish. He was the first to break that frightening look and apply the same anguish to the study of a large rose embroidered on a footstool in front of the other armchair: her armchair, if they had been seated together in harmony, but she was standing, ready to serve him. In his feeling of doom there was also a good portion of pity for her, stabbed to death in the act of her first wifely duty.

Why was she waiting so long for the first final question? There would be many, covering everything, even the cufflinks, but he would answer none of them. As for what he would do next, his mind felt the nearness of that black future, as one feels the tempest raging beyond the windowpane, while still within the protection of home.

"You are too tired and angry and I shouldn't talk about these matters now," she said, but she seemed strangely happy, and he almost sent up a furtive glance to investigate this, but didn't quite dare. Refined methods of torture, he concluded.

"But how do you know she hasn't slept a wink, if you haven't seen her?"

"Did I say that?"

"Of course you didn't, but this proves that she was right both times: this morning and two nights ago."

There was another rose on the carpet, partly hidden by the footstool, and he wondered if the rose on the footstool knew it was crushing the rose on the carpet with the front-right lion's paw of the footstool. And there was an itch inside his left shoe, because of the heat. He decided to let that bother him, as part of the general punishment to come; on the other hand, the one thing he could still do without losing face, before losing his head in a public execution, was to remove that foot from the fireplace and try to scratch it invisibly against the other foot. Which he did, and in the course of this secret operation, he sighed and yawned, not invisibly, alas.

"But I see you're bored. Obviously, this is not the moment to tell you, even though certain considerations are more important for me than anything else. Not for you, I know that already; I should be resigned to it by now."

"No, no, they are, they are," he said, speaking almost in a dream and wondering whether he was already as insane as everybody else in this strange world. "Please tell me."

"Then I will, very briefly. These are facts, and one cannot argue with facts: When she came to my room yesterday morning, Adriana said, 'Miss Mary, that new husband of yours, he's not a doctor, he's a saint, one of those people who can make you recover from any disease just by telling you that you're not sick. He came to the kitchen, I was boiling some water to make camomile tea, because I couldn't sleep, he just said to me, my girl, you're not sick, what's this nonsense. And I recovered. Then he saw me going into Kostia's room and he followed me there, and the moment Kostia saw him he had no asthma any more. I think he's a saint.' Are you listening, my love?"

"Yes, I am."

"Don't look so cross, I'll be brief, but I must tell you, this is all true. Kostia recovered, and since you saw him he had an attack twice and it was gone the moment he heard that you were coming. So I told him all about our plans, and he can't wait to have you as his new pappa. But about Adriana—you know, last night I told her I wanted her to come with us to Switzerland, and she said no. I asked her why, she said she has to look after her mother. But I know she will be very unhappy without me and Kostia. We've been like sisters for years, and if I ever died, she would be the only person to whom I could trust Kostia. I cried a great deal last night, and she did, too, and I made her promise to reconsider. This morning she came back looking very pale and sick; she had a temperature, she cried, she said she had thought it over all night, but still it was no. And I know very well that the main reason for her feeling so sick is that she wants to say yes, she needs me and Kostia in her life, she has absolutely no one on earth, since she made the awful discovery that her husband, whom she had adored above all other beings on earth, was a vulgarian, a carnal animal. I won't even begin to tell you what he did to her . . . in church, of all places. Too horrible for words. But for her it was the end of all hope of children. From that day on she's hated all men indiscriminately, and she lives only for us: for Mamachen, for me and for Kostia. And I feel I must force her out of her suicidal decision. She's a saint—like Mamachen. She lives only for others. I suspect she was trapped by that terrible younger sister of hers into believing she had to look after her. And why? Because Cefala envies her, Cefala doesn't want Adriana to have a pleasant life abroad, she wants to go abroad herself, that's her dream, and she would do anything to have it come true. And since no one would ever want her around, not even for a minute, she takes pleasure in destroying the one chance her poor sister has of having a new life for herself. So now I've given you the whole intricate background, please help me, please go to her room now and talk to her, tell her you want her to come with us. She trusts you so much, she could never say no to you. I know it's true, even though she hasn't told me so herself. You with your psychic powers can do anything to people, I mean anything good, because you're the bearer of good things. For example, you just guessed that she hadn't slept at all. How could you know this, unless you had magic powers?"

Leonardo had reached an important decision: he had decided that the rose on the rug wasn't suffering at all from the murderous pressure of the lion's paw on its very heart, therefore he didn't have to do anything drastic about it, such as displace the footstool so the four paws stood on blue sky between roses. He sighed with relief, but still he didn't dare let the two roses out of sight, as a good doctor will not leave his patients when they are just recovering from a major crisis: one never knows what may develop. And in the dreamy voice of someone absorbed in other worries than those of the person standing in front of him, he said: "Nonsense, Mary. I said it just to say something, I don't even know why I said it, probably to be done with the whole question."

"But that's it, my love: psychic persons DO act that way, they are born mediums, the truth borrows their voice to express itself. They never know what they have said, or why they have said it. This is a proven scientific fact: Mamachen and I have been studying metapsychics lately with the famous Doctor Richet of Paris."

"Meta . . . *what?*"

"Metapsychics. The psychological counterpart of metaphysics."

"Ah."

"You don't believe in it, do you?"

"Definitely not. They're all charlatans, those people. I do believe in human empathy, of course, because that is as normal as sunshine.

Love between two human beings is part of that phenomenon."
And he began to worry about the rose again: perhaps it did need
urgent intervention, to save it from being asphyxiated. But in the
outer regions of his mind, beyond the poor rose in its sickroom, he
did recall his love for Mary as having had that quality. No longer. In
recent days he had felt it, and refused himself permission to think
about it, but since he had last seen the two sisters together under
that umbrella, and even earlier, he had realized what had destroyed
his love for Mary: her flushed face, her burning ears, which contrasted so unpleasantly with the sunny gold of her hair. She seemed
vulgar, while it was her two maids who were extremely distinguished. And with his love gone, how could he face all those other
difficulties that had seemed complicated enough before, when Mary
was still his ideal woman?

"Well," said Mary, kissing him stormily on the mouth, and he
cringed at the contact, "I see that your *farouche* honesty makes it
impossible for me to tell you anything good about yourself. But
then, since our love is of that miraculous variety, will you do it for
love of me?"

"Do what?"

"Go to Adriana's room and speak to her?"

"No, Mary, I won't." And now he looked up to face the sad
evidence of his lost love. If only Gennariello would materialize from
thin air and take her away from him . . . No such chance now, he
knew.

"And why won't you? To spite me?"

"No, Mary, I won't, because—"

"Why do you always have to call me Mary? There's something
ominous in all this. You've stopped loving me."

"Nonsense."

And he pushed away the footstool just in time to save the life of
his patient.

"What is irritating you so this morning?"

"Mary . . . my love, I mean . . . consider my case, please: I
come here all dripping with rain, have hardly slept at all—and now
I ᴅᴏ know what I'm saying—add to this that I have been robbed
of all my money by that bastard coachman, and, if all this weren't
sufficient, that bastard Tegolani—"

"Just a moment, my love, it's all my fault. I should have told you the instant you came in that Mamachen wanted you to tell Tegolani how much money you need, and he'll give it to you."

"Tegolani? I don't accept money from anyone, but even if I were starving to death, I would never accept anything from him."

"But it's our money, not his."

"Then where does he come in?"

"As an administrator. We never touch money, we never pay bills, he does all that, and does it very efficiently."

"How nice of him. And I suppose he does it all for free."

"It's part of his job as our lawyer and administrator. You know how dishonest the Romans are. . . ."

"Yes, beginning with him."

"Why do you say that? Mamachen will be very hurt if she hears. She trusts Tegolani. You've only just met him, we've had him in our service for years and years. But if you hate him so, I can ask him to give the money to me, and I'll give it to you."

"I said I don't accept money from anyone, and I forbid you ever to talk about money again."

He knew this would bring good results. But it didn't.

"Darling, I'm so proud of you. And Mamachen will be too. You're exactly as we are: you hate the very mention of money. I swear I'll never mention money again. Is that better?"

"Of course it is." And his heart sank into his shoes, making them feel icy again: proof that his heart was icy too. How can one be so stupid? he asked himself, meaning himself and these two crazy women interchangeably. In a desperate attempt at relaunching the subject he said: "If I need money, I know where to go."

"Where?"

"Back to work."

"You mean back . . . home?"

She had spoken the word hesitatingly, but it hit the mark. A ray of hope against all hope brightened his face: perhaps the Rubicon could still be crossed on his way back, to recapture his lost dignity. Even Giovanna looked desirable now, not as a woman, God forbid, but as a piece of furniture, yes, the shabby furniture to which he was accustomed: quite a contrast to this private museum here, but at least something he had earned and could pay for.

Now the rose was in danger again, from exposure this time. Too unprotected: it had been used to that footstool for years, and perhaps it had been a mistake to remove it altogether.

"LEONARDO?"

"Yes?"

A long, long silence. He went back to the footstool and rescued it just as it was about to fall into the sky, pulled it back into place, and felt that the underrose was now strong enough to support it. In fact, both roses immediately felt better.

"LEONARDO?"

She might as well have called him Doctor: the tone was icy enough.

"Yes?"

"Why don't you answer me? Why do you look so cheerful?"

"I? Cheerful? Not at all."

"Yes you do. You ARE. That word HOME struck a chord of nostalgia in your heart. You long for your homely environment, things you paid for with the money you earned, while all this is a private museum, and it not only frightens you, it demeans you. I know you, I know EVERYTHING. I, too, am psychic when it comes to those I love. That's why I know so little about the Monster. I never felt psychic about him. And I knew this was coming. Quietly, like the approach of death I felt it during the night. I couldn't sleep either. After Adriana had told me of her betrayal (and what other word is there for what she's done to me?) I knew: HIS betrayal comes next. Now I am all alone in the world." (Thank God she didn't mention suicide. Or did one thank God for that? The rose was suffering again.)

A very long pause, in which the Infallible One spoke ex-cathedra and in bronze: eight o'clock. He lifted his eyes slowly, very slowly, and there she stood: Lady Cefala (not Cefala the half-breed, with the hands and the voice and the mentality of a servant girl). And what had wrought the miracle was a vascular factor he, more than anyone else, should have diagnosed earlier, because he had studied it for years; in fact, he had made it the subject of his first contribution to the *Policlinico*, the most authoritative journal of clinical medicine in Italy. This was heightened blood pressure, with its concomitant phenomena of extreme anxiety, mental delusions and even hallucinations in women whose sex life has been suddenly interrupted, either by the death of the partner or by a sudden incompatibility. Why hadn't he recognized it in Mary, if he had recognized it in Adriana? Because he had been conditioned to think that any woman who enjoyed sex was a whore, potentially at least, therefore a very bad risk for a husband. But here the risk was minimal, given her lack of intelligence in matters of everyday interest, in which inferior women usually excel, plus her total infatuation with him. And besides, he had crossed the Rubicon, so everything was perfect. The psychological trigger was suddenly released and his passion for Cefala transferred itself instantly to Mary. He knelt down on the carpet in front of her and said: "My love, *you* are my home, your body is the home of our future children, and when I say home otherwise I only mean a place where I am not a kept man, where I earn my daily bread and can take care of others less fortunate than I am; I definitely do not mean my former wife or my sisters and their children, I mean the disinherited of the whole world, and if my experience of suffering mankind has so far been limited to Laterza, this is not to be held against me as a sign of ill will, or, still worse, treason."

Lady Cefala disappeared like a vision of Paradise, and a flushed, sex-hungry female sat down heavily on both roses, driving her fingernails into her hands, and moaning quietly as she stared at her love.

"Let's find a room where we can . . ."

Alas, the morning hours are inimical to stolen sweets unless you have your own *garçonnière*. A discreet knock on the door, and Bernhard appeared, dressed up for Dust, as a priest for low Mass: no gold on his uniform, a jacket that looked like a mattress with bands of pink stripes, heavy white gloves, a green apron, a magnificent episcopal *flabello* in green cockfeathers with a long mahogany handle, and a soft yellow suede cloth in his left hand. Behind him, an acolyte, with his liturgical instruments, consisting of a three-step mahogany ladder, which he placed in front of the first shelf, mounted it silently (he was wearing dust slippers) and began to take out the huge leather-bound volumes from the top shelf, which volumes Bernhard dusted lightly as if he were blessing them, then handed back to the acolyte who replaced them with great care in their original order.

There was only one thing Leonardo knew about all these books in foreign languages, and it was something he knew that the servants knew too: there was no speck of dust on them, which alone would be sufficient to make this library different from any other library. It had never been used, it could never have been used by two women who were constantly busy helping their servants at the great task of leaving them alone, so that in their solitude they could think of more orders to give them, so they could be left alone even more. He became fascinated with this religious ceremony, a real Mass of Purification.

"Do they have to keep busy doing nothing?" he asked Mary in a whisper.

"Darling, if you don't take good care of a house every day, it turns into a stable."

"There is a long way to go from here to a stable. Send them to hell, give them a free morning for once."

"Darling, if you start breaking the rules, you'll have complete anarchy in two days."

"A palace revolution, you mean."

He had hardly finished pronouncing these words, when a waiter came in and whispered something in *romanesco* to the acolyte, who answered angrily, "I can't. Don't you see I'm working?"

"Get down from that ladder and do it. I can't, don't you see I'm not shaved, and I'm not wearing my uniform?"

"Go shave and dress for duty, it's after eight, what do you think you are: a prince?"

"It would take time, and breakfast is ready. Someone must announce it, send the German Turd to do it."

"The German Turd doesn't announce breakfast, and he isn't wearing the right clothes for it either. Why are you late *and* unshaven *and* dirty?"

"Because I'm working with the gardener."

"And all the others? What are they doing?"

"They're taking the frames off the paintings; they can't wash and put on their uniforms."

"And Adriana?"

"Adriana is sick in bed."

At this moment the butler hissed in terrible Teutonic Italian: "Don't talk so loud, don't you see that our masters are watching you?" Leonardo looked at Mary who had been looking at him for quite some time in obvious embarrassment, fearing God knows what Apulian development from all this, so he asked: "What is it? Don't you think it's funny?"

"Funny?" she whispered into his ear, almost in terror. "Please don't say anything, let's slip out and go into the music room."

"Why not into the dining room since breakfast is ready?"

"Sssshhht, darling. Let's give them a chance to decide who must announce it."

"This is ridiculous," he said aloud. Then, to the waiter: "We heard you: breakfast is ready, thank you very much." And, taking Mary by the arm, he led her quietly into the dining room where breakfast was indeed ready, but not officially so: the coffee pot was being placed on a hot plate in one corner of the room and covered with a huge cupola, this one in embroidered silk; dishes were being piled up on the same plate to keep them warm, the alcohol lamp under the vast samovar was being lit, butter was being curled up into little baroque shapes and distributed onto the various butter plates on the table, flowers were being put into small vases and placed beyond the butter plates—one rose for each guest—and a strange iron instrument in the shape of the iron bed used to roast St. Lawrence was being held over the fireplace, to toast bread, while the twenty-four chairs around the table were being lined up like soldiers in dress uniform before being reviewed by the king. All of which intricate details of what constitutes breakfast requires a staff of at least five servants, plus an orchestrator, all in uniform and white gloves. Instead, they were still in their morning fatigues, gloveless, chatting comfortably among themselves, some in a tone of happy gossip, others of unhappy recrimination, but the entire over-ture against or about their dear mistresses and their Cafone gigolo. Leonardo hastily withdrew, dragging Mary with him in his shameful retreat beyond the breakfast Rubicon, but not quickly enough to avert total disarray and anarchy among the five servants and their breakfast orchestrator. They all ran out into the corridor and from there into the library to attack the two breakfast heralds for not announcing to them that breakfast had been announced, and thus Mary and Leonardo, running into the library for shelter, found themselves once again where they should not have been: at a revolutionary rally of various subversive parties—the butler and his acolyte accusing the unshaven waiter of desertion, he accusing them of sabotage, because the Dust-Purification Ceremony was—he claimed —the most cowardly sinecure ever invented by lazy servants to fool their idiot masters, "but you can't fool us, we're the real workers, you sonsofbitches," and more along those lines. At which Leonardo stepped in, granting general amnesty to all the conflicting revolutionary factions, provided they all took a vacation.

"We can make our own toast, even our own coffee, if we need to. Thank you, and don't lose your tempers. Life is short enough as it is, without ulcers and heart attacks to make it shorter. So, think of your health and keep well."* But now Mary took over and said firmly: "Please let's not do that. We can wait another five minutes for them to come and make the formal announcement, and then go into the dining room. If we went now, there would be no end of wars in the kitchen, and no one can go there and put them in their place. That's their kingdom. And besides, do you want to lower yourself to *their* level?"

He felt deeply hurt and asked: "Would that include your sister Adriana?"

"Of course not. That's why I can't give her up. And I know you can help me, but you won't."

She was very upset again and very pale. Lady Cefala was back in all her sovereign beauty. "Look, darling," he said, "let me explain something to you that will clear the air once and for all and stop all these recriminations. You said this was my home."

"Can you doubt it? How many times must we repeat it? It is your home and you are the absolute Czar in it: we are all your humble subjects."

"I don't want to be a Czar, I only want to be a husband. So, if this is my home—"

* A purely Neapolitan expression, only recently adopted in central and northern Italy, perhaps under Italo-American influence.

Another light knock on the door prevented him from completing his sentence.

"Come in," shouted Mary imperiously, and the butler appeared, still in his dusting uniform, for which he proceeded to apologize, or so Leonardo understood from his gestures of helplessness. The angry Teuton was exhibiting his gloves and his apron as if they were chains, or instruments of torture. He seemed almost eloquent in his guttural sputtering, to which Mary replied in her imperious high soprano until the German language sounded like two different tongues spoken by angry kings at the border in a last-minute attempt to settle their dispute in civilized terms, before launching another Thirty Years War.

Finally, Mary won, and her enemy bowed out, almost in tears. Before reaching the door he turned his back and left the room like a beaten old man.

"What was all *that*? Translate, please."

"Well, if you insist. I told him you were the master of the house now, and as such had full authority to announce to me that breakfast was ready. The two servants had taken this as a personal rebuff—it's their first day in service here—"

"But aren't we leaving today or tomorrow?"

"Not quite, unfortunately. But even if we left today, we would still have to close house."

"Well, you have twelve servants already, can't they close it for you, or is the key so heavy it takes fourteen to lift it? This is like a fairy tale."

"My love, you don't realize that closing a house means a lot more than turning a key in a keyhole. If we closed this house, there would be endless problems reorganizing routines, cleaning—"

"Cleaning? What this place needs is a bit of dirt to begin with. Without it the servants will feel useless, which will lead to disenchantment, suicides, madness, all sorts of calamity, even bloody revolution."

Mary looked at him in ecstasy: "You see? I was right again and so was Adriana: you've guessed exactly what Mamachen always thinks, but never says out loud."

"Why doesn't she? Or why doesn't she act accordingly, if this is what she thinks? Cut the staff by nine tenths . . ."

They were interrupted by a pale Bernhard in his admiral's uniform and white gloves mournfully announcing that breakfast would be ready in exactly five minutes, would they please forgive him for this final delay, but there were reasons.

The five long minutes passed in silence between Mary and Leonardo. He held the watch in his hand and she stared at him. As they walked towards the dining room, Mary said: "You will be pleased to know that your orders have been obeyed: I instructed Bernhard to leave us alone, so we can prepare breakfast for ourselves as if we were having a picnic."

"A what?"

"A p-i-c-n-i-c. It is an English word which means eating outside, in total contact with nature, like little animals or savages. Just imagine: toasting our own bread and making our own omelets on the open fire. Please, darling, make an effort and smile when you see what Bernhard has done." And indeed the good butler had done his best to surprise his new master: pastoral nature was rampant. The white tablecloth had been changed for one with wildflowers, baskets of wheat and butterflies embroidered all along the margins, and each individual napkin bore the same pastoral decoration. And of course the entire elaborate flower arrangement that the butler's assistants had completed half an hour earlier was now gone: in the place of individual roses in baroque vases, there were porcelain figurines of shepherds and shepherdesses, goats, sheep, cows, wild horses, working horses harnessed to haywagons, even dogs silently barking at each and every cup and dish and coffee pot on the table—all entirely new of course, a pastoral service in pale pink, decorated with bucolic scenes. Even the table silver Leonardo knew so well from having had such trouble using it had been replaced with porcelain knives and forks, and spoons, all decorated with flowers and vegetables. As a centerpiece, instead of the heavy silver tray with a mirror for a base and a huge flower vase on top of it, there was a porcelain pond in the most beautiful light blue, surrounded by porcelain trees and blades of grass, and on the pond were porcelain ducks and swans. At either side of the pond, two huge porcelain trees filled with porcelain birds and porcelain fruits had replaced the two heavy silver candlesticks that had so irritated him during that endless dinner two nights previously.

But the butler had also made an honest effort at pastoralizing himself and his assistants: they were all dressed up in beautiful silk clothes and kerchiefs that made them look just like the shepherds on the table. That is, for the butler it was easy to look like a porcelain doll, but not for all the Sicilian bandits: they looked even more like themselves than usual. Leonardo knew these travesties only too well: he had been a choirboy himself, and had taken part in the procession of the Corpus Domini or the Passion Plays for years. Of course, he had never seen such precious porcelain statuettes and painted china on a private dinner table—only under glass in the museum of Naples or at the royal palace of Caserta.

He couldn't smile, he couldn't even look at the butler. Mary smiled nervously for him and conveyed to the butler a very kind German interpretation of Leonardo's southern Italian silence, then reinterpreted for Leonardo the butler's Teutonic nonresponse: "He is so moved by your gratitude he can't utter a word. And now, darling, let's make our own omelets. Or do you prefer fried eggs?"

"Omelet for me," he said somberly.

"For me, too," she said joyfully, with another long explanation in German of how deeply moved Leonardo was by this simple, rural picnic. But not even Bernhard was so stupid as to accept this comedy. "May I be excused?" he asked, in his clumsy Italian, looking icily at Leonardo.

"With the greatest of pleasure," was the answer. "You and the whole Corpus Domini." Then, to Mary: "All right, let's make that omelet. Where are the eggs?"

At that moment Sophie entered the dining room and everybody froze into a catatonic ritual of respect. Obviously, she was not in a good mood, and they all felt it. This confirmed in Leonardo the vague suspicion that she was angry at him, and it filled him with terror. "Good morning again," she said, as if he had disobeyed her order to have a good morning already. Then, to Mary: "Don't be upset. I said I was not going to have breakfast with you, and I won't. You must be alone, the two of you. But why wasn't I informed that you were going to have a celebration for Kostia?"

"For Kostia?" asked Mary, stricken. "Kostia is having breakfast in his room, with Luther."

"Is having, you said? I had hoped he had had it already. It's a little late for his breakfast."

"Yes, Mamachen, it is. In fact, he must have had breakfast almost an hour ago."

"But then why this carnival? Who ordered it?"

"Didn't I tell you?" said Leonardo reproachfully to Mary, to which Sophie replied: "Don't get up!" making both him and the servants aware that he had failed to greet her correctly, but when he started to rise, pushing the two servants away from his sides (he couldn't have seen that they were closing in on him from behind like pincers, clutching instruments of torture), she repeated, with restrained anger: "I just told you not to get up! I _knew_ this would happen." And just as she had rightly foreseen, the instruments of torture fell and broke: one of them was a tray with a frying pan on it, and the other an egg, which the right-hand servant had been holding in his white glove.

Now, of course, Leonardo had to get up in order to help clean the mess on the rug, but he hadn't calculated the risk of moving too fast when your legs are caught in the folds of a tablecloth reaching to the floor. All the porcelain trees came tumbling down on a whole population of pastoral figurines, cattle, chicken, geese and dogs, even on castles in the French countryside, which were split open as if by lightning.

"Blood of the Holy Virgin! Thirty thousand lire's damages, at least," shouted one of the servants, quickly joined by Tegolani, who came storming into the room shouting: "Thirty thousand? Fifty thousand at least! Those were all from the personal service of Marie Antoinette!"

"Get-out-of-here!" shouted Sophie, throwing more cups and figurines at the head of the impertinent servant, who ran out of the room with both hands over his ears, and then, to Tegolani: "And you, how dare you mention money in my dining room? If I want to destroy all I own, that's my business," punctuated with another cup thrown on the floor, "my pleasure," and another cup was gone, "my privilege," a third cup flew at the windowpane and broke it, "and whoever dares tell me what these things cost can get out of this house and stay there! The only man in this house who has the right to express his views on the way I spend my money is right here: Doctor Claudi, for your information. You have been in my service for nine years, MISTER LAWYER, therefore I expect you to know how I detest hearing money mentioned in my house. Have that servant paid his wages for a month, and send him to hell."

"At your orders," said Tegolani, bowing out very humbly, then, before he left the room: "And at your orders, too, Doctor Claudi."

As soon as the door closed on him, Sophie sighed with relief: "*Gospody*," she remarked. "One more word from that imbecile and I would almost have lost my temper!" Mary was sobbing quietly, shaking from head to foot; her ears were flaming red again, which disturbed Leonardo more than anything he had done to the precious china, but as soon as she saw that her mother was not pleased with her reaction, she paled under that glance and became beautiful again, more beautiful than Cefala, which allowed Leonardo to feel sorry for Mary rather than himself. Sophie's eye took in all these changes in his expression, and seemed to have understood their cause: "Don't be upset, Doctor Claudi—I mean . . ." (she swallowed her pride) "my future son-in-law. Let's be cheerful. Life is sad enough as it is, why should we allow a few broken shards of crockery to ruin our picnic? Or don't you want me to join you for a brief moment? Just for an omelet?"

"How can you *ask* such a question?" said Mary, flinging herself bodily into her mother's arms, while Leonardo took advantage of the very brief moment he had to discharge all his pent-up anger on the one pastoral brigand still left in the room. "What are you doing here?" he hissed at him in Sicilian, "listening in on our conversations? Get out of here, quick."

Sophie overheard him and yelled: "No!" Then, to Leonardo: "I don't want to hurt Bernhard's feelings. He has done so much to make this picnic a success, poor darling, let's show him that we appreciate his good will."

"Yes, yes," said Leonardo, sitting down again, observing the destruction that was still encumbering the table. Sophie sat down too, and it was only at this moment that she seemed to realize the extent of the damage. "My God," she said, laughing, "he was right: Marie Antoinette's entire service!!!! Isn't it priceless? Hahaha . . . haha . . . hahahahahahahaha . . ."

Mary was quickly infected by her convulsive laughter: "Haha-haha, Mamachen, look at the French Revolution . . ."

This made Sophie even more hysterical: "Wonderful . . . fan-tastic . . . Not even Robespierre or Danton would have thought of such a mass execution. . . . Hahahaha . . . Men, women, chil-dren and cattle . . . hahaha . . . birds, too . . . hahahahahahahaha . . . and trees . . . and castles, mountains . . . hahahaha . . . mmm clouds . . . Haaaahahahahahahahaha . . . a picnic on a battlefield . . . hahahaha . . ."

And Mary, choking with merriment and all red in the face: "No, on Judgment Day . . ."

In the meantime Leonardo sat quietly fighting back his tears with heroic self-control. He was not sorry for himself now, being tied to a madwoman like Mary, and of course he wasn't sorry for the dolls he had destroyed; he was sorry for the artisans who had made those statuettes in the years before 1789: they had put love into their work, and even if the Queen of France was such a beast (and he hated her for her remarks to the hungry in Versailles) the destruc-tion of objects is also the destruction of life, and even worse per-haps: it is desecration, a senseless rage against the dead, therefore blasphemy under any theological cluster of gods in the heavens. And these two women laughing at his act of desecration to make him feel better (he knew) should instead have cried in despair and insulted him, or even struck him and then asked his forgiveness—"Here is your chance to forgive us, we are equals in sin." But laughing, showing that desecration is in reality a joke, what for-giveness is that? What generosity? The offender can never kneel down and ask to be forgiven by such creatures: he remains trapped with his shame and his tears, and they with their indifference to the destruction of wealth. Is that a way to show that you are superior to wealth? Oh no: this is wealth at its worst—God's gifts in the hands of little children. So, when he saw the brigand in white gloves coming at him with an egg in one hand and a small silver knife in the other, and realized that a new porcelain frying pan had already been placed in front of him, his hands began to tremble, and he said: "No, please, you do it, but out there and not here, and not for me. I'm not hungry. May I be excused?"

He didn't quite dare push his chair away from the table, nor disentangle his legs from the folds of the tablecloth; he had learned that much at least. He was just humbly asking to be allowed to disappear and cry in some corner, away from it all. The two mad-women froze into the same catatonic attention that the entrance of one of them had caused before, but for Mary it was natural, while for her mother it was not. Mary was anguished but pale and beauti-ful, while her mother was purple in the face, and it was she who now couldn't control herself. First her fat cheeks began to wobble, then her huge eyes to water, and it was she who now stared at the battlefield, crying over the death of her dolls.

"Mamachen," cried Mary, getting up and upsetting some of the corpses on the table, "Mamachen, don't be angry, Leonardo doesn't mean it that way: he has a headache, he didn't have a wink of sleep all night."

"You don't have to tell me, you silly little girl, I know. I am just sorry for poor Bernhard, who thought he had done what you asked. . . . But never mind," she said, blowing her huge nose into so tiny a handkerchief that Leonardo wondered how she could do it. Then she smiled politely through her tears, pushed her own chair away and surged up monumentally like the red moon over a site of car-nage, and said, "I'm sorry. Please lie down anywhere, the house is yours, but I suggest that you have breakfast served in your room. Your headache may be due to an empty stomach. I shall see you both later, when Mr. Schultz arrives."

Thus ended the picnic, and thus began the search for rest.

"On the library couch, I'll bring you breakfast there," said Mary, but Bernhard was still dusting the books with the help of his assis-tant. He excused himself in German and Mary begged him not to hurry. In the music room the Avvocato was discussing the price of picture frame gilding with an expert in the art, who seemed an-noyed at being interrupted, because he lost his inspiration, "and you know how artists are," whispered Leonardo into Mary's ear, to amuse her. Then, to Tegolani, in the polite tone of a master ad-dressing a slave: "How long do you think this will take?"

"Not longer than twenty minutes," answered the obedient ser-vant looking at the artist for confirmation, and the artist answered:

"Five, if I'm given the time to concentrate." And the slave, most
obediently, translating from the mysterious language of the arts into
the humble language of religious worship: "Five. That gives you
fifteen, because in twenty minutes the secretary will be here with
her dictating machine."

"Dictating machine? Does she take dictation from a machine?"

"Yes, sir."

"How amusing . . ." Leonardo was learning the uses of this
word he had just acquired in connection with the loss of a huge
amount of capital, caused by his own humble person. "May I take
three more of your precious minutes and ask you to describe the sex
of the dictating machine?"

"I'm so sorry, I didn't quite catch the question."

"There are three sexes: male, female and clerical, which invests
both the male and female clergy, and I was wondering whether they
had invented a fourth sex for dictating machines and perhaps . . .
lawyers." He savored the effect of this stab, which seemed to
amuse the artist, then said to Mary: "Let's not disturb Benvenuto
Cellini." And then, with a most Jesuitical reverence, he bowed out
of the room, followed by a blushing Mary.

In the drawing room Bernhard was washing the green hands of
the huge palm trees with a wet cloth, while one of his assistants was
waiting for him to be finished, so he could offer him another wet
cloth, and after this a third cloth to dry every single one of the
thirty or forty fingers—but this time was not being wasted by the
assistant, because the first wet cloth had to be washed in a pail of
soapy water and then rinsed and squeezed, the second in a pail of
clear water, and the third hung to dry in front of the fireplace,
where several dry cloths were waiting for their chance to come in
handy. But this was not all: another assistant on top of a ladder
(not the same one used for the library, which never left the library;
this was a normal ladder such as is kept in the servants' quarters
when not in use) was paring the fingernails of the highest palm
hands. The fourth assistant, who was directing the nail triming
from a strategic vantage point, fixed his attention on Leonardo and
looked worried, lest he had made a mistake.

Mary asked the butler, with many apologies, how long it would take them to finish their work, and translated his answer: "He says they still have to trim the lower leaves of both plants, because, as you can see, they are . . . disturbing."

Leonardo noticed that in fact this was true: on one side a hand was tickling the marble nose of Leonardo's former-future father-in-law, and on the other the left ear of his present-future mother-in-law. He said nothing, because he understood that the subject was dangerous. "We can of course go back to the library," said Mary.

But in the library they were rolling up the rug, and there was already a great deal of dust on all the furniture. "Oh, I see: time is money," said Leonardo. "And I, who thought your house needed dust. There is enough dust here to keep five servants busy for a whole week. Add to this the dust that has already kept two servants busy for an hour this morning, and you will see what a rich time these people have. We country doctors, who must spend so much time and so much money to learn the profession, and more time and more money in dust and mud to pay house calls in distant places, and often wait years before our bills are paid, we learn the lesson that money is time, too much of it to make it worth our while."

"Oh, my love," said Mary, in ecstasy, "what prophetic words. I must write them down and memorize them."

"Nonsense, Mary, let's find a place where I can have a cup of coffee and lie down. I'm at the end of my tether."

"Oh yes, my love, of course."

They tried the dining room, but the French Revolution was still being cleared away and the props for another stage setting being brought in: different flower vases with different flowers and china to match, while a woman, who turned out to be Giovanna, was kneeling on the rug, surrounded by small basins with soapy and clean water, and working so hard that she had to wipe her brow and her nose every other minute. She rose to greet Mary who embraced her and kissed her: "Oh, Giovanna, I'm so glad to see you. How is Adriana?"

"Not well, Miss Mary, not well at all. She keeps crying, she doesn't want to eat or drink anything, and she refuses to see a doctor."

"Not even this doctor here?"

"Not even him, I'm afraid. Mother asked her several times, and she said no."

"Perhaps because she doesn't want to disturb him, but if he appeared in her room unexpectedly, do you think she would refuse to see him? I don't."

"I do," said Leonardo, blushing against his will, and becoming emphatic, to justify his blushing. "If she were really sick, she would be the first to ask for a doctor. I don't know her, of course, but she looks to me like a very healthy person, who cares for herself properly. Probably what she needs is to be left alone, absolutely alone, without anyone disturbing her."

"But how strange," said Giovanna, "that's exactly what she keeps saying: Leave me alone, I'm quite well, I care enough for my health to call a doctor when I need one, leave me alone, just pretend I'm not here at all. You must be a great doctor, they all say that in the kitchen."

"Nonsense," replied Leonardo angrily. "Any country doctor could tell you that much. I see you're still trying to get that stain out of the rug, I'm so angry at myself for causing all that trouble."

"No trouble at all," she said, "the stain is gone; what I'm doing is reviving the threads, so the pile of the rug will stay even, with all the threads up."

"And why? So that anyone coming in from the street can flatten it again and cake it with all sorts of dirt? They tell me that in Japan people must take off their shoes before entering a house. That's a civilized country for you: all the rest of us are barbarians. What Europe needs is to be invaded by Japan, perhaps then we may learn how to live."

Mary looked apprehensive, as did Giovanna, and he understood that he had probably said the wrong thing.

"Tell me, Giovanna," said Mary, "where can we find an empty room? The doctor must lie down for a moment, he has a headache."

"The little study room next to the entrance door. No one ever goes there."

"Oh, you're right, I hadn't thought of it. Thank you, and give Adriana a kiss from me. Tell her—"

"Don't tell her anything," said Leonardo, "leave her alone. And thank you for suggesting that room."

"There's even a couch in there, and we can lock the door," whispered Mary as soon as they had left the dining room.

"Wonderful, where is it?"

"That door there."

Leonardo ran to it, opened it—and there on a couch next to the fireplace, under a strong lamp, was Count Jahn-Rusconi's sister, skirts lifted to the knee in front of the fire, hat, raincoat, white gloves and umbrella hanging on the back of a chair. She had earphones on like a telephone operator, and was scribbling away on her lap. Somewhere in the dark, beyond the circle of light: the dictating machine.

"What kind of behavior is this?" she shouted, pulling down her skirts at once. "Couldn't you knock before entering?"

"It's my fault," said Mary, "please forgive us. . . ."

"Oh . . . it's you. . . . I'm sorry, but I can't see anybody now. I have to finish this by nine thirty."

"What's she doing here?" asked Leonardo, as soon as they had closed the door.

"Working for Mr. Schultz."

"You mean employed? As a secretary?"

"A translator. She also translates books, she needs money, poor girl, she runs about town every morning, giving Italian lessons to foreigners."

"To men as well?"

"Men or women, what's the difference?"

"What do you mean *what's the difference?* And her brother allows this?"

"Allows it? He's very grateful: they don't have a penny to their name."

"Why doesn't he work instead?"

"He's too lazy, he gets up at noon and spends his days loafing about the city with Prince Potenziani, his bosom friend."

"Don't they have a mother?"

"The mother had a very hard life: she was her father's assistant after he was exiled and excommunicated for being a member of the Mazzini cabinet; they lived in London for years in total poverty, he translated all of Shakespeare into Italian, and then they came back, she married a poor and untitled relative of the Duchess of Mecklenburg, a German painter, who died right after his son was born, and so Margherita, who's a very brave girl, began to work when she was barely fifteen."

"But then why all the smugness?"

"You may also ask 'why the title,' since they are no longer Rusconi but Jahn, being the last descendants of that family. Well, this is Rome. They have to keep up a façade. They have to ride in a coach with their own coat of arms on the Corso every day, and so the King allowed the old lady to add Rusconi to her name, and to resume the title her father had renounced to call himself Citizen Rusconi. But let's find another room for you to rest in."

They thought of Kostia's room, but could hear his governess giving him his daily lesson in German history, so Mary said: "Let's try my bedroom."

"Your bedroom?"

"I don't have one, I share it with Mamachen, but we can ask her." Sophie was sitting in her boudoir, holding court. Leonardo stayed outside the door. He could hear a variety of feminine voices in a variety of foreign languages, which by now he could clearly distinguish, thus acquiring a more diversified ignorance (how like Adriana). Soon Mary emerged again and he had a glimpse of his future mother-in-law with one hand given over to a kneeling young woman, who looked as if she were sculpting it or painting it (it was his first experience of a manicurist at work), the other hand being observed from varying distances by a jeweler who had just delivered a couple of rings to be worn on different occasions and at different hours of the social day; her head meantime was in the hands of yet another young woman, who was fitting tiny baby bonnets on top of her majestic hairdo and tying them with ribbons under one of her three chins, while still another young woman whose face he couldn't see, because she had her back turned to the door, was holding a large mirror in front of the whole coronation, so the sovereign could see what was being done to her public image up there. And the entire cosmopolitan court was either standing or seated across from her, all with their backs to Leonardo, exercising their sovereign rights to criticize or applaud, not the sovereign's opinions, but the outward manifestations of her power. He almost learned the words for *hat, ring, becoming* and *unbecoming* in at least four languages, but he wasn't quite sure which of the sounds were nouns, which adjectives and which superlatives; he only knew that they applied to the crown or to the rings, because huge female hats, *lorgnons* and index fingers were turned in the direction of the head or the hand in an accompanying mime that expanded upon each utterance. As for the sovereign herself, she had become an entirely different person—not that she looked different since Leonardo had last seen her, just that she was looking differently at the mirror from the way she looked at other nonreflecting objects, or at people. What modesty, what awe, what true love in those great eyes, and how eagerly she seemed to entertain other people's opinions! No, Leonardo's mother had never been that way: oh, in her youth, perhaps, but youth ends for a woman the moment she has children, and this woman had grandchildren. Lots of them.

Finally, Mary reappeared, but became flustered as soon as she realized that Leonardo had been observing her mother. "I'm sorry I left the door open," she said, closing it, "but you shouldn't have looked."

"Why? I wasn't the only man there, I saw at least two."

"Yes, a jeweler and a bootmaker: what kind of men are they?"

"Thank God, we're here, now you can give me a kiss," she said, once they were safely in the bedroom, but it was a very brief kiss, because all sorts of ancestors and ancestresses were looking at them sternly from the walls, the dresser and the night tables, more and more of them; wherever Leonardo looked, he encountered paintings, miniatures and photographs of these proud people, either dead or prepared for the day when their images would be left alone on earth, more deserving of pity and attention than their own children, because children change and pictures don't.

He sat down on the bed to take off his shoes, but Mary stopped him: "Not here, that's mother's bed, my bed is there," and she pointed to a tiny couch, much too short for her, and tilted back so that it looked more like an elongated armchair than a couch, let alone a bed.

"How can you fit on this? Your feet must be sticking out at one end."

"They do, but at night I close in this end with that chair there, so that my feet rest on the chair."

"And the sheets? Where do you tuck them in?"

"I don't."

"And how long have you been sleeping like this?"

"For a year and a half, since I stopped living with the Monster. I usually spend the nights here, instead of at Via Sistina."

"But . . . isn't it uncomfortable?"

"Oh, Mamachen likes it this way. I can see her as she sits up in bed, she can see me, the best parts of our evenings are spent talking like this, from bed to bed, and I feel as if I were a little girl again. She reads to me, she even tells me fairy tales sometimes."

"Oh, now I understand why you wouldn't want to leave without your mother."

"I couldn't in any case, because of Kostia."

"Yes, but I meant if we left with him."

"That would be impossible. Mamachen couldn't survive a day of the separation."

"Does she feel the same way about her other grandchildren?"

"Oh no. She doesn't even know them all, doesn't care how many there are, and if they're all still alive."

"Why?"

"Because she doesn't approve of the mothers."

"And how about your sister's children?"

"There are none. My sister Katia ran away from her husband and is now in an insane asylum in Berlin. Pierre put her there to steal all her jewelry, and in the meantime she really did go insane. And my two other sisters aren't married yet. But let me bring you some breakfast, and then you must sleep."

"No breakfast, only a cup of strong coffee."

Mary left, after covering up his feet with a soft fur blanket. He put his hands behind his neck and began to meditate, while his eyes followed the distant lines of the Cupolone, now brightened by sunshine, now darkened again by gray clouds, constantly drawn and erased and redrawn by nervous lines of rain on the window. What a wonderful wife she will make, once her mother is dead! And it can't take too long: the old tyrant is huge, has all the signs of a heart case and eats far too much. And once this kingdom is all mine, think of the good I'll be able to do. . . . First I'll dismiss all the servants but one, then with the salary of the other eleven for six months I'll offer my poor people an aqueduct. . . . Think of the gratitude . . . Then we'll build a hospital . . . a public library . . . scholarships for the talented. . . . How's that for a kept man? And how sweet, to be forced to accept all this by the one woman who understands me: Adriana. It was all her doing and I bear no blame at all.

When Mary arrived with coffee, he was trumpeting the snore of the righteous.

That image of the Treasure of Christianity beyond the windowpane, those sudden flooding bursts of sunlight amid the general deluge—classical elements in all religious paintings, where the stream of beatitude rains obliquely from heaven onto the chosen object, be he the village patron saint or the village he's praying for—informed the outer edges of his dream, while the interiors were informed by the image of the quiet fireplace behind his back, which became visible on the windowpane only when the rain was so intense as to cancel all visions of beatitude.

"You are the master in this house. . . ." The phrase surfaced in his mind just as he was falling asleep, and in the dream he saw for the first time in his life that Mary was right, more than right, prophetic in reverse, proving that he had been the master of the house even back in his childhood, when he had learned that in his house there were no masters or mistresses: only servants, doing the same work and sitting at the same table, then washing the same dishes and sleeping under the same roof, but not putting the same money in the bank and marrying the same people.

The dream was about a window in the house of his mother's great-uncle, the Padrone di Paranze,* Don Poseidone Navigabene; his solid home stood like a lighthouse on a high cliff above the sea— and a lighthouse it was, even though its signals were directed not to

---

* I.e., the owner of the Paranze, or twin fishing boats typical of the Adriatic. They are painted in many different colors, and some have an image of the sun on the sails, in red or yellow.

passing ships, but to the Christian God who had replaced Poseidon and all the other Olympians too. (In correct terminology, this heavenly abode was an old church perched on top of a family house.)

It was Don Poseidone who by providing the services of the Mazzieri (beaters) had guaranteed the election of the famous Piedmontese Prime Minister Giolitti in exchange for a series of governmental decisions in favor of the rich landowners or shipowners against their farmhands and deckhands, who of course made up the majority of the population. Yet, when they went to Rome, these rich members of the Malavita* never appeared as oppressors of the poor because they dressed like them, they talked like them, and their habits were almost as frugal. It was therefore easy for them to impress their protectors in high places with the fairy tale that they and they alone represented "the People," and that the real oppressors were the absentee landlords of the feudal nobility (who oppressed no one, because they were either already ruined and living in debt, or were in the process of ruining themselves with the help of this new rising class from which came their loans and eventually their downfall). As for the people themselves, they were regarded as dangerous subversives, with the result that they had begun to behave as such, or at least to listen attentively to the Socialist orators who were trying to teach them how to fight the moneyed Malavita.

If there was one man Don Poseidone hated, it was his neighbor Don Ilarione Salvemini. Salvemini had a son in Rome, and this son, Gaetano, was not only a brilliant professor of history who had become famous overnight with his discovery of the Socialist nature of the political strife between the Magnati (Big Ones) and the Popolani (People's Party) back in Dante's time, he had recently run for Parliament on a Socialist ticket, and had been elected.

Don Poseidone hated the Salveminis, and his peers hated Don Poseidone. He was a tyrant. In his rich house, as in all the rich houses of the region, there was no heating, no wood to burn and no fireplaces, because in the hearts of working people there was no room for soft habits, such as sitting by the kitchen stove and day-

---

* A general term, meaning Evil Life, applicable both to the Mafia and the Camorra.

dreaming. At least the women, for whom such softness was not shameful (being a woman was shameful enough), cooked meals and mended socks or ironed shirts while sitting by the fire. But what would a young boy, a future man, do by the fire all day long? Study books? And what books are worth studying after the age of seven, when you have learned how to read, write and recite your prayers? Ledger books? But these are for public accountants, an inferior race of men, usually cripples and certainly weaklings. What was left but the study of religion, becoming a spy for the devil (that is, a voyeur for the Church, which was the devil triumphant)? Of course, women need the supervision of a man, and thus priests are, at their very best, self-appointed eunuchs, whose manly task consists in self-sacrifice, or daily self-castration. That was why Poseidone's brother, Eolo, who was gentle by nature but not very intelligent, had been forced to study for the priesthood, while Poseidone, who was very acute indeed, trebled his fortune every year at a time when everybody in Apulia, Calabria, Campania and Sicily was losing his savings or his job in the two terrible crises of 1884 and 1896. Leonardo's family, too, had lost a great deal of money and had been helped by his mother's Uncle Poseidone with a substantial loan. Neither she nor her husband nor the children liked Don Poseidone, but they tried to keep on good terms with him, because they had seven daughters to marry and a large almond tree grove to look after and a son to keep at the Jesuit seminary of Matera, in the hope that he might some day become a good priest, perhaps even a Cardinal or a Pope. And this was what Don Poseidone had bet his money on. Leonardo knew it, and when he decided to give up his career in the Church in order to become a physician (and a MODERN, anti-clerical, antisuperstition physician), he knew that he was endangering the family and condemning his seven sisters to perpetual poverty, perhaps even as wives of day-laborers, because Don Poseidone would never give one penny to the family of such a heartless egotist. But in the long years while this major decision was ripening in Leonardo's adolescent mind, he often sat in Uncle Poseidone's "church," watching the sea from the window. And Don Eolo liked to sit there too and just stare at the sea until he fell asleep. But on those cold winter days, which often lasted well through April and May, when the wind and the rain knocked too loudly on the glass, it

meant that God was sick in His mind, He was in one of His destructive rages again, and must be reminded that there were people
out at sea, honest Apulians, who hadn't done anything bad, so it
was for Don Eolo to raise his voice and teach God from the pulpit
how to behave. But Don Eolo happened to love God and tended to
grant him the benefit of the doubt. Persuasion, yes, but on a free
basis, as between friends discussing their opinions, and even that
was a great effort for Don Eolo, whose instinct was for resignation
to God's will, almost as if God, and not Don Poseidone, were the
head of the family.

It was usually Leonardo who warned Don Eolo of the coming call
to prayer; and soon enough the whole family, and the families of
sailors out at sea, would be regurgitated from the narrow stairway to
sit in their pews, while Don Poseidone's voice urged them to make
haste. "Every minute counts, God won't wait for you to snivel out
your prayers of intercession before killing your husbands and
brothers and fathers and sons!! Get going!!!"

Don Eolo would begin to sing Mass (Don Poseidone didn't care
if the True Church allowed Mass only in the morning and on an
empty stomach: in an emergency, all the rules break down).

And he would interrupt his brother after a matter of seconds:
"No, no, and no! Too soft, too whining, remind Him that these are
His words. . . . Stop it! Let me do the talking."

And he would say something like this: "Dear Lord, Our Friend
and Protector, what do You think You're up to? No one here has
done anything wrong, as far as I can tell, but if he has, punish him
individually right now, don't punish all these innocent people who
love You and obey You and work hard to keep their families alive.
If You are good and omniscient, and we all know You are, You
must also know that if Don Poseidone loses his fleet, the poor will
starve more quickly than the idle and degenerate rich, because no
one but Don Poseidone will feed the poor, and house them and
send them a physician for free. . . . But Don Poseidone cannot
keep feeding everybody for free, unless You allow him to make
some profits—not just puny profits, big profits, because our population has grown, and so have their needs. . . . Don Poseidone isn't
God, YOU are God, that's why I am speaking to You, in true
humility. Look at my ledger books: I'm holding my profits way

down, so just compare my ledger books with those of my fellow merchants before You sink my ships. . . . The sea is so big, can't You have that storm somewhere else?"

Here he would whine and even cry, and only then did he allow Don Eolo to play his role in the traditional style—and in Latin, of course.

The local population preferred Don Eolo's services to those of their own parish priest because here they could pray directly to the sea, *and* keep an eye on the possible answer to their prayers: Don Poseidone had widened his window until it looked like a shop front in a large town. Besides, when the service was over, Donna Addolorata always served food and wine for everybody, so it became a village feast.

On very rainy days, the congregation saw more of themselves than of the sea reflected in that mirror of a window, since the candles were kept away from the glass so that they wouldn't be blown out if the panes broke. The glass never did break, but it trembled, and that became the true image of wealth in Leonardo's eyes as a child: something that separates you from the world, but by an artifice so thin that the next gust of wind may destroy it. So when Don Poseidone lifted his fists at the storm behind his brother's back and shouted, *"Enough!"* Leonardo was always surprised that God didn't answer at once with a huge tidal wave shattering the window and annihilating the entire family. He *knew* that the poor assembled there in prayer would not be killed; even if God sank every single ship, their relatives would be saved, while his parents, his sisters and himself would be killed. But he also knew that the first ones of all to die would be his parents, because they had come for dishonest reasons; they hated Don Poseidone and they loved his money. How could *they* claim they loved God? But nothing happened; nothing ever happened. Could this go on forever? In 1902, when Leonardo was dreaming of him, Don Poseidone was still alive and well and richer than ever before, but Leonardo's parents were both dead. They had been very sick for a long time before dying, his sisters were all unhappily married or even more unhappily widowed, their daughters were either unhappily waiting for a husband who would never show up, because they were poor, or unhappily married to Christ, after seeing what beasts their fathers were: and this was all

his fault, because he had refused to become a Cardinal or the Pope
to satisfy Uncle Poseidone. As a result, cousin Crocifisso Di Santo
instead had received Uncle Poseidone's assistance in his ambitions
to become a professor, and was now the personal eye doctor of the
King and the Pope.

I must look up Crocifisso, he decided. If worse comes to worst
here, he will help me. But I must not forget to find out where he
lives and where he works, BEFORE I GO TO BED TONIGHT. And thus
the dream brought him back to the window. Now the "church" was
outside the window, and in him was a sea of troubles, wrecked ambitions and the bodies of his parents somewhere in the frothing
waves.

Sophie had become Don Poseidone, and from the top of St.
Peter's Cupola she was shouting through her bedroom window:
"What are you doing? What have you done? You have killed your
poor parents, ruined your life, deserted your family and your duty,
dishonored my name, raped my servants, and now you even want to
sleep in my bed? Get out of there, quick, before I have you arrested
for adultery and packed off to Laterza, where you belong!" And he
was trying to wake up, but couldn't, because Don Poseidone was
focusing a mirror on him, like Archimedes when he set fire to the
ships of Marcellus, and his eyes were being burned out like the eyes
of Oedipus.

He woke up with a headache, and saw that someone in a window across the street was playing with lenses, trying to focus them
on him. He rose from the bed and went to the window, just in time
to see a little boy disappear behind the windowsill. "Damn fool," he
said, looking at his watch. He had only slept twenty-five minutes,
but he felt completely restored, and also in urgent need of the
bathroom. He dressed, combed his hair, and went out into the
corridor.

There stood Sophie with Tegolani. It was quite obvious that he
had nothing important to tell her and that she wanted to be rid of
him—but she couldn't because, as Leonardo suddenly learned to his
surprise, the rich can talk "importantly" about unimportant things
to unimportant people. It is both an act of charity towards the
people they can't help humiliating all the time by the mere fact of
being rich, and also a form of atonement for their wealth: they feel

they must pretend to take an interest in the price of the most minute things (especially in the maintenance of precious things) in order not to make their servants feel inferior to their humble tasks. And the servants who know this can keep their masters busy for hours without fear of the slightest reproach, even though they know perfectly well that they are being hated for it. It is their best revenge, and also their best strategy. Because the moment this torture is over, a kindhearted master will sigh with relief and say: "What a bore, but what an excellent servant."

Leonardo decided to intervene, but the moment he appeared in the corridor, Tegolani, noticing sudden relief on the face of his mistress, said: "Before I forget, my mother sends her best wishes to the young couple. She has prayed for them day and night."

"Oh, how touching," said Sophie, then, to Leonardo, "did you hear that?"

"Yes," said Leonardo, blushing, and then blushing even more because he was ashamed of blushing. "Yes, I heard that."

"And don't you think it's touching?"

"Yes, I do." And, after clearing his throat, but not his face, which looked as if he were about to vomit: "Thank you very much."

"Don't look at me," said Sophie, imploringly, making an effort to smile. "Look at our friend here when you thank him."

Leonardo tried to obey, but he couldn't focus his eyes. He smiled at the floor near Tegolani's feet, he smiled at the walls around him, at the ceiling above him, blinking and making little Jesuitical reverences, then finally managed to adjust his eyes, but the effort was so great that he had to close them. His face contracted, his upper teeth bared themselves, and he looked like a dog ready to bite.

After which, feeling that he had done his duty, he said proudly: "I have thanked him. May I go now?"

"No, not for serious business, ever," said Mr. Schultz to the gray-haired old woman who was standing before him, her hands filled with telegrams he was reading and annotating with a strange instrument which looked like a pen but was obviously not a pen. He was seated at the desk in the library, but he was doing his work on his knees, because the butler was dusting the desk and shaking his head in utter dismay at the amount of dust that could accumulate on a desk in such a short time.

"Please, dust that there too," said the gray-haired old woman, pointing to a smaller desk near the window.

"Yes, yes," said the butler, in his Germanic accent. "Have done everything this morning, and now dust again everywhere. Terrible, terrible."

"Oh, here you are," said Mr. Schultz to Leonardo, without smiling. "I said nine thirty; it is ten to ten. Twenty minutes late for your lesson. Never mind, don't apologize, that too is a convenient way of wasting time. This is Miss Panzironi, the one person in Rome who knows the value of time. She is never late, never loquacious, never content with the amount of work she's done, and yet it's remarkable what she manages to do in one working day. We can talk freely in her presence, she's an old friend. I recommended her to the Russian ambassador as a teacher of Italian thirty-five years ago, yes thirty-five, isn't it, Miss Panzironi?"

"Eighteen hundred sixty-seven, Mr. Schultz, almost thirty-six," she replied while bowing to Leonardo in order not to waste time in useless introductory chatter.

"Indeed, indeed, almost thirty-six . . . how time flies. . . . Well, Miss Panzironi, who began studying languages at the age of ten, all by herself—her father being a cook in the household of Prince Gourchakoff in Sorrento—was asking my permission to call my customers on the telephone, and I said no. Nothing can replace the written word. The telephone, the telegraph may give you the information you need to reach a sound decision, but the actual decision needs a letter, because that's where the mind must face itself as in a mirror. Don't you agree, young man?"

"I don't know," said Leonardo. "My decisions are reached on the bodies of my patients."

Mr. Schultz didn't like this, and it showed on his face as he greeted Mary and Sophie at the door and told them to sit down. "Yesterday we interrupted our debate on the subject of truthfulness in human behavior, and I mentioned George Washington. I was pleased to realize that this young man shared my antipathy for *furberia*, the Italian way of getting ahead in the world: Machiavelli's evil shadow, still haunting the halls of power in this corrupt country. I promised him Andrew Carnegie's book, *The Gospel of Wealth*. Of course no Italian publisher would have such a book in translation, so I requested that Countess Ottavia Rusconi and her daughter translate it for me. That will be my wedding present to you, young man. As the whole book won't be ready for another few months, I gave instructions that they first translate the chapter where I am mentioned—not by name, of course, but by argument, so to speak. It will be ready in a few minutes, and I want you to read it carefully and comment on it in writing. You won't be allowed to leave Rome before I am satisfied that you have done your homework. . . ."

"But . . ."

"Don't interrupt me, please. This goes for you too, Sophie. You asked me to examine this young man's fitness to become Mary's husband, and I am doing it. Back to you, young man. What alarmed me particularly was your idea that we should learn from the poor."

"Didn't we discuss that yesterday?"

"No. We talked about Tolstoy, that dangerous subversive who nonviolently lays explosives under the very foundations of society, then asks us to follow his example for the sake of world peace. Let me ask you a question, Doctor, and remember, you are now in the classroom and I am your teacher. Have you read Marx's *Philosophy of Poverty?*"

"I haven't read a single word by Marx, but I happen to know by mere chance that he never wrote that book. Pierre Joseph Proudhon —never read a word of his, either—wrote it, and Marx replied with a book called *The Poverty of Philosophy.*"

"I have no time and no taste for semantic skirmishes between two such criminals. They are twins in their attempt to undermine society."

"It wouldn't seem so, from their writings."

"How do you know, if you haven't read either of them?"

"And how do you?"

"I don't have to. Facts are facts: open the papers and you find plenty of them: your king was killed by an anarchist two years ago, that was two years after the Empress of Austria, who was murdered two years after the President of France, who was murdered two years after five policemen died trying to defuse a bomb in a crowded theater in Paris. . . . Spain, England, France have all been hit by anarchy, my friend Frick was almost killed by an anarchist in Pittsburgh. . . . Marx may disagree with Proudhon and even proselytize against him, but they would never kill each other. Their differences are the fights between highwaymen over their booty, or over technicalities in the execution of some crime. Tolstoy of course doesn't see it this way: he titles his novel after a book by Proudhon called *War and Peace*. Did you know that?"

"No, but I still think that you and I should read Marx and Proudhon before we discuss them."

"Who tells you I haven't read Proudhon? Tell me: who said that property is theft?"

"I don't know."

"Proudhon. And now tell me: do you believe that property is theft?"

"No. I believe that property is the object of theft. It attracts thieves the way honey attracts flies. I see property as a disease-favoring condition—a syndrome, to use the correct term. We need property, just as we need arsenic, nitrates, carbon monoxide: all the poisons that are present in our physiology—but of course beyond the barest minimum trace, they become lethal. So does property. When people are too rich, they should be bled of their excess in wealth; they would only lose worries and enemies, the causes of apoplexy, while acquiring friends, pleasures and all the other conditions for a long and happy life."

Mary and Sophie smiled, which angered Mr. Schultz.

"A most dangerous theory, a crazy Utopia," he shouted, pounding the desk with his fist, "because it makes you love poverty."

"What's wrong with that?"

"When you love poverty, you become poor."

"Richer, it seems to me."

"I know, I know: the usual super-idealistic nonsense. Are you a Superman? I hate Nietzsche as I hate Tolstoy, and I respect Saint Francis, but you are not Saint Francis. You use medical instruments that cost money. You take official trips to Rome to plead for an aqueduct that costs millions. You feel these are your sacred rights.

Why don't you wear a cassock and go around begging and telling
your constituents that they should love Brother Sun and Sister
Moon, Cousin Cloud and her child Rain?"

Leonardo sank his head in shame.

"This said, I agree with you that the rich should be bled of their
superfluous wealth, but not by the poor, who know nothing about
money. It takes experts to do that, people who have given evidence
that they can *make* money. Only the rich can bleed themselves
without killing themselves—that is, without depriving the poor of
their sustenance. Does Marx know how money is made? No, and he
doesn't want to know. He lets his daughters starve to death, while
he goes on scribbling his venomous tracts in the British Museum
library, and his wife, the noble and idealistic Baroness von West-
phalen, sits at home and tells the creditors that the Herr Doktor is
not home. She sees her daughters wilt away, but she goes on believing that her first loyalty is to the enemy of her own kind, and of
humanity in general. As for Proudhon, he believes in petty property,
on the level of near starvation. Now *you* tell *me* how your parents
paid for your medical studies, before you sing the praises of poverty.
I see you can't answer. Never mind. Let me teach you that economy
begins with waste, with excess profits, offered for free to those
worthy few among the poor who early in life reveal an excess of
inventiveness, which, duly fed by that same excess of wealth, results
in all the great conquests we have seen in the field of science,
art—any of the things that make life worth living. Radium, recently
discovered, will work wonders in medicine. Do you know what it
costs to produce one milligram of radium? I happen to know, because Doctor Curie and his wife are my personal friends, and on my
personal recommendation they can help you a great deal in your
scientific endeavors. But would you deprive people like the Curies
of the money they need for their research, to give each starving
individual (and not even everywhere on earth, only in one small
city) a little more food or clothing for one year? Charity doesn't
breed science, it only breeds hatred the moment it ends, and so,
would you have all the rich keep all the poor as their personal pets
forever, and let the Discoverer, the Savior of Mankind, the Builder
of a Better World, starve for the money he needs to do his work?

How about discovering some new source of nourishment, some miraculous cure of disease, perhaps some means of getting more out of the stingy soil of your dry regions down South? Would you prefer to feed the unworthy, the damned, the doomed, for a few months, or to help all mankind for all time to come, through the concentrated financing of our finest minds?"

Leonardo stood silent, transfixed by this fairy tale. Mary and Sophie were smiling, and Mr. Schultz went on, as if he had noticed nothing (but he had, and he sounded more secure): "We are both scientists you and I, Doctor, because the discovery of money as a living thing was the beginning of all modern science, and Capitalism is the science of sciences, because it makes all the rest of them possible. Tolstoy and Saint Francis are thieves: they steal the bread from the poor by stealing their incentive to earn money. Inertia alone is the great modern evil. With transportation, which doesn't just mean steam engines and boats, but first and foremost transportation of values from one form of investment to another, anyone who doesn't keep things moving is an enemy of life and of the future. If I hadn't—"

He was interrupted by the arrival of a telegram which he excused himself to read. It obviously contained bad news, for he grew purple with anger and summoned his secretary. She opened her shorthand pad and sat down next to his desk, ready for dictation.

"Sir," he dictated, in a fit of anger, then, after listening to a burst of advice in Russian from his secretary, he corrected himself: "All right. Change 'Sir' to 'Your Excellency.' . . ." But he couldn't go on. He shook his head in angry denial, then resumed his dictation: "Your Excellency . . ." A heavy silence fell upon him, crushing him so badly that he failed to notice that it had revived everyone else after the deluge of his words. "No, not 'Your Excellency,' he doesn't deserve it. . . . Damned Italians . . ."

Miss Panzironi interrupted her reading of new telegrams to cast an angry eye at him.

"What is it? More bad news?" he asked, as he saw that his secretary was now gloomily reading yet another telegram. "Give it to me, Miss Panzironi, what are you waiting for?"

He repeated the same question in Russian, but Miss Panzironi answered him in Italian, looking sternly at Leonardo: "I think, Mr. Schultz, it would be better for your audience if you read these other telegrams later."

"What do you mean, later? I am for complete sincerity, like my adopted daughter Sophie, and this is a family reunion, in which matters of vital importance for the future of this new family are being discussed. Give me those telegrams."

Miss Panzironi obeyed, very reluctantly, and waited for the storm. It broke soon enough.

"Whaaat? I never gave orders to my London office to buy those shares. . . . Who did? Who took such liberties with my hard-won earnings? Could it be . . ." He gulped down his suspicion and looked wildly at Sophie. In the meantime Miss Panzironi was putting another telegram on his desk. "My God, it's your son again, Sophie! . . . But this time I *am ruined*. He used all of my capital, without my permission, to buy the most bankrupt shares in the world. . . . A thief, a swindler, he must have faked my signature, a murderer, that's what he is." Then, with a superhuman effort, he smiled and said: "I apologize. But you see in front of you a man who must start again from scratch, for the third time in his life. . . ."

"Mr. Schultz," said Sophie, with dignity. "You don't have to start from scratch. My money is yours, all of it, without any conditions."

"No, Sophie, thank you. I have never accepted anyone's help."

"But it's yours anyway: you persuaded my father not to disinherit me, and you lent Vladimir the capital he needed to buy his partnership with Baron Knoop."

"Yes, my darling daughter, yes, and it was a thousand times worth it. I grew rich on it, richer than he did, but even if I had lost my last penny, it would still have been my best investment ever. But this madman here . . . this criminal of a son of yours . . ."

"Will you bring him to justice?" asked Sophie.

"No, Sophie, I will not. I feel a great responsibility to the workers in the factories, the employees in both our banks, his and mine, but especially to the investors . . . people who thought they had made money at long last, after years and years of untold sacrifices, and now . . . their hard-won riches are all gone like a mirage. And this within the short lifespan of hard workers like myself and poor Vladimir, who was killed by his work."

"By his children, you can say!!!" screamed Sophie, then slammed the door behind her, sobbing aloud.

"I shouldn't have said that," Mr. Schultz whispered. "I'm sorry, but I am so upset. . . . Yes, Doctor, he was killed by his ungrateful sons in the fortieth year of his life. But still, I can only pray that Pierre has been right once more. God preserve his genius, and preserve us from his friendship. . . . Jail, no, but the end of our partnership in business, yes!" He pounded the desk with his fist several times, making all the objects on it jump and tremble, then passed his hand over his forehead in an effort to remember something, but couldn't, and so he asked: "Where was I?"

Silence from the audience.

"Help me, please, where was I?"

"Do you really want to know?" asked Leonardo.

"Of course I do."

"You were . . . er . . . You were . . . hating poverty!"

An even longer silence, in which everyone looked away from Mr. Schultz, mostly at the floor. Finally he realized this and said: "Why should I be ashamed of my feelings? Or deny my whole view of life, in the face of disaster? Especially as it was the right philosophy and I knew it? Yes, Doctor, if I hadn't hated poverty I wouldn't be so secure now, so . . . capable of judging the needs of millions from a privileged point of observation, and let me add without any false modesty, so universally respected by my business associates throughout the world!"

Mary and Leonardo took refuge in the music room.

"When are we going to leave?"

"I don't know, in a few days, soon . . . I can't stand it any more."

"How do you think I feel? But why in a few days? Why not tomorrow?"

"Ask Mr. Schultz, darling. He wanted to examine you thoroughly. You heard him. But I think you passed the test with flying colors."

"Hm . . . What does your mother have against me?"

"Nothing, my love, she's tired. She's impatient to leave."

"Then why don't we just leave? You both treat him like dirt most of the time, then you let him install his office in here, and you act like frightened little girls. *In your own house* . . ."

"We can't. Making fun of him is one thing, but walking out on him is quite another. Shhh . . . He's coming."

And in fact, Mr. Schultz was coming into the music room, but they only saw his hand and his arm holding the door open, then he closed it again and in another second they saw him in the entrance hall, talking to Tegolani in whispers. Tegolani left the house, and at the same moment a tall gentleman came in.

"I was told you were here," he said, shaking hands with Mr. Schultz.

"Yes, to supervise an inventory and for other family reasons. Tell me, how did it go?"

"We lose everything. The Queen Mother takes the palace, and the government pays us by canceling our debt of two million lire with the bank. That palace alone is worth at least five million, but go discuss these matters with the government."

"Thieves . . . real thieves. Listen, I'll see you this afternoon about the business in London. I'm waiting for a telegram, I'll know more in a few hours."

"Very good. Shall we say five?"

"Five will do. At the club."

"No, at my place."

"Very good. At your place. No, let's make it tomorrow morning at nine. I won't be through here before late tonight, I fear."

As soon as the tall gentleman was gone, Miss Jahn-Rusconi came out of her little room with books and notepads under her arm, like a schoolgirl. "Ready?" he asked, and led her by the arm into the library from which he emerged five minutes later, holding his head in his hands. He went straight to the sofa, sat down and sighed. "I have had enough. At my age, I should be able to think of myself sometimes, and not always about other people."

Leonardo sat down next to him, and patted him on the back, while Mary gasped, frightened at such familiarity.

"Thank you," said Mr. Schultz. "You are a good man. Never mind me, I'm old, I'm tired. Oh, if I could only trust *one* man in my business." He paused, looked up, smiled, then said: "Can you imagine what she said to me, that stupid little girl? She said she couldn't translate that blasphemous book. 'Why blasphemous?' I asked, and she says, 'Because there is no gospel of wealth, only a gospel of poverty.' See how dangerous it can be, when you try to share your philosophical thinking with women? *You* said more or less the same thing, but you never refused to read the book."

Mary intervened, saying, "Don't bother with her, she's the daughter of a painter, what can you expect?"

"Shame on you, Mary, for saying such a thing. I'd like to hear you repeat it in the presence of your admirers Degas and Monet. What would they think of you?"

Leonardo turned pale: "Who are they?"

A long, sad look from Mr. Schultz and a shadow in Mary's eyes made him aware of his blunder.

"Who are they?" he repeated. Then angrily: "Painters? All right, so I'm ignorant. Does that make me unworthy of marrying Mary? Am I now to pass an exam in art history?"

Mr. Schultz laughed. "I like you," he said, caressing his head. "I like your spontaneity, your honesty. And I like our free exchanges of views on life. I hope we will have more of them when I come back from London next week."

"Next week? Why can't we leave before then?"

"Because of this damn inventory, and Sophie has to be here, only she knows what she owns—or perhaps she doesn't, but they're all her belongings, so she has to be present."

"Look, Mr. Schultz, since you like me, and I like you very much too, let me be honest with you: no one needs this inventory."

"What? You too believe in squandering wealth in order to prove your Tolstoian purity?"

"On the contrary, I firmly believe in administering it wisely, and that is why as a first measure of defense I would dismiss that administrator. In my opinion, he's a thief."

"You too find him . . . unpalatable?"

"Unpalatable? Revolting. False . . . er . . ."

"Go on, I'm listening."

But Sophie, too, was listening, and the terrifying spectacle she made at the door made him duck down, as if she were about to smite him. "What right have you to criticize a man I trust?" she shouted. "Even if you were right—and I know you are *not*—your excessive preoccupation with objects, precious as they may be, belies your whole philosophy, and makes me wonder if you believed a word of what you were saying so splendidly before. I was so proud of you; now I am *very* disappointed!"

Mr. Schultz rose from the sofa and hurried towards Sophie, taking her by the arm. "Calm down, my child, don't be unjust. We are here to air our opinions freely, and you cannot stop Leonardo from expressing his doubts about a man I myself have never liked, and like even less now that I see him every few minutes."

As with the proverbial wolf in the fable, there was a soft knock on the door and Tegolani appeared, smiling and humble as ever.

"I'm glad you came," said Sophie. "We need your opinion."

"Absolutely not," said Mr. Schultz. "This is a family reunion, we need no outsiders for the moment. You may go, Mr. Tegolani, I'll call you when you are needed."

Tegolani withdrew in good order, and Mr. Schultz said: "Now, Sophie, please have Leonardo tell you why he mistrusts your administrator, and answer him, not me."

Like an obedient little girl, Sophie blushed and said: "You have the floor, Doctor. Speak, please."

Leonardo too blushed up to his ears—with anger this time—then said, quietly: "What I dislike about him is first of all his eavesdropping, but more even than that, or at least on the same level, his cowardliness about the smallest, most innocent things, which makes him tell so many unnecessary lies, puny lies that build themselves up into mountains. . . . And all that drama about his mother . . ."

"How can you be so inhuman as to reproach a man for loving his mother?" asked Sophie with frightening self-control.

"He can't love her, or he wouldn't always be telling us that she's about to die. When you love someone, that is your most secret fear." There was a long silence, then he went on: "But this is only one of his symptoms. He is the typical Italian *furbo;* namely, a stupid man who has no belief in simplicity and frankness. To be more precise: he doesn't believe in himself, but he wants others to trust him."

"Well spoken," said Mr. Schultz. "But what do you suppose we should do if we dismiss him? How could we protect this house?"

Leonardo braced himself not to betray his deep emotion, then pronounced the terrible word that had been buried in his heart for so long: "Adriana can take care of everything. You need no lawyers and no administrator here."

"But she's a woman," said Mr. Schultz.

"She is superior to a man in judgment and strength of character."

"That's something to consider," said Mr. Schultz. "Now, Sophie, what is your opinion?"

"I am glad that Leonardo appreciates the extraordinary qualities of our dear Adriana, but I can't understand why he has taken such a violent stand against poor Tegolani, whom he doesn't know at all, while I have known him for over ten years and have never had the slightest reason to suspect him of dishonesty. He is of course *furbo* —all Italians are, Leonardo is the only exception to this rule—but Tegolani's *furberia* is so innocent, so open, I may say, that it's quite funny to watch. Isn't that true, Mary? We laugh for hours in bed over his latest trick. And he's really a dear, I swear to you; a real darling."

In the silence that followed there was a quick exchange of glances between Leonardo and Mr. Schultz. Leonardo was so relieved by Sophie's referring to him by his name again, after having withdrawn to the coldest form of address several times that morning, that he felt he could speak openly now: "Sophie, Mr. Schultz, I have been told several times this morning that this is a family council of some sort, and I have been told many times since my first day here that I am the master of this house. Both contentions are wrong, or, to use a more correct term, grossly exaggerated. You are Russian—or whatever you are . . . English?" A long glance at Schultz, who blushed like a child, and said: "Well . . . yes, no . . . I mean . . . German by birth, Russian by education, but English by choice, and now possibly American: in other words, a Jew, and a Jew's only fatherland is the country where people are not judged by their accent or the shape of their noses, but by their love of humanity in general, and their willingness to share what ancient wisdom they possess with people risen to humanity much later from monkeyhood or stone-age sociability. Does that answer your question?"

Leonardo was so moved that instead of replying, he ran over to

Mr. Schultz and embraced him, kissing him on both cheeks. Sophie
and Mary locked them both in an embarrassing embrace, like big
children playing a silly game. When this comedy was over, Leonardo continued: "So, you are foreigners, and I am a native, which
means that no Italian liar can lie to me: he is my brother, millions
of the same lies used for thousands of years by our uncountable
ancestors unite us, while the only thing that divides us is my personal revolt against our common tradition. By refusing to be *furbo*,
I become *fesso*, a term not to be used in polite society, but one that
any Italian knows and no foreigner does. It means a man who hides
nothing from anybody, because he's not ashamed of his origins or
his stupidity. Now, I'm telling you that your darling Tegolani and
his brother the priest, whom I haven't met and hope I never will,
are both the slimiest of liars, spies and slanderers; they steal other
people's trust, and anything they can lay their hands on, given half a
chance. The only reason Tegolani may not have stolen from you is
because he doesn't *have* to: in this house waste is so much the rule
that thieves never even have the chance to practice their art.
They're too busy emptying the wastebaskets into their pockets. This
is all I have to say."

This time there was no embrace, only a handshake, extended by
Mr. Schultz, of the type a great businessman or statesman offers a
man he acknowledges as his equal, after having formerly treated
him as his inferior: "Here, let's shake hands: on the very day I had
been given one more reason to mistrust a young man who still is, in
spite of everything, dear to my heart, I have my first reason, my son,
to give you all my trust. Sophie was right in saying you are the
master of this house. If you say Tegolani must go, he will go. I
confess I was taken in myself, not by him, but by his brother, whom
Sophie wanted me to meet, so I would get an idea of what these
people are like. And I must say the brother did impress me as an
intelligent, liberal priest. Very understanding towards the Jews and
the Protestants, to the point where he even praised Andrew Carnegie's book. . . . What could be more liberal than that? Anyway,
I think we can only recognize Leonardo's authority and act accordingly. What do you say to this, Sophie?"

Sophie looked as if she were about to have a heart attack; she could hardly breathe: "Do you realize what you are doing to that poor, ailing old woman? Even if her son is a hypocrite, she exists, she's no lie, she is a person, and a good, kindhearted person, I assure you, Leonardo. I wish you could see her, speak to her, and see her sons with her, not so much the Monsignor, who is a bit of an egotist, but this one of ours, who may have all the bad qualities of the Italians, but he has the good ones, too, I assure you. Please, don't kill his poor mother. . . . Please!!!!"

"I'm sorry, Sophie, but I think you're exaggerating. I'm sure the old woman is not a monster like her sons . . ." Leonardo had to interrupt himself, because even Mr. Schultz seemed to cringe at the mention of the family slogan, but he went on, pretending he had noticed nothing: ". . . but I am equally sure that she must have been wondering for a long time how her darling little baby aged sixty or sixty-five could get away with such puny lies about all his evil doings. They must both think you a gullible *straniera*, an old *Inglese*. And I wouldn't be surprised to discover that they have a good laugh about you every time they meet. As for the Monsignor, he is the kind of priest who wouldn't last three days in a Jesuit college without being made the target of spitballs and every kind of practical joke by the students."

Sophie's cowardly answer was to appeal to Schultz in Russian. But even if Leonardo couldn't understand a single word, he understood a great deal from the tone of her voice, the lightning bolts in her eyes, and the mime (a straight index finger pointed first at Mr. Schultz, then at Leonardo, as if to say: "And is this the man I'm supposed to obey?," then again at Mr. Schultz, with words that sounded like the cackling of turkeys and the yelping of Pekinese dogs, but that could only mean: "You, with all your authority, how can you accept such an imposition?").

As a result of which unfair procedures, Mr. Schultz straightened his necktie, cleared his throat, and said to Leonardo, with a faint quiver in his voice: "As the natural head of the family council, owing to my very advanced age, may I suggest that you give Tegolani the benefit of the doubt. You have no proof of Tegolani's dishonesty, other than your own exceptional purity of soul, which makes you shun all lies, no matter how 'necessary' or diplomatic.

For which purity of soul we all love you, please rest assured that
Sophie is so grateful for the very presence of a rare person like you
on earth, she has been thanking God every morning and every night
in her prayers. But since Mr. Tegolani has been in her service for
almost ten years, and he couldn't do more damage in the next two
weeks than he has done in those ten years, I suggest we postpone all
drastic decisions until after the inventory is finished and sealed. Of
course, that means you will have to stay here for another two weeks."

"Another two weeks?"

"At a bare minimum, yes, another two weeks."

"But . . . Mary and I cannot wait another two weeks. . . ."

"That's what Sophie just told me, and she said she couldn't wait
either. She says she has left this place for months every year, and
nothing was ever missing from it. She agrees Tegolani is a liar, if we
must use so strong a term, but she adds that people of your high
standards of morality are extremely rare, even in Germany, even in
England; and we won't mention Russia, because Russia is a country
of comedians, who don't know vice from virtue, black from white, or
the sun from the moon. And she made me aware of the fact that
even I, who pride myself on recognizing none but the highest standards of truthfulness and honesty, go on keeping her son in my bank
and in my industry (not for long, I assure you, but she retorts that,
if this latest gamble proves successful I will go on keeping him, and
she is right), . . . so, why don't you make an exception and accept
the sad reality that not everybody is like you?"

"I? . . . But I never set myself up as an example."

"You are wrong there. But since you seem to be so understanding, shall we say you . . . agree not to adopt drastic reforms in your
staff before you leave? Later of course, I'll be the first to act on your
behalf, once you are gone, because I must come back to Rome at
least once a month. But, if you agree to this compromise solution
. . . I don't see why you couldn't leave . . . tomorrow, or perhaps
in two days. . . ."

"Oh, darling," shouted Mary, flinging herself into Leonardo's
arms, much to the scandalized amazement of Mr. Schultz and even
of her mother, "darling, let's leave as soon as possible, who cares
about objects anyway? We'll win the Nobel Prize with your discoveries, and we won't ever have to thank anybody for guarding our

earthly possessions. It's the Spirit that counts, and you are the Spirit. . . ."

This was the moment, he felt, to assert his authority with Sophie, through Mary, for the benefit of the one friend he had found in that strange world. He pushed Mary gently aside and said: "Mary, please, no human being is the Spirit, and no object on earth is contemptible, especially if earned by work, but even if it isn't, an object, an art object, for example, is always evidence of the artist's hard work, and to know this you don't have to know everything about art. *You* know everything about art but nothing about human respect for man-made objects.

"As for that so-called administrator, I stand by my judgment and you do as you please, but I insist that, even if you don't dismiss him, you should deprive him at once of any further right to hire or dismiss servants, and that all these new men he has hired for all sorts of nonexistent tasks be dismissed at once, on *your* order, Sophie, not on *his* orders, and also that the servants *you* trust— namely, that . . . what's her name . . . Adriana, yes, and her mother—be the official custodians of the house, not he."

Sophie became frantic again: "But how can I tell him any such thing?"

"Mr. Schultz can. I can. In fact, I'd love to. He crawls to me like a little dog. I'll tell him it's being done for his mother's sake, so he can devote more time to her before she returns to her Maker."

At that moment there was the usual discreet knock on the door, and the butler's face appeared. The name he whispered acted like the strings on a row of puppets, sending all their limbs suddenly flying. Here the puppets also had voices, facial expressions, emotions, even thoughts, all of which Leonardo knew very well by now and even knew how to pit advantageously one against another, but what utterly defeated him at this point was the sudden unanimity of reactions. To confirm him in his sudden confusion, there now appeared in the doorway a small woman of more than mature age, less imposing than Sophie on first sight—in fact, almost Italian- looking in her helplessness—but there was something half hidden in that tiny bundle of black velvets, furs and silks like a tiger in the thick of a tree: one piercing eye barely visible under a heavy lid, while the other looked blankly, not at you, but at its fellow eye.

The only thing Leonardo remembered suddenly as a warning indication of who this woman might be was Mary's strange sentence of the previous day: "We are poor."

Mr. Schultz's behavior confirmed it. He looked like another Leonardo, and the thought that came to Leonardo's mind was: I wonder whether this man will be able to hold his knife and fork if this woman stays for lunch? . . . If she stays, I leave.

He had counted on lunch, in fact he knew that even if he didn't succeed in unseating Tegolani from his financial position, he had at least conquered his own seat at table and he had intended to use it, even holding his fork the wrong way.

The third thing he understood was that his whole concern with Tegolani and objects had become a big joke, and yet it still mattered. The fourth thing he knew was that fighting with Tegolani was the same as fighting with Peppino and Liborio. What he owed them was to stay *in* this fairy tale, so they could boast they were his friends, whereas what he owed himself was to stay *out* of it.

While all this was taking shape in his mind, his own image was being recorded in the mind of the black tiger out there on the sofa. She had installed herself with Mary and Sophie on either side, her short arms around their shoulders, like the arms of the rising Aphrodite in the Ludovisi throne of recent archaeological excavation, and if they were not treating her as a goddess, it was only because they knew they were goddesses too. But Mr. Schultz was acting like a man who, if he didn't treat her as a goddess, might lose something—Leonardo didn't quite know what, but it must be something important; perhaps as important as *his* place in the fairy tale was to Peppino, Liborio and Tegolani.

But the thought that worried him most of all was: I'm hungry and penniless, and WHERE AM I GOING TO EAT LUNCH? This was interrupted by Mr. Schultz, who took him by the arm and led him to a window while the ladies shrieked and yelped and cackled in Russian. There, in the presence of the old Cupolone, now again bright with sunshine amid fluffy clouds against a backdrop of pine trees, he heard the great revelation: "This is Madame Morosoff, our biggest steel and textile industrialist, the kind of woman only Moscow can produce: thirty thousand workers, all under her personal command, like soldiers under a general, but not just any general, one greater than Napoleon. *She* fights for peace, not for personal glory. She doesn't kill and maim and destroy entire families and cities, she *forms* them, keeps them together, united in the one ideal of honest, constructive work, as my friend Carnegie would say, and all this, ever since her husband died. He was rich and of course powerful, but his empire was disintegrating under competition. His death was her emotional undoing, even though she would never admit it—in this she is like Sophie, stubborn in her great sorrow, an example of undying loyalty even long after the death of her companion—but she is utterly unlike Sophie in the manifestations of that sorrow. She does not squander everything as a revenge against the Almighty who has deprived her of her loved one's presence. Madam Morosoff has become a man in her husband's image, and a better one than he was. She has a whole army of engineers at her command, engineers from every country in Europe, and the Russian ones she hires she sends abroad for an extensive training period. Her own sons are among them, but at work they are treated like all the others, they must wait their turn before they are admitted to her presence: short visits, no personal problems discussed, and let me tell you, between you, me and the gate-post, as they say in England, Russian men must be treated that way, there is an innate weakness in them which makes them somewhat contemptible, the whole lot of them. Which explains drunks like Klagonov or crooks like Pierre." Here he stopped, to put his face in his hands again and mumble: "God, what he has done to me today . . . My dear Leonardo, I am speaking to you as to a brother: I am ruined, I fear . . . and once you're ruined in my business, there is no coming back: not from this kind of ruin, that exposes the lowest instincts of the pure gambler."

Leonardo squeezed his arm and said: "Mr. Schultz, if I can be of any assistance, count on me, please. I will take care of your health until you have recovered from the shock, and Mary will write letters for you, read, translate, do anything, and I am sure that the people who have trusted you until now can't fail to continue. You are too rare a person to be easily overlooked or cast aside."

"May the Lord hear you and bless you, my brother. . . . Just a moment, they're calling me." And he hurried over to the three ladies, while Leonardo sighed and shook his head in disapproval,

thinking how bleak the countryside looked just one step beyond the
Rubicon: a real no-man's land, there was no reason to believe it
might grow any more human as he advanced deeper into it. . . .
But here was his new "brother" rushing back again, hands waving in
the air like a clown.

"Good news! good news! Just imagine, *she* suggested buying those
shares. She *knows* they'll go up tomorrow, and if there is one person
who should know, it is she. . . . Can you imagine what she just
said? She said: 'If I were rich enough to gamble, I would have
bought them yesterday myself, Pierre is a genius.' That's what she
said, and she despises him: 'Keep him on a leash like a dangerous
dog,' she said immediately afterwards. You can bet I will, the goddamn wolf. . . . I'm rich again, Leonardo, I can help you and I
will: now, about bacteriology? Mary insists I put you into partnership with Madame Curie, but Mary is a baby, she thinks *she* can
discover something like radium, can you imagine anything sillier?
The field of scientific discovery is almost exhausted, two or three
more and we have it, the next step is to find out how life can be
produced in the laboratory, and that's the field I think you should
specialize in. . . . Don't think I would refuse to help you if you
insisted on radiology, it isn't that I'm against spending that kind of
money: it's yours, I'll help you invest it wisely, but I also want to
help you invest your genius in productive research because let's be
realistic, if you work in radiology, no matter what new applications
you come up with, or where you may be working, the credit will still
all be hers, and let me warn you: she's Polish, which means a Slav,
and beware of Slavic women, you don't ever dare antagonize them,
if you want to live a long life. . . . By the way, don't tell anybody
you know about the Nobel Prize, it's still a great secret—not to me,
of course, because I go to Sweden every three months and have two
small factories there and a small bank, nothing important, just toys
of mine, but toys that allow me to keep in touch with whatever
happens in that country. . . . Just a moment, they're calling me
again."

And he was gone, but this time Leonardo was dazzled by visions
of himself with a large laboratory at his command: he would never
treat his associates like machines, nor would he ever work on mak-

ing life in test tubes. The Catholic Church may be wrong, but
Moral Geometry exists, and nothing good can come of men who
sink into the quicksands of hubris. . . . "Yes? I'm coming."

He had heard his name twice in the course of this reverie; and the
third time it was Mary's sweet voice calling him, so he knew he was
wanted. But as soon as he turned his back on St. Peter's and saw
that half-closed eye in the thick of that black tree, he stopped,
shivers running down his spine.

"Come, darling, come," said Mary rushing to him and taking him
by the hand like a child. He followed her, dragging a bit, and caught
a glimpse of satisfaction in the tiger eye. She must be used to that
kind of response, he thought. What kind of privilege is it to wait on
line for your turn at the guillotine? These are the Protestant Jesuits:
first they behead you, then they sew your head back on, praising you
for your repentance, then the moment they see that your head is
erect again, it's time for another beheading.

"Stop," said Leonardo, in the middle of the room. He was looking at something very strange. They had called in Tegolani, and he
was listening to the tiger and bowing all over the place while the
other two looked on and smiled.

"Come on," said Mary.

"Are you crazy? Is she going to force some sort of reconciliation
between me and Tegolani?"

"Oh, come on, my love, it's nothing of the sort. She wants to buy
a *pied-à-terre* in Rome, and Tegolani knows all about them."

"A *what?*"

"A . . . foot on the ground."

"She wants to buy a foot?"

"No, darling, a small place of her own, so she doesn't have to go
to a hotel."

"Why, is she going to settle down here?"

"Of course not. She lives in Moscow. She hasn't been here for
thirty years, and she wants to come back at least once every year."

"For how long?"

"Oh, never more than a week, just for a breath of air."

"And for that breath of air she needs a place in Rome? Fully
staffed, I imagine. Fourteen servants in uniform."

"No, just a handful to keep the place clean. But why are you asking all these questions? Aren't you happy we can finally leave in two days?"

"Can we?"

"Of course, my love, you're such a spoilsport with your eternal pessimism. She said it was all right for us to leave, even if Tegolani is a fox."

"And how does she know?"

"Oh, she knows everything. One glance, and she can give you a complete picture of a person's psychology, morality, family background and personal weaknesses. Isn't she sweet?"

"Sweet? She's a gorgon!"

"Darling . . . how can you? She's Mamachen's closest friend. . . . Are you really dead set on *tegolanizing* everyone in the whole world?"

"On what?"

"Making Tegolanis of people." She had tears in her eyes, and Leonardo was subdued. One more glance and a frightening "Come here" motion from the sweet tiger's little hand, and Leonardo walked, pale and trembling, to his doom.

But it wasn't his doom any more than it was his triumph: he had overlooked the fact that, in the presence of money, the rich are humbler than the poor. Andrew Carnegie was right, he concluded as he swallowed the insult of not being noticed at all, although he had been seen by them all, Tegolani included. Both Sophie and Mr. Schultz were paying court, acting as interpreters, and the first thing Leonardo heard as he joined them was their duet (why should they both be saying the same thing? But then that was like asking why Sophie needed two horses to her cab): "Nothing palatial, please, she doesn't want to spend more than a million."

Leonardo translated this aloud into his own terms: "Three Apulian Aqueducts . . . Blood of the Holy Virgin!!!"

He might as well not have spoken. Not even the blasphemy shook Tegolani's indifference. "One million?" he said, rolling the points of his mustache. "One million is a little low for the cottage I mentioned."

"Too low?" shouted Leonardo. "Are you crazy? You can buy the whole Vatican for that!"

Said the tiger to Tegolani: "One million was the price you were asking a year ago, when I wanted that place for my daughter."

"That's true, but prices have gone up. Don't forget the crisis and the inflation."

Mr. Schultz translated this into Russian, and the sweet tiger seemed unimpressed. She murmured something which was quickly translated as: "How much are they asking?"

"Two million fivehundredthousandfifty: a real bargain if you ask me."

And Leonardo, aloud: "Seven and a half aqueducts; equals one Niagara Falls or two Vaticans with live Pope included." But even this went unnoticed.

"May I show you the blueprints?" asked Tegolani, and the answer was yes, so he went away to get them. Now Leonardo felt the tiger's eye both on him and inside him. She was reading his entrails like an ancient Pythian priestess, and he trembled at the thought of what she might discover.

"May I speak now?" he asked, but Tegolani was coming back with a huge black portfolio under his arm, and Mr. Schultz was busy: he had to find a table low enough to hold the blueprints without disturbing the two ladies. He found one, and from his corner of the room he motioned to Leonardo for help, so here the two masters of the house were, waiting on the crook, who didn't move an inch: he just stood there, holding the arsenal of his new weaponry for the projected burglary.

"Thank you," he said to his two masters, when they presented him with the surface he needed. Eight eyes were staring at Tegolani's hands as he slowly untied the strings of the portfolio, and they didn't seem to notice that his hands spoke louder than words: they were indeed the hands of a thief.

Boring questions ensued on the size of the rooms, the number and efficiency of the toilets, the coal furnace, the kitchen, the oven, the wine cellar, and Tegolani was now perspiring abundantly because he grasped that the fish wouldn't bite. As a last bait he showed them many photographs of the villa, the park, the view from the villa, but still the comment was always: "She says it's too expensive."

"I can try and talk to the owner, but I'm afraid I won't be able to

get a price much lower than, let's say . . . two million fourhun-
dredfiftythousand."

"No."

"Very well," he said, and started arranging the pictures and the
blueprints so they wouldn't stick out of the portfolio, while the
eight innocent eyes looked on in dismay. Suddenly, the tiger's eye
caught a glimpse of something in a photograph she hadn't seen
before.

"She wants to see something in one of the pictures," was the
translation. So they were all displayed again, and when she found
what she was looking for, she jumped up like a child: "*Eti, eti . . .*"
she yelped, pointing to little sticks in one corner of the garden.

"Oh, those," said Tegolani, "those are spring peas: the owner
loves peas, and he put this tiny plot right in the middle of the lawn
in front of the villa. But it can be taken out in a matter of minutes."

After this was translated into Russian, the tiger jumped up and
made a long speech which was summed up as follows: "She says it
would be insane to destroy spring peas. They probably grow very
well here."

"Oh yes, they do. My mother loves Prince X's peas. He always
sends her some."

This message was also duly translated, and back came the reply:
"She wants to know if spring peas are expensive, now that all the
prices have gone up."

"Very, very expensive."

A long discussion followed, after which came the verdict: "She
thinks it would be very convenient not to have to go and buy peas
on the market. She wonders whether one could transform the whole
lawn into a vegetable garden. Would Roman lettuce grow well?"

"Roman lettuce, my dear Mr. Schultz, is Roman to begin with.
This is the best, the only place on earth for Roman lettuce!"

After another long debate, the final offer: "She says that if you
can find a reliable vegetable gardener, she will take the place, but
only for two million. Not one cent more."

Tegolani sighed with such relief that he had to mention his
mother, in order to ascribe his sigh to sadness. "That's the end of

another beautiful Roman villa," he said to Mr. Schultz. "I don't dare tell my mother that the garden she loved so much will be destroyed to make room for more city streets and modern buildings . . . just like the Villa Ludovisi." Sophie overheard him and became agitated: "What? Why should it be destroyed, if the Prince can get two million for it? These Roman barbarians . . ."

"Because the real estate speculators are offering him almost three million for it. He's making a great sacrifice to keep it intact at the low price I mentioned. So don't call him a barbarian, my dear Signora."

"Wait a moment," she said, and quickly translated the sad message into Russian. The tiger became very attentive, looked straight into Tegolani's eyes, went up to him and shouted a few words into his face, which neither Sophie nor Mr. Schultz volunteered to translate, but she insisted, while Tegolani pretended to be almost overcome with sadness, and moved away, sniffling and wiping his eyes.

"Don't go," shouted Sophie, and he stopped in front of the closed door, without turning around, like a frightened little boy.

After a lively discussion between the three Russians, Mr. Schultz went up to Tegolani and said: "The lady wants you to know that she is leaving in two days, and if you accept one million and a half, she will buy it sight unseen. If not, she will buy something else that has been offered her this morning for a much lower price. The time limit for an answer is three hours; that is: two p.m. I advise the Prince to accept, I know the place, and I know that the lady would find lots of things to object to if she saw the place, just as my daughter did, and then she would lose interest."

"Impossible," said Tegolani.

"Don't tell *me* now: tell *her* in three hours."

"Out of politeness, yes. I can tell the butler now to come back here at two and say the answer is no."

"By all means do so and thank you."

After Tegolani was gone, Leonardo asked Mary: "What was it she said to him that they wouldn't translate?"

"She said: 'You stupid little comedian, if we were in Russia I'd have you whipped on your bare backside in the presence of all the other servants to teach you a lesson.' " She laughed, then added:

"Now you know, darling, why we don't like to live in Russia. When an absolute angel like Madame Morosoff can say such a thing, you can imagine what ordinary people will do."

"Why, doesn't she ever have her servants whipped?"

"Oh no. They all worship her. One glance from those beautiful eyes, and they all rush to obey her. She was just telling us that the governor of Moscow, who is the brother of the Czar, offered her military assistance at the factory in case of a revolution, and she refused, saying: 'What strange ideas you have. I assure you that my workers will start a revolution only with my consent.' The next day she summoned all her workers and said: 'My boys, I promised the governor you would be good, therefore please honor my promise, don't make me into a liar for the first time in my life.' And they all shouted: 'We will be good, don't worry!' Isn't that wonderful?"

"Is it?" asked Leonardo, cheerfully.

Mary couldn't answer, because Mr. Schultz was coming towards them. "My dear Leonardo," he said, "since we have become such friends, I must tell you something you ought to know. Tegolani's answer to our offer will be yes."

"If you think I don't know that, my dear Mr. Schultz, you're a babe-in-the-woods."

"I know you know that, but what I want you to know is something else: Madame Morosoff is very proud of her business sense, because she got the place for a song."

"Some song!!!"

"We are not discussing that. What I want you to know is that, if I had bargained on my own initiative—and I almost did—she would have refused, because these are 'Jewish methods.' "

Mary reacted violently: "I forbid you to say that Madame Morosoff is anti-Semitic!"

"Not more than you, Mary, or your mother. Or you, Leonardo, who met your first Jew in this room two nights ago, and almost fainted. You all live in a fairy tale; we are the only ones who don't because we do all the suffering . . . and not as outcasts, but *incasts*. There are two ways of casting the Jew *in*, and I'll let you decide which is the worst, Leonardo, because your people suffer the same kind of fate in the Protestant countries, especially America. One is the prejudiced way, the other the progressive way. The *prejudiced* way is followed by those who kill us regularly by the thousands, or even one by one if we happen to have no master—just as if we were cats or dogs, prey to the dogcatcher or the simple housemaid who drowns a litter of kittens in the river at birth, saving the two nicest to give the children as pets. Then of course there are the pedigreed varieties of our species, who command high prices and are not allowed to mate beneath their class. All the kings on earth have their court Jews. Some marry them off to other court Jews, to breed house tutors, privy councilors and artists. We pedigreed ones live well, but we are either mated according to plan or castrated. If a Jew is a favored court pet, he must never have feelings for his own people, even if he saw his own parents die in a pogrom, as I did when I was a child. For us Jews to associate with our court equals is always dangerous. Which is why we became anti-Semitic, to be able to help other Jews. From a distance, but never too openly. To give you an example: when I decided to become an English subject, my own master, the brother of the Emperor, arranged for me to be 'advised' against it in private audience with the Autocrat, who said to me: 'Why ever do you want to do it? The English are all Jews!' I was meant to be grateful, because he had excluded me from his metaphor *on purpose*. But, alas, I disappointed him. I was never forgiven for it, although I was still used as a financial adviser and for other secret family services. I was never received by His Majesty again. . . .

"Yet it was in England that I discovered the delights of being a *progressive* incast. This situation is of course totally reversed: instead of divorcing yourself from your own people, you marry them—ALL of them. His Britannic Majesty, who is of course a cousin of His Russian Majesty, received me frequently, and still does, in spite of the fact that Marx and Engels were Jews, as are many of the other subversives who inhabit the reading room of the British Museum. Nothing is ever said, because the English don't talk: they just hold their breath for a minute, to make sure you hear their unspoken disappointment, which translates itself as: 'I had expected more of you.' Thus, while Mary can say she hates the Russians, and you can say you hate the Italians, I can have no such . . . prejudices . . . against my own people. I must be *progressive*; the whole world ghetto and many of the world's prisons and insane asylums are my personal responsibility. Frankly, I prefer your stupid, Catholic, bureaucratic anti-Semitism, in which either we take out Christian papers—baptism is a certificate—or we are accused of killing Christ, as we certainly did. . . ."

"NO!" shouted Mary, who was almost in tears. "The Romans did!"

"What do *you* know, my child? The Romans washed their hands of it—let the schlemiels do it."

Leonardo frowned. "Just a moment . . . I never heard that name before, and I know my Church history."

"Neither did I," said Mary.

Mr. Schultz explained. "You couldn't. But the schlemiels are the tribe that killed Christ and would do it over again if . . ."

"Oh, *here* you are," said Sophie, as if they had been hiding miles away and she hadn't known where to look for them. The tiger in the meantime was hunting bargains: she was staring at some tiny bronze statuettes she had taken out of a china cabinet, as if her eye could melt them, then taking them to Sophie and asking her questions about them in Russian; if she was satisfied with the answer she would nod, not at Sophie, but at the statuette *in person*. But if she was dissatisfied, she would sneer at it and growl like a little dog before putting it back into the cabinet and repeating the entire performance with another bronze object. Sophie seemed amused, but also a little frightened.

"You have conquered her heart, Leonardo," Sophie went on. "She asked me to repeat to you the story of what happened between her and the governor of Moscow during the recent rev—"

"I told it to him already," said Mary proudly, and Sophie seemed a little disappointed that Leonardo wasn't more impressed.

"But do you realize what that means? The courage it takes? Thirty thousand wild beasts, such as only Russia can produce . . ."

"I know, I know, the entire population of Laterza, men, women and children."

"Yes, but her workers are all or almost all married and have large families."

"I know: the entire population of Rome. But tell me two things I *don't* know: what is she doing with all those things? Does she want to buy them?"

"No, of course not: she is admiring them, she knows everything about bronzes—Greek, Egyptian, Chinese, Japanese—her knowledge of art is universal."

"Just a moment," said Schultz. "Tell him honestly that she is also asking what you paid for them and that you are somewhat appalled by that kind of curiosity. If I had shown it, you would have said: 'How Jewish of you . . .' "

"Eberhard Sacharovitch, how can you say such a thing?" asked Sophie, almost in a whisper, for fear lest her tiger friend suddenly develop a knowledge of Italian.

"I am teaching Leonardo about my own people." Then, to Leonardo: "Have you read *The Merchant of Venice?*"

"I have no time to read novels, but if you recommend it, I will."

The tiger put an end to this embarrassing episode by coming over, bronzeless now, and taking Leonardo's head in both hands, not to detach it and ask its price but to stare into his eyes and yelp at him in many different tones, then motion to Sophie for a translation.

"She says you are the only person in the whole world from whom she would take orders. You are like her, she says, if you told all the drunks in your care that you had promised they would never touch vodka again, they would never touch vodka again, to honor your word. They wouldn't want this to be your first lie, and she did the same with her thirty thousand workers."

More yelping, which Sophie promptly decoded as: "Between the two of you, she says you could reform the world and put the Socialists and the anarchists to shame. She also wants to know what you would like for a wedding present."

Without waiting for Leonardo's reply, she engaged in a lively exchange of yelping with the tiger, and came back to him with the following: "She insists on giving you a hospital, but I said this was going to be my present. I'm sorry I can no longer surprise you with it, but I didn't know how I could avoid mentioning it after she had. What else can I say you want?"

"I want nothing, especially no hospitals: a job in one, yes, but not in your hospital, or hers, please. One thing I do want is to know what she means when she says she's too poor to gamble." Leonardo was still thinking of the shares the tiger had advised Pierre to buy.

"You can't ask her such a question," said Schultz.

"Why?"

"I'll tell you later, not now."

Leonardo was very irritated, as Schultz saw, but this made Leonardo more stubborn and not less; this was his revenge for having been discovered ignorant on the subject of those damned painters and that damned unknown author of *The Merchant of Venice*. Here he was on his own ground: poverty was the thing he knew all about from personal observation.

Mr. Schultz had found his natural refuge in the vicinity of the tiger, whose every movement he knew like a good circus trainer, and Leonardo was left with his two women, who were more than eager to answer his question.

"Darling, she is too poor because she is a saint, but a real one, not like those dolls the Catholics pray to."

"But that's nonsense: Saint Francis may not sit in heaven, but he did live on earth, and gave up everything he owned. This saint here pays two million lire for a dish of peas and Roman lettuce, and still pays the salaries of thirty thousand workers. Where's her poverty?"

"Darling, let me—"

Sophie interrupted her: "No, let *me* explain: do you know what a budget is?"

"I should say I do; I'm a mayor."

"Well then; you know what it means when the budget is all taken up by the needs of the people."

"Yes, but then I would not say I was too poor to gamble: *too honest*, is the correct term."

"But that's what she meant. Her budget is all taken up by the needs of her workers."

"And by young peas at two and a half million lire a pound, but let's not digress. That word *poor* betrays a feeling of envy. . . . But I see she wants to know what we are talking about. Translate, please."

Sophie could do nothing but obey, trapped as she was between the tiger and the barking little mutt, and the tiger came over and kissed the mutt on both cheeks, then made a big sign of the cross on his forehead with her fat little hand, and Sophie had to translate the following: "She says you're right and you're a saint. And she wants you to know that she is ashamed of having been envious. Only Certain People gamble."

These last words were translated after Sophie had made sure that Mr. Schultz was not within hearing distance, and Leonardo felt that in fairness to him, he must make his words audible, so he shouted: "Certain People Who? The Jews?" He was disappointed to realize that Mr. Schultz had just left the room. But Sophie was extremely relieved, and this gave her a chance to seek the tiger's help. The tiger listened to the whole story, then laughed in a high falsetto, kissing Leonardo again, and talking at great length to Sophie, who paraphrased it all: "She's so fascinated with your honesty that she has asked whether she can stay for lunch. Of course I am delighted. She will bring her guests, one of them is the future mayor of Rome, who is also a Jew: Mr. Nathan."

"For lunch? But I can't stay for lunch."

"Why?"

"I have to see my cousin."

"WHAT cousin?" asked Sophie in anger.

"The doctor."

"Ask him too. This is your house, you should see your friends or relatives here, if they . . . I mean yes, in any case. I told you many times we were eager to meet him."

"I can't. He's very timid, and he wants to discuss some extremely delicate personal matters with me."

"Plenty of time after lunch."

"But . . . it will take me time to find him, he lives a long way from here, and . . ."

"The coachman is entirely at your service, lunch will be very late, because the mayor can't have lunch early, he's a delightful person, and there will be other people here who are counting on seeing you: Miss Ambron, who promised to bring Marinetti, you can have a fight with him, it will be most amusing, then Mommsen's son-in-law, Willamowitz, may come too, and probably a few others, who all know about you. . . . But in any case, now that my friend has changed all her plans entirely for your sake, you can't say no."

"I'm sorry, but . . ."

"But what?"

"I have no right to decide for him. If he says yes, we will come, if not . . ."

Again the tiger was eager to hear everything, and she took Leonardo's defense with such energy that Sophie seemed almost resigned. "She says I have no right to interfere with the head of the family, she is sorry you won't meet her daughter, who is a rare beauty, a most fascinating young girl . . ."

Mary joined in: "Yes, darling, why don't you stay and meet her? She's such a beauty you will be stunned."

"I don't care to meet beauties, you are my beauty, and—"

"Darling, I know, which is why I'm not jealous. But she's one of my closest friends, although she's much younger—"

But Sophie stopped her: "Don't interfere with him, Mary. He is a man of principles, he must have his reasons."

"But don't we count at all?" asked Mary, very resentful now.

Leonardo didn't know what to do. On one side was the tiger, staring at him proudly, and holding Sophie by the hand like a younger sister, and on the other was Mary, pleading. He had already decided to give up another meal for Mary's sake, but what was slowing down his reactions was sheer hunger. Beyond those doors that were constantly being opened and closed, there loomed, suspended in midair like a divine presence, an aroma of good cooking that weakened every moral resolve and principle. Where else will I find such a meal, if I leave this house now, without a cent in my pocket or a friend in this city?

Alas, he didn't know that Mary was observing him while he was being torn by these doubts and ascribing his hesitation to her *unforgivable egotism*. There is beauty in self-sacrifice, she remembered, because this was her mother's guiding moral principle. He will love me all the more if I don't make it any harder for him to help his poor needy cousin. This decided in the depths of her conscience, she moved towards Leonardo at the very same moment he was moving towards her to tell her he had decided to stay on, and she said: "Whatever you are going to tell me, let me talk first: I understand. You want to sacrifice your principles to me, but I will not accept. I am proud of your loyalty to that poor cousin of yours who is in such pain today, while we are so happy. I want you to go, I insist, in fact, I *order* you to go. Do it for me, more than for him. Give me a chance to prove to you that I can be altruistic too, the way Mamachen always has been. In fact, let me tell her."

She was dragging him by the hand; he still hoped it might all end with his deciding to stay on and being applauded for it, but he hadn't counted on those imponderable elements that can change the whole course of history. Tegolani came in to announce to Madame Morosoff that the answer was yes, she could have her peas and lettuce once a year for the modest price of a million and a half. The tiger was so happy that she discharged the overflow of her happiness onto her childhood friend Sophie, who had no time for Mary's moral victories over her selfish nature. "All right, all right, but don't expect to be praised as a heroine for this right now. Can't you see I'm busy? And you, Leonardo, don't keep your cousin waiting. Go, and if you can come back with him, so much the better, but if you can't, tea is at five and dinner at nine tonight, with all the same people, and a few more at the Russian embassy. We must celebrate. A million and a half is a real bargain. Isn't my friend wonderful? See how happy she is? She loves the simple things of life: young peas, a vegetable garden, birds in the trees . . . And now, before you go, please thank Tegolani for this beautiful present he's offering Mary and you." And she showed him a French book with lots of gold and bright colors on the cover, a balloon and the blue sky and the moon in the distance. "Jules Verne's trip to the moon. A book Mary adores. Look how beautiful." The tiger also commented with loud yelps, and Sophie translated in a hurry: "She says that this is no fantasy, it is being studied by serious scientists as a real possibility, and she invites us all to be the first passengers. But go now, go, don't let us keep you here with our silly chatter."

And before he could offer to stay, he was already cut off from their universe, as if they had really all left for the moon in that stupid illustration: five or ten lire at the most, a generous gift from the man who had just robbed them of at least half a million.

"Your carriage is ready," said the doorman, taking off his hat.

Leonardo didn't even bother to answer. He was a poor man in a poor hat and a rich overcoat with no money in his pocket and nothing to eat in a big, foreign city.

As he reached the street, feeling weak, he closed his eyes. Too much sunshine, too much joy in the air, too much loneliness in his heart. What am I doing here? he asked himself. Am I not crossing the Rubicon again in retreat? This is madness.

"Where do you want to go?" asked the coachman.

"Where do I want to go? Nowhere. Back upstairs, my friend. That's where I want to go."

And without even noticing how baffled the poor devil was, he walked slowly in the direction of the Scalinata, but stopped short so as not to be seen by the beggars. If I went back to the hotel, I could order a meal just as grand as the one I just missed, and eat it alone in comfort, then come back.

The project seemed sound, because it could even include the long nap he certainly needed, almost more than food, but the thought of being all alone in his self-imposed banishment saddened him so much, he felt a sob rise in his throat. He walked thus, very slowly, until he reached the fountain, and stood there watching St. Peter's from this less familiar point of view. He was so used to seeing it from his new home that this rekindled all his nostalgia and sadness.

Suddenly a brilliant thought came to him. He could go and see the Cardinal. Indeed, this would be a highly moral and charitable thing to do, both towards the Cardinal and towards Mary. He could tell him the truth; namely, that Gennariello had been Mary's invention to make her husband jealous, when she still cared to save appearances for her child's sake and also for the sake of the faith she had embraced. This would restore Mary's image in his eyes. After all, he was a priest, he had converted her to Catholicism, and he liked Mary very much. And, of course, it would help Leonardo to talk everything over with a man of the cloth, who was also very much a man of the world, and whom he admired.

Why didn't I think of it before? And of course he will ask me to stay for lunch. This is called mixing the useful with the delectable. If anyone in Rome knows what good cooking is, he does; and in his presence I can eat as I damn please. It will be a general confession.

With these thoughts in mind he entered the Villa Medici and asked if the Cardinal was at home.

"Of course he is," said the doorman. "Whom may I announce?"

"Doctor Claudi, and please tell him it's very urgent because I'm very hungry."

The doorman looked rather amused, so Leonardo corrected himself: "I mean it's almost lunchtime, I am awaited elsewhere."

"No hurry," said the doorman. "Here in Rome it's never lunchtime until you actually sit down, even at five or six."

The large entrance hall to the Villa Medici was very cold, in contrast to the world outside. It seemed as if winter had retired indoors. The uniformed guard at the French Academy had done his duty towards his foreign employers and their new native visitor by standing obediently behind his little desk and dispatching a young boy (also in uniform) to announce him to the Cardinal. He had also done his duty by offering Leonardo a large choice of gold-crested chairs or gold-crested baroque benches to sit upon and wait. Leonardo chose a huge papal chair, on which he sat, trying to look dignified enough to impress that dignified uniform and the poor serf inside it. But after only a minute of this silent scene, the doorman excused himself with a deep bow, and took his chair outside to lean against the wall and close his eyes, saying: "Aaaaaah, thank God, summer is near! There's such a draft in there! Winter's getting more French than the French—it's certainly colder than the French ambassador, the director of the academy and the Cardinal all rolled into one!" Leonardo couldn't see the person he was talking to, but he soon realized it must be an elderly lady, from the way she laughed and coughed as the doorman went on: "You were right to bring your chair here, it's the best spot in all Rome: even on the coldest winter days you can sit here in the sun as if it were high summer."

Leonardo knew this only too well, and was tempted to go out again and wait in the sunshine, but he feared the wilting effect of the sun on his enthusiasm, and since in reality he had no real reason to see the Cardinal, he had already begun to ask himself: What am I doing here? What do I have in common with that paradox-mad old lecher? Nothing. So why didn't I stay home? Why, indeed, but here he was, and he was beginning to hope that the Cardinal would have no time for him, because this would allow him to go home and say he hadn't found his cousin, or had found him and had made an appointment for five, any useful lie, or even no lie at all: his presence would make Mary so happy that with her sitting beside him he might even handle all the knives and forks and ask her advice in case things became too difficult.

Five minutes passed, then ten, and winter seemed to claim even that single chair on which he was sitting, so he bundled himself up in his overcoat, hid each hand up the sleeve of the other arm and closed his eyes. After a minute of this he got up from his bed and closed the window, then went back to bed. But still his legs felt cold, so he mumbled: "Stop pulling the blanket away, Adriana. I want to sleep, too." But he had hardly finished saying this, when he found himself back in Matera with Adriana in his bed, and the Prefect of Studies looking at him in horror, while all his classmates laughed. It was five in the morning, reveille was still ringing, his clothes had been taken away, Adriana was all naked, and the Prefect was taking out his whip.

"What's the matter? Are you ill?" asked the doorman.

"Nothing, nothing," said Leonardo, waking up. "Just a bad dream, I haven't slept all night, and I'm leaving tomorrow . . . never mind, it's nothing."

"Poor son," said the old lady who had been waiting outside, "you mustn't overdo it. You look very tired and pale. What is it?"

"Nothing, I assure you."

"I don't believe it, but I don't want to be indiscreet. Come out and wait in the sun, it's very cold in here." And she suddenly laughed.

Now Leonardo knew he must have been shouting in his nightmare; perhaps he had even called Adriana aloud, and he knew from his all too frequent experiences of the last few days that he was in real trouble again. But the kind lady realized this with that fine intuition only an Italian mother can have, and said: "Poor son, you must be sick, God knows what tribulations have brought you to see His Eminence, and here I am laughing at you. Please believe me, I wasn't making fun of you. . . . But I was very stupid, will you forgive me?"

This language was so new to him, and there was such real pain in
that voice, so much true humility, so much motherly care, that his
heart melted, and tears came into his eyes. He tried in vain to stop
but the shame of it all brought more self-pity welling up from his
heart, and down through his nose, and a first sob made itself heard
in his breath, which allowed the kind lady to open her arms and
take him in as a beloved, long-lost son. He cried abundantly on that
welcoming shoulder, slightly disgusted by the smell of old age,
which becomes funerary as it impregnates clothes, hats and hairpins: it is a mixture of last year's perspiration plus last year's cleaning fluids and mothballs, plus this year's perfumes aimed at killing
them all, but since you can't kill dead things the smells of yesteryear
come back like horrid ghosts to make old people more disgusting
when they are clean than when they are dirty.

The doorman had withdrawn from the scene, not so much out of
respect, but because his lunch was arriving in the form of the classical plate hidden in the classical white napkin and carried by the
classical barefoot and starving street boy who runs errands for a
penny. But hidden though it was, the food spoke its own sweet
name into Leonardo's ears by way of his nostrils, saying: "*Porchetta*
is what I am, come and eat me if you can."

As if to make this message even more painful, the old lady kept
saying: "Poor son, poor son," while patting Leonardo on the back
to make him stop crying.

Leonardo finally emerged from his miserable tearbath completely
refreshed with his hopes restored, but again he couldn't name the
true reason for his hope; namely, the hope of a much better meal
upstairs, and with much better wines than the one he was now
being offered by the doorman. "*Vuól favorire?*"*

"No, thank you," he said. "I need a bit of sunshine; if His Eminence calls, I'll be here in the garden."

"Make yourself at home," said the doorman, sitting down at his
table, without paying the slightest attention to the elegant people
who were passing his desk on their way in or out, and this too made
Leonardo feel better, because it canceled every trace of his momentary weakness from the very air in this place. He was glad he had

* "Want to share?"

cried and was grateful to the old lady, but no more than the soil is grateful to the raincloud, once the sun shines again. Alas, he hadn't reckoned with a widow and a mother, who probably hadn't held a man (let alone a weeping man) in her arms for so long, not to grab the occasion and hold on to it with all the strength of her own silent despair. Too proud to cry herself, she was grateful to him for shedding tears in her presence, something he realized too late for his own good: this was his own mother reborn, and if there was any gratitude left in him by now, it was to God for having put an end to her long illness. He had cried then, too, for false reasons: not so much her departure, as the slow fading away of all his hopes of becoming a professor of clinical medicine, as he spent days and nights and months and years by her bedside.

"Look out, look out, there's a puddle there, don't wet your feet," she chanted, running with tiny tottering steps behind him and coughing miserably as she ran.

"Thank you, thank you, I've seen it," he chanted back, trying to put as much affection into his chanting as he had put into his sobs, but sobs come richly and for free, like rain in spring, while gratitude comes hard and costs dear.

"You're walking so (cough, cough) fast. . . . Too (cough, cough) fast for (cough) me . . ."

"Sorry," he said, and slowed down.

"I didn't . . . (cough) mean to interfere. . . . I just wanted to explain why I was laughing earlier. You see, the doorman said: 'The winter is more French than the French.' He keeps forgetting that I'm French, I'm not Italian."

"Oh? You don't sound French at all."

"Because I was born here, and my father was born here, but we're French. My grandfather came here with Napoleon, unwillingly, I want you to know, because he was for the old regime. La Vieille France. And so of course was his brother, the famous Monsignor Bienaimé, who became Cardinal *in pectore*, but never in the open, because the Pope died of a heart attack just as he was about to dictate the Monsignor's name for the new list. As we say in French: C'EST LA VIE."

"Italy owes a great deal to France."

"You're the first Italian ever to say such a thing. Thank you."

"Well, I always try to give everyone his due. We are the Latin
Sisters: Italy and France."

"How true. But try to make the Italians see this. They stubbornly
refuse. Have you known the Cardinal long?" She was observing his
fur coat.

"Oh," he said, trying hard to remember, "let's see . . . it feels as
if I've known him all my life. Which isn't true, of course, but he is
such a remarkable person."

"Remarkable is not the word. A saint."

"Exactly!"

"And not just ANY saint. A very great saint."

Leonardo was so hungry and so impatient to get back to his own
new family of worshippers that he would have gone on with this
orgy of stupidity by answering: "Yes, a French saint is what you
mean," but luckily or unluckily for him, someone else in the garden
was extolling the Cardinal in terms that made the old lady sound
reserved. "I tell you, the Cardinal is an absolute genius," said this
new voice, which Leonardo recognized and hated at once, "the
greatest mind that ever was, and I can prove it to you: he agrees
with me. When I gave him your project to read, he said: Let me see
this worthy priest, I want to tell him what I think of this idea."

And the priest thus addressed answered with a priestly voice:
"That's all very fine, my young friend, but my previous experiences
with him don't confirm your enthusiasm. I have always found him
narrow-minded, nasty—in a word: French."

"Oh, I know, you don't have to tell me, there is French and
French: he is my grandfather's cousin, he's an exception, he belongs
to the highest French aristocracy. I'm half French too, after all, and
look at me—would you call me narrow-minded?"

"You?" asked the priestly voice with even greater priestliness.
"You have an open mind, you are like me; in fact, you remind me
of myself as a young man. . . ."

Leonardo turned around, saying: "I know that young man," just
as the old lady did the same, saying: "I know that priest: he's my
father confessor." They walked towards the entrance hall as fast as
they could to make sure that the doorman wouldn't let the newcomers pass through first, but they didn't succeed, and all they saw
were two backs disappearing into the arch of a very steep staircase.

"Too bad," said the old lady, shaking her head in resignation.

"Too bad, my foot," shouted Leonardo, staring angrily at the doorman, who was picking his teeth and chewing whatever bits of meat he could still dislodge from the cavities. "We were here first, and we both have urgent business: why did you let those two in ahead of us?"

Without saying a word, because he was too busy making horrible salivating, sucking noises with his tongue, the doorman picked up three large silver coins from the desk, showed them to Leonardo before putting them into his pocket, and finally remarked by way of comment: "As you can see, they had urgent business too."

"Don't worry," said the old lady, laying her hand on Leonardo's sleeve. "I can wait, your business is more urgent than mine."

"Oh no, no, I can wait, my business isn't urgent at all, only a bit long, and I would hate you to have to wait for me, you go first. I'll take another short walk in the garden."

"What an excellent idea, I'll go with you," she said, but he moved faster this time and didn't stop until he found himself protected by a huge oak and a thick wall, from behind which he could see the old lady in the distance, and while she searched for him in vain, he relieved himself and decided that in any case the Cardinal would not be free to have lunch before having dismissed Monsignor Tegolani and that arrogant German count who had toasted Mary on red wine and been so badly treated by Mommsen.

What a beautiful garden it was. . . . What gigantic trees, what abundance of flowerbeds, fountains, birds in the new foliage, clouds in the sky . . . these were not like the clouds of Apulia: these were shaped by Bernini or Michelangelo, to decorate views of baroque Rome. . . . If only we could spend the rest of our lives in this beautiful city . . . I could work in a hospital here and do all my research work at the university, and we could live in Madame Morosoff's villa, eating peas and cabbage for free . . . and Adriana could live with us. . . . An important man like the Cardinal must have ways of getting around the law; he could give us our divorces with the full consent of the Pope. Another reason for my coming to see him.

With these pleasant thoughts in mind, he went back into the

villa and reached the old lady just as she was slowly beginning to climb the stairs. Could he refuse to help her?

"Oh, how kind of you," she said, "but you are in a hurry, and I am so slow that by the time I get to the top, you'll have told your long story to His Eminence. . . ."

"Oh no, my story is much longer than that, and besides, I could never let you climb without my help."

"Oh, how I wish my own son were like you," she said, sighing.

"I'm quite sure you have no reason to complain about your son."

"You're right, he's wonderful, but I so rarely see him."

Because he was free of his own mother, he felt he could afford to be filial to this one, and loyal to her son, whoever he might be, by preserving his indifference as a superior form of affection.

"Your son must think of you all the time, and if he doesn't boast about you, it is out of sheer modesty and respect."

"How can you tell? Do you know him?"

"I feel it. Observing you is sufficient—I am a doctor and the mayor of a large town, thirty thousand inhabitants—to know that the son of such a woman can only be a good man." She embraced him again, now weeping herself, which instantly filled him with a deep sense of shame for his own earlier weakness. He knew now, for the first time in his life, how disgusting it is to be seen crying by people who are not themselves in a similar state. But now every thing was different, and he suddenly understood why: not Mary, but the promise of a new life of scientific research, that supreme luxury of the mind inaccessible to him until this very morning, when his new friend Schultz had first spoken to him about it. . . . "Madame," he said, patting her on the back so that she would stop crying, "Madame, your son wouldn't want you to indulge this kind of weakness. Please control yourself: you have no reason to cry, if the people you love are all alive and in good health. Are they? That is the question to ask, and if the answer is in the affirmative, then your tears are displeasing to God, or, in correct terminology, tempting to the fates, who are superior to the gods, as everybody knows."

These words had a most unexpected effect on the old lady. She recoiled from him, disentangling her arm, and made several signs of the cross, mumbling prayers to herself. Then she addressed him in horror: "A freethinker? An atheist? A reader of Renan? Don't you come near me. . . ."

"Madame," he said, in the same quiet voice he had used with his mother on similar occasions, after similar remarks, "when I speak of the fates, I speak of God the Father, and when I speak of the gods, I speak of Jesus Christ, who believed that His father had forsaken Him; please rest assured that I am not here to harm you, but neither am I here to discuss intricate questions of theology. Come, let me help you up this staircase."

Quietly, like a scolded child, she accepted his arm and climbed a few more steps, until they reached the landing and stopped to have a look at the view.

The large window was open on the most grandiose view of Rome imaginable. In front, the two belfries of the baroque church of Santa Trinità dei Monti, almost exactly aligned, so that one seemed an extension of the other in a curious optical illusion—and behind it, echoing behind the garden separated by a thick wall from the panoramic road and the fountain and the obelisk Leonardo had admired in moonlight only yesterday, another and most delicate of gardens, with green lawns and romantic benches covered with ivy leaves. Ancient cypresses showed their naked torsos way up into the thick of their fresh green manes, and there were oak trees even rougher and older, their manes even thicker: trees that had grown into living fossils, still transmitting life to the tenderest branches way up in the sky, columns therefore, not trees, parts of a temple that had not been destroyed or put to a different use after the fall of an ancient religion: still the same temple serving the same heathen gods under the noses of Cardinals and Popes and parish priests, and, what seemed more surprising, with their knowing consent. There were monks, churchmen from many countries, nuns from the Sacred Heart and a sprinkling of Cardinals coming and going among the trees and benches, mixing freely with French artists from the academy and their shapely Roman models; here and there he saw society ladies with their long white gloves and fluffy parasols and their morning-coated suitors in tall cylinder hats or casual English berets.

Beyond this metropolitan "nature," what one saw of the city was like a formal garden of stones, invaded here and there by bits of private "nature": the roof gardens of Rome, so many of them, so small and yet so rustic, real vegetable gardens and vineyards with tiny peasant houses half hidden by new seedlings and shrubs, the whole thing perched on top of somber rocks: Roman palaces with the deep crevices around them; the Roman streets. And in those streets, fountains of all sizes and voices, a distant chorus, louder at times than Roman church bells. Even the Cupolone looked like a fountain in the blue midday haze.

"Look at all this, just look, and thank the Almighty for such glory!"

"Yes, yes," she said, "the world is beautiful, but life is not."

What a bore, he thought, trying to locate the roof under which Mary was now thinking of him. He found it, and could not keep this discovery to himself. "There's Via Gregoriana, you see? And that roof with those vines and those tables and chairs, that's the top of number forty-two."

She looked at him in terror, which he didn't notice, but he did notice her silence, and it bothered him. "Aren't I good at recognizing places in a big city like this?"

"Yes, yes."

"From every single window in the palace you can see the Cupolone."

"Holy Mother of God, have mercy on us sinners," she sighed, and repeated the whole thing under her breath, in Latin, with closed eyes. When the prayer was finished, she said: "The trouble with my son is that he is married to a terrible woman."

"Aren't we all?" he said cheerfully.

"My poor husband wasn't."

"I mean present company excluded, of course."

She said nothing, but he knew she was hurt by his blunder, so he tried to correct it by saying: "Those we have loved are more present to us after they have departed. My poor mother is more present to me now than at any time in the past . . . and yet, I was constantly near her."

"You are married," she said, staring at his wedding ring.

"I was," he said, bracing himself to tell the whole truth, "but . . ."

"I understand. A widower."

He didn't answer, but for the first time in his life, he felt that he wasn't compelled to explain.

"Any children?"

"No."

"Well, in a way . . ." She interrupted herself to look at a man in the park who was waving at her, then, with a very sad smile: "I'm sorry, for a moment I thought that was my son. He must be waving at you."

"At me? No, I don't know him."

But the man had recognized him, and when he called, Leonardo recognized his voice: it was the crazy American sculptor, who was shouting: "See you at Mary's for lunch."

"No," he shouted back, "I must see someone here."

"Oh," shouted Hazeltine, "you know where to find the best cooking in Rome. Give my love to the Cardinal." And he was gone, running after a young woman on her way out of the garden.

They reached the top floor, and from there a much steeper and narrower flight of stairs led them to the attic where the Cardinal lived. They were received by a French priest; Leonardo realized that the old lady's French was almost as bad as his own, but she insisted on speaking it, and the young priest insisted on repeating her questions in Italian: "You want to know if His Eminence remembers he had an appointment with you. His Eminence does." More of her French, then: "Yes, Madame, I think I understand. You want to know if there will be enough time for you too. I can assure you that His Eminence finds time for everybody. Please be seated here in this room. His Eminence will be here in a minute."

They were led into a very large library with a low ceiling and windows almost to floor level. From the next room came the voice of the young German, speaking French, followed by the Cardinal's voice sounding particularly sharp: "My young German grand-nephew and cousin and whatever else he is thinks that you and I need an interpreter, but we do not: neither interpreters, nor professors of theology, don't you agree, Monsignor Tegolani?"

"Of course, of course, Your Eminence. But it's the enthusiasm of youth that makes Count Sandroxyll so . . . eloquent."

"Eloquence is not the word I would use. Nor enthusiasm. Arrogance, rather, and verbosity, both typical of the young, but not of all who are young. Only of the uneducated young. Yet I know he received an excellent education both from his mother and from his tutor, let alone his grandfather, who was truly a great scholar. Though obviously it wasn't *such* a good education, if the results are so poor. Anyway, he claims that you seem to be shocked by my repeated rejection of your pet project, because it means that I don't want the public to pity Our Lord and Savior in His hour of torture and crucifixion."

"No no no no, Your Eminence," stuttered the Monsignor, "this isn't, this isn't, this isn't at all what I said, oh no, no, no, young man, I mean sir Count, not at all, not at all, I never said that."

"Oh, but you did, don't lie," shouted the Count, and the Cardinal stopped him: "Come now, what's this? How dare you talk that way to a priest? Apologize to him at once, and allow me to answer him." There was a murmur of apology from the Count, followed by more stammering sounds from the Monsignor, then the Cardinal's voice was heard again: "Of course I'm against the Passion Play as a form of religious education, and I particularly detest the Bavarian Passion Play that you seem to find so uplifting. And of course I don't want the public to be feeling pity for Our Lord and Savior, tortured and crucified by His enemies. This is perfectly true, and I owe you an explanation: in my opinion, it is not the drama of Christ, but of His enemies, and our pity belongs to them if we want to be His disciples. We cannot pity Him *and* want to be like Him. The crucifixion was His triumph: what right do we have to weep for Him? Wouldn't we rather weep for Judas, Peter or Pilate, who betrayed Him, each in his own way? His enemies deserve pity because they are shadows, dust, the absence of light. He is the opposite of all these things, and having said that much let me add that your concern was not in the least religious but overtly political, because you wanted an Italian Passion Play financed by the French government, to counteract the Bavarian Passion Play, which is propaganda for Germany. Much as I am committed to defending the interests of my country, I do so only because German arrogance is far worse than our own. An alliance between German culture and Italian ignorance would spell the end of the civilized world as we have known it. Good day."

The door was suddenly flung open, and a very red-faced Monsignor Tegolani emerged, followed by a very red-faced Count Sandroxyll; their dual embarrassment seemed even greater when they saw Leonardo and the old lady. Leonardo's reaction was cruel: he smiled and said, "Great man, the Cardinal," as if expecting them to agree with him, so of course they hastened their flight, but the old lady's reaction stopped them in their tracks. She seemed to want to embrace them, so they both tried to shake hands with her. The Monsignor had precedence, but as he didn't let go of her hand after shaking it, the Count grabbed her other hand and shook it independently, then held it against his heart, and the Monsignor did the same.

"What is this?" asked the Cardinal, suddenly appearing in the doorway.

No one dared answer him; all eyes, except Leonardo's, were looking down at the floor.

"Is the Monsignor your father confessor?" asked the Cardinal, and the old lady whispered, "Yes, Your Eminence."

"Very well. Do you want to go with him, or do you want to talk to me first?"

"If I may have one second with Your Eminence . . ." She kept looking at the Monsignor for approval.

"Please go, don't mind me," said he, bowing out and dragging the Count with him. The French priest had disappeared, so they opened the door by themselves and the usual comedy began: "You first, Count."

"No, Monsignor, after you."

The Cardinal became angry: "Monsignor Tegolani, it is for you to go first, and you, Achaz, close the door. We're freezing." Then, to Leonardo, still very angrily: "What do you want here?"

"Nothing. Only to give you good news."

"Your good news can wait. Make yourself at home. And you, Madame, wait for me in here, or wait for me in there. I must talk to my cook, but I'll be back in a minute."

He disappeared through a red curtain that hung behind a red chair, and, as Leonardo heard a door being opened and closed, he knew that Hazeltine was right: a scent of cooking came from there, so delicious that he had to close his eyes and sit down because he

felt faint. When the Cardinal came back, Leonardo didn't even
open his eyes; he did so only after he heard the Cardinal closing the
door and beginning a conversation with the old lady. But his hunger
was still unbearable, so he tried to concentrate on something—anything—else. He began to observe the room. Its apparent disorder
concealed a secret order of precedence, both in time and space, but
more especially in elements unclassified because unknown, such as
the processes of thought co-existing with those of physiology—
which, as Leonardo knew only too well, are knowable only in their
definitions, not their essence. Even the books, all neatly classified by
subject on their shelves, became entangled in this other network the
moment they were taken off the shelf and placed on the desk with
books from totally unrelated subjects and shelves: it was clear that
they belonged together in some mysterious climate of thought,
which itself was subject to hours, lights and smells even, and most
certainly to different organic impulses, but for what reasons and by
what magic agencies was unknown to anyone but the Cardinal
himself.

This network of orders constituted a natural defense against outside intrusions, much as the dry weeds on a beach hold it together
and allow it to grow dunes, defending it against the onslaught of the
sea. How much more manly and intelligent and dignified this apparent disorder than the all too apparent order in Mary's library.
Here, under the Cardinal's eye, even a speck of dust had its reason
to live and multiply, if its removal threatened the order of some
island of thought on the desk. And yet elsewhere, not only on the
shelves, but on that very desk as well, there was clear evidence that a
hand had passed with a cloth and furniture polish. It was obvious
from these signs that no lighthearted observation, no stupid paradox
could enter that world and make its home without being detected
and questioned at once in the light of older theories or observations,
which had more force even now after tens of centuries, than any
revolutionary thought invented yesterday. In Mary's house this tight
control did not exist, because most of her books had never been
touched, except once a day by the Servants In Charge. Mary and
her mother knew why they wanted those books in their house, but
didn't know *how* to want them, there was never any time, any

climate of thought, because they only tolerated their own climate, in fact, they made it and unmade it, and changed it every day, every hour of every day. . . .

The minutes passed. He looked at his watch, and was frightened to realize that for the first time since his father's death, it had stopped. He had simply forgotten to wind it the previous evening, or that same morning, as he usually did, when (rarely enough) he forgot to do so before going to bed. Had his life really changed so much? A superstitious fear stilled his hunger for a moment; images of a lone belfry in a city destroyed by an earthquake, marking the hour of its death; images of a dead landowner at the bottom of a precipice, his watch marking the hour of his death: the only clue by which his murderers could be found, and the police never caught them; other such images of the life he had known in the time of that watch, and now the watch was dead. He knew this must have been the moment he had left his previous life behind forever. The Rubicon. Yes, Adriana had mentioned it at the very moment he would usually look at his watch in the morning.

Suddenly, a timid knock on the door, the door from the kitchen: how was it possible? But he didn't have to wait long: a yellow face surrounded by white hair from top to bottom appeared trembling from inside the folds of the red curtain, like the stage manager in all provincial theaters to see if the audience is thick enough to warrant the raising of the curtain.

"May I come in?" asked the old gentleman in a gentlemanly whisper.

"Of course," said Leonardo. "I'm not the master here."

"Oh, I know you're not the master here, but then you must be a friend. No one ever is allowed to stay alone in this room unless he's one of us. May I introduce myself? Amedeo Mauri."

"Amedeo Mauri? Not THE Amedeo Mauri? . . ." Leonardo had suddenly recognized the face of the famous physician he had seen, week after week, in the illustrated magazines, after Mauri's son had murdered a young woman and been jailed for life. Had anyone told Leonardo he was going to find himself alone in the same room with Mauri, he would have said: "These things only happen in fairy tales." Meantime, Mauri had taken it for granted that his name would cause some wonderment, and had simply sat down at the

desk, and put his hand on one of the towers of books representing a
"moment of order," and begun to dismantle it like an expert watch-
maker who fumbles with a watch, unscrews all the tiny wheels and
lets them fall out, knowing he can put them together again in a
minute. Finally, Leonardo cleared his throat and said: "I am a
physician, graduated in 1893 from the University of Naples, *summa
cum laude*. I wrote my dissertation with Rummo, I studied your
lectures and know them still by heart."

In great confusion Mauri let the delicate mechanism collapse on
the table and said: "Rummo? A pupil of Rummo? How is my
master Rummo?"

"I don't know, I haven't seen him for years, he wanted me to go
on working with him and become a professor of clinical medicine,
but circumstances prevented me from returning to Naples from my
home village, and that's where I remained, a modest country
doctor."

"The best thing that—"

"One moment, let me finish: Rummo always spoke of you as *his*
master. He used to interrupt his lectures in anguish and say: 'I
wonder what my master Mauri would say about this hypothesis.
Remember, this is not his idea, but my modest way of groping in
the dark, in search of him.'"

A bright smile made the old man's face suddenly young. "How
silly, but how delightful. And how typical of my master's modesty:
what does a difference of forty years matter in our field, or in any
field, for that matter? Now, for example, Biscard is also my master,
and yet he considers me *his* master. We have come to the conclusion that we are both pupils of Empedocles. . . ."

"Empedocles? But he has always been MY master."

"Then that makes three of us."

"But who's Biscard?"

"Oh, you don't know? I'm surprised. Biscard is his intimates'
nickname for Bistolphe, Cardinal d'Escarande—I mean his bookish
intimates, not his society intimates. He has a taste for frivolity,
which is, in my opinion, as much part of his scientific mind as his
huge culture, but very few people have the faintest notion of *that*
except of course for those who exploit his mind, as I do all the time.
But before I show you some of his immense scientific work, let me

finish my sentence, the one you interrupted to tell me about
Rummo's devotion—and I am glad you did—but all the same, what
I wanted to tell you is this: Don't complain that you are a country
doctor; it is the safest role for a scientist today, because the problems remain what they are, as they recur in all their tragic entirety,
day after day, while in hospitals and laboratories, young physicians
have too many magazines to read, and I mean boring clinical magazines, with boring learned articles, and their minds are led astray.
After only two years of this, they begin to feel that unless they
become discoverers of a new bacillus, like Koch, or a new substance,
like Curie, they are not real, modern doctors. Nonsense. These
people live in the moon. The world is not a laboratory, rather its
opposite, chaos, and if a young physician doesn't learn to cope with
chaos, in chaotic conditions, on chaotic people, he is not a real
doctor, but only a magician. Medicine in America already seems to
be oriented that way, and we Italians, with our provincial eagerness
to be part of the big city, the big Concert of Nations, are apt to
disregard the true medical practice of poverty, *on* poverty, *with very
poor means,* as being unworthy of our age. Go back to your village
as soon as you can."

"Oh, thank you, Professor. I believe you, and, in fact, I stayed in
my village as just that."

"Very good. Now let me show you Biscard's work. See this carton
under the table? It's full of tiny reference notes which, put together,
may constitute the magnum opus on the medicinal qualities of
herbs and the ways they were used in the neolithic age. He has
conducted his studies on peasants in France, China, India, Mo-
rocco, the Congo and South America, reconstructing a lost science
from whatever is still remembered as superstitious practice, and of
course no medical school would take him seriously today, but he
isn't even trying to become known, let alone accepted. He works for
the pure love of science and for his friends, provided their love of
science is as pure as his own. When I decided to disappear into total
oblivion, which you understand, I went to see Biscard, whom I had
known as a patient, and I became *his* patient, and finally his assistant. It saved not only my life, but my soul, or, as he likes to say, my
death. He is right. Isn't death our greatest blessing, if we know how
to face it? Now let me show you that carton there: in it you will

find anything you need to know about socialism, starting with the days of medieval Florence, but probably even earlier, I don't know, it isn't my subject. Our best scholars come here to replenish their minds or their own files. In that corner there, you see two cartons: the one on top contains files on the history of paintings in the Renaissance, the one below is all about Byzantium: art, history, law, religion, gossip. Here on the left of this desk, see this little drawer? Open it."

Leonardo opened it and found it full of coins—copper, silver, gold, Italian and foreign—and a few banknotes. "What's this?" he asked.

"Money. Any one of us who needs money comes here and takes what he needs. If he happens to make a lot of money, he will come here and fill the drawer. It's a bank, the One Hundred Percent Interest Bank, as he calls it. Nothing but interest fills it and nothing but interest empties it. Do you need some?"

"No, thank you," said Leonardo, blushing.

"Don't blush; if you are here, this is part of your oxygen. Does anyone deny you oxygen in the place where you live? Come on, have some."

"No no, I happen to be very rich at the moment. That is: my wife is rich. My future wife, I mean."

"Well, in that case you may wish to contribute."

"With pleasure, yes, but after my marriage, not today. In more correct terminology, my present state of solvency is not such as to justify extravagant projects."

"All right, all right, you've made your point, I'm sorry I mentioned it at all."

And with these words, Mauri withdrew into himself, as if Leonardo's answer had turned off a light. If he had looked like a luminous ghost before, now he looked like an alabaster statue.

I must have hurt his feelings, Leonardo thought, and tried to explain: "Professor Mauri?"

"Yes?"

"I didn't mean extravagant projects, I meant admirable, beautiful, very idealistic and, as such, highly commendable . . ."

"All right, all right, one more reason to help us, but don't tell _me_, tell your rich wife."

This time Mauri didn't look into his eyes, but examined his body, from the neck down to his calves, the whole length of his overcoat, then quickly glanced away in disapproval, and went on sorting his papers, as if he were all alone in the room.

Leonardo knew that look only too well: it reminded him of his own horrified expression when he detected the unmistakable signs of smallpox on the naked body of a patient.

He took off his overcoat and threw it angrily on a chair, while preparing a detailed explanation of the circumstances that had imposed such a strange garment upon him. He was also going to invoke the Cardinal's authority as a witness, but he didn't dare interrupt the great man in his work. A few seconds passed, then a few more, but the great man seemed to be more and more absorbed, so Leonardo cast a few rapid glances around at the rest of the room; without ever losing sight of that venerable head and those venerable hands on those venerable papers.

There was a large sofa in one corner, but it couldn't be used, because a frameless painting had been put on it, held in place by two reclining bronze vases. Two more paintings had been placed on the floor, and they blocked all access to the couch. Piles of books were keeping them from slipping, and it was obvious that the maid was never allowed to move them. Two comfortable armchairs were similarly occupied and surrounded by paintings held in place by yet more objects: bronze statuettes, porcelain vases, books. The walls were dirty, with clean patches where paintings had once been hanging, probably for many years; but then they must also have been gone for as many years, because dusty overcoats were now hanging on their nails. Empty cases with the names of French wines stamped on them were now obviously used as substitute chairs, because even the few chairs that existed were all occupied by books, some even by smaller paintings, balanced without any protection on top of the shaky pyramids. Leonardo was surprised that the room had seemed so splendid to him at first, and he concluded that his expectation had probably preceded him and transformed the place into a replica of the splendor he was accustomed to in Mary's house.

Suddenly the bell rang: a tiny silver bell placed over the door.

"Will you kindly open it?" asked Mauri, still without looking up from his work, and Leonardo obeyed. A tough, unshaven adolescent in shirtsleeves, with a filthy shepherd's hat and the typical *ciocie**on his naked feet and legs, pushed his way in. Leonardo grabbed him by the arm before he could advance any farther, saying: "Just a moment, what do you want here?"

"And who the hell are you?" asked the adolescent, rolling up his left sleeve with his right hand and clenching his big fist for the blow, while Leonardo withdrew in great haste.

"Oh, Giovanni, come in, come in," said Mauri without lifting his head, and Giovanni, tamed like a dog that has heard his master's voice, gave Leonardo a friendly pat on the back and moved over to the desk, saying: "Hey you, don't work so hard. Any cash for me?"

"Don't take it all, Giovanni, you know Biscard doesn't like it."

"But I'm hungry."

"Go to the kitchen and eat. Here, five lire for you."

"Ten."

"Six. Not one cent more. You took some yesterday when I wasn't here."

"I spent it all."

Giovanni pocketed the money and squeezed himself through behind the professor's chair, then lifted the red curtain, causing another whiff of divine aromas to invade the place, and disappeared, to reappear a minute later holding a leg of lamb, which he began to chew. A tiny old woman with glasses appeared suddenly from behind the curtain, shouting angry words in French, but Giovanni had already reached the center of the room, and, before leaving again with his loot, he stuck it under Leonardo's nose and said: "Want some?" Then, laughing at Leonardo's pale face, he took a second bite at the meat, and ran out of the room without saying goodbye.

"That's Giovanni," said Mauri, chuckling, but still without interrupting his work; then, hearing voices on the landing, he asked: "Is the door open?"

"No, I'll open it," said Leonardo, hiding behind the door as he

---

* *Ciocia* (plural *ciocie*): ancient Roman footwear. Ciociaria is now the name of the region where the Ciociari live.

did so. This time it was Donna Ersilia, followed by a tall and very elegant-looking young man. They went straight to the desk, and Mauri rose from his seat to greet them with delight.

"My nephew, Leone Caetani," she said. Mauri seemed very pleased.

"How wonderful. So you're going to read us your paper on the history of Arabic medicine."

"It would be pointless. Biscard knows more about it than I do."

"Nonsense, he was telling me yesterday that—" There was a sudden interruption, caused by Donna Ersilia's frightened gasp as she saw Leonardo.

"We must leave at once," she said. "I refuse to stay in the same room with that creature. The Cardinal should have warned me." And without listening to her nephew's protests, she bustled out as she had come, so all he could do was let her go and shrug his shoulders.

"Well, you have enemies in high society," said Mauri, laughing. "That's a good recommendation, although I like that woman, in spite of her intellectual manias."

"It's not my fault at all," said Leonardo, with a tremor in his voice, "I can explain . . ." But now people were streaming in—six young men who looked like poor university students, and a short, angry-looking red-haired young man, whom Leonardo for a brief instant mistook for Mary's husband, but he was immediately re-assured and cheered as he heard the young man speak in his own Apulian accent: "Hey, Mauri, what are you studying today?"

"Oh, I'm just . . ."

"Whaaaat?" shouted the young Apulian, staring at Leonardo's overcoat on the chair: "Who the fuck owns a sable-lined overcoat here?"

"Goombà, let me explain," said Leonardo, coming towards the man, arms open for a brotherly embrace, but before he could speak another word, the young man shouted: "My name is Gaetano Salvemini. What's yours?"

"Salvemini? The Marxist?" These words, spoken in terror, might alone have sufficed to brief Salvemini on the nature of his "goombà," but Leonardo's frightened eyes left no doubt as to his feelings, and thus, before he could think of anything else to say,

Salvemini was shouting and rolling his eyes exactly like another
Leonardo, but an Old Testament Leonardo, not one mollified and
rendered more understanding by the Gospels (Sophie's good tidings
in his favor): "I have no desire to break bread with rich landowners
who starve my people and deny them an aqueduct!" Whereupon he
turned his back on Leonardo and walked proudly downstage to
thank his silent audience with silent little gestures of the head for
their silent little gestures of approval. Leonardo was so thunderstruck by this ghost of his recent, uncompromising self, that he
paled and gasped for air, but no one noticed him, and what he
heard next from the very mouth of his revered master confused him
even further: "Ladies and gentlemen," said Mauri, "before we hear
our Socialist speaker explain to us why his native Apulia is so politically backward and still without water, we shall hear Prince Leone
Caetani on the subject of Arabic medicine." But Leonardo jumped
up like a lion, shouting: "I alone here can speak for Apulia, because
I came to Rome officially, as mayor of my hometown, on invitation
from the Senate of the Kingdom." "Shut up, Cafone!" shouted
Salvemini, and everybody laughed. Leonardo slumped into his chair.
Caetani's voice reached him as the joyous cries of children playing
in a schoolyard may reach a convict in the nearby jail. "Ladies and
gentlemen, Arabic medicine is hardly a fit subject for today's reunion: that place is reserved for medieval cooking, as your noses
have already told you. We are about to eat the very delicacy which
would have sent Pope Martin the Fourth to hell, together with the
Florentine banker Ciacco and several other famous gluttons, but for
Dante's weird sense of justice. He placed Pope Martin comfortably
in Purgatory and tells us of him only that 'He came from Tours,
had the whole church on his arms, and is atoning here by severe
fasting for the eels of Bolsena and the Vernaccia.' An ancient
chronicle explains Dante's reference as follows: 'Pope Martin,
former treasurer of the cathedral of Tours in the land of Brie' (we
are also going to have an excellent Brie, I hear from Luisette, the
cook), 'was very sinful in matters of gluttony. He loved eels fished
from the lake of Bolsena and liked to see them drown in Vernaccia
wine, then had them roasted, and ate them, and he was so solicitous
of that taste that he asked for them all the time, and even had them
drowned and roasted in his own bedroom. He had no table manners

nor knew any limits to his gluttony, and when he was completely
bloated and unable to move, he used to say: *O Sanctus Deus,
quanta mala patimur pro Ecclesia Sancta Dei. . . .'** At his death,
the following verses were composed in his honor:

> *Gaudent anguille,*
> *quia mortuus hic jacet ille*
> *Qui quasi morte reas*
> *ecoriabat eas*

(let the eels rejoice because here lies dead he who . . . er . . .
skinned those sinners alive)."

Roars of laughter greeted this reading, and Leonardo was feeling
even more abandoned in his corner, when, to his great surprise,
Prince Caetani came over to him and asked, very politely, showing
him the document he had just read: "Do you by any chance know
the correct translation for the whole verse?"

Leonardo looked at it, hoping to God that his famous proficiency
in Latin might lead him to victory against the hated Salvemini, but
he too was baffled by that ablative floating in the void, and he
began to blush and stutter like a schoolboy in front of his teacher.
Salvemini sneered and his audience followed suit, but Caetani
seemed determined to help him and said, ever more politely: "I
suppose none of us can . . . but let me ask your opinion: what do
you think of this as a present for Biscard? It does look like a page
from an ancient missal with all that gold lettering and parchment
and illuminated decoration, doesn't it? Do you think he'll like it?"
Leonardo was so overwhelmed he couldn't utter a word for the
lump in his throat. He nodded, restraining an impulse to throw
himself at the feet of this great prince and say, "I am your humblest
subject and you are my king." But he didn't have to; the truly regal
behavior of the Prince was universally interpreted as an order to
follow his example and accept him into the group. Except, that is,
for Salvemini, who continued to growl like a dog. When he saw
that his growling wasn't impressing anyone, he barked, "On with

---

* O Holy God, how many ills must we suffer for the sake of Thy Holy
Church. . . .

the meeting! ᴅᴏ you or ᴅᴏɴ'ᴛ you want to hear about the woes of my people?"

They all did, even the Prince, who abandoned his newly acquired subject to rally obediently to his revolutionary overlord. And the overlord snarled:

"The real tragedy of Apulia is this: that we, the Socialists, the *only* ones who can help these poor wretches by teaching them a bit of good English-style Socialism, are prevented from doing so—not by the police, the army or even the sable-coated thieves, but by the poor wretches themselves!!! Try to tell them that they have rights, that feudalism ended in seventeen eighty-nine, they will laugh in your face and tell you you're living in the moon. Why? Because slavery is normalcy to them. Eight centuries ago the Popes gave us the appalling feudalism which is still intact today, and no railroads, no telegraph, no telephone, no modern science can destroy it. And yet before then, under the Swabs and the Normans, the nobility and the clergy were strictly controlled, even *oppressed* by the king, who defended his people against his own courtiers, and the small landholder thrived. The population was larger than it is today, we had hospitals, we had aqueducts, and today we have neither."

Leonardo was beaming, but no one noticed.

"In the rest of Europe the feudal class has gradually lost its privileges to the rising bourgeoisie, thanks to a flood of new religious and philosophical ideas. But no such thing happened in our stagnant world under the Sablecoats. Changes came frequently, very frequently indeed, but only in the form of foreign invasions, and the only things that were allowed to change—such as the name and language of the new king—changed *nothing* in the terrible lives of the poor. The sable-coated guardians of their poverty saw to it that the tradition of ignorance and resignation was kept intact. They ᴀʟᴡᴀʏs betrayed king and country, if the foreign invader seemed strong enough to warrant the risk, and offered him their services before he could ever give battle. Which the foreign invader found extremely convenient, and so did they, because this allowed them to maintain the position their families had occupied for centuries. Thus they served the Durazzos, the Anjous, the French, the Spaniards, the Austrians, the Bourbons, Napoleon, then the Bourbons again, and now the Savoys. And if we Socialists should win tomorrow in the North, we would find in the South a ready-made Socialist regime, complete with all the verbal trimmings and theories, under the control of the selfsame reactionary Mafia of landowners and priests who have sucked the lifeblood of the poor for eight centuries."

"I agree with you one hundred percent," shouted Leonardo, "because now at long last I'm on your side, although . . ." He couldn't continue; his words were drowned in an explosion of laughter. When the laughter died down, Salvemini pointed at him. "Didn't I tell you? Ten minutes ago, to this noble landowner, I was a dirty Marxist!"

"I am not a noble landowner, I'm an impoverished, bourgeois landowner, and I still hate and despise you, you Marxist hoodlum. I've read your antipatriotic writings and I've seen your disruptive pranks and criminal vandalism with my own eyes in the classrooms of the University of Naples, when I was there on my father's last pennies trying to do some serious work. I hate and loathe the Church, I hate and loathe the nobility, but I *devoutly* believe in the *nobility* of work, in the *nobility* of my medical calling, and I stoutly defend all of my *noble* colleagues who, instead of taking to political subversion, rose from abject poverty to the heights of the liberal professions!"

"They are the worst!" shouted Salvemini, trying to recapture his audience from a triumphant Leonardo.

"Why the worst?" asked Caetani.

"Because they are the most reactionary exploiters of the poor, the most capitalistic capitalists. . . ."

Leonardo had taken the floor, and was brandishing a rolled up manuscript as a stick in Salvemini's face: "*This* is the speech *I* delivered in the Senate three days ago, attacking the Church and the landowners and the learned archaeologists who expropriate the poor to let Etruscan ghosts live in their houses."

"You did that?"

"That and much more!!! As mayor of Laterza, when someone denounces a poor farmer to me for destroying some Roman mosaic he found while tilling the soil, I denounce the Italian state to the denouncer and to the whole population, that's what I do."

"But then, Goombà, you're a Socialist at heart," said Salvemini, coming to him with open arms.

"Don't use that obscene word on me." Now it was Leonardo who was barking, in an exact replica of the earlier Salvemini.

"It's *you* who have used obscene words to me," barked Salvemini in return, "and I who have deliberately disregarded them. . . ." Then, to Caetani: "You be the judge."

"You are both wrong," was Caetani's haughty pronouncement. "But you, Gaetano, were wrong first for using words that are the fruit of advanced studies, which only your Socialist comrades understand. Right!" Caetani was now developing his verdict. "I for one cannot fathom why you, a university professor, should take such a violent stand against your own kind, calling them the worst capitalist exploiters of the poor when you know that they themselves are the poorest, most exploited and most generous public servants in the entire country."

Salvemini first swelled with anger, then exploded, but with a great smile that bared two lines of huge white teeth, making him look like a child: "It is disgusting!!" he shouted. "I thought that the five years I spent with all these loathsome Florentine aristocrats debating their loathsome ideas had at least taught me some of their good manners, but obviously I am *still* the same Apulian Cafone I was when I first got there. How disgusting of me! I apologize! This said, let me be brief and to the point: All the South, like all Gaul, is divided into Three Parts: large landed property, small landed property, and God's property, alias the sea, which, for the purposes of Socialist action amounts to nil, because the seafarers spend most of their time with the winds and the waves, have a language all their own, still count in Bourbon currency, and until they marry are mere floating scum, so their highest ambition is marriage, because that allows them to become captains at sea. The wife is taken, sight unseen, on Mamma's choice, seen once on the wedding day, then once a year every year after that. On the other hand, the Adriatic Sea is rich, and the seafarers don't fare badly. There is only one political cause they would be ready to die for: the yearly fiesta of their protectress, the Madonna of the Martyrs. Promise them we'd celebrate that fiesta twice a year, and they'd all become militant

Socialists in an instant. Now to the farmers. They don't live in the
country, they are day-laborers who walk miles to and from work, can
work only when it doesn't rain and are all starving. As are most of
their foremen. On to the big landowners, unwilling Socialists at
heart: here we have one of them, Prince Caetani, perhaps the only
one in the whole South. The others all hate us, and are driven by
fear—of learning anything new from books or from experience—
and by greed. They are infinitely greedier than the poor. For one
penny of profit they would starve the whole country, yet they themselves will *never* do a stitch of honest work. Instead, they all sit in
Parliament and in the Senate. What Italy needs is a big slash in the
military budget, a kick in the ass to the leeches in the Royal Palace,
the Royal Senate, and the Royal Parliament, and an intelligent,
English-type Socialism or American-type democracy. But do the
members of our learned proletariat understand the whole message?
No. They only understand that someone must be kicked in the ass,
and so they preach Socialism by attacking peaceful citizens, breaking windowpanes and smashing up classrooms in the universities of
Palermo and Naples, where, incidentally, I never spent one single
day of my life. They write obscenities on walls, they disrupt work in
libraries and laboratories, and the moment they go back to their
villages, they join the ranks of the Monarchist Party, or become
killers for the Mafia in the War Ministry, the Senate, the Parliament and, needless to say, the Vatican. Can you blame me for not
wanting these people in the ranks of our party? In eighteen ninety-
eight, when we opened a Socialist club in the town of Gravina,
hoping to win maybe twenty new members after weeks of solid
propaganda, we had one thousand applications on the very first day.
For once I was grateful to our murderer of a Prime Minister for
outlawing the club at once. But then in Bari, we made one mild
speech and again a thousand or so converts applied. How could they
all be sincere? These kinds of people are crooks, and we cannot
allow our party to become the last refuge for crooks! Thank God for
this member of the liberal professions who takes offense if anyone
calls him a Socialist . . . he is one, and to him goes my brotherly
embrace."

With these words, amid general applause, Salvemini embraced

and kissed Leonardo, who was not ashamed to let the emotion show as he thanked his new friends, especially Mauri, who had seemed so hostile until then. "Tell me how you fare as a doctor," said Mauri, while Salvemini was avidly reading Leonardo's speech to the Senate. "Badly," said Leonardo. "Twelve hundred lire a year and ten thousand poor to care for. My predecessors cured only the rich. Of course on election day someone takes care of the poor; that is, they get them drunk and take them by the coachload to vote for the Mafia candidate and if they don't vote as they're told, they're beaten to a pulp: that's where the doctor comes in. But after the elections, if a destitute goes to the doctor, he's thrown down the stairs. That's why I entered politics and became mayor, but I still spend most of my time caring for the poor. I let my two assistants take care of administrative matters, and then I review them."

"But this is exactly what Salvemini was describing in his famous study on the township of Molfetta. Haven't you read it?"

"I'm so busy, I have little time to read."

"Imbecile," said Mauri, pulling him gently by the ear. "Instead of coming to Rome and pleading with your enemies for an aqueduct you'll never get, you should read the Socialists' writings. Salvemini used that book and then his speeches in Parliament to propose that the state pay for two doctors per town at a salary of three thousand lire each on condition that they cure only the poor; after three years' probation the two doctors would hold office for life, so as to free them from all political temptation. The mayor would be required by law to control their performance."

"But that's wonderful!!!" Leonardo cried. "Let me go and thank him."

"But didn't you know that this is the law everywhere in Italy but in the South?"

"No, all I read in the papers was that the Socialists had an *unrealistic* project that would have turned the whole state into a philanthropic organization, and of course we can't afford it."

Mauri smiled and said: "I can tell what papers you've been reading. But let's talk to Salvemini. I have a project: I want you to become an agitator for the party in your town. With your wife's money you can do things that neither Salvemini nor I could ever hope to do."

This word "agitator" made Leonardo cringe, but two things were drawing him towards Salvemini: his smile as he read Leonardo's speech, and the fact that Luisette, the cook, was bringing out trays of tidbits which the crowd were already devouring.

But before they could interrupt Salvemini in his reading, he himself was interrupted by the sudden arrival of a hunchback monk with a long white beard, bare, dirty feet and worn-out sandals, followed by four young men, obviously students. As the students embraced Salvemini and kissed him, the monk (whom Salvemini had spurned with the same air of disgust Leonardo knew so well by now) straightened his back, lifted his heavy cassock over his head and threw it high in the air, revealing his undershirt and drawers, stripped off his beard and threw it onto Leonardo's overcoat, and finally removed his wig, to bare a youngish, clean-shaven head that brought shrieks of joyful recognition and embraces from the entire company, Salvemini included.

"He made it, he made it!!" they screamed until a door opened in the distance and the Cardinal's face appeared.

"Silence there!" he shouted, then closed his door again. Trousers, shirts and a jacket were instantly produced from under the overcoats that hung on nails along the wall, and thus, summarily reclothed, the young man was ready for Salvemini's anxious question. "Tell me all about Nicola." "No," said the former convict somberly. "I have no time. We must be on the next train to Geneva, but I'll write to you. What we need is warm overcoats and money." Instantly, money was produced from the drawer in the desk, and the few overcoats on the wall were hastily tried on by the five young men and accepted after using a windowpane as a mirror. "My cassock is warmer," said the ex-friar, "but I think the police have been alerted, so I'd better not use it."

This was Leonardo's great chance. Throwing the false beard on the floor, he came forward with his overcoat on his arm. "Take this," he said. But everybody laughed, and the young man rejected it impatiently, saying in a loud, angry voice: "Too expensive, can't afford it."

"But it's a present."

"Some nice present: I'm trying to escape from the police; this will get the entire police force after me."

"Why? On the contrary . . ."

The young man huffed with impatience. "Will *someone* explain to this rich idiot that if the police don't arrest me for looking like a thief, they'll be offering me unwavering protection from some imaginary one?"

Everyone laughed, and Salvemini intervened to say to Leonardo: "*Tu hai perduto il vizio e non riesci a perdere il pelo,*"* which brought down the house, leaving Leonardo worse off than he had been in that entire short hour.

After the five men were gone, Salvemini sought out Leonardo again.

"What's your name, by the way?"

"Leonardo Claudi."

"Not the great-nephew of that old sonofabitch Don Poseidone Navigabene?"

"Exactly, and he ruined your father, Don Ilarione Salvemini."

"He did not. The government did. Eight centuries of history did. But let's talk about your speech in the Senate. First of all, what's this name and address scribbled on the back of your manuscript?"

"It's the name of the Senator who invited me and the address of the Senate."

There was a long silence before Salvemini spoke. "This Senator is the greatest single enemy of your entire project and of all suffering Apulians, and the address is the address of the Hunter's Club, the most aristocratic club in Rome, so you actually harangued an assembly of dozing idiots, if not an empty room—which is just as well, because your sonorous, generous, onerous speech is the typical high school composition that gets the prize and a handshake from the prefect of police representing His Majesty the King. Shall we tear it up, as a symbolic act of your divorce from your former radical self?" And with these words, Salvemini tore the precious manuscript into shreds, and threw them into the wastebasket.

Leonardo felt the tearing noise rip his heart several times over.

---

* "You've lost the vice but can't lose the coat"—a reversal of the proverb: "The wolf loses its coat but not its vice."

He couldn't utter a sound, didn't dare lift his eyes from Salvemini's shoes, which, he noticed, were old and cracked beyond repair. He then observed Caetani's shoes, which looked better even than Bernhard's or Mr. Schultz's, and moved on to observe everyone else's shoes, and discovered that they all looked more or less as bad as Salvemini's.

In the distance, Salvemini's voice: "You members of the Radical Party are all angelic at heart, but stupid, because you fear any association with us as if we were the devil incarnate. You say here you are the mayor of a town of thirty thousand inhabitants. It isn't true: you are the mayor of a town inhabited by no more than a dozen or so women, perhaps a few male imbeciles, two or three priests and a few corpses—let's say two."

"Why do you have to insult Laterza?" he moaned, lifting his head again and looking Salvemini straight in the eye.

"I'm not insulting Laterza, nor its mayor. These are facts. Tell me: how many brothers and sisters do you have?"

"No brothers, only seven sisters."

"That makes seven instead of twelve female citizens. Their husbands don't count, and your wife doesn't count. Parents both dead?"

"Yes."

"Two corpses, I was right. How many priests?"

"One great-uncle."

"That's one too many. These are the people you must not hurt, whatever you do as mayor. The priest gave you the election, because he needed a decent front to keep fooling the illiterate population, and perhaps even the press, if some of his crimes come to the light. This allowed you to live in the moon, or in some fairy tale about yourself as the David who defeats Goliath. But Goliath, my poor friend, is not *one* giant, Goliath is billions of microbes that infest the air of Italy and make *you* drunk with romantic delusions that you can be an honest public servant while acting only as a private individual. Do you know the Greek term for a man who banishes the community from his actions and thoughts? IDIOTES; in German: *Privatmann*. Another fact, not an insult: IDIOT!!! This won't do, Goombà Leonardo, even if you have a rich wife to finance the

fairy tale for God knows how long. You heard me ask the fake
monk about Nicola. I'll tell you his story, and it's no fairy tale.
Nicola Barbato was the founder of the Sicilian *Fasci*. Before resorting to public action, he lived for years as a noble, upright citizen—
like you—until he realized that his honesty was being turned to
stupidity or even dishonesty in the hands of the state and the
Church, and would continue to be, unless he CREATED a public
of honest people acting and living as he did. He never killed anyone,
he only protested against the slow and premeditated murder prac-
ticed by the state, for which he earned fourteen years at hard labor
in the same jail from which those four students helped the false
monk escape. They couldn't help Barbato: he's kept in maximum
security, perhaps he's even dead, we don't know, I'll hear from
Geneva in a few days. . . . But you are going to join the Socialist
Party right now, and I'll make an exception of you, and let you run
for office, provided you—"

He was interrupted by the sudden arrival of the Cardinal, who
was trying to shelter the old lady from view; she was sobbing abundantly. Everyone backed away in reverent silence while the Cardinal
escorted the poor woman to the door, but when the door was closed
on her, faces brightened up again, throats were cleared and voices
began to circulate. "Biscard," said Leone Caetani, "two nights ago
we heard the tocsin from Saint Peter's. Unfortunately, it turned out
to have been one of the lesser Scagnozzi in the College of Cardinals, but it gave me the idea of presenting you with a certificate of
fitness to ascend the Throne of Saint Peter's, and here . . ."

"Just a moment," said the Cardinal, unsmiling. "I still have to see
this . . . *gentleman*," as if the word "gentleman" were coming to
him with an effort. And without even looking at Leonardo, he
pointed the way to the same door from which he had emerged with
the old lady.

Leonardo looked to Salvemini for help, but Salvemini seemed to
have turned to a pillar of salt. No one uttered a word, so the former
proud mayor of a town of thirty thousand inhabitants and orator to
the Senate of the Kingdom walked ahead of the Cardinal, like the
old high school student he had become again.

As if the many emotions of the last three days hadn't been enough for a mind already confused by lack of sleep, food and moral serenity, this new room was so frighteningly familiar to Leonardo as to make him forget the new world he had seen in the library. It was the bedroom of a poor village priest and the bedroom of a degenerate Spanish Grandee, all rolled into one. First of all, the slanted roof seemed more slanted here than in the library, the large beams larger and of much rougher cut, the smaller horizontal beams so poorly shaped and twisted and decayed that some had been replaced with freshly cut branches of trees, still with their leaves attached, and of course dry and dusty. In one corner, a rusty washbasin of the kind used in Laterza by the poorer people—but not by their doctor and mayor, nor any of his assistants, not even by Liborio and Peppino. Even the pail for the discharge of dirty water was cheap; first of all, it didn't match the basin or the pitcher underneath, and besides, it had even larger patches of enamel missing. Beyond this rustic washstand was another red curtain like the one that separated the library from the kitchen and dining room, and one could see that it served as a clothes closet for a poor parish priest, as Leonardo instantly knew, identifying the clerical garments hanging there, and the clerical shoes aligned against the wall. But on either side of that poverty, what opulence poured in through the two windows. . . . Where else on earth could one have such a bird's eye view of St. Peter's, the Scalinata, the fountain and the oak trees around it? One could even see the man down there who had given Leonardo his last free meal as an advance payment for a favor Leonardo had already forgotten, and remembered now with a feeling of shame. This, from one window. But the other was no less magnificent: it focused on a corner of the garden Leonardo had not seen from the library: a most intimate corner between a box-hedge and a wall covered with ivy. A broken column and a baroque fountain mask dribbling onto a delicate beard of lichens, which underlay the water all the way down into the marble basin filled with red fish, gave it that unmistakable stamp of a private princely garden which is still retained by public parks—but only in a great city, not in the provinces (Laterza had such a fountain in a park, but the fountain mask was dry, the ivy dead, the flowerbeds destroyed and the broken columns corroded and tarnished by excrement). On a bench, a young couple in passionate loveplay: the man had his tongue on the tits of the woman, which were clearly visible from up here, as were her naked legs, twisted around the sleeve of his overcoat. Leonardo pretended not to notice, and focused his attention on the brocade baldaquin above the Cardinal's bed: very princely looking indeed, but in the manner of the bedrooms of the French or German kings in the royal palace of Naples, now a museum—dust everywhere, huge golden crowns with huge patches of gold missing, baring the plaster skeleton of all this pomp; discolored red linings under discolored tatters of ancient brocade, discolored brocade armchairs with white stuffing popping out from all sides, caked and slicked with grease on the arms and back, and a few broken springs showing below the stocky legs. The night table loaded with open books, one on top of the other, and the iron bedposts festooned with rosaries in all colors and substances, also with icons of all epochs and dimensions—just like votive chapels in the poorest country churches, where the flimsiest bits of gold are often found hanging together with truly precious jewels that exposure to poverty more than to time has tarnished beyond recognition. That this was the bed of a great nobleman could be seen from the gold crown on top of the baldaquin, the tattered coat of arms on every piece of the brocade, and a porcelain chamber pot under the bed with the same coat of arms painted on it.

Seeing that Leonardo seemed attracted by the bed, the Cardinal changed tone, as if the only reason for ordering Leonardo into the room had been to show him his icons: "Some of these are the most beautiful in the oriental church," he said. "The ones here in this row come from the Lubomirski collection. My grandmother was a Lubomirski, although actually she was also the daughter of Louis Quinze, who secretly gave her part of his wife's collection of icons. The images are inspired, aren't they?"

Leonardo had the greatest contempt for all Byzantine art, as being too childish and utterly untrue to nature, but he pretended a great interest in the icons that were placed in his hands. "You're not looking," said the Cardinal, taking them all away from him in a fit of impatience. "Why didn't you tell me that you hate them?" He laid the icons on the bed instead of hanging them back on the bedpost, and said: "Out with your good news."

After a brief hesitation, Leonardo made a great effort to feign the same enthusiasm he had felt earlier for his "confession," and said: "It's about Mary." Then, with another great effort: "I am proud to be able to report that Mary is not the kind of dishonorable woman you thought. . . ."

"I thought?"

"Yes, you even said so."

"I said so?"

"Yes, you did. I am no child: when someone tells me that a married woman intends to commit divorce and run away with her lover, I know what that means. You spoke about a rich Neapolitan lover of hers, a widower . . . or don't you remember?"

"I remember everything very clearly, but go on, tell me what that means, because, if you are not a child, I am."

"Well . . . that means she is an unfaithful wife, a woman of loose morals, like all these degenerate women of the aristocracy."

"Oh, I see . . . I see. Go on."

"You don't seem to believe me, but I assure you that the rich Neapolitan lover never existed."

"I don't believe you. Is it true? Do you have evidence?"

"Mary's word. She never lies to me. He never existed!"

The Cardinal seemed stunned. "Can you swear to this?"

"On my mother's grave. She invented him to make her husband jealous. But she was always faithful to me, all these years, she loved *no other man,* and if she married that Monster, that immoral, lurid creature, it was only to escape from the immoral advances of another lurid man, an old man, and an aristocrat, of course: the Marchese Carlo Tempi. She never originally intended to marry the Monster. She did it to spite her mother. I confess that I find this kind of reasoning very weak, but then women are women, and—"

"Just a moment: are you a confessor?"

"No, I'm not a priest."

"But a confessor all the same, a new type of confessor: one who confesses for the sinner. Interesting. Go on."

"Did I hurt your feelings?"

"Go on, I said."

"Well, that's all."

"And what makes you think I judged her as severely as you seem to be judging her?"

"I am not judging her. I love her and I respect her, because she never betrayed her husband, even though she hated him."

"I see. Go on. And so you . . ."

Leonardo couldn't go on. He had seen two things that appalled him; outside, Giovanni was sitting on the same bench where the two lovers had been sitting before, and he was kissing a man. He recoiled from the spectacle only to find the Cardinal completely transfixed by the same sight, and suffering all the pains of the jealous lover. Since he couldn't know that Leonardo had seen Giovanni in the library, he didn't reveal his alarm, but just pretended he was gazing at the buildings or the clouds in the distance, his eyes glued on the bench, and his face registering pain. "Go on with your story," the Cardinal said, in a rather distant voice.

"That's all," said Leonardo.

"I'm so glad. Do go on." The Cardinal had heard nothing. One could see that he was making a great effort. He walked away from the window and began to pace the room with his hands behind his back, as if he were alone with his thoughts. Finally he remembered Leonardo, and turned to him with a completely calm expression on his face: he had obviously won a great battle with himself.

"I am waiting for the rest of your story."

"There is no rest to the story. I've told you everything."

"You have? All right, if you don't want to go on, I'll go on for you: you have now come to rescue Mary from that bad marriage."

"Exactly."

"And how do you intend to rescue her?"

"By marrying her."

"But she is married, and so are you."

"Yes, but we will get a divorce."

"And why have you come to tell me these things that any normal person would keep to himself?"

"Because I trust you. You are the only person I truly trust in Rome, and . . ."

"And perhaps I may suggest some way of getting this divorce by the usual Italian method, i.e., personal recommendation. Is that why you came?"

"Not exactly, but . . . if you think that such a way can be found, why of course I'd prefer it. I don't like to go against the law."

"But around the law to save appearances. Am I right?"

"Yes."

"Well, you've come to the wrong place. I am a priest, you know?"

"But you yourself said you believed in divorce."

"I see, I see . . ."

The Cardinal's face seemed to become more and more serene, and Leonardo knew he had been right to hide nothing from this man. Perhaps now the demands of his stomach, too, would be finally heard and accepted.

"Well," said the Cardinal, with a deep sigh of relief, "the ways of the Lord are indeed strange at times. . . . You have brought me both good news and bad news. Let's begin with the bad news: what you've just told me proves that my famous intelligence service, for which the French government has agreed to pay me a salary, is worthless. Trusting my informers, I had believed there *was* a rich Neapolitan widower, and the old Dragon had come here from her castle in the Black Forest to arrange for Mary's elopement with him and the child, I even knew she had retained the same lawyer in Switzerland as the Queen of Saxony, whose divorce is the scandal of the day. So, when I heard that the rich Neapolitan widower was in Rome, I simply announced myself as a guest at the dinner given for Mommsen. There I met you and liked your fresh intelligence, even your frank provincialism. You told me you were neither rich, nor a widower, your accent told me you were not Neapolitan, so I thought: this is the man we can use *against* the rich Neapolitan widower. Mary is in love with this man as she was with my young friend Angelo. . . . Yes, don't make those eyes at me: as you see, the story is not altogether as romantic as you imagined. Mary *did* love the young painter who rescued her from Carlo Tempi's advances, and for a while it really was a happy marriage. He ruined it soon enough, but so did she, with her pestiferous Russian temper.

But on with my story. My only fear was that you might learn about the rich Neapolitan widower, and ruin yourself by killing him or Mary or both. So I dealt the blow myself, knowing that I could help you in your distress. I am familiar with these problems: I started my career as a tutor in the Royal Family of Naples—they're distant cousins of mine—in eighteen fifty-eight. . . . Unfortunately for you and for our friendship, later that evening you did something dreadful, so beneath a gentleman's dignity, that I decided you would *never* set foot in this place, *never* become one of my friends. God willed it otherwise and sent you here to help me in *my* distress: only a few minutes ago I gave my solemn word to Mary's mother-in-law that I knew you were not the rich Neapolitan widower. . . . What is it? Are you fainting? Didn't you realize that was Mary's mother-in-law? Obviously not, because you told her everything about yourself. . . . Discretion is not an Italian virtue, I must say: when it comes to women, the Italian follows only the dictates of his vanity. Angelo is that way, too: he boasted to Mary about his conquests. No wonder Mary grew to detest him. . . . So, as I was saying, I swore to his mother that I knew Mary would not elope with you. I know you feel like the proverbial cook who broke the eggs in the basket and tried to use it as a frying pan, but this is the best thing that could have happened to you."

"To me?" cried Leonardo. "My life is finished."

"Nonsense, it's only beginning. It was finished before, when you thought a woman could save you. This is the typical Dante syndrome of all romantic Italians: they dream of Beatrice, to escape from their wife and children. True: Dante had all those children and a good wife he never mentioned, not even in passing, but at least his Beatrice was dead, and he did write a great poem, in which the only ugly verses are those describing his encounter with her . . . my God, what an orgy of masturbatory self-pity that is. . . . Still, the deification of woman was a very serious matter in those days. Modern romantic love instead is a travesty of love, a Protestant transaction to cover moral bankruptcy, a form of self-love deposited in someone else's banking account: *Love me, because I hate myself.* Which is why it all ends in suicide. If you ask me, it all *begins* with suicide, and people rot away in happy second marriages, filling the world with the stench of their dead souls."

Leonardo looked up at him like a beaten dog and muttered: "So you condemn Mary to moral and physical sterility, to save a rotten marriage: two, in fact, because I, too, married the wrong woman and want no children from her."

The Cardinal shook his head and smiled sadly: "*Condemn* . . . *Save* . . . *The Wrong Woman*, the *Right Man* . . . What language to use . . . Are you the right man to save the right woman from the wrong man? Is she the right woman to save you from your wrong woman? Obviously not, because you both made wrong decisions, and life is not a modern department store where you can exchange the merchandise if you feel you've been cheated. Life goes on: you can't set the clock back and start living nine years ago *again*, under different stars, because you're not alone, and your personal pleasure is not the only thing that exists on earth. You have your patients, your constituents, your aqueduct, Mary has her son, and I am not here to condemn your past or save your future, only to prevent further damage to that child, who had the misfortune of being born to such parents. The father isn't fit to have children, only mistresses: he's so proud of his manliness, he sounds like a boy of fifteen. He will remain fifteen until he dies, just like *his* father. And Mary is not fit to be a mother. She *did* reject her mother in anger eight years ago only to call her back the moment she became pregnant, and of course the old Dragon was happy to come back and accept the new toy Mary had made for her, because she herself was too old to make toys of her own. Mary is an actress, what she needs is a stage, but try telling that to the old Dragon or to a vain provincial male like you. This said, let me add that the Dragon, too, was unfit to have children. The Dragon is ruining that grandchild, who speaks four languages, but hardly any Italian at all, so when his father talks to him, he doesn't understand, and when his other grandmother, who at least can talk French, says nice things to him and kisses him, the child undergoes a process of mental and physical disinfection at home: first of all, he's scrubbed and washed down with alcohol, before his One and Only Grandmother touches him, and then he is asked to repeat whatever he has heard from *that woman*, which is then ridiculed and proven wrong. As a result of this, every time he sees the Dragon or even hears her voice, he has an attack of asthma."

"He doesn't when he sees me."

"Which is all to the good. You can do a great deal for that poor child."·

"By giving him illegitimate brothers and sisters? Is that Catholic morality?"

"No, sir, it is your *personal* immorality to think only of yourself, while pretending you love a woman. The true value of a man is determined by what he is able to give up. Unless love makes you a better person, it won't make you a good father. Mary needs guidance, a man to confide in, more than a man in bed. And that child needs *his* father, whom he worships, and his other grandmother, the *human* one, whom he worships, too, while he's driven insane by that goddess of Digestion, that permanent earthquake on wheels, that mass of international proteins and useless knowledge, who is still crying for her own mother whom she lost when she was three. That child and he alone needs a divorce—from *her*! What *you* can do for her is show her that you are a man, and not another piece of clay she can mold at her will. Say no to her, kindly but firmly, and *from a distance*. This alone may cure her. Of course self-sacrifice is no pleasure at first, but it becomes a pleasure as you train yourself to it. And besides, good things happen to those who expect them least, while they elude the eternal child whose only aim in life is to satisfy his passions. Give yourself three years of chaste love and self-sacrifice, and something good may come your way."

"Yes," said Leonardo, smiling bitterly: "my wife's death and the death of Mary's husband . . ." Then, in anger: "I don't want to be tempted by evil thoughts."

"Then why not by *good* thoughts? Why not think that *you* may die soon, and that your dear memory will teach these poor women to do something for others at long last? Go back to your hometown *today*, and from there write to Mary, and either tell her the truth that you came here and spilled the beans (and she may hate you), or tell her that goodly lie which *will* become the truth, little by little, with God's help: 'Dear Mary, let's not think of ourselves but of your child and my patients. I have other obligations too, but my love for you can only be strengthened by this very hard decision, et cetera.'"

Leonardo instantly felt both better and worse: the fairy tale was finished and everything was as it should be—boring and hopeless. In other words, he was back home, where nothing good happened, not even by mistake. In this anteroom of hell, everything purely physical was heaven, so now, despite the sadness he knew he would feel over the loss of Mary, he felt hungry. And since he couldn't say: "I want a dish of eels in wine," he said, feigning utter despair: "I want children now."

"Children now?" shouted the Cardinal. "Are you insane? Don't you realize that *children now* means to see them die in war or live like criminals in twenty years' time? The world is finished. You may wonder why I continue to fight for a better Europe. I don't know why myself: hope for a lesser evil, I suppose. But children? Innocent creatures, bearers of good tidings, *now*? Insane! Where is your healthy Apulian pessimism?"

A faint knock on the door, unnoticed by the Cardinal, a brief pause, a whiff of the most delicious smells on earth, and Salvemini's bright smile, then his voice: "Your Eminence, we're hungry."

"Go ahead without me, I'll join you in a minute, I'm just saying goodbye to my friend."

Now Leonardo knew there was no hope, and he wept—timidly at first, then, helped by thoughts of Mary, with violent sobs. In vain did the Cardinal caress his head and promise him aid, friendship, long letters, even an aqueduct, paid for by Sophie. "She will, I know she will. . . . Just think of the triumph of your mission. . . . And you'll have to come back to Rome frequently, and you'll see Mary." Nothing could console him. He wanted his eels in wine, like Pope Martin the Fourth. "Stop that nonsense," said the Cardinal finally, "and tell me why you behaved so basely in Mary's house the other night."

The sinner's tears, almost his very heart stopped instantly, and he mumbled, head low: "Because the flesh is weak."

"Oh." And the Cardinal blushed, then shook his head and smiled bitterly. "I don't know and don't want to know. I am neither Mary's confessor nor yours. I really don't know why I still bother to talk to you at all. . . . I suppose Angelo's mother was right: I care more for you than for her. No wonder: you are young and intelli-

gent, she is old and stupid. I defend her against you, because that is
part of my pastoral duty, but to defend you against yourself is part
of my Socratic amusement, which can become dearer than life, as
Socrates himself said when asked by his judges why he went on
subverting the young, in full knowledge that this might cost him his
life. Or don't you remember the Apology?"

"I do," boasted Leonardo with a big smile, happy as he was to
have been saved from a ruinous confession, and he quoted Socrates's answer in Greek: "Because there is amusement in it."

"At long last," said the Cardinal, opening his arms, and Leonardo
fell into them, then withdrew as quickly, horrified by the sudden
doubt: Am I giving up my manhood for a mess of pottage?

But the Cardinal seemed more eager to express indignation than
love: "And now tell me: why did you sin against politeness?"

"I? When? How?"

"By recommending an illiterate museum guard for the post of
librarian."

"Oh, *that*?" And he shrugged his shoulders.

"Yes, *that*, which shocks me more than whatever you did with
Mary. Physical passion is a natural thing and it may harm only one
person, but what you did shows a savage, cold contempt for society,
and harms everyone without exception. How can a healthy community exist, if you bestow academic titles and important positions as
favors to your clients? Would you have recommended that despicable clown for a medical post, without seeing his credentials? No,
because you have respect for your profession."

"But he lied to me. . . ."

"He did not. He is a public lie, and you should have known that.
He is the uncle of a poor unwed mother, now a prostitute, here on
the steps of Trinità dei Monti. I know her story, she trusts me
because she thinks I'm the Pope. He tried for years to have her
deported, instead of helping her, and he has money. They call him a
professor; in fact, very few people know his real name, I for one
don't. Here is how it all began: look at this picture." And he went
to a drawer, and pulled out a large photograph of a chair between
two statues. "This is the famous Chair in Ancient Greek Sculpture,
occupied by your friend. The picture was taken by my friend Count

Primoli at the Torlonia museum, and the title was a joke by the American sculptor Hazeltine. Here the Professor sat for years, under this statue with the figleaf, judging the conduct of museum guides and visitors by comparing their interest in statues *with* the fig leaf as opposed to statues *without* it. When they stopped too long in front of the latter, especially if accompanied by women, he accused them of immorality. It became his crusade, and if he wasn't removed from his post it is only because people were amused by him: he became a museum exhibit all by himself. Yet you not only were blind to such evidence, but even invented the sob story about his being a brilliant student ruined by poverty or God knows what, probably women."

"But that's what he told me."

"He did not. I questioned him, I suspected something fishy and went to the Baron's yesterday at noon, and when I saw him appear I knew my suspicions were correct. He told me you had offered him the job as a bargain against some cufflinks you had given him by mistake, before you learned how precious they were. True or not?"

"That's a long story."

"Long or short, I don't want to hear it. Please think about these matters on your way to Apulia tonight, and write to me from home. Now go, I am late."

"But I can't go home," said Leonardo, in a last, desperate attempt to get at those eels.

"Why? Need money? I'll give it to you."

"No no, I have plenty of money . . . but . . ."

"But what?"

"First of all, there is no direct train before tomorrow morning. . . ."

"All right, leave tomorrow morning, but without going to Mary's again. Promise?"

And now came the basest of all lies: "But if I leave tomorrow morning they will come after me, and force me to leave with them by boat, from Naples, on the way to Egypt."

The Cardinal seemed annoyed for a moment, and said: "Let's see . . . I can't have them arrested without evidence, they travel with that child all the time. . . . Well, there's a solution, but you must give me your word of honor, as one man to another, that you will not be seen in Mary's house for the next five days. I know it's a great sacrifice to ask, but I'm very busy, and I need time to think. If I tell that woman that she was right about you, she will have you arrested at once, and I won't be able to help you. You'll be ruined forever and Mary and Sophie, who can't be very pleased after the Baron told them the whole story last night, will never want to see you again, because of course their names will be in the papers too, so you see how important it is that you go into hiding until I find a solution. Trust me. And now give me your word, man to man."

He extended his hand, and Leonardo shook it, saying, "Thank you," in tones of the utmost sincerity, while completing the rest of the sentence deep in his heart: . . . thank you, that is, for not asking me on my word of honor if I hadn't seen Mary already this morning. But the Cardinal was still holding his hand and gazing into his eyes with genuine affection. "You don't have to thank me. I love you like my own son. Now go. You know where the door is. . . . I still have something to do here."

Leonardo left, dragging his feet but trying to seem in a hurry; that is, absorbed in urgent thoughts, so as not to lose face if Salvemini asked him why he wasn't staying for lunch. Salvemini didn't. He just said: "At long last! Now we can eat! You must sit next to me. I want to give you precise instructions before you go back to Laterza."

"I'm afraid I can't stay," said Leonardo feebly.

"Why? Do you have some other urgent engagement?"

"Nothing *really* urgent, but . . ."

"Then you can leave immediately after lunch."

"If the Cardinal invites me . . ."

"You don't need an invitation. Everyone who comes here eats lunch before he goes. The others are already in the dining room. I waited for you, because I wanted to tell you how you can expose those bastards down South. It has to become a real national scandal, and you are in an ideal position to demonstrate what happens to a public official who puts his trust in the government. And I will write an article such as I and I alone know how to write!"

"We'll see," said Leonardo. He was terrorized by the entire prospect, but the nearness of food made him feel dizzy, and he would give anything to be seated at table before the Cardinal appeared. They passed the chair on which the accursed overcoat was lying, and Leonardo suddenly realized that two unsavory characters were inspecting it with greedy eyes. Instinctively, he scowled at them, and one of them hastily said by way of apology: "I used to work in London; I was a tailor at Huntsman's before I became a political activist, and I've just won a bet with my friend here. I *knew* this coat was made by Huntsman: they make the best coats in the world—and the most expensive!" But suddenly Leonardo knew that there was something else that mattered more, and he knew it without even having to turn around: the Cardinal had arrived, and the Cardinal was furious with him. The entire atmosphere changed; an icy silence isolated him even from Salvemini. Looking at Salvemini as if Leonardo didn't even exist, the Cardinal said: "Come along, let's go into the dining room. I want you to sit next to me." And Salvemini actually disentangled himself from Leonardo and began to follow the Cardinal. The treason! The slur on his honor! "Salvemini!" Leonardo almost whined: "But you wanted *me* to sit next to *you*. . . ."

The Cardinal turned back, eyes wide and glittering. "Hand him that garment, please," he ordered the tailor. Salvemini blushed, hurried to help Leonardo into his coat, and started whispering Apulian whispers that would have drowned a hissing locomotive. "What can I do . . . he doesn't seem to want you to stay . . . but then what do you care? . . . Go to a restaurant and I'll meet you after five at the Caffè Greco."

And before Leonardo could make up his mind whether to say yes or no, or even *how* he should say it, he was all alone in the big library and cheerful voices hailing the arrival of food were echoing to him from a long, long way away, as in a nightmare. Both dead and alive, in a waking dream, he left the room he had most loved in his life.

But we cannot live our death for more than a split second. Breathing itself is resurrection and forgiveness for the sins we committed in an earlier life. Thus with his first step down that steep staircase, a completely new Leonardo was born: one who was hungry for food, but also for an enemy other than himself. He stopped at the end of the first landing, where he had stood at the window with Kostia's other grandmother, and the moment he set foot into that rhomboid of sunshine that was warming the bricks on the floor, his feet felt warm, then the warmth climbed up to his knees, it touched his pelvis, then his stomach, his chest, and finally his face. To hell with sodomist Cardinals and Socialist princes and their Socialist lackeys . . . to hell with the lot of them! I'd rather be the fool I am. . . . And to think I was ready to flatter a degenerate and become a traitor to King and Country, all for the sake of a mess of pottage. . . . So my reality has always been a fairy tale, has it? . . . But Mary and I are no fairy tale, Science is no fairy tale, and what I need right now is advice from someone who has his feet right on the ground. . . . To the police! With these thoughts, he took a deep breath redolent of sweet spring flowers, but instead of feeling stronger, he felt weaker again, because of the same hunger that had made him come there and ruin himself in the first place. Lonely again, more lonely than ever, because he had lost friends he had never imagined existed, he resumed his descent, trying to look as dignified as possible for the benefit of the doorman.

He passed the doorman, who bowed deeply, then suddenly remembered that he not only didn't know where to go, but didn't have the strength for a long walk, nor the money for a cab. So he turned back, and, with an air of great disdain, he asked the doorman: "How do I get to police headquarters?"

"It's a long way from here, sir, but your coachman is out there, he will know."

"Oh yes, my coachman, that's right." Leonardo was baffled, but maintaining the same air of disdain, he walked outside. Sure enough, the good coachman was there, dozing on top of his cab, probably mumbling the Miserere to himself. Poor devil, was this the man Mary and her mother had suspected of spying? . . . *I am the spy* . . . He tried to send this ugly thought back to the depths of hell where it belonged, and touched the coachman's foot, to awaken him.

"Oh, it's you, sir. . . . Madame said I was to follow you, in case you needed me. . . . Where do you want to go?"

"To police headquarters."

"Very good. Shall I open the door for you?"

"Of course not. I can open it myself."

"Thank you. There were two gentlemen asking for you, but I think they've gone."

"Two gentlemen?" A deep feeling of unease came over him, but before he could recieve an answer to his questions or decide what to do, here they both were, arms wide, loud voices calling.

"Whaaaat?" he shouted angrily, stepping back to avoid Peppino and Liborio and their disgusting embraces: "What are you doing here? Why aren't you at your desks back at Town Hall in Laterza?"

"Why aren't you at your desk?"

"me? I'm finished with Laterza."

"So are we."

"Oh no you're not. I have a reason to be here."

"And so have we. Why should you be the only one to find happiness in Rome? You promised to introduce us to Mary's sisters, or to her friends, if she has no sisters."

"How dare you say such things? I never promised anything of the sort, and I forbid you to use that name as if you knew her. Get out of my way and go back to your duties, or I . . ."

"You what? You'll denounce us to the police? You know very well you can't. You're the mayor, we're only your assistants. We follow your example, we—"

"You go to hell and leave me alone. I'll have nothing to do with you."

"You go to hell, you pimp."

"How dare you?"

There was a brief respite: the two men were consulting in whispers. Then one of them said: "If you want us to go back, give us some money."

"I have no money."

"Do you expect us to believe you? Look at that overcoat."

"D'you want this overcoat? Here, take it."

"What would we do with that silly overcoat? It's an overcoat for women anyway."

"You can sell it, you can give it to your wives."

"We're just as fed up with our wives as you are. Why should you be the only one to have a right to your freedom?"

But he was interrupted: "Come on, Liborio, don't talk to that prick. Can't you see he's been totally corrupted by money?" Then, to Leonardo: "A curse on you, your bitch mistress and all your future children."

"Fuck you and your whores of mothers, wives and daughters." This was too much: they both came at him with clenched fists, but the coachman aimed his whip at them and let them have it on the hands, while Leonardo took refuge in the coach. Pursued by whip and horses, the last two characters of his ancient reality fled from him like scared chickens.

"Here we are," shouted the coachman into the china cabinet. Leonardo woke up from his nightmarish nap and prepared to get out. His first impulse was to leave his overcoat behind, but on second thought he decided to take it along as a sure passkey to all doors in a government office. And besides, he felt cold, so he quickly put it on before confronting the two armed Carabinieri in front of a somber-looking palace.

"Where are you going?" asked a voice of purest Apulian, the purest *faccia da galera** Leonardo had ever seen, leveling a bayonet against him, while his counterpart, the purest *faccia di fesso*,† was slowly lifting his rifle to imitate his colleague.

"To see His Excellency the Capo Questore. Personal business."

The intimidating effect of this magic formula made Leonardo feel better. He looked at the two bayonets contemptuously as they quickly withdrew from his chest, then he allowed the two sentinels to admire his overcoat as he slowly entered the building. The memory of the Cardinal threatened to destroy his self-assurance, but he pushed it back, and gave himself an even haughtier countenance as he confronted the next sentinel, this time a plainclothesman seated behind a desk, pen in hand, and with that air of embarrassment that illiterates have when confronted with paper and ink.

"*Documenda*," barked the poor idiot, also in the purest Apulian, and again Leonardo felt at home, but this time gravely insulted in his official dignity. "Where is it written that a personal friend of the

---

* Literally: face worthy of a jail.
† Face of a fool.

Capo Questore is supposed to obey such idiotic injunctions from a mere flunky?" he asked, lifting his chin to make it clear that he was speaking not to an equal but to a very low inferior.

"In the new regulations, which, verbally speaking, were redacted by His Excellency the Minister for Grace and Justice in person, after they killed our defunct monarchist king by premeditated regicide with a fire-weapon which a murderous hand brandished treacherously on purpose from America, where the scum of the earth produces such vultures which plunge the mother-fatherland into eternal mourning for a king named The Good, as befits His fulgid memory."

Leonardo was stunned by this peroration, and didn't know what to answer, when a flunky slightly less miserably dressed than this one came storming in from a side corridor: "Be gone, you fool. Don't you see you're talking to a person of the highest distinction?" Then, to Leonardo: "He doesn't know a gentleman from an anarchist. I had to go to the toilet, as I have frequent miction due to an incipient prostate syndrome, and I asked this imbecile to sit here for a few minutes and not let any dubious characters by." Then, again to the flunky: "Couldn't you see who he is from his overcoat? You think that, just because you've memorized His Excellency's speech on the tragedy, you can repeat every word of it. Well, I'll have you know that you quoted it all wrong: you are an illiterate, and this gentleman here has at least three degrees and four titles and is probably even a baron or a count. Or a prince? . . ." he asked, timidly eyeing Leonardo again.

"No such nonsense. Just Doctor Leonardo Claudi, mayor of Laterza: thirty thousand inhabitants and no aqueduct." These last words were spoken with an air of reproach that made the head flunky even humbler. He couldn't know that the reproach was for Leonardo himself and for the absent Salvemini.

"How right you are. . . . I can't even begin to tell you how right you are, because I know nothing about aqueducts. The town where I come from, in Calabria, has plenty of water—purest mountain water. Yessir, and we don't realize how lucky we are. Of course here in Rome the water is plentiful and excellent. What do you think of the mineral waters of Fiuggi for the urinary tract?"

"Absolutely perfect," said Leonardo, "and so is Bagni di Chianciano. And Montecatini in Tuscany. Italian waters are the best in
the world."

"That's what I always say. And do you think that urotropine is a
good medicine for my condition?'

"I don't know the state of your genito-urinary system, but as a
general rule, urotropine is the only good substance found so far that
doesn't have side effects on the kidneys, the way sandalwood has in
the cure for gonorrhea. But may I ask you to let me go to the Capo
Questore? I'm in a hurry."

"Of course, of course."

"Here is his personal calling card, he gave it to me two days ago,
and told me to come and see him any time."

The head flunky took the paper Leonardo was handing him,
studied it carefully, then said: "You don't want to see the Capo
Questore, you want to see Commissario Tuttolomondo. Next corridor to the left, back stairs, fourth floor, seventh door on the right."
These words contained a certain contempt which Leonardo sensed
at once, so he said, very sternly: "I want to see the Capo Questore,
as indicated by that card."

"But, my dear sir, this is no visiting card. This is a leaflet torn
from the agenda of the Capo Questore, a thing that Commissario
Tuttolomondo should never have done, because it is forbidden by
the new regulations, to save paper. And also to avoid unpleasant
misunderstandings like the present one. Go to the fourth floor."

"I am not going to the fourth floor, and I want to see the Capo
Questore. This card was given me when I met this gentleman escorting the Queen Mother. How can a simple Commissario escort
the Queen Mother?"

"My dear sir," said the flunky, beginning to look rather impatient, "Her Majesty herself would not wish to be guarded by the
Capo Questore, now that her royal husband is dead. The Capo
Questore would of course escort His Majesty the new king, because
as you know better than I, an anarchist or a Socialist would want to
kill the new one, not the widow of the king they've killed already."

"I am not interested in details. I am not going to the back corridor and the fourth floor. I want to see the Capo Questore, and I

know where to go." And he turned his back to the flunky, walking towards the main staircase, which was large, luminous and dignified, with the red carpet and the brass stair rods he had become accustomed to in his hotel and in Mary's house.

But he didn't get very far, because the flunky shouted: "Stop! You have no right to use those stairs." And as Leonardo gave no indication of obeying, a lesser flunky grabbed him roughly by the arm and said: "Obey orders."

All of the rage, the sadness, the hunger, the confusion he had been suppressing for so long exploded in a major scene which was heard all over the palace. Faces of uniformed policemen and plain-clothesmen, even of female secretaries, appeared along the entire ramp of the main stairway to look down with passionate interest: something new at least to break the monotony.

No one had ever seen a man so expensively dressed treated that way by the flunkies, nor had anyone ever heard such an Apulian accent used to express such imperious demands. (Had the accent been English, German or French, even Italian murdered beyond recognition, everybody would have understood the so-called Latin and acted accordingly; namely, by showing the greatest respect for the protester.)

While Leonardo was fighting with the flunkies, who were pulling at his coat, the alarm was sounded from on high: another flunky appeared on the landing, shouting: "His Excellency!!!" Which meant that His Excellency the Capo Questore was about to come downstairs and go home to lunch. All the curious onlookers instantly disappeared from the landing, and the personal flunky of the *piano nobile*—namely, the one who announced other Excellencies to his own Excellency, and had the power to keep Excellencies waiting for hours if he wasn't satisfied with their importance —came down to test the way; namely, to see that His Excellency's eyes be spared the sight of his inferiors. He had heard the loud Apulian voice, and was anxious to have the trespasser arrested at once. But as he descended like an eagle on this rebellious southern lamb, his expert eyes fell on Leonardo's overcoat and he shouted: "Stop, for God's sake, Hands Off!!!! He is an Excellency!"

Leonardo was instantly released, but he couldn't be stopped from

venting his anger at everybody including his rescuer, in a language
not worthy of his overcoat. At that moment His Excellency himself
appeared at the top of the stairs, and Leonardo suddenly undersood.
There walked, on the stout body of a small Southerner like himself,
an overcoat that might be similar to his own in pretension, but not
in quality; rabbit, not sable, was what emerged from that black
tunic, and the proud wearer of that rabbit could no longer be
proud: he was silently envious and reverent, as only a male can be,
when sartorially self-conscious.

"I must apologize for my men," he said, stretching out his hand.
"With whom do I have the honor?"

Leonardo introduced himself very humbly and began to explain
how he had met the Commissario who had led him to believe that
he was the Capo Questore, but he didn't have to go far.

"I know everything," said His Excellency. "I know the lady you
were with, I know that Her Majesty the Queen Mother offered her
the flowers she had bought for herself, and I am at your service for
whatever may have brought you here. Please come into my office,
this is no appropriate place to discuss confidential matters."

"But Your Excellency was probably going out to lunch, and I
would hate to cause any delay in—"

"No delay at all: my lunch can wait."

"But we can discuss it on the way. . . . I, too, must go to dine at
my hotel, in fact, perhaps—"

"Not at all, not at all: my time is yours." Then, to his personal
flunky: "Please call my wife and—"

"It's already been done," answered the flunky, meaning he
would do it immediately, so Leonardo dragged his aching stomach
and his tired legs into another office. It must have been a dining
room in its more glorious days: frescoes of live venison decorated
the walls, more frescoes with garlands made up of apples, pears,
cherries and grapes decorated the ceiling, and a banquet of gods
served by fat little angels and naked nymphs occupied the whole
vault. Modern science, alas, had interrupted the banquet by tearing
the tablecloth, the scant veils and even the live flesh of the deities
with nails and sockets holding thick electric cords; the very mouth
of Father Jupiter vomited the chain around which the main cord

was twisted. A large dusty enamel plate with a dirty green fringe served as a lampshade above His Excellency's desk, and a telephone, also connected with wires and sockets that scarred and effaced both venison and mountains of fruit, stood right under the lamp on His Excellency's desk.

"Please sit down. Let's take off our coats."

Leonardo slowly obeyed, and now their roles were reversed: he looked like the provincial Apulian he was, despite his cravat and shirt, while His Excellency looked like a real Excellency in his gray suit obviously cut by an excellent tailor.

"I shall be very brief," said Leonardo, "because I know you must be hungry, and I myself am both hungry and tired. Early this morning I had to go to the house of a man who has robbed me, cheated me and done me a great deal of damage, but alas, he had left Rome, gone back to his village down South, and all on my money!"

"How horrible. Tell me all about it, we will have him arrested at once. I can telephone any large city in the country, and have anyone pursued in any province by the police. Modern efficiency."

"Thank you. His name is Luigi Schillasi, and he—"

"You mean the retired museum guard who always goes to the Caffè Greco? The so-called Professor?"

"Yes, why, do you know him?"

"Very well indeed, not personally, of course, he's a nobody, but he does happen to be a friend of the Commissario who was escorting Her Majesty when you met him, and he has a son who's a Carabiniere in Sardinia, just beginning his career. I hesitate to believe that he actually cheated you; he's a bit of a bore, and a bit of a clown, but otherwise an honest man, a patriot, a man of integrity. . . . I am sure that when he comes back he will repay you. His wife is well-off: she was a cook in the household of a Roman prince, and married a baron who left her all his money. We shall look into the matter, however, and whatever else we can do for you, we will do with pleasure. Is that all?"

"No, I would like to ask you some confidential information."

"Of course, of course, and you may rest assured that it will be kept strictly confidential."

"Do you know the Cardinal d'Escarande?"

"I know of him, but I never had the honor of being introduced to him. A very high-minded prelate, a prince of the Church, of course . . ."

"Do you think he can be trusted?"

"He is too much, that is, too much of a moralist, a very strict disciple of His Holiness in matters concerning the recent encyclical *Rerum Novarum*. What a disaster for the Church and for all Catholics . . . Why should His Holiness rage against all things new? What's so sinful about the telephone or the bicycle? Or the Singer sewing machine? My wife went straight to the Pope to ask him if it was dangerous for her salvation to use it, and of course the Pope was furious. But it's his own fault. *De Minimis non curat Praetor*, says the Justinian law . . . But your Cardinal is even worse than the Pope when it comes to scientific progress. He thinks it's all immoral."

"So he is also against divorce."

"Absolutely."

"And yet . . . he's very baffling. Let me explain: I met him at dinner at my friend's house the other night, and since he spoke at length about his belief in the necessity of legalizing divorce—"

"Did he? That surprises me a great deal, but then, of course, a Frenchman . . ."

"Yes, and so this morning I committed the great blunder of going to see him and asking him about the possibility . . ."

"Well, you may have shocked him, but I don't see why you should worry. The person you're going to marry is so rich and so powerful that she can obtain everything for you, even a divorce. Anything else?"

Almost against his will, out of timidity, Leonardo asked: "Isn't the Cardinal . . . a bit of a degenerate?"

"Oh, that definitely—but then, what can you expect of a Frenchman? They're all rotten to the core—*and* a subversive, too. He surrounds himself with Socialists, anarchists, all sorts of unreliable elements."

"Right, I've noticed that too. But you don't think he might denounce me to the police, do you?"

"For what?"

"For abduction of a minor."

"What minor?"

"The son of the person I'm going to marry."

"But the person you are going to marry has sons aged thirty or even forty, and—"

"Oh, all that business about the old lady again."

"She isn't old, she's still very young and attractive, but she was married very young, and—"

"I'M NOT MARRYING HER! I'm marrying the daughter."

"Oh, the daughter. A great beauty, a perfect amazon, very popular in the highest social circles, but always very moral. . . . Congratulations. But, if I'm not mistaken, Miss Ludmilla isn't married. Unless she married recently, in Paris where she now lives."

"I don't mean *that* daughter, I mean the one who lives here."

"But she's married to an Italian! Do you mean to say she would divorce her husband and take her child away from him? If she does that, we'll certainly arrest her, both for abduction of a minor and for adultery."

This took care of Leonardo's hunger. No pangs in his stomach, no shameful readiness to agree with his enemies or court the mighty of this world; no desire to live, either. He was a finished man and he knew it. Or, in his own correct terminology, he was an adolescent idiot, and he wondered how this man could put up with his presence here. Why didn't he just kick him out, as his flunkies had begun to do earlier? "With your permission," he said, getting up from his chair and picking up his stupid overcoat, perhaps his worst enemy on earth, after himself.

But to his great surprise, His Excellency now became infinitely more servile than before. "Please, my dear friend, don't take offense, let me explain. I never intended to offend you, please sit down and let me explain."

"But there is nothing to explain. You were right and I was wrong. Forgive me, rather, for disturbing you. Good day." And without even looking at His Excellency, he slowly made for the door. "Wait, wait, don't go . . ." panted His Excellency, struggling to extricate himself from the soft depths of his red armchair, "please be reasonable, my dear friend, and sit down for a moment."

Out of sheer physical weakness, Leonardo obeyed, and His Excellency began: "From what you said about the Cardinal, I understood at once that you are a man of high principles, a good Italian, a patriot. And of course a good Christian, i.e., a Catholic: let's not deny our Mother Church any more than we deny our Mother Fatherland. Do you need a divorce? A divorce is a scandal, for our Mother Church and for ourselves and even more for the woman we marry than for the woman we leave. A divorced woman has a stigma attached to her past that no force on earth can erase, while a woman who has a lover is universally respected, not only because she keeps her feelings to herself, but also quite particularly because she respects the Holy Sacrament of Matrimony, the domestic hearth, the unity of the family, her husband and her children. You can be very discreet about your love affairs, but not about divorce, which immediately involves the children in an open debate about the moral worthiness of both their parents. That undermines the foundations of society, my friend. I have seen many cases of Italians married to foreign women who eventually divorced them and ruined *both* husband and children. The children felt suddenly independent, because they had passed judgment on their parents, and they all married early, not for love, but for the fun of getting a divorce. One divorce leads to another, and then what is left of a man's honor? If the woman stays married, on the other hand, and finds herself a respectable lover—I mean one with no syphilis or gonorrhea—no one will dare slander her for, if anyone did, both husband and lover would defend her, because although they had never met and would never become friends, they had one thing in common—the one thing that keeps the Family and the Fatherland together: their honor. You are extremely lucky, in that you have found a lady who has never, not once, been the subject of gossip. This, in a place like Rome, is a record worth considering. Everyone knows she doesn't love her husband and the husband has mistresses all over the place. If he wants to waste his life and endanger his health that way, that's his business, but for as long as he actually lived with his wife, he had only one mistress: a highly honorable and healthy woman. This is one thing I and I alone can tell you. As the head of the Roman police and a personal friend of her father-in-law (and we were more than friends, Don Teofilo and I, we were like arse and shirt, we shared mistresses ever since we were young), I am in a position to know things no one else possibly could. Let divorce come in like a stroke of lightning to disturb this peaceful situation, and what do you have? Dishonor, slander, unending open warfare, and, of course, crime on all sides: your adultery, hers, to which you add the intent to commit one more crime, the most unforgiveable of all—abduction of a minor. Even suppose it all comes to pass as you had planned it—because, given money, there are thousands of ways to circumvent the law—what hope, what guarantee do you have that your own children will respect you in the future, after what you have done to another man?"

"All very well, but how am I to have children out of wedlock? I don't want bastards."

"What is a bastard? Just a word, and if you knew how many bastards there are in the best families in Rome, and how filial their devotion to their illegitimate fathers, and how bastardly the attitude of legitimate children to both parents, you would thank God on your knees that your son will be the one to discover some day he was born a bastard, and not *you* to discover that he *became* one at the age of fifteen."

"Yes, but the name? Why should my children go about under another man's name?"

"What's in a name? Names can be changed. It's what people say that counts, not what you think. You lack humility, you consider your feelings more important than the voice of the people, which, as you know, is called the voice of God. If you have bastards, the honor is all yours: it's for the cuckolded man to feel dishonored. And this particular man is superior to such trifles. He has accepted his fate, but he would never stand being dishonored in the courts by a divorce. And, mark you, a former husband can damage a woman's reputation in devious ways a cuckolded husband would never resort to, for the sake of his good name."

Leonardo let all this eloquence flow over him as a drowning man lets the waters close above his head. This worried His Excellency, who went into a new spin of explanations and apologies: "You understand, this isn't cynicism, this is what the Germans call *Realpolitik*. You come to me and tell me all your secret plans for the conquest of the fortress. If you had been more politically minded than you are, you would have kept away from me and surprised the police with what the French call a *fait accompli* (and I want you to notice that both these foreign theories I mention were invented by

Italians, and illegally appropriated by foreigners). Now, some
people might call you mindless for what you did."

"I do, I do . . ." sighed Leonardo in an outburst of despair and
gastric distress.

"—but I don't, because I have known everything about you for
some time, and now that I have met you, I know that my informers
were right: you are a genius, a man of great intellectual and patri-
cian distinction. And the proof is that a superior mind like Her
Royal Majesty the Queen Mother gave you the flowers she had
bought for herself."

"She did not. She gave them to my future mother-in-law . . .
but what am I saying? My future nothing, that's what she is,
thanks to my utter mindlessness!"

"Not at all, not at all, she's your future warhorse, yes, that's it;
don't you see? Convert her to the True Faith and you'll be famous
instantly! The Church will never dare touch you then."

Leonardo couldn't help laughing, despite his dejection, but His
Excellency took him to task at once: "You are a man of little faith,
if you laugh at such matters. Why didn't you come to me right
away, instead of going to the Cardinal? First of all, the Cardinal is a
Frenchman, therefore not to be trusted, because he wants the
papacy for France, and you can see what a disaster that would be for
us. And, secondly, he's a narrow-minded conservative, and an anarchist, don't ask me how these two positions can be combined in one
person, because an ambidextrous person can be anything. You
should have come to me, because I have all the best Cardinals in
the palm of my hand. I have a personal file on every one of them,
and they know it, but in addition to this basic . . . base of opera-
tions, I have done personal favors for every one of them, and none
of them knows this about any of the others because I'm no fool and
I know how to handle such matters. Machiavelli was an Italian,
after all. The ancient institution of Furberia was invented by us, not
by the boors in our former Nordic colonies. What is power worth, if
you don't abuse it? HOW you abuse it, that's the secret of real
power. You must abuse it in the interest of a Good Cause. And, of
course, for altruistic reasons, such as helping a friend in need. What
reasons do I have for helping you? Because I like you, and I recognize your genius, and don't want it lost to our national history. You

must make your discoveries here, not in France, Germany or Russia. Here, in the Eternal City of Genius."

Leonardo was completely undone. He just sat there dejectedly; the combined effect of all this and his hunger had brought about an invincible somnolence, and in a supreme effort to keep his eyes open, he frowned, he stared, feigning a total fascination with the nonsense he was hearing. His Excellency took it as such, and was eager to fascinate him even more. "You see in front of you a man who, by mere force of will power—and God's Grace, of course: what would we be without His guiding hand, His fatherly care of every minute, His Divine Providence, in one word?—a man, I was saying, who, by mere dint of will power has risen from the humblest ranks, without ever using his native nobility to get ahead, and is now, thanks to Divine Providence first and foremost, one of the highest, if not the highest official in the government of this Eternal City. Do you realize that, if anyone wanted to start a real revolution—not a mock one, I mean a *real* one—one that replaces one ruler with another, all he would have to do is corrupt *me*? Who knows every single move, every personal weakness of the ruling sovereign? The chief of police, of course. These people are lucky God allows them to have *me* here, instead of a bad man. What would they do, if I suddenly turned bad? Yet look at them: does one of these courtiers, one of these high government officials, one"—here he lowered his voice and leaned close enough for Leonardo to notice pyorrhea and two rotten teeth—"in the Royal Family itself, treat me as I should be treated; namely, as a human being? The answer is no: they order me about like a simple Commissario, they even call me that at times; sometimes when they feel they have to treat me a little better than a Commissario, do you know what they call me?"

"No," said Leonardo, if only to exercise his voice and stay awake a little longer.

"I'll give you a thousand guesses: *Cavaliere*. A title that has almost become an insult in Italy. Who isn't Cavaliere in Rome, may I ask? Here, under me, I have thirty-six Cavalieri and, in the whole Italian government, certainly more than five hundred, counting the different branches of the administration. Not only that: I have absolute authority over ninety-seven Commendatori all over the country; I, and I alone, give the final agreement before anyone receives such a title in Rome; I could stop it—in fact, I could ruin a whole career with one single innuendo. But that's not all: I have been an Ufficiale di Gran Croce three times since eighteen ninety-six, I am one of the very few men in Rome who can boast such high titles both from the King and from the Holy See. I am an Excellency twice over, TWICE. And yet, comes the official occasion, inevitably, unfailingly, with a regularity that would drive anyone insane, what am I called in the presence of my own lowliest underlings? Cavaliere. Confess that you don't know whether to laugh or to cry. . . ."

"I confess," said Leonardo, wishing to God the Cardinal were present to hear him.

"Not that I care to dine with princes. I was raised among princes and dukes in Sicily, and proudly said goodbye to all that at the tender age of sixteen. But do these Roman princes ever ask themselves what kind of a heart beats under the clothes of a policeman? If they did, the answer would be: the heart of a poet—an epic poet, of course. How could any other kind of poetry spring from this Eternal City, as once again it is reasserting itself as the Capital of the World? I never show my epic poems to anyone, because I am too shy, but I do show them my epitaphs."

"Your . . . what?"

"My epitaphs. I'm the best writer of epitaphs in all Italy. Of course, no one knows which ones are by me, because it isn't done to mention the name of the author. Too bad, because some day posterity will realize that some epitaphs are better than others, and then who will know under what name they should be published? I keep copies of them here, in my safe and also at home, so if anything happens in a war or a revolution, one of the two copies will be saved. I do the same with my poems, of course. Do you want me to read you some of my epitaphs?"

"Not now, thank you. I really think I must be going, I'm rather hungry."

"Oh yes, of course, it must be late." He consulted his watch and said: "My God, it's almost three, what am I doing? And I haven't even told you how I shamed Prince Caetani, who once claimed to me he knew the entire *Divine Comedy* by heart, but couldn't quote the verses I had chosen for a speech to the policemen of Rome on the occasion of the King's birthday. It's a long story, I'd better keep it for another day. Let's go."

On the stairway, Leonardo suddenly found himself in the company of an entirely new man and his surprise was so great that he forgot his hunger altogether again, for the third time in the course of a matter of hours. This transformed character grabbed him by the arm and began to continue a conversation the beginning of which Leonardo had never even heard. "You understand my game, in view of the coming Conclave—it may come sooner than we think: His Holiness is not in good health. I now have eight Cardinals in my hand: you know which ones I mean. From these will come the one to be elected to the Throne, and therefore you and I will be able to influence the papal game on the chessboard of history."

"I?" asked Leonardo, as if proclaiming his innocence in front of a judge.

"You, too. Indirectly, of course, through our friend Mrs. von Randen. Have you met her personal banker?"

"Y . . . es."

"Very important pawn in the coming balance of power in Europe. You know of course that he is not the father of our dear Marchesa Tempi."

"I don't know his daughter."

"She is not his daughter. She's the daughter of a Russian grand duke. And her conversion to our faith was the work of one of my Cardinals, when he was still a humble Monsignor. Brilliant, brilliant theologian. I wish he were working on the foster father now, while you are working on Mrs. von Randen. You can't convert two persons at one blow. And you are too busy with your own estates and other personal responsibilities."

Here he stopped to reflect on some other great problem concerning them both, and Leonardo had the time to observe the effect of this cheap comedy on an audience of flunkies and minor officials, all gathered downstairs now as if this were a regular part of their duties. People who were coming in from outside with their own worries and complaints were quickly briefed by the flunkies on the importance of the occasion: His Excellency was going out to lunch, and the gentleman with him was also an Excellency or something similar in rank. In vain did Leonardo try to make it clear with grimaces of distaste, amazement, even amusement, that he had nothing to do with this vulgar performance: the audience turned against him and he didn't dare look beyond the footlights, lest he provoke both his old and his new enemies to action. So he played his part bravely, even eagerly, for Mary's sake, and was pleased when His Excellency stopped for the seventh time (each step had already been a stop, and the lower they came, the longer these became) and said, taking his arm: "Do you know that Mrs. von Randen was here once?"

"Was she?"

"Yes, she came on purpose, to see where I worked. She had been introduced to me at the Russian embassy, by the ambassador in person: an old and very intimate friend of mine. He promised me one of the highest decorations in the Russian Empire; but then he was recalled. But I wouldn't know where to pin another decoration on my dinner jacket; when I go out on formal occasions I have so many, and you know what those high awards all weigh! Yes, she was introduced to me by him as the richest and most extravagant member of the Russian colony in Rome, and indeed I soon discovered it was true. She took a fancy to me—I mean a highly moral one, nothing sentimental about it: she is a woman of the Spirit, a writer and a scholar—so she took a fancy to me because, she said, I was a great original, and she wanted to put me into a novel she was writing about Rome. Ask her when you see her today whether she has finished it and tell her that one of her humblest admirers takes the liberty of sending her his greetings!"

Leonardo swallowed a great deal of saliva, cleared his throat and said humbly: "Yes, yes, of course I will."

"And did you meet the widow of His Excellency, the head of police, two days ago?"

"No, why, have they killed the head of the Italian police now?"

"Lord, no, that would mean me. . . ." And he made an obscene gesture which brought respectful giggles from the audience, while Leonardo excused himself, blushing: "I'm so sorry, I should have known, you mean the Russian Minister of the Interior."

"Another Excellency gone, killed in the line of duty! What a
tragedy! His Imperial Majesty should be very careful now, remembering how his grandfather died. I always care about the sovereign
in my custody, while many of my colleagues do not. They only care
about themselves and their puny medals and honors. What are
honors, I ask, in the face of God's greatness? Nothing. *Memento
mori*, says the Latin tag. *Memento quia pulvis es et in pulvere
reverteris*. That's me: ready to die at any moment, with the name of
my God on my lips."

They had exhausted all the steps, now they were on a level with
the flunkies and the public, and His Excellency all at once became
very reserved. But somehow he nevertheless allowed them to overhear one of the highest interexcellential conversations they had ever
been party to. "This," said His Excellency, disentangling his arm
from Leonardo's and caressing the fur on his collar, "this is the kind
of lining I should have for my overcoat. As you can see, I wear the
cheapest, falsest fur to be found, because in my professional capac-
ities it's always safer for me not to dress up. This must be Russian
ermine or zibeline."

"I don't know. It isn't mine, I . . ."

"Zibeline, zibeline, I'm sure," shouted His Excellency to cover up
Leonardo's imprudent words. "His Imperial Majesty William the
Second was wearing one when I accompanied him to the Capitol, in
eighteen ninety-six, for an informal visit to the museum. None of
our Excellencies wear it, except for the Excellency in Foreign
Affairs, who is, like me, a connoisseur of furs: all the others wear
fox. How much did you pay for it?"

"I told you, it isn't—"

"You don't know of course, because it was a present from our
mutual friend, eh? I know, I know . . . but this is worth at least
four thousand lire . . . in rubles, of course. I'll have to order one
from Russia."

"Do you want it? I'll give it to you and you can give me yours."

"I could never accept such an exchange. You might be taken for a
nobody—which is the reason I wear this kind of fur—and I might
be taken for a Royal Highness and shot by anarchists."

"I don't care," said Leonardo. "If you want it, I'll give it to
you."

"My dear Highness," said His Excellency, feigning absent-mindedness, then, seeing that Leonardo's face was darkening, he shouted: "Just a moment . . . I was forgetting . . ." (his fingers were snapping in an effort to recall something important, and his hand was forcing Leonardo to walk faster, away from the two senti-nels) ". . . what was it I wanted to tell you? Something very, very important." When they were out of the sentinels' earshot and eye-sight, His Excellency's face became normal again, but not Leo-nardo's: in fact, he looked even gloomier now, as he spoke.

"Why do you call me Highness, when you know very well I am not?"

"Did I?" His Excellency's ears turned purple. "I wasn't aware of it. Sorry. And thank you for the offer of your overcoat, which, of course, I cannot accept."

"Why not? It will be too long for you, but it was long for me and they had to take it up. Ask your wife to do the same, or your maid, if you have one, and you can even have a cape made for your wife out of the rest."

"But how can I repay you for such a generous gift?"

"I'm not in the fur business, and, as I told you, I paid nothing for this. Do you want it? Give me yours, I'll give you mine."

"Here? Why don't you come to my house for a modest meal?"

"No, thank you. If you want to change in my coach, there it is."

"That's an idea."

They walked to the coach, His Excellency climbed in while Leo-nardo was undressing, then His Excellency's hand emerged with his coat, Leonardo took it with one hand and gave him his own with the other. Two seconds later His Excellency emerged with Leo-nardo's overcoat on his arm, and watched Leonardo with a certain apprehension: the cheaper garment was too wide and too short.

"No, no," said His Excellency with a slight tremor in his voice: "It doesn't fit you, it never will, I can't take advantage of you."

"I don't care," said Leonardo. "Keep that thing, I don't want it. This will do for me."

"But how can I thank you?"

"You don't have to."

"Well, it was a pleasure to meet you, and I'm sure that the

Conclave will come sooner than we think. But in any case you may always count on my friendship and eternal gratitude."

With a warm handshake they parted, and Leonardo slumped down in his seat, shouting to the coachman: "To the hotel, please."

It was only when they passed Piazza di Spagna that he realized he had totally forgotten to plead the case of the *porchetta* man.

Back at the hotel, he ordered himself a big lunch to be served in his room, and the answer was yes, but not in your bedroom: "You have a dining room, why not there?"

"All right, the dining room, but when can I eat?"

"In a half hour, no earlier."

Another agonizing half hour . . . He dragged himself upstairs, threw his new overcoat on the floor, and himself into bed, falling asleep almost instantly.

But a few minutes later he was awake again. He was too tired: morally tired, eager to leave that bed, with its memories of Adriana and his fears of having made her pregnant. But he was also too tired to get up; he dreamed that he had got up only to realize that he hadn't, so he tried to get up again, and again did so only in his dream. And every time the dream became more luminous and credible, and lasted longer, and his breathing became quieter. When he finally opened his eyes, he heard whispers, and saw Mr. Schultz talking to a waiter at the door leading to the dining room. At first he found this perfectly normal, and believed he had been asleep in Sophie's bedroom, where he had slept that morning, but then he recognized his hotel room and remembered all the circumstances of his agitated day, but couldn't understand why Mr. Schultz, of all people, should be in his bedroom, and why he should be holding Leonardo's new overcoat on his arm, as if it were his intention to walk away with it. He closed his eyes again, to hide, not like a child, or the proverbial ostrich, but like a former student for the priesthood who sees the Father Censor look through his overcoat pockets while he is asleep, and knows that he has no right to surprise the Father Censor and ask him what he is doing.

As if this thought had suggested the action to Mr. Schultz, Leonardo heard the ruffling of papers and quickly opened one eye, to catch Mr. Schultz putting on his glasses and reading some tiny bits of paper he had found in one of the pockets. A few more rapid blinks allowed him to photograph the face of Mr. Schultz looking rather baffled, then frowning and shaking his head, then walking towards a wooden coat rack that stood in a corner, and hanging the overcoat there with the efficiency of a good servant. He didn't know whether to wait for him to leave, or to open his eyes officially and act surprised. He didn't have to do either, because Mr. Schultz softly called, "Leonardo?"

The effect of that timid voice, and of his name pronounced in that foreign accent, melted his heart, and he opened his eyes, pretending to be very surprised and a bit hazy.

"Your lunch is ready, don't you want to eat it? Your guest hasn't arrived yet, and I am going to leave before he or she appears. But after you've finished, send for me, I'll be in my room: I must talk to you."

"But I'm not expecting any guests; let me tell you why I ordered lunch here instead of coming home. . . ."

"No explanations needed, or asked, for that matter," and the voice seemed just a little resentful, which upset Leonardo at once, as he jumped to his feet and rearranged his cravat in the mirror.

"But I feel the need to explain; please listen. I . . . er . . . I had such a busy morning that I couldn't find a moment to eat anything, and when I finally got back here I felt so dizzy and tired that I took the liberty of ordering some lunch, because I didn't eat anything, even last night, and this morning I skipped breakfast, and I was so dreadfully tired that while I was waiting for my lunch I just threw myself on the bed and fell asleep."

Mr. Schultz became pensive, while Leonardo watched him with a slight recurrence of tension, which was soon dispelled, thank God, by the broad smile that appeared on that distinguished old face: "But that suits me very well: I'll join you and have a bite myself. I haven't eaten either, except for a cup of black coffee this morning at five, when I got up, and I feel rather hungry now."

"But . . . didn't you have lunch at the house?"

"Well, in a way . . . but you know how it is, when so many important people gather for a meal: the host has other things to do than enjoy his own food. And besides— But I'll tell you everything later. You begin, because you must be starving, I'll go back to my room and make an urgent telephone call, then I'll join you, and we will have hours to talk undisturbed. Does this seem acceptable?"

"Excellent, excellent, I have so many things to discuss with you."

"And I with you, so that makes two of us. See you in a minute."

With these words he was gone, and Leonardo sighed with relief. Not another meal with supervision of an expert in the handling of knives and forks . . . He went into the dining room, sat down, dismissed the waiter and began to eat so quickly that when Mr. Schultz reappeared, he was almost ready to eat only soup, or ice cream, or bread—the easiest foods to handle—and he had gulped down half a bottle of an excellent French wine, which made everything in his life appear easy. Of course, the experiences of that long morning still seemed ugly, but at a distance, and as he knew that in two days he would be leaving Rome, the only thing that worried him was a problem of timing, but he already had a workable plan: ask His Excellency the policeman to dinner at Mary's for two days after their departure. What a blow to the idiot's vanity . . . Of course this would mean open warfare, lawsuits for abduction of a minor and all that, but since this was what Mary and her mother wanted and were ready to fight from abroad, why should he care? His disgust with Rome was such that he wished he could leave that very night, and forever. The only thorn in his heart now was that precious fur coat: not that he loved it, all of a sudden, but to have given it to such a despicable person was indeed unforgivable. *Pazienza*, he said to himself, thinking how lucky he was to have found a friend like Sophie. If she has forgiven so much, she will certainly forgive me for the loss of that and those cufflinks too. I owe her a complete explanation, and I shall begin with Schultz right now. "As you see, Mr. Schultz, I have eaten already, but I can still eat more, to keep you company."

"But how kind of you, how generous," said Mr. Schultz with a broad smile. "So, here we are at long last without the ladies. We can be frank with each other, don't you think?"

"Why yes, of course, that's exactly what I was going to say. Because, you see—"

"Just a moment, let me ask you first: did you have a good time with your cousin?"

"What do you mean by a good time? I would have had a better time at home. I saw him because I had to see him."

"Did you see him immediately after you left the house?"

"No, not immediately. I had to see someone else first. In fact—"

"Please, don't elaborate. I'm not a father inquisitor. My only question is: why didn't you ask your cousin for lunch, as Mary and her mother had suggested?"

"Well, he was in a hurry, he was in no mood to meet new people, we had family matters to discuss. . . ."

"I see, I see. But you also bought a new overcoat."

"No, I did not. That . . . that was an exchange."

"An exchange? With whom, if I may be so inquisitive?"

"Ho-hum . . . With my cousin."

"Oh, I see. He's short and fat."

"Hm-hn . . . yes."

"Shorter than you."

"Hahaha . . . yes. It was a mistake, because this overcoat doesn't fit me, but . . . he liked it so much . . ."

"I understand. Generosity is our first trait, isn't it?"

This time Leonardo neither answered nor coughed, nor giggled. A strange current of cold air seemed to be coming from Mr. Schultz, as if he had suddenly vanished, leaving nothing but an open window through which darkness came in instead of afternoon sun. It is usually light that chases away darkness: here the opposite. Mr. Schultz, materializing again instantaneously, put his hand into his pocket and took out the famous missing moonstone cufflinks, which he placed next to Leonardo's plate.

"Like your generosity with these?"

Leonardo sighed with relief; the dark night was beginning to melt, and he said cheerfully: "If you promise to believe me, I will tell you the whole truth. In fact, that's what I wanted to tell Sophie and Mary, and you too, of course, because you are part of the family."

"How kind of you to include me."

"It's not kindness, it is the verification of a fact. *I* am the new-comer here, so it is with humility and awe that I dare—"

"Enough of your Italian pleasantries. State the facts."

"The facts," said Leonardo, feeling the blood rush to his neck, "are simply these: I didn't have a cent in my pocket, and I tried to explain this to a poor beggar woman with a sick child on the Scalinata; she didn't believe me and began to abuse me; I ran away, met the man Schillasi on my way down, and he wanted me to denounce her to the police for robbing me. I just couldn't persuade him that she hadn't. Later we went to a café together—"

"Where you told everybody that you were Sophie's lover."

Leonardo jumped up from his chair shouting: "I DID NOT!"

"Reason talks, guilt shouts, says the old French proverb."

"But I tell you—"

"Not so loud, please. I'm here, not down there in the piazza."

"But you don't seem to believe me, and you promised . . ."

"I never promised anything. That was entirely *your* assumption, and entirely a falsehood. Or can you find a better name for it?"

"Falsehood, truthhood, what big words to use . . . It was an assumption—all right, what's wrong with that? How can a conversation begin between two gentlemen?"

"It cannot, because you are not a gentleman, and if you had given me time to prove it to you, I could have spared you your tragedy which I have known for days in all its minutest details."

Now the whole room was dark. Objects were visible as they must be to cats, who provide their own light, or so superstition says. Leonardo lifted his eyes and saw the face of Mr. Schultz, standing out from all reality, past, present and future; it was a face he knew because he had seen it often enough in the mirror, and any earlier differences between him and Mr. Schultz disappeared, together with the "assumption" of friendship and humanity. He recognized and of course loved his own face in the mirror, with a feeling of envy such as he had never believed possible, because how can a young man wish to look so old and decaying? He can, indeed he must, because that face had earned its right to grow old: his never would. Yet even the damned in the *Inferno* are allowed to tell their tragic story, and so Leonardo spoke again, while Mr. Schultz sat, nonplussed by his daring.

"I know you saw Schillasi, I know everything about you and the Baron and the Cardinal, and it was my mistake, for which I must humbly apologize. I believed all his lies about being a professor, I would never have done what I did, if I had known. I was guilty of stupidity, provincial contempt for the conventions of the world, but I say and repeat and swear on my own mother's grave that I never, never, never said or even vaguely thought of saying that Sophie was my mistress. That's horrible . . . and I cringe at the thought that you, a man of the world, you, who have known me and seen me frequently over the last three or four days, should have believed any such vulgar, horrible slander."

"Easy, young man, are you accusing me?"

"No, I am only describing my reactions at the thought that you *might* have believed it, so I assume you really didn't in your heart of hearts."

"I wish you were right, and I can't tell you how grieved I was when I was confronted with the truth."

"The truth?"

"The truth. How do you explain that at least three different people have reported the same thing as having been said by you at the Caffè Greco, and a fourth person heard you say it elsewhere?"

"Names, please. If you are not a father inquisitor, don't use their methods."

"You Italians say: name the sin, not the sinner."

"Well, if you yourself admit that they sinned in reporting such nonsense, then I may also assume they were all liars."

"Why not assume that you were the liar, since you are one? Why should a sick old woman, who has never even heard of you, invent this story, with names and everything? Why should the mother of Avvocato Tegolani slander you? She didn't know who you were, but she heard what you said, and she described you exactly as you are, or rather, as you were then, in your expensive fur coat, which your cousin will have to cut in half, to fit him, judging from this overcoat of his, and she even identified your accent, as you were boasting of your conquest to a man who sells *porchetta* right under her bedroom window."

"But that's all a misunderstanding, I *swear* to you—please give me the benefit of the doubt."

"I wish I could, but a man caught lying once has lost all possible credit. I'm a banker, you know, I deal with people's means of livelihood all the time, I know how sacred they are to *them*, and I don't mean the rich, whose love of money I have always despised, I mean the very poor, who earn their money sweating blood, as you Italians so aptly say, and it is because I understand and love the poor, the *honest* poor, I mean, that I must draw a line where my trust ends. You have told us not one, but many lies, useless lies, as you so eloquently described them this morning, and—again in your own words—you don't deserve to be believed. I can say it does look like a misunderstanding. I can go even further: the episode at the café may even look like a misunderstanding. In fact, I had reached that conclusion myself, and had decided to spare you any unpleasant confrontation with witnesses, but that was yesterday—what a terrible day for poor Sophie, how she suffered, how nobly she overcame her disgust for this man who had cheated everybody . . . Yes, what is it? I see you flashing your famous Italian eyes . . . spare yourself the effort, no one is impressed . . . cheated everybody, I say and yet . . . and yet, we both said to ourselves: he doesn't know any better, he deserves the benefit of the doubt. . . . And we gave it to him."

With this word "him" Mr. Schultz thought he had driven the knife home and could rest for a moment. But he hadn't counted on Leonardo's candor: "And I'm grateful to you for this favor, which I am trying to deserve."

"Too late. You seemed to have more than deserved it this morning, with your beautiful words, which won you my friendship, and the complete devotion of a person as noble and uncompromising as Madame Morosoff, but your later lies of today . . ."

"What lies? You haven't given me the time to tell you the whole truth: I went to see the Cardinal. That was a stupid thing to do, and I don't even know why I did it, I was nervous, with all those Russians around."

"Spare yourself another lie and spare me another unpleasant truth. I just gave you the time to tell me the whole truth, and now you're using it to tell me another lie, which will be followed by still another lie, on and on incessantly."

And he rose from his seat, in a great hurry to leave. Leonardo rushed after him and grabbed him by the arm.

"You must let me talk. Please, don't go away like this. . . ."

"I am not going away. Go back there and sit down; take my advice, you will soon need a chair to slump into. Go, I say!"

They were on the threshold of the bedroom, and Leonardo knew what was coming: Adriana must have forgotten some intimate garment, and this was the end. He hesitated for a second, but as Mr. Schultz seemed determined not to be followed into the other room, he walked slowly back to his chair, feeling the eyes of the Father Censor on him as he went.

"All right," said Mr. Schultz, as Leonardo timidly looked at him again from his chair. "Now wait." Leonardo saw him go to the coat rack and come back with the "new" overcoat. This was such a relief that he couldn't help smiling as Mr. Schultz solemnly folded the overcoat inside out, while walking back into the dining room, then showed him the name of the tailor embroidered on a label, and under it, also neatly embroidered, the words: *His Excellency Gennaro Ramirez, January 3d, 1900.* "Whose coat is this?"

A long silence, and a smile on Leonardo's face, followed by a light shrugging of the shoulders, and a sigh of impatience.

"You seem amused. You're even worse than I thought. No answer? Well, let me tell you the truth, then, since you seem unwilling to talk: you went from the Cardinal's house to police headquarters, where you stayed a whole hour and emerged with that man, arm in arm, like two old friends. The coachman didn't tell me about this exchange of overcoats, he is a very stupid man, and probably didn't even notice it, but I noticed at once that Pierre's overcoat had disappeared from your room, and this one was lying on the floor. Let me tell you two details: Pierre's overcoat was worth more than one thousand even of these cufflinks, and the person of Mr. Ramirez is worth precisely nothing. He is one of the lowest creatures in all Rome, lower by far than your so-called cousin Schillasi. If you knew German, you would be able to read a most telling description of Ramirez in a book by Sophie titled *Sketches*. He is not only an illiterate fool with social ambitions and pretenses of nobility, like almost all the Italians I have known—"

"Not me!"

"Granted, not you, but you are still a liar, and a more vicious one than Ramirez, who only lies about his noble ancestors. Still, Ramirez is more disgusting than you in other ways: for an invitation to dinner he will sell his own mother. No one ever receives him, nor pays any attention to him, and you go to this man and talk to him for a whole hour, about God knows what, I'm not asking you, I don't want to know—or, rather—I do know, because it is easy to imagine, and then you even give him a present such as I would consider too extravagant for myself, and in my old age I could well afford to buy myself that kind of an overcoat. See mine over there, on that rack? If you knew anything about furs, you would recognize it as the type of fur almost anyone can afford. But, no matter. I do want to ask you one question, before you leave. . . ."

"I am not leaving."

"Yes, you are. We'll talk about that later. Now answer my question: how long have you known Mary's mother-in-law?"

"I didn't even know she was Mary's mother-in-law. I met her by absolute chance, in the Cardinal's anteroom, downstairs."

"Absolute chance, downstairs . . . never known her before . . . One doesn't cry on the shoulder of a lady, especially a lady like that, the quintessence of timidity and suspicion, unless one has known her for years."

"But I swear to you . . ."

"Yes, yes, I know. Circumstances, again. How about the circumstance that you hate Mary's child and Mary's mother, and would find it convenient to be rid of both, and are trying to find means to arrange for all that?"

"That is the most lurid slander I have ever heard in my life, the stupidest, weirdest fairy tale ever invented by a sick mind."

"Easy, young man, easy. I may not know the exact mechanism of your secret plans, but I know that some plan of the sort must exist. There is no other explanation, and I am not going to wrack my brains in search of one. I hate mysteries. Nor do I want any further explanations from you. I am just telling you that I will not allow my adopted grandchild Mary ever to see you again, let alone marry you."

Leonardo felt almost relieved. Now he knew that Mary and Sophie were still for him, and that his real enemy knew nothing about Adriana. So he could still dare something, and he did: "Yet you allowed your adopted granddaughter Mary to run away with the lowest of clowns in all Rome, much lower, in fact, than Ramirez, who worships him as a genius. At least Ramirez didn't try to rape Mary, but your own son-in-law did. That's why Mary threw herself into the arms of a fool you call the Monster: to flee from a real monster. And if she lied to her own mother, it was only to protect the innocent wife of *that* monster, and of course you. Will you call her a liar too, or just a martyr to your own pride and moral imbecility?"

Mr. Schultz reeled, collapsed, and hid his face in his hands. Leonardo looked on in sheer delight, and felt so liberated that he grabbed the carving knife, slowly rose from his chair, and when he found himself behind Mr. Schultz, he looked at that bent neck, then turned his back to it and, cutting himself a huge portion of white meat from the turkey on the contrebuffet, ate it with his hands, then licked his fingers. When he sat down again, still chewing noisily and picking his teeth with his golden toothpick, Mr. Schultz lifted his head and looked at him with disgust. But it was not the disgust of the winner: there was fear in that look too, and, in a way, a profound admiration, which embarrassed Leonardo.

"Come on," he said, "what's wrong with being wrong for once? No one is perfect! It's not the end of the world. Mary survived both that bastard of a son-in-law of yours and that bastard of her husband, and by God she's going to marry me and take her child with her. I know how, but you don't. And I won't tell you how. I've had enough of being called a liar by someone who's no better than I am."

"I never tell lies . . . never, and I don't go about censoring others as you do. . . . Leave me alone with my grief, can't you see what you've done to me?" And he hid his face in his hands again.

"I'm sorry," said Leonardo timidly. "I was only trying to be helpful."

"Helpful, he calls it. . . . I don't take my errors lightly."

"Neither do I, but it all depends on what errors. If I killed one of my patients through ignorance, of course I'd be a finished man, but if I disappointed you, my God, that's just too bad; after all, I'm not a thief. Mary's brother is a thief, and you not only survived, but helped him go on stealing."

"Enough, enough, enough, you're a devil. . . . I mustn't weaken a second time. I know you're wrong, because you are clever, and I am only stupid."

"You are the first person on earth to call me clever. Today, of all days in my life . . . Hahahaha . . . Hahhahhaaaahhaaa . . ."

"Stop being so cynical, you—Italian comedian."

"Take care, you international clown."

There was a tense moment, in which neither of the two seemed willing to say the next word, then Mr. Schultz began to nod his head, as if listening to some inner voice, and said: "I have found the solution. For the third and last time, I shall give you the benefit of the doubt. But I shall also put you to a test. You must answer me honestly, and if you do not, you're finished. Do you have anything else to conceal? Any other lies you told us recently? Any dishonorable actions to confess?"

Leonardo felt it coming and lowered his head, concentrating his interest on a crumb hidden under the rim of his plate, like a bird under a roof in a hailstorm.

"Take your time," said Mr. Schultz now, almost in a whisper, then after an effort adding: "Leonardo." Then, after another pause: "I know it's hard, and if you think I'm against you, you are wrong. I was, two days ago, or was it yesterday? My God, how time DOESN'T fly, when it swells our hearts with sorrow. . . . Yes, it was yesterday that I said no to Mary, in her mother's presence, after the Baron came and told us. I had seen Schillasi before, on the Scalinata, as you exchanged waistcoats with him. I passed right by you, you didn't notice me. I had followed you out of the house. And I saw the scene between you and Angelo, but from a distance: I just caught Schillasi and stopped him in the piazza. He said he was in a hurry, but he agreed to sell me the cufflinks for five hundred lire: they're worth *two* maximum; in fact, they were bought by Mary's grandfather in Piazza di Spagna, in eighteen forty-nine, I was with him. That was the year of the Roman Republic, we had lunch with the president, Giuseppe Mazzini, and with his foreign minister, Count Carlo Rusconi, whom I later helped in London, for years I helped him and his daughter Ottavia . . . how time flies when it swells our heart with joy. . . . So, I went back to the house and told Mary what kind of a cousin you had, and she was very hurt, but her mother seemed proud. They both knew that stupid clown; he's the brother-in-law of an old manservant in the household of Countess Lovatelli, known as Amore e Pizziche—Donna Ersilia wrote a book on Love and Psyche, and he boasted everywhere that his mistress had written *Amore e Pizziche.** . . . Sophie was all proud of your relationship with those low people, and of course Mary was proud too, once she saw her mother's reaction. Then came the blow. We had just returned from the Russian embassy, when the Baron arrived and told us that your famous scholar was none other than Schillasi. Now the roles were reversed: Sophie was hurt, and Mary was proud, and that was the first time I saw Mary win Sophie over. But I was quite determined to put an end to the whole thing, and so this morning you found me with my office installed in the house. And it was the first time in my life I saw *myself* being won over by a person I didn't respect. Your beautiful speech . . . I have it right here, I brought it with me, Miss Panzironi took notes and copied them while we were talking with Madame Morosoff. . . . I'll reread them to you, so they may help you find the strength to confess."

"No, please."

But Mr. Schultz had already put on his glasses and was searching among the letters and telegrams he had taken out of his pocket, so Leonardo went back to his crumb and wished he were it.

"Here we are: 'Now, for example, this habit of telling unnecessary lies is what I find particularly detestable in my dear countrymen. And you must have lived with them, been brought up under this lower kind of wisdom, to recognize it. . . .' I'll spare you the rest. Are you ready to confess?"

Leonardo looked up, and decided not to say anything for a while.

"All right, you take your time and I'll go on talking. But there will come a point where I have nothing more to say and it will be too late. Shall I go on?"

No answer.

"Very well. So, where was I? Oh yes, after you left to see your cousin, Adriana's husband came in. You may not know that Adriana has a husband who worships her and who comes to the house all the time to see her, though she refuses to see him. This morning

* *Loving and Pinching*, in Romanesco. In Italian it would be *pizzichi*.

she didn't, even though she was sick, or probably because she felt so
sick and unhappy. You don't know that Adriana and Mary are like
sisters. Or did you?"

"No," said Leonardo, without looking up from under that roof.

"And Adriana came to me. She got out of bed, pale and feverish
as she was, dressed in a hurry and came to me. We talked for only a
few minutes in the music room, while the others were in the library,
and what she told me almost gave me a stroke. I thought I was
going to die right then and there. I couldn't believe my ears, I kept
asking her if it was the truth, but I couldn't doubt it, she was so
upset, she could hardly open her mouth. I sent her back to bed and
went to join the others—but I simply couldn't bring myself to tell
them that Adriana's husband had actually seen you crying in the
arms of that old idiot we all so cordially detest."

Leonardo looked up and saw that the hailstorm had passed. Birds
were chirping festively again and the chicken was again crossing the
road. . . .

"Are you ready to confess?"

"But I have nothing to confess."

"Are you so sure? We'll see. It's getting late, late in the story, I
want you to know."

Leonardo stayed under the roof, but only out of *scaramanzia.**

"All right, your choice. I'll give you more chance than you deserve. . . . So I went back to the library and said nothing, but
Sophie noticed the state I was in and she asked me to follow her
outside, which I did, and there I told her. It was her turn to feel ill,
and this time I had to escort her to her room. We stayed there for a
half hour, trying to understand this whole nightmarish mystery, but
couldn't. Finally we both decided that we must force ourselves to go
back, for the sake of our guests. Mary of course noticed nothing,
which was good, but we both felt so pained whenever we saw her
that it made the next hour a real torture. Then came the next
blow. . . . Are you ready to confess?"

"But I have nothing to confess."

"Your choice, but time is getting very, very short. Ready?"

---

* The antidote to the evil eye: i.e., touching wood.

Leonardo was looking sleepy, and Mr. Schultz stared at his eyelids as he fought off the temptation to close them.

"Well . . . I don't know what to say at this point. Why give you so much time? All right, I promised, and I never go back on my word. So after that terrible hour came the next blow, just as the butler was getting ready to announce dinner. He heard the doorbell and, thinking this was another guest, told one of the younger boys to open up and send the new guests to the library. At that point I was leaving the library, because my distress was such that I needed to be alone for a while, and what do I see? Two of the most vulgar-looking individuals and one of the new waiters, all embracing one another and laughing and talking, I am sorry to say, in *your* accent. I couldn't understand what they were saying, but I knew this was enough, and I shouted: 'What's all this?' Our waiter instantly excused himself by saying one of the men was his cousin, but the two new arrivals didn't seem in the least embarrassed. One of them asked me, 'Are you Mary's Pappa? I'm Leonardo's cousin, how are you, Goombà?' And before I could say a word, he was kissing me on the mouth. At which moment, Mary appeared, and asked him: 'Where is Leonardo? Why isn't he with you?' 'He'll be here soon enough,' said this barbarian. 'Are you Mary?' 'I am,' she answered, and so he kissed her on both cheeks, which I couldn't prevent, because she seemed quite willing, and then the other barbarian kissed her too, before she could ask him who he was. And Mary, innocently of course, wanted to take them into the library with her. At this point I said: 'No. You two, come with me in here, and you, Mary, leave us alone.' As you will easily grasp, Mary didn't even think of paying any attention. She joined us, but the two barbarians wouldn't let me talk. Your cousin began to ask Mary if she had a sister he could marry, then the other barbarian said: '*Two* sisters, one for me too.' At this point Mary was beginning to be really upset; she kept asking: 'But why isn't Leonardo with you? What happened to him?' And they just giggled and said: 'Never mind, he's in no danger, but will he be surprised to find us here!' So I shouted: 'Enough. You, Mary, leave us alone, and you two, tell me where Leonardo is and why you dared to come here without him.' This seemed to sober them down, and they were about to answer me, when Sophie appeared at the door and asked not your cousin, but the other man: 'Are you Leonardo's cousin?' 'No,' he said, 'I'm the cousin of the boy who opened the door. Leonardo's cousin is that one there.' And your cousin opened his arms to embrace Sophie—luckily I stopped him in time—and said: 'No, I'm not his cousin, I'm his wife's cousin, but I'm fed up with my wife too, and I want a divorce and a new wife as pretty as Mary.' At which point Sophie fainted. Not completely: she is a remarkable woman and has unbelievable control over her emotions. She just sat down hard and put both hands over her face, while Mary knelt by her side and tried to help her. I felt this was the moment to give Mary the shock she needed, and I, said to your cousins or whatever they are that they must talk to me alone and answer all my questions, starting with why you were not with them, and how they had dared come to the house by themselves, without being invited. So they did. Will you take over from here? This is not a confession, I know what went on between you, because they told me, of course. I just want to see whether your version corresponds to theirs, and perhaps once you have overcome that unbelievable coy timidity of yours you may even regain your gift of theatrical eloquence, and tell me what your assistants didn't know: namely, why you went to see the Cardinal, why you are on such intimate terms with the old lady, and why you had to rush off to the chief of police."

"But it's not my fault if those two barbarians, as you so aptly describe them, whom I hate far more than you do, overstayed their time in Rome and—"

"Stop right there. I don't want justifications, just the facts. I am the judge and I am asking you, the accused, to tell me your version of the facts that led to your arrest. I know that with Italians this is the only system that works. It doesn't guarantee that they will tell you the truth, but their lies will be that much more difficult because they know they'll be in jail the moment they're found out. . . ."

"The reason I went to see the Cardinal—"

"No! I said, continue from where I left off. You met them . . ."

Leonardo was back under his roof, blushing and suffering.

". . . as you were coming out of the Cardinal's house, and what did you say to them?"

Leonardo rolled his eyes and huffed with impatience, and Mr.

Schultz said: "Don't roll your eyes and don't huff with impatience. See how patient *I* am. Pretend you're telling a lie, perhaps that will allow you to be as eloquent as you are when you pretend you're telling the truth. Come on: you met them and you said . . . ?"

"I asked them why they—"

"No. The exact words."

"I said, 'Why aren't you back at your desks?' "

"Right. And they said . . ."

"They said, 'Why aren't you?' "

"Right. And with this our interview is closed. Consider it my last question to you: Why aren't *you* back at *your* desk? If it is a matter of money, I can pay for your ticket. Not the first-class tickets I offered your assistants—who turned out to be perfectly decent villagers, whose fantasies had been inflamed by your tales of money and splendor and elephants and maharajas and czars . . ."

"That's a lie, I never, never said such things. They invented them years ago, and I have no control over their minds."

"I see. Was that the reason you ordered our coachman to whip them in public?"

"I swear I did not. The coachman can testify to that."

"I am not going to ask the coachman. I asked Adriana and she told me everything about what went on in the kitchen and in the changing room that evening."

Leonardo left his refuge under the roof to slide out of sight under the table. There he sought refuge between his knees, then his eyes slid down to his shoes, and the shoes slowly began to recede into the distance, growing smaller and smaller until they disappeared in a dark hole, and the next thing he knew his forehead was wet. Mr. Schultz was holding a corner of the napkin over Leonardo's forehead, and water was dripping onto his face and down his collar. Some drops had reached his chest. He opened his eyes and Mr. Schultz withdrew, saying: "It's over. Yes, young man, I know it's hard on you, I know you are suffering, but so am I, so are we all. The harm you have done to every one of us, including poor Adriana, is incalculable. It can never be forgotten. It will sting for years. You mentioned Pierre. Pierre never hurt me that way, because Pierre couldn't hurt me. I never liked him. You I loved like a son from the first moment I saw you. I was attracted to you, because you seemed so simple and so direct. I made an effort to seem inimical, because I owed it to the memory of Sophie's father, my great benefactor. But I was always ready to accept your arguments, and I do so wish I hadn't. The horror of it all keeps coming back to me every minute: here, I say to myself, is a man who has taken advantage of the love we have all given him so blindly, so confidently; in our own house, under our eyes, he began to conspire against us with the one person he had been warned against: the coachman. Adriana told us everything: how you disappeared with him into the changing room and how he emerged announcing to everyone in his usual stupid way that you were his closest friend. So obviously you had a plan in mind, and now that you know, please tell me. For the last time, answer my questions: Why did you go to the Cardinal and why were you so happy to see the old lady? You must have had an appointment with her. There is no other explanation."

"Yes," said Leonardo joyfully, stretching his arms because his heart felt so much lighter. "Yes, there *is* an explanation, and it may even amuse you. I went to see the Cardinal because I was hungry and I had never once been able to eat in that palace in peace—ask the Cardinal, he can tell you—the reason being I never learned to hold a knife and fork the way you do."

Mr. Schultz frowned, he stared at Leonardo for a moment, then said: "And why, if this is to be believed, didn't the Cardinal ask you to stay? Why the sudden rush to the chief of police, the one person in Rome, incidentally, who would favor Angelo's mother against Mary's."

Leonardo smiled happily again and said: "I know it sounds strange, but the Cardinal was angry at me because of Schillasi, very angry in fact, and so I decided to go to the chief of police, thinking he was the man I had met with the Queen Mother. Ask Sophie, she can tell you. The plainclothesman guarding the Queen gave me his visiting card, when he discovered I came from Laterza. . . ."

"Another cousin, I imagine."

"No, but a friend of friends, a goombà, as we say. And I was hoping he would invite me to lunch. But he was away, and so . . ."

"And so you went to see our greatest enemy, not knowing him at all."

"That's right. I wanted to denounce Schillasi anyway for the cufflinks."

"How intricate, how like a cheap mystery. And that explains another mystery: that, in spite of your intimate friendship with the chief of police, so intimate that you exchanged overcoats, as one only does among old schoolmates or brothers—in your case, I should say cousins—in spite of all that, he didn't ask you to lunch, and so you came here, where you would have come anyway directly from the Cardinal's if hunger had been your motive."

"Well, the truth is that I detested him so much I refused to go to his house for lunch, and so I came back here. The reason I didn't come here directly was that I would have felt so lonely; in fact, when I left the Cardinal's house, I was thinking of going back to Mary's and saying that I had seen my cousin and he couldn't come."

"Oh, oh, I see. Now we begin to uncover still more little tricks. Your famous cousin, of course, the only one you *did* have a right to claim and never even saw. And yet you knew he was in Rome, your assistants told you as much, and you told them he was the personal physician of the King and the Pope. . . ."

"They said that, I never did."

"*You* told *us*. If you had reasons to distrust those poor villagers who invented stories about elephants and maharajas and czars, why did you so readily believe that particular fairy tale? Anyway, they say you told them, and I prefer to believe them than you, especially since I spoke to your cousin."

"What? You . . . *spoke* to my cousin?"

"He came to the house, he's there now."

"He . . . *is* there *now*? Why didn't you tell me? Let's go home, he'll confirm . . ."

"Confirm what? That you never asked your assistants for his address, but went on boasting that he was what he is not? He doesn't want to see you, but even if he did, Sophie has given strict orders that you are not to be admitted to the house again, ever."

"Why?"

Mr. Schultz looked at the walls and spoke to them: "Still he asks why. . . ." Then, turning to him: "Because the cup is full. If you had voluntarily confessed that you had used him in such a shameful manner to conceal all your contacts with the enemy, Sophie might even have forgiven you, provided of course your reasons became at least understandable in human terms. But this way we only have the choice of considering you a pathological liar and an idiot, or a cheap operator, in it either for money or the political intrigue all you Italians from the South so relish—and you can see that in both cases you would prove totally unacceptable. Mary of course may still believe in you, but I doubt it. We will see how she feels when she emerges from her shock. She lost consciousness when your cousin finally arrived and told us he had never laid eyes on you these last four days, and it's lucky that it was your cousin. He seems to be an excellent physician, not only an eye specialist. He's now sitting by Mary, watching the slow progress of her shock. He's confident that she will be out of it soon, and when this happens, they will all go to Baden-Baden or to Paris for a while; your cousin has accepted Sophie's invitation to go with them. I personally have to leave for London tonight, and will be back after they've gone, but I will join them later. In the meantime I advise that you clear out of here as soon as you can and go back to your hometown, your intrigues, your wife and your cousins. I wish I could order you to leave tomorrow morning. I know all the trains to Laterza by now: there is one at five thirty, but I promised Sophie I would tell you—not on her part—let it be clear that she doesn't want any semblance of direct contact with you, *everything is to be done through me*—I promised I would tell you to take your time. She's too much of a lady to kick you out as an intruder and an enemy. But I advise you that, if you want to act as a gentleman at least once in your life, you should not take excessive advantage of such an offer. I therefore trust that, when I come back to Rome in two weeks' time, I shall be spared the notion that you are still our unwelcome guest. The porter has been instructed to buy you a third-class ticket to Laterza whenever you ask him. I sent your assistants home first-class. They deserved it, you don't. Goodbye."

Leonardo's first reaction was one of disbelief. This man is an idiot, he always hated me, now he hates me even more because of what I said about his son-in-law, but Sophie doesn't want me to leave, and Mary fainted because she was so worried about me. I

can't allow that bastard Crocifisso to believe he can just step into
my place. I must talk to Sophie—but how, if she's given orders . . .
or, rather, this beast has? . . . Dante will help me.

As he rang the bell, he noticed an envelope on his plate. He
opened it; there were fifty lire in it, left by Mr. Schultz: a very large
sum. So he, too, had had second thoughts. But then money seems
to do nothing but create second thoughts. If I had had fifty lire in
my pocket the first day, none of this would have happened. I would
have given money to the prostitute, bought food and coffee for
myself without meeting Schillasi, found that bastard Crocifisso in
his hospital, bought the flowers for Sophie without meeting the
Queen Mother and that bastard policeman, and now there would be
no problem. . . . But why isn't anybody coming?

He rang the bell again, and again fell into second thoughts about
money: If I had had money in 1893, Mary and I would have got
married, by now we would have eight children, at least, and none of
these problems would ever have existed . . . what's the matter
with that waiter?

He rang a third time, and began to write on his prescription pad:
Dear Sophie . . . But then more second thoughts began to attack
that familiar appellative: If I could only explain *before* having to
write her name . . . She was angry this morning, and yet all she
knew about was Schillasi. . . . What's the matter with these
damned servants?

At this point he finally arrived, the same waiter who had been so
humble before, but he didn't even ask what was wanted of him: he
just began to clear the table and brush the crumbs off the tablecloth
with a half-moon-shaped brush and a silver scoop.

"I rang for you three times, didn't you hear me?"

"Nossir, I was busy."

"Where is Dante?"

"Dante who?"

"Dante, the man who washes the floors and the bathtubs."

"Not here in the afternoons."

"Where does he live? I need him urgently."

"I'll find out and let you know."

"But he lives in the hotel with his mother, the old chambermaid
for this apartment."

"Oh, THAT Dante. I'll call him."

"When?"

"As soon as I've cleared the table and taken away the dishes."

"But I'm in a hurry."

No answer. Leonardo tried to master his anger and began to rewrite his short note. But he couldn't just begin in impersonal language, and then explain that this was due to his feelings of unworthiness until he had explained that he was innocent. Nor would he now assume that she might like the familiarity which she herself had denied him first thing that morning. The waiter finally left and Dante arrived, and when Leonardo saw that familiar face from happier days, he almost broke down. "Dante, my friend, I'm so glad to see you. I need your help, urgently. I'm in great trouble. My heart is" (another sob formed in his throat) ". . . so heavy."

But Dante didn't seem to understand. He stood there, blinking, as if Leonardo were speaking in some foreign language.

"Do you understand me, Dante? Will you go to Mrs. von Randen at once and give her a note from me, personally?"

"I can't, sir, I'm busy."

"But I'll give you a generous tip. In fact, I still owe you money from yesterday morning, here it is."

"Nossir, you don't owe me anything."

"Take it anyway, it's fifty lire: I owed your mother something from the first day. . . ."

"Nossir, you owe her nothing."

"Give it to her, please."

"I can't, sir. We are at the service of Mrs. von Randen, we can't take tips from strangers."

And with this he was gone, without even saying goodbye. "Strangers?" The memory of that brotherly embrace of the first morning began to throb.

Pacing the room is one way to bridge gaps in your soul. You don't want to walk outside, so you walk your cage like a lion, and you walk as if at the end of those five or six steps you could finally walk through the wall and go wherever your heart belongs. Leonardo paced the room in all directions, around chairs, between chairs, from window to window, then from one room to the other, from bed to bathroom door, from bathroom door to bed, trying not to remember: You once had a future, then something happened, and you're left with the past. . . . Here you are, entombed . . . but wait a moment, what do you see? The famous telephone that made you laugh so much the first day. Why not use it?

He sat comfortably on the bed, imagining himself already in Sophie's presence, and combed his hair and his beard before taking the two heavy receivers into his hands. "Signorina . . ."

The concierge answered: "What do you want?"

"Connect me with Mrs. von Randen."

"Mr. Schultz gave orders that only calls authorized by him could be made through this phone."

"But this is for him, he asked me to call."

"If you say so. It's your responsibility, I warn you. . . ."

"I tell you, it's very urgent, he will be angry if you don't."

"As you say."

After some bickering with the female operator, the bell rang, and Bernhard answered. "Urgent, for Madame, from Mr. Schultz," shouted Leonardo, trying to sound Roman, and of course the idiot didn't recognize his voice. Oh, what a violent heartbeat, while waiting for her to come to the phone. . . . What will you say first? Ask about Mary's condition or about your own? How do I stand in your heart? Can you still give me a chance to justify myself? No, I shall give her no time to think. I shall just tell her—

A click, then Sophie's anguished voice pouring forth in the highest soprano . . . in Russian.

Leonardo listened in silent terror, then heard more bickering between Sophie and the operator who was being asked to connect her again with Mr. Schultz, very urgently, he must have been cut off, and then suddenly, Sophie's voice came again: "No no, he's here, thank you." Down went the receiver, and Leonardo put down his own. When a few seconds later his phone rang, he didn't have the courage to answer, and it kept ringing and ringing, until it stopped. He was still sitting on his bed panting, when there was a knock on the door, and the concierge appeared before Leonardo could say come in.

"What do you think you are doing, sir? You are endangering my job. Mr. Schultz gave me hell, he said it was my fault, he won't believe me."

Leonardo looked at him, then rose from his bed while the man was repeating his boring litany, took the envelope with the fifty lire in it and gave it to him, saying: "Fifty lire for you."

There was a brief silence, then the roles were reversed: the man bowed and wagged his coattails like a dog, mumbling words of eternal gratitude. "Listen," said Leonardo, "I have had enough of your servile manners. I order you to tell Mr. Schultz I have given you that money in his name. Thank him, but don't you dare return it to him, or I will have Mrs. von Randen kick you out of here when she changes her mood, which may be any minute now. Understand? You have been warned."

"No need to, sir, no need, we have so many Russians here, I know their moods. . . . Thank you, thank you a thousand times."

After the man had left he felt better. There's nothing like anger to restore our wounded honor. Yes, but is it restored? In the world of the concierge, yes; but memories still sting. What happened? Where did the future die? Will it ever be reborn? Is Mary awake now? And is that bastard with her? Will he take her away from me? Will she be swayed? The only thing to do is kill him. Kill them both, and then myself. Why not kill myself now, to punish them all? But first write the truth. No, I'm tired. What is the truth here, anyway? Adriana is the truth, and she, too, is against me. No, the truth is fatigue. I was tired; that first night without sleep made Adriana possible, that second night without sleep made Cefala possible, then Adriana again, then . . . No, not just fatigue: there was also lack of food, and of course money.

These thoughts that came in circles gradually thinned until another truth seeped in: he had been dishonest. Clever, *furbo*—no, stupid—yet the intention was to be clever. . . . "But where can I go now? Not home, of course, but where? Death, of course, death . . ." He was repeating these words aloud to himself, babbling them from trembling lips, as he tried to push the pencil across his notepad for a letter of insults to Schultz, but they became a lullaby: "To market, to market, to buy a fat pig . . . Home again, home again . . . No, not home, ever, death, yes, death . . . there's no other place for me in the world. . . ." Soon the name "Mary," which had been dormant in his mind, came back to him

with that quiet image, a little faded, yet sacred, that he had kept in
the church of his heart all those years while in bed with Giovanna.
"Mary, where is my Mary? I don't know. I love you, Mary. You are
the woman of my life. I shall never love any other woman but you."
This was like the last post sounded in barracks, ordering all the
soldiers to sleep. He got up from his chair, staggered towards his
bedroom, shunned the bed as remindful of the slavery of conjugal
life, and, as he often did at home, lay down on the floor in the
granary and fell asleep at once, hiding his face in the crook of his
arm.

Leonardo woke up after a most restful dreamless sleep, in the
granary of his own house, and his first thought was to heat some
water for shaving, make fresh coffee, harness his horse and be out
on his rounds before daybreak. That this wasn't possible he learned
all of a sudden from the smell of furniture polish and . . . of
wealth in general, and the whole fairy tale with its unhappy ending
struck him full in the face, causing him to lie down on the floor
again in utter agony. Three thirty in the morning. All that energy
ready for a good day's work now to be wasted in useless sufferings
and humiliation. She hadn't called, probably she hadn't regained
consciousness. The only comforting thought—but for how long?—
was that his cousin couldn't have spent the night there, so he wasn't
there now, but would probably be back in the morning, to see
how HIS patient was doing. HIS PATIENT . . . From MY GODDESS,
to HIS PATIENT. His future wife, perhaps. He wasn't married, he
wasn't a liar, he was, in fact, the victim of the same liar who had
so ruined Mary's life. Did Mary think so? If her mother did, so
did she; if not now, she would soon, just give her time to recover from her great disappointment. I must see her, I absolutely
must see her, before she recovers. This is inhuman. She hasn't
called, she hasn't sent . . . (only at this point did Adriana come
back into his life). Oh, how I hate her. . . . It was all her fault,
filthy creature . . . unfaithful servant, traitress. . . . She's trying
to drag me down to her own level. How can I get to Mary without
going through her, or through my other enemies? Mary doesn't even
know about her, and yet, she hasn't called. . . . He had to remind
himself that she was probably still unconscious, that's why she

hadn't called. But why should she suffer so much? What have I
done that was so terrible? I haven't betrayed her with another
woman—she doesn't know about it, so it doesn't exist—so why?
The pain was so great, he had to talk to Mary directly, which he
did: "Why make such a tragedy out of a few silly lies? Think of
what I've lost by coming here, think of my humiliation, my suffering. . . . I'm betraying my duties, both as a mayor and a physician,
a family man, an uncle, a brother, . . . you can leave out the husband, but I'm a good uncle and a good brother and also a good
mayor and a good doctor . . . I gave up all this for *you*, and you
make such a mountain out of a molehill. . . . I needed a good
night's sleep, and now that I've had it, I can answer all those silly
accusations in a minute. ONE MINUTE . . . Oh, why was I so tired
yesterday? You stupid rich people only know how to waste your
time. I'm a working man, I use my time to help others, I must
go to bed early, or I won't know what I'm doing. And now, when I
could be working, you keep me idle here, you've ruined my life,
you've killed me . . . I'm only pretending to be alive, this is no
life. . . . Where shall I go? What can I do? Do you think I'll let
you go abroad without me? With that bastard idiot cousin of mine?
Like hell, I will. You'll find me at the station, with my gun. . . ."
But his gun was in Laterza, and here he had no money to buy one.
"Action, action . . ." What he meant was words: he had the power
to destroy the whole castle of lies on which Sophie had always lived,
indeed he *had* to do it now, because now his ideas were clear, and at
the hours when these people began to think, he was ready for bed.
He grabbed the phone. After a very long wait, filled with a frying
noise, the night porter answered, in a sleepy voice: "What is it?"

"Connect me with Mr. Schultz."

"All right."

Another very long wait, then the same sleepy voice: "No answer.
He must be asleep."

"No, he's not. He left for London tonight."

"Oh, yes, that's right. At midnight. I helped him, what a fool I
am to have forgotten— But you knew, so why are you disturbing me
to call him when he's no longer here?"

"I . . . er . . . I . . ."

"You're crazy, that's what you are. *Mannaggia alli mortacci tua. . ."** And with this litany the frying noise ended.

Gone were the days when Roman insults could awaken in him the proud mayor of Laterza, or the proud laureate in medicine and surgery. Now they awoke in him the memories of the beaten man he was, and the reasons for that beating.

Now they'll come and pack my suitcase for me, the way they do with bad boys in college, when they're being kicked out and sent home to their unworthy parents. But I'll kill myself, rather than go. . . . He listened, his ear at the door: no noise outside. Then, remembering what Schultz had said, he realized that Sophie would never forgive them if they sent him away. This was *her* place, his last foothold in her world: his lost Atlantis. But having momentarily reached this comforting conclusion, he found it poisoned by the very next thought: But if she wants me not to leave, why doesn't she speak to me? What are they waiting for? Do they think I can accept any humiliation? I'm not the Monster, who married for money. . . . And again this moment of defiance was submerged in a mass of embarrassing memories not yet refined and sharpened to their lacerating edge. But he knew they soon would be; in fact, this was his future, the only future he could think of with passion: everything else had lost all meaning.

He decided to go out. Twenty-four hours exactly since the wild beating Adriana had given him! The first in that long day . . . How clear everything becomes in the memory of pain.

Klagonov's boots were outside, as they had been the first day. A distant snoring noise slid under his door and faded into the stuffy air. He walked downstairs, and a breath of cold oxygen gave him new energy, which he instantly used to fuel his indecision. Do I want to go out? Where shall I go? Why did I leave my room? Yet the unreasoning body of a person accustomed to his share of human woes and their total evaporation in the early morning air drove him out in spite of his knowledge that this was no time for hope. But then negative pleasures help, too: the night porter was asleep in his corner, the doorman snoring somewhere on a sofa in the hall. Why

---

* Typical Roman curse upon the dead, unknown elsewhere in Italy.

not rebel in his loneliness? He walked past them and they did not stir. But once outside he felt cold, and didn't dare go back in again, lest they wake up and inspect him to make sure he was a guest and not a thief.

What a guest . . . But the coachmen were sensitive to the smell of their prey, and they all woke up together to offer him their services. How like yesterday morning . . . Only a bit earlier. He just raised his hand in denial, without lifting his eyes from the ground.

A brief hesitation in the middle of the square: should he go right, towards the open countryside, or left, towards Via Gregoriana? Isn't the solitude of nature more soothing to the pains of lost love than the cold corridors of city streets? But here medical instinct guided him infallibly: the city is sick, the whole city is sick, it's suffering terribly and needs a doctor's science. . . .

He walked briskly, as if he were in a hurry to get there, and this gave him the illusion that this was true, and that everything was normal again.

He passed the dark corridor of Via del Babuino, under the shadow of its various roofs, some protruding more, some less, out over the middle of the street, which was reserved for the moon, and when he emerged into Piazza di Spagna, the whole splendor of Rome was spread out in front of him and collected into corners of beauty, like the precious furniture and draperies in Mary's drawing room. On his left, the Via San Giuseppe, with the tent of the *porchetta* man closed for the night, the steep hill, and the tall cypresses above the level of Villa Medici; on his right, Via della Croce, black and white with shadows and moon, and in front of him Via Due Macelli, ending in another steep hill with high cypresses and oak trees against the sky, but halfway between him and the trees, this side of the dark corridor of Via Due Macelli, the singing fountain, and on its left, Jacob's dream of a ladder to heaven: the Scalinata, flooded with moonlight. Everything was in its normal place, so why not Mary's feelings? There is a peace in masonry that denies war and suffering so strongly that one can easily understand why war begins and ends with the destruction of buildings. Human beings are such impermanent creatures that their war and their peace otherwise are never clearly defined.

As he came closer to the fountain, he saw the two belfries of Trinità dei Monti with their tiny hollow eyes full of that veiled darkness created by the moon.

Only the goddess of the night, "the woman who rules here," was abroad, dancing a slow dance of shadows around that marble boat down there; inside it was the moon liquefied into ribbons of water, water pulverized into a haze of moonlight. And the earth singing to itself for music. As he mounted the stairs, watching his shadow as it was being swept under his feet, he retraced his whole fairy tale from the very beginning, and by the time he reached the heap of rags under which Schillasi's niece and her child, and probably the other beggars, were snoring, he had already identified the root of all his troubles in the sudden confrontation between Mary the Image, and Mary the Reality. Why had he never told her how much he had worshipped that image? Why? How he regretted it now, how clearly he saw that if he had *acted* he would never have had the time to notice his inadequacy at table or in the drawing room, nor felt the urge to go out, where he had met with trouble. Why? Because he had only been on the receiving end of new impressions, new material for memories and not for action. This is the fate of those who have become resigned to their fate, and in this Mr. Schultz had been right: all Italians lived by memory and were resigned to their fate. And he, the fool, who had begun to worry because this or that gift of the gods had not resembled his model of perfection, his lost future!!!! Who was living in the moon here, if not he? What right had the Cardinal, or Mr. Schultz, or Schillasi, or anyone, to offer him advice, and criticize him for not heeding it?—the right he himself had given them. That was why they all liked him so much, not because he was better than the rest of mankind (which, to his horror, he now realized he had begun to believe). His fault, then. *Mea culpa, mea culpa, mea maxima culpa.* One doesn't ask honest advice, because one doesn't ask honestly, ever. We ask advice and pretend we will follow it, when we know it is going to be offered anyway with threats and controls. We ask for advice, in order to gain time, and lull our advisers into sleep.

He walked quietly away and mounted the last steps towards Via Gregoriana. Another scene was awaiting him there: the stage of his evening adventures with Marinetti, the Cardinal, the Queen of Saxony, and of course Mary. Even up here, I courted the Cardinal, the Baron, the Prince and Duke, the Count, the Queen—everybody in the world but Mary.

He turned away and looked at Via Gregoriana. An immense, fiery, noisy silence was streaming out of the dark palaces to crush him under its weight. How could so much silence be concentrated in one place? Why were those windows closed? Why were they dark? Why was one darker than the others, with the shutters wide open? But wasn't that the window he had opened three nights ago, to let Kostia see the moon?

Only now did the worst of all possible blows come down upon him: Wasn't I called the sun, and she the moon, as in the old fairy tale?

Mary's window was frowning with shutters, as were all the other windows in the palace. The *portone* was solemnly closed, its two brass rings like instruments of torture hanging at rest and shining in the dark. And all the other palaces he had never noticed while walking down the street were equally silent and threatening. A whole city, closed up for the night behind its walls, but still ready to defend itself against the enemy. He wanted to call out to Mary, to remind her of their pact, of her submission to his solar superiority, but he didn't dare. She was in bed with her mother, probably huddled against her and in pain, but determined to stay faithful to her who never told lies, and not to him, a liar down here in the street come begging for his victory.

As if by secret signal, a dusky candlelight began to flicker behind the dirty basement window, then disappeared, to flicker again between the iron bars of a small window next to the *portone*, then a loud noise of keys and padlocks was heard echoing high into the vaulted entrance hall *now closed to him forever*. Forever? But that couldn't be possible. It hurt too much. . . . He had to leave quickly, run away in the dark, before the big doors opened.

But Leonardo stayed on, tempted by habit. How can that door, so huge, so generous, not allow a small man like me to come home again? O habit, even though you be young, please consider how faithful I have been to you these last four days: never have I known any other habit in this house, please let the doorman greet me in his accustomed way and say, They're waiting for you upstairs. . . .

They were awake all night, go, hurry upstairs. . . . D'you want the key?

In the thick of that huge wooden wall within the stone one, a tiny door is being opened: so tiny the doorman has to bend his head very low and lift his foot very high to get outside. Behind him there's a woman. . . . Giovanna? Or Adriana? They're talking.

"I told you it isn't him," he says and she says something Leonardo can't hear. Can it be *him* they mean?

The doorman steps out into the street, he's a bare three feet from Leonardo, but he's not looking at him, he's looking towards the Scalinata and waiting.

And Adriana, yes, Adriana comes out and asks: "Is he coming?"

"No, he's not."

"I can't believe it," she says, "he's so late this morning, he should have been here hours ago."

"Hours ago? Why hours ago? You know he has his hours. When he comes he will knock."

And he moves back towards the tiny door. But Adriana shouts: "You haven't looked, I think I hear him."

"It's too cold, I don't want to catch pneumonia just because you're impatient."

"It's not me who's impatient, it's Signorina Mary. She asked me twice already."

"So you tell her to be patient. When he comes he will knock."

But Leonardo is knocking, can't they hear his heart pounding against his rib cage? It shakes him so, he cannot speak.

"Isn't that him?" asks Adriana, who has gone back inside, shivering in her black shawl.

The doorman looks again, but again not at him and says: "No, it's not."

Leonardo comes forward, clears his throat, coughs, but cannot speak a word.

The doorman squints to identify the source of the cough; Leonardo says: "Good morning." Adriana calls from a distance: "Isn't that him?"

"No," shouts the doorman, turning his back on Leonardo, without even acknowledging him, "that's not him."

"Who is it?"

"Nobody."

With this terrible word, he lifts his knee again and bends his head, climbs back into his little box, and with a bang the wooden wall is black. No one would ever know that it concealed a secret door for Mary's secret friends, but not for him: Nobody.

Nobody is not expected, but somebody is keeping Mary awake at that hour.

Yet Nobody's heart is still knocking so desperately against his own shaky wall that he wishes a door could be opened in it by some miracle, to let his heart leap out and die there in front of that other door, so that the next time they come out for that mysterious guest, they will step on his heart and the blood will spurt up into their eyes. Then indeed they would have to report to the traitress upstairs that Nobody can't have so much blood and such a big heart, and she will know his name at once, and cry it aloud so that the whole city will hear: Leonardo, my love, my heart, my sunshine . . . where are you? But nobody would answer her desperate cries.

His heartbeat slowed. Leonardo was living again to savor sweet revenge, and he sneered savagely in the dark, thinking of Croci-fisso's rage when he found himself rejected, chased away by the doorman on orders from upstairs, not knowing why. . . . But before that fairy tale comes true, my dear cousin, you'll be confronted with a real man, whose fists will disfigure your fat face, whose outstretched fingers will close around your fat throat, and whose feet will crush your skull with joy. "Ha . . ." he shouted, posting himself for the attack: he had just seen him in the distance. Croci-fisso had just turned the corner, but he was not alone. . . . Never mind: I can kill two, I'm the worthy son of the man who could kill a bull with his bare fist.

"You go, I'll wait for you here," said an Apulian voice, or were these just sounds he had heard in the sudden morning wind? He waited, and the wind also withdrew, holding its breath. And now slowly, from the deserted stage up there another shadow emerged, calling to this shadow against the wall: "I'll wait down in the piazza."

A tinkling of metals, an opening of other tiny doors farther up the Via Gregoriana, and Leonardo knew this was the milkman. What a relief. Now he felt cold again, for it *was* cold. He rubbed

his hands and tried to warm them with his breath, while he heard
the doorman's voice again, calling to Adriana: "He's coming." And
it was good to feel indifferent, although the wind was cruel.

Once back on stage, he heard the goats down on the Scalinata
and, in the distance, the old voice of the Infallible, struggling
against the wind to carry the message: Five Thirty.

For the first time since he had arrived in Rome, he used the left
wing of the Scalinata to go down to the piazza, not only to avoid
the beggars, who were now getting their milk from under the goats,
but deliberately to establish a different tradition. Obviously, his old
habit of taking the left stairs to go up and the right ones to go down
was not the correct way in Rome. Now that he had reversed the
course of his fortune, things would go better. As he reached the
piazza, he stopped for a moment to look back at the whole scene,
while the belfries up there and others all over Rome echoed the
Infallible Dictate. It was cheerful music, and the goats with their
tinkling bells were cheerful too, but still, from the palace up there,
came such a stubborn silence that it choked every other voice,
making the very birds mournful, the moon useless, the fountain
indifferent.

SIXTH DAY

To be strong and heroic is not enough for victory: you must first have an enemy other than yourself. This is why the first enemy of the person who discovers himself to be his own worst enemy must be the person he loves and wants to win back. "It was all a mistake," he will say to himself, but he can't say it just to himself, without acting upon it like a man: he must say it to her, or he won't win the war. Leonardo had never been rejected: it was fate, in the person of Sophie, that had destroyed Mary's dream. For years he had mourned a lost love that he had never even begun to find. In his own conscience, it had been an ideal excuse to marry cold-bloodedly and cold-bloodedly to ruin many other women, always for the valid reason that his ideal love was elsewhere. For a former intended priest, it was the perfect formula for continuing in holy orders without any of the burdens, not even the burden of faith. Once he had been a strong man, an atheist, a man who had a secret. And now, suddenly, he was a weak man and his secret was everybody's gossip. Mary must pay for this, and, after she had paid, he would take her back, but he wouldn't let her know this until the very last minute. Had he been a writer or a poét, he would have rushed back to his hotel to write her a poem or a long letter, but he was a man of science and of action.

First: I must hate her, despise her whole world. I am doing this for her, for all of them: they must learn that you cannot treat the whole world as if you own it. Once I have taught them this lesson, I'll look around for something better. Or I may just exploit my acquaintances here, even Ramirez, because I cannot let these barbarians ruin me altogether. As for Crocifisso, I'll take care of him too, for daring to say he wouldn't see me. Who the hell does he think he is?

He almost spoke these words aloud as he was entering the hotel again and immediately felt better, because it was so warm and clean and luxurious. Which constructive mood, of course, gave him the strength he needed to pass the desk without deigning to give the uniformed servants a glance.

"Sir, sir . . ." the night porter called, as he was running up the stairs.

"Sir? . . ."

He didn't bother to turn back, and the night porter chased after him with a piece of paper in his hand.

"What is it?" he asked, feeling his heart beat faster at the sight of the paper.

"You're wanted on the phone. They tried to reach you twice, since you left."

"From Rome or from outside Rome?"

"From Rome."

"From . . . Mrs. von Randen?"

"I think so, the telephone Signorina didn't tell me. She only said it was extremely urgent."

"Then why do you say that it's from Mrs. von Randen?"

"I never said it was, I said I *think* so, because they always call *urgent*, no one else does."

"Tell the Signorina I am back, I'll wait in my room."

He ran upstairs, entered his room, and it was a different room again. The mere thought that he could have suffered as much in it as he had since yesterday afternoon seemed so absurd it made him smile. How stupid can one be? Why all the worry? *Amor Omnia Vincit*, didn't I know it? There are no other two lovers like us, and if I made a few mistakes, I won't ever make any more in the future, so let's forget about those, too.

Aaaah, what a relief to be able to breathe again. The only point that still hurt was his encounter with the doorman and with Adriana. Perhaps he didn't recognize me, or perhaps he hasn't been told, and still believes what he heard yesterday—not from THEM, they wouldn't talk to their servants, not even to Adriana . . . and *she's* been turned against me by that swine of the old bastard. . . . But thank God, in a few minutes everything will be clear, and I can have a real breakfast again, and this time, who the hell cares how I hold my knife and fork?

He lay down next to the phone, ready to jump up the moment it rang, and covered himself up with the comforter, but his hands were freezing, and there was no way to warm them. In a few minutes even this will be over, and I'll be able to take a hot bath and shave, before going home.

But a whole hour passed, and no one called. He tried to call the concierge, who said he couldn't call the operator, because she didn't know where the call had come from: "It can only have come from Mrs. von Randen, they'll call back."

"You think they will?"

"Of course they will. They always do."

"So you advise me to be patient."

"By all means."

"Thank you. You're a real friend. You know how it is, when the heart is involved."

"I know, I know, we all have hearts."

"How true. Thank you from the bottom of my heart. You're a real friend."

"At your service, sir."

But another hour passed and no call came. He paced the room until he was dizzy, then it occurred to him that he could order breakfast, since he was no longer honor-bound to refuse everything except for the room itself, and so he ordered breakfast and ate abundantly, and very slowly, while another hour passed. And still no one called. So he called the concierge again: "I think I'm going to take a bath and shave, but if they call, keep ringing until I come to the phone."

"I will."

"You think it's a good idea for one to take a bath and shave?"

"An excellent idea, sir."

"You're such a good friend, I can't tell you how grateful I am to you."

"Too kind of you, sir. Count on me to let you know if they call."

"Thank you a thousand times."

"At your service."

He took a bath and shaved, dressed again and now lay on the bed rather less comfortably than before, because he had put on a new shirt with a very stiff collar. In a few minutes she'll call, and I'll go straight there, so it's better if I keep myself ready.

By two o'clock in the afternoon, he had begun to have a headache and shivers. That'll teach her to keep me waiting here for so many hours, without calling back. Who does she think I am? Her humble servant?

At that moment the phone rang. The metamorphosis from murderous resentment to the most Christian generosity was instant: "My love," he cried, "all is forgiven, I'm coming home."

But the contact was broken, and it took the concierge a good ten minutes to call the Signorina-operator again. The operator was busy on a very important call to a cabinet minister and could pay no attention to any lower type of call from private citizens. Leonardo finally put down his receivers and ran downstairs to announce that he was ging to Via Gregoriana on foot: it would be quicker than waiting for a new telephone call.

"No, no, please, sir, don't go, don't move from here, it's coming, just a moment, the Signorina is through with the cabinet minister, it is he who is going to see *his* party on foot, so don't give up this chance while you have it. Go back upstairs."

Meekly, Leonardo went back to his room and waited another hour and a half, and finally the call came through: "Darling," he sobbed, "I can't take it any more, I'm—"

"You are talking to *me*," said the Signorina, "keep your passion in harness for another few minutes, please. I can't take it any more either, everybody's calling me darling, I never had such good treatment in private life, my husband never called me darling, not even twenty-five years ago, when we were married."

"I've had enough of you," shouted Leonardo, beside himself with rage.

"Please let me explain," answered a male Apulian voice.

"What is this?" shouted Leonardo, "why are you intruding?"

"I am not." It was Crocifisso. "I'm calling you to explain. I shall never touch Mary, even though everything between the two of you is finished. I consider her still yours, because that is the rule between honorable men, at least for a few months after the end of the affair, and besides, I don't like her. It's her sister I'm in love with. Can you tell me in full confidence—is she *illibata?*"*

Leonardo's reaction was one of profound shock at hearing Crocifisso, profound relief upon being so honestly reassured and profound anger upon being so insulted.

"How dare you allow yourself such an assumption?"

"What assumption? That the sister would have me? The mother says so, and she seems to be a very respectable person. But can you trust the young today, with waltzes and steam engines and speaking French, and other corrupting influences? I wouldn't want to wake up a cuckold one nice day after my marriage. Don't forget, I'm a descendant of Saint Thomas Aquinas. I owe something to the family saint."

"Fuck your family saint, I won't answer your question before you've answered mine. How dare you assume that everything between me and Mary is finished?"

"She said so herself."

"What did she say and when?"

"Last night after dinner."

"What? Did she have dinner with you? Where?"

"At her house . . ."

"But wasn't she ill?"

"That didn't last long. When I went back for dinner, at nine, she was normal. A bit pale, not too cheerful, but normal. I asked her about you, offered her my help, and she said: I don't want to talk about him, please."

"Of course she said so, because you're a stranger and you were trying to intrude, but nothing has changed between us, because nothing can. I want you to know our love is stronger than the fire of God Almighty."

"And I couldn't be happier to hear such good news. Did you talk during the night?"

---

* Literally: untasted in libation; i.e., untouched, pure.

"We began, but these damn telephones are impossible. We were interrupted. But she'll call again, I'm sure. Why don't you come here instead of keeping the line busy?"

"Because I promised her mother and that English gentleman, her uncle, or her step-grandfather, whatever he is, not to contact you, because it seems you told them lies, even about me. . . ."

"You're the liar. I was told that you didn't want to see me, because you thought I had invented all that nonsense about your being the private doctor of the King and the Pope, when it must have been you who told Liborio and Peppino . . ."

"I swear on my poor father's grave I never did."

"Then why did you believe I had?"

"I didn't for one split second. I *had* to."

"You had to? What forced you?"

"That old Protestant banker, and of course her mother. You ought to know how these Protestants are: unless you agree with them onehundredpercent, they won't even begin to talk to you. So I had to admit I was angry that you had never got in touch with me, and there I wasn't lying, because I most certainly was angry, but when I realized I would get nowhere by taking up your defense openly, I applied the methods of our Jesuit schoolteachers: first pretend you agree, to get your foot in the door, then slowly dismantle their fortress of pride and show them that even they can be wrong. Does that seem to make sense?"

"Y . . . es, it does, but all the same . . . Come here and talk to me. I want to ask you a few questions, and I can't leave, because Mary will call any minute."

"And I can't come, because I promised the old man I wouldn't."

"He left for London last night."

"Oh, he did?"

"Yes, take my word for it. He told me so himself. What time did you leave the palace?"

"At eleven."

"Were there other guests for dinner?"

"Some very respectable Russians, who spoke Russian, of course."

"All right, come over at once."

As Leonardo hung up, he felt both relieved and desperate. Relieved, because he had finally heard a friendly voice from home, and desperate, because of the terrible things this voice had told him about Mary not wanting to talk about him: worse, Mary being able to talk, to have dinner in his absence, smiling, laughing even, as if he didn't exist: he, her sun, she, his moon. . . . Had it all been a fairy tale? Why all this? Still because of those innocent lies? If it had been for some real reason, like Adriana, he could have understood, but those perfectly innocent lies . . . How could she be so stupid, so cruel, so unjust?? He must write her a letter. . . . No, perhaps she would call, but no, she would not; in the meantime, to know that in a few minutes Crocifisso would come, and time would pass in pleasant or unpleasant conversation with a person he loved or rather detested, was the greatest possible relief: give time time, so that Mary's decision to call him would ripen all by itself, and come as a surprise, because nothing is worse than waiting in the void for something that may happen and again may not, something probably terrible but perhaps not. . . . A new kind of pain, discovering that you can wait impatiently for a person you don't like, and who can bring you nothing good. Expectation is blinder than love: anyone, please let anyone come and take away my anguish. . . .

When Crocifisso arrived, Leonardo was unhappily happy to see him. "Come in, come in, sit down here, this is my bedroom, or do you want to sit in the dining room?"

Crocifisso was so stunned by the splendor of the place he couldn't speak, but when he did, he expressed it very cogently: "If these people are so respectable, and they're ready to marry their daughter to me, there must be something wrong with her. . . . Wouldn't you say so?"

"How do you know they're respectable? Perhaps they're not." (What a relief, to hear his own voice form such a sentence.)

"How do you mean they're not? Look at this private apartment in this most respectable hotel. And of course you must have seen the palace. . . ."

(What an insult: "You must have seen the palace. . . .")

"Yes, I have seen the palace, and plenty more besides, but what does that mean? Respectability has nothing to do with money." (Shades of Don Poseidone . . . But Crocifisso didn't catch on.)

"Morally speaking it doesn't, but in reality . . ."

"But then respectable for you means rich."

"You'll never change, Leonardo, you're still more of a priest than a man."

"What do you mean, I'm not a man? This has nothing to do with either priesthood or manhood: this is a question of grammar. If they are respectable, then your question is answered; if they are not, your question is another one; namely: How can I like these people without running the risk of being corrupted by their wealth?"

"You see? I was right: you speak of corruption, as if you could see the devil everywhere. You remind me of the Father Prefect. Has it ever occurred to you how much good one can do with money?"

(Why did he have to say that?)

Since Leonardo didn't answer, Crocifisso went on: "The English banker also thinks that you would make a good priest, but not a good husband for Mary."

"Did he say that?"

"Twice in the course of our first conversation."

"Was Mary present?"

"No, this was before she came, and when she came . . ."

"I know, you don't have to repeat it."

"You're suffering, I can see, but why did you do it?"

"Do WHAAT?"

"Tell lies. You know how these Protestants are: they live a lie, which is their denial of our Church, but they never *tell* lies, so they always hurt people, while we, who have our Latin wisdom, live the truth of our holy religion, and tell lies to protect our beliefs from heretics."

"So that's why you pretended you didn't want to see me."

"We already discussed that, and if you don't believe in my brotherly feelings, I'd better go."

"No, please don't. But you have to understand my feeling that if you had been a bit more courageous in my defense, the old bastard would never have talked to me the way he did. Never mind; Mary loves me, and that's all that counts. We've overcome so much in these nine years, we can overcome more."

"I'm glad to hear you say so. . . . Cheer up, don't act as if you didn't believe it."

"You're right, Crocifisso, you are right. The fact is that, at times . . . even these silly misund—" He couldn't go on. He buried his face in his hands and cried and cried and cried, while Crocifisso patted him on the head, saying: "You mustn't cry this way. . . . She wouldn't like it."

(That made things worse: now his sobs could be heard out in the corridor.)

"You look pale and drawn and really sick. You frighten me."

(Worse still.)

When he had cried so much that his hands turned stiff, he felt better and smiled through his tears. "I'm an imbecile, you see, but I can't live without her, and she, of course, can't . . ." (Why did YOU have to say that, when you know it isn't true? Now cry, you fool, cry for your lost love.)

This time his entire arms went numb, and his mind was so confused that he felt truly better and sighed with relief.

"That's good," said Crocifisso. "Now tell me: is Ludmilla a virgin?"

"I don't know, I've never even seen her."

"But you must have heard about her from them. You're about to be the new man in their family, you must be informed."

"No, with these people it doesn't work that way." (Oh, Leonardo, don't you wish THEY were here to listen to your noble, PROTESTANT words?)

"You mean you would agree to become the brother-in-law of a dishonored woman and the laughing-stock of the man—or MEN—who dishonored her? I'm surprised at you."

"Of course I wouldn't, and I happen to know that Ludmilla is absolutely pure."

"Then why didn't you say so at once? What do you mean by pure, a virgin?"

"Of course, what else?"

"You never know with these Protestants, and you seem well on your way towards becoming one yourself. To be against the priests is one thing, but to betray our holy religion is another. So reassure me again: she's a virgin, you say."

"Yes, as far as I know."

"Then you do doubt it."

"No, I don't but . . . is one ever sure of anything in life?"

"That is the one thing in life of which a man can and must be sure. In a respectable family the sister knows about the sister, even if the brothers are indifferent, as I imagine they are, owing to their false religion. Is Mary sure that her sister is a virgin?"

"Yes." (You cringe, Leonardo, why did you say it?)

"Are you cringing?"

"No, I'm cold, I'm tired . . . I . . ."

"Now now now . . . don't start crying again. Listen to me, when this storm has passed—and I am sure it will—why don't you explain to Mary that it is better for her honor and yours—mine too, if I decide to marry her sister—that there be no divorce? Your divorce would of course be a terrible scandal, but hers would be an indelible stain on everyone concerned, it would mar even your profession. What honest man would allow you to take care of his family, knowing that you are the husband of a divorced woman? If they knew you were the lover of a married woman, that wouldn't disturb anyone, that's your business; in fact, it would be to your honor that you were faithful to an unhappy woman. But a divorced woman is a constant threat, a real sword of Damocles over your head. I'm told that Mary's husband is a perfectly decent fellow, in good health and a real man, with many mistresses. I'm sure he would welcome the moral support of a respectable member of the liberal professions in his complex family situation. But a divorce—treason, desertion of the conjugal roof, destruction of the domestic hearth . . . Just think how many acts named by the penal code that would imply."

"How do you know her husband is in good health?"

"I asked; as a physician it wasn't difficult to discover who his doctor is. I did it for you. If I had discovered that he was syphilitic, I would have interfered at once, to warn you. But I was able to ascertain that he doesn't even have gonorrhea, so what could be safer? And why harm such an ideal . . . 'partner,' to use the correct term for once? Do it for me, I beg you, if you want us to become brothers-in-law. . . ."

Leonardo smiled sweetly: "How can I become your brother-in-law if I don't marry your sister-in-law? What you mean is assistant brother-in-law."

Crocifisso didn't like this. "I'm glad to see you've got over your depression. Good for you, but spare me your funny remarks. Think how much I've done for you."

"All right, all right . . ."

"Do you agree with me, or don't you, that a divorce would be a stain on your honor?"

"Yes, yes." (You're tired, Leonardo, you want to sleep.)

"Yes, yes, is too vague. I want a frank YES."

"YES!"

"And now another thing, it's rather delicate, but since it can no longer hurt you . . ."

"What is it?"

"Don't be so nervous, or I won't be able to tell you. It's against my nature to . . . to . . . intrude."

"What is it? Tell me at once."

"Well, it seems that . . . or, rather, let me put it this way—er—you don't actually have to worry about sparing poor Giovanna's feelings: she has a lover back in Laterza."

"A . . . WHAT?"

Leonardo's heart stopped dead for a moment. He turned white, his hands began to tremble, he couldn't speak.

"Yes, a lover."

"Who is he?"

"Does it matter?"

"I have a right to know!"

Crocifisso named him, and Leonardo roared like a lion: "The traitress!!! The whore!!! So it was for *him* that she spent all my money on clothes and hats!!! For him, not for me!!! And that was why the traitor insisted I come to Rome on this official mission!!! All for her, not for me! They'll pay for it!!!"

Mary had vanished. The telephone had vanished. All he felt was a wild thirst for revenge.

"Since when has this been going on? And since when have you known about it, and from whom? And how many people in Laterza are aware of it? I want to know everything, now! And if you don't tell me the truth . . ."

"Hey, listen, don't talk to me that way. I'm not in the habit of making trouble among married couples. I told you for your own good."

"My own good? What can I do after this? At this tragic moment in my life?"

"Nothing! But it will keep your mind off Mary, so that you won't do anything foolish to win her back. Time is the ultimate healer in these extramarital situations. And since you hate Giovanna, what do you care?"

"What do I care? My honor has been dragged in the mud. . . ."

"One more reason for you not to marry a divorced woman, and not to ask for a divorce. What do you want to do: kill the man? Kill Giovanna? Land in jail for the rest of your life? Of course not. You are here, you learn about this, and you decide to act like a true gentleman: you ignore the sinners, and resume an old dream of love that was interrupted by your marriage and Mary's, all without resorting to scandal. You help Mary abide by the oath she has taken before God, you help her forgive her disloyal husband, and you start a new life in Rome. Everybody will respect you for this, everybody will help you, starting with Mary's husband. This is the advantage of living in a metropolis. I, too, have a *situation* with a married woman from a very respectable family; she offered me a divorce, which I couldn't accept, because if I married her I would lose standing in the hospitals, and my career would be ruined. Besides, my poor mother would be very unhappy. So you understand that Mary's divorce would make me a cuckold. I can't afford it. I love Ludmilla more than my own life, but . . ."

"How can you, if you've never even seen her?"

"I saw her picture. That was enough. So I'm leaving Rome tonight, to go to my mother and ask for her advice, and also to be away from Ludmilla and her picture as long as I don't know whether she's a virgin or not." He smiled triumphantly, then said: "Were you about to ask me something?"

"No."

He was, he had been, but Crocifisso's question stopped him just in time. What was the point of asking the same questions again? Who cared who had told him and how long Giovanna had been betraying him? Crocifisso was right, but Crocifisso was wrong—*as Crocifisso* he was wrong, all wrong, from head to foot, from the top of his hat to the tips of his patent-leather shoes, the kind of shoes Leonardo detested so much; wrong to his manicured, polished fingertips, and wrong again around his fat waist, and wrong in his flabby cheeks, his blondish beard, and his ass-arse mouth. . . .

While these thoughts were purging his angry mind, Crocifisso was staring in awe at His Excellency's overcoat.

"Like it?" asked Leonardo.

"It's marvelous, tailor-made, very expensive, I can see, and superb fur. I can tell you that my chief, who had the honor of treating both the last sovereign Pope and the first sovereign King, Victor Emmanuel the Second, is the only eye doctor in Rome who can afford such a coat. Splendid. Mary's present?"

"No. An exchange I stupidly made for a Russian fur coat twenty times more expensive than this one."

"Whaaat? Why?"

"Because I'm a fool."

"And with whom?"

"Look at the name inside."

Crocifisso looked and was speechless. "His Excellency the chief of police? You know him personally?"

"Much too well for the safety of my last meal. A sewer."*

"He can't be, if he's the chief of the Roman police. You're always finding fault with everybody on earth. Name me one person in high places you respect."

"God, if he existed. But I respect those who invented him."

Crocifisso shook his head and smiled condescendingly. "I always said you should be a priest or a hermit."

"Right. Do you want that coat?"

"What do you mean: WANT it . . . ?"

"I mean WANT IT. Do you?"

"Leonardo, is this a symptom of despair? In that case, of course not."

"Take it as a symptom of hope and a token of friendship."

"In that case, how can I refuse? But . . . isn't it too much of a sacrifice?"

Leonardo just nodded condescendingly, and Crocifisso kissed him in tears.

"I can't tell you how grateful I am. I always knew you were a noble soul. There *is* some of our blood in your veins, after all. Well, I wish you good luck. And remember my advice: save your honor

---

* Typical Neapolitan expression. *Una chiavica.*

and the honor of the Church. I don't believe in anything either: how can you, after modern science has shown us the truth? But whether we're believers or not, you must admit that the Catholic Church is the only solid institution in our troubled times. And besides, it's part of our national heritage. Think of the art: Raphael, Michelangelo, the whole bunch of them . . ."

With these words, and with the fur coat on his back, which fitted him perfectly ("Thank you again, just look at this label . . . my God, people will be impressed back home. . . . Thank you thank you thank you . . . I must rush, I promised the English banker to find a specialist for the little boy's asthma, and I must take care of it, if I want to take the night train. First-class sleeper, of course, I owe it to my name, but God it's expensive . . ."), he was gone.

Crocifisso's visit had been useful. Now Leonardo knew what to do. He opened the curtains, the window, the shutters, let the glorious afternoon sunshine in, sat down at the precious desk next to the window, took out his prescription pad, placed it in front of him, let the sun warm his hands and his sleeves, then lifted the heavy lid of the enameled Russian inkwell, seized the heavy gold and ivory pen, looked at the golden nib, dipped it into the purple ink, and wrote, in his large, calligraphic script:

March 19th, St. Joseph, return of the swallows, End of Mary, INCIPIT VITA NOVA.

Twenty drops of Pythagorean Logic, three drops of Empedoclean Medicine, one drop of Ascetic Acid, diluted in a sea of fresh courage, take AD LIB *before, during or after a seizure.*

Doctor Leonardo Claudi

(Here a moment of hesitation: should he write Laterza, Province of Brindisi?)

R O M E.

With this last word he had completely broken with his past. He no longer lived in Laterza, he lived in Rome. How? Where? That was something to be studied after a long night's sleep, before which he must have dinner. He rang the bell, and, when the waiter appeared, he said in an authoritative voice, without even looking at the serf's face: "A very large serving of spaghetti with tomato sauce made with olive oil, not butter. Salad, lots of provolone, mozzarella, black bread, ricotta with sugar, whatever fresh fruit there is, red wine, of course, the same I had for lunch yesterday, and I want it all served immediately. No waiting on table, please."

In the same breath, but not in the same voice, he looked sternly at the telephone in the other room and whispered: "I'm not afraid of you." Then he looked out of the window again, into the square below, and felt no fear of the ladies and gentlemen in their open or closed carriages emerging from the Corso, turning at the obelisk and going back for the evening parade. Nor the ladies and gentlemen on foot who emerged from the Corso and went back again, without leaving the sidewalk. Quietly, he admired the pink clouds of sunset, the whistling swallows swooping through the sky, the pink light on the twin cupolas of the churches guarding the Corso and the Babuino, then turning away from the spectacle of worldliness, he followed the sunlight as deep as he could inside himself, without even noticing that he now considered Sophie's private dining room in Rome's most expensive hotel as the natural setting for his renunciation.

The sunbeams reflected by framed etchings under glass, by glass doors of china cabinets, by silver trays on shelves, plus more sunbeams refracted into a myriad of colors from diamond-faceted crystal stoppers of decanters and wine jugs on the table, plus the sunshine pinpointed in the samovar, the coffee pot, the chocolate pot, the cream jug, the sugar bowl—all this ordinance of the constant war on hunger with which the room had been so richly equipped—detached him even more from the pleasures of the flesh. When dinner was finally served, he had almost lost his appetite. Indeed, he accepted it only so as to prevent those parasitic servants of Sophie's from charging her for an expensive meal he hadn't eaten. His mood was so spiritual that he was already seeing himself as a hermit of the Franciscan order in the sanctuary of Camaldoli. (He had never been there, but he had seen photographs of it in the office of the Father Prefect in Matera.) As he ate, he reinforced his mystical state by firing all his spiritual batteries against the Fortress Mary, while her material resources were busy conquering his hunger. "If Mary were suddenly to die," he told himself aloud, with his mouth full of her food, "I would of course accept her death as God's Will. But by God, I will not accept her rejection. I shall tell her exactly what I think of her and her mother, but instead of becoming her lover, as that swine Crocifisso advised, I shall refuse myself to her and go to Camaldoli. There alone can I exercise my calling without being defiled by the shadows of my past shame, as I would be in Laterza now. I shall offer free medical services to the poor and the rich also, provided they pay the poor, not me. I shall tell them where and how they should spend their money. And if Mary wants to reform, she can join me in spiritual marriage, as Santa Chiara joined San Francesco, from a distance. And now, to bed, Fra Leonardo!"

Of course, a hermit cannot sleep in a soft bed, especially if that bed has been enjoyed by him in the company of a woman (and what a woman). Fra Leonardo would sleep on the cold floor. That the nearness of the telephone on the night table might have something to do with this decision never occurred to him. He had regained the adolescent innocence of the days when he really dreamed of becoming a saint. . . .

A light knock on the door, and all sainthood went to hell at once.

"Who is it?" he roared, his heart in his throat.

"The maid, to close the windows and turn down your bed."

"I can do that myself, thank you. I don't want any service in this room as long as I'm here. Understand?"

"All right," and discreet steps moved away. Worldly thoughts came again; should he sleep in his clothes or take them off? But if he took them off, he would have to take a blanket from the bed, and that was a compromise with the riches of this world, THEIR world. Yes, but could he afford to catch pneumonia? Or to ruin his clothes, which he HAD to treat gently, as long as he wasn't wearing a rough cassock? Of course not. So he undressed both himself and the bed, put on a nightshirt and wrapped himself in a beautiful, huge, soft blanket. The rug of course was also softer than the hard earth of Camaldoli would be: But one thing at a time: this is still Rome, this isn't my NEW home.

One more irreligious thought: How will I stand it, surrounded by superstitious monks and even more superstitious villagers, who identify all modern science with the New Things forbidden by the Papal Encyclical. I don't even believe in God. . . .

Then, after a few minutes of soul-searching: Pending the glorious reunion between Science and Religion, is there anything wrong in behaving as if I still believed? I'll be doing it for purely philosophical reasons, my reward is in my conscience. . . . So good night, Fra Leonardo, tomorrow you will take your first step away from here and towards Camaldoli. You will write to Mary's husband, ask his forgiveness, and return her to him; that is, tell him what he must do if he wants to win her back. The Cardinal will be so surprised by your sacrifice that he will come and ask your forgiveness on his knees. And you will say to him: My son, all is forgiven. Mend your ways, too, that's all I have to say to you. . . . And, for the first time in his life, he will be speechless.

With these noble thoughts he fell asleep, and when he woke, the moon was on the carpet. The long shadows stretching from the chairs and the thin legs of the dresser looked like trees against a white sky, and the sky itself, seen through the open window from underneath, looked like a pond reflecting another white sky with a few stars and a moon just out of sight. Cheerful voices of strollers from the heights of the Pincio, noises of plates and knives and forks and more voices from the restaurant kitchen downstairs, timid chirping of birds, a few stray swallows whistling through the night sky, all contrasted painfully with the silence that fell upon his head from the night table above him. That damned black beast: the Pope was right in the encyclical of his. . . . Why should telephones be allowed into a house, anyway? Telephones are for post offices and police stations. Perhaps Marx is right too, these capitalists use all the instruments of public power for their own private ends. . . .

He couldn't go back to sleep with that silence barking over him like Cerberus over the damned buried in the ice. He got up and sat

on the bed, staring at the black telephone with its two heavy ear-
wings hanging lifeless on either side of its body, like a bat with the
mouth of a sea monster: "Why don't you tell her to lift your
brother's wings up there, so that I may lift yours? What is she
waiting for? Doesn't she know I've been abandoned even by my
wife? Where can I go? What can I do? Doesn't she care enough to
ask?" How could he become a hermit and help Mary if she had
forgotten him already?

The very thought that she might be out strolling like everybody
else in Rome at that hour, or eating in a restaurant, or enjoying the
moon from her open Victoria, hurt him as the greatest blow he had
ever endured. How could she be so indifferent to his suffering? So
inhuman, so barbaric, so . . . Russian? Here he was suffering the
pains of hell, while she was enjoying the moonlight, not even thinking of him. Perhaps she was even looking for a substitute: Count
Jahn-Rusconi? Marinetti? Count Sandroxyll?

Now he was pacing the room, clad only in his nightshirt, dizzy
with anguish and with the constant going around in circles and
semicircles. Suddenly he saw a smaller telephone on the dresser and
became frightened, but then realized it was an optical illusion created by the stethoscope that had been lying there since Adriana had
gone to bed with him. What hurt him was not the thought of
Adriana, whom he passionately detested by now, but the image that
came to mind: A *hermit with a stethoscope?* The whole conflict
between science and religion appeared to him in all its tragic grandeur. Who better than he knew the stubborn stupidity of those
monks, who put strange green mold onto open wounds and claimed
it was the best disinfectant in the world, and that it had worked
wonders since the days of Empedocles and Pythagoras? Was there
any reason to think that modern science would fare much better
against twenty-five centuries of superstition in the hermitage of
Camaldoli? Not even his threats of police intervention, ordered in
his capacity as mayor of Laterza, had forced a monk in a neighboring village to desist from such filthy practices.

Mary had been *right* to destroy Giovanna's wedding present, but
why, oh *why* didn't she come and join her own replacement for it
and help him now?

Thus ended the Vita Nova of the New Pilgrim of Love, Fra
Leonardo of the Franciscan sanctuary of Camaldoli.

On to the reconquest of Mary. "Beauty alone shall be my
weapon!"

He turned on the light, but alas, what he saw in the mirror was
not likely to charm anyone: swollen, reddish eyes, a puffy face, a red
nose from too much crying. Where was the dashing mayor, the
Man of Principle who had so impressed all those people yesterday
morning? Yet in the moonlight perhaps these miseries would be
concealed by a romantic pallor. He dressed in a hurry; all the noises
from the outside were calling him to battle: cheerful feminine
voices, proud male voices, songs, the brisk clatter of horses trotting
through the night, birds, distant dogs barking at the moon. Everybody seemed active, even the new leaves spoke silently but loudly of
spring and love.

He ran all the way up to the Pincio, then all the way down again,
because a carriage he had seen seemed to contain Mary and her
mother, then up again, because another carriage had exactly the
same two female figures in it, then he followed Mary and her
mother on foot forever, only to find out he was wrong, then he
followed carriages again, then stopped at the top of the Scalinata
where he had stopped with them three nights before, then he ran to
the fountain, because they were certainly there, this time there
could be no doubt, but no, there was no doubt they weren't part of
the crowd, and he strained his neck, his eyes, his legs, he was sweating, his necktie was out of place, it was a nightmare, and finally he
realized that everybody, even men, looked from a distance like Mary
and Sophie. Yet all this happened in a haze, because above all the
voices, the carriages, the human steps, the birds, the church bells
and the wind, there was still that cold current of silence coming
from that frightening street, and he alone could hear it, as a dog
hears noises no human ear can perceive, and gives warning. How
Leonardo wished he could bark, howl, bite until someone killed
him . . . Thus he ran into the forbidden street and saw lights in
the library and in the drawing room and in the dining room. Was it
possible? Lights? Cheerful lights? How many people were there who
could see Mary now, while he could not? Gasping for breath, he

leaned against the wall of the house across the street, saw the doorman having dinner, saw the dark entrance hall with the lantern under the arch, and closed his eyes in pain.

"*Fratellissimo carissimo!!!*" Before he could decide what to do next, Klagonov was smothering him with kisses. He wasn't alone. Crocifisso was there too.

"What? You . . . here? . . ."

"Yes," said Crocifisso, "I thought it wouldn't be nice to leave Rome without saying goodbye or at least sending flowers, so I brought the flowers myself, and they were very pleased and asked me to stay for a bite. Which was very fortunate, because I met the one person who could tell me the truth you didn't seem to know."

"Yes," said Klagonov, squeezing Crocifisso's arm with mournful affection. "Great consolation in tragic sorrowfulness mine that so good and noble a person, Aquinas Saint Thomas Philosopher descendant he, Ludmilla's love receive will and return back for life. Ach, *fratellissimo carissimo* in tragedy, we now united in cry, they in laugh and joy." And he began to sob on Leonardo's shoulder, which instantly cured Leonardo of all desire to do the same.

"You understand," said Crocifisso in Apulian to Leonardo: "She turned him down, even though he's a prince, and very, very respectable. And she is an absolute virgin, he says so. Aren't you happy for me?"

"Yes, yes," said Leonardo, to put an end to the torture, staring at those windows from which he could see the silence streaming through the windowpanes to search him out in the dark. He could hardly breathe. "Who else was there?" he asked.

Klagonov obliged: "Marinetti, Count Rusconi, Count Sandroxyll, and Count Keyserling."

"Who's he?"

"Old suitor Mary he, but no luck. Mary love you."

"How do you know?"

"I imagine. Of course now angry she, your name forbidden mention of is, but I know what to do you must to she take again."

"What?"

"Metallicize yourself, learn from Marinetti. Great man he, I his pupil and God's, have become cured, every now and then not, every then and now yes, takes time, and now fortunately found real worthy of Ludmilla person in this man here, allow me introduce him you."

"We've met before," said Leonardo in a painful whisper, but Klagonov's words were beginning to help.

"My dear prince," said Crocifisso, holding out his hand, "I'm sorry, but I must go. If I want to take the first train home, I must go to bed now. Thank you for entrusting Ludmilla to me. I already know that she will make me happy, and I will try my best to make her happy too. I love her so much, I can't wait to meet her!"

Klagonov embraced him and kissed him, sobbing aloud with joy, then Crocifisso embraced Leonardo and said: "I hope everything will be for the best in your life too. If it isn't Mary, you'll find someone else. And you can always count on me." With these words he was gone, and the two *fratellissimi* were left alone in their sorrow.

Slowly they walked away, Klagonov still talking drunkenly about his lost love, and lost indeed it was, he couldn't find it again, he was ready for bed, while Leonardo wasn't, he was ready for suffering and yet eager to leave that place of torture. They walked away, Klagonov looking drunkenly at the moon, Leonardo trying to look at nothing long enough to feel the sting, but at that hour even the dirt on the square was a monument of beauty, with its tiny, clear shadows scattered by the moon. And the fountain was murmuring away its tale of woe, tiny birds under roofs were answering tiny birds in the sky, and the Infallible out there, in his own raucous voice, was calling, not from across the Tiber, but from inside every room in Mary's house, that it was late, late in the night and late in life and nothing else but late, forever. . . .

"When do you want your ticket for?" asked the concierge very politely, and Leonardo said: "I'll let you know."

"Why?" thundered Klagonov, who had been snoring as he walked, leaning on Leonardo: "You not leaving?"

"Yes, not tomorrow, not the next day, but very soon."

"Not allow I," shouted Klagonov, falling onto the concierge across the desk. "He my only support in spiritual pain of communion of pain," and after a long burp: "is." Then, after another long burp: "Forbid I you accept his order to ticket buy for away. He here as long as need I he."

"At your orders," said the concierge, without looking at Leonardo. Klagonov climbed the stairs on his hands and knees, moaning: "Metallization . . . Metallization . . . Bronze Age, Iron Age, Tin Age. Metal, tin too . . ." Then, after the usual long pause: "is." Another few steps, then: "Also prick must of steel be. Hahaha . . . hahaha." He couldn't stop laughing. Then he noticed Leonardo's angry face, rose to his feet and said: "Hit me. I unworthy divine Ludmilla am. But I swear not of her body thought visited me. All same, unworthy I, please hit me, spit on me. Please, do as favor."

"Go to bed."

"Unworthy even spitted upon to be I? True. Unworthy. No metal. No, no." Then, stumbling into his room and falling onto the bed, he began to sing:

All'idea di quel metallo . . .

laughing and burping and crying, all in one.

Leonardo left him there and ran to his room.

He locked the moon out of his new Vita Nova, by closing the window and drawing the double curtains. Then he went to the dining room, drew the curtains there too, so as not to see the Piazza del Popolo, sat down at Sophie's desk, and began to write a long letter . . . to Mary's husband.

But alas, Leonardo had never been a letter writer. What with his "correct terms" and "correct terminologies" and "as I was sayings," and *"insomma" and "non so se mi son bene spiegato,"** daylight came, and he had only written *Dear, Eminent, Illustrious,* or plain *Sir,* then torn up the sheet and thrown it angrily away, so that the room was strewn with little white paper clouds on the carpet, and he up there, like Jupiter the maker of good and foul weather, was still trying to find the right beginning for the rightest of letters ever written by one Italian *galantuomo* to another Italian *galantuomo,*

---

* "I don't know if I've explained myself properly."

both having lost their honor in opposite ways, one because he had interpreted his stupidly, the other because he had stupidly believed one could live without it—and how can two such *galantuomini* find a common terminology for their uncommon woes?

So daylight came, and the night having brought no good counsel, because good counsel is delivered in sleep and he hadn't slept since the hermit interlude, he did the stupidest thing in his life by opening the window and breathing the clean morning air as if he had deserved it and could act wisely in this new day of his new Vita Nova. But it was NOT a new day of his new life, it was only a new day in his old life, and he realized it too late for his own good.

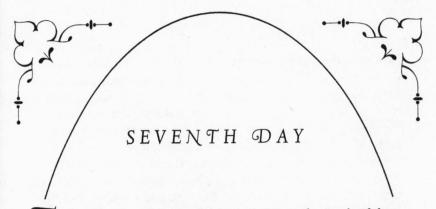

SEVENTH DAY

The goatherds were returning from their rounds, one herd from Via del Babuino, one from Via del Corso, one from Via di Ripetta, the three streets that lead fanwise into the heart of Rome from all of northern Europe, and so for a moment the noble Piazza del Popolo was a square in a very small village in the poor South: Apulia, Calabria, Campania, Sannio. The variety of dialects disappeared in the uniformity of goat-language, to which all shepherds on earth answer with human goat-sounds. Add to this conference between animals and humans the smells of both, so similar in the lower strata of society, and you have the kind of world over which the Holy Image of Mary, the blond virgin from Russia, had reigned supreme, guiding the country doctor on horseback across the steep cliffs of the poorest countryside on earth. It was that same doctor who ran out of the room now, oblivious to the fact that this was not home, this was Rome, and in Rome no one who lives in the most expensive hotel goes out in his shirtsleeves, unshaven, without even a starched collar and an appropriate necktie. All of which Leonardo did, running past the concierge who might have stopped him, had he been awake. He ran out, he crossed the whole square, mounted the ruined marble steps that led to the farms along the Tiber, and there he begged his own people, his dear, simple people, for a tin of fresh milk, promising he would pay by giving them free medical assistance any time. "I live right there, see that window across the square? That's where I live, my name is Doctor Claudi, ask for me and come right up, I'll see you and your children for free, if you give me some milk and some of that good peasant bread you have. I ran out without my wallet, that's why I can't pay you."

He knew, while he was uttering these words, that the Virgin Mary of Laterza (and Russia) was watching him from above:

hadn't she done so for nine years? Perhaps she would intercede with the married Mary in Rome, and make her understand that she was being too cruel. And he obtained his milk, his bread, even some olive oil and salt to eat it with, ate with joy, thanked his new "friends," and walked back "home," to make himself presentable for his last days of a false life among false people.

Back in his room, he shaved, dressed and resumed his difficult letter, using five more pads of precious monogrammed paper (the monogram was in silver—huge, baroque, and Cyrillic) and again little clouds of white paper covered the floor. He was still at the first word. Suddenly, a knock on the door. It was the director of the hotel in person, to notify him very politely that his ticket to Laterza would be ready for tomorrow morning, would he please pack his belongings, so that the hotel carriage could take him to the station at four, because third-class always being so full, it was advisable that he get there in time. Before he could say yes or no, or why, the director was gone. Now he felt he couldn't write his letter at all so he walked out, blushing up to the ears as he passed the director behind his desk. How could he go back to Laterza without a penny for the porter and for the carriage to take him the few miles from Laterza station to Laterza village?

This was obviously an order from Sophie. They must have asked her. Lost in these thoughts, he found himself face to face with Adriana, so close in fact that he opened his arms to embrace her. "Adriana, my friend, I need your advice."

She was obviously upset, she couldn't utter a sound, her hands were trembling as she motioned him back without touching him, but she found the strength to recoil, turn her back to him, and run away. He ran after her down the stairs and out of the hotel and finally grabbed her by the arm, crying: "You can't do this to me, you've got to listen. . . ."

She turned on him like a viper and hissed: "A man who goes to the police to denounce my Signora, when I told him to stay away from the police, a man who is in conspiracy with the Monster and his mother and the Cardinal is no friend of mine." And she spat in his face.

He made no effort to erase the sign of its insult because he didn't want to let go of her, and the sight of what she had done upset her so that she could barely hold back her tears.

"Listen to me, Adriana, it was all a misunderstanding. . . ."

She lifted her other arm and hit him so violently in the eye that he almost fell backwards, but he still didn't give up and ran after her again, and managed to grab her arm once more.

"If you don't let me go, I'll call the police," she shouted, and then, seeing a crowd assemble, she went on: "Shame on you, a gentleman, to molest a decent girl in the street. Go to the whorehouse if you need women so badly!"

This time it was his turn to run, because the crowd was becoming voluble, and when he got back to the hotel, his hands were trembling, his eye was smarting, his walk unsteady. Again, all the personnel watched him disapprovingly, and he heard one of them say: "Thank God we'll be rid of him tomorrow." The others agreed, but he couldn't hear them, because he was back in his room. Again he closed the window and sat down at the desk, this time to write a letter to Sophie, and again the first line took twenty sheets of her monogrammed paper.

Sophie . . . Madame . . . Dear Madame . . . Dear Sophie . . .
After an hour he gave up and went to the mirror to examine his eye. It hurt. It looked very, very red. He didn't want to meet Mary that way. And how would he justify it to her, in the unlikely event that she hadn't heard all about it already? Adriana was not to be trusted, by now he knew that for sure. And tomorrow, the end? Without ever, ever seeing Mary again? Impossible. Impossible also because of the money: two reasons then, not just one. He couldn't leave, he *wouldn't* leave! What the hell, if they had been given orders by her, this time he would have a chance to face her and tell her. Tell her everything: from his fear of exhibiting his table manners to . . . to everything, except for Adriana and Cefala. These were things between him and his conscience. Enough of this Protestant pride . . . Who the hell did they think they were? And this was the first thing to insist on in a letter: who the hell do you Protestants think you are?

Back to the desk, a new sheet of paper, pen in hand: *Madame . . .*
No.

Illustrious Lady . . .

No. Reads like an envelope. It's offensive, un-Christian, Protestant, in fact. After all, I am still her guest.

My very, very dear lost friend Sophie!

Tears came to his throat, then to his eyes, then fell right onto these kind words, making them into an unreadable mess. *If you only knew why these first words are blotted out,* he wrote, knowing very well these were not the correct terms for a letter. But what *were* the correct terms?

There are no correct terms, there is no substitute for the eye and the touch, even with people you don't love THAT way. If she only could see me, hear me cry . . .

There was a discreet knock on the door, and he KNEW this was Sophie. "O my God, I thank Thee." He spoke to Him in whispers, not to her. Let her knock twice and come in on her own, to see what SHE has done.

"Sir?"

The director again.

"What the hell do you want? Who authorized you to come in?"

"Sir, if you use that kind of language I will have no choice but to call the police and have you thrown out by force, you and your filthy luggage."

So this was the language of these uniformed lackeys once the allurement of money was gone. He wiped his tears, but his hands were trembling so, his heart beating so, he couldn't utter a word. He stared wildly, mutely, at the offender, who now said:

"Sir, what is this new idea of yours, to have all the milkmen of Rome come here with their families, to see you, their 'good doctor'? What do you think this is, a consulting room for derelicts? This is a first-class hotel. . . ."

One glance outside the window confirmed Leonardo's suspicion: the whole square was teeming with shepherds and their families, all coming towards the hotel. HIS MOMENT HAD ARRIVED.

"You lackey," he said quietly, looking the director in the face. "Who are you to prevent me from exercising my profession as I see fit, and to insult me in my own quarters? As long as I stay here, this is my house, not yours, and if you dare call the police, you will find that my personal friend His Excellency Ramirez will teach you a lesson such as I wouldn't dare teach you now, because I'm too angry to control myself. In my hometown, an upstart bastard like you would have his face smashed to a pulp. And if these orders stem from Mrs. von Randen, tell her that as long as I am her guest here—that is, until tomorrow morning at four—she has no right to behave this way, and I shall shame her in the presence of the whole civilized world. Go now, and let my patients come to me this instant!"

The director paled, gasped, trembled and disappeared without another word. Minutes later the first goatherds came in, and he began to use his stethoscope on them, on their wives, on their children, taking in their acrid stench as the purest oxygen he had tasted since his arrival at that accursed hotel.

For at least another hour it continued to seem that indeed his time had come: he was living his honest reality in the world of his dishonest fairy tale. What triumph, to transform the Hotel de Russie into his surgery in Laterza, in his own father's house! Alas, what brought this reality to an abrupt and unpleasant end was not the hotel staff, whose arrival he was dreading at every moment (he knew they had the right to kick him out, no need of the police for that)—what came to destroy his new reality was the most ancient of the fairy tales against which modern science was now fighting, the same fairy tale he had fought in Laterza: that green mold, and the belief that it was a more powerful disinfectant than alcohol and iodine and hydrogen peroxide. Perhaps he was too nervous because of his fear of the servants, which made him jittery every time he heard someone enter his bedroom (he had improvised his surgery in the bathroom, which was so vast, so clean, so well provided with alcohol, water and soap). When he tore the first such green dressing from an open wound, bandaged with the filthiest handkerchiefs ever seen, he said nothing, but when the second such dressing came under his eyes, he exploded and called it a crime. "What are you trying to do: murder your child? This is no disinfectant, this is infection, one of the worst sources of infection, in fact! Off with that dirt!!!"

The father of the wounded child protested, other goatherds forced their way into the bathroom to see what was happening, and

in a matter of seconds they were calling him a fool, a false doctor, a
doctor for the rich, a doctor for laughs, and then they left, all of
them, urging even the newcomers to go, proclaiming aloud in the
corridor and all the way along the crowded stairs that he was an
idiot, a doctor for the English, not a real, Italian doctor.

Fairy tales disappear cleanly and discreetly like dreams. Realities
do not: they leave a trail of dirt and disorder, but none so great as
this one. The goatherds had defiled the soft blue carpet with their
filthy boots, they had even rested them on his bed, leaving brown
seals of goat manure and mud that carried the imprint of their nail-
studded soles or their raffia-laced *ciocie*. One *ciocia* had even been
left on his bed (it belonged to the child with the bandaged foot).

Left alone with this ruin, Leonardo did the same thing he had
always done in the thick of reality back home: he rushed to open
the windows and let the clean air in. But who would clear away the
dirt? Who would repair that broken crystal glass in the dining
room? That torn silk curtain? Who would wash those lace curtains
on which the barbarians had wiped the dirt from their hands? It
was a miracle they hadn't stolen his watch, which still remained on
the dresser. But they had emptied the liquor from the decanters in
the dining room, and left a trail of green, sugary stains on the
precious wood and on the precious carpet.

Realizing finally that this was his greatest blunder to date, Leonardo knew that he must atone for this at least, or kill himself at
once. So began his Via Crucis.

Before leaving the room he closed his eyes to concentrate on his
next step without having to take in any more of the devastation he
had caused, then prayed to Mary's Image, then slowly walked
downstairs along the same trail of stench and dirty rugs he had just
left behind. His fists were clenched behind his back, he was trying
to steel himself (metallicize? he thought, with bitter irony) to receive even physical blows without flinching. Subdued faces greeted
the Repentant. No one moved, except for the few foreigners who
were watching the scene with amusement. He walked straight to the
door of the director's office, opened it and stood there, his eyes to
the ground, after a glimpse to make sure that his enemy was ready
to receive him. He was more than ready: an unknown, very distinguished Italian gentleman was standing by him, also silent.

"I have no words," said Leonardo, "to express my shame and my horror. Tell me what I can do to repair such immense damage. I have property in Laterza, I have money in the bank, anything you may ask I can pay within a matter of days: the time it takes to arrange for such a transaction."

The director said nothing, but the unknown gentleman smiled and said: "No need for reparations. Madame von Randen takes on herself the sole responsibility for whatever damages we suffered. I am the owner of this hotel, please sit down." And he stretched out his hand, which Leonardo dazedly took. "His Excellency Ramirez sends you his best wishes, by the way, and says he'll be in touch with you in a few days. He had to leave Rome on urgent business."

"Thank you," said Leonardo, feeling very slightly better. "And who spoke with Mrs. von Randen?"

"No one, as far as I know. At least I didn't. . . ." Then, to the director, who suddenly seemed absorbed in his work: "Did you, by any chance?"

"I? How would I dare? That's why I sent for you."

"Oh yes, of course, that's why he sent for me. The decision seemed important enough, so I consulted with her administrator, and he agreed with me that it wasn't important enough to risk disturbing her. She often has guests in that apartment who seem . . . how shall I put it? . . . possessed, yes, that's the word, possessed by the same . . . generous urge to do something for the lowly, or for mankind in general, you know what I mean; in fact, you must know her, so I don't have to explain: she's that way herself, she can't stand the thought that there is poverty, unhappiness, anything less than ideal conditions on earth, and she rushes to help, to devote herself, to expose herself, shall I say? Just as you did this morning, yes, to expose herself to great physical dangers, even, God forbid, to what some might call ridicule (which is not, mark you, not MY opinion, I'm like that too: an idealist, an overgenerous soul; there are very few of us left, my dear sir, very very few . . .). So, as I was saying, she, you, I, we all live in peril to help our neighbor—and see what our neighbor does to us in exchange . . . The fact, the sad, horrible yet true fact is that we all live in the moon and the others, the cynical, dishonest, unspeakable people live on earth, with both feet solidly planted on the ground so it is they who always win in the end. You have seen it yourself this very morning: you tried to help the lowly, the sick, the disinherited, and they called you a false doctor. And why? Because you tried to save them from their barbaric superstitious practices, which are worthy of cavemen, not of twentieth-century man, the man of science, who travels on trains, uses telephones, knows about disinfectants, and has found the cure for rabies, scurvy, pellagra, smallpox, et cetera—in short, like you: great scientists all, but at the same time the dupes of anyone with less salt in his brains, and more dishonesty in his heart."

Throughout this whole speech, Leonardo kept watching the director, wishing he would say something too, but the director seemed satisfied with the nonsense being invented by the hotel owner, and at the same time almost amused by it, thus showing his contempt for the fool who was supposed to accept it as genuine. A difficult situation for Leonardo to deal with, since he was infinitely grateful for being treated so kindly, and at the same time so humiliated and ashamed. He waited for the director to look his way, but the director did not, even when he rose from his chair and tried to get out of the office without having to ask Leonardo's permission. They attempted to get around one another as people do in a narrow street, dodging this way and that and finally the director, looking impatiently at Leonardo's shoes, apologized to *them* for being in a hurry, and Leonardo apologized to *him:* "I'm sorry." Then, as the director was already at the door: ". . . I mean, not only for this, . . . I . . ." And as the director rushed to close the door behind him, so that he wouldn't have to hear, Leonardo completed his sentence to the hotel owner: ". . . I intended to apologize to him for the . . . the most unfortunate words uttered by me in a moment of . . . lack of presence of mind, . . . words dictated by my . . . uncivilized, SOUTHERN short-temperedness, . . . which, as you well know, . . . at times . . . "

"No need, my good sir, no need, no need, no need whatever . . . It was for him to apologize to you, for assuming you had decided to leave tomorrow morning, which, I assume, you probably do not intend to do, at least for the moment; none of his business, none of my business to inquire about the precise date—"

"Oh, no no no, absolutely not, I mean, yes, it is your business—I

mean, your right—to know, and I'm glad to be able to tell you that
the precise date . . . the precise date . . . I mean, if we want to
be precise . . . is not yet absolutely settled, but don't worry, please,
it will be, the moment I will have had a chance to . . . how shall
I put it? . . . SPEAK calmly for a few minutes with my distinguished and most hospitable hostess, you know how it is, especially
in these close bonds of friendship and affective . . . I mean, family
relationships, I . . . I can't discuss matters that concern not only
me, but her and . . . others in the family, you understand, I hope.
. . . Reasons of discretion . . ."

"You don't have to tell me, my dear sir, I understand and of
course respect the private character of those reasons."

"I am so very grate—"

"Just a moment, my dear sir, what I wanted to say is that, if that
is the only reason you can't give a precise date for your departure, I
can ask the telephone operator to call Madame von Randen, and let
you talk to her right now from this office. . . . I'll just leave you
and close the door. . . ."

At this moment the director opened it, as if he had been listening
at the keyhole, and said: "She's not in Rome, I think she left last
night."

Leonardo began to tremble like a leaf. He gasped and went so
white that the director froze into silence, and the hotel owner
rushed towards him to save him from falling over, but Leonardo
smiled sadly and said in a very shaky voice: "That's impossible, I
SAW her last night. . . ."

"Oh, you DID?" said the director, growing pale and worried in
turn. "I'm sorry you did, I mean I'm sorry I didn't know, but I
thought I knew for certain that she had left last night for Germany."

"I would know if she had . . ." gasped Leonardo, and the director ran out of the room again to roar at the concierge. "Didn't
you say Mrs. von Randen had left last night?"

"I never said any such thing," answered the concierge defensively.
"It must have been someone else."

"Oh, the night porter . . ."

"Maybe, but that's not me. Ask him, before you accuse. . . ."

"But he's not here."

Leonardo had slumped into a chair and covered his forehead with his hand.

"What is all this chitchat about?" asked the hotel owner in a fit of rage. "Call and find out."

"Call and find out?" asked the director.

"Yes, call and find out."

"But . . . it will take an hour. I'll send a bell-boy over."

"Send a bell-boy, send two, send three . . . don't ask *me* what you should do. Do it, for God's sake. . . ."

"Yessir, I will."

At that moment Dante's voice called to the concierge from the entrance hall: "Say, why don't you ask people who know? She can't have left, she has thirty-five guests for dinner tonight. . . ."

"Oh, does she?" asked the hotel owner, speaking to the concierge through the open doorway.

"Don't ask me," said the concierge, "ask him."

"I told you," shouted Dante from the other end of the hall. "She has thirty-five people for dinner."

"Thank you, Dante," answered the hotel owner; then, putting his hand on Leonardo's shoulder: "You were right, she can't have left Rome. In fact, you'll obviously be seeing her tonight, so take your time and tell us as soon as you know."

"You're right," said Leonardo, trying to smile and getting up from his chair. "I'll certainly see her tonight, in fact, I'd quite forgotten. . . ."

With these words, which he regretted at once because they made everyone smile in a way he didn't like at all, he bowed out and staggered back to his room, trying to hold his head high, his hand firmly on the banister, in order to keep himself from falling.

Three maids unknown to him, and a "Dante" who wasn't Dante (as he realized only when the man lifted his face from scrubbing the bathroom floor), were putting his apartment back into shape. All sorts of filthy objects had been collected in no less than five pails next to the door.

"We'll be through in a minute," said one of the maids. "Do you want me to call the porter for your luggage?"

"Let him do his packing first," said another maid, then, to him:

"Sir, will you please avoid sitting on the bed as you pack your belongings? We've just changed it, and we'd hate to have to change it again, if you put your feet on the bed cover the way you did before."

"I never do such things, and I am not leaving anyway," he said, in a firm voice.

"I beg your pardon."

"I told you I never do such things."

Now they were all lined up in front of him, as if expecting a tip.

"May I have your names, and I will send you a little something when I have cashed my money at the bank?"

"Oh . . ."

"Oh, but you don't have to . . ."

"No need, no need, sir . . ."

But the man in the bathroom called: "Gregorio is MY name; remember, don't give it to Dante, sir, he'll never give it to me."

"That's right," said the three maids, "don't give it to anyone else, please, especially not to Dante's mother or Cefala: they always pocket everything. They think they own this place. My name is Elisabetta."

"And mine, Giggia."

"And mine, Agata."

"Very well," said Leonardo, taking out his prescription pad and writing down all their names with an air of grave concern. "You'll hear from me soon, and thank you again. You've done a wonderful job."

"How nice he is," said Elisabetta to the others. "No one ever talks that way to us. Thank you, sir."

But the other two said nothing, they hardly smiled as they left, and Gregorio even scowled. Once they were out in the corridor, Leonardo could hear their comments:

"You're such a fool, Elisabetta. The others don't use nice words, but they pay, this one here never will."

And Gregorio: "He will, he will, if the old lady gives him the cash, but if she doesn't, he won't, because he has no money himself. Have you heard about his train ticket and . . ." The rest of this revelation went to the people downstairs, the voices were already too faint, but Leonardo heard the three girls giggle in the distance as he closed and locked the door.

His isolation from the world was now complete. He was not only a man without roots, but without branches, leaves or flowers, let alone fruits. Yet for the moment he at least had this beautiful apartment all to himself, so he could go on nursing his sorrow like a child.

He opened his bedroom window in order to close the shutters so that he would never see the moon again, nor the morning sun—not even this morning's, which was still claiming one tiny triangle of the windowsill. Leonardo touched the tiny triangle and it warmed the tips of his fingers and his nails too, but the second joint of each finger was already back in winter. He stretched out his whole hand, palm down, like a bishop offering his hand to the congregation for the kissing of the pastoral ring.

"Look at him, look, he's blessing the crowds, he thinks he's the Pope," shouted Gregorio's voice from the garden, and the three girls laughed. He withdrew his hand as if it had accidentally caught fire and angrily closed the shutters but smiled with satisfaction when he heard the concierge shouting from inside the hotel: "Hey, you, what are you doing out there? Taking it easy? Don't you know that five Russian princes plus families and servants are arriving today?" The slaves ran back inside, but Leonardo didn't dare open the shutters again. Mary's dinner guests, obviously, he thought, and it hurt, oh how it hurt. . . . And how strange, to feel nostalgia for Russians, any Russians, he who had never even known what their language sounded like until four days ago. Or was it five? Yes, five. Five and a half, corrected the Infallible from the other side of the house, echoed by the cliff Leonardo was watching through the slits in his jail window. Soon all the lesser churches answered the Infallible's order to glorify noontime. A group of masons who had been building a wall somewhere in the neighborhood (it was easy to guess: first the sound of the scalpel scraping the brick clean, then the slap of wet plaster on it, and then the wooden handle of the scalpel hammering it lightly into place and shaving the wall clean of

whatever plaster had oozed out under pressure) stopped their bricklaying instantly and with it the lazy chanting or whistling that inevitably accompanies bricklaying, with cheerful cries of "Lunchtime!!!
Pass the bread!! Pass the wine, pass the knife!!!" How lucky they
were, to belong in this beautiful city and have the dignity of a job,
and no one to court or to thank for room and board. . . .

He closed the window, pulled both sets of curtains, then went
into the dining room, from which the only daylight now stole into
the darkened bedroom, pulled the curtains there, so as not to be
seen by the coachmen outside as he opened the window to close the
shutters, and went back again to the bed bumping into chairs and
tables and doors, before he could find the lightswitch. Ah, what joy
to have abolished the entire day. He decided not to ring for lunch,
and immediately felt calmer, more spiritual, as in his college days
when he would enter into a period of fasting and spiritual exercises.
But he also decided to treat himself well, with all the luxuries he
was entitled to so long as he didn't have to leave for destinations
unknown. He ran himself a hot bath, then undressed and from the
bathtub enjoyed the bright colors of the Pincio and the sky, guessed
more than seen through the milky screen of the curtains. Outside
noises and voices were muted by the closed window: they became
memories, a fitting condition for all his experiences from this moment on. After his bath, he put a large bath mat on the carpet next
to his bed, fetched a blanket and a pillow, and thus began his long
night of despair, to which he exposed himself as if it were a cure
prescribed by a doctor.

His first dream was about leaving by boat for Egypt, from the
seaport of Brindisi. Mary was waiting for him across the Adriatic,
and he could see her, although he knew that she was hundreds of
miles away. It was a big ship, a real ocean liner, but as he got closer
to it, the ship became smaller, and just as he was about to climb
aboard, it turned into the kind of paper boat children make out of
pages from their notebooks. He still hoped to be able to board it,
but the moment the ship touched water, it unfolded, and the loose
sheet of his notepad floated away into the distance.

He woke up; he had only slept an hour. His fatigue was so great
that he went to sleep again at once, and had a dream about the big

dinner party at Mary's house. Her palace was so huge that the main stairway was the Scalinata, and yet the moment he walked towards it he couldn't find it. Fortunately there was the service entrance with a spiral staircase leading to the ballroom, which echoed with voices and sounds of cheerful music. He climbed the stairs, but when he got close to the floor from which the noises were coming, the stairs became smaller and smaller until they disappeared into the wall, and he found himself only a few feet below his goal, trying in vain to climb a perfectly smooth surface. Again he woke up, but this time the whole room had become the Piazza di Spagna, and he knew there was a moon, he knew Mary and her mother were nearby, but he could see nothing because his eyes were so tightly closed that he couldn't open them. He tried and tried, he even tried with his hands to lift the upper eyelid or lower the lower one: only darkness came into his eyes, and yet he knew that everybody else could see.

Other dreams he could only remember because they all took place in the landscapes of grief, but what the dreams were about he couldn't recall: meanings and faces and actions changed so rapidly that he was exhausted by the mere effort of trying to keep track of them, so he gave up and endured as many dreams as beats to his pulse. He woke up with a high temperature, which gave him great happiness. Now he knew he was going to die, and so he dreamed about his death, and at long last he had a chance to talk to Mary and to Sophie, and everything seemed clear again; the three of them took a long walk in the moonlight, and it was such a long walk that his legs turned numb and he couldn't keep up with them. He called and called: they were too far away to hear him. He lifted his legs, but could advance less than an inch at every step. When he woke up he was so tired that he couldn't even move to get some water from the bottle on the night table. Finally, after another long dreamless sleep, he woke up rested, and it was three in the morning. From under the door came sliding in an echo of piano music and songs, then laughter, then Klagonov's drunken voice, sounding as if he were talking in his sleep, with those long pauses between words that drunkards use when sleeping aloud. But the words were all in Russian and French and other languages, against a background of women's voices, laughing and chattering. He got up, went to the

dining room and sat down at the desk, to begin a new letter to
Mary's husband. This time he wrote seven pages, and when he
realized that what he had said made sense (in fact, he cried with joy
over the beauty of his arguments) he dozed off again and slept
soundly until noontime.

EIGHTH DAY

*D*iscreet knock. Without speaking, without a pang of fear, he slowly got up from his mat, went to the door and opened it, imagining it must be Klagonov. It was Schillasi. He was delighted, although he pretended to be the opposite.

"What do you want? How dare you show your face at all after what you've done to me?"

"Goombà, a friend is always a friend."

"You think so? How interesting. Come in and sit down and explain to me what kind of a friend you are, because I want to know."

Schillasi did and did and did (come in, sit down, explain). "If I hadn't pushed you, you would have gone back to Laterza the day after we met, or don't you remember you were going to write a letter to Mary and explain everything?"

Leonardo remembered. How could he have forgotten his senseless fears of that first day? He remembered everything, and in every instance everything had been his fault, so he was deprived even of the one catharsis available to the heavyhearted: the self-righteous logorrhea that allows them to discharge their guilt on others. Yet what other use could he find for such a vulgar person? Schillasi shook his head: "I see that you can't answer me, which is a good sign. You're beginning to learn. In life, you see, one must be practical, even cynical at times. Idealists like you always drown in their own shit, because they have no time for such vulgar devices as bathrooms. You've no friends left now but me. Does anyone else come to see you these days?"

"What do you know about my life?"

"Plenty. You've become the laughing-stock of the Caffè Greco."

"How could I, if no one knows me there?"

"Everybody does, you made your position quite clear the one time you were there. Do you know what they say about you at the Greco? That you were Sophie's lover, and that Mary's husband said to Sophie: 'Either you give up him, or my son and my wife. I can't have such immorality going on in your house.'"

"The bastard— Is that what they say he says?" ·

"Yes, I'm glad to report; in fact, I was silently praying that's how they would interpret you, because if they had guessed the truth, you wouldn't be alive by now. Mary's husband may be a philanderer, he may hate her guts, but being cuckolded is something else. No husband likes that, and no husband lets it happen to him, especially if he hates his wife. One more reason to double all the controls. When you love your wife it's easy to control her: you're always with her, and you care. It's when you don't care that it becomes a police job."

Leonardo buried his face in his hands, and cringed with shame.

"Goombà, why this strange reaction? What do you care, since you hate Rome and are not going to live here, ever?"

"And where shall I live? In Laterza? Do you know what happened to me there? Exactly what you would expect from a fool like me: my wife has a lover, and everybody's known for years except me. A kind soul told me yesterday, or was it two days ago? I've lost all sense of time, but what does it matter anyway?"

Schillasi frowned and became very comforting: "What a tragedy . . . I take sincere part in your sorrow, my heart bleeds in unison with yours."

Leonardo couldn't help laughing. Then, seeing that Schillasi didn't quite know how to interpret this, he added: "I don't care, except for the fact that now I don't know where to go. As long as I didn't know about it, Laterza seemed the only possible place for me, but now . . ."

"Why do you keep talking about going back? How about Mary? What does she say?"

Leonardo lifted his eyes to the ceiling, lowered them to the window, closed them to retrace the beam of silence all the way back to its source, and said, with a final sob in his voice: "I don't know . . ."

"What d'you mean, you don't know? . . . Come on, answer me, don't start crying again: be a *man*, for God's sake. Ask her!!!"

"They won't let me."

"Poor, poor friend . . . I know who can help you."

"You do?"

"Yes, I do. But let's go out and have lunch."

"No, let's have lunch here."

"Can you?"

"Yes, and I can have guests."

"Here? In this room?"

"No, there, in the dining room. But you will eat, I won't."

"Come on, I can't eat alone, you must be starving, you've lost weight, you look terrible, you're shaking all over."

"It's nothing: just a little temperature from overexertion. But I can't eat."

"You will, and we'll have Champagne. I've never had Champagne in my life. This will be a celebration."

"Only if you tell me right away who it is that can help me."

"I'll only tell you after I've seen you eat and drink."

"I won't drink, but I may eat something."

He rang the bell, and when the waiter came, he said: "Lunch for two, please, with Champagne."

"Oh," said the waiter. "I'll have to send the head waiter for that." And he was gone.

"Now tell me who can help me."

"A woman."

"A friend of Mary's?"

"Not altogether, although she is in a way."

"Who? Her maid?"

"Oh no, a lady, a real lady."

They were interrupted by the head waiter, who said impertinently: "Sir, I'm sorry, but you are not supposed to have guests."

There was a long silence, then Leonardo asked, humbly: "Why not?"

"Orders. I don't make the rules here."

"But I only want one lunch served, I don't eat."

"All the same, sir. You are supposed to eat alone, or not at all.

And I can't give you Champagne, unless I have an order from the administrator, or from Madame in person."

There was another long silence, which seemed to irritate the head waiter, who said: "I'm afraid I can't stay here any longer, I have fifty-five new guests downstairs and I'm alone in the restaurant. If you want to eat downstairs, you can, but then you pay. At your orders, sir."

And he was gone.

"That's the rich for you," said Schillasi. "The moment they can't use you for their own purposes, you're thrown out like a squeezed lemon. I tell you what we'll do: we'll go out to lunch, then I'll take you to this lady."

"Who is she?"

"Angelo's mistress."

"The new one? I know her, I've met her, she seemed to like me very much."

"Where did you meet her?"

"On the Scalinata, when he took my hat and whirled it on a stick.

"Oh . . . you'd better forget her at once, and not even mention her name, because the person I have in mind is the old mistress, the one who liked you so much at the Greco."

Leonardo looked at him incredulously and laughed.

"What's so funny about that?"

"Goombà, I appreciate your good will, but how can the discarded mistress of the man whose wife I was about to take away from him do anything for me?"

"If anyone on earth can, she can."

"Have you spoken to her?"

"Yes."

"When?"

"This morning. I met her in the street. She asked me about you, I said I didn't know if you had left, I told her what I knew, and she said she knew everything already, I didn't have to repeat it, she only wanted to know where to find you, because she couldn't ask the hotel people here, they're all devoted to Mary. So I offered to help her, and this is why I came."

Leonardo rose to the occasion. "She's a beautiful woman, I like her, she's as unhappy as I am, and for the same reasons, so what do I stand to lose? Nothing. The only thing against her is that she has been discarded by Mary's husband. There's no glory in picking up your enemy's leftovers." He sighed. "All right, let's go." Then, after a moment's hesitation: "Let me just look at something."

He went to the desk and reread his letter to Mary's husband, found it excellent and conclusive, so he added one formal last sentence and signed it, then put it in its envelope—and suddenly remembered he hadn't shaved. After ten minutes he was back, cleanshaven, neatly dressed and ready to go. But before they went, he reread the letter very carefully yet once more, then with a sense of satisfaction, because it was so noble, he said: "Let's go." What now made him so eager was the thought that if Angelo did heed his warning (and how could he not, after what Leonardo had written?), he would have less time for his new mistress (who had so little time for him anyway that she would soon leave him) and he would go back to his first mistress out of despair. Therefore, she wasn't a leftover, and it paid to cuckold him.

"Goombà, don't come out like this, it's cold today, put on your elegant fur coat."

"It's gone."

"Where?"

"Never mind. Another stupid thing which cost me my happiness."

"Who has it?"

"I said, never mind." He was cringing at the memory of why he had gone to the chief of police.

"All right, let's take a carriage then."

Once in the closed carriage, Schillasi pulled a few gold coins out of his pocket and tried to put them into Leonardo's, but Leonardo wouldn't let him. "Not after what I've done to you," he said, thinking of the police again, but Schillasi insisted: "How about what *I've* done to you? Let me make amends, please."

"No, I can't."

"You have no money, I received five hundred lire from the English banker for those cufflinks, they were worth very little."

"Thank you." He was furious: he was being offered less than five percent of the five hundred.

After a few minutes they were there. "You wait here," said Schillasi. "I want to make sure she's alone. She asked me to take care. You never know: Mary's husband may have taken a fancy to seeing her just as a friend, and if he saw you here, it wouldn't be so good. Wait for me in that café there. Eat something, now you have money. You need food."

Leonardo obeyed, but ate nothing, because he found the pastry too expensive. The twenty lire was what he would have needed to go back to Laterza third-class, tip the baggage man at the station and pay for the stagecoach. Not one penny left, and even though he knew he would never go back, as of now this remained his only possibility.

Schillasi wasn't gone long. "All clear," he said. "She's anxious to see you, and she says she can help you with Mary. I won't wait. You can thank me later."

Thus they parted, and Leonardo walked up the dark stairs of an old Roman house, the first house in his Roman experience not much better than any of the boardinghouses where he had lived as a student in Naples: greasy walls, a greasy rope for a banister, pungent smell of cabbage from every landing, windows open on laundry hanging across towards the houses on the other side of the street. He realized how quickly he had become used to living in splendor, and this saddened him again when he thought of his immediate future.

Five landings, ten whiffs of the same cabbage soup from ten apartment doors, then the eleventh whiff, emanating from the attic, and there, behind a half-open door, waited the beautiful woman who looked like Mary. Or who once had. Now, alas, she looked like a woman who had cried a great deal, and tears had washed all the beauty from her face. She had aged ten years in five days. She was all dressed up with makeup on her cheeks, under her eyes, on her lips; she looked like a whore, and five days ago she had looked like Mary! . . . How could I have sunk so low as to find a resemblance between them?

She smiled, sadly, with an effort that made her look even uglier, and observed him with a certain cruel joy he registered at once, sensitive as he had become with grief and fasting. "And so we meet again, in a different mood," she said. "Come in." And she preceded him. "Sit down." And she showed him to a sofa that seemed as broken-down as the two of them; the springs creaking and meowing and chirping until the whole thing cringed and collapsed under Leonardo's thin body as if he had weighed a ton.

She sat across from him and looked worried for a second: the tall mirror which the sofa was bracing up was leaning dangerously over him, threatening to kill him. He followed the direction of her eyes. "Never mind," she said, "the thing is old but solid. They knew how to build sofas in those days. Now that they make them without frames, they won't last more than five years: this one is eighty years old, it comes from France, it used to be in the d'Escarande castle at Lalande."

"Oh," he said, just to say something, because he had already lost all hope in her capacity to help him, "I think I've heard that name before."

"Of course you have, that's the name of the Cardinal, and this sofa belonged to his branch of the family. See the crest here and here and up there? That's the Lalande crest." She had to stop. "Forgive me . . ." and she cleared her throat, tried to breathe more freely, then began to recite: "In field of gold, two lions at rest" (a sob marked the sadness of the lions) "under a tree of green which charges the Head of the Second." (She was now crying openly, tears streaming down her flabby cheeks, but she had to recite it all, as if it were a sacred duty, such as only feudal lords could understand and carry through.) "Crusader's arm, bent, with Saracen sword in the First . . ." (this was almost too much, but she went on) ". . . four doves in the sky above the Second, signifying the four hopes of the House of Lalande to reconquer Citoges from the Normans." (This, not her own twentieth-century sorrows, made her break down completely.) Leonardo had resisted until now but the absurdity of those tears caused by the four doves in the sky above the Second, representing the four hopes of the House of Lalande to reconquer Citoges, did it: he broke down too and began to sob quietly all by himself, but after a few seconds, his sobs became so violent that the four hopes of Lalande, plus the two lions at rest and

the Second charged by the tree of green, all came tumbling down
on his head and rolled under the table.

"Never mind picking up the pieces," she said. "I'm sorry I cried,
the fact is that I haven't used that sofa for years: ever since Angelo
came here the first time and we became lovers that same night,
from then on we always went directly to bed, without even looking
into this room. And do you know how many years ago that was?"

"How could I?"

"Fourteen. He was so beautiful, so true to his name, with his red
hair and fiery character."

"You mean long before Mary arrived?"

"Oh, long, long before. Ours was the real marriage, not the one
she forced him into."

"She did not!"

"She did, she did. To forget you, of course, but she did. And who
made it last so long? I did. Mary doesn't know, of course, she's too
much of an egotist to know anything but her own immediate
whims, but the truth of the matter is that, without me, she would
never have had a husband for more than a few months. He gave in
to her because she was rich, and because she looked like me, and on
both counts he was wrong. She isn't rich: her mother is rich, but
she must beg for every cent, and pay for it in blind obedience.
Which is like saying suicide. That's what killed even the resemblance between us, which was deeper than you think. Mary is a
born actress, like me, and a born can-can dancer. She would be
perfect singing the song that made me famous in Paris twenty-five
years ago." And she began to sing, in a rather lovely, tender voice,
while lifting her skirts and showing her beautiful naked legs:

"When I wear blue stockings and panties, the sky seems blue to
you . . . When I wear gold stockings and panties, the sun seems
gold to you . . . When I wear white stockings and panties, the
moon seems white to you . . . But when I take off my stockings
and panties, then the whole world turns red . . . So, come here,
my love, it's time for bed. . . ."

Leonardo was so shocked he closed his eyes and slumped into the
low armchair she had just vacated. "Thank you," he said, very firmly
and primly, "thank you very much indeed. Schillasi had said you
might help me with Mary, and you have. I'm beginning to see that

she doesn't deserve any of the torments I've been going through the
last two nights and three days. You're not the first person to tell me
she was a born actress. No one dared to say cabaret dancer: you did,
and you must know. And you also said something else which seems
more credible and less . . . offensive: you said she can't see beyond
her own egotistical whims. I know you're right. In correct medical
terminology, that is an egomaniac with paranoid tendencies. Look
what she did to me: until two days ago, if I showed less than mad
passion all the time, she felt betrayed, unloved, forsaken, suicidal.
But the moment I needed a sign of reassurance from her: complete
silence. She did try to call me once but she got scared, perhaps her
mother came in, and she never called again or wrote. Nothing,
absolutely nothing. Well, so be it. Who cares? I feel better already.
So thank you again. Now I must go."

"No, you must not!" she shouted, turning on him like a snake.
"And you're a conceited fool!!! It's not for her to reassure you, it's
for you to reassure her, after what you've done!"

"What *have* I done?"

"Never mind. You know and I know."

"What do *you* know?"

"What the Cardinal told me."

"The Cardinal?"

"The Cardinal. He was here yesterday afternoon. And he told me
everything . . . everything. . . ."

"And you believe that degenerate hypocrite?"

"Why degenerate? And why a hypocrite? He's one of the
healthiest and most outspoken men I know. If it's his homosexual-
ity that shocks you, let me tell you he's a better lover than any
Italian I've known in my life. He initiated me into the arts of love
when I was sixteen, and I shall never forget those wonderful moments. Kind, understanding, generous, and *manly*. And don't you
misunderstand his interest in you for that kind of an interest. He
never talks openly to his young lovers as he did to you or as he
would to any person he loves intellectually. He saw rare qualities in
you, just as I did, from a distance, when I saw you making a fool of
yourself at the Greco. And he decided to help you, to guide you, to
rescue you from the sewers of your backward provinces down there.
You don't know what kind of a teacher he is. . . . Of course, I

don't agree with his idea of what you should do about Mary. He is a priest, after all, and a highly religious priest, too."

"A priest of belly-dancing, that, yes. There are primitive religions in which—"

"Idiot, imbecile, ignoramus. Do you know what the Latin word for bishop is?"

"Yes, *Praesul.*"

"And do you know what it means?"

"Director of the mysteries."

"No, of the dance."

"That's what you say."

"That's what he says, and I believe him rather than you. But no matter: he's a priest and a friend of Angelo's mother. You didn't have to spill the beans to him, and then he would never have spoken to you as he did. Nor tried to interfere with your actions. I believe you should leave with Mary, you and she are absolutely made for one another. Besides, if you left her now, where would you go? Back to your silly wife down there?"

There was a long, long silence. Leonardo was staring at the broken coat of arms under the table.

"Idiot. Give me that letter."

"What letter?"

"The letter you've written to Angelo."

"How do you know I wrote to Angelo?"

"One thousand guesses: the Professor, of course. That's why he kept you waiting downstairs: to tell me he'd read it."

"When?"

"While you were shaving."

"The bastard! And I thought he was a friend! He's cheated me again!"

"It's you who cheat yourself again and again and again. . . . Come on now, give me that letter."

Leonardo shook his head, deliberating silently, then said: "I'll read it to you, then you will see how good it is."

"All right."

She sat down on the small table in front of him, and he began to read, holding up the letter as a screen so as not to have to see that puffy, aging face:

"Dear Angelo, Allow me to use this friendly appellative, which is justified by the fact that we do have a great deal more in common than we would ever wish to admit: masculine vanity, which all of us Italians have in common, is one of these elements, but, still more than—"

She tore the letter away from him and ran off. He ran after her, shouting: "Hey, give me that letter, if you don't, I'll . . ."

But he never finished his sentence. The letter was burning under a large pot on the kitchen stove, and she kept stirring the coals, to consume it more quickly.

"You had no right to do that, you've destroyed days and nights of the most painful work. I'll never be able to do it again. . . ."

"And you have no right to destroy my work of fourteen painful years, to satisfy your masculine Italian vanity! Since you want to give up Mary, you can't stand the thought that she might take another man: she must go back to her jailer, whom she hates. That's the heart of the matter. Why didn't you spend one half hour of those days and nights writing a love letter to Mary?"

He was stunned, as if the idea had never crossed his mind. Then he remembered that it had, and he said whiningly: "She would never have read it."

"Why?"

"Because she hates me, they made her hate me."

"A woman always reads the letters of her outgoing lover, no matter how much she may hate him."

"How do you know?"

"I am a woman, if you please. Of course, you Italian males know everything!"

He shook his head again in distress, then said, almost in a whisper: "Why YOU ITALIANS: aren't you Italian yourself?"

"No, French."

"With that Roman accent?"

"Do you want to hear me talk in *your* heavy accent?" she replied in the heaviest Apulian cadence, then: "In a Florentine accent?" (in Florentine), "Venetian? Sicilian? Neapolitan? Spanish? I can imitate all the accents on earth, and so can Mary, Angelo tells me. Does that make her less Russian than she is, or me less French?"

He seemed sleepy, his eyes were blinking.

"Let's eat now, you must be hungry."

"No."

"Your choice, if you want to play the sulking little boy, I must eat. I'm hungry, I haven't eaten for two days."

She put two plates on the marble table, threw two heavy silver spoons out of a drawer, took two glasses from a shelf and a bottle of red wine, lifted the pot from the stove, opened it, and it smelled good: peasant bean soup.

"Doesn't it tempt you?" she said, filling his bowl first.

"No."

"Sit down at least and watch me eat."

He did, and she began to eat without looking at him. Suddenly she cringed as she heard him sniffle; she beat the glass on the table and shouted: "Stop being a baby! Enough of those crocodile tears!"

Which made things worse: now he couldn't control himself, and buried his face in his hands.

She grabbed both bowls and threw them on the floor, then put her arm on the table and wept on it so violently that the whole table trembled on its weak legs. One minute later they were crying in each other's arms, in spite of her efforts to prevent it: "Go, go, leave me alone, I'm too ugly. You're ugly too, oh my God, how ugly we both are. . . ." More sobs, then: "Why, oh why, must pain make everything more difficult? See those who are happy, how easy it is for them to look handsome . . . and look at us now—who would want to look at us?"

He certainly didn't, but his hands were beginning to feel the breasts under her dress, and she was letting him do it.

"Let's go to bed," he whispered, and they did, no longer crying, but each in his own way: she solemnly, as if readying herself for major surgery, and he very nervously, as if he were afraid of being caught and beaten. He was: it didn't work. He whimpered out of humiliation, still trying to force himself, and she spoke to him quietly: "Lie down, you're hungry, do you think the body can be treated as a slave?"

"But I swear to you that this has never happened before. . . ."

"I don't believe it and I don't care. How old do you think I am?"

"I don't know," he said, covering up and settling in the bed beside her.

"Forty-nine. And you're thirty-two, Angelo's age, and, like Angelo and all Italians, a man from your waist down, and a woman, a vain, hysterical woman and a liar from your waist up. Prederasts, that is: pre-pederasts, the Cardinal calls you, and he's a real man. Sleep now, I'll clear up the mess in the kitchen and make us some lunch, a good lunch, that's the first thing you'll need if you want to find Mary again."

She disappeared into the kitchen, and he got dressed. When she heard him arrive, she wiped her eyes in a hurry and sighed, as if she had been sobbing again. He said nothing, sat down and began to eat bread.

"You certainly made a mess of your life," she said, filling a new bowl with soup and putting it in front of him; then, after filling her own and sitting down: "But not of Mary's life, yet. You *will*, the ground is ready, her mother has prepared it for you, so she expects to be ruined by you. She wants it. Angelo didn't ruin her enough; in fact, he never even tried. Tell me: have you ever asked yourself during these days and nights what you could do to win back Mary and her mother?—You must win them back together, or not even try. Have you?"

"Yes, but it would take years."

"No. One minute."

"One minute?"

"Less: the time it takes to read a name in an envelope that comes with a bunch of red roses."

"That's a French idea: you don't know them, they're Russian."

"They are women. Beautiful roses, and lots of them, or perhaps other flowers, but there must lots, and well presented."

"And who has the money?"

"I do. I'll give it to you after lunch and you will go to the most expensive florist in Rome; it's not far from here. Order thirty-six red roses, write your name on a card the florist will give you; DO NOT write a word on the envelope, but give their name and address to the florist, and a large tip. Then don't go back to your hotel, because if you do, you will spoil everything by waiting for an answer. You will come here and spend the night with me. Tomorrow morning, and not too early either, you will go back to your hotel, and Mary will be back, either waiting for you there or at home."

Leonardo looked at her incredulously, but said not a word, because he liked the idea, as one likes a theme for fantasies of things unobtainable: *What would you do if you had all the money in the world? or . . . if you were a magician?*

But she noticed that his features were settling down into their normal proportions, with no more puffy areas indicating local death.

"You're happy," she said, with an air of reproach, and he felt driven to deny it, as an act of Christian charity.

"Oh yes you are," she insisted, "I know it: you're turning beautiful again, the way I remembered you. But I'm not."

"You have always been beautiful."

"I know it, but not since the evening I met you, when Angelo told me he was going to leave me for that woman. He came here and told me just like that, and expected me to understand. In fact, he left without even noticing that I was fainting; he must have thought I was pretending. But I did faint, and I didn't wake up until the next morning at three, here, seated at this table, with my head on my right arm. At first I didn't know what had happened, then I remembered everything, and I knew that my life was finished. My blood stopped circulating, and I became all bloated."

"The blood doesn't stop circulating, and you will become normal again."

"Which means I am abnormal."

"Well, you do look different, and you said it yourself: pain is fatal to our looks. But as soon as he comes back to you, and I do feel he will . . ."

"What makes you say that? I know he won't. He only likes older women."

"But the woman he has now is very young."

"You've seen her again, I know. And you think she's young?"

"She looks it."

"She does not. Only a country boy like you would think so: she's fifty-three."

"Whaat?"

"Fifty-three, probably fifty-five. Embalmed. And vivacious, of course, witty, elegant: a real Frenchwoman of our generation. And

she betrays him, and he doesn't see it. I told him so at the beginning of our last conversation, and he said nonsense. But he wasn't
thinking of her that evening: he was thinking of Mary. You had
made him madly jealous, so I told him how I had heard you boasting about Mary's mother, your rich mistress. . . ."

"But I never said any such thing."

"I know you didn't. I invented it. I even told the Cardinal, before
coming home that same evening, because he's such a gossip he can't
keep a secret for five minutes. And I told Angelo that I was going to
snatch you away from her, because I found you charming. Which is
true, but I had no desire to leave Angelo, only to make him jealous.
And I did, for a few minutes: men are always vulnerable on that
score. But then, all of a sudden, he shrugged his shoulders and said:
'Well, anyway, what do I care, since I'm going to leave you for
Christine?' 'Christine?' I said, 'but Christine goes to bed with the
first person who walks into the room, she's famous for that.' And he
said: 'That's a lie. She does not. She just told me she loves me, and
I promised I would move in with her tomorrow. So don't expect to
see me again.' And then he saw that I was rather upset, so he said:
'What is it? Didn't you know this was going to end, sooner or later?
But let's remain friends. Why don't you dine with me and Christine tomorrow night?' I felt faint, I heard him say something unpleasant that sounded like a reproach, but I couldn't understand
what it was. So—that's the whole story. And afterwards the Cardinal came, because he felt that something must be wrong with me,
he always knows when I'm not well, he's such a dear, thoughtful
friend. He came and found me crying. . . ." She began to sob
again, but restrained herself instantly. "Enough. I must learn to
bear it. Let me give you the money." She rose from her seat and
left. When she came back, half an hour later, Leonardo had finished eating all the soup in the tureen and all the bread on the
table, and felt strong again.

"Here are sixty lire for the flowers and five for the tip. And here
are twenty lire I found on the carpet in my room. Could they be
yours?"

"Oh, oh . . . yes, I'd entirely forgotten," he said, blushing up to
his ears. "Schillasi gave me this money because I had none on me,

and I swear I never gave it another thought. I'll only take the five
lire for the tip."

"But you need at least sixty for the flowers."

"No, I can always discuss the price."

"Not with that florist. He's English."

"But Schillasi gave me this money. . . ."

"But you didn't give it to yourself for flowers, because in the
opinion of a little Abbot like you, flowers are a frivolity. Come, take
it and go now, quickly. And come back any time before dinner, and
don't go to the hotel. On your word of honor."

"My word of honor," he said, remembering this was the second
time he had given it lately, but that it was the first time he intended
to keep it.

The moment he entered the flowershop, he knew that happiness
was back. "Does the gentleman need help?" asked the distinguished
Englishman in Mr. Schultz's accent.

"Help, indeed," mumbled Leonardo to himself, looking at the
fantastic prices.

"What was that again?"

"Nothing, just looking."

"At your service, sir. When you have chosen, call me."

Forty lire for a dozen red roses. Fifty for yellow roses, twenty for a
branch of almond blossom, such as any street child in Laterza could
steal from Leonardo's garden without being punished, just threatened with a spanking if he ever did it again. And here, the owner of
those beautiful almond trees was asking him to pay the entire price
of his ticket back home for flowers much less rich than his own.
And why should an Englishman come all the way down to Italy to
sell flowers to the Italians: their own flowers at that? "This is plain
theft, this isn't commerce."

"Sir?"

"I'm not ready yet."

"At your service, please make yourself at home."

"What a formula to use: I AM at home, it is you who make me
feel a foreigner in my own garden!"

A quick glance at the Englishman, who was busy skinning an old

lady alive, made him aware that the Englishman was judging the
Italian eccentric. A nice new combination: poor *and* eccentric . . .
Besides, why send flowers to people who had dozens of fresh
flowers every morning in every corner of the house, and in the
middle, and on every table in between?

Suddenly, Bernhard walked into the shop, and Leonardo hid in a
corner behind a huge plant, ready to run the moment Bernhard
turned his back on him, but, it was to be hoped, not on purpose as
all the other servants had done in the last four days. He slipped
outside, waited, walked a little farther down the street, and there in
front of a church he saw a poor woman selling beautiful roses,
branches of almond blossom, violets, all sorts of fresh flowers.

"How much for these roses?"

"Well, my good sir, today they're still a little expensive, so you'd
better not buy them: tomorrow they'll be cheaper."

"But how much are they, anyway?"

"I'm ashamed to tell you sir, don't ask me."

"I want to know."

"Five lire a dozen, but if you insist, I can give them to you for
three fifty."

"I'll pay you six, and take two dozen."

"Sir, but that's insane. You must be in love with the lady."

"I am."

"Then God bless you and bring you good luck, these roses will
bewitch her. One whiff, and she'll faint from sheer longing for you.
Don't you think that six fifty would be a decent price for them?"

"Seven."

"My God, I've never seen such love!"

"The address to which they should be sent . . ."

"Ah, no, sir, I have no one to send them, I'm all alone in this
world since my poor husband died last year in May. Yessir, May
second, at five in the morning. And now I'm all alone."

"Wait a moment," he said, and ran back to the flowershop,
entered it, went straight to Bernhard, who was ordering basketfuls
of flowers for a number of people whose names were on a list in his
hand, and said, calmly but with authority: "Bernhard, wait for me
here, I have a package for you." Bernhard, who obviously knew
nothing of the change in his fortunes (or was he so polite as not to

think at all?), bowed and nodded and stood there, instead of leaving after having delivered his list. Leonardo bought three dozen of the beautiful roses from the woman in front of the church, at seven lire a dozen, and brought them to Bernard in his arms, getting his jacket and waistcoat all wet. When the Englishman saw him come in with the flowers, he said: "But, sir, this isn't done . . . *we* sell flowers."

"Yes, I know, but your prices are very high. Look at the bargain I got: seven lire a dozen." And before the Englishman could protest, he said to Bernhard, "Find some paper to wrap these in, please, and a card with an envelope."

At this point the Englishman knew that the Italian had a right to his eccentricity, because he was probably a house guest of his best client, and offered him the card and the envelope, and even a fountain pen to use.

"Thank you," said Leonardo, and he sat down at a desk, and wrote: *From Leonardo, who loves you both more than his own soul.* On the envelope he wrote: *For Sophie and Mary,* then gave the envelope to Bernhard, plus a tip of two lire, which Bernhard accepted with profuse thanks, as if it had been ten. After this, he thanked the Englishman, gave him back his pen and walked out as quickly as he had come.

The fact of writing the note reawakened all the passion he had been unable to feel in the presence of the flowers with the English price tags, and he went back to his own florist to buy three dozen more roses for his hostess and near-miss mistress.

If it is true that the prick wants no worries, as Leonardo had discovered to his great humiliation earlier that day, it is equally true that happiness is wanted by the whole body, and in vain does the puritan mind try to restrict that happiness to the one person designated by the heart as the image on earth of the One and Only God we worship in Heaven. When religion is gone, people don't lose their monotheistic habits and beliefs; on the contrary, they try to find on earth what they have lost in heaven. Now that he had found his happiness again, he could go back to that place of humiliation with all the generosity of happiness, and not with the worries of lost love and revenge. Which is why he bought flowers for his hostess, whose very name he still didn't know, and when he found her crying again in the kitchen, exactly where he had left her, with her purse open on the marble table, the dishes unwashed and the wine still untouched in her glass, he was determined to stay faithful to Mary, and to use his sexual failure of that day as an excuse for his genuine lack of interest. Why not tell her the truth, as frankly and candidly as Mary would have done, had she been a man? All he wanted to give her was some hope, and the comfort of a kindred soul such as he had missed so terribly during the last three days. He put his hand on hers, with a cheerful expression on his face and made her partake of his rediscovered purity of heart: "Be of good cheer, my dear friend, and rest assured that your woes are my woes, so don't cry, for you have a real friend here." She looked up at him and, seeing all the flowers cradled in his other arm, she seized his friendly hand and kissed it with passionate gratitude. "You're the first person on earth to speak gently to me when I am in pain. . . . The first and only . . . Oh no, what am I saying? Bistolphe is the first, but until now I thought there would never be another one, and now I've found one and I'm happy again. Thank you, thank you, oh, thank you a thousand times, you're so generous. You've spent all your money to let me share in your happiness. Angelo never did such a thing, he's a real Italian like the rest, but you're different, you're a saint, yes, a real fool, God's fool. . . . Oh, how I love you."

And getting up from her seat, she took him in her arms, squeezing the roses between them, but gently, so they wouldn't fall, and buried her face in their freshness, breathing their scent with delight, while Leonardo, holding his head back, observed the miracle: her ugly features became beautiful again; Mary, whom he hadn't seen for three long days, emerged from this mass of vulgarity like the sun at the bottom of the cliff where all the excrement and garbage of Laterza came to rest, transforming that filthy brook into a torrent of gold every morning. How could he still recoil from her and deny her the one little kiss she was asking?

When he detached his face from hers again, it was three in the morning; she was snoring heavily, and he breathed discreetly, so as not to take in any more of that air, so thick with sin and French perfume, the same scent he had first inhaled amid many other scents in Mary's drawing room, his very first moment in that house, and then traced home to the beautiful bottle with its diamond-faceted stopper on Mary's dresser in Mary's bedroom—obviously a twin bottle to the one that had stared at him reproachfully from this woman's dresser in her bedroom on the previous afternoon, the first afternoon of his second Vita Nova in three days.

O Moral Geometry, have thy divine circles in the heavens been perturbed by the motions of sin in this room? Has the harmony of the spheres been interrupted by the obscene noises and sighs which I have sung and moaned and grunted and farted, by the attraction between my sex organs and hers . . . what is her name? I still don't know it. How is that possible? And how vulgarly proud I was to have finally proven to her, not that she had a friend, but a lover she could trust to perform as her own vulgarity demanded and indeed received. Taide is her name, for "Taide is the whore who answered her fucker when he asked: 'Do I perform well?' 'Marvelously.'" As this quote from *The Divine Comedy* came back to his mind, so also did the vague recollection that he had opened his eyes sometime before, during that blissful night, calling Mary, and that this nameless woman had struck him on the face, shouting: "No sir, I won't let you say that name here. It happened once before, and if you could have seen *his* face that night, you'd call yourself damn lucky you got away with one little slap." How could he have forgotten that? By making love again as he had.

Out of here, he ordered himself silently, and began to slide out from under the blankets into the cold air of the room. But finding his clothes wasn't easy, and when he did, there was still one sock missing, and he knew, after a long and careful search, that it must be under the blanket somewhere, so he was now confronted with a question of manners: should he awaken her by calling her darling? He had tried to shake her, first very gently, then more energetically, but she just muttered: "Let me sleep; I'm so tired."

"Darling . . . where is the lightswitch?"

She turned on the light and, seeing him all dressed, asked: "Were you trying to leave like a thief in the night, without saying goodbye?"

"No."

"You mean yes. All right, I should have expected it but don't go back to your hotel so early. It's dangerous."

"Why?"

"Suppose they haven't answered your message? You'll get frantic again, and that's not good. By the time they reach you, you may act as stupidly as you did with the Cardinal, spilling the beans when no one had asked you to do so."

"So you think there may be no answer yet? That means you suspect there won't be one at all. Tell me the truth, you do suspect it, don't you?"

"I'm not inside their skin, I don't know what they may do. With Russians no one can ever be sure. But if they're anything like normal women at all, they should have answered you at once. There is, however, a good chance that they may have gone out to dinner and come back so late that they won't see the flowers before ten or eleven this morning."

"My God . . . So you really do believe this may not work!"

"I never said that. Come back to bed and sleep some more, you must be tired."

"I'm not tired, I'm anxious. What if you're right in your doubts —you never mentioned them yesterday—and the silence continues? What shall I do? Where shall I go?"

"You come here and live with me. I'm not poor, but what's more important, I have excellent connections in town, and I can get you a very rich clientele in a matter of weeks. You could even repay me in a short time, if that's your main worry."

This prospect seemed to have erased all trace of fatigue from her face and her voice. As for yesterday's sorrow, it seemed like the ghost of a bad dream at sunrise.

Far be it from him as he sat there, remembering only too well what she had looked and sounded like in grief, to dare plunge her into that hell again (which, he still desperately hoped, was no longer his hell too). And yet how dare he make such an assumption when he had nothing to support him but her words of yesterday, when he *was* in exactly that same hell himself, when indeed they were wedded by the same grief into a kind of communion? How

dare he? How dare I? he kept warning himself, to prove to the
Powers that Be that he was not trespassing.

She didn't notice the struggle that was tearing him apart: between cruelty and charity, fear of fear and hope of a vanishing
hope.

"And you know what's really funny?" she went on. "This would
be the first time in years I could count on the Cardinal's approval.
He told me so last time he came here (and it was the first time he'd
mentioned the matter at all: until then, for the whole time I was
married to Angelo—and it was a true marriage, I want you to know,
complete with infidelities and all that—the Cardinal never gave me
a single word of reproach). I knew he disapproved, because he
worried about Angelo's mother and later, little Kostia, and also
about Mary, but never, never, never a direct word from him. He's
so discreet, you feel like becoming a practicing Catholic out of sheer
gratitude. Luckily, other priests make you aware of the dangers
involved. . . . So two days ago, when he came here, he said: 'Ah,
my poor child, if only Divine Providence could unite you and Leonardo . . . Wouldn't that solve all your problems and mine?'
These very words . . . And if we were living together, he himself
would help you find a position in Rome. You must change your
opinion of him. He is of course an endless talker, but underneath all
that there's a great heart, and a genuine intelligence of a truly
universal nature. . . . But you're not listening. Come to bed,
you're still tired."

"No, thank you, I'm not. Let me find that other sock I was
looking for, and then I think I'll go out for a walk."

"But it's cold, my love, you have no overcoat, you'll catch pneumonia, and then you'll die, and I'll be all alone, truly alone this
time. . . ."

He cringed and looked at her with terror.

"Well," she said, as if suddenly discovering the new abyss under
her feet, "well, . . . I should have known I was deluding myself
again. . . . How could I have made such a stupid mistake? You
love Mary and that's that. Who am I to interfere? You're both
young, you have a long story of romantic dedication behind you. I
shouldn't interfere and I won't. Forgive me for building my little
castles in the air."

And she sighed heavily, as if to take in the oxygen her lungs were beginning to miss under so heavy a heart.

"You're not well," he said, with a detached participation typical of the family doctor who is afraid of being detained by his patient after the house call is finished.

"Never mind, it's nothing."

"Let me give you a glass of water. Or would some massage of the neck be of help? . . . A cup of strong coffee? . . . Something to eat? That's it perhaps: you ate nothing for dinner last night. I'm an excellent cook, let me go to the kitchen and . . . will eggs do?"

"No, darling, it's nothing. I assure you. Leave me alone for a moment."

But her voice was quivering, and her eyes shining with tears.

"Er . . . *darling* . . ." he said, taking her face into his hands as if to examine her eyesight. "I worry . . ."

"YOU worry . . . Of course you worry," she replied, with a firm voice but damp cheeks, "but I tell you, Mary is yours, she has never for one second stopped loving you . . . even if she hasn't called or sent for you, she certainly will, first thing in the morn . . ."

The effort was too great, now she was crying again without restraint, and he was afraid that his irritation might show.

"I wasn't thinking of these things, I was thinking about you."

She laughed. "No lies, please. I'm an old woman, an old bitch, in fact, and I know all the lies by heart, even before they're spoken. I felt yours in the air, and I didn't want to recognize it for what it was. . . . My fault . . . But what am I complaining about? I had a day and a night of bliss, it had everything I could have wished for: amusement, friendship, and then . . . this . . ."

And she jumped out of bed as if it were on fire, tearing the blanket off to cover herself.

"Do you realize, darling, that you haven't even asked me my name?"

"I . . ."

"Do you know my name?"

"Nnno . . . , but . . ."

"But it wasn't necessary, of course, you're right. Now it will be. Not that I expect to hear from you ever."

"I'll write to you."

"You don't have to and you don't mean to, either. And you're quite right. Find your sock, put it on, and go out for a walk if you really want to, but come back here around seven, no later, for . . . oh, nothing, you don't have to come back at all. My name is Luisa Bontemps, and don't ever mention it in Mary's presence, because she would know at once that we were lovers."

"Why?"

"She's a woman, and you are . . ." She smiled, took his face into her hands and looked at it lovingly, then said: "You are a fool, a dear, dear fool, who believes he's clever. That's the only thing that prevents you from being a holy fool like Christ, but there's such a dear innocence in your eyes that it melts my heart. . . ."

She sniffled for a moment in his arms, then disentangled herself to look at the clock.

"It's almost five. You may go now. But promise you won't telephone Mary this early or do anything senseless."

"I promise."

He couldn't say more, he was too ashamed of his happiness. "Let's have coffee, I'll make it, you find your sock and join me in the kitchen."

Left alone, he found his sock again, along with his egotism, which he intended to defend against all onslaughts of Christian charity. The only way to do this was to adopt the hypocritical methods he had always used with the Jesuits; namely, their own: act as if his good fortune were a burden, a temptation of the gods who were ready to punish him out of sheer envy, and as if he, little boy that he was, knew nothing of these forces that were threatening him from all sides, even beckoning to him with promises of happiness.

"Here I am," he said, cheered by the odor of coffee. "Let me fan the coals," and he took the half-burned and dirty straw fan out of her hand. She said nothing, sliced big chunks of black peasant bread and put them on a grill, which she held close to the coffee pot, so that the bread would toast more quickly. No words were exchanged for a while, both had their eyes fixed on the coals, as if that were the oracle from which they were awaiting information and divine guidance. Every now and then he would glance furtively at her face, which seemed calm enough to reassure him, but he withheld all expression from his own, because he felt too happy. In a few hours,

Mary would be his again, and this woman out of his life forever.
The thought of leaving Rome now appealed to him, suddenly and
intensely, and so new worries were beginning to take shape on the
distant horizon: What to do about the Cardinal worried him more
than anything else. If only science could free man from his promises
. . . What a silly thought to have, and yet, how true it seemed,
that a clear conscience was essential to health. Not MENS SANA
IN CORPORE SANO, but the opposite, because the body functions
better when the mind is not burdened by shame or remorse. These
thoughts absorbed him so completely that he forgot to spy on her,
and his eyes spoke happiness, tempered by a profound desire to
be worthy of it. Would this be, at long last, the Vita Nova he had
begun so many times already in so many wrong ways?

The coffee pot began to spout: she turned it quickly, leaving the
toast too close to the fire, and the bread began to burn. He noticed
neither of these facts, and went on looking into the future up in the
sky, through the black chimney.

"Darling, why don't you take off the toast, while I get the butter
from the windowsill?"

"Oh yes, of course."

He did, then scraped the burned slices with a knife, and breakfast
was ready.

"Marmalade?"

"No, thank you. I prefer my toast with oil and garlic."

"Not if you're going to be reunited with your love after a tragic
separation: it could mark the beginning of the end. Let me give you
fresh mozzarella with oil and pepper and salt, or ham, if you prefer.
Or ricotta with sugar?"

He hesitated, and she said cheerfully: "Let's have a real dinner,
we didn't eat anything last night."

"Yes, let's."

Was this to be his last meal without fear? Her table manners
were, thank God, very informal, but his fear of her unhappiness
paralyzed him more even than his old fears of knives and forks. She
looked gloomy underneath all that show, and so he tried to behave
with less energy than she did.

"Darling, you don't have to pretend you're not happy. I know you are. But don't forget to shave as soon as you get back to the hotel. And to make up a lie for Mary."

"What lie?"

"If she tried to reach you yesterday, she'll ask you where you spent the night."

"Oh, so you think she may have?"

"I don't know, but you must have your lie ready and rehearsed. So now: where did you spend the night?"

"At the hotel."

"Idiot, I just told you it's impossible. So where did you spend the night?"

"At my cousin's."

"Does this cousin exist, or is he an . . . Italian cousin?"

"No no, he exists. He left for home yesterday morning."

"Does Mary know him?"

"Yes," he said, feeling the sting, and with it the renewed fear of disaster.

"All right, so now let me give you some money."

"But I have money."

"I don't believe it, and in any case you ought to pay back the Professor. You should never have dealings with that kind of person. Here it is, and . . ."

"But I can't . . ."

"You obey Mamma; she knows best. And now go."

He was surprised by this sudden release, and didn't quite dare take it seriously.

"I say go. Get up and go. I thought it all out, while you were dreaming of your future in front of the kitchen stove. I don't want you, I want Angelo back. Without me he's a lost soul, just like you, perhaps more so—anyway, all men are lost without a woman who loves them. But she must be a real woman, not a spoiled little girl like Mary, or a goose and a whore like the woman he has now. And I know I can win, because God is right. And God knows I love him and she does not. And the moment you and Mary leave with that child, that will teach him a lesson. He will realize then how little the goose cares for him and how much I do. Because he worships that child, although he never sees him. And he knows that no other person on earth cares as much as I do, and understands his sorrow as much as I do." She looked both evil and calm. They didn't kiss on parting. He had braced himself for it, as a last toll to pay for his freedom, and when she said, "No, please," he felt very grateful.

But when the door was closed behind him, he was almost overcome by pity. Here is one disease that science can't cure, he concluded: Life itself.

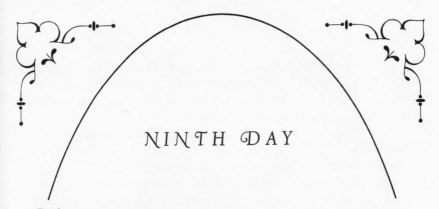

NINTH DAY

$\mathcal{T}$he morning was bright, the morning was clean, the morning was soothing, invigorating, mild and violent, the morning was all the good things a morning must be after a night of great confusion. We carry with us the very things we are escaping from, because that, too, is the disease of life: only after death will there be a clean break with the past, but it's the spirit that counts (vague word, but what better term can you find for that harmony between yourself and the universe? Harmony, of course, the harmony of the spheres), and so the harmony of the spheres at last incorporated him again, as of the moment he walked into the open air. In it was buried all his anguish of yesterday, along with many other things that weren't his and that science couldn't cure because science is human, and therefore part of the disease. But in nature there is health, even though nature is full of people like ourselves: the very fact that we can't know them helps us know God through the mystery they represent and that He has so well shielded from our knowledge. And besides, there are birds in the morning, gloriously joyful birds that brush the sky, tearing through it from top to bottom, from the highest of clouds to a few feet above the street pavement under our very feet as we walk. They are there before us and leave before we catch up with them; in the time we take to advance one more step towards that shiny cobblestone which so many generations have trodden before us, they have already swooped upwards again to disappear beyond the rooftops, calling excitedly like children at the close of school.

Five more steps, and they're back, down and then up again, tracing a long dotted line of bodies in the dark air.

Why didn't he mention the swallows, if he used so many birds all the time? (Leonardo was now thinking of Dante: *Inferno*, Fifth

Canto: two similes with birds in the space of six verses.) Because the swallows are so happy, so active, so sure of where they're going (in pursuit of food, and their food wanders aimlessly, often striking our eyeballs by mistake and drowning there in a single tear), while Dante's birds seem lost and unhappy, crying their woes much higher than we can cry ours, as they serve his comparison with the souls of those damned to torment—the carnal sinners. . . .

He thought he was going to find himself in the Piazza del Popolo, and was in fact trying to walk very slowly, when he suddenly emerged in front of the Caffè Greco. The first rays of the morning sun were coming down the Scalinata, straight along Via Condotti, and the café was open. A waiter in his shirtsleeves, with a long, green apron covering his legs like a skirt, was polishing the brass knobs, and it was a joy to see them glitter in the sun.

"Open?" asked Leonardo.

"Yes. Do you want to sit down?"

He went inside, and loved the place, so empty of all the bad people who had made life so difficult for him. But then he had also found Luisa there. He suddenly saw her as an eternal treasure in the archives of his soul: all beauty and joy. The darker aspects of his experience had come away like the fingerprints and dirty stains on those doorknobs under the experienced hand of their keeper. Indeed, we always carry over our sins into heaven-on-earth, but what would our new life be like, without the memory of the old? Even Schillasi became part of his memories of Rome, and he liked him. Now he could say he knew Rome really well, and he already saw it as the ideal place to live. Perhaps someday, who knows? But what he liked especially about the Greco was that he could sit down and order coffee, and pay for it and tip the waiter who had recognized him and was very respectful now.

While sipping his coffee he stared at the table where Luisa had sat with her lover and lost him. He studied all the ghosts of those people in the space they had occupied and then emptied, and the memory of their faces, their lies, their efforts to delude themselves and one another made the honesty of the morning even greater by comparison. He knew that the waiter was a better man now than he would be this afternoon, and beckoned to him, paid for his coffee and gave him a large tip.

Out in the street again, he walked to Piazza di Spagna and leaned against a wall around the corner from the Greco, to bask in the sunshine and wait for the right time to go to his hotel. The day was mild, but not yet established in the spaces occupied by the night; the shadows were still cold, and Leonardo who had so joyfully leaped into that freshness to acquire new strength for this truly new life, now felt a pleasant torpor which left him almost asleep on his feet, as he was offering his face to the kiss of the sun (how much more honest and soothing than the kisses of Luisa, who had meant well at the beginning, but was carried away by the devil of sensuousness, . . . the same devil that was in me at that moment).

Early risers passed in front of him, casting a brief shadow onto the orange curtain of his closed eyelids, and the slightly longer shadow of their worries over the silence that covered his own. And there were plenty of people passing by, and plenty of worries, but his biggest one was: Will I find a message at the hotel? And if not, will I ever get one at all?

He was trying not to think of this worry, not to revive the worries about his future, even about that little boy in Laterza whose health depended on him and who might as well be dead by now. He was also trying to think of the lie he would tell Mary, of the lies he had been told by Giovanna so successfully and for so long, but the Great Mother Worry kept sending her messages into the forefront of his conscience: How can two dozen roses make all the difference between life and death? And if it can in the minds of two eccentric Russian women, how can it in the Great Mind of Moral Geometry? Right is right and wrong is wrong. So there will be no message. The silence continues.

And here, the shadows of other people's worries: ". . . you see, I told my husband to watch out, but he wouldn't listen, and now he's lost his job. . . ."

He opened his eyes to see who had spoken, and saw two women in rags and slippers disappearing across the square in the gold dust of the sun. They were going towards the Scalinata and starting up the steps. Back to his lesser worries: I have to shave, and then I must pour a lot of that toilet water in my bathroom all over my clothes, in case Mary recognizes Luisa's perfume. . . . But of course there won't be any Mary, because there can't be any message.

"Five lire? But that's more than my husband makes in a whole day, and we have nine children to feed, plus my mother and his father. . . ." Again he opened his eyes: two very decently dressed women walking towards the fountain and stopping there, instead of climbing the Scalinata. Back to his lesser worries: Why aren't they climbing the Scalinata? And he suddenly realized they were busy washing flowers in the fountain: a boy was helping them, and a pushcart loaded with fresh flowers was waiting nearby. Perhaps these were the florists from whom the Queen Mother had purchased those flowers the first day. Will Mary have received my roses? Of course, but it won't make any difference, because Moral Geometry Must Be.

"You don't know her: she's stubborn, she's cruel, and she ruined my whole night. . . ."

Two men, going the other way, towards Piazza del Popolo and his hotel. That voice sounded strangely familiar: could it be Mary's husband?

"I did, Father, but God has no time for the worries of the poor."

A woman and a priest, also going that way.

"My wife? No, she knows nothing. But listen to what . . ."

Two young men, coming from the fountain and disappearing into Via Condotti.

Seven o'clock from Trinità dei Monti, San Giuseppe, other churches right and left, all of them except for the Cupolone. A coincidence? A sign that he would never hear the Cupolone again from Mary's house? Of course I won't, because there will be no message.

He lifted his eyes towards the two belfries up there and the first palaces of Via Gregoriana, but saw nothing but sun dust, shot through by the darting black swallows. And if I wait too long here and they come down to meet me and find me all reeking of perfume and still unshaven?

He moved slowly towards his hotel, but each step was more difficult than the last, paralyzed by fear. So, when he arrived at the end of the square, and saw on his right the *porchetta* vendor busily working on his field kitchen and his wife hanging chunks of new meat on the hooks under their sunlit tent, he felt suddenly hungry and decided to stop there for a quick meal before going back to his hotel. He had the money now, he could pay, but then the memory of the promise he hadn't kept made him hesitate. So he looked at the street on his left, and noticed that it was called Via Vittoria. He decided against it at once: that would have been like tempting the fates. He walked to the next street and it was called Via della Croce. Instinctively he chose to go all the way down the Way of the Cross, because *that* came before Resurrection, and what he was hoping for was resurrection from the pits of despair and sin into which he had fallen since he had attended a play called *Resurrection*. He stopped at another *porchetta* place at the corner of what was an obviously disreputable street, judging by the kind of women who were beckoning to him from the windows and doors of several filthy row houses. He paid for his *porchetta* and ate it strolling down the Way of the Cross thinking that it was perhaps a mistake to waste so much time instead of rushing back to shave, take a bath and baptize himself with toilet water. At the end of Via della Croce he saw a large church across the Corso and instinctively entered it to hear Mass. If God exists, He will be pleased to see that when I'm in trouble, I return to Him. If He doesn't exist, there's no harm done. And the Church received him as generously as it always had in the past, giving him sadness in place of despair. In anguish and confusion, he knelt down before the altar but instead of praying, he recited the most beautiful version of the Lord's Prayer (by Dante, of course).

When he came to the point where Dante (much to the horror of even his best commentators, *if* they are Catholics, that is) says:

> *Deliver onto us our daily* manna
> *Without which in this ample desert*
> *Backwards go those who most strive to walk*

he burst into tears, and, a church being the appropriate place for tears, he made no effort to conceal them, only buried his face in his hands.

Thus he cried over everything in his life and the life of the world, from the death of his mother, to sacrificing Mary's love to go and finish his medical studies, to Giovanna's betrayal, to everybody's betrayal in the matter of the aqueduct, to Mary's betrayal . . . NO,

NOT BETRAYAL, just lack of faith in him, or, rather, stubborn indifference; that is: silence . . . but WAS IT STILL THERE? He didn't dare move, and waited until he could find the courage to pray, and then prayed to the Working Hypothesis of God. And suddenly, before he knew it, a priest came to him with the Blessed Host in his hand, on the working hypothesis that he was fit to receive God, after due confession and absolution.

He was horrified, but before he could open his mouth to whisper his apologies and leave, he had opened it to God, and received God into the filthiest of houses ever prepared for such a guest (the correct term for whom is Host, he immediately thought, as he got up and left). As he sat down in the first pew he could find, still horrified by his unspeakable sin, he noticed that the only other persons who had taken God with him were the three members of the Jahn-Rusconi family: mother, daughter and son. They stopped at his pew, where they had left their belongings, and of course didn't look at him, because this was not the right moment for social contacts, but no sooner had he left the church and was still standing in front of it, aghast at what he had done, than they came out and greeted him with the kindest of smiles.

"Beautiful day," said the young Countess, offering him her hand to shake, thus embarrassing her brother who seemed rather hesitant. And he still was, as he mechanically did the only right thing; namely, offer his hand to Leonardo and say: "Good morning, Doctor, how are you?"

"Very well, thank you, and you?"

"Oh, very, *very* well, indeed . . . er . . . hm . . ."

At this point the sister intervened, not talking to him, only talking on THE HYPOTHESIS that he was still there, as in fact he was because he didn't have the presence of mind to leave: "Mother, may I introduce Doctor . . ." and she finally looked at him, like a teacher who will go just so far and no further in suggesting the right answer to the class idiot.

"Claudi," he answered, coming forwards and daring the first formal social handkiss of his life.

"I have heard a great deal about you," said the old Countess, from the height of her absolute superiority, and Leonardo corrected her: "You have also seen me at least once before."

"Have I? Not that I know of."

"Yes, you have, a few mornings ago on the Scalinata."

Both her children withdrew and turned their backs, obviously so as not to be seen laughing; they came back with red faces, pretending to be clearing their throats, while their mother, with half-closed eyes, was saying:

"I can't recall the occasion."

"But I do, very well," insisted Leonardo, "and in fact, I—"

"You MUST be mistaken."

"Oh no, I have an excellent memory. And I know why I remember: because it was no pleasure for me."

Their strange expression made him aware of his *gaffe*, and he corrected himself: "I mean the occasion, not the fact that I saw you, but let's not talk about it."

"That's right," said her daughter, rather curtly, "let's not talk about it. Goodbye." And she tried to pull her mother by the arm, but the old lady resisted: "Just a moment, please." Then, turning to a very embarrassed Leonardo: "But whether I have seen you or not, allow me to wish you the best of luck in all your endeavors. Life is a trial for all of us, I am an old woman, I know."

"You are right," he said, "young people always make fools of themselves, . . ." then, noticing the suppressed laughter again, "present company excluded, of course, except for me. I always make a fool of myself. I only wish I knew why."

This melted the daughter's heart, but made her brother even more reserved.

"May we offer you a ride in our coach?" she asked. "Where are you going?"

"Not far, thank you. Only to my hotel."

"Which is?"

"The Hotel de Russie."

If he had said "I am a royal highness" the effect could not have been more miraculous. "But of course we'll take you there, it's on our way."

It was not, as the position of the coach and the coachman's question indicated: "To the Villa Doria?"

"No, the Hotel de Russie first," said the Count, showing that he too could speak in a tone of command.

This helped Leonardo forget his sin until he arrived in front of the hotel and clumsily bowed his way out of the coach, but the terrible silence that greeted him inside was a clear indication that his sin had not been forgotten where sins are computed and stored away for future reference. The voice of God is only heard in silence; in fact, it is the silence of all other voices on earth. And the silence was still there! He didn't even glance in the direction of the desk, but walked upstairs very slowly, to give the concierge his last chance to call him and say: "Sir, there is a message for you."

He even stopped twice on the way, but nobody called. "Luisa was right," he said to himself, "they'll call later," as he tried to go into his room, forgetting that he needed a key and that the key was downstairs. But when he was forced to remember the key, he couldn't find the strength to go downstairs, and looked around for help. One of the rooms was open, and a maid could be seen airing a bed.

"May I disturb you for a moment?" he asked, and the maid answered: "Of course, sir, at your orders."

"I forgot my key, could you please fetch it for me?"

"No need, I have a passkey here."

She opened the door and he gave her a large tip, not out of kindness, out of despair.

Luisa is right, she MUST be right. It's only eight, they won't call before ten. And he decided to take a long bath, shave, baptize himself with toilet water and then . . . Then hang myself, if this goes on.

The bathtub was flooded in sunlight, so he let the water fill the tub very slowly, then watched the sun reflected in it, shaved, took his bath and closed his eyes. After a pleasant nap he realized it must be nine o'clock, because if he knew anything at all, he knew the position of the sun in that room after these six horrible days. But the Infallible Voice corrected him: TEN O'CLOCK. Was it possible? TEN, and no answer? He dried himself slowly, very slowly, while measuring THEIR time not his, in a working hypothesis of a long evening out (which already made him suffer: how COULD they stay out so late, when they knew nothing of his condition or his whereabouts?), or perhaps Mary hadn't gone out at all, but then, *how could the servants* not have known that those flowers with that message were so important to her? No. None of the working hypotheses worked, but the Truth of Moral Geometry did, and that was a hypothesis he dreaded.

In the bedroom he dressed slowly, very slowly, after baptizing his clothes with more than just a sprinkle of toilet water. TEN THIRTY and the silence was louder than ever. He didn't dare go out again, so he decided to pace his two rooms once more, as he had done during the worst moments of that worst period of his life.

He opened the door to the dining room—and saw Mary. She was seated at the desk, writing.

She looked up, their eyes met, and the silence fell upon them, bounced back on them from the floor, circled them and choked them until they gasped for a last breath of air; only then did they fall into each other's arms.

After a frantic repetition of the words: "No, it isn't true, it isn't possible, I can't believe it . . ." Mary detached herself from him and asked, angrily: "Where did you spend the night?"

"Here, my love."

"HERE? But we've been here since five this morning. . . ."

"I left at three."

"But the bed wasn't touched."

"I slept on the floor."

"But they told us downstairs that you had been out since yesterday morning."

"Yes, at three, yesterday morning."

"But you said last night . . ."

"No, love, you asked WHERE DID YOU SPEND *the* NIGHT, not *last* night."

"Swear?"

"No need to swear, the concierge can tell you. He did, in fact: I left yesterday morning."

There was a silence, then Mary asked: "And LAST night? WHERE did you spend it?"

At that moment a shriek from the bedroom made them aware that Sophie had arrived.

"Why wasn't I told?" she asked, pale as death. "What IS this? Were you here all the time, alone with Mary?"

"Of course not. I came in at eight."

"At eight? This morning at eight?"

"Yes. I don't . . . Yes."

"Are you ready to repeat this in front of the hotel director and everybody else downstairs?"

"Absolutely. I was driven back here by Countess Jahn-Rusconi and her two children."

"Countess Jahn-Rusconi. That *Catholic*? And her *children*? WHAT children, I ask? There have been no children in that family for generations. They're all Egyptian mummies, they look it, too. . . ."

"I know nothing about them."

"Then how come you were driven home in their coach? They're such snobs, even though they're penniless, they wouldn't ask anyone into their coach unless he were at least a prince!"

"I know nothing about them, I'm only telling you . . ." He didn't dare use the word *truth*, so he said: ". . . what I know."

"What *do* you know?"

"I mean what happened."

"Did you spend the night at their house?"

"I don't even know where they live. I met them in church."

"In CHURCH?"

"In church."

"YOU, in CHURCH???"

"Yes."

"What were you doing in church?"

"Waiting for the right moment to come back. I had been told—"

"Come back from WHERE?"

"From my cousin's house."

Sophie gasped, Mary lifted her arms in the air and shrieked: "ANOTHER COUSIN?"

"No, the only true one, the one you know."

"But if the police waited there all night for you and came back this morning at five to report you hadn't been found. . . ."

Leonardo stopped breathing, a fainting spell came over him again in that same room, almost on the same spot where it had attacked him earlier, under the same cruel grilling by Inquisitor Schultz. The whole room became smaller and smaller, Mary and Sophie began to recede, still standing there with their pale faces, their quivering lips, their panting chests, their insane eyes, while the birds went on singing outside, cleansing the sky with their high notes. . . . Leonardo tried to resist, he knew this was the end, but still he tried and tried, until the light came slowly back, the room, the furniture, the objects on the table and the two female Inquisitors all grew back to size, but they were still waiting for his answer, and he was still without it, but he did know one thing: namely, that calm is the first sign of superiority, so he stayed calm, absolutely motionless, like Farinata in hell WAITING FOR HIS OWN ANSWER AS INSPIRED FROM ABOVE; and it came: "Of course they wouldn't find me there. The police are so stupid, they always go to the doorman or the doorwoman, and my cousin, who's not like me—poor and a total fool—but rich and astute, is not about to expose himself to the vulgar curiosity of gossips like that. He lives there and works there, of course, but he has another apartment in town, where he entertains without being spied on, and as he was leaving for home, to see his mother about marrying your daughter Ludmilla, he came here first and finding me in a state of utter despair, because I had had no word from you and didn't know what you thought of me, since Mr. Schultz had treated me like a real criminal, without giving me a moment to justify myself, my cousin said to me: 'If you stay here you'll go insane or commit suicide out of sheer despair. Here's the key to my other apartment, I'm going away for a week, but, before I go, I want to see Mrs. von Randen again to give her the name of a good doctor for that child: he has asthma. In fact, why don't you come with me? It'll do you good to walk, you need air, you need a change.' So I walked out with him, all the way up to Via Gregoriana, and then I was left outside like an animal one doesn't take indoors. I walked all over town like a madman that night, I probably circled all Rome twice, maybe even three times, impossible to tell, because I never moved from Via Gregoriana, just up and down, up and down like a sentinel in front of a tomb. It was cold, I was freezing and feverish, I had no overcoat, because I had stupidly given it away, and I did *that* because I'm a poor man, and that expensive overcoat on me was a lie and a provocation to thieves, policemen and especially gossips like that ninety-five-year-old witch who spends her dying days at the window, and who gossiped about me, and said indecent things I wouldn't want to repeat, but then you know them all already: Mr. Schultz, the Grand Inquisitor, reported them to you, unless of course they were reported by his assistant Tegolani, the worthy son of that worthy old gorgon. So, I was all alone and ill, out in the cold, and when my cousin came out in the company of that drunken Russian prince who lives across the hall, he told me all was well for him but not for me. He said my name was not a welcome sound in your house, and I had better go back to my hometown forever. But in the meantime he allowed me to stay in his apartment. . . ."

There was a long silence; and for the first time in centuries it was not crashing down on him from above, but crawling up from below, and he simply disregarded it. Then suddenly, Mary asked in a sharp voice: "With one of his mistresses?"

"Of course not, what do you think?"

Sophie turned on Mary like a snake: "I forbid you to mention such things."

"You don't know the Italians, Mamachen. This is common practice here among friends."

"If that is what you think," said Leonardo, "all that remains for me is to pack my belongings and move back there altogether, until Crocifisso comes back. What I will do aft—"

Sophie's hand was on his mouth, firmly but lovingly. "I will not hear of such a thing. Come, my prodigal son, and be forgiven. . . ."

But Mary stood motionless and cold, and Leonardo didn't dare move either.

"Tell me immediately," she asked, with fiery eyes, "the address of that place."

Another spell was coming, and Leonardo just had time to answer, in the dark: "Via Vittoria."

Mary's shriek revived him at once, if not in fighting condition, but her words did the rest: "Not THAT name . . ."

"Why, Mary? It's the name of a street not far from here."

"It is also the name of a woman you conspired with against us. . . . Or have you forgotten?"

"What woman?"

Sophie answered for Mary, and she seemed less forgiving now: "The Monster's mother."

"That was exactly the question Mr. Schultz flung at me as an

answer, in the usual inquisitorial style of all such hypocrites, and I
want you to know that I fainted right there, on that chair, under his
inhuman questioning that admits of no hesitation, because time is
money. . . . Until this very moment I had no idea that her name
was Vittoria, and of course I couldn't guess who the old lady was
when I first saw her. I fell asleep on one of those big chairs in the
hall of the Villa Medici waiting to be received by the Cardinal.
And so you want to know *why* I fell asleep? Because I had had less
than an hour's sleep the previous night, out of worry about those
cufflinks. At five a.m. I had got up to go to Schillasi's house, and he
wasn't there, he had left on a pleasure trip with his wife, on the five
hundred lire Schultz gave him for those cufflinks worth two lire."

"We want to know why you went to the Cardinal."

"I'll come to that. First let me tell you that when I came to your
palace I couldn't sleep there, because in every room there were
servants busy doing nothing, because time is money again, and
where the servants were not earning *their* money on *your* time that
way, Mr. Schultz was wasting *my* time to impress me with the
power of *his* money—or yours, who cares? So Miss Rusconi was
working in one room on *The Gospel of Wealth,* Miss Panzironi in
another, and you, Sophie, were being kind to milliners and jewelers
and shoemakers, and to other worshippers of *your* money on *their*
time, but not to me. You called me Doctor Claudi, you were distant
and hard, and you only melted when you asked me to be kind to
Tegolani, because his mother, besides spying on me from her window and telling lies about me, had been so kind as to send us her
good wishes. . . ."

"We still want to hear why you went to see the Cardinal."

"I'm coming to that. . . . At your dinner party, I couldn't even
eat. If it hadn't been for the Cardinal, who was sitting next to me
and who gave me his ice cream, I would have starved that night, but
at least I had ice cream."

"And why couldn't you eat?"

"Because I was jealous. It was the first night I was—"

"Why talk about the *first* night, if not to waste our time? I still
want to know why you insisted on seeing your cousin, after we all
begged you to stay, and even our new guest had changed her schedule to become better acquainted with you."

"Why? To see the Cardinal."

"And why did you have to see the Cardinal so urgently?"

Leonardo's mind was blurred again, and a terrible headache was beginning to pound at his temples, but could he mention THAT at this point?

"Why did I have to see the Cardinal?" he asked, in a weak, dreamy voice, then, as if suddenly inspired: "Ask Adriana."

"Adriana?" they both said, in the same breath, in the same voice. "Why Adriana?"

And he, still in a haze: "Yes, why Adriana?" Then, before fainting: "This is it. This is Moral Geometry. The Truth wants to be known, because the Truth is Knowledge."

When he opened his eyes again, the two women were kneeling at either side of his bed, and a man, he faintly saw, was just leaving the room.

"Who is that man?" he asked, then closed his eyes again, trying to remember if he had confessed everything.

"That's the doctor," said Sophie. "He says you're exhausted, but it's nothing, just a fainting spell."

He sat up, staring at her without even looking at Mary, and Sophie said: "This is truly miraculous. The moment you lost consciousness, Adriana knocked on the door. She too believed you had never come back, because no one had seen you come in. You must have come in when the concierge was in his office. So poor Adriana had been told we were here, and wanted to comfort us. And she cried with joy when she saw you, and of course we told her you had said she could answer our question, and she did."

"What did she say?" asked Leonardo, very, very quietly, so as not to betray any emotion.

"She said you didn't know how to use your knife and fork, and the Cardinal was the only person you trusted."

"But that's exactly what I *told* you, and you wouldn't believe me."

"You said nothing of the sort, my love," said Mary, embracing him. "And of course it's clear now why you fainted before you saw the Cardinal, and that horrible old woman took advantage of you, pretending she was being nice to you—and everything else is clear too. Of course you couldn't have stayed at the Cardinal's for lunch. You must have noticed what kind of a person he is. So you went to the police for advice, Mamachen remembers your meeting the police agent you knew. Isn't that right?"

"Not for advice. For lunch! And my friend wasn't there, so I was taken to see Ramirez . . ."

"Of course, darling, he's such a damn snob, he must have known all about you."

"He did. And you can understand why I didn't accept *his* invitation to lunch. And I came here because I had no money. . . ."

"Of course, darling, I know, you were so proud, so magnificent, when you refused to take money from Tegolani."

"Nothing magnificent about it, I have my dignity, after all."

"Of course, darling, of course . . . And you're not as clever as you think, says Mamachen: you're a fool!"

Leonardo was startled. Could this be Moral Geometry again? But he was quickly reassured: "Oh, how lucky we are to have found a fool in Italy! Mr. Schultz swore to us that you were astute— FURBO—but you're not. We've won! Mamachen, isn't it wonderful that we've won?"

"I never doubted it," said Sophie, "but you gave me a difficult time, Leonardo. Couldn't you have called, or written?"

"I tried, *Mamma-Chinn*, but I couldn't. I'm not a writer, like you or like Mary. Is that clear, *Mamma-Chinn*?" They shrieked with joy, they laughed, they kissed him passionately. In a word: they were defeated forever—or so he thought, until he realized what he had done. He had stepped into the sacred language no one but family members can share, even after they have been called crooks in the presence of foreigners; it was therefore NOT the sacred language of endearment, which is open even to foreigners, even to recognized crooks, even to servants, once they have made one laugh: "You're a perfect dear, you're so amusing." (Their correct term was LUSTIG.) But from the sacred language, there was no appeal.

"Oh, darling," said Mary, "you have all the virtues: you are even funnier than Tegolani. Isn't it true, Mamachen?"

"Yes," sentenced Mamachen, who had decided to put an end to merriment by classifying it as such in German: "*Sehr lustig*, but," she continued in Italian, for the sake of this *lustig* foreigner, "when

I admit someone to the honor of calling me 'my beloved little mother,' I have a right to exact a little more of him than I would of a clown like Tegolani, or Klagonov, or MISTER DOCTOR Crocifisso Di Santo. That may be all right for Ludmilla, but not for us, wouldn't you say so, Mary?"

"Yes, Mamachen."

"Well, then . . . my dear son-*un*-law, you COULD indeed have written, even if you are not a writer."

"I tried to telephone," he said timidly.

"I know you did, I was told so by Schultz, and was duly angered by your typical Italian superficiality, if I may say so, since I'm now speaking to my son. *Anyone* can telephone! When you have broken the rules of politeness, you *write* to apologize."

"But I was told by Schultz *not* to write."

"He did it on purpose and he was right. He acted on the logic that, if you had been accused unjustly, you would find words that would endure, not flimsy words that die with the sound that gave them birth. Those are too circumstantial to be taken seriously by anyone. They don't mend broken hearts, they don't restore broken friendships. Even servants, when they quarrel, write a letter, and it's usually a good one. There isn't a person on earth, if you ask me, who hasn't written at least *one* good letter in his life, I mean a great literary page, worthy of being reprinted in an anthology. And if they're illiterate, they go to a scribe and dictate it to him. They see it being put into script by someone who knows script and who would certainly refuse to do so if he judged the words unsuited to the message. Our darling Adriana wrote a very noble letter to her husband when she decided to leave him, although the actual account of her reasons was as unprintable as it was amusing, I must say. Mary and I found it *lustig*, and she didn't object to our laughing while she told us all about it, but if we had laughed when she showed us the letter she had dictated to the scribe, she would have been extremely unhappy. She asked us to read it to her, and it was she who accepted it; we dared say nothing, we just read it to her, and *after* she had accepted it, we concurred in her opinion, and added our own approval, which of course pleased her very much."

These words were spoken on almost the exact spot where Adriana had spoken almost the exact same words, and Leonardo blushed, avoiding Sophie's eyes, lest she read the truth in them.

"Mamachen," said Mary, "can't you see that he's suffering?"

"I do, my daughter, but I have seen you suffer so horribly for so many days, minute after minute, hour after hour, AND putting on a civilized appearance for guests, that I MUST say these things. If I didn't let them come out now, they would burn inside me for days. Indeed, I had decided to ask Leonardo not to show himself in the house for another week or so, because I needed time to recover. When you were born, Mary, people traveled by train. Also when I was born, come to that, but we didn't find it natural, so I still belong in an epoch in which people didn't use speed as an excuse for being impolite." Then, to Leonardo: "Now you are authorized to come to the house whenever you like. In fact, you are its master, and the head of our family. We owe you respect and obedience."

"Thank you," said Leonardo. "And I shall try to deserve them."

He knelt in front of her and kissed her hand. She let him do so as a sign of obedience, while looking at Mary, who understood her wish and knelt down too, kissing her other hand.

"That will do, children, let's not exaggerate. I'm not a tyrant, I'm your friend."

"Yes, Mamachen," said Mary, and he just nodded, straightening himself and then straightening his necktie.

"I'm ravenous," said Sophie, "but I need rest even more than I need food. Let's go home."

"May I stay?" asked Mary.

"Of course not. Don't you agree, Leonardo?"

"One hundred percent."

"See? Your husband orders you to go home. He will come whenever he wants, but you too need a rest."

"Quite right," he said. "She's pale and drawn. I too need a rest. What time is lunch?"

"What time is it now?"

"Eleven thirty," he said, letting his father's watch have its word, too.

"Two thirty, sharp," she said. "Please be punctual."

"I will be."

And thus they parted, without even a kiss, because it would have seemed scandalous in such a formal atmosphere. He remembered the rules of politeness and kept bowing to them from the top of the landing as they went downstairs, and was so pleased when it was all over that he sighed "Aaaaaaah!!!!!" aloud then went back to his room to savor his happiness.

And he had reason to. Happiness is nothing unless it is shared, but it must be shared with our fellow convicts first, and only later, much later, with our dear liberators. Even if the outside world hasn't changed in our absence, our absence has changed it for us: our presence is all in here, attached to these bandages: tear them off and you will have reopened an old wound, which calls for more bandages as solid as those that have been discarded.

He was tired, because he felt relaxed, but since he felt happy too, he couldn't relax as he had in jail: his happiness focused on ever tinier things in his room: this chair, which must be sat upon in happiness, that other chair at the desk, the chair next to the window, the floor next to his bed, the irregularity in the floor tile under the bed, the threads coming off the rug between the wall and the left hind leg of the bed, the bit of enamel that had come off the bathtub, the whining noise of that faucet on the right, even the toilet seat on which he had sat crying instead of doing what he was supposed to do. But he was busy visiting the outside world too, AS SEEN FROM HIS JAIL: a quick glance at the sky in the direction of Via Gregoriana. The hemorrhage of silence had stopped, birds crisscrossed freely, the clouds drank in sunshine; one would hardly have believed the sky had been so deeply scarred by that silence for days and nights on end (and to think that HE had been reproached for sending HIS silence to THEM . . .). But even this parenthetical consideration was a source of new happiness: future happiness, that is. He would cope with it all, while looking after the children and making his scientific discoveries, perhaps even finding time to go back to his beloved archaeology. . . . Who knows?

But even the future shrank visibly under his mind's eye and focused on tinier projects and hopes: the project to ask of Ramirez what he had promised to obtain for the *porchetta* man, the promise of a generous present to the poor prostitute on the Scalinata, but then there were such nasty and negative projects as not returning one cent to Schillasi: on the contrary, getting more of the money back that Schillasi had "earned" by returning those cufflinks, and then there was the project of writing to Giovanna to let her know ᴡʜʏ he wasn't coming back, and how much happier he was with ʜɪs mistress than she would ever be with the kind of men ꜱʜᴇ could catch with ʜᴇʀ charms. . . . He knew of course that this was a very ignoble project, but the thought of it, instead of correcting him, begot one even worse: the thought of ruining Crocifisso's chances with Ludmilla by using his power of veto as head of the family. There must be a punishment for what Crocifisso had done to him while he was too weak to notice, and for what Don Poseidone had done to his mother. Further ignoble tiny projects: letting all those flunkeys downstairs know that he now lived permanently in two places: Via Gregoriana *and* the Hotel de Russie. Ah, what a joy, to come back here tonight for a real, honest sleep, or even later this afternoon for a good nap . . . And what a relief not to have any women tonight, or tomorrow night . . .

With these noble thoughts in mind, which did nothing but purify his love, he decided to go out and was about to leave, when he noticed a small box on the dresser with the words *To the Sun from the Moon*, in Mary's handwriting. Smiling with pride and love, he opened it and found it full of gold coins, mostly twenty lire pieces, and a small note with the following words: *This is our money, not mine, so if it hurts your pride to accept it, you may pay yourself back some day; not me, and not now.*

He put a handful of coins into his pocket and was about to leave, when the thought came to him that any of the servants might come in and be tempted. Where should he hide it? Under the mattress? Or under the china cabinet? In a suitcase? Or under the carpet? Thus he began in the fullness of his years to play hide-and-seek with an imaginary thief. Disgusted with himself for this exercise in those antisocial feelings he had always hated in his parents, his sisters, everyone in Laterza, he decided to risk at least some of the gold, and put a few coins into the bed, another few under the mattress, still more under the carpet, and the rest in flower vases, cups and sugar bowls, even in the big samovar on the teatable near the dining room window. And then he left.

His first decision, as he passed the desk, was to give nothing to the concierge, because his attitude had changed so radically since Sophie and Mary had been there. "Sonofabitch," he muttered, waving to him with one hand, and clutching the gold coins in his pocket with the other. "And nothing for you, either, sonsofbitches," he muttered again as he acknowledged the servile greetings of the doorman, the bell-boys, the porters and the coachmen outside.

He then moved slowly towards the center of the piazza, to be out of the last morning shadows and also to be seen by the houses, the three churches, the obelisk, the cobblestones and the clouds in the sky, in his present state of happiness. They had seen him in such a state of despair lately that it was only fair of him to let them know. But before these inanimate objects on earth or vapors in the sky could feel his presence and tell him that they had understood what it meant in terms of eternity, all the coachmen in the piazza felt his presence as a potential customer, and this angered him. "Leave me alone," he shouted. "I don't need you; I don't want to be disturbed."

"Have you become a tourist?" asked one of them. "Are you drunk?" said another, and a third shouted to his colleagues: "Just look at that prick: he thinks he's an Englishman!"

Well, he thought, walking swiftly away, clenching his fists around the gold coins in his pockets. Schultz is not entirely wrong when he says that the lowly don't deserve to be helped. Only science can help them, and that from a distance.

He walked lazily along the sunny side of Via del Babuino, thinking of nothing and everything at the same time, as befits a rich man who can choose to think whatever he wants, whenever he wants. In this pleasant state of vagueness, he visited the corner where he had been so distressed earlier that same morning, and imitated himself standing there in the sun, his back against the wall, listening to the birds and the people passing by. But the day too had grown richer in sunshine, birds and passersby, whose shadows and voices overlapped, forming a murmur of meaningless sounds in a haze of shapes and colors. Traffic was growing heavy too: horse carriage after horse carriage, top-hatted coachman after top-hatted coachman (with or without the blinding reflections from the white parasols and veils and hats and gloves worn by elegant ladies with artificial gardens on their heads) made spring appear as a creation of milliners, jewelers, carriage-makers and tailors, aided by architects and sculptors—anything but the simple thing it is: a return of mother earth from the regions of death and despair, into the warm bed of the Sungod who will make her pregnant again.

Leonardo crossed the square, stopped in front of the fountain to see the sun become water and the water turn to sunshine again, reached the first steps of the Scalinata, where he bought all the flowers a poorer Leonardo had been unable to buy the first day (hence all his troubles), and began to climb, feeling the rich heaviness of spring in his legs. As he reached the beggar woman, he stopped, pulled his hand out of his pocket with a jumble of coins he didn't even count, opened his hand and said to her: "I do keep my promises, this is for you."

"For me? But dear sir, this is more than even the Pope gave me last year. It's too much."

"You deserve it, and you'll get more in a few days, provided you promise to take your child to a doctor whose name I will give you, and have him examined and taken care of. It won't cost you a cent, but if you refuse, it will cost you a great deal, because I'll never help you again."

"For you, my dear sir, I will do anything, and I'm going to church right now, to pray for you and your dear ones."

"You don't have to do that: just do what I ask: no more."

He relished the effect of this scene on the few passersby, and wished Schillasi could see him, then resumed his lazy walk until he reached the top and tried to find some place for his elbows to rest for a few minutes, but the whole balustrade was occupied by lazy Romans, looking at the same spectacle of lights and shadows that had fascinated him, and they all seemed lost in the same meditation upon nothing, their eyes half closed, their breath almost an audible snore. There were young priests next to pretty young girls, distinguished ladies next to bearded ne'er-do-wells, one Carabiniere in uniform with rifle and sword next to a criminal who might have been his brother but for the uniform that placed one in charge of the law and the other in charge of breaking it. The rite of mother earth returning to her spouse and master made them all unaware of one another, all equally blessed by the same love engulfing the earth and the heavens. At the windows of palaces, hotels and convents, the same faithful attending the same service, elbows solidly claiming the same space on the same windowsills, faces exposed to the same bliss from above, while the Infallible One under the marble crinoline of his spouse raucously invited the flock to take gastronomic communion.

One or two housewives left the balustrade, and Leonardo found a place for his elbows. There he stood and relaxed, his face hidden in the warm and humid flowers he had bought. If he could only walk to the Villa Medici now and have lunch with the Cardinal. But he knew that day would soon come and felt encouraged. How good, how civilized, to go there with Mary some day and talk to Mauri, to Salvemini, learn something new, develop even more than he had in these few days away from home. This *was* the fairy tale, and it *wasn't* absurd, and it was only just beginning.

How things happen to you when you don't move at all! He would never have known that this was the beginning, not of a fairy tale, but of a new life, the new life he could never officially inaugurate so long as he kept making it a great moral resolve and a test of his will power.

Two o'clock, says the Infallible. Another good half hour of this view that you don't even have to look at. And Leonardo thinks: the tourist knows he has come here to see the most beautiful sights in the civilized world. He looks at everything like a scholar at a book, to understand it all and remember it later. The native knows he's here. He doesn't have to look, he won't have to recall this sunshine in the fogs of the North. Two fifteen, says the Infallible, and slowly some of the lazy Romans lift their elbows from the balustrade and go home for lunch. And so does Leonardo, because now he has a home again.

In these few days of suffering Mary had lost so much weight that she looked nine years younger again, and Leonardo recognized that he had not recognized her at all since their first meeting at the theater, he had forgotten what Santa Maria di Laterza looked like. Now she was here, now everything that makes up a home was here in Via Gregoriana, except for all those servants, Adriana above all, who belonged in a fairy tale. THIS WAS REALITY.

Sophie, too, had lost weight, and looked less overwrought than usual, so the Cardinal was right again: it had all been a blessing in disguise.

"How beautiful you are," he said to Mary, and she replied: "It's the first time I've heard such words from you."

They ate alone. The servants were hardly ever seen; the food was brought in and left on the table: Mary tried to pass it around, but Leonardo wouldn't let her. He was the new butler for the two ladies. All during lunch, Sophie looked at the flowers while she talked, and she talked a great deal about medicine, showing a knowledge that stunned Leonardo, who was proud to confirm that her questions were pertinent, her hypotheses plausible, her terminology correct. Mary said nothing and looked only at him, but this did not prevent him from eating in his accustomed way.

After lunch Leonardo looked at the paintings as if he had never seen them before, and fell in love with a small view of Albano over Sophie's writing desk. He was told it was by Corot, and Mary was so proud of him for having recognized that it was beautiful. Then Mary played the piano while he smoked a cigar and listened to strange music he didn't like at all, but pretended to find beautiful, and again Mary was proud that he had understood Beethoven, and wanted to play him some Chopin.

"No, thank you," he said. "I would like to express a wish, if I may."

The two women laughed. "If you may?" said Sophie. "It is for us to ask you if we may do something to please you. You are the master of the house: it is so good to be able to obey orders again, after so many years."

"Well then," he said, "my wish is that we go to Albano tomorrow, and tonight to the Corso in your open carriage."

Sophie gaped, and Mary said: "But tonight we're leaving for Geneva."

"Tonight? Why?"

"To begin our new life, darling."

"And to escape from our enemies," said Sophie. "I thought you knew."

"No, I knew nothing."

"You did know that we were going to leave two days after you came here the last time, and then everything seemed to become impossible, but now that we can leave, why wait another day?"

"I . . . thought . . ."

"You thought what?"

"Nothing."

"Darling," said Mary, in a state of agitation again, "you ARE thinking of something. What is it?"

"But I assure you . . ."

"You can't fool me. Speak openly, you're the master here, and we are here to obey your orders. Why don't you want to leave?"

"I never said I didn't want to leave."

"But that was what you really wanted or you wouldn't have asked to go to Albano tomorrow and to the Corso tonight."

"No, no, I only thought that, since we were in no hurry to leave . . ."

"But we *are* in a hurry to leave. Do you want to fall victim to your emenies?"

"What enemies?"

"What do you mean WHAT ENEMIES? The Monster, his mother, the Cardinal, the chief of police, all these people who stand in the way of our happiness . . . Or do you believe in the immorality of doing as the Romans do, who are delighted if their wives have lovers, and the wives equally delighted if their husbands have mistresses?"

"No, I find it horrible."

"Mary," said Sophie, restraining herself, but very much on edge, "when will you learn to understand the will of your superiors instead of questioning it?" Then, to Leonardo: "I am sorry, my poor Leonardo, and apologize for my daughter whom I have trained so badly in the arts of obedience. I quite understand your reactions, my dear son, and once more I am full of admiration for your truly divine foolishness." Then, to Mary, pointing to him as a teacher of zoology would point into the lion's cage: "Here is Leonardo, the Lion, God's Lion, the Biblical Lion of Judah, as reinterpreted correctly only by the New Testament: a lion in the spiritual sense; namely, a lamb to the wolves who inhabit this base world. He is so

good, so superior to their level of intelligence—namely, to *furberia*
—that he once more exposes himself, and us, and your poor child,
to the greatest of dangers because he cannot conceive that people he
has seen and loved, like your mother-in-law—WHAT LAW, may I
ask?—may be more evil than any snake in the grass." Now again
turning to the lion in the cage: "My Divine Lamb, how can you
imagine that the Cardinal and the chief of police will not act on the
precious information they must have gathered from you? After
speaking to you this morning, I decided we must leave tonight, and
have ordered my railroad car to be readied for the fifth time in these
few troubled days, but this time irreversibly, because I know I am
interpreting your will. So I called for my knave Tegolani and asked
him: 'What shall we do to circumvent the forces of Evil with which
you are so familiar?' And the knave said to me: 'I anticipated your
question, and I have had my answer ready for several days; I was
going to put it into effect without letting you know, but since you
ask me, here it is: we shall invite the Cardinal for a big dinner party
to be held here several days after you plan to leave, and we shall
send the same invitation to many other people of our acquaintance,
so he will hear from them that the party really is going to take place.
And on the eve of that day we shall send out urgent notes saying
you are not well and have not returned from the waters of Chianciano. Only then will they hear from your lawyers in Geneva that
divorce proceedings have been initiated.' And I said: 'What a perfect plan. How clever, it's worthy of the Trojan Horse. But are you
sure it will work?' And he said: 'I tried it out five days ago, by
sending out invitations for the night before last, which were canceled that same morning, saying you were not well.' What do you
think of this, my lamb?"

The lamb, who had now truly become a skinned *porchetta* ready
to be chopped and roasted in public, piece by piece, for each individual customer, said: "It's a most wonderful plan, but couldn't we
leave in another two weeks? I so want to see the sites portrayed by
Corot in that beautiful painting. I also feel it's highly unfair to the
Romans not to let them see Mary in this beautiful new outfit, with
this marvelous hat, this new hairdo, this perfect symphony of grays
and whites . . . these gray pearls . . ."

And Mary fell into his arms, saying: "Darling, my love, this is my wedding dress. I was trying it out in the hope you would like it. Why should the Romans see it?"

"Mary is right," said Sopie. "And besides, it would be highly immoral for a married woman like Mary to be seen with you in her carriage, as if you were her lover. They can see her in Switzerland, if they care to do so, under the aegis of a more moral law: the law that permits a woman to reject her past mistakes and try again on a clean slate."

Leonardo said nothing, and Sophie asked: "What are your orders?"

"Orders? I have no orders to give. Tegolani gives orders."

"Don't be childish, Leonardo. That's like saying that the coach-man gives orders to the horses. He interprets in horse-language the orders given him in his own human language. Even a servant is human, but he must deal with horses in the language of horses. Clear?"

"Yes."

"So, what are your orders?"

"That . . . you should obey Tegolani, so he can steal in peace. Why don't we wait for the return of Mr. Schultz at least?"

"Materialistic considerations, eh? I can't believe it. This is not you speaking. Try again."

". . . When is the train leaving?"

"THAT's the right answer."

"I'm sorry, I would call it a question."

"I love your courage. The train leaves at . . . when *does* the train leave?" She rang the bell and Bernhard appeared. The question was asked in German, and it seemed to cover many pages of small print, to which many more pages of small print were offered in reply; the result was "Ten fifteen, but we ought to be at the station not later than nine, because our car will seemingly be at-tached to the local train for Chianciano, which leaves at ten after nine, to be hooked on later to the Paris Express farther out of the station. This takes time and great secrecy. All arranged by darling Tegolani. So, what are your orders?"

"I must pack my suitcase. It will take time."

"Ten minutes. We can send Adriana to help you."

"Absolutely not."

"But she will love to do it. Just a moment." Sophie went out of the room, and Mary was upset again: "Tell me the truth: is there another woman?"

"Absolutely not."

"Two perhaps?"

"I said no."

"Swear it on your mother's grave."

"Doesn't my word suffice?"

"Do you realize, my love, that if I were to find out later, I would kill myself?"

"Don't I know it. . . . That's why I prefer not to speak."

"Oh . . . then there is something to talk about. . . ." And she grew terribly pale.

"No, Mary, there is nothing, but words keep evoking more words until no one understands what he's saying. It isn't *realistic*, that's what I intended to say."

"But that doesn't prevent you from swearing on your mother's grave that there is nothing."

"I suppose so."

"Then do."

He did, with mental reservations, hoping that Moral Geometry would stop at that. Mary seemed relieved, and when Sophie came back she was serene again.

"How perfectly extraordinary," said Sophie. "Adriana is unwell, she must leave for the Sabinian mountains tonight to see her aunt, but she said immediately: 'Why do you have to leave tonight? What's all the hurry?' "

Mary was very upset. "So she is leaving for the mountains . . . And I still hoped she would join us. How can I live without Adriana? Who will dress me? Who can advise me on a million things as well as she does? Let me go and try to persuade her."

"All right," said Leonardo, "and I will go and pack my suitcase."

"How manly of you," said Sophie, very proudly. "Facts, not words!"

Leonardo felt like saying: The words are all yours: all I can do is obey. But he was so scared they might read his thoughts, that all he said was, "Tell me where I must be and at what time, please."

"Back here in a few minutes. The coachman can wait for you at the Russie."

"All right. Goodbye."

He let the coachman take him back to his hotel without speaking a word, before, during and after the trip. He was now the rich man wrapped up in his hurry, a stranger in his own house. And the coachman withdrew into himself, as if he had never known him before. It had all been a parenthesis, like those acquaintanceships one strikes up on trains, which are suddenly interrupted by a nap and must be started all over again when one wakes again, because the thread was too thin, cut off with the closing of an eye.

Back in his room, he packed his old suitcase with his old things, leaving out all the new shirts and cravats Mary had bought for him. He intended to pack these in the new suitcase, the one Adriana had used for her seduction scene. It was empty when he opened it, but out of it tumbled the precise image of each item it had contained that night. He dismissed the whole memory as the shadow of a dream and stood there sadly, thinking nostalgically of Mary, not Adriana. Mary so beautiful, so fit for the splendors of the Corso, yet denied to the Romans, because it was immoral that she be seen without protection from the Protestant law that allows you to divorce your whole past and start again, as if it had never existed. But it had: Kostia was the proof of that, and Kostia's asthma proved that he couldn't divorce his small self and live. His mother's future had nothing to do with his own tiny past, which ought to be respected. The Cardinal was right. He needed a divorce from his grandmother.

While entertaining these thoughts that did not entertain him very much, Leonardo was pacing his apartment and saying goodbye to the things that had been so faithful to him at a time when he had no friends on earth. How could he leave them? He began to look for ideas, as one looks for objects, in drawers and closets. He found a screwdriver and began to unscrew one of the beautiful bronze doorknobs, then a windowknob, and put both into the empty suitcase. Then he took all the soap he could find in the bathroom closet, and then even the soap in the bathtub and on the washstand,

and packed them away in clean towels. He closed the suitcase and carried it out himself, lest the servants discover what he had taken and denounce him. But in the corridor he found Dante, who was obviously waiting for him. Shall I give him a tip? he asked himself, and the answer was: No: not after the way he behaved to me, when I was all alone and desperate. He was already downstairs, with Dante carrying his two suitcases, when he remembered his *spolverina* and his hat, and ran back up to get them. The coachman was already waiting outside, so the rich man, all wrapped up in his hurry, left without giving a cent to the knaves who had served him so badly, and they all thanked him anyway (while they had treated him so badly when he had truly been generous with them). The thought that a great deal of money, gold money, was hidden everywhere in his room, even in his bed, never occurred to him. The hurry of the rich had erased every notion of his previous conception of economy, which belonged to an age of rural values and the slow pace of Nature.

"All packed? But how wonderful, how perfect!" said Sophie, who received him in the dining room, seated in front of the tea-battery like a pilot at the wheel of a large ocean liner, in a room full of delicate instruments. "Poor Mary is very upset, she's still trying to talk Adriana into joining us, or even into coming later, but Adriana seems to have decided to enter a convent. It makes us both so angry, because we know it's not her idea, it's the devilish plan of that little upstart bitch of a Cefala. . . . Cefala, indeed; can anyone be more A-cefala? It's she who 'wants' to enter a convent, and it will serve the Church right if it lets a bitch like that pretend she has a true vocation. And she dragged Adriana along with her, just to prevent Adriana from having the life she wants; namely, with Mary, her true sister. Who does she think she is, that upstart little bitch? I hate her so. And I pity her poor mother, who gave in to the entreaties of some bastard Roman prince to beget that little monkey! Doesn't she look like a monkey? Pure Mongol face. Well, that's life. Thank God we're leaving this damned country forever! When they elect a Protestant Pope, that's when I'll come back. Lemon or cream?"

"No tea at all, thank you."

"You must learn to drink tea, it's good for you. You can't go on an empty stomach between now and dinnertime."

"Do you mean we'll have dinner on the train?"

"No, here, at seven, early dinner tonight."

"Well, it's almost five."

"All right, do as you please, you're the master of the house, but I'm going to have my tea anyway."

She had hardly begun to destroy a huge chocolate cake with the help of a few cups of very strong tea, when Klagonov stormed in.

"*Fratellissimo carissimo,* I a failure am. Metallicize myself I not can, an impossible possibility is, without Ludmilla. You lucky, you of steel made are, and now you happy with Mary. Crocifisso here with you is?"

"No."

"He of your tonight trip informed is?"

"No."

"He suffer will. I glad am, even though this no Christian thought is. I coming with you tonight am."

"You are?"

"Not in your compartment, I never dare would such a thing do. But Sophie in company of, play cards with her and of philosophy speak about will, Tolstoy, Marinetti, Beethoven . . ."

"Beethoven?" asked Leonardo proudly. "But isn't he a musician?"

"Is. But of music philosophy in soul his great foundation of profundity suffused is, as demonstrate can, and will to Sophie, if not she dishes and glasses and cups on my head break will in defense her philosophical NO against my YES."

A torrent of Russian words from Sophie stopped Klagonov, who thanked her profusely in Russian and kissed her hand several times, to prove how grateful he was. Mary came in. Her eyes were red, she was still wiping them as she said: "My sister is gone. She will pray for us. I do so hope she loses her faith and comes back to work for me."

"So do *I*," said Sophie, "in fact, I'll pray for it. Did the mutt leave too?"

"Of course."

"Did *she* dare say she would pray for us?"

"Yes, but I found her much better today. She's not such a bad girl."

"How can you say such a thing, Mary? She is a . . . an individual."

"No, Mamachen, she is a person."

"Not at all: an individual." Then, to Klagonov: "Lemon or cream?"

She realized too late that she had asked him in Italian, and this amused everybody, even Klagonov, who couldn't stop laughing.

"Champagne," said Klagonov, "that will one a bit calm. I need it too."

They drank Champagne, then more Russians arrived, and finally Leonardo said: "I want to take a walk with Mary. May I?"

Sophie became pensive, then said: "Not to the Corso."

"No, no, in front of Villa Medici, to the fountain and back."

"Let's see . . . Perhaps you can. The coachman will follow you."

"Absolutely not."

"With his carriage, of course, and from a distance."

Leonardo agreed. He didn't want to miss his last sunset in Rome.

They went out. Even in the entrance hall they could hear the loud hissing of the swallows as they swept by the hundreds in front of the house. Again the balustrade was all occupied by lazy Romans with their eyes half closed and their elbows firmly implanted on the yellowish travertine. There, too, the swallows made such a noise that they could hardly hear their own voices. But they had no need to communicate with voices. Each communicated with his own vision of the other in the glaring afterlight of the sunset, which remains brilliant orange for a while, then fades to yellow, and stays yellow for a long, long time, indeed long after the first stars have come out, so that the various tints of ochre and gray and old and brown that constitute the bulk of ancient Rome stand out in the night as sources of a soft yellow light, reflections from the clouds that have died out already in the sky, but not on earth.

The stars were bright, but Villa Medici was brighter still with the past day's sunshine. The fountain was still talking, and the blazing white Cupolone still mincing thin slices of time like state secrets that the Pope would make known Urbi et Orbi as soon as He saw fit.

"You are so beautiful," said Leonardo.

"Well, here they are again—my young friends," said the Cardinal, appearing from nowhere and putting his hands on their shoulders. "Mary is so elegant tonight. She ought to be on the stage. Can you imagine her success? Madame Sarah would go into hiding. Well, children, goodbye. I must run. I'm late."

And before they could say anything, he had vanished inside the ghostly yellow edifice.

"Sit down," said Sophie to Leonardo.

"But didn't you say we must go? It's eight thirty, isn't it?"

"It is, and we must indeed leave in a hurry. Sit down."

He sat down, but still couldn't understand. Everybody had sat down, family and guests and servants, all in the music room, some ready to leave with their overcoats on, others ready to stay and carry the luggage downstairs, and yet they all sat down because she said so, and they seemed perfectly calm, as if no one were leaving at all.

"It is a Russian habit," said Sophie. "Before we take a trip, we sit down and photograph in our soul the last moment of peace we have enjoyed before leaving. It ensures a happy return, or so they say, but it certainly ensures happy memories, which can always be recalled, unscathed by the worries that have caused our departure."

So they all sat in silence, as if no one else were present. No one cried, even though tears were very close behind everyone's eyelids, until finally they broke the spell, and tears began to flow freely, together with words.

Everybody embraced everybody else, symbolically or genuinely, but even true embraces became strangely symbolical, and thus there was no class distinction and no trace of unkindness. Klagonov, completely drunk, but beautiful, with his red nose shining above his clothes, looked like an orchestra conductor making wide blessing gestures.

"Take the Corot with you," said Leonardo, still wiping his eyes after crying in everybody's arms, and Sophie replied: "Absolutely not. That would be tactless. It would be like telling the knave we think he's a thief."

"But he *is*."

"Leonardo, such evil thoughts at such a sacred moment!"

Leonardo said nothing: he was only the master of the house. Now Sophie addressed Klagonov very violently in Russian, and he cried, nodding and kissing her hand. "He's going home to bed. He's drunk. Shame on him."

Klagonov nodded as he embraced Leonardo, saying: "Too much champagnization, too little metallization, that is what happened has. Goodbye, *fratellissimo carissimo*."

"And now," said Sophie, "we must all go to the station separately. A measure of prudence, dictated by the highest strategic reasons."

Leonardo was glad to go alone. He knew how to get there, and it was his last walk as a free man. But when he got to the station he had forgotten what train he must ask for, and became very agitated. In a panic of doubt, he went to the police, right there in the station building, and said: "I am the mayor of Laterza, and am supposed to leave secretly with a person whose name I can't reveal for reasons of discretion, and since, for reasons of prudence, they have hooked her private car onto a train which is not the one to Geneva we are supposed to take later, I don't know where to go."

"No problem," said the Commissario. "I know all about it. You are the lover of the married Russian lady with the rich mother who lives in Via Gregoriana?"

". . . er . . . in a way, between you and me, yes."

"Track eleven. You'll see the sign: INCOGNITO: *Private Car*."

"Thank you so much."

And he ran to his train. He was about to board the beautiful blue sleeper when a railroad employee stopped him.

"You can't go here. Incognito."

"I know, but I AM Incognito."

"Prove it. Your name."

"How can I prove it, if I'm supposed to be Incognito?"

"Are you poking fun at me in the exercise of my functions? I'll have you arrested—sir."

"But I wasn't poking fun at you. I only—"

"Yes, you were, I'm no fool, I wasn't born yesterday."

"Neither was I, and I forbid you to—"

"You don't know who you're talking to."

"Neither do you."

"All right, jail for you."

Two Carabinieri were called. Leonardo was beginning to fight them off when Tegolani materialized from nowhere and said: "Let him free. He's 'the person.' "

"I'm so sorry, Doctor Claudi," said the railroad employee, "I didn't know if you were the right Incognito. I HAD to find out."

"No matter," said Leonardo, without greeting Tegolani at all.

But Tegolani ran after him and said: "They haven't arrived yet. I'm so glad I was able to help you."

"That's all right. What time is it?"

"Still quite early. You have at least half an hour. This train is leaving late. In fact, it may leave later than your train, so you can safely go to the right track, which is track seven. There's a sign there: PARIS EXPRESS."

"Thank you very much."

And he walked proudly away.

Here was the blue and golden car of the Jupitress, here the toad-prince, waiting for his beautiful princess with her child, there the thief of all thieves, and all around them the poor mortals who knew nothing and traveled third-class, carrying their cheap luggage and their poor dreams which consisted in finding a hard seat next to theirs not occupied by any new passengers during any of the seventy stops between here and Laterza, or here and Milano, here and any distant place where workers go to see their miserable dreams miserably fulfilled or regally ignored. Leonardo recognized everybody: they were all Leonardos, or Leonardo's sisters, at various stages of their lives: in childhood, adolescence or early middle age (thirty-two). And they all carried their suitcases by themselves, and stopped here and there to change arms, and to relax a bit. . . . And I dare climb into my rich fairy tale here, while they all suffer?

But here came a great commotion of railroad employees and policemen: the Great Incognita with her Incognita daughter and grandchild, maids, butler and governess, travel agent, lawyer-administrator and a small following of Russian friends was advancing in secret through the crowds, looking desperately for the most Incognito of them all, whose name was being called aloud.

He heard it and ran to the fairy tale coach to apologize, as the master of the house should, and was instantly forgiven.

Finally the car left. One side of it was occupied by the Jupitress with some of her friends and most of her servants, and the other by no one but Mary and Leonardo.

Late at night, when the train stopped in Florence, Leonardo heard that fabulous name heralding that fabulous place, and he prudently raised the black curtain, then prudently opened the window, so that some of the air of Dante's hometown (and much of the blackest coal of his hell) came into his sleeping compartment. The station platform was empty but for a few employees and workers, one of them passing in front of every car with his huge hammer and testing the wheels, which resounded like church bells in the night. No one spoke Florentine at all, and he waited in vain for a sound of that divine language as spoken in the right place. Only at the very end, as the train got under way, did he hear blasphemy in the right accent, telling the engineer that he could set the locomotive into motion again. A long whistle, a few puffs, the train left the station and for a moment he caught a glimpse of a dark shape under the starlit sky: the cupola of Brunelleschi. "Mary," he called. "Come and see: it's the sister of *our* Cupolone." She did, and together they watched the silent monument pass by beyond a network of wires and telegraph poles. Above it, in the sky, a tiny trace of moon, the last slice, so thin that it looked like the paring of a baby's fingernail. It did look a little Turkish, with that star in its curve, but it was still the moon of Tolstoy's *Resurrection*.

And in that moon they lived happily ever after.

A Note on the Type

The text of this book was set in Electra,
a type face designed by William Addison Dwiggins
for the Mergenthaler Linotype Company
and first made available in 1935. Electra cannot be classified
as either "modern" or "old-style." It is not based
on any historical model, and hence does not echo any particular
period or style of type design. It avoids the extreme contrast
between thick and thin elements that marks most modern
faces, and is without eccentricities that catch the eye
and interfere with reading. In general, Electra is a simple,
readable typeface that attempts to give a feeling of
fluidity, power, and speed.

W. A. Dwiggins (1880–1956)
began an association with the Mergenthaler Linotype
Company in 1929 and over the next twenty-seven years
designed a number of book types, including the Metro, Electra,
Caledonia, Eldorado, and Falcon.

Composed by American Book–Stratford Press, Inc.,
Brattleboro, Vt.
Printed and bound by The Haddon Craftsmen, Inc.,
Scranton, Pennsylvania.
Design by Margaret McCutcheon Wagner

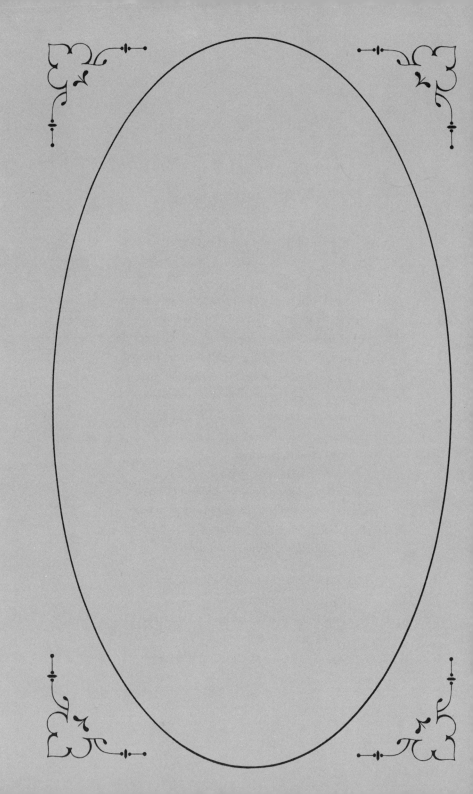